"The Vera Wright trilogy stands out as the most ambitious and most accomplished work in Elizabeth Jolley's oeuvre.... From the Modernist novelists of the generation before hers, Ford Madox Ford and James Joyce and Virginia Woolf in particular... she absorbed the essentials of the narrative method so strikingly deployed in the trilogy. They also confirmed in her her sense of the self as the shifting and evanescent issue of a dialectic between memory and the fabulating intelligence."

—J. M. Coetzee,
from the Introduction to the Australian edition

"Jolley is one of the best writers of the twentieth century.... Just open this book to any page to see the strange, beautiful music she makes out of the raw material of her own life, from her days of nursing training during the Second World War to the derelict farms of western Australia to her green-lit sojourns with Mr. George in his wheelchair.... [She] transports us to 'the twilight between the fact and the imagined,' where the ruthlessness of Vera's self-examination is tempered everywhere by humor, joy, and surprise. Vera's voice is mordant, charming, alive, and candid in a way that made me feel less alone as I read, and almost personally understood.... She can focus on details as small as the nape of Mr. George's neck and show us what is vulnerable about our own existence."

—Karen Russell, author of
St. Lucy's Home for Girls Raised by Wolves

"Although I had read the novels singly as they came out, I wasn't prepared for the impact of reading them as one work.... The formal achievement is awesome ... it is a work that expands what we are able to understand as real." —*Australian Book Review*

(continued on next page)

My Father's Moon

Cabin Fever

"One of her best—sharply observed, heartrendingly funny, profoundly serious. . . . [Jolley] is one of the preeminent novelists writing in English today."   —*Los Angeles Times Book Review*

"Psychologically astute, this is Jolley writing with masterful power."
                                        —*Publishers Weekly*

"Some may be reminded of Jean Rhys . . . Others may well think of Paula Fox. . . . The pathos and humor of wartime London, the lonely courage of Vera, the sorrowful figure of her child and the quirky generosity of the novel's minor characters . . . make *Cabin Fever* a poignant celebration and farewell."   —*New York Times Book Review*

"[Jolley] writes with vividness and assurance, even while she shies away from conventional storytelling."   —*Times Literary Supplement*

The Georges' Wife

"A sparely written, deeply meditated account of the lamentations of a life spent in an open-eyed attempt to persevere with love, whoever the object, whatever the cost . . . fiction of a sufficiently high level to be considered a form of truth."   —*The Australian Weekend Review*

"As I wait for my invitation to the fabled desert island motel, I think this is one of the contemporary novels I would like to bring along."
                                        —*Australian Style*

THE VERA WRIGHT TRILOGY

ELIZABETH JOLLEY

THE VERA WRIGHT TRILOGY

My Father's Moon

Cabin Fever

The Georges' Wife

A Karen & Michael Braziller Book
PERSEA BOOKS / NEW YORK

For Leonard Jolley

The individual novels of *The Vera Wright Trilogy* were previously published in Australia and in the United States, as follows: *My Father's Moon* in 1989 by Penguin Books Australia and by Harper & Row, New York; *Cabin Fever* in 1990 by Penguin Books Australia and by Harper & Row, New York; *The Georges' Wife* in 1993 by Penguin Books Australia.

The present three-in-one volume of *The Vera Wright Trilogy* was published for the first time anywhere in the world by Persea Books, New York, in 2010, and includes the first U. S. publication of *The Georges' Wife*.

To request permission to reprint or to make copies, and/or for any other information, please write to the publisher:

Persea Books, Inc.
853 Broadway
New York, NY 10003

Library of Congress Cataloging-in-Publication Data
Jolley, Elizabeth, 1923–2007.
The Vera Wright trilogy : My father's moon, Cabin fever, The Georges' wife / Elizabeth Jolley.— 1st ed.
p. cm.
"A Karen & Michael Braziller Book."
ISBN 978-0-89255-352-5 (trade pbk. : alk. paper)
1. Nurses—England—Fiction. 2. World War, 1939–1945—Fiction. 3. English—Australia—Fiction. 4. Domestic fiction. I. Title.
PR9619.3.J68V47 2009
823'.914—dc22
       2009018051

Designed by Rita Lascaro. Typeset in Minion.
Printed on acid-free, recycled paper by The Maple-Vail Book Manufacturing Group, York, Pennsylvania.
First Edition

Contents

I would like to express my thanks to the Curtin University of Technology for the continuing privilege of being with students and colleagues in the School of Communication and Cultural Studies and for the provision of a room in which to write. I would like, in particular, to thank Don Watts, Peter Reeves, Brian Dibble, Ian Reid, Anne Brewster, and Don Grant. In addition I would like to thank John Maloney, John de Laeter, Don Yeats, and Ross Bennett.

A special thanks is offered to Nancy McKenzie who, for a great many years, has typed my manuscripts. She is endlessly patient.

I would like as well to thank Kay Ronai, an especially thoughtful and sensitive editor.

THE VERA WRIGHT TRILOGY

MY FATHER'S MOON

Author's Note

It comes as a surprise to realize that time has gone by and that there are now people who are no longer familiar with the abbreviations which were once a part of everyday existence.

ATS was the abbreviation for Auxiliary Territorial Service. ARP stood for Air Raid Precaution, NA was Nursing Auxiliary (or sometimes Naughty Annie). The abbreviations were always used. They were part of the idiom. I never heard the words spoken in full. Similarly RMO and RSO were always said for the Resident Medical Officer and the Resident Surgical Officer respectively.

Elizabeth Jolley

Fairfields

⌘

"Why can't the father, the father of your—what I mean is why can't he do something?"

"I've told you, he's dead."

"How can you say that, he was on the phone last night. I could tell by your voice, that's who it was."

"He's dead. I've told you."

At last the day has come when I must leave for Fairfields. It is all arranged. I have been there once already and know it to be a place of grated raw vegetables and children with restless eyes. It is also a place of poetry and music and of people with interesting lives and ideas.

"I simply can't understand you. How could you with your education and your background breed like a rabbit—"

"You're always saying that, for years you've said it. I've told you, rabbits have six, I only one."

"How can you speak to me, your mother, like that."

"Oh shut up and remember this. I'm never coming back. Never!"

"And another thing, Helena looks like a miner's child dressed up for an outing!" My mother does not like the white frock and the white socks and the white hair ribbons. I tie Helena's hair in two bunches with enormous bows and do not remind my mother that she bought the white frock, and the white socks and the white ribbons.

"She'll get a headache, her hair pulled tight like that. And why white for a train journey, two train journeys. Oh Vera!" My mother, I can see, has tears in her eyes. "Leave Helena here with me, your father and I would like to have her here with us, please! Besides, she is happy with us."

But I will not be parted from my child. I throw a milk bottle across the kitchen, it shatters on the tiles, and I am pleased because my mother is frightened. "What's wrong with miners and their children and their outings?" I shout at her.

Perhaps Helena would be happier with her grandmother. I do not want to think this and it is painful to be told.

My father comes with us to the station.

"That's a nice coat," he says, carrying it for me. It is my school winter coat, dark green and thick. It would not fit into my case so I have to carry it or wear it.

"It's a new coat, is it?" he says feeling the cloth with his hands. I don't reply because I have been wearing the coat for so many years.

We are too early for the train. The platform is deserted.

"It looks like a Loden," he is still talking about the coat. "Like an Austrian Loden cloth." He is restless, my father, very white faced and he holds Helena's hand and walks up and down the platform, up and down. The coat on his other arm.

Always when my father sees off a train he is at the station too soon. And then, when the train is about to leave, when the whistle is being blown and the doors slam shut, one after the other down the whole length of the train, he rushes away and comes back with newspapers and magazines and pushes them through the window as he runs beside the now moving train. As the engine gets up steam and the carriages clank alongside the platform my father increases his speed, keeping up a smiling face outside the window.

His bent figure, his waving arms, and his white face have always been the last things I have seen when leaving. I know too from being with him, seeing other people off, that he stands at the end of the platform, still waving, long after the train has disappeared.

Walking up and down we do not speak to each other. The smell of the station and the sound of an engine at the other platform remind me of Ramsden and of the night several years earlier when I met her train. Ramsden, staff nurse Ramsden, arriving at midnight. There was a thick fog and her train was delayed.

"I've invited Ramsden to come and stay for a few days," I said to my mother then, assuming a nonchalance, a carelessness of speech to hide Ramsden's age and seniority.

"Why of course Vera, a nursing friend is always welcome . . ." There had been a natural progression from school friend to nursing friend. My father never learned to follow, to keep up with this progression.

"And is Miss Ramsden a good girl?" would be his greeting, a continuation of, "and is Jeanie a good girl?" He would say it to Ramsden without seeing the maturity and the elegance and without any understanding of the superior quality of her underclothes.

"My parents are looking forward to meeting you." I invited Ramsden knowing already these other things.

Ramsden, with two tickets to Beethoven, in our Town Hall, prepared herself to make the long journey.

Putting off the visit, in my mind, from one day to the next, reluctantly, at last I was in the Ladies Only waiting room crouched over a dying fire, thin lipped and hostile with the bitter night. My school coat heavy but not warm enough and my shoes soaked.

Ramsden, who had once, unasked, played the piano for my tears, arrived at last. I could see she was cold. She was pale and there were dark circles of fatigue round her eyes. She came towards me distinguished in her well-cut tailored jacket and skirt. Her clothing and manner set her apart immediately from the other disembarking passengers.

"Miss Ramsden will have to share the room," my mother said before I left for the station, "your sister's come home again." Shrugging and blinking I went on reading without replying. Reading, getting ready slowly, turning the page of my book, keeping one finger in the page while I dressed to go and meet the train.

Ramsden came towards me with both hands reaching out in leather gloves. At once she was telling me about the Beethoven, the choral symphony, and how she had been able to get tickets. There was Bach too, Cantata eighteen. Remember? She said. *For as the rain cometh down and the snow from heaven*, she, beating time with one hand, sang, *so shall my word be that goeth forth out of my mouth* . . . In the poor light of the single mean lamp her eyes were pools of pleasure and tenderness. She did not mind the black-out she said when I apologized for the dreariness of the station. "Ramsden," I said, "I'm most awfully sorry but there's been something of a tragedy at home. I couldn't let you know . . . I'm so most awfully sorry . . ."

"Not . . . ?" Concern added more line to Ramsden's tired face. I nodded turning away from the smell of traveling which hung about the woolen cloth of her suit.

"Oh Wright! I am so sorry, Veronica." It was the first time she had spoken my first name, well almost the first time. I glanced at her luggage which stood by itself on the fast emptying platform. The case seemed to hold in its shape and leather the four long hours of traveling, the long tedious journey made twice as long by the fog.

There would be a stopping train to London coming through late, expected at three in the morning the porter said as Ramsden retrieved her case from its desolation.

A glance into the waiting room showed that the remnant of the fire was now a little heap of cold ash. Perhaps, she suggested, even though there was no fire it would be warmer to sit in there.

"I'm so sorry," I said, "I shall not be able to wait for your train." So sorry, I told her, I must get back, simply must get back.

"Is it . . . ?" More concern caused Ramsden to raise her dark eyebrows. The question unfinished, I drew my arm away from her hand's touch. I thought of the needlework and embroidery book I had chosen from her room, too nervous with my act, then, to read the titles when, to please me, she said to choose a book to have to keep, as a present, from her shelf. The badly chosen book I thought, at the time, made me feel sick. I began that day, almost straight away, to feel sick.

We walked along the fog-filled platform. "I've come to you all the way from London," Ramsden, drawing me to her, began in her low voice. "I'd hoped . . ." I turned away from the clumsy embrace of her breathed-out whispered words knowing her breath to be the breath of hunger.

"I'm sorry," I said again stiffening away from her, "but I'll have to go."

"To them," she said, "yes of course, you must." She nodded her understanding and her resignation.

"I am sorry I can't wait till your train comes. I can't wait with you. I'm most awfully sorry!" Trying to change, to lift my accent to match hers.

She nodded again. I knew from before, though I couldn't see them, what her eyes would be like.

I had to walk the three miles home as there were no buses at that time of night. The fog swirled cold in my face. The way was familiar but other things were not. My own body, for one thing, for I was trying, every day, to conceal my morning sickness.

I turn away trying to avoid the place on the platform where Ramsden tried to draw me towards an intensity of feeling I could not be a part of that night.

"She wasn't on the train," I told my mother the next morning standing on purpose behind her flowered overall and keeping to the back of her head which was still encased in metal rollers. She was hurrying to get to the Red Cross depot. Her war effort.

"It was a dreadful night for traveling," my mother said, not turning from the sink, "perhaps your Miss Ramsden will send a letter. You can invite her again, perhaps in the spring, we'll have more space then, perhaps by then your sister will be better."

My father, running now beside the moving train, pushes a magazine and a comic through the window. I, because I feel I must, lean out and see him waving at the end of the platform. Helena, clinging to my skirt, cries for her Grandpa.

Unable to stop thinking of Ramsden I wonder why do I think of her today after all this time of forgetting her. I never write to her. I never did write even when she wrote to me saying that she was still nursing and that she lived out, that she had a little flat which had escaped the bombs and if I liked to stay she would love to have me stay as long as I liked, "as long as you feel like it." I never answered. Never told her I had a child. Never let her into my poverty and never let her into my loneliness.

London is full of people who seem to know where they are and to have some purpose in this knowing. I drag my case and the coat and Helena and change stations and at last we are traveling through the fields and summer meadows of Hertfordshire. The train, this time, is dirty and has no corridor and immediately Helena wants the lavatory. I hate the scenery.

At last we are climbing the steep field path from the bus stop to the school. Fairfields, I have been there once already and know the way. The path is a mud path after it leaves the dry narrow track through the tall corn which is turning, waving and rippling, from the green to gold, spotted scarlet with poppies and visited by humming hot-weather insects. I have seen before that the mud is caused by water seeping from two enormous manholes in the trees at the top of the hill. Drains, the drains of Fairfields School.

"Who is that?" Helena stops whimpering. And I see a man standing quite still, half hidden by trees. He does not seem to be watching, rather it is as if he is trying to be unseen as we climb together. He does not move except to try and merge into a tree trunk. With the case I push Helena on up the steepest part of the path and I do not look back into the woods.

In the courtyard no one is about except for a little boy standing in the porch. He tells me his Granny will be coming to this door, that he is waiting to be fetched by her. "My Granny's got a gas stove," he tells me. I think suddenly of my mother's kitchen and wish that I could wait now at this door for her to come and fetch me and Helena. Straight away I want to go back.

Miss Palmer, the Principal, the one they call Patch, I know this too from my earlier visit, carrying a hod of coke, comes round from an outhouse.

"Ah!" she says. "I see you mean to stay!" She indicates my winter coat. "So this is Helena!" She glances at my child. "She's buttoned up I daresay." I know this to mean something not quite explained but I nod and smile. Patch tells me that no one is coming to fetch Martin. "He's new, he hasn't," she says, "adjusted yet."

She shows me my room which I am to share with Helena. It is bare except for a cupboard and two small beds. It is bright yellow with strong smelling distemper. There is a window, high up, strangled with creeper.

"Feel free to wander," Patch says, "tea in the study at four. Children's tea in the playroom at five and then the bathings. Paint the walls if you feel creative." She has a fleshy face and short, stiff hair, gray like some sort of metal. I do not dislike her.

"Thank you," I say, narrowing my eyes at the walls as if planning an exotic mural.

Helena, pulling everything from the unlocked case, intones a monologue over her rediscovered few toys. I stare into the foliage and the thick mass of summer green leaf immediately outside the window.

Later the Swiss girl, Josepha, who has the room opposite mine, takes me round the upstairs rooms which are strewn with sleeping children. We pull some of them out of bed and sit them on little chipped enamel pots. There is the hot smell of sleeping children and their pots.

Josepha tells me the top bathroom is mine and she gives me a bath list. The face flannels and towels hang on hooks round the room.

Josepha comes late to breakfast and takes most of the bread and the milk and the butter up to her room where her sweetheart, Rudi, sleeps. I heard their endless talk up and down in another language, the rise and fall of an incomprehensible muttering all night long, or so it seemed in my own sleeplessness.

The staff sit at breakfast in a well-bred studied shabbiness huddled round a tall copper coffee pot and some blue bowls of milk. Children are not allowed and it seems that I hear Helena crying and crying locked in our room upstairs. Patch does not come to breakfast but Myles, who is Deputy Principal, fetches prunes and ryvita for her. She is dark-eyed and expensively dressed like Ramsden but she has nothing of Ramsden's music and tenderness. She is aloof and flanked by two enormous dogs. She is something more than Deputy Principal. Josepha explains.

"Do not go in," Josepha points at Patch's door, "if both together are in there."

When I dress Helena I take great trouble over her hair ribbons and let her, with many changes of mind, choose her dress because I am sorry for leaving her alone, locked in to cry in a strange place. I have come to Fairfields to work with the idea that it will give Helena school and companionship and already I have tried to persuade her, to beg her and finally rushed away from her frightened crying because staff offspring (Myles' words) are not allowed at staff meals. I take a long time dressing Helena and find that Josepha has dressed all the children from my list as well as her own. I begin to collect up the little pots.

"No! Leave!" Josepha shouts and, tying the last child into a pinafore, she herds them downstairs. Moving swiftly Josepha can make me, with Helena clinging to my dress, seem useless.

Josepha does the dining room and I am to do, with Olive Morris, the playroom where the smaller children have their meals. Mrs. Morris has a little boy called Frank but Helena will not sit by him. She follows me with a piece of bread and treacle and I have to spend so much time cleaning her that Olive Morris does the whole breakfast and wipes the tables and the floor. She does not say anything only gets on with ladling cod-liver oil, which is free, into the children as they leave the little tables.

I discover that Olive Morris has three children in the school and that Josepha feels it is morally right that Olive should work more than anyone else because of this. Josepha is always dragging children off to have their hair washed. She has enormous washing days and is often scrubbing something violently at ten o'clock at night. The smell of scorching accompanies the fierceness of her ironing.

"Do not go in there," she points to the first-floor bathroom, "when Patch and Tanya are in there and," she says, "do not tell Myles!"

Tanya teaches art. She looks poor but Josepha says she is filthy rich and wears rags on purpose.

Tanya, on my first day, was painting headless clowns on the dining-room walls. She stepped back squinting at her work. "They are going to play ball with the heads," she explained bending down over her paint pots as if she had been talking to me for years.

"What a good idea," I said, ashamed of my accent and trying to sound as if I knew all about painting.

That day she asked me what time it was, saying that she must hurry and get her wrists slashed before Frederick comes back from his holiday.

Later, in the pantry, she is there with both arms bandaged. "Frederick the Great," she says, "he'll be back. Disinfectant, fly spray, cockroach powder, and mouse traps. He will," she says, "ask you to examine his tonsils."

Olive Morris looks ill. Sometimes when I sit in my room at night with an old cardigan round the light to keep it off Helena's bed I think of Olive and begin to understand what real poverty is; her dreadful little bowls of never clean washing, the rags which she is forever mending, and her pale crumpled face from which her worried eyes look out hopelessly.

I have plenty of pretty clothes for Helena. And then it suddenly comes to me that this is the only difference. My prospects are the same as Olive's. I have as little hope for the future as she has. It just happens that at present, because of gifts from my mother, Helena, for the first years of her life, has been properly fed and is well dressed.

One hot afternoon I sit with the children in the sand pit hoping that they will play. There are only two little spades and the children quarrel and fight and bite each other. It is hard to understand why the children can't enjoy the spacious lawns and the places where they can run and shout and hide amongst the rose bushes. Beyond the lawn is deep uncut grass bright with buttercups and china-blue hare-bells. I am tired, tired in a way which makes me want to lie down in the long grass and close my eyes. Helena, crying, will not let me rest. The children are unhappy. I think it is because they do not have enough food. They are hungry all the time.

I do lie down and I look up at the sky. Once I looked at the sky, not with Ramsden but after we had been talking together. I would like to hear Ramsden's voice now. It is strange to wish this after so long. Perhaps it is because everyone here seems to have someone. Relationships, as they are called here, are acceptable. And I, having no one, wishing for someone, vividly recall Ramsden. She said, that time in the morning before I went for my day off to sleep among the spindles of rosemary at the end of my mother's garden, that love was infinite. That it was possible, if a person loved, to believe in the spiritual understanding of truths which were not fully understood intellectually. She said that the person you loved was not an end in itself, was not something you came to the end of, but was the beginning of discoveries which could be made because of loving someone.

Lying in the grass, pushing Helena away, I think about this and wonder how I can bring it into the conversation at the four o'clock staff tea and impress Patch and Myles. I practice some words and an accent of better quality.

Because of being away from meadow flowers for so long I pick some buttercups and some of the delicate grasses adding their glowing tips to the bunch wondering, with bitter uneasiness, how I can get them unseen to my room. I can see Patch and Myles at the large window of Patch's room. Instead of impressing them I shall simply seem vulgar, acquisitive and stupid, clutching a handful of weeds, ineffectually shepherding the little children towards their meager plates of lettuce leaves and Patch-rationed bread.

In the evening there is a thunder storm with heavy rain. I am caught in the rain on the way back from the little shop where I have tried to buy some fruit. The woman there asks me if I am from the school and if I am, she says she is unable to give me credit. In the shop there is the warm sweet smell of newspapers, firelighters and cheap sweets, aniseed, a smell of ordinary life which is missing in the life of the school. Shocked I tell her I can pay and I buy some poor-quality carrots as the apples, beneath their rosy skins, might be rotten. I will wash the carrots and give them to Helena when I have to leave her alone in our room in the mornings.

The storm is directly overhead, the thunder so loud I am afraid Helena will wake and be frightened so I do not shelter in the shop but hurry back along the main road, through the corn and up the steep path. I am wet through and the mud path is a stream. The trees sway and groan. I slip and catch hold of the undergrowth to stop myself from falling. When I look up I see that there is someone standing, half hidden, quite near, in the same place where a man was standing on that first afternoon. This man, I think it is the same man, is standing quite still letting the rain wash over him as it pours through the leaves and branches. His hair is plastered wet-sleeked on his round head and water runs in rivulets down his dark suit. He, like me, has no coat. He does not move and he does not speak. He seems to be looking at me as I try to climb the steep path as quickly as I can. I feel afraid. I have never felt or experienced fear like this before. Real terror, because of his stillness, makes my legs weak. I hurry splashing across the courtyard and make my way, trembling, round to the kitchen door. Wet and shivering I meet Olive Morris in the passage outside my room. She is carrying a basin of washing. Rags trail over her shoulder and her worn-out blouse, as usual, has come out of her skirt.

I tell her about the man in the woods. "Ought I to tell Patch?" I try to breathe calmly. "It's getting dark out there. He's soaked to the skin. I ought to tell Patch."

Olive Morris's shapeless soft face is paler than ever and her lips twitch. She looks behind her nervously.

"No," she says in a low voice. "No, never tell anyone here any-thing. Never!" she hurries off along to the other stairs which lead directly up to her room in the top gable of the house.

While I am drying my hair, Olive Morris, in a torn raincoat, comes to my door.

"I'm going down to post a letter," she says putting a scarf over her head. "So if I see your stranger in the trees I'll send him on his way—there's no need at all to have Myles go out with the dogs. No need at all."

My surprise at the suggestion that Myles and the dogs might hunt the intruder is less than the feeling of relief that I need not go to Patch's room where Myles, renowned for her sensitive nudes, will be sketching Patch in charcoal and reading poetry aloud. They would smile at each other, exchanging intimate glances while Patch pretended to search her handbag for a ten shilling note as part of the payment owing to me, Myles had looked up gazing as if thoughtfully at me for a few minutes and then had resumed her reading of the leather-bound poems.

Josepha is on bedroom duty and the whole school is quiet. Grateful that Helena has not been disturbed by the storm I lie down in my narrow bed.

Instead of falling asleep I think of the school and how it is not at all as I thought it would be. Helena stands alone all day peering through partly closed doors watching the dancing classes. She looks on at the painting and at the clay-modeling and is only on the edge of the music.

There must be people who feel and think as I do but they are not here as I thought they would be. I want to lean out of a win-dow in a city full of such people and call to some passer-by. I am by my own mistakes buried in this green-leafed corruption and I am alone.

My day off which Josepha did not tell me about till all the children were washed and dressed was a mixture of relief and sadness. A bus ride to town. Siting with Helena in a small cafe eating doughnuts. Choosing a sun hat for Helena. Buying some little wooden spades and some colored chalks. Trying to eat a picnic lunch of fruit and biscuits on a road mender's heap of gravel chips. I can hardly bear to think about it. As I handed Helena her share and saw her crouched on the stones with her small hands trying to hold her food without a plate I knew how wrong it was that she was like this with no place to go home to.

I think now over and over again that it is my fault that we are alone, more so than ever, at the side of the main road with cars and lorries streaming in both directions.

There is a sudden sound, a sound of shooting. Gun shots. I go into the dark passage. From Josepha's room comes the usual running up and down of their voices, first hers and then his. I am afraid to disturb them. A door further down clicks open and I see, with relief, it is Tanya.

"Oh it's you Tanya! Did you hear anything just now?"

"Lord no. I never hear a thing m'dear and I never ask questions either so if you've been letting anyone in or out I just wouldn't know darling."

I tell her about the shot.

"Lord!" Tanya says. "That's Frederick. Back from his leave. Frederick the Great, literature and drama. Room's over the stables. Never unpacks. Got a Mother. North London. Cap gun. Shoots off gun for sex. The only trouble is darling," Tanya drawls, "the orgasm isn't shared." She disappears into the bathroom saying that she's taken an overdose and so must have her bath quickly.

I go on up the next lot of stairs to Olive's room. I have never been there. I must talk to someone. Softly I knock on the door. At once Olive opens it as if she is waiting on the other side of it.

"Oh it's you!" Her frightened white face peers at me.

"Can I come in?" I step past her hesitation into her room. It is not my intention to be rude, I tell her, it is my loneliness. Olive catches me by the arm. Her eyes implore. I am suddenly ashamed for, sitting up in bed wearing a crumpled shirt and a tie, is a man. The man I had seen standing with sinister patience in the rain.

"Oh Olive, I am so sorry. I do beg . . ."

"This is Mr. Morris, my husband. This is Vera Wright, dear," Olive whispers a plain introduction.

"Pleased to meet you I'm sure," Mr. Morris says. I continue to mumble words of apology and try to move backwards to the door.

The three Morris children are all in a heap asleep in a second sagging double bed up against the gable window. Washing is hanging on little lines across the crowded room and Mr. Morris's suit is spread over the bed ends to dry.

"Mr. Morris is on his way to a business conference," Olive begins to explain. I squeeze her arm. "I'll see you tomorrow," I say. We are wordless at the top of the steep stairs. She is tucking her blouse into her too loose skirt. It seems to me that she will go on performing this little action forever even when she has no clothes on.

"No one at all knows that Mr. Morris is here," she says in a breaking whisper.

At breakfast I wish I had someone to whom I could carry, with devotion, bread and butter and coffee. I could not envy Myles because of Patch, or Josepha because of Rudi. Tanya must be feeling as I feel for she prepares a little tray for Frederick and is back almost at once with a swollen bruised bleeding nose and quite quickly develops two black eyes which, it is clear, will take days to fade.

It would be nice for Olive to sail into breakfast and remove a quantity of food bearing it away with dignity to the room in the top gable.

"I suppose you know," I say to Patch when we meet by chance in the hall, "that Olive Morris's husband arrived unexpectedly last night and will be with us for a few days."

Patch says, "Is he dear?" That is all.

Mr. Morris, who is a big man, wears his good suit every day thus setting himself somewhat apart from the rest of us. He comes to supper and tells us stories about dog racing. His dogs win. He tells us about boxing and wrestling. He has knocked out all the champs. He knows all their names and the dates of the matches.

He knows confidence men who treble their millions in five minutes. His brothers and sisters teach in all the best universities and his dear old mother is the favorite Lady in Waiting at Buckingham Palace. Snooker is his forte, a sign, he tells us, of a misspent youth. He sighs.

Patch comes to supper every night. Josepha stops shouting at Olive. Mr. Morris calls Olive "Lovey" and reminds her, for us all to hear, of extravagant incidents in their lives. He boasts about his older children regaling us with their exam results and sporting successes. Olive withers. She is smaller and paler and trembles visibly when Patch, in a genial mood, with mockery and amusement in her voice, leads Mr. Morris into greater heights of story telling. While he talks his eyes slide sideways as he tries to observe us all and see the effects of his fast-moving mouth.

Mr. Morris, we have to see, is the perfect husband and father. During the day he encourages his children and the other children to climb all over him. He organizes games and races, promising prizes.

He gives all sorts of presents, the table in the kitchen is heaped with chickens and ducks, ready for the oven, jars of honey and expensive jams, and baskets of apples and fresh vegetables. Patch prepares the meals herself. Our vegetarian diet was only because the local butchers, unpaid, no longer supply the school.

Frederick, refusing to come to meals, refusing to leave the loft, has a bucket on a string into which Josepha, he will not take from anyone else, puts chicken breasts and bread and butter and a white jug of milk. Tanya says if there is any wormy fruit or fly-blown meat Frederick the Great will get it. He, she explains, because of always searching for them, attracts the disasters in food.

"Where is Mr. Philbrick?" Patch asks correcting quickly what she calls a fox's paw, a slip of the tongue. "Mr. Morris? Why isn't he here?" She is carving, with skill, the golden chickens and Myles is serving the beans and baby carrots which shine in butter. Olive can hardly swallow a mouthful.

"What's keeping Mr. Morris?" I ask her loud enough for Patch's ears. "Anything wrong?" devouring my plateful. "Is someone ill?"

"No. No—it's nothing at all," she whispers.

Towards the end of the meal Mr. Morris comes in quietly and sits down next to the shrinking Olive. Patch, with grease on her large chin, hands a plate of chicken to him. Thick-set, stockily at the head of the table, she sings contralto as if guarding a secret with undisturbed complacence.

There is a commotion in the hall and the sound of boots approaching.

"It is the Politz!" Josepha, on bedroom duty, calls from the stairs.

Mr. Morris leaps up.

"Leave this to me dear Lady," he says to Patch. And, with a snake-like movement, he is on his way to the door.

We follow just in time to see Mr. Morris, suddenly small and white-faced, being led in handcuffs to the front door and out to a car which, with the engine running, is waiting.

I want to say something to Olive to comfort her.

"It's better this way," she says, "better for him this way, better than them getting him with dogs. And the children," she says, "they didn't see anything." I don't ask her what Mr. Morris has done. She does not tell me anything except that Mr. Morris finds prison life unbearable and that he has a long stretch of it ahead.

Patch walks about the school singing and eating the ends off a crusty loaf. When the bills come addressed to her for all the presents from Mr. Morris she laughs and tosses them into the kitchen fire.

One of the little boys rushing through the hall stops to glance at Tanya's latest painting.

"How often do you have sexual intercourse?" he pauses long enough in his flight to ask.

"Three times a week." Tanya steps back to squint at her work. "Never more, never less," she says.

Tanya says that Frederick the Great is coming down from the loft and will be at supper. I wash my hair and put on my good dress and go down to the meal early rejoicing that it is Olive's night to settle the children. I am looking forward to meeting Frederick. Perhaps, at last, there will be someone for me. Olive scuttles by with her tray which she must eat upstairs. I hear the uproar from the bedrooms and smile to myself.

Frederick is bent in a strange contortion over the sink in the pantry. He is trying to see into his throat with a torch and a small piece of broken mirror stuck into the loose window frame. I am glad to be able to meet him without Josepha and Tanya.

"Would you mind looking at my throat," he says straightening up. He is very tall and his eyes enclosed in gold-rimmed spectacles do not look at me. "I've been trying a new gargle." He hands me the torch and I peer into his throat.

"Is it painful?" I feel I should ask him.

"Not at all," he says, taking back the torch.

In the dining room Frederick has a little table to himself in the corner. He eats alone quickly and leaves at once. I sit in my usual place. One of the children is practicing on the pantry piano. I listen to the conscientious stumblings. Ramsden played Bach seriously repeating and repeating until she was satisfied and then moving on to the next phrases.

In my head I compose a letter to Ramsden . . . *this neck of the woods,* this is not my way but it persists, *this neck of the woods is not far from London. Any chance of your coming down one afternoon? Staff tea is at four. I'd love to see you and show you round . . .*

There is so much I would tell Ramsden.

For as the rain cometh down, and the snow from heaven, and returneth
not thither, but watereth the earth, and make it bring forth and bud,
that it may give seed to the sower, and bread to the eater:
so shall my word be that goeth forth out of my mouth:

I want to write to Ramsden. After that night and after almost five years how do I address her? Dear Ramsden? Dear staff nurse Ramsden? She might be Sister Ramsden. She might not be nursing now though she did go on after the end of the war. She might be married though I think that is unlikely, perhaps she is on concert platforms . . .

Dear Ramsden I have no way at all of getting away from this place. Please Ramsden can you come? Please?

Patch and Myles come in to supper. Ignoring me they devotedly help each other to mountains of grated raw carrots and cabbage.

My Father's Moon

Before this journey is over I intend to speak to the woman. *Ramsden*, I shall say, *is it you?* The train has just left the first station, there is plenty of time in which to contemplate the conversation; the questions and the answers and the ultimate revelation. It is comfortable to think about the possibilities.

The woman siting on the other side, diagonally opposite, could be someone I used to know. A long time ago. In another place. Her clothes are of the same good quality, the same materials, even the same colors. It is the tilt of the head which is so remarkably similar. She looks like someone who is passionately fond of the cello. Fond of listening to the cello. I look at her hands and feel sure she plays the piano. When I look at her hands it is as if I can hear her playing a Mozart sonata or practicing something from Bach. Repeating and repeating phrases until a perfection is achieved. I am certain, as I go on looking, that she plays Cyril Scott's *Water Wagtail*.

For some time now I have traveled by suburban train to and from the places where I work. This evening I am on the earlier train. I caught the earlier train on purpose even though, because of this, I arrive too soon . . .

The unfamiliar early train travels, of course, through the same landscape, the familiar. There is nothing remarkable in this. It is my reason for taking this train which makes the journey remarkable. The train stops at the same stations but naturally the people getting in or out are not the same people as those on the later train.

I sit staring out of the window at the same meeting places of unknown roads, at the backs of the same shabby houses and garden fences, at the same warehouses and the same smash repair yards and at the now well-known backs of the metropolitan markets.

About once a week I catch the earlier train for a special reason. Every week it is the same. Every week I think that this time I will speak to her. This week I am on this train in order to speak to her. I will cross from my seat and sit by her and I will speak to her. I always sit where I can see her from the side and from the back and I sit close enough to hear her voice if she should speak. I long to hear the voice, her voice, to know whether it is the same voice. Voices and ways of speaking often remain unchanged.

This time I almost brought the violin case with me though I am not now accustomed to carrying it when I go out. If Ramsden saw the violin case, if the woman saw it, she would remember.

"They're both in good condition," the man in the shop said. "Both the same price. Choose your pick," he said. "Take your time."

I could not make up my mind, and then I chose the violin case. The following week I went back for the camera case but it had gone. The violin case had once been lined with some dark red soft material, some of it was still left. I only opened it once and it was then I saw the remains of the lining. I carried the case whenever I went out.

The first time I saw Ramsden the sentry at the hospital gates had his bayonet fixed. He looked awkward and he blushed as he said, "Who goes there!" Surprised, I told him my name and my identity-card number, it was the middle of the morning and we were challenged, as a rule, only after dark. I supposed the rule must have been changed. A dispatch from HQ, I thought, seeing in my mind the nimble motor cyclist arrive.

Ramsden, on her way out, gave a small smile in the direction of the violin case and I was pleased that I had bought it. On that day I had been at the hospital for seven weeks.

Two people sitting behind me are talking in German. I begin to listen to the animated conversation and grope for meanings in what they are saying in this language which was once familiar. I begin to recognize a few words: *eine Dame . . . keine Ahnung . . . langsam . . . Milch und Tränenbäche . . . mein Elend . . . zu grosser Schmerz und so weiter.* But I want the words of cherishing spoken in German. I want those first words the child remembers on waking to the knowing of language. I wish now in the train to be spoken to as *du . . .*

The woman sitting on the other side is looking calmly out of the window. Naturally she sees the same things that I see. It is quite comfortable to know that I have only to lean over and touch her sleeve.

I never worked with Ramsden. I saw her sometimes in the dining room. There are several little pictures of her in my mind. The doctors called her Miss Ramsden. She did the penicillin syringes too. One nurse, usually a senior, spent the whole day cleaning and sterilizing the syringes and the needles, setting up the trolley, giving the injections, and then clearing the trolley and cleaning and sterilizing and checking all over again. Whenever I passed the glass doors of the ward where she was I saw her in the sterilizing room seriously attending to the syringes and needles for the three-hourly injections.

"Ramsden," I said, "this is the part we like isn't it? This part, this is it, we like this . . ."

"It's the anticipation," she replied, "it's what is hoped for and then realized." She was sitting on the edge of her bed.

"This part, this . . ." I said once more. I pointed with one finger as if to place the cello somewhere in the space between us. "This going down part," I said, "is the part we like best."

Ramsden nodded. She was mending a stocking. Her stockings were not the usual ones, not the gray uniform stockings which were lisle and, after repeated washing, were hard to mend. Ramsden's stockings, I noticed immediately, were smooth and soft and they glistened like honey. Dark, honey-colored stockings. Ramsden's stockings were silk stockings. She was oversewing a run at the ankle. Her sewing was done so carefully I knew the repair would be invisible. She had invited me into her room to listen to a record.

"Do you know why you like it?" she repeated an earlier question. The cello reminded me of her. How could I tell her this. It shook my head. Staff nurse Ramsden, she was senior to me. When she listened to music she sat with her legs crossed over and she moved her foot very slightly, I could see, in time to the music. How could I speak to her about the downward thrust of the cello and about the perfection in the way the other instruments came up to meet the cello. How could I say to her that I thought someone had measured the movement of the notes controlling carefully the going down and the coming up in order to produce this exquisite mixture. There were other things too that I could not speak about. How could I say to her what I thought about the poet Rilke, about his face and about how I felt when I looked at his photograph in the book she had. She knew his poems, understood them. I wanted to tell her that when I looked at Rilke's face I felt clumsy as if made of wood. Even the way he stood in the photograph had something special about it and when I read a poem of his to myself I wanted to read lines aloud to her. "Listen to this, Ramsden," I wanted to say, "listen to this."

> But hand in hand now with that God she walked,
> her paces circumscribed by lengthy shroudings
> uncertain, gentle, and without impatience.
> Wrapt in herself, like one whose time is near...

There were other things too from *Orpheus*, but she knowing his poems might have felt I was intruding. When I read Rilke everything I was trying to write seemed commonplace and unmusical, completely without any delicacy and refinement. I never told Ramsden I was trying to write because what I wrote was about her. I wanted to write about Ramsden. How could I tell her that?

Later when she talked about the music she said the soloist was innocent and vulnerable. She said the music was eloquent and that there was something intimate about the cello. She was very dignified and all her words seemed especially chosen. I wanted her to say them all again to me. The word *intimate*, I had never before spoken to anyone who used this word. She said the cello, the music of the cello, was intimate. Ramsden's discipline prevented her from repeating what she had said. She continued to oversew her stocking and we listened once more to the second movement. When I listened to a particular passage in this movement I seemed to see Ramsden walking ahead of me with great beech trees on either side of her. Magnificent smooth trees with their rain-soaked branches darkened and dripping. Then we were walking together, I imagined, beneath these trees, with the wet leaves deep round our ankles. Ramsden, I thought, would have small ribbed socks on over her stockings . . .

Lyrical, she said the music was lyrical and I was not sure what she meant. She said then that, if I liked, I could borrow her records.

When I played the record at home my father, not knowing the qualities of the cello, asked if I could make the music a bit quieter. It was my day off, most of it had been wasted because I slept and no one woke me. My father asked was there a piano piece, he said he liked the piano very much. I told him that staff nurse Ramsden played the piano and my mother said perhaps Miss Ramsden would come some time and play the piano for us. She said she would make a fire in the front room and we could all sit and listen . . .

Because I caught the earlier train I have an hour to spare before it is time for the clinic to open. The people who attend this clinic will be setting off from their houses in order to keep their appointments.

I walk to a bus stop where there is a bench and, though I am in a familiar place, I feel as if I have come to a strange land. In one sense there is a strangeness because all the old houses and their once cared for gardens have gone. In their place are tall concrete buildings, floor upon floor of offices, all faced with gleaming windows. Some lit up and some dark. The buildings rise from parking lots all quite similar but unrecognizable as though I have never seen them before. Small trees and bushes planted as ornaments offer a few twigs and leaves. The new buildings are not at peace with their surroundings. They are not part of the landscape, they are an imposition. They do not match each other and they have taken away any tranquility, any special quality of human life the streets may have had once.

The Easter lilies, uncherished, appear as they do every year with surprising suddenness, their pink and white long-lasting freshness bursting out of the brown, bald patches of earth at the ends of those places which have been left out from the spreading bitumen.

If I had spoken in the train I could have said, "Ramsden," I could have said, "I feel sad. Lately I seem unable to prevent a feeling of melancholy which comes over me as soon as I wake up. I feel nervous and muddled and everything is accompanied by a sense of sorrow and futility." Should I join a sect? I could have asked her. A cult? On TV these people, with a chosen way, all look light hearted. They dance carrying bricks and mortar across building sites. They jive and twist and break-dance from kitchens to dining rooms carrying wooden platters of something fresh and green neatly chopped up. Perhaps it is uncooked spinach. Perhaps it is their flying hair and their happy eyes which attract, but then the memory of the uneasiness of communal living and the sharing of possessions and money seems too difficult, too frightening to contemplate. In real life it won't, I could have told her, it won't be the same as it is on TV. Probably only the more sparkling members of the sect are filmed, I could have said this too, and something is sure to be painted on the spinach to make it look more attractive. Food in advertisements, I could have been knowledgeable, food in advertisements is treated before being photographed. I left the train at my station without another glance in her direction.

Perhaps the lilies are a reminder and a comfort. Without fail they flower at Easter. Forgotten till they flower, an unsought simultaneous caution and blessing.

It seems to me now, when I think of it, that my father was always seeing me off either at a bus stop or at the station. He would suggest that he come to the bus or the train just as I was about to leave. Sometimes he came part of the way in the train getting out at the first stop and then, waiting alone, he would travel on the first train back. Because of the decision being made at the last minute, as the train was moving, he would have only a platform ticket so, as well as all the waiting and the extra traveling, he would be detained at the other end to make explanations and to pay his fare for both directions. All this must have taken a lot of time. And sometimes in the middle of winter it was bitterly cold.

The strong feeling of love which goes from the parent to the child does not seem a part of the child which can be given back to the parent. I realize now with regret that I never thought then of his repeated return journeys. I never thought of the windswept platforms, of the small smoldering waiting-room fires and the long, often wet, walks from the bus to the house. I simply always looked ahead, being already on my journey even before I set out, to the place to which I was going.

The minutes which turned out to be the last I was to have with my father were at a railway station. When it was time for my train to leave even when the whistle was being blown my father went on with what he was saying. He said that if we never saw each other again I must not mind. He was getting older he said then, he was surprised at how quickly he was getting older and though he planned to live a long time it might be that we should not be able to make the next journeys in time. It is incredible that I could have paid so little attention then and the longing to hear his voice once more at this moment is something I never thought of till now.

He had his umbrella with him and when the train began to move he walked beside the moving train for as long as he could waving the umbrella. I did not think about the umbrella then either. But now I remember that during the years he often left it in trains and it traveled the length and breadth of England coming back at intervals labeled from Liverpool, Norfolk, St. Ives, and Glasgow to the lost-property office where he was, with a kind of apologetic triumph, able to claim it.

The huge Easter moon, as if within arm's length, as if it can be reached simply by stretching out both hands to take it and hold it, is low down in the sky, serene and full, lighting the night so that it looks as if everything is snow covered, and deep shadows lie across pale, moon-whitened lawns. This moon is the same moon that my father will have seen. He always told me when I had to leave for school, every term when I wept because I did not want to leave, he told me that if I looked at the moon, wherever I was, I was seeing the same moon that he was looking at. "And because of this," he said, "you must know that I am not very far away. You must never feel lonely," he said. He said the moon would never be extinguished. Sometimes, he said, it was not possible to see the moon, but it was always there. He said he liked to think of it as his.

I waited once for several hours at a bus stop, a temporary stop on a street corner in London. There was a traffic diversion and the portable sign was the final stop for the Green Line from Hertford. It was the long summer evening moving slowly into the night of soft dusty warmth. A few people walked on the pavement. All of them had places they were going to. A policeman asked me if everything was all right.

"I'm waiting for someone," I told him. I waited with Helena for Ramsden.

In the end, in my desperation, I did write my letter to Ramsden asking her to help me to leave Fairfields, the school where I had gone to live and work taking Helena with me. It was a progressive boarding school. There was not enough food and I was never paid. In my letter I told Ramsden everything that had happened, about my child, about my leaving home, about my loneliness, about my disappointment with the school. I had not expected, I told her, such fraudulent ways. My poverty, I thought, would be evident without any description. After writing the letter I was not able to wait for a reply from Ramsden because, when I went to give notice that I wanted to leave in a fortnight, Patch (the headmistress) replied in her singing voice, the dangerous contralto in which she encouraged people to condemn and entangle themselves, "By all means but please do go today. There's a bus at the end of the field path at three o'clock." Neither she nor Miss Myles, after exchanging slightly raised eyebrows with one another, said anything else to me.

I sent my letter to the last address I had from Ramsden almost five years earlier. She was, she said then, still nursing and had a little flat where I would be welcome. Five years is a long time.

I told her in my letter that I would wait for her at the terminus of the Green Line. As I wrote I could not help wondering if she was by now playing the piano in concerts. Perhaps on tour somewhere in the north of England; in the places where concert pianists play. I tried to think of likely towns and villages. As I wrote I wept, remembering Ramsden's kind eyes and her shy manner. Staff nurse Ramsden with her older more experienced face—as someone once described her—and her musician's nose—someone else had said once. She had never known what there was to know about the violin case I carried with me in those days. It had been my intention always to tell her but circumstances changed intentions.

I begged her in the letter and in my heart to be there. Five years is a long time to ignore a kind invitation from someone. A long time to let pass without any kind of reply. With failing hope I walked slowly up and down the pavement which still held the dust and the warmth of the day. I walked and waited with Helena who was white faced and hungry and tired. Sometimes she sat on our heavy case on my roughly folded school winter coat. I tried to comfort myself with little visions of Ramsden playing the piano and nodding and smiling to Helena who would dance, thump-thump, on the carpet in the little living room. I seemed to remember that Ramsden said in the letter, sent all those years ago, that the flat was tiny.

"You'd best be coming along with me." It was the policeman again. He had passed us several times. Helena was asleep on the folded coat and I was leaning against the railings at the front of an empty house.

The woman in charge of the night shelter gave me a small huckaback towel and a square of green soap. She said she had enough hot water if Helena and I could share a bath.

"She's very like you," the woman said not trying very hard to hide her curiosity behind a certain sort of kindness. She gave us two slices of bread and butter and a thick cup of tea each. She handed me two gray blankets and said Helena would be able to sleep across the foot of the bed she was able to let me have for one night. The girl who had the bed, she explained, was due to come out of hospital where she had been operated on to have a propelling pencil removed from her bladder.

"The things they'll try," the woman said. "I or anyone, for that matter, could have told her she was too far gone for anything like that. All on her own too pore thing. Made herself properly poorly and lorst her baby too." She looked at Helena who was eating her bread and butter, crusts and all, neatly in what seemed to me to be an excessive show of virtue.

"There's some as keeps their kiddies," the woman said.

"Yes," I said avoiding her meaning looks. The night shelter for women carried an implication. There was more than the need of a bed. At St. Cuthberts the nurses had not been too sympathetic. I remembered all too clearly herding A.T.S. girls into one of the bathrooms every evening where they sat naked from the waist down in chipped enamel basins of hot water and bicarbonate of soda. In her lectures the Sister Tutor reminded often for the need to let patients be as dignified as possible. The hot basins defied this. Many of the girls were pregnant. Some women, the Sister Tutor said, mistook the orifices in their own bodies. All this, at that time, belonged to other people.

Later my own child was to be the embodiment of all that was poetical and beautiful and wished for. Before she was born I called her Beatrice. I forgot about the A.T.S.

Grateful for the hot bath and the tea and the promised bed I addressed the woman in charge as Sister.

Did the Sister, I asked her, ever know a staff nurse called Ramsden? The woman, narrowing her eyes, thought for a moment and said yes she thought she had—now she recalled it. There was a Ramsden she thought, yes she was sure, who joined the Queens Nurses and went to Mombassa. I tried to take comfort from the doubtful recollection. Yes, went to Mombassa with the Queens Nurses. Very fine women the Queens Nurses. And one night, so she'd heard, the cook in the nurses' quarters was stabbed by an intruder. Horribly stabbed, a dozen or more times in the chest, the neck and the stomach. Apparently the murder was justified, brought on by the cook's own behavior—him having gone raving mad earlier that same day. But of Ramsden herself she had no actual news.

I understood as I lay under the thin blanket that she had been trying to offer some sort of reply to my stupid and hopeless question. Perhaps the cook in Mombassa was often murdered horribly in these attempts to provide answers.

I tried to sleep but Helena, accustomed to a bed to herself, kicked unbearably all night.

Being at a bus stop, not waiting for a bus, and with the dusk turning quickly to darkness, I think of my father's moon. This moon, once his moon and now mine, is now climbing the warm night sky. It hangs in the branches of a single tree left between the new buildings.

The journey to school is always, it seems, at dusk. My father comes to the first stop. This first journey is in the autumn when the afternoons are dark before four o'clock. The melancholy railway crawls through water-logged meadows where mourning willow trees follow the winding steams. Cattle, knee deep in damp grass, raise their heads as if in an understanding of sorrow as the slow train passes. The roads at the level crossings are deserted. No one waits to wave and curtains of drab colors are pulled across the dimly lit cottage windows.

At the first stop there is a kind of forced gaiety in the meetings on the platform. Some girls have already been to school and others, like me, are going for the first time. My father watches and when the carriage doors are slammed, one after the other, he melts away from the side of the train as it moves slowly along the platform gradually gathering speed, resuming its journey.

I sink back at once into that incredible pool of loneliness which is, I know now but did not understand then, a part of being one of a crowd. I try to think of the moon. Though it is not Easter, my father said before the doors had all slammed, there will be, if the clouds disperse, a moon. He pointed as he spoke towards the dome of the railway station. Because he pointed with his umbrella I felt embarrassed and, instead of looking up, I stared at my shoes. I try to think about his moon being behind the clouds even if I cannot see it. I wish, I am wishing I had smiled and waved to him.

In the noisy compartment everyone is talking and laughing. We are all reflected in the windows and the dark, shadowed fields slip by on both sides.

The school bus, emblazoned with an uplifting motto, rattles through an unfamiliar land. The others sing songs which I have never heard before. There is no moon. The front door of the school opens directly on to the village street. Everyone rushes from the bus and the headmaster and his wife stand side by side in a square of light to receive us.

"Wrong hand Veronica. It is Veronica isn't it?" he ticks my name on a list he has. "Other hand Veronica. We always shake hands with the right hand."

When I unpack my overnight bag I am comforted by the new things, the new nightdress, the handkerchiefs and the stockings folded carefully by my mother. Especially my new fountain pen pleases me.

Almost at once I begin my game of comparisons, placing myself above someone if more favorable and below others if less favorable in appearance. This game of appearance is a game of chance. Chance can be swayed by effort, that is one of the rules, but effort has to be more persistent than is humanly possible. It is a game of measuring the unfamiliar against the familiar. I prefer the familiar. I like to know my way, my place with other people, perhaps because of other uncertainties.

I am still on the bench at the bus stop. My father's moon is huge and is now above the tree in a dark-blue space between the buildings. A few cars have come. I have seen their headlights dip and turn off and I have seen the dark shapes of people making their way into the place where my clinic is. They will sit in the comfortable chairs in the waiting room till they are called in to see me. Unavoidably I am late sometimes but they wait.

At the other place where I work there is a scent of hot pines. The sun, beating down on a nearby plantation all day, brings into the warm still air a heart-lifting fragrance. There is a narrow path pressed into the dry grass and the fallen pine needles. This is the path I take to and from the railway station. Sometimes I suggest to other people that they walk on this path. The crows circling and calling suggest great distance. Endless paddocks with waving crops could be quite close on the other side of the new tall buildings. The corridors indoors smell of toast, of coffee, and of hot curries. It is as if there are people cooking at turning points on the paths and in corners between the buildings. It is as if they have casually thrown their saris over the cooking pots to protect them from the prevailing winds.

From where I sit it seems as if the moon is shining with some secret wisdom. I read somewhere that it was said of Chekhov that he *shows us life's depths at the very moment when he seems to reflect its shimmering surface.*

My father's moon is like this.

But the game. The game of comparisons. Before meals at school we have to stand in line beginning with the smallest and ending with the tallest. The room is not very big and the tallest stand over the smallest. We are not allowed to speak and our shoes and table napkins are examined by the prefects. It is during this time of silence and inspection that I make my comparisons. Carefully I am comparing my defects with those of my immediate neighbors. I glance sideways at the pleats of their tunics and notice that the girl next to me bulges. In my mind I call her Bulge; her pleats do not lie flat, they bulge. She is tall and awkward, taller than I am and more round shouldered. I try to straighten my back and to smooth my tunic pleats. I can be better than Bulge. She has cracked lips and she bites her nails. I try not to chew my nails but my hands are not well kept as are the hands of the girl on the other side of me. She has pretty nails and her hair is soft and fluffy. My hair is straight but not as greasy and uneven as Bulge's. Fluffy Hair's feet turn out when she walks. My feet are straight but my stockings are hopelessly wrinkled and hers are not. We all have spots. Bulge's spots are the worst, Fluffy Hair's complexion is the best. She is marred by a slight squint. We all wear spectacles. These are all the same except that Bulge has cracked one of her lenses. My lenses need cleaning.

It is the sound of someone closing a case very quietly in the dormitory after the lights have been turned off which makes me cry. It is the kind of sound which belongs to my mother. This quiet little closing of a case. My nightdress, which she made, is very comfortable. It wraps round me. She knitted it on a circular needle, a kind of stockinette she said it was, very soft, she said. When she had finished it she was very pleased because it had no seams. She was telling our neighbor, showing her the night-dress and the new clothes for school, all marked with my name embroidered on linen tape. The cabin trunk bought specially and labeled clearly "Luggage in Advance" in readiness for the journey by goods train produced an uneasy excitement. My mother, handling the nightdress again, spoke to me:

> *ein weiches reines Kleid für dich zu weben,*
> *darin nicht einmal die geringste Spur*
> *Von Naht dich drückt . . .*

"Shut up," I said, not liking her to speak to me in German in front of the woman from next door. "Shut up," I said again, knowing from the way she spoke it was a part of a poem. "Shut up," I crushed the nightdress back into the overnight bag, "it's only a nightgown!"

When I stop crying I pretend that the nightdress is my mother holding me.

On our second Sunday afternoon I am invited with Bulge and Fluffy Hair and Helen Ferguson and another girl called Amy to explore a place called Harpers Hill. Bulge is particularly shapeless in her Sunday dress. My dress, we have to wear navy-blue serge dresses, is already too tight for me and it is only the second Sunday. Fluffy Hair's dress belongs to her Auntie and has a red lace collar instead of the compulsory white linen one. The collars are supposed to be detachable so that they can be washed.

I wish I could be small and neat and pretty like Amy, or even quick like Helen Ferguson who always knows what's for breakfast the night before. Very quickly she understands the system and knows in advance the times of things, the difference between Morning Meeting and Evening Meeting and where we are supposed to be at certain times, whose turn it is to mop the dormitory, and which nights are bath nights. I do not have this quality of knowing and when I look at Helen Ferguson I wonder why I am made as I am. In class Helen Ferguson has a special way of sitting with one foot slightly in front of the other and she sucks her pen while she is thinking. I try to sit as she does and try to look as if I am thinking while I suck the rounded end of my new pen.

During Morning Meeting I am worrying about the invitation

which seems sinister in some way. It is more like a command from the senior girls. I try and listen to the prayer at the beginning of Meeting. We all have to ask God to be in our hearts. All the time I am thinking of the crossroads where we are supposed to meet for the walk. Bulge does not stop chewing her nails and her fingers all through Meeting. I examine my nails, chew them, and, remembering, sit on my hands.

Between autumn-berried hedges in unscratched shoes and new stockings we wait at the crossroads. The brown plowed fields slope to a new horizon of heavy cloud. There are some farm buildings quite close but no sign of people. The distant throbbing of an invisible tractor and the melancholy cawing of the rooks bring back the sadness and the extraordinary fear of the first Sunday afternoon walk too vividly. I try not to scream as I screamed that day and I try not to think about the longed for streets crowded with people and endlessly noisy with trams. It is empty in the country and our raincoats are too long.

The girl, the straw-colored one they call Etty, comes along the road towards us. She says it's to be a picnic and the others are waiting with the food not far away. She says to follow her. A pleasant surprise, the picnic. She leads us along a little path across some fields to a thicket. We have to bend down to follow the path as it winds between blackberry and under other prickly bushes. Our excited talk is soon silenced as we struggle through a hopeless tangle of thorns and bramble. Amy says she thinks we should turn back. Bulge has the most awful scratches on her forehead. Amy says, "Look, her head's bleeding." But Etty says no we shall soon get through to the place.

Suddenly we emerge high up on the edge of a sandy cliff. "It's a landslide!" I say and, frightened, I try to move away from the edge. Before we have time to turn back the girls, who have been hiding, rush out and grab us by the arms and legs. They tie us up with our own scarves and raincoat belts and push us over the edge and down the steep rough walls of the quarry. I am too frightened to cry out or to resist. Bulge fights and screams in a strange voice quite unlike any voice I have ever heard. Four big girls have her by the arms and legs. They pull her knickers off as she rolls over kicking. Her lumpy white thighs show above the tops of her brown woolen stockings.

"Not this man but Barabbas! Not this man but Barabbas!" they shout. "She's got pockets in her knickers! Pockets in her knickers!" The horrible chant is all round Bulge as she lies howling.

As quickly as the big girls appeared they are gone. We, none of us, try to do anything to help Bulge as we struggle free from the knotted belts and scarves. Helen Ferguson and Amy lead the way back as we try to find the road. Though we examine, exclaiming, our torn clothes and show each other our scratches and bruises the real hurt is something we cannot speak about. Fluffy Hair cries. Bulge, who has stopped crying, lumbers along with her head down. Amy, who does not cry, is very red. She declares she will report the incident. "That's a bit too daring," I say, hoping that she will do as she says. I am wondering if Bulge is still without her knickers.

"There's Etty and some of them," Helen Ferguson says as we approach the crossroads. It has started to rain. Huddled against the rain we walk slowly on towards them.

"Hurry up you lot!" Etty calls in ringing tones. "We're getting wet." She indicates the girls sheltering under the red-berried hawthorn.

"I suppose you know," Etty says, "Harpers Hill is absolutely out of bounds. So you'd better not tell. If you get the whole school gated it'll be the worse for you!" She rejoins the others who stand watching us as we walk by.

"That was only a rag. We were only ragging you," Etty calls, "so mind you don't get the whole school gated!" Glistening water drops fly from the wet hedge as the girls leap out, one after the other, across the soaked grass of the ditch. They race ahead screaming with laughter. Their laughter continues long after they are out of sight.

In Evening Meeting Bulge cannot stop crying and she has no handkerchief. Helen Ferguson, sitting next to me on the other side, nudges me and grins, making grimaces of disgust, nodding in the direction of Bulge and we both shake with simulated mirth, making, at the same time, a pretense of trying to suppress it. Without any sound Bulge draws breath and weeps, her eyes and nose running into her thick fingers. I lean away from her heaving body. I can see her grazed knees because both her stockings have huge holes in them.

Before Meeting, while we were in line while two seniors were practicing Bach, a duet on the common-room piano, Bulge turned up the hem of her Sunday dress to show me a large three-cornered tear. It is a hedge tear she told me then while the hammered Bach fell about our ears. And it will be impossible, when it is mended, she said, for her mother to lengthen the dress.

I give another hardly visible but exaggerated shiver of mirth and pretend, as Helen Ferguson is doing, to look serious and attentive as if being thoughtful and as if listening with understanding to the reading. The seniors read in turn, a different one every Sunday. It is Etty's turn to read. She reads in a clear voice. She has been practicing her reading for some days.

"Romans chapter nine, verse twenty-one." Her Sunday dress is well pressed and the white collar sparkles round her pretty neck.

> *Hath not the potter power*
> *over the clay, of the same lump*
> *to make one vessel unto honor*
> *and another unto dishonor?*

"And from verse twenty." Etty looks up smiling and lisping just a little,

> *Shall the thing formed say to*
> *him that formed it, Why hast*
> *thou made me thus?*

Etty minces from the platform where the staff sit in a semi-circle. She walks demurely back to her seat.

"These two verses," Miss Vanburgh gets up and puts both

hands on the lectern, it is her turn to give the Address, "These two verses," she says, "are sometimes run together."

"Shall the clay say to the potter why hast thou made me thus . . ."

Bulge is still weeping.

Miss Besser, on tiptoe across the creaking boards of the platform, creeps down, bending double between the rows of chairs, and, leaning over, whispers to me to take Muriel.

"Take your friend out of Meeting, take her to . . ."

"I don't know her. She isn't my friend," I begin to say in a whisper, trying to explain, "she's not my friend . . ."

"To Matron," Miss Besser says in a low voice, "take Muriel."

I get up and go out with Bulge who falls over her own feet and, kicking the chair legs, makes a noise which draws attention to our attempted silent movement.

I know it is the custom for the one who leads the other to put an arm of care and protection round the shoulders of distress. I know this already after two weeks. It is not because I do not know . . .

I wait with Bulge in the little porch outside Matron's cottage. Bulge does not look at me with her face, only with her round and shaking shoulders.

Matron, when she comes, gives Bulge a handkerchief and reaches for the iodine. "A hot bath," she says to Bulge, "and early bed. I'll have some hot milk sent up. Be quick," Matron adds, "and don't use up too much hot water. Hot milk," she says, "in half an hour."

I do not go back into Meeting. Instead I stand for a time in a place where nobody comes, between the cloakroom and the bootroom. It is a sort of passage which does not lead anywhere. I think of Bulge lying back if only for a few minutes in the lovely hot water. I feel cold. Half an hour, that is the time Matron has allowed Bulge. Perhaps, if I am quick . . .

The lights are out in our dormitory. I am nice and warm. In spite of the quick and secret bath (it is not my night), and the glass of hot milk—because of my bed being nearer the door the maid brings it to me by mistake—(it has been sweetened generously with honey) in spite of all this I keep longing for the cherishing words familiar in childhood. Because of the terrible hedge tear in the navy-blue hem and, because of the lumpy shoulders, I crouch under my bedclothes unable to stop seeing the shoulders without an arm round them. I am not able to weep as Bulge weeps. My tears will not come to wash away, for me, her shoulders.

At night we always hear the seniors, Etty in particular, singing in the bathroom. Two of them, tonight, may have to miss their baths. Etty's voice is especially noticeable this night.

> *little man you're crying,* she sings,
> *little man you're blue*
> *I know why you're crying*
> *I know why you're blue*
> *Some-one stole your Kiddi-Kar away from you*

The moon, my father's moon, is too far away.

Recha

∝

The constant sound of television might be for a great many people what a mountain stream was to Wordsworth. Instead of these I have the sound of doves.

There are times during these golden afternoons when I know that I am not hearing the doves. It seems impossible that I should not hear them when they sidle to and fro, back and forth, along the edge of the roof above my window, endlessly scraping and tapping and rustling along the tremulous gutters. If I do hear them it is only because I hear them all the time, even when they are not there. Their voices are like the voices of a family, heard still even though this family has ceased to exist.

The little guest, on heat, I remember quite clearly, all those years ago, replete with more than food, stuffed, they would say now, took away with her my silk frock and the Swiss cotton embroidered pillow-slips with which my mother, to honor and please a visitor rather than to offer mere shelter to a homeless refugee, had made the bed.

She, the little guest, tipping forward on high heels, walks to and fro on the kitchen floor busily scraping left-over morsels of food on to saucers. Scraps of fried bread and bits of chopped-up liver. She carries them one by one to the pantry shelf. As she walks she lets slip from her person little swabs of bloodstained cotton wool. These catch on her heels and are trodden, back and forth, mottling the tiles as if with squashed strawberries.

"It is as if she is in heat," my mother says.

"The expression, this expression," my father corrects gently, "is not, as a rule in English, applied to a human being."

"Bloodstain," my mother complains, "everywhere a bloodstain. Look! Wherever she goes. People, when they grow up, should be able to look after themselves. They should be able to look after their *monatsfluss.*"

Later my mother comes to me.

"Lend Recha your dress, the new one," she says, persuading. "Lend her the new dress, the one with the little blue flowers."

"The one with the forget-me-not flowers? But it's my Liberty silk. It's my good dress. I haven't worn it yet."

"Yes. Yes. I know but Recha has an interview. She has to go for an interview. You know, she might find for herself a post as a housekeeper. She has no home now. She must find herself a home. We must help her."

"But she's not my size. The skirt will be much too long."

"I know this. We can gather it up at the waist. You understand. With a nice sash. You have some ribbon . . ."

"Why hasn't she got a home then? A house. She's here now in England. She's got a husband. An English soldier, isn't he? He was here with her, in my room, in my bed. Why can't she go? With him? She's safe now."

"He is in a camp," my mother explains. "I don't need to tell you. She has to find somewhere to live. He has to go back to Salisbury, to his camp."

"But he must have a family, her mother-in-law why can't she . . . ? "

"Be quiet now," my mother says quickly, "she is coming downstairs again."

Recha stands in front of the long mirror in my mother's bedroom twitching the soft folds of my dress over her plump body. She pulls at her black hair frizzing it out on her forehead. Her cheeks are red and shine as if about to burst.

"Senk you," she says to me. I have never seen her before. She is already, with her husband, in my room when I come home from school for the summer holiday. My sister tells me straight away that there are people in my room. It is her room too. She has a bed in our mother's room. She tells me that for ages now people have been arriving, sometimes on the night train from London, arriving and going to bed at once, sleeping and sleeping and then talking in whispers and crying.

"The crying is the worst," she says. She says she heard one woman crying all night. Even our father was not able to stop her crying.

"He walks to the station in the night," my sister says. She says that he has given away his winter coat and that it's all right for now but what will he do in winter.

"These people," my mother says, "they have nothing. Recha must have packed the things in her luggage with her rags and bits of cotton wool." She explains the treachery in her soft up-and-down voice. "Perhaps she thought they were gifts from us." Her voice is like a stream running. "The time!" she says to my father, "it's time for you to leave for the station. Look!" she says, "Look at the time!"

Two more people are arriving. They will have our bedroom. My sister and I move our bedclothes once more.

"The oil-cloth on here is so thin the horsehair's prickling through," I complain to my sister.

"I'll have the sofa then," she says. "I'll sleep there."

"Oh no. It's all right." We slide off the sofa laughing as we did when we were little. One of our old games.

I am ashamed because I have been robbed. This is the strange thing about it. When one is robbed there is this feeling of being ashamed. I do not want to admit to anyone that my silk frock has been stolen. And, even more, I do not want my father and mother to admit that they have been deceived in any way. Especially by people they are trying to help, and in their own house.

But of course they do not even think they have been deceived or robbed.

"Recha," my mother is saying to my father in the kitchen, "Recha has never done any housework or cooking in her life. How will she manage as housekeeper? She has such beautiful hands."

Simply, my mother and father are seeing impossible suffering, especially people being separated from each other or making hurried marriages in order to escape from something they are not able to endure, something they must, at all costs, get away from.

"It is an irony, is it called irony?" My mother's soft voice reaches the horsehair sofa. She is talking still to my father. "Is it called irony? If it was once a joke," she says, "for a bespectacled shrimp of an intellectual, a Jew, to be an officer in a Red Cossack regiment during the Polish campaign of 1920, is this the same joke, if it can be called a joke, which is being repeated now twenty years later?" I have heard her before talking about these men, the gray beards, she calls them, with their gold-rimmed glasses and flying side curls, desperate to disguise their accents and their hand movements, marching or trying to march, walking on thin bent legs, their narrow shoulders and their intellectual superiority, "bowing," she is saying it again "to the healthy pink flesh of the English Tommies."

My father's voice, like a boulder in a wild mountain stream, interrupts her. I can hear his deep voice soothing.

It is not like my mother to use a word like Tommy. If English people use it they say Our Tommies, Our Boys, not English Tommies. I pull my sheets back over the inadequate horsehair. I think, in the morning, I will correct my mother so that she need not make a mistake of this sort in front of the neighbors.

Bathroom Dance

꼿

When I try on one of the nurse's caps my friend Helen nearly dies.

"Oh!" she cries, "take it off! I'll die! Oh if you could see yourself. Oh!" she screams and Miss Besser looks at me with six years of reproach stored in the look.

We are all sewing Helen's uniform in the Domestic Science room. Three pin-striped dresses with long sleeves, buttoned from the wrist to the elbow, double tucks and innumerable button holes; fourteen white aprons and fourteen little caps which have to be rubbed along the seam with a wet toothbrush before the tapes can be drawn up to make those neat little pleats at the back. Helen looks so sweet in hers. I can't help wishing, when I see myself in the cap, that I am not going to do nursing after all.

Helen ordered her material before persuading me to go to the hospital with her. So, when I order mine it is too late to have my uniform made by the class. It is the end of term, the end of our last year at school. My material is sent home.

Mister Jackson tells us, in the last Sunday evening meeting, that he wants the deepest responsibility for standards and judgments in his pupils, especially those who are about to leave the happy family which is how he likes to think of his school. We must not, he says, believe in doing just what we please. We must always believe in the nourishment of the inner life and in the loving discipline of personal relationships. We must always be concerned with the relentless search for truth at whatever cost to tradition and externals. I leave school carrying his inspiration and his coziness with me. For some reason I keep thinking about and remembering something about the reed bending and surviving and the sturdy oak blown down.

My mother says the stuff is pillow ticking. She feels there is nothing refined about nursing. The arrival of the striped material has upset her. She says she has other things in mind for me, traveling on the continent, Europe, she says, studying art and ancient buildings and music.

"But there's a war on," I say.

"Oh well, after the war."

She can see my mind is made up and she is sad and cross for some days. The parcel, with one corner torn open, lies in the hall. She is comforted by the arrival of a letter from the Matron saying that all probationer nurses are required to bring warm sensible knickers. She feels the Matron must be a very nice person after all and she has my uniform made for me in a shop and pays extra to have it done quickly.

Helen's mother invites me to spend a few days with Helen before we go to St. Cuthberts.

The tiny rooms in Helen's home are full of sunshine. There are bright-yellow curtains gently fluttering at the open windows. The garden is full of summer flowers, roses and lupins and delphiniums, light blue and dark blue. The front of the house is covered with a trellis of flowers, some kind of wisteria which is sweetly fragrant at dusk.

Helen's mother is small and quiet and kind. She is anxious and always concerned. She puts laxatives in the puddings she makes.

I like Helen's house and garden, it is peaceful there and I would like to be there all the time but Helen wants to do other things. She is terribly in love with someone called David. Everything is David these few days. We spend a great deal of time outside a milkbar on the corner near David's house or walking endlessly in the streets where he is likely to go. No one, except me, knows of this great love. Because I am a visitor in the house I try to be agreeable. And I try to make an effort to understand intense looks from Helen, mysterious frowns, raised eyebrows, head shakings or noddings, and flustered alterations about arrangements as well as I can.

"I can't think what is the matter with Helen," Mrs. Ferguson says softly one evening when Helen rushes from the room to answer the telephone in case it should be David. We are putting up the black-out screens which Mrs. Ferguson has made skillfully to go behind the cheerful yellow curtains every night. "I suppose she is excited about her career," she says in her quiet voice, picking up a little table which was in Helen's way.

Everyone is so keen on careers for us. Mister Jackson, at school, was always reading aloud from letters sent by old boys and girls who are having careers, poultry farming, running boys' clubs and digging with the unemployed. He liked the envelopes to match the paper, he said, and sometimes he held up both for us all to see.

Helen is desperate to see David before we leave. We go to all the services at his mother's church and to her Bible class where she makes us hand round plates of rock cakes to the Old Folk between the lantern slides. But there is no David. Helen writes him a postcard with a silly passionate message. During the night she cries and cries and says it is awful being so madly in love and will I pretend I have sent the postcard. Of course I say I won't. Helen begs me, she keeps on begging, saying that she lives in the neighborhood and everyone knows her and will talk about her. She starts to howl and I am afraid Mrs. Ferguson will hear and, in the end, I tell her, "All right, if you really want me to."

In the morning I write another card saying that I am sorry about the stupid card which I have sent and I show it to Helen, saying, "We'll need to wash our hair before we go."

"I'll go up first," she says. While she is in the bathroom using up all the hot water, I add a few words to my postcard, a silly passionate message, and I put Helen's name on it because of being tired and confused with the bad night we had. I go out and post it before she comes down with her hair all done up in a towel, the way she always does.

Mrs. Ferguson comes up to London with us when we set off for St. Cuthberts. Helen has to dash back to the house twice, once for her camera and the second time for her raincoat. I wait with Mrs. Ferguson on the corner and she points out to me the window in the County Hospital where her husband died the year before. Her blue eyes are the saddest eyes I have ever seen. I say I am sorry about Mr. Ferguson's death, but because of the uneasiness of the journey and the place where we are going, I know that I am not really concerned about her sorrow. Ashamed, I turn away from her.

Helen comes rushing up the hill, she has slammed the front door, she says, forgetting that she put the key on the kitchen table and will her mother manage to climb through the pantry window in the dark and whatever are we waiting for when we have only a few minutes to get to the train.

David, unseen, goes about his unseen life in the narrow suburb of little streets and houses. Helen seems to forget him easily, straight away.

Just as we are sitting down to lunch there is an air-raid warning. It is terrible to have to leave the plates of food which have been placed in front of us. Mrs. Ferguson has some paper bags in her handbag.

"Mother! You can't!" Helen's face is red and angry. Mrs. Ferguson, ignoring her, slides the salads and the bread and butter into the bags. We have to stand for two hours in the air-raid shelter. It is very noisy the A.R.P. wardens say and they will not let us leave. It is too crowded for us to eat in there and, in any case, you can't eat when you are frightened.

Later, in the next train, we have to stand all the way because the whole train is filled with the army. Big bodies, big rosy faces, thick rough greatcoats, kitbags, boots, and cigarette smoke wherever we look. We stand swaying in the corridor pressed and squeezed by people passing, still looking for somewhere to sit. We can't eat there either. We throw the sad bags, beetroot soaked, out onto the railway lines.

I feel sick as soon as we go into the main hall at St. Cuthberts. It is the hospital smell and the smell of the bread and butter we try to eat in the nurses' dining room. Helen tries to pour two cups of tea but the tea is all gone. The teapot has a bitter smell of emptiness.

Upstairs in Helen's room on the Peace corridor as it is called because it is over the chapel, we put on our uniforms and she screams with laughter at the sight of me in my cap.

"Oh, you look just like you did at school," she can't stop laughing. How can she laugh like this when we are so late. For wartime security the railway station names have been removed and, though we were counting the stops, we made a mistake and went past our station and had to wait for a bus which would bring us back.

"Lend me a safety pin," I say, "one of my buttons has broken in half." Helen, with a mouthful of hair grips, busy with her own cap, shakes her head. I go back along the corridor to my own room. It is melancholy in there, dark, because a piece of black-out material has been pinned over the window and is only partly looped up. The afternoon sun of autumn is sad too when I peer out of the bit of window and see the long slanting shadows lying across unfamiliar fields and roads leading to unknown places.

My school trunk, in my room before me, is a kind of betrayal. When I open it books and shoes and clothes spill out. Some of my pressed wildflowers have come unstuck and I put them back between the pages remembering the sweet, wet grass near the school where we searched for flowers. I seem to see clearly shining long fingers pulling stalks and holding bunches. Saxifrage, campion, vetch, ragged robin, star of Bethlehem, wild strawberry, and sorrel. Quickly I tidy the flowers—violet, buttercup, King cup, cowslip, coltsfoot, wood anemone, shepherd's purse, lady's slipper, jack-in-the-pulpit, and bryony...

"No Christian names on duty please," staff nurse Sharpe says, so, after six years in the same dormitory, Helen and I make a great effort. Ferguson—Wright, Wright—Ferguson.

"Have you finished with the floor mop—Ferguson?"

"Oh, you have it first—Wright."

"Oh! No! by all means, after you Ferguson."

"No, after you Wright."

Staff nurse Sharpe turns her eyes up to the ceiling so that only the whites show. She puts her watch on the window sill saying, "Quarter of an hour to get those baths, basins, and toilets really clean and the floors done too. So hurry!"

"No Christian names on duty," we remind each other.

We never sleep in our rooms on the Peace corridor. Every night we have to carry our blankets down to the basement where we sleep on straw mattresses. It is supposed to be safe there in air raids. There is no air and the water pipes make noises all night. As soon as I am able to fall asleep Night Sister Bean is banging with the end of her torch saying, "Five-thirty a.m. nurses, five-thirty a.m." And it is time to take up our blankets and carry them back upstairs to our rooms.

I am working with Helen in the children's ward. Because half the hospital is full of soldiers the ward is very crowded. There are sixty children; there is always someone laughing and someone crying. I am too slow. My sleeves are always rolled up when they should be rolled down and buttoned into the cuffs. When my sleeves are down and buttoned it seems they have to be rolled up again at once. I can never remember the names of the children and what they have wrong with them.

The weeks go by and I play my secret game of comparisons as I played it at school. On the Peace corridor are some very pretty nurses. They are always washing each other's hair and hanging their delicate underclothes to dry in the bathroom. In the scented steamy atmosphere I can't help comparing their clothes with mine and their faces and bodies with mine. Every time I am always worse than they are and they all look so much more attractive in their uniforms, especially the cap suits them well. Even their finger nails are better than mine.

"Nurse Wright!" Night Sister Bean calls my name at breakfast.

"Yes Sister." I stand up as I have seen the others do.

"Matron's office nine a.m." she says and goes on calling the register.

I am worried about my appointment with the Matron. Something must be wrong.

"What did Matron want?" Ferguson is waiting for me when I go to the ward to fetch my gas mask and my helmet. I am anxious not to lose these as I am responsible for them and will have to give them back if I leave the hospital or if the war should come to an end.

"What did Matron want?" Ferguson repeats her question, giving me time to think.

"Oh it is nothing much," I reply.

"Oh come on! What did she want you for? Are you in trouble?" she asks hopefully.

"Oh no, it's nothing much at all." I wave my gas mask. "If you must know she wanted to tell me that she is very pleased with my work and she'll be very surprised if I don't win the gold medal." Ferguson stares at me, her mouth wide open, while I collect my clean aprons. She does not notice that one of them is hers. It will give me an extra one for the week. I go to the office to tell the ward sister that I have been transferred to the theater.

Had I the heavens' embroidered cloths,
Enwrought with golden and silver light,

O'Connor, the theater staff nurse, is singing. She has an Irish accent and a mellow voice. I would like to tell her I know this poem too.

The blue and the dim and the dark cloths
Of night and light and the half light,

In the theater they are all intimate. They have well-bred voices and ways of speaking. They look healthy and well poised and behave with the ease of movement and gesture which comes from years of good breeding. They are a little circle in which I am not included. I do not try to be. I wish every day, though, that I could be a part of their reference and their joke.

In a fog of the incomprehensible and the obscure I strive, more stupid than I have ever been in my life, to anticipate the needs of the theater sister whose small, hard eyes glitter at me above her white cotton mask. I rush off for the jaconet.

"Why didn't you look at the table!" I piece together her angry masked hiss as I stand offering a carefully opened and held sterilized drum. One frightened glance at the operating table tells me it is catgut she asked for.

"Boil up the trolley," the careless instruction in the soft Irish voice floats towards me at the end of the long morning. Everything is on the instrument trolley.

"Why ever didn't you put the doctors' soap back on the sink first!" The theater is awash with boiled-over soap suds. Staff nurse O'Connor, lazily amused, is just scornful enough. "And," she says, "what in God's Holy Name is this!" She fishes from the sterilizer a doll-sized jumper. She holds it up in the long-handled forceps. "I see trouble ahead," she warns, "better not let sister see this." It is the chief surgeon's real Jaeger woolen vest. He wears it to operate. He has only two and is very particular about them. I have discovered already that sister is afraid of the chief surgeon, consequently I need to be afraid of her. The smell of boiled soap and wool is terrible and it takes me the whole afternoon to clear up.

Theater sister and staff nurse O'Connor, always in masks, exchange glances of immediate understanding. They, when not in masks, have loud voices and laugh. They talk a great deal about horses and dogs and about Mummy and Daddy. They are quite shameless in all this Mummy and Daddy talk.

The X-ray staff are even more well-bred. They never wear uniform and they sing and laugh and come into the theater in whatever they happen to be wearing—backless dinner dresses, tennis shorts, or their night gowns. All the time they have a sleepy desirable look of mingled charm and efficiency. War-time shortages of chocolate and other food stuffs and restrictions on movement, not going up to London at night for instance, do not seem to affect them. They are always called by pet names, Diamond and Snorter. Diamond is the pretty one, she has a mop of curls and little white teeth in a tiny rosebud mouth. Snorter is horsey. She wears trousers and little yellow waist coats. She always has a cigarette dangling from her bottom lip.

I can't compare myself with these people at all. They never speak to me except to ask me to fetch something. Even Mr. Potter, the anesthetist who seems kind and has a fatherly voice, never looks in my direction. He says, holding out his syringe, "Evipan" or "Pentothal," and talks to the others. Something about his voice, every day, reminds me of a quality in my father's voice; it makes me wish to be back at home. There is something hopeless in being hopeful that one person can actually match and replace another. It is not possible.

Sometimes Mr. Potter tells a joke to the others and I do not know whether I should join in the laugh or not.

I like Snorter's clothes and wish that I had some like them. I possess a three-quarter-length oatmeal coat with padded shoulders and gilt buttons which my mother thinks is elegant and useful as it will go with everything. It is so ugly it does not matter what I wear it with. The blue skirt I have is too long, the material is heavy, it sags and makes me tired.

"Not with brown shoes!" Ferguson shakes her head.

It is my day off and I am in her room. The emptiness of the lonely day stretches ahead of me. It is true that the blue skirt and the brown shoes, they are all I have, do look terrible together.

Ferguson and her new friend, Carson, are going out to meet some soldiers to go on something called a pub crawl. Ferguson, I know, has never had anything stronger than ginger beer to drink in her life. I am watching her get ready. She has frizzed her hair all across her baby round forehead. I can't help admiring her, the blaze of lipstick alters her completely.

Carson comes in balancing on very high-heeled shoes. She has on a halo hat with a cheeky little veil and some bright-pink silk stockings.

"What lovely pink stockings!" I say to please her.

"Salmon, please," Carson says haughtily. Her hair is curled too and she is plastered all over with ornaments, brooches, necklaces, rings, and lipstick, a different color from Ferguson's. Ferguson looks bare and chubby and schoolgirlish next to Carson.

Both of them are about to go when I suddenly feel I can't face the whole day alone.

"It's my day off too," I say, "and I don't know where to go."

Ferguson pauses in the doorway.

"Well, why don't you come with us," Carson says. Both of them look at me.

"The trouble is, Wright," Carson says kindly, "the trouble is that you've got no sex appeal."

After they have gone I sit in Ferguson's room for a long time staring at myself in her mirror to see if it shows badly that I have no sex appeal.

I dream my name is Chevalier and I search for my name on the typed lists on the green baize notice boards. The examination results are out. I search for my name in the middle of the names and only find it later at the top.

My name, not the Chevalier of the dream, but my own name is at the top of the lists when they appear.

I work hard in all my free time at the lecture notes and at the essays "Ward Routine," "Nursing as a Career," "Some Aspects of the History of Nursing," and "The Nurse and Her Patient."

The one on ward routine pleases me most. As I write the essay, the staff and the patients and the wards of St. Cuthberts seem to unfold about me and I begin to understand what I am trying to do in this hospital. I rewrite the essay collecting the complete working of a hospital ward into two sheets of paper. When it is read aloud to the other nurses, Ferguson stares at me and does not take her eyes off me all through the nursing lecture which follows.

I learn every bone and muscle in the body and all the muscle attachments and all the systems of the body. I begin to understand the destruction of disease and the construction of cure. I find I can use phrases suddenly in speech or on paper which give a correct answer. Formulae for digestion or respiration or for the action of drugs. Words and phrases like gaseous interchange and internal combustion roll from my pen and the name at the top of the lists continues to be mine.

"Don't tell me you'll be top in invalid cookery too!" Ferguson says and she reminds me of the white sauce I made at school which was said to have blocked up the drains for two days. She goes on to remind me how my pastry board, put up at the window to dry, was the one which fell on the headmaster's wife while she was weeding in the garden below, breaking her glasses and altering the shape of her nose forever.

My invalid carrot is the prettiest of them all. The examiner gives me the highest mark.

"But it's not even cooked properly!" Ferguson is outraged when she tastes it afterwards. She says the sauce is disgusting.

"Oh well you can't expect the examiner to actually eat all the things she is marking," I say.

Ferguson has indigestion, she is very uncomfortable all evening because, in the greedy big taste, she has nearly the whole carrot.

It is the custom, apparently, at St. Cuthberts to move the nurses from one corridor to another. I am given a large room in a corridor called Industry. It is over the kitchens and is noisy and smells of burning saucepans. This room has a big tall window. I move my bed under the window and, dressed in my school jersey, I lie on the bed for as long as possible to feel the fresh cold air on my face before going down to the basement for the night. Some evenings I fall into a deep and refreshing sleep obediently waking up, when called, to go down to the doubtful safety below.

Every day, after the operations, I go round the theater with a pail of hot soapy water cleaning everything. There is an orderly peacefulness in the quiet white tranquility which seems, every afternoon, to follow the strained, bloodstained mornings.

In my new room I copy out my lecture notes:

... infection follows the line of least resistance ...

and read my school poetry book:

> *Through the thick corn the scarlet poppies peep,*
> *And round green roots and yellowing stalks I see*
> *Pale pink convolvulus in tendrils creep;*
> *And air-swept lindens yield*
> *Their scent ...*

I am not able to put out of my mind the eyes of a man who is asleep but unable to close his eyes. The putrid smell of wounded flesh comes with me to my room and I hear, all the time, the sounds of bone surgery and the troubled respiration which accompanies the lengthy periods of deep anesthetic ...

> *Oft thou hast given them store*
> *Of flowers—the frail leaf'd, white anemony,*
> *Dark blue bells drench'd with dews of summer eves*
> *And purple orchises with spotted leaves ...*

... in the theater recovery ward there are fifteen amputations, seven above the knee and eight below. The beds are made in two halves so that the padded stumps can be watched. Every bed has its own bell and tourniquet ...

St. Cuthberts is only a drop in the ocean; staff nurse O'Connor did not address the remark to me, I overhead it.

Next to my room is a large room which has been converted into a bathroom. The dividing wall is a wooden partition. The water pipes make a lot of noise and people like to sing there, usually something from an opera.

One night I wake from my evening-stolen sleep hearing two voices talking in the bathroom. It is dark in my room; I can see some light from the bathroom through a knot-hole high up in the partition. The voices belong to Diamond and Snorter. This is strange because they live somewhere outside the hospital and would not need to use that bathroom. It is not a comfortable place at all, very cold, with a big old bath awkwardly in the middle of the rough floor.

Diamond and Snorter are singing and making a lot of noise, laughing and shrieking above the rushing water.

Singing:

> *Give me thy hand O Fairest*
> *la la la la la la la*
> *I would and yet I would not*

Laughter and the huge bath obviously being filled to the brim.

> *Our lives would be all pleasure*

> *tra la la la la la la*
> *tra la la la la la la*

> *tum pe te tum*

> *tum pe te tum*

"That was some party was it not!"

"Rather!" Their rich voices richer over the water.

I stand up on my bed and peer through the hole which is about the size of an egg. I have never looked through before, though have heard lots of baths and songs. I have never heard Diamond and Snorter in there before—if it is them.

It is Diamond and Snorter and they are naturally quite naked. There is nothing unusual about their bodies. Their clothes, party clothes, are all in little heaps on the floor. They, the women not the clothes, are holding hands, their arms held up gracefully. They are stepping up towards each other and away again. They have stopped singing and are nodding and smiling and turning to the left and to the right, and, then, with sedate little steps, skipping slowly round and round. It is a dance, a little dance for two people, a minuet, graceful, strange, and remote. In the steam the naked bodies are like a pair of sea birds engaged in mating display. They appear and disappear as if seen through a white sea mist on some far-off shore.

The dance quickens. It is more serious. Each pulls the other more fiercely, letting go suddenly, laughing, and then not laughing. Dancing still, now serious now amusing. To and fro, together, back and forth and together and round and round they skip and dance. Then, all at once, they drop hands and clasp each other close, as if in a private ballroom, and quick step a foxtrot all round the bathroom.

It is not an ugly dance, it is rhythmic and ridiculous. Their thighs and buttocks shake and tremble and Snorter's hair has come undone and is hanging about her large red ears in wispy strands.

The dance over, they climb into the deep hot bath and tenderly wash each other.

The little dance, the bathroom dance, gives me an entirely new outlook. I can't wait to see Diamond and Snorter again. I look at everyone at breakfast, not Ferguson, of course (I know everything there is to know about her life) with a fresh interest.

Later I am standing beside the patient in the anesthetic room, waiting for Mr. Potter, when Snorter comes struggling through the swing doors with her old cricket bag. She flops about the room dragging the bag:

And on the beach undid his corded bales

she says, as she always does, while rummaging in the bag for her white wellington boots. I want to tell Snorter, though I never do, that I too know this poem.

I look hard at Snorter. Even now her hair is not combed

properly. Her theater gown has no tapes at the back so that it hangs, untied and crooked. She only has one boot on when Mr. Potter comes. The unfairness of it all comes over me. Why do I have to be neatly and completely dressed at all times. Why do they not speak to me except to ask for something to be fetched or taken away. Suddenly I say to Snorter, "*Minuet du Salle de la Bain*," in my appalling accent. I am surprised at myself. She is hopping on one foot, a wellington boot in her hand, she stops hopping for a moment.

"*de la salle de bain* surely," she corrects me with a perfect pronunciation and a well-mannered smile. "Also lower case," she says, "not caps, alters the emphasis."

"Oh yes of course," I mutter hastily. An apology.

"Pentothal." Mr. Potter is perched on his stool at the patient's head, his syringe held out vaguely in my direction.

Night Runner

⚭

Night Sister Percy is dying. It is my first night as Night Runner at St. Cuthberts. Night Sister Bean, grumbling and cackling, calls the register and, at the end, she calls my name.

"Nurse Wright."

"Yes Sister," I reply, half rising in my chair as I have seen the others do. The Maids' Dining Room, where we eat, is too cramped to do anything else.

"Night Runner," she says and I sit down again. The thought of being Night Runner is alarming. Nurse Dixon has been Night Runner for a long time. All along I have been hoping that I would escape from these duties and responsibilities, the efficient rushing here and there to relieve on different wards; every night bringing something new and difficult.

The Night Runner has to prepare the night nurses' meal too; one little sitting at twelve midnight and a second one at twelve forty-five and, of course, the clearing up and the washing up.

Every night I admire Nurse Dixon in the tiny cramped kitchen where we sit close together, regardless of rank, in the hot smell of warmed up fish or mince and the noise of the jugs of strong black coffee, keeping hot, in two black pans of boiling water. We eat our meal there in this intimacy with these two hot saucepans splashing and hissing just behind us. The coffee, only a little at the bottom of each jug, looks thick and dark and I wonder how it is made. Tonight I will have to find out and have it ready when the first little group of nurses appears.

When I report to Night Sister Bean in her office, she tells me to go for the oxygen.

"Go up to Isolation for the oxygen," she says without looking up from something she is writing. I am standing in front of her desk. I have never been so close to her before, not in this position, that is, of looking at her from above. She is starch scented, shrouded mysteriously in the daintily severe folds of spotted white gauze. She is a sorceress disguised in the heavenly blue of the Madonna; a shriveled, rustling, aromatic, knowledgeable, Madonna-colored magician; she is a wardress and a keeper. She is an angel in charge of life and in charge of death. Her fine white cap, balancing, nodding, a grotesque blossom flowering for ever in the dark halls of the night, hovers beneath me. She is said to have powers, an enchantment, beyond the powers of an ordinary human. For one thing, she has been on night duty in this hospital for over thirty years. As I stand there I realize that I do not know her at all and that I am afraid of her.

"Well," she says, "don't just stand there. Go up to Isolation for the oxygen and bring it at once to Industry."

"Yes, Sister," I say and I go as quickly as I can. The parts of the hospital are all known by different names; Big Boys, Big Girls, Top Ward, Bottom Ward, Side Ward, and Middle, Industry, Peace, Chapel, and Nursery. I have a room on the Peace corridor, so named because it is above the chapel and next to Matron's wing.

Industry is the part over the kitchens. There are rooms for nurses there too. Quite often there is a pleasant noise and smell of cooking in these rooms. The Nurses' sick bay is there and it is there that I have to take the oxygen.

I am frightened out here.

For one thing, Isolation is never used. It is, as the name suggests, isolated. It is approached by a long, narrow covered way sloping up through a war-troubled shrubbery where all the dust bins are kept. Because of not being able to show any lights it is absolutely dark there. When I go out into the darkness I can smell rotting arms and legs, thrown out of the operating theater and not put properly into the bins. I gather my apron close so that I will not get caught by a protruding maimed hand.

When I flash my torch quickly over the bins I see they are clean and innocent and have their lids firmly pressed on. In the torchlight there is no smell.

The sky at the end of the covered passage is decorated with the pale moving fans of search lights. The beams of light are interwoven with the sounds of throbbing engines. The air-raid warning might sound at any moment. In the emergency of being made Night Runner so suddenly, I have forgotten to bring my tin hat and gas mask from the Maids' Dining Room.

I am worried about the gas mask and the tin hat. I have signed for them on arrival at the hospital and am completely responsible for them. I will have to hand them back if I leave the hospital or if this war comes to an end. Usually I never leave either of them out of my care. I have them tied together with thick string. I put them under my chair at meal times and hang them up in the nurses' cupboard on the ward where I am working.

It is hard to find the oxygen. My torch light picks up stacks of pillows, shelves of gray blankets, rolls of waterproof sheets, and some biscuit tins labeled Emergency Dressings, all with dates on them. There are two tea chests filled with tins and bottles. The chests are marked Emergency, Iron Rations, Doctors Only in red paint. There do not seem to be similar boxes marked for nurses or patients.

At last I find the oxygen cylinder and I rush with the little trolley up to Industry.

Sister Percy is dying. She is the other Night Sister and is very fat. She is propped, gasping, on pillows, a blue trout with eyes bulging, behind the floral screens made by Matron's mother for sick nurses.

It is the first time I have seen someone who is dying. Night Sister Bean is there and the RMO and the Home Sister. They take the oxygen and Sister Bean tells me I need not stay. She pulls the screens closer round Sister Percy.

In the basement of the hospital I set about the secrets of making the coffee and having it come only so far up the jugs.

Later Night Sister Bean comes and says why haven't I lit the gas, which, when you think about it, is a good thing to say as they will surely want that potato and mince stuff hot. Before she leaves she makes me get down on my knees to hunt behind the pipes for cockroaches. She has a steel knitting needle for this and we knock and scrape and rattle about, Night Sister Bean on her knees too, and we chase them out, the revolting things, and sprinkle some white powder which, she says, they love to eat without knowing it is absolutely fatal to them.

It is something special about night duty, this little meal time in the middle of the night, with everyone sitting together, even Night Sister Bean, herself, coming to one or the other of the sittings. She seems almost human, in spite of the mysterious things whispered about her, at these meals. Sometimes she even complains about the sameness of them, saying that one thing the war cannot do is to make these meals worse than they are and that it is sheer drudgery to eat them night after night. When I think about this I realize she has been eating stewed mince and pounded fish for so many years and I can't help wishing I could do something about it.

This first night it takes me a long time to clear up in the little pantry. When at last I am finished Night Sister Bean sends me to relieve on Bottom Ward. There is a spinal operation in the theater recovery room just now, she says, and a spare nurse will be needed when the patient comes back to the ward.

On my way to Bottom Ward I wish I could be working with staff nurse Ramsden.

"I will play something for you," she said to me once when I was alone and filled with tears in the bleak, unused room which is the nurses' sitting room.

She ran her fingers up and down the piano keys. "This is Mussorgsky," she said. "It's called Gopak, a kind of little dance," she explained. She played and turned her head towards me nodding and smiling. "Do you like this?" she asked, her eyes smiling. It is not everyone who has had Mussorgsky played for them; the thought gives me courage as I hurry along the unlit passage to the ward.

There is a circle of light from the uncurtained windows of the office in the middle of the ward. I can see a devout head bent over the desk in the office. I feel I am looking at an Angel of mercy who is sitting quietly there ready to minister to the helpless patients.

Staff nurse Sharpe is seated in the office with an army blanket tucked discreetly over her petticoat. Her uniform dress lies across her lap. She explains that she is just taking up the hem and will I go to the kitchen and cut the bread and butter. As I pass the linen cupboard I see the other night nurse curled up in a heap of blankets. She is asleep. This is my friend Ferguson.

I sink slowly into the bread cutting. It is a quiet and leisurely task. While I cut and spread I eat a lot of the soft new bread and I wonder how Sharpe will manage to wear her uniform shortened. Matron is so particular that we wear them long, ten inches off the ground, so that the soldiers do not get in a heightened excitement about us.

Sharpe comes in quite soon. She seems annoyed that I have not finished. She puts her watch on the table and says the whole lot, breakfast trays all polished and set, and bread and butter for sixty men, must be finished in a quarter of an hour. I really hurry up after this and am just ready when the operation case comes back and I have to go and sit by him in the small ward. I hope to see Ferguson but staff nurse Sharpe has sent her round changing the water jugs.

Easily I slip into my dream of Ferguson. She owes me six and sevenpence. I have written it on the back of my writing pad. I'll go out with her and borrow two and six.

"Oh Lord!" I'll say, "it's my mother's birthday and I haven't a thing for her and here I am without my purse. Say, can you lend me two and six?" And then I'll let her buy a coffee and a bun for me that will bring it to three shillings and I won't ever pay it back and, in that way, will recover some of the six and sevenpence.

"Cross my heart, cut me in two if my word is not true," I say to myself and I resolve to sit in Ferguson's room as soon as I am off duty. I'll sit there till she pays me the money. I'll just sit and sit there till it dawns on her why I am there.

The patient, quite still as if dead, suddenly moves and helps himself to a drink of water. He vomits and flings the bowl across the room. He seems to be coming round from his anesthetic. I grope under the bedclothes. I should count his pulse but I am unable to find his wrist.

"Oh I can't," he groans, "not now I can't."

He seems to be in plaster of paris from head to foot. He groans again and sleeps. Nervously I wait to try again to find some place on his body where I can feel his pulse.

High on the wall in the Maids' Dining Room is an ancient wireless. It splutters and gargles all day with the tinny music of workers' play time and Vera Lynn plaintively announcing there'll always be an England. Sometimes in the early mornings, while we have our dinner, the music is of a different kind. Sometimes it is majestic, lofty, and sustaining.

"Wright!" Staff nurse Ramsden calls across the crowded tables. "Mock Morris? Would you say?" she waves a long-fingered hand.

"No," I shake my head, "not Mock Morris, it's Beethoven." She laughs. She knows it is not Beethoven. It is a little joke we have come to share. It is the only joke I have with anyone. Perhaps it is the same for Ramsden. She has a slight mustache and I have noticed, in her room, an odor, a heaviness which belongs with older women perhaps from the perfumed soap she has and the material of well-made underwear. Her shoes and stockings, her suits and blouses and hats have the fragrance of being of a better quality. Ramsden asked me once about the violin I was carrying. She has said to me to choose one of her books, she has several in her room, as a present from her to me. Secretly I think, every day, that I admire Ramsden. I love her. Perhaps. I think, I will tell her, one day, the truth about the violin case.

A special quality about working during the night is the stepping out of doors in the mornings, the first feeling of the fresh air and the sun which is hardly warm in its brightness.

We ride our bicycles. Not Ramsden. There is a towing patch along the river. I, not knowing it before, like the smell of the river, the muddy banks, and the cattle-trodden grass. Water birds, disturbed, rise noisily. Our own voices echo.

Though we have had our meal we want breakfast. Ferguson hasn't any money. Neither has Queen. Ferguson says she will owe Queen if Queen will owe me for them both. We agree and I pay. And all the way back I am trying to work out what has to be added to the outstanding six and sevenpence.

Ferguson's room, when I go to sit there, looks as if it should be roped off as a bomb crater. Her clothes, and some of mine, are scattered everywhere. There is a note from the Home Sister on her dusty dressing table. I read the note, it is to tell Ferguson to clean her hair brush.

Bored and sleepy I study the note repeatedly, and add "Neither a Borrower nor a Lender be" in handwriting so like the Home Sister's it takes my breath away.

I search for Ferguson's writing paper. It is of superior quality and very suitable. I write some little notes in this newly learned handwriting and put them carefully in my pocket. I continue to wait for Ferguson, hardly able to keep my eyes open.

I might have missed my sleep altogether if I had not remembered in time that Ferguson has gone home for her nights off.

I do not flash the torch for fear of being seen. I grope in the dark fishing for something, anything, in the cavernous tea chest, and hasten back down the covered way.

Night Sister Bean says to me to go to Bottom Ward to relieve and I say, "Yes Sister," and leave her office backwards, shuffling my feet and bending as if bowing slightly, my hands, behind my back, clasping and almost dropping an enormous glass jar.

It is bottled Chinese gooseberries, of all things, and I put one on each of the baked apples, splashing the spicy syrup generously. Night Sister Bean smiles, crackling starch, and says the baked apples have a piquant flavor. She has not had such a delicious baked apple for thirty years. "Piquant!" she says.

Staff nurse Sharpe sits in the office all night with nursing auxiliary Queen. Queen has put operation stockings over her shoes to keep warm. Both Sharpe and Queen are wrapped up in army blankets. Sharpe has to let down the hem of her dress. Sister Bean asked her to stay behind at breakfast.

Whenever I come back to the office Sharpe says, "Take these pills to bed twelve" or "Get the lavatories cleaned," and "Time to do the bread and butter—and don't leave the trays smeary like last night."

At the end of the ward I pull out the laundry baskets and I move the empty oxygen cylinders and the fire equipment; the buckets of water and sand. I simply move them all out from their normal places, just a little way out, and later, when Sharpe and Queen go along to the lavatory, they fall over these things and knock into each other, making the biggest disturbance ever heard in a hospital at night. Night Sister Bean comes rushing all the way up from her office in the main hall. She is furious and tells Sharpe and Queen to report to Matron at nine a.m. She can see that I am busy, quietly with my little torch, up the other end of the ward, pouring the fragrant mouth wash in readiness for the morning.

The tomato sauce has endless possibilities. The dressed crab is in such a small quantity that the only thing I can do is to put a tiny spoonful on top of the helpings of mashed potato. Night Sister Bean is appreciative and says the flavor seeps right through. Tinned bilberries, celery soup, and custard powder come readily to my experienced hands.

I do not see staff nurse Ramsden very often. She has not asked me in to her room again to choose the book. Perhaps she has changed her mind. She is, after all, senior to me.

There are times when an unutterable loneliness is the only

company in the cold early morning. The bicycle rides across the heath or along the river are over too quickly and, because of this, are meaningless. With a sense of inexplicable bereavement my free time seems to stretch ahead in emptiness. I go to bed too soon and sleep badly.

I am glad when Ferguson comes back; very pleased. In the pantry I am opening a big tin, the biggest thing I have managed to lift out so far. I say "Hallo" to Ferguson as she sits down with the other nurses; they talk and laugh together. I go on with my work.

"Oh, you've got IT," I say to Ferguson. "Plenty of S.A. Know what that is? Sex appeal, it's written all over you." And seeing, out of the corner of my eye, Night Sister Bean coming in, I go on talking as if I haven't seen her.

"How you do it beats me Fergie," I say. "How is it you have all the men talking about you the way they do? You certainly must have given them plenty to think about. They all adore you. Corporal Smith's absolutely mad about you, really!" Unconcernedly I scrape scrape at the tin. "He never slept last night. Sharpe had to slip him a Mickey Finn, just a quick one. He's waiting for another letter from you and I think he's sending the poem you asked for. Who on earth is your go between?" so I go on and scrape scrape at the tin.

I know why there is silence behind me. I turn round.

"Oh, here you are at last Sister," I say to Night Sister Bean. Ferguson is a dull red color, pity, as she was looking so well after her nights off.

"Here we are Sister," I say, "on the menu we have Pheasant Wing in Aspic. Will you have the fish pie with it?" I serve all the plates in turn. The coffee hisses and spits behind us.

"Matron's office, nine o'clock," Nigh Sister Bean says to Ferguson.

"Yes, Sister."

Ferguson is sent to Big Girls for the rest of the night and I am to relieve, as usual, on Bottom Ward. I wake Corporal Smith at four a.m. and urge him to write to Nurse Ferguson. "Every day she waits for a letter," I tell him, "she'll get ill from not eating if you don't write." Staff nurse Sharpe finds me by his bed and sends me to scrub the bathroom walls.

"And do out all the cupboards too, and quickly," she says.

In the morning when I see Sharpe safely in the queue for letters I rush up to the Peace corridor and find her room. I cram her curtains into her messy wet soap dish and leave one of my neatly folded notes on her dressing table.

Do not let your curtains dangle in the soap dish. Sister.

There is not much I can do with cherry jam. I serve it with the stewed mince as a sweet and sour sauce. It is a favorite with the Royal family, I tell them, but I can see I shall have to risk another raid on my secret store.

The next night I have a good dig into both chests and load myself up with tinned tomato soup, a tinned chicken, some sardines, and two tins of pears.

Nurse Dixon is mystified. Her eyes are full of questions.

"Where d'you get all . . ." her lips form whispered words.

"No time to chat now, sorry," I say. I am hastily setting a little tray for Night Sister Bean. I have started taking an extra cup of coffee along to her office. It seems the best way to use up a tin of shortbread fingers. Balancing my tray I race up the dark stairs and along the passage to Night Sister Bean's office.

"Bottom Ward," Night Sister Bean says without looking up. Again I am at the mercy of Sharpe.

"Wash down the kitchen walls," she says, "and do all the shelves and cupboards and quickly—before you start the blanket baths." She gives me a list of the more disagreeable men to do; she says to change their bottom sheets too. All the hardest work while nursing auxiliary Queen, who is back there, and herself sit wrapped up in the office, smoking, with a pot of hot coffee between them on the desk.

I go into the small ward and give the emergency bell there three rings bringing Night Sister Bean to the ward before Sharpe and Queen realize what is happening.

"Is it an air raid?" Queen asks anxiously.

"Nurses should know why they ring, Nurse," Sister Bean says and she makes them take her round to every bed whispering the diagnosis and treatment of every patient. Night Sister Bean rustling and croaking, fidgeting and cursing, disturbs all the men trying to find out who rang three times.

"Someone must be hemorrhaging," she says, "find out who it is."

Peering maliciously into the kitchen, Sister Bean sees me quietly up the step ladder with my little pail of soapy water. The wet walls gleam primrose yellow as if they have been freshly painted. She tells Sharpe and Queen to report to Matron's office nine a.m. for smoking on duty.

Once again Sharpe is in the letter queue. I take the loaded ash tray from the Porters' Lodge and spill it all over her room.

Your room is disgusting. Take some hot water and disinfectant and wash down, Sister.

The folded note lies neatly on her dressing table.

I try listening to Beethoven but it reminds me of my loneliness. I wish Corporal Smith would write to me. I wish someone would write to me. Ferguson is going to The Old Green Room for coffee. She is popular, always going out.

In my room I have a list.

1. Listen to Beethoven.
2. Keep window wide open. If cold sleep in school jersey.
3. Ride bicycle for complexion. (care of)
4. Write and Think.

"I can't come out," I say to Ferguson. "I'm listening to Beethoven," I say, ignoring the fact that she has not asked me.

"It's only one record," she says, "you've only got one record."

"It's Beethoven all the same." I beat time delicately and wear my far away look.

Ferguson goes off out and I add number 5 with difficulty to

the list. The paper is stuck in at the side of the dressing-table mirror and uneven to write on.

5. Divide N.S.B.'s nature and discover exactly the extent of her powers.

I take my white windsor, bath size, to the wash room and fill a basin with hot water to soften the soap. I set to work with my nail file and scissors. I'll take my torch tonight, I'm thinking, a tin of powdered milk would be useful. Whipped up, it makes very good cream; delicious with the baked apples.

The likeness is surprising. It is the distinction of the shape and the tilt of the cap, the little figure is emerging perfectly. I work patiently for a long time. I am going to split the image in half very carefully and torture one half keeping the other half as a control, as in a scientific experiment, and observe the effect on the living person.

The idea is so tremendous I feel faint. Already I foresee results, the upright, crisp little blue and white Bean totters in the passage, she wilts and calls for help.

"Nurse Wright! Help me up, dear. What a good child you are, so gentle too. Just help me to that chair, thank you, dear child. Thank you!"

The Peace corridor is very quiet. Another good thing about the night duty is that we all may sleep in our beds during the day. Every morning I long for this sleep. Up until this time, I, like the others, have had to carry bedclothes down to the basement every night because of the air raids. There are no beds in the basement, only some sack mattresses of straw. There is no air there either.

I love the smell of the clean white windsor. I am sculpting carefully with the file. The likeness is indeed perfect. My hands are slippery and wrinkled and I am unable to stop them from shaking. I feel suddenly that I possess some hitherto unknown but vital power to be able to make this—this effigy.

And then, all at once, Night Sister Bean is there in the door-way of the wash room, peering about to see who it is not in bed yet and it is after twelve noon already. Because I am thinking of the moment when I will split the image and considering which tool will be most suitable for this, the sudden appearance of Sister Bean is, to say the least, confusing.

I plunge my head into the basin together with Her I am so carefully fashioning, saying, "Oh, I can never get the soap out of my hair!," delighted at the sound of weariness achieved.

She says to remember always to have the rinsing water hotter than the washing water. "Hot as you can bear it," she says.

"Thank you Sister."

She is rustling and cackling, crackling and disturbing, checking every corner of the wash room, quickly looking into all the lavatories, saying as she leaves, "And it is better to take off your cap first."

So there I am with the soaked limp thing, frothed and scummed all over with the white windsor, on my head, still secure with an iron foundry of hair grips and useless for tonight. My work of art too is ruined, the outlines blurred and destroyed before being finished. It is a solemn moment of understanding that from a remote spot, namely the door, she has been able to spoil what I have made and add a further destruction of her own, my cap.

My back aches with bending over the stupid little sink. These days I am missing too much sleep. In spite of being so tired I go down to the ramp where the milk churns are loaded and unloaded. It is the meeting place of the inside of the hospital with the outside world. The clean laundry boxes are there, neatly stacked. Fortunately Ferguson's box is near the edge. I open it and remove one of her fresh clean caps. My box is there too but I don't want to take one of mine as it will leave me short later in the week.

The powdered household milk is in the chest as I hoped, tins of it and real coffee too. I find more soup, mushroom, cream of asparagus, cream of chicken, vegetable, and minestrone. I am quite reckless with my torch. Christmas is coming, I take a little hoard of interesting tins.

I discover that Night Sister Bean has a weakness for hot broth and I try, every night, to slip a cup along to her office in the early part of the night before I start on anything else.

Several things are on my mind, mostly small affairs. For some time I have Corporal Smith's love letter to Ferguson, sixteen pages, in my pocket. It is not sealed and her name does not appear anywhere in the letter. It is too long for one person so I divide the letter in half and address two envelopes in Corporal Smith's handwriting, one to Sharpe and one to Ferguson. Accidentally I drop them, unsealed, one by the desk in Night Sister Bean's office and the other in the little hall outside Matron's room. We are not supposed to be intimate with the male patients and I feel certain too that Corporal Smith is a married man, but there is something else on my mind; it is whether a nurse should send a Christmas card to the Matron. It is something entirely beyond my experience.

In the end I buy one, a big expensive card, a Dutch Interior. It costs one and ninepence. I sit a whole morning over it trying to think what I should write.

A very Happy Christmas to Matron from Nurse Wright
Nurse Wright sounds presumptuous. I haven't taken an external exam yet. She may not regard me as nurse.

A very Happy Event . . . that would be quite wrong.

A very Happy Christmas to You from Guess Who. She might think that silly.

Happy Christmas. Vera. Too familiar. *Veronica.* I have never liked my name.

A Happy Christmas to Matron from one of her staff and in very small writing underneath *N/V Wright.*

I keep wondering if all the others will send Matron a Christmas card. It is hardly a thing you can ask anyone. Besides I do not want, particularly to give Ferguson the idea. She will never think of it herself. And who can I ask if I don't ask her?

I put the card in Matron's correspondence pigeon hole. The card is so big it has to be bent over at the top to fit in. I am nervous in case someone passing will see me.

Again I am relieving on Bottom Ward. Always it is this Bottom Ward. This time I have to creep round cleaning all the bed wheels.

"And quietly," Sharpe says, "Nurse Queen and I don't want everyone waking up!"

The card worries me. I will take it out in the morning. The message is all wrong.

One of her staff! I can't bear to think about it.

The card is still there, bending, apologizing, and self conscious in the morning. I want to remove it but there are people about and correspondence must not be tampered with.

Twice during the day I get dressed and creep down from the Peace corridor, pale, hollow-eyed, and drab, all night nurses are completely out of place in the afternoons. I feel conspicuous, sick nearly, standing about in the hall waiting to be alone there so that I can remove that vulgar card and its silly message. It is still bending there in the narrow compartment.

Even when the hall is free of people there are two nurses chattering together by the main door. Whyever do they stand in this cold place to talk? I have to give up and go back to bed, much too cold to sleep. Ferguson has my hot-water bottle for her toothache. It seems I can never get even with her. Never ever.

The card is still there in the evening when we go down to the Maids' Dining Room for breakfast. I can hardly eat as I am thinking of a plot to retrieve the card.

The register is finished.

"Nurse Wright."

"Yes Sister?" half rising in my chair as we all do in that cramped place.

"Matron's office nine a.m. tomorrow."

"Yes Sister," I sit down again. It can't be to thank me for the card as it hasn't been received yet. A number of reasons come to mind, for one thing there are the two deep caves of dark emptiness; perhaps they have been discovered . . .

In spite of a sense of foreboding I go, with my little torch hidden beneath my apron, up the long covered way. I need more powdered milk. The path seems endless. The night sky has the same ominous decoration; throbbing engines alternate with sharp anti-aircraft guns and the air-raid sirens wail up and down, up and down. The soft searchlights move slowly. They make no noise and are helpless. I feel exposed and push my hands round the emptiness of the nearest tea chest. Grabbing a tin of powdered milk I rush back down past the festering bins and on down towards an eternity of the unknown.

I have a corner seat in this train by a mistake which is not entirely my fault. The woman, who is in this seat, asks me if I think she has time to fetch herself a cup of tea. I can see that she badly wants to do this and, in order that she does not have to go without the tea, I agree that, though she will be cutting it fine, there is a chance that she will have time. So she goes and I see her just emerging from the refreshment room with a look on her face which shows how she feels. She has her tea clutched in one hand and I have her reserved seat because it is silly, now that the train has started, to stand in the corridor being crushed by army greatcoats and kitbags and boots, simply looking at the emptiness of this comfortable corner.

I have some household milk for Mother, it is always useful in these days of rationing. I have the tinned chicken also. At the last minute I could not think what to do with it as Night Sister Bean will not be naming the next Night Runner till this evening, and, of course, I shall not be there to know who it is and so am not able to hand on either the milk or the chicken.

There is too the chance that the new Night Runner might be my friend Ferguson. It would not do to give her these advantages.

This is my first holiday from St. Cuthberts, my nights off and ten days holiday. Thirteen days off.

"Shall I take my tin hat, I mean my helmet, and my gas mask?" I ask Matron.

"By all means if you would like to," she says and wishes me a pleasant holiday and a happy Christmas.

The tin hat and the gas mask are tied to my suitcase. My little sister will be interested to see them.

My father will be pleased with his Christmas card. He has always liked the detail and the warm colors of a Dutch Interior. He will not mind the crossing out inside. The card will flatten if I press it tonight in the dictionary.

For some reason I am thinking about staff nurse Ramsden. Last night, in the doorway of the Maids' Dining Room, I stood aside to let her go in first.

"Thank you," she said and then she asked me what my first name was.

"First name?"

"Yes, your Christian name, what is it?" her voice, usually low, was even lower. Like a kind of shyness.

I did not have the chance to answer. We had to squeeze through to our different tables quickly as Night Sister Bean was already calling the register.

If Ramsden could be on the platform to meet my train at the end of this journey I would be able to answer her question. Perhaps I would be able to explain to her about the violin case. I would like to see Ramsden, I would like to be going to her. Thinking about her and seeing her face, in my mind, when she turned to smile at me, the time when she played Mussorgsky on the piano in the nurses' sitting room, makes me think that it is very probable, though no one has ever spoken about it, that Night Sister Bean might very well be missing her life-long friend Night Sister Percy. Missing her intolerably.

Lois

This is a piano concerto, Lois. Lois, listen! Listen to the way the piano rushes in. It's the Emperor Concerto, Lois. It's not really hard to listen to, is it? Is it? But Lois, wait. Listen. All the same. Listen to this.

Ashes of Roses, the perfume is called that. No, not perfume really, Lois. It's only scent. Little bottle of scent to take to boarding school. Ashes of Roses to bring to the hospital.

Lois, you'll never believe this. I was so unhappy at boarding school to begin with. My mother put scent on my handkerchief for me to take back and hold when I went to sleep.

Silly but it's real. Lois, you like the scent, do you? You did say you liked the scent. You told me you liked the fragrance. You smell nice, you said that to me once. It's Ashes of Roses. I told you, it's the Ashes of Roses.

Tango Bolero now. Not the Emperor. The Tango. I'm glad you asked to share with me Lois when we had the chance to change.

From this high window the world is out there. The trees. You could paint the trees, Lois. The park is over to the right and on this side there's the railway and the canal. Did you notice this evening, Lois, how the water shines as the rest of the world gets dark? And last week, Lois, did you see that, in the moonlight, the water shines all night? Did you see that? Can't put a black-out curtain over the canal, can you? All those places out there, the buildings, the warehouses, and the railway and the dark streets. All dark, in darkness. People inside those houses don't know who can see their upstairs windows and their roof tops.

Tango. Tango Bolero. Lois. Listen! Someone's coming!

"What is that noise? Nurse? Whatever is that terrible noise?"

"It's music, Sister. It's the Tango Bolero."

"Tango. Fango. Turn it off this instant! I never heard such a noise in all my life. Do you know what time it is?"

"No Sister. Sorry Sister."

"It's practically midnight! Where is the music? For heavens sake. Where is it coming from?"

"It's in the wardrobe, Sister, I'll turn it off."

"And Nurse! Where is your nightdress? You've got nothing on! Why haven't you got your nightdress on?"

"I, er, I was too hot Sister."

"Well child! For heavens sake open the window. And put the black-out back. If you're careful, slip your hand behind the curtain, put a book or something to hold the curtain down."

"Yes Sister. Thank you Sister."

"Why aren't you on duty Nurse?"

"We're, I mean, I'm on nights off Sister."

"I see. Nurse! I never saw, in my life, such an untidy room. Your room is a disgrace and the beds! Is that your pillow? Pull the pillow out and put it back where it belongs. And try to remember that others want and need their sleep. And another thing, Nurse, it is not healthy to sleep without your gown. See that you put it on at once."

"Yes Sister. Thank you Sister."

"Has she gone? The old witch?"

"Yes. That was close. Yes, she's gone."

"I was suffocating under all that heap. Who was it?"

"Home Sister."

"Yep. I know that. But how? Which witch?"

"Morton."

"Forget her! Let's put the tango on again. Don't put your

nighty on. Here, push the towel in the gramophone and this blanket over the top and close the wardrobe this time."

"And listen! Let's open the window and take down the black-out so if she comes back she can't switch on the light."

"Good idea. And put the chair against the door."

Ashes of Roses. Tango Bolero. Like this. Put your arms round me. Like this. Tango.

Of course at a time like this, I know, it is not right to actually think of anyone, I mean to really think of another person just now. But there is just this, that that witch Morton might be on her way back up here. And if I go on thinking of another person the awful thing is that Sister Bean might be coming up with her.

The Hunt

The early morning sunlight filters through the bushes outside my window making tremulous patterns of light and shade on the wall opposite. This partly shaded shadow-moving light makes the room serene and tranquil. I try to prolong the tranquility by keeping my thoughts as peaceful as possible. Sometimes I have a wish to keep on staring into the leaves and the small branches out there until I disappear into them. Once I saw a hand in the leaves. It seemed to be reaching towards me, it was my own hand. I often hold out my hand now towards the bushes in order to see this enticing reflection. I wish too, often in the evenings, for an elixir, an ancient potion with magic qualities. A provider of energy and enlightenment.

Os innominatum Ilium Ischium Acetabulum and the Symphysis Pubis, the poetry of anatomy. It's like poetry I want to tell them, this anatomy, this usefulness of the pelvis. We are studying together, in the room I share with Lois, for our exams. *The Ilium presents two surfaces, external and internal, a crest, two processes, anterior and posterior, and an articulating surface for the sacrum.* I want to tell them, Trent and Ferguson, that I am going to a house party at Dr. Metcalf's. Lois has just come in so I do not say anything. Dr. Metcalf gave me the invitation in Magda's purple handwriting this morning on the ward. I have missed the opportunity. I can't tell them now.

"Any cigs?" Lois asks, knowing that none of us smokes and knowing too that I will have a packet of State Express 333 especially for her. State Express is her favorite. Ferguson does not like Lois. Lois does not seem to notice Ferguson.

"The crest of the ilium is curved and surmounts the bone, here it is," I say quickly, the point of my pencil hovering over the bone on the page. And with the other hand I pull the present for Lois out of my pocket slipping it to her sideways. Trent raises her eyebrows.

"I can read you like a book," she says to me out of the corner of her mouth. "Dead Loss," she says, "brother to Joe Loss." She makes me laugh.

I do not say anything about the invitation. I shall be coming in very late. I shall have to sign the book and ask the night porter to unlock for me. I wonder whose name I should sign. Ferguson's or Trent's? If names appear too often in the late pass book it is a question of appearing on Sister Bean's list for Matron's office at nine a.m. I would never use Lois's name. I have some feelings for her which I am not able to define. I feel happy when she comes into the room. Her clothes amuse me. I have a great wish to protect her and to do things for her. I like giving her small presents and seeing her pleasure. I make up my mind, as Lois shrouds us in smoke, to put Helen Ferguson in the book. It is Sunday. It is my day off. I did not go out because of the party tonight and because of the forthcoming exams. I wanted to go on sleeping too, on my bed in this room I have with Lois. We only sleep in the basement now if there is an air-raid warning. There was a prolonged one last night.

The night porter, because it is Sunday, will be a relieving one. He will not know me. I can be H. Ferguson for him.

"Describe the acetabulum," Trent says, "and do it without looking at the book."

"A deep, cup-shaped cavity, formed by the union of three bones . . ." Helen Ferguson's voice reminds me of our first days and weeks at the hospital, of the first Sunday here . . .

On my first Sunday I had the evening off. I wanted to be on my bed. The bed wasn't even made up. The bedclothes were rolled neatly in readiness for carrying downstairs later on. It was late afternoon towards the end of summer. A narrow shaft of sunshine came through the little space where the black-out curtain was tied up in a loop. It was very quiet and then someone started playing the organ in the chapel below. I liked the music and I tried not to sleep. I wanted to hear the organ but could hardly keep my eyes open. Images, one after the other in that familiar ritual of oncoming sleep, crowded my thoughts. Images from the children's ward, the noise, the big black trays on which we carried little tin plates of mince and potatoes and the baked apples swimming in yellow cream and covered with the shining crystals of brown sugar. "Good food," staff nurse Sharpe, who was teaching me, said, "is essential in their treatment. You must see that every child eats the dinner." Images from the children's ward, the occupational therapist moving slowly between the beds and the frames like a walking sewing basket. Twice in one morning one of the boys cut her scissors off and she had to find a new piece of string. Staff nurse Sharpe explained that she kept the scissors tied to her overall. She seemed, with her white hair, to be elderly but Sharpe said no it was because all her family were killed when their house was bombed and her hair had gone white overnight. In all the noise of shouting and crying and dropping tin plates or cups and the boys throwing conkers, the therapist played the piano in the middle of the ward and some of the little ones, rolling their heads from side to side, sang.

> The good ship sails on the anny anny O
> The anny anny O
> The good ship sails on the anny anny O . . .

We have stopped studying for a few minutes as Trent is making some toast and cocoa in the little kitchen at the end of the passage. Lois says have I still got some cake left.

The children in the ward, when they sing, can only roll their heads from side to side because of being strapped on to their frames. Mrs. Doe, the wardsmaid who is unable to read and write, crashes the tin plates, Sharpe says they are aluminum, into the sink. I envy Mrs. Doe. She says she goes to the pictures with her old man Fridays. I envy her because she can go home at night. She cleans the floors and washes up and comes and goes through a back door. She says exactly what she thinks about us. She calls it giving us a piece of her mind.

And all the time while the work is being done, all through the terrible noise and rush, Vera Lynn is singing on the wireless. She sings "There'll always be an England" and something that sounds like "There'll be blue birds over the white cliffs of Dover." I like the therapist but we have no reason to talk to each other and I don't know her name or where she lives.

It seemed to me during the first few days that there was a smell of disease, of tuberculosis, and when I asked staff nurse Sharpe about this, in a moment when she seemed approachable, she said no the disease did not smell. She thought it was the little woolen shawls the children all had, they probably needed washing and it was something I could get done on the first fine day.

When I lay on my bed that first Sunday evening someone came along the Peace corridor knocking on all the doors, opening and closing them. Tap tap of heels on the floorboards, knock knock open door click close door click all the way along.

Now it is my door. I keep my eyes closed. I hope whoever it is will go away. It is my first Sunday in this place and I am tired. I have never been so tired. My hands and arms up to the elbows are all chapped and sore. My feet hurt. I would leave if I knew how to.

"Time for chapel Nurse!" It is Sister Bean. Why isn't she in bed? She is the Night Sister. "Time for chapel Nurse!" as if she is wound up for these words. She closes the door and I hear her tap tap knock knock to the end of Peace and back tap knock open click close click all along the other side. And then tap tap back to my door knock open click.

"Time for chapel Nurse!"

"I am a Quaker, Sister."

"Time for chapel Nurse!"

In candlelight and incense and the music of the organ Father Bailey, the portly one, and Father Reynold who is hungry and red-nosed pass, in their robes, to and fro, up and down the aisles between the rows of pretty nurses. All have on fresh clean caps and aprons. All, with devout expressions, are bending their head down, repeating *I believe.* It is called the creed. I have never heard it before. At the door I was given an unfamiliar little book. It is nicely bound in leather and the pages are edged with gold. I would like to keep it. There is a squat tuffet thing for me to kneel on. We kneel and sit and kneel and stand and sit and when we all move there is a rustling like leaves falling in autumn. There is a chanting and murmuring of believing. I am not sure what I believe and, unless I read in the little book (if I can find the page), I do not know the words. At school prayers were silent in our own words in our hearts. I see two nurses, two of the ones I have been working with, they are very pious.

On their dressing tables they both have silver-framed photographs and every day their conversations, in well-bred voices, ripple across the Peace corridor.

"Oh Mandy Darling, have you heard from Derek lately?"

"Yes Darling, simply adorable letter this morning."

"How heavenly Darling! I adore his big ears."

"Barrington Darling have *you* heard from Rojji Rogère?"

"Mm yes Darling, this morning. He's on a Brenn Gun Carrier."

"Oh Wizard!"

It is Nurse Mandy who holds the crying children, the little boys, over the jet of icy water in the sluice room every morning to punish them for wetting their cots. They go on crying and crying, their voices hoarse from crying. She is saying this "*I believe,*" she believes in a whole list of things and I am trying to keep my eyes open . . .

"What's in the *acetabular fossa?*" Ferguson's question—it's her turn after answering correctly—is for me.

"Fat," I say. They laugh but it is correct.

"What and where," it is my turn to ask Trent, "what and where is the *ligamentum teres?*"

It is not possible to compare, to make comparisons, between this room which is Dr. Metcalf's and any of my mother's rooms. On the ground floor she has the back room and the front room and the kitchen. In this house, which is the Metcalfs' house, I cannot begin to know how many rooms there are, parts of the house are unknown to me. All the same I am making comparisons. Dr. Metcalf has a carpet; at home we have linoleum and a rug, a black rug in case the coal spits and burns. There are some books at home, here the walls are lined with books. This room is Dr. Metcalf's study. It is not very light, there is a shaded reading lamp. The electric light at home hangs in the middle of the room on a flex from the ceiling. My father likes bright light.

"Don't read with a bad light," he is always saying it, "you'll spoil your pretty eyes. Don't spoil your pretty eyes."

This is a much bigger house, a better house, there are more rooms than we have at home. Perhaps I should have gone home instead of coming here. It is a whole week since the party. Dr. Metcalf had to leave in the middle of it as he was wanted at the hospital. I wanted to leave then to go with him but Magda would not hear of it.

"Precious child stay!" she cried all across the room. "You simply can't go yet. I'll pop you in a taxi." And then she asked me to come the next free evening I had because she was going to be away, "and Jonty must, simply must have some good company," she said. "He wants to play some music called *The Hunt*," she said. I told her I'd like that very much and all the guests thought this very funny.

"Oh! Isn't she just a pet," Magda cried then. "Come here precious pet!" She told me she wanted to hug me and kiss me forever.

On the way to the Metcalfs' this evening I keep hoping that Dr. Metcalf will answer the door. I do not like Mrs. Privett, the housekeeper. I think I am afraid of her. Magda calls her Mrs. P. Really it is more that Mrs. P dislikes me. Magda encourages Mrs. P in her disapproval of everything because, she says, when Mrs. P is hating she works terribly hard and polishes everything and scours the saucepans, haven't I noticed how shiny they are.

Mrs. P does let me in and she opens the door only a little way so that I have to step in sideways.

"Dr. Metcalf is expecting me," I say, my voice all silly and shaky with nervousness. It seems a long time that I am waiting for him to come and I worry in case he does not really want me to come or that he has forgotten that I am coming. I try to work out how much in pounds, shillings, and pence his curtains and chair covers will have cost. I look up and down the walls and the books and at the furnishings adding value and subtracting.

Dr. Metcalf, when he comes in, is very nice and gently helps me off with my coat. He winds up the gramophone and puts on the record. But there is something wrong with it. We can hardly hear it. I feel I should say it is nice but we both know something is wrong. He stops the gramophone and takes off the record. He explains it is a quartet by Mozart, it's called The Hunt. He says he is sorry it's a flop and I say it doesn't matter. There is a silence between us which I feel I must fill.

I kneel down and look along the book cases hoping to recognize a title and make some intelligent remark but all the books are strange to me. I read aloud some of the titles. Dr. Metcalf looks amused.

"Which would you like to read?" he asks after a little silence. I tell him that I'm afraid I don't know. He bends down and takes a book.

"Try this one," he says, and kneels beside me.

My clumsy skirt is caught all round my legs as I struggle awkwardly to my feet. The book is *The Voyage Out* by someone called Virginia Woolf.

"A lady writer," I say and feel ashamed to have said such a stupid thing. "Thank you," I say. I like his hand, the feeling of it, as he gives me the book. I tell him I am afraid it might be too difficult for me.

"Try it," he says getting up. He says he thinks Mrs. P is going out but she has left us some supper and, if I like, we can have it by the fire in his study. Would I like that, he wants to know.

"Yes," I say, glad that Mrs. P is going out, "that would be nice."

A patient has given Dr. Metcalf some rhubarb. He shows it to me in the kitchen and I offer to cook it for him. He sits on the edge of the table while I wash it and cut it up. I try to do this neatly and not to strip it too much. It needs a lot of sugar I tell him. It is a moment of authority which I enjoy. But when we look for the sugar there isn't any. Mrs. P must have had it all in her tea he says and I wish I had brought my ration with me but of course I didn't know about the rhubarb.

The kitchen is transformed, that's how Dr. Metcalf puts it, by the fragrance of the stewed rhubarb. He will eat it, he says, for breakfast. He carries our supper through to the study.

We do not eat much. I am shy sitting there with a tray between us. I hardly notice what there is to eat. Some sort of salad with pears in it. I feel I have said silly things about his books. Because he is quiet I talk, feeling all the time that I am talking too much.

"I suppose it's about six miles, I go there on my bike, I like the ride, it's country there, hawthorn berries and rose hips on both sides of the road, the wild roses when they are out are so pretty. Her house is in the middle of a field. Hens, she keeps hens." I am telling Dr. Metcalf about Gertrude's Place. "I could," I tell him, "bring some eggs, one time, for Magda, perhaps next time," I say, "I go there on my days off but if I don't go Mother goes on the bus."

Dr. Metcalf is always quiet, I suppose, it does not show, this quietness, so much when Magda and the others are there. In one of the silences we hear Mrs. P returning. Dr. Metcalf says she has come back earlier than usual. In another of the silences I say that I am thinking it is time for me to go back to the hospital. When I say this Dr. Metcalf says he will take me back. And I say oh no I would not dream of him coming out again. He says a walk would be nice. He feels like a walk. Should we walk to the hospital? Or do I prefer to go by bus?

"Oh a walk would be lovely," I say.

Outside the front door, to our surprise, there is a thick fog. It is impossible to see even one footstep ahead. It is as if a cold damp wall is right up against us. Slowly we go forward. I feel along the wall with both hands. We can follow the wall I say but Dr. Metcalf reminds me that the wall does not go beyond the corner of the street. We come to the end of the wall. I feel completely enveloped. My scarf, coat, and gloves are wet. I try to go back. I reach for the wall but am not able to find it. I can't breathe. I stumble off the unseen edge of the pavement. There is a silence so terrible it is as if the world has ceased to exist. I feel terrified and try to call out to Dr. Metcalf and find he is near me. He puts his arm round me and says it is no good, we'll have to find our way back to the house and it will be best for me to sleep there and go in to the hospital in the morning.

Mrs. Privett has already gone to bed but Dr. Metcalf taps on her door and asks if I can sleep in her sitting room. He explains about the fog and that we have had to leave our wet things in the kitchen. He brings a mattress from one of the spare beds upstairs and puts it on her sitting-room floor. Mrs. P, who looks more sour than usual in her dressing gown and curlers, hands me two sheets. Dr. Metcalf brings down an armful of blankets. He says goodnight to Mrs. P and me in a most formal way. I can hardly bear this and I want to drop the sheets and rush along the passage and into the hall and up the big staircase after him. I want to be upstairs in his part of the house, even though he is alone up there. I don't want to be an unwelcome guest in Mrs. Privett's sitting room.

"Can I have a glass of water please," I ask Mrs. P. She brings me half a glass which she holds out to me round the door before closing it. I make up a sort of bed on the floor.

Mrs. Privett's sitting room is crowded with her things. There is only just room for the mattress between the chairs and the table and the sideboard. There is a dark red plush tablecloth with an immense fringe all round it. She has some china shepherd and shepherdess figures on the mantelpiece and two stuffed birds under glass covers. There is a mirror over the mantel and a great many photographs in bone frames. One forbidding face glares from the cruet on the sideboard. I examine the room to try to overcome my uneasiness and the wishing to be with Dr. Metcalf. When we were in the fog he was close to me guiding me with his arm round me and his body close to mine. I try to recapture the feeling of his arm being round me. Does he suddenly not want me? I wonder if he is in bed or whether he will come downstairs again. I open the door a bit but it is dark and quiet. Upstairs in one of the pretty bedrooms I would be near him. The time goes by very slowly. I am cold. I don't want to put out the light. Oh come down again please.

I feel I can't breathe when the light is out. I am too near the floor. Mrs. P's horrible face seems to be in the room, disagreeable, when the light is off. I struggle up off the mattress and put on the light again. I check her black-out curtain and knock something over on the other side of the curtain. Perhaps a plant in a pot. I don't dare move the curtain to look. When I try to crawl back into the tunnel of bedclothes I knock over the water and it makes a wet patch on the carpet and soaks into the side of the mattress. The room is getting colder.

I am not asleep and, though I have kept on most of my clothes, I am cold. Right through my whole body I am cold. I wish I was at home and not here. I wish I had gone home. And another thing, I do not know where Mrs. P's bathroom is. I want my mother. This is such an unusual wish that I weep a bit in a sort of despair. It is only a quarter to two. A great many hours till the morning. My mother would not like the Metcalfs. I wish I could be warm. Dr. Metcalf obviously does not like me much.

The place where I lived as a child is a place of small mean houses in terraces in mean little streets. All around are pit mounds, some black with fresh slag from the mines and others covered with coarse tufty grass and the yellow weed called coltsfoot. There are small triangles of meadow with partly derelict barns and farm cottages. Sometimes there are a few cows and chickens. The bone and glue factory is not far away and at the end of the street where we once lived there are the brick kilns.

One night when I am walking home with my mother we hear someone crying in the darkness ahead of us. The lane is shut in by dark slag heaps and there is, as if relieving the endless smell of bone and glue, a sharp fresh fragrance from the elderberry bushes which are, at intervals, along the roadway.

"Who is it?" my mother calls in her soft voice. But no one answers. "Who is it crying?" my mother calls again, her voice like a flute in the night. "Who are you? Why are you crying? Don't be afraid. Tell me what is the matter." My mother, holding my hand, stands still in the middle of the road. After a bit a girl comes out from the black patch of elderberry. She is still crying. She tells my mother she is Sylvia Bradley and her father has turned her out with only a shilling. We walk on together, slowly, while the girl tells my mother. The fragrance of the snapped-off and bruised elderberry is left behind and the smell of bone and glue seems stronger. With a heaving roar the blast furnace on the other side of the town opens and the sky is filled with the familiar red glow. We can hear the wheels at the mine shaft turning as one cage of men comes up and another cage goes down. "Where will I go," Sylvia Bradley cries, "I've got nowhere to go."

My mother never lets us play with the Bradley girls. There are nine of them and they do not wear any knickers. Emily Bradley, the next eldest, knows a shop where the woman makes rum and butter toffees. If you eat them they make you drunk, she tells us.

I must have been asleep, or nearly asleep. Sylvia Bradley. She was the one who cried so much that night. All along the road my mother tried to comfort her and to persuade her to go home again. "When your baby is born," she said to Sylvia Bradley, "your mother and father are sure to love your baby. You will see, they will not turn you out. Go back home to them."

I want my hairbrush. I struggle up from the mattress. It is colder than ever in the room. There is a draught along the floor. My back aches. I want the bathroom. I don't know at all where the bathroom is in Mrs. P's part of the house. I go as quietly as I can, feeling my way along the passage to the door which leads into the wide front hall. The black-out curtain for the fan-light window over the front door has not been put up and a faint light comes through. Perhaps it is the fog making a mysterious misty light. It must be getting on for morning. I feel my way to the staircase and go up as quietly as I can. There is a landing where the staircase turns. The lavatory, which has an ornamental stained-glass door, opens off this landing. Magda explained once that it was there because it was added to the house.

When I come out, instead of going down, I go on upstairs and along the thickly carpeted passage. I can smell Magda's perfume. It is dark and all the doors are closed. There is no sound from behind the closed door which is Dr. Metcalf's. I go to the top of the stairs again and make my way back to the sitting room. It is airless and colder than ever. I don't suppose Mrs. P ever uses the room and I'm sure she never has a fire in it. I crawl back into the cold damp bedclothes. The fog must be seeping in through the walls. It is not even three o'clock. My hair needs brushing. I wish I had my hairbrush. I am used to brushing my hair before I go to bed. I have not been able to clean my teeth either. Trying to sleep in my clothes is awful. I'm tired and everything I will have to do tomorrow rushes in on me. I'll never manage. Because it is silly to wish for my hairbrush and for my mother I can't help crying a bit more.

I am afraid to go to sleep. I am frightened of being asleep when Mrs. Privett comes in here in the morning. I don't want her to come into her sitting room and find me asleep.

Of all the girls at school, apart from Ferguson of course, Bulge is the one I seem to remember most. It is not that I am always thinking of those times, but when I do, I seem to remember Bulge.

The first and only nice thing I ever do towards Bulge is when I visit her after her appendix operation in the hospital at Oxford. I have to be taken there to have my ear examined and dressed and bandaged. Bulge is lying back on her pillows with her washing bowl beside her. She is supposed to have washed her face. It is not visiting time but I am allowed in because of being brought to the out-patients' department. Bulge is the only schoolgirl in the women's ward. She has her doll and her doll's clothes on the locker by her bed. The other patients seem to like Bulge. Even the nurses seem to like her and they even have little jokes with her. They all call her Muriel. No one except me knows the name Bulge. She does not know it herself.

The ward is long and narrow and the beds are all stripped on to chairs and the patients are washing themselves in bowls like the one Bulge has. She looks different. Her face seems white and clean, like wax, and she seems to have lost her spots. She looks tired and, without her spectacles, she seems more childish. Her face, I have never noticed before, her face is round. Her hair has been brushed back off her face and this makes her look different. She even seems pretty.

"Have you finished with this?" I indicate the bowl and she says yes and will I put it with the others on that high metal trolley. When I lift the bowl the water splashes up everywhere. I have lifted it too high. I thought it would be a heavy bowl by the look of it but it is light, much lighter than I imagined. I put too much effort into lifting it a nurse says as she goes by. I feel confused and ashamed and the nurse says she had done the same thing years ago, not knowing the bowls were so light.

"I brought this for you to read," I say to Bulge as I place *Treacle Wins Through* on the sheet. "Here," I say, "I thought you would like to read this."

"Oh! I say! Yes rather! What's it like?" Bulge raises herself a little bit. She looks in an eager but short-sighted way at the book.

"Haven't read it yet, not all of it."

"Oh. You finish it first. After all, Mummy and Chris gave it to you. When they came to school that day, they brought it for you."

"Yes, well, I know, but they're your parents. And you are in hospital. I'll finish it after you. They are your parents—it was jolly decent of them to give me a present. They are your parents, after all."

"Only half. Chris is Mummy's Friend. Remember."

"Yes I know. But you have it first. Go on." I push the book with Treacle's boarding-school adventures, which I am longing to read, nearer to her.

I can tell Bulge is pleased. She fingers the book and smiles.

It's the first and only nice thing I have ever done . . .

I'm shivering. I fold up my blankets and the sheets. I let myself out of the front door of the Metcalfs' house. It is still dark but the fog has lifted. I set off to walk to the hospital. It is still not light as I climb the hill to the service entrance. The night porter will be somewhere near there. He has the key to the special door in the basement. There is a passage down there through to the part of the hospital where the nurses have their rooms.

The night porter believes my story about the fog. He says not to bother about signing the book. He says the fog is the best anti-aircraft there is.

"There's been no bombs," he says. His wife is nervous in the night, in the air raids, but this time she'll have had a good sleep. I have never thought of the night porters, or any of the porters, having wives, and perhaps children, at home. Suddenly I feel ashamed because, before I found him, I was remembering that I had no hair clips, no hair nets, and not one apron button. I was thinking that Lois, and even some of the others, Ferguson in particular, must have been helping themselves to my store of these. These shortages, as they are called, seem more important than the progress of the war. Even that phrase, the progress of the war, because people say it all the time, seems to have no meaning. As I follow close behind the night porter I feel ashamed of my own small selfish brain. His wife is probably alone every night scared stiff. And I cried for my hairbrush and then centered my thoughts on a hair clip.

We go down in the lift to the lower ground floor. As we walk past the glass doors of Lower Ground Radium I catch sight of staff nurse Ramsden. She is sitting in the ward office with a small shaded light beside her. She is bent over the desk, writing, probably some of the night report. She must have been moved there recently. I wish she would look up and see me and smile at me. I have to hurry to keep up with the porter.

"Ramsden," I could say if I could speak to her just now. "Ramsden, do you know *The Hunt*?" and Ramsden, her eyes suddenly bright with some memory of the music, would say, "Ah! Yes. Mozart, the quartet. *The Hunt*. It's K458 in B flat major."

As it is a quartet, and, if all four instruments leap in together on the opening notes, it would be too difficult for her to sing the first few bars. From what I managed to hear, when Dr. Metcalf tried the record, I feel it would not be possible for the human voice, by itself, to produce the sounds. If I could speak to Ramsden just now I feel sure that is what she would explain. I would like to talk to Ramsden now about the way in which the musicians, in a quartet, play towards each other, leaning forward as if to emphasize something in the music and then, pausing, they lean back allowing the phrases of music to follow one another, to meet and join, to climb and cascade. I would like her to agree with me and to say that she knows about the serious expressions the musicians have while they play and that she has noticed too the way they have of drooping their wrists and showing the vulnerable white backs of their hands.

The porter, with his key in the lock, is waiting for me.

"You know Roberts," Lois says at breakfast.

"Roberts? Roberts?" I say putting my plate of fried potatoes on the table. I am hungry.

"Yes Roberts. Roberts—Nurse Roberts." Lois lights a cigarette. She never eats breakfast. I move her tea cup nearer to her elbow. "Well listen!" Lois says. "Roberts. She's been throwing up all over the place. Can't keep a thing down. Diet kitchen of all places. Can you imagine! It's the powdered egg. Just the sight of the packet is enough to make her throw up. She's fainted during Report too, twice." Lois, after a deep breath, exhales a cloud of smoke. She nips out her cigarette, squeezing it quickly between her thumb and forefinger, as Sister Bean, clutching the registers to her flat white apron, marches across the dining room.

"Abbott Abrahams Ackerman Allwood . . ." Nurses in various parts of the large room are answering to the rapid barking of their names. Some half rise from their places at table. "Arrington and Attwood . . ."

"Nurse Arrington!"

"Yes Sister."

"Matron's office nine a.m."

"Yes Sister."

"Nurses Baker Barrington Beam Beamish Beckett . . ."

"Anyway," Lois says looking at me, "long time no see, where were you last night?"

"Nurses Birch Bowman D Bowman E Broadhurst Brown Burchall . . .'

Gertrude's Place

When I see the visiting nurse cross the lighted veranda of the house opposite I recall without wanting to the navy-blue uniform of the district nurse as she dismounted from her bicycle. Pushing through the long grass and weeds she climbed slowly up to a small house in the middle of a field where scattered hens were industrious and apparently independent.

At that time I watched from higher up the hill, leaning heavily on my own bicycle, assuring myself that other people, for example, Madame Curie, had safely ridden bicycles right up to the time of confinement. As the nurse made her slow journey I thought of the illness in the house and how I could go down there and tell her that I could do all that had to be done. "I can stay. Tell me what needs to be done. I will do all that needs doing." Easily I could do this.

The nurse did not leave. After a short time I saw smoke rise from the chimney; she would need a fire to have some hot water. I remember that I wondered then whether the nurse would know to shut up the hens for the night. As I watched from high up on the hill I thought of foxes.

I remember now, unwillingly, all kinds of things. One small thing only, the sight of an unknown nurse going in to an unknown patient across the road, is needed to bring back memories mysteriously stored in such a way that all seem fresh and whole as if they belong now at the present time, perhaps yesterday, the day before yesterday, or this morning . . . one of these memories being the schoolgirl game of comparisons which I continued to play, silently watchful, observing my companions noticing the quality of their hair, their complexions, their finger nails, their uniforms especially the condition of the starched caps and collars and all the time secretly placing myself above or below a standard which I regarded as acceptable. When I stood then in the queue for letters I noticed the fat stomachs, the thick waists of some of the nurses, and how their aprons were pulled tight across this bulging roundness. My own apron, at that time, was neat and flat and the memory of the sudden realization, one morning that this could not always be so is so intense now that I remember clearly the unfamiliar nausea which accompanied this thought.

Other things come back in quick succession, the wedding ring for sixpence, the way in which I heard what had happened to Dr. Metcalf, the attempts I made to retrieve a letter I had written. On that day, in the bleakness, I saw little Nurse Roberts, alone and portly under her winter coat, standing at the bus stop with her suitcase on the pavement beside her. And then there followed the whispered reasons for her running away. Always a great deal of whispering.

The daylight, that evening when I watched the district nurse pushing her bicycle up the steep lane, faded quickly and quite soon the dusk became night. Across the field I saw the light in the window of the little living room and I wished then for the times when I was in that room beside the hearth. I thought with longing of the times I had spent there and how it was a long time since I l had been there. I remained for some hours in the damp cold, undecided. I did not go down to the place that night and, because of what was happening to me, I never went back there again.

One evening as the lift goes up and I am waiting, it passes the floor where I am standing and I see through the little glass window staff nurse Ramsden in the lift. Really I see her polished shoes, I know they are hers. Her shoes are of better quality and she has narrow feet, narrow at the heel and the shoes fit perfectly as if made especially for her.

I never hear anyone call staff nurse Ramsden "Penicillin Peggy" though she is very often the one in charge of the syringes and the needles, cleaning and sterilizing them, and giving the three-hourly injections. Everyone calls Ramsden Miss Ramsden, even some of the patients. Because she understands and speaks other languages, she is often asked in to translate for a prisoner or perhaps a Polish officer who can speak some sort of German. This morning during the surgeon's ward round I can see her laughing with a German P.O.W. He looks at her with admiration in his eyes and he carefully repeats some of the words and she, in her quiet way, laughs softly again and translates for Mr. Bowen, the surgeon, and he laughs too. Ramsden is not at all nervous with Mr. Bowen, she bends over to unfasten the bandage and to remove the dressing and the prisoner closes his eyes and grips the head rail of the bed till his knuckles shine white.

Ramsden reads Rilke in German. I have heard her read. Perhaps it is that which makes me invite her.

"Ramsden," I say, "my folks," this is not my way but I say it, "my folks would be very happy if you would visit, you know, if you would care to come and stay with us sometime."

Ramsden says she would like that very much and she thanks me.

My mother would like someone who can read these poems in her language. I am always trying to think of ways to comfort my mother and it seems to me that I can offer Ramsden to her.

"Infection takes the line of least resistance, sing that to la," Trent says, "a peptic ulcer is an ulcer which occurs anywhere in the alimentary canal—repeat after me—a peptic ulcer is . . ." This evening we are all trying to revise for our exams. Trent, with her uniform unbuttoned, is on circulation, Ferguson has turned up varicose conditions, and Lois wants to go over the preparation of trolleys for mastoid dressings, lumbar puncture, and washing a patient's hair in bed. Of course I cannot tell them that I shall be inviting staff nurse Ramsden home later on when we have some holidays. I can't help thinking about my invitation with a mixture of excitement and plain worry.

For one thing where could staff nurse Ramsden sleep in my mother's house?

"Now gels, heads up, throw out your chests." Trent opens the window. "Mind the black-out," someone says. It is impossible to study with Trent in the room. She makes a joke out of everything. She sings and dances and dresses up in bath towels. She pretends to give elaborate intimate treatment to imaginary patients. She pretends she has made dreadful mistakes and kneels before an imaginary ward sister . . .

We have all started having cold baths every morning. Trent has one too but we have all noticed the steam coming under the partition . . .

Lois says to me later that she has worked with Trent on the wards and that if she, Lois, were ill it would be Trent she would want to have to look after her. This is considered to be the highest praise one nurse can give another nurse.

Because of the war some wards are badly overcrowded to enable us to prepare others to be quite empty in readiness for the wounded. It is impossible to imagine a life which is not in the war.

"O'course we couldn't go to bed or anythin'—they had ladders great big long ones up the wall to our winders an' we hid under the bed, we didn't have any candle for fear they would see it and our shadders on the curtings an' all along the mantelpiece we had these big paint tins full of rusty old nails to rattle about and throw should any of 'em come right up and bosst in through the winder."

I am at Gertrude's Place. Gertrude is telling me about what she calls the raids when she was a girl. She lived then, she tells me, in a Place called Netherton or near there just out of it somewhere where the chain shops were, and the women (her mother was one of them), with great big muscles for swinging a sledge hammer, made chains. Gertrude had to take her little baby brother to be fed, he was on the breast, she says; "The women all set theirselves comfortable against the wall to feed the babbies and us girls we played skip rope an' hopscotch an' clay allys and such till it was time to take the babbies back home and put the taters on the hob to boil." The women, she tells me, wore big overall dresses and they did not bother much about any knickers. Her mother, she says, did not know any life except the chain shop. There were different gangs she explains and they were always raiding. She says having to put black stuff over her window now at night because of the air raids even though she is in the country reminds her of when she was a girl and they didn't dare to show any light. "I thought," she says, "that bein' here in the fields and with the spinney so close a light would not show but they, the wardens, they keep comin' to say they can see a light from my place. The wardens come here you see . . . reminds me of them gangs years ago . . ."

I am at Gertrude's Place, it is the country. I came on my bicycle. My day off. I have two days off. "I'll come again tomorrow," I say. She is pleased. She is always waiting for me to come. She writes letters in big black handwriting on paper used for wrapping boiling fowls. In places her pen digs up the paper.

> . . . If you can come Tue or Wed . . . I shall be home. If too tired for the bicycle you can get the eleven a.m. bus to the Holly Bush and walk down by the spinney it's about a mile but it don't seem that long and you can have a good rest . . . I'll have some eggs . . .

In the rush of work on the wards I am always thinking of Gertrude's Place and how I will get out there first thing on my day off.

I have been cutting out a frieze of wallpaper with rosebuds on it and we have pasted it round her back kitchen wall. Against the blue distemper the pink and white looks nice. Gertrude says she is pleased. I can see the way her eyes are shining that she is pleased. She is sunburned and seems old and she always looks clean even though she can only wash with a bit of rag wrung out in a basin of hot water. She does not have a bathroom. In one room there is a billiard table and the incubators and a harmonium which she plays while she sings hymns. She and her husband don't go to bed at night she explains on one of my visits. They sit one each side of the fire with the kettle singing. They sit there and sleep the night, she laughs when she tells me, and says that the kettle there on the hob is ready and boiling every morning. A big oil lamp on three chains hangs low over the table in the living room. The table is so littered with things never put away that they have become, as she says, so much rubbish. She clears a space on the corner of the table so that I can eat the egg she has boiled for me. She cuts the loaf on a folded piece of newspaper and hands me slices of white bread spread with real butter.

"It must be all your butter ration," I say.

"There's plenty where that came from," she says. And I describe the little string bags which all the nurses carry with them; "a little jar for sugar, one for butter and one for jam or marmalade." I tell her about the tin baths of jam made in the hospital and ladled into our jars. She can't imagine, she says, us all lining up once a week. I tell her about the black-out shutters for the tall windows in the ward and how these have to be put up early shutting out the sun and the fresh air. We have exams I tell her in about two weeks time. She says can I eat a second egg if she puts one on and I say yes if she can spare it. This makes her laugh.

I want to tell Gertrude about Lois, my friend, being jealous of my new friendship with Dr. Metcalf and his wife. I want to tell her that I bought Lois a pretty nightdress so that she would not mind my going to Magda Metcalf's parties and how Lois never wore the nightdress but gave it to her ugly, stupid mother who is so greedy she would take everything. If I tell Gertrude that I buy cigarettes for Lois and that I minded dreadfully about the nightdress she might think that I am too fond of Lois or something. If I tell her about the games at the Metcalfs' party she might think I am in what she calls bad company. Magda is very generous. She tells everybody that I saved her life and she is always giving me expensive things like the silver bracelets which I can't wear. For some reason bangles look all wrong on my arms and, in any case, people would wonder where I got them from.

She has given me some pure silk blouses which don't really suit me. I don't know what to wear them with and then there's other things like chiffon scarves and lace-edged hankies and a jeweled comb. As well as all this she is giving me something else which I can't explain about to Gertrude. Magda tells me to come round whenever I'm free because they love having me there.

I can't exactly explain to Gertrude how they show me off to their friends in the strange way that they do. Magda calls me Darling in front of everyone and Dr. Metcalf actually called me by my first name on the ward the other day. How can I tell Gertrude about these people; they are very nice and they want me to be with them. Of course I didn't save Magda's life. She was admitted to Casualty one night while I was relief nurse there. She was in an attack of asthma, it looked pretty fearful, and because I didn't know what to do till the RMO came I dragged in the big oxygen cylinder and Magda got better straight away at the sight of it.

"Since when," the Night Superintendent said later, "since when, Nurse, has oxygen been the remedy for asthma? And by what miracle, Nurse, can an empty cylinder be of use to anyone?" How can I tell anyone that? And Lois says do I realize that Dr. Metcalf has made eleven nurses pregnant and don't I know what it was that caused Sister Green on chests to suicide.

I think I love Dr. Metcalf. Certainly I love Magda, she is kind and full of ideas. All her friends love her and they dress up and cook wild meals and dance and, though I mostly watch, I love being at their house especially when Dr. Metcalf lends me books or suggests that we listen to music. Sometimes he looks very tired and one night I thought he was looking at me as if he loved me and when he walked to the bus with me he caught my hand quickly as the bus came and quickly kissed my fingers . . .

Gertrude brings me my second egg and watches me eat it. Perhaps I will tell her next time and then give up all that she thinks is bad company. I think from what little she says that she does not much care for Lois. Lois smokes all the time and never has any money. Once when I mention the money side of things

Gertrude says that she must have some because if the hospital is paying me twenty-eight shillings a month they must be paying her too.

"They wouldn't give to one and not to another," Gertrude says. Which is, of course, perfectly true.

The sky always seems nearer at Gertrude's Place. It seems to come down, rain soft and swollen, the clouds rosy at the edges and shining as if pearls are sewn into their linings, to the top of the grassy slope which goes straight up from the windows of the living room. The feeling I have of being able to reach out to take the sky in both hands is one of the most restful things I have ever known. I sit there knowing about the nearness of the sky, not reaching out but, at the same time, pleased about the possibilities. These possibilities are connected in an undefined way with Dr. Metcalf and how I feel towards him, and then there is Gertrude sitting across on the other side of the table. Two separate people but joined together because of how I feel about them.

The fowls are dotted white and brown all over the slope of the field. Gertrude has an old bucket on its side out there on the grass. She can tell at once when it starts to rain because of the splash marks the first drops make on it. A rooster struts by and Gertrude, with her little laugh, says to always watch that one. "Keep a eye on him," she says, "don't trust him, not a inch, he'll be into you where you least expect it." She laughs again. "Roosters!" she says, "they can be something wicked!" Afterwards we put the eggs ready for me to take home. Lovely smooth large eggs, their shells glowing a cream apricot color or pure white with a translucence which makes them seem frail. We wrap the eggs in threes in torn-off pieces of a magazine. They are black-market eggs and my mother, anxious always about provisions, has said to me to buy as many as Gertrude can spare. She lets me have three dozen. She has two dressed fowls for my mother too, one of them she explains has had a fox get to her but not much taken, just a wing and a bit of breast. She has neatened the fowl, she says, with her dressmaking scissors. "Tell mother," she says, "I'm sorry about that old red fox."

As we work I have a great wish to talk about Dr. Metcalf, to tell Gertrude about his quiet gentleness and about his brown eyes. I want to tell her about Magda and how fond she is of her beautiful dog, how the dog lies in bed beside her, a Red Setter, and how Magda talks to him and fondles him. I could tell Gertrude I feel sorry for Dr. Metcalf, that I want . . . Gertrude says what about a game of billiards or cards. Games bore me but I play because I know Gertrude likes to play. We play racing patience, Gertrude calls it "pounce," it is her favorite. We play three games and she wins them all.

The long summer evening is beginning to get dark and Gertrude comes down through the damp grass and nettles and cow parsley to the road with me. I walk with my bicycle. I tell her I will come back in the morning to scrape and clean out the hen houses as usual. I almost say, "I'll have to leave early because I'm going to a party," but I can't say the words.

"Two nights off," she says, "Eh? but that's nice!"

I turn round as I coast down the long hill just before the road bends round and I see her standing alone and waving. I wave and switch on the bicycle lamp grateful that my father insisted on lending it to me.

When I come home there is a telegram for me from the hospital telling me to return at once. The nurses' hours are being rearranged.

"I suppose it's wounded men," I say to my mother, "a convoy." My face is burning pleasantly with the fresh air. She is upset and makes a parcel with a fruit cake and some hard-boiled eggs for me to take back.

"There's a train at nine-twenty," my father says, and he says he will come to the station.

In the gray half light I walk up and down the platform with my father. He always comes to the train if he can. He tells me, "You are doing God's work." He tells me to remember:

"Der Herr ist mein Hirte, mir wird nichts mangeln . . .

Remember," he says; "*The Lord is my Shepherd . . . und ob ich schon wanderte im finstern Tal, fürchte ich kein Unglück; denn du bist bei mir, dein Stecken und Stab trösten mich . . .* verse four," he says and he holds my hand.

"Not in German," I say in a low voice, glancing quickly to see if the other people waiting for the train have noticed. For my father it is not the language of the enemy but is the language for cherishing. I feel his hand holding mine and I want to cry and go back home with him. I am afraid.

"I don't want to go," I tell him.

"It's God's work," he says again.

The notice board in the deserted front hall of the Nurses' Home is covered with neatly written timetables. I am on duty at four a.m. I go up to the room which I share with Lois. I go in very quietly as she will be asleep. But her bed is empty. The black-out curtains are not drawn and the window is open. From this window, high up, I can lean, it seems, right into the black darkness which is the world. There is a sweetness, a faint fragrance of crushed grass as if it has come with me from Gertrude's Place. It is probably from the park. When I try to breathe it in once more it is not there. There are no lights anywhere only the canal shines in the light of the rising moon. The moon and the moonlit water are inextinguishable. Two tiny points of yellow light far below are moving and stopping and moving on again slowly. It is a bus. A faint roar, as of breathing, comes to me across the black shadowed roof-tops. I close the window and fix the curtain.

Trying to sleep I think of the tranquility of Gertrude's field scattered with hens.

"Darling, you are such a pet!" Magda said the other evening when I arrived late (after evening duty) at her birthday party. "Isn't she just a pet," she called out, turning me round and round in front of her roomful of guests. "Isn't she sweet to come after work. You Darling!" she kissed me. "And you still wear your school coat. I love it! I wish I had it." She buried her face in the dark-green nap. I was not sure whether she was laughing or crying.

"You could have it," I said, "but I seem to need it!"

"She seems to need it," Magda cried. "Oh isn't she just perfect. A natural perfect! Jonty," she called Dr. Metcalf, "take this dear child somewhere and undress her. Help her out of this coat." They were all laughing.

If I tell Gertrude she will see how generous and kind Magda is. But Gertrude might think she is being generous with the wrong things. I do not want to give back the special thing I am being given. Gertrude I feel sure will tell me not to take.

I turn over. I am afraid because I can't sleep. Then the rumbling starts. I have heard this noise before. I know what it is. I watched one morning with Lois. From our high-up window we could see a long train of mysterious carriages and wagons winding across to the station nearest the hospital. This is what I can hear now. The wagons, some of them will be marked with a red cross, are bringing wounded soldiers. I can hear the brakes squealing as the train draws up and stops and then, jolting, pulls along a bit more to stop again to allow the stretchers to be unloaded into the waiting ambulances. Quite soon I hear the first of these ambulances, like on that other morning, come slowly up to the hospital. They come steadily one after the other. The empty beds we have prepared will fill again with men who have fear and pain in their eyes. They do not really sleep but lie with their teeth clenched and their hands clenched and their eyes half open. Some of them are not able to close their eyes in sleep.

I do not see Lois at all or Trent. We leave little notes for each other. We are working an eight-hour shift, eight hours on and eight hours off. There is no time off. We eat and sleep and work and eat and sleep and work. Some of the nurses get ill and we are short of staff. The ward where I am is all split beds for amputations. Every bed has its own electric bell and its own tourniquet, some beds have two.

Gertrude, waiting for me to come, writes to me. I queue for letters and am pleased when I see her black handwriting;

Queenie has her pups you'll be pleased to know little balls of fat tumbling about you'll love 'em. If you miss the eleven am bus there's another at one. We would have a bit less time that's all—

and

Have you ever seen the pig's meat salted down you'll see it up at Violet's when you come they've killed a pig up there you should taste the pork pies. I'll have one ready all wrapped for you . . .

One of the men, he is only a boy really, as well as having both legs amputated above the knee, has a terrible wound in his stomach. I try, while I am dressing it, not to show that I can't bear it. One day he asks me to put the gold cross from round his neck into the wound but I tell him I can't do this. He begs me and I say no I can't because it isn't sterile. He has tears on his face and my own eyes fill with tears so that it is hard to see what I am doing. I brush something small and white out of his bed. It seems to roll up like a soft bread crumb. As I swab the wound it seems something is moving in it. It is a maggot. I pick it out quickly with the forceps trying not to show my shock. Suddenly I see there are maggots everywhere. It's as though he is being eaten alive. They are crawling from under his other bandages and in and out of his shirt and the sheets. I lean over him to try to stop him seeing and I ring the bell, the three rings for emergency. I have never done this before. I try to cover him but the maggots have spilled on the floor and he has seen them. I see the horror of it in his eyes.

The charge nurse comes round the screens straight away. "Fetch a dustpan and brush nurse," she says to me "and ring for the RSO." As I go I hear her raised voice as she tries to restrain him and to say words of comfort—that the maggots have been put there on purpose, that they have cleaned his wounds and yes of course she'll put the gold cross wherever he wants it— yes, she'll put it there now—

Magda, who has a bad toothache, telephones me on the ward. Her face is horrible, all swollen, she says. She wants me to go with them to their little shack on the river. An easy journey she explains, a bus every hour on the hour. It is awkward taking the phone call in the ward office. I tell her I am not free. "Well Darling," she says, "next week then, as soon as you can manage. We'll be there. Just shout from the bank and we'll bring the punt to get you."

"Oh lovely!" I say, trying to get my voice as like Magda's as I can so that Ferguson, who has come into the office in a hurry for the thermometers, can hear, "Oh lovely!"

All evening while I am cleaning locker tops and making beds and giving out the soup and bread the men have for their supper I think about the river shack, a holiday bungalow which is a part of a rich person's life. I can imagine it clearly, low on the bank close to the quiet water. It will be painted white and there will be a small landing, a wooden jetty, belonging just to that cottage. I have seen these places, very private with grass coming right up to the walls. And all night it will be possible to smell the river water and to hear the soft sounds of it. I can imagine too the pleasure of being on the private jetty, of sitting there with my feet in the water as rich people sit looking as if they own that particular part of the river while ordinary people can only go by during an hour's paid-for pleasure trip in a boat owned and hired out by someone else . . .

Gertrude writes to say she is renting the field next to her place and it is for me. I can have some fowls of my own there and she'll look after them while I am at the hospital. She is buying some bricks too. She adds a p.s., "p'raps we could build us a pig pen and have a pig between us, a sow, we'd make a lot from the litter. I've always wanted to keep a pig."

I can't sleep and I try to read and I find a passage written by George Eliot to Caroline Bray after she has started her life with George Lewes. She writes:

> *I should like never to write about myself again; it is not healthy to dwell on one's own feelings and conduct,*

but only to try and live more faithfully and lovingly
every fresh day . . .

I like this very much and I sit on the edge of my bed and write a letter to Gertrude. I tell her that I like the idea of the field and the pig sty very much. I want to write to her about the maggots, I keep seeing them in my mind, but I write about Magda, all about her, about her face swollen with the bad tooth and how she says she is such a cold person and when you go to see her she is all crouched over a fire with little heaps of underclothes arranged all round the hearth to warm. I write some pages about the excitement of being invited to a doctor's house and how Magda is the daughter of a leading surgeon and that this is a good thing for Dr. Metcalf—everyone says so. I tell her about the all-night parties and how Magda and her friends call me "darling." And then I write about Dr. Metcalf and tell her that I think I love him. I end the letter telling her that I'm coming over to her place on my next day off to clean out the hen houses and to see my field and I tell her that I want to see her more than I want to see anyone else. I try to end my letter with a sentence from the quotation from George Eliot but do not know which part of it to include.

The next morning I address the letter and post it.

Tetanus typhoid diphtheria and gas gangrene. Relatives, mothers, and fathers traveling the length and breadth of England arrive at the hospital too late. They sit in corridors waiting for the first light of the morning and for the first trams . . .

Our examinations are postponed indefinitely.

I have a day off at last and I sleep all night and, because no one wakes me, I sleep all day as well. Unable to have these hours again I feel as if I am wasting the whole of my life.

I wait in the queue for letters. There is one for me from Gertrude, it is the longest letter I have ever had from anyone. I read it quickly—wondering what she will say in answer to mine.

I am ever so grateful, she writes, *for the fowl pen cleaning out but I feel very guilty as well. I am very concerned about your health, I will own up, I know you are a lot thinner than you should be it gives you a Ethereal Look and you should have the Perfect Health Look and not be overburdened with life. I should like you to have a few weeks out at grass . . .*

As I read it seems I can smell the potatoes boiling on the hob at Gertrude's Place and it is as if her voice is speaking telling me how a horse when he is overworked is put in a good meadow field, in good green pasture, where he can rest and eat and wander with other horses in safety and complete freedom. She writes:

I should like you to have a time of no worry and no burden. I am thinking such a lot about you and want you here so I can get you better. I could clear out the other room and make a nice bed where you could sleep quiet and comfortable. Of course I know I can want this for you and you might not want . . .

The slope of grass outside the window seems very close as I read on; it is as if she is speaking;

I will say that you occupy a place in my thoughts and in my Heart and life no one else will ever fill. Chiefly I am so grateful it will always seem so good of you, a person like yourself, to be friends with someone like me. I know I have to finish in this page and not be saying more in this letter it's nearly like saying Goodbye when I don't want you to go. I just want one more word. I don't know if you know it or not but there is something about you so refined and nice. Pure Gold or should it be Diamonds.
It is lovely to know one is loved and treasured and

I want to say I am so Happy to think of you being so kind and willing to know me and to come and see me and write to me. I want nothing but love and happiness for you and complete Reliance in the spirit of one who loves you   from your loving friend

Gertrude

Though I am reading the letter in the hospital dining room it seems as if I am in the twilight in the living room at Gertrude's Place with her sitting across the table from me—the packs of old cards ready for our game. I seem to be in the silence of the late afternoon at her place. I am wishing to be there and I think how I will go on Sunday, my next day off. I will get up early and be there the whole day and examine the rented field and decide where the pig pen should be. Gertrude, in her answer to my letter, has not said anything about Magda or Dr. Metcalf. It is as though they no longer exist.

"Long time no see." Lois has plonked herself in the chair opposite mine. She has spilled her tea in her saucer. "How's tricks?" she says lighting a cigarette and squinting at me through the smoke.

Every day I re-read Gertrude's letter. I carry it with me in the pocket of my uniform and while I am working I can feel its bulkiness. Perhaps when Ramsden comes to stay she will like to come out to Gertrude's Place, not on a bicycle of course, we can take the eleven a.m. bus to Holly Bush and walk down by the spinney, it's about a mile across the fields. Ramsden will not be coming for a while. By the time she comes we might have the pig and if you have something like a pig it is nice to be able to show it to someone.

At last it is Saturday and I have the evening off before the Sunday which is my day off. When I leave the ward Dr. Metcalf is waiting by the lift. He tells me that Magda has had to go off to visit her mother but the invitation to the cottage on the river still holds.

"What about tonight?" he asks. "I'll meet you at the bus stop in about half an hour. A lazy day," he says, "on the water tomorrow. Magda will be coming later on," he says.

"Yes," I tell him. "Yes, thank you, that will be lovely."

Up in the room I share with Lois she is there, half dressed, smoking and flipping the pages of a magazine. I change and tie my hair in two bunches.

"How come," Lois asks, "how come the red ribbons?"

"My better-half," I say, "my better-half likes my hair this way."

Ramsden

It is just like Ramsden, I mean, it is just the kind of thing Ramsden would say. She isn't saying it to me. She is saying that Bach must have written one of the Brandenburg Concertos in such a way that when a school orchestra drags through it it does not matter.

Which Brandenburg Concerto, I want to ask. But I am not in the conversation. Staff nurse Ramsden is talking to staff nurse Pusey-Hall. From the few paces behind them I can hear and listen to their words. It is clear that they have been to a concert together. A recital or a concert.

Bach dragged his violins as if on purpose. Only Ramsden could say something like this. So that, however badly the school orchestra played, it would not show. Ramsden and Pusey-Hall laugh in their well-bred way along the corridor. Like me, both of them are, in fresh white aprons, going on duty. Their long lacy caps seem to me to be exceptionally delicate, white and beautiful. We are all going to different places but this first part of the corridor we all share. Their voices are rich with amusement and tender at times as if intimate. I like the idea of the tender intimacy of their voices. I quicken my pace to keep up with theirs.

Ramsden is on the lower ground floor, a men's surgical ward down there, officers and men, men in the main ward and officers in the small wards. She kneels, at night, in the main ward to say the Lord's Prayer and the men, for those few minutes, hold up their housey-housey and wait in silence while Ramsden says the prayer and then they go on calling the numbers of the game. I have never actually seen Ramsden kneel down in the middle of the ward. I have only heard about it but can picture it well to myself. We are all meant to do this but not many staff nurses do. So far I have never been in charge at night but I try to memorize the Lord's Prayer. *Our Father which art in Heaven*, so that when the time comes I will be able to kneel and pray for the men.

Perhaps Ramsden and Pusey-Hall have been to something in the Town Hall. Perhaps the Sunday afternoon concert. Something quite beyond my reach. What did I do on Sunday? Of course, I remember, I went to sleep. More often than not it seems that I am sleeping away my whole life.

"An exploration of the twentieth-century religious belief and conviction . . ." Snatches of their conversation reach me still. "A need for the heroic response . . ." I miss the next bit, "the eternal suffering of . . ." Whose suffering? Did Ramsden say Christ?

I am not at all on the same intellectual level. I think Ramsden and Pusey-Hall read widely, especially the work of philosophers, and they have been to a concert.

Miss Robson, at school, had damp dark patches under her arms when she was conducting. There was one boy, the leading violin, the only one of us who could really play. White-faced, I think his name was Mottram, something like that. It does not matter.

I think I know what Ramsden means about the Brandenburg Concerto. Everyone playing at their own pace, some ahead of others. It is nice to know what Ramsden means. I can imagine her at the concert. She will have seen the gleaming black piano keys thin and sleek on the white ones, and she will have seen the pianist's surprisingly short fingers. The hands dimpled and like frogs falling above and below each other along the keyboard. She will have seen his serious pouting mouth and her head will have moved slightly in time with his head movements. Perhaps it was a quartet or a trio, the players leaning towards and away from each other, the pianist breathing lightly with the sound of the cello. Then there will have been the repeats with changes from a major key to the minor and then back to the expected and hoped for major. The pianist will have flipped the pages, before the page-turner could lean forward to do it, to glance quickly at the bottom of an earlier page before bowing his head and playing softly, this time without needing to look at the music. And all the time the ardent violinist climbs with feathery notes and the cellist plucks his strings.

Miss Robson, at school, had a little rod, a bâton. She tapped it to start and to stop the orchestra. She used it to make us lift our wrists at the piano.

The pianist on the concert platform can let his wrists drop. His galloping fingers can be flat, splayed out, or arched. He can choose.

Ramsden and Pusey-Hall will know all this. Close behind the rustle of their uniforms my own uniform makes its little starched sounds. They have been to a concert, probably on Sunday afternoon.

River Shack

∞

I have never wanted to spread out my pages to show to anyone, not even when I have been asked to. I have never told anyone about the little mark, the little cross, at the top left of every page. I never write a page of anything without first putting this little mark, without first asking a Blessing. How can I tell anyone this?

"I'll ask a Blessing," my father always said before a meal. Because he was hungry he was always sitting down first. And, with his hand shading his eyes, he would bend his head down as if ashamed that he had started, to eat before anyone else and before praying.

"Always ask a Blessing," he said, "before you do anything, before you undertake anything, and then remember, always, to pray again and offer thanks.

The little mark which is a tiny cross is on everything I write. I do not want to tell people about the little cross. People are suspicious. They suspect. They are superstitious too. They might be afraid of what they think of as the sentimental or the religious. This makes it harder to explain things. I have put the cross there for years. I never spoke of it, even in an imaginary conversation, with Ramsden. Perhaps one day it will be the right time to try to explain and, at the same time, to give up the secret of the harbor. The sky harbor, the exact place in the Brahms where the soprano sings with sustained serenity, her voice rising above a particular group of trees on a certain road known only in this pattern of events to me.

If I think now about the fowls at Gertrude's Place and if the nurse did, in fact, shut them up early that afternoon when I watched from higher up the hill leaning on my bicycle, unable to make up my mind to go down to the place where Gertrude was lying ill—if I think now about them, it is clear that, shut up early and left, it would be some time before they were let out. They would be like the prisoners in *Fidelio* when they are brought out suddenly from the darkness into daylight, let out from the dungeon, at Leonora's request, half blind in the sunlight, groping for each other's shoulders as they try to walk round in a circle. It will be all that the hens can do if, like the prisoners, they have been confined in the dark for too long—just stumble about the field falling over each other...

If I think now of foxes it is to think more of their coloring than of their habits. Magda's hair is often the color of fox, the golden red fox. A vixen. Gertrude would think of her as a vixen but not the vixen prowling for food for her partly weaned cubs or lying in a half circle of dust sunning herself and her offspring. Gertrude would see Magda as a huntress, perhaps hunting for herself, something stealthy and, though surrounded by people, alone.

When I hear about Dr. Metcalf's death, a death without any sense I cannot believe it but I have to. The whole hospital is talking about it. He never even got to the front. That is what they are all saying...

I always lift lavatory seats and peer under them. It was Bulge, at school, who said to do this. It was when we were in the school sanatorium together, isolated with German measles. She said it was because there might be a snake under it. She said in Madagascar, when she was a little girl, her nurse there was very careful to make sure there was no snake under the seat. Bulge's real father was dead, she explained. He had been a missionary.

So now I lift the wooden seat in the lavatory behind the river shack. There is no snake. The door does not close properly so I keep my foot against it, but no one comes. It is possible to sit here and look out across the meadows. The early morning mist takes a long time to lift and disperse. And, in the evenings, long shadows lie along the grass.

I was not kind to Bulge when we had German measles. When she talked to me I did not answer and I lay down with the bedclothes pulled up to my head. She was sorry for me and thought my ear ache must be bad. It was embarrassing to be ill just with Bulge.

Matron seemed to like Bulge. Bulge did not seem to be getting better. She had pains in her stomach. The pains made her cry out aloud. She wanted me to call Matron . . .

Magda's body is beautiful.

"You are beautiful," I tell Magda. She is standing naked on the river bank and Dr. Metcalf is pouring buckets of water over her. She seems taller without her clothes and I am surprised at her hips. I am surprised too about the size of her breasts. She is sunburned, a lovely golden brown, all over. The bodies of rich people are always suntanned and handsome. Dr. Metcalf is brown too. It is because they can be in places where they can take off all their clothes. They do not have to look out of tall windows and see the sun and not be out in it because they have to work. The black-out shutters at the hospital are put up at five o'clock blocking out the daylight and the sun. People like me are always white. Even if there is a sunny day and I can lie in the sun I simply get hot and I stay white. My face is gaunt with the dark circles of night duty for ever round my eyes.

Ferguson and Trent go up on the hospital roof, the flat part, one day. They do not mean to sleep but just to have an hour of summer sun up there. They do sleep and both are still red. Ferguson's blisters are only now beginning to be less painful and Trent is peeling horribly.

"Nurse Ferguson and Nurse Trent," Sister Bean said at breakfast. They both half rose from their chairs.

"Yes Sister?" as if in one voice.

"Matron's office nine a.m.," Sister Bean said.

When I tell Magda she is beautiful she laughs and says, "Isn't she sweet, Jonty, to tell me that? I'm old Veronica dear," she says to me, "can't you see how I *sag* everywhere. Look at all my saggings darling! Oh! *Quelle horreur!*"

When she describes her saggings she makes them sound desirable. Next to these magnificent people, when I make my comparisons, I seem to be badly made. These other people look as if they are the result of years of fine breeding. They are well-bred not only in their manners but in their bones and in their skin.

Dr. Metcalf has his shorts on. He is bigger in his partial nakedness than in his white coat on the wards.

"Strip orf darling!" Magda yells at me. "Let Jonty shower you." We are washing ourselves with white windsor soap at the edge of the river. The smell of the soap out of doors has a curious effect and, if I close my eyes, it is as if I am in the night nurses' bathroom at the row of small basins, fashioning Sister Bean in white windsor . . .

"Oh isn't she shy and sweet, closing her eyes!" Magda cries. "Take everything off Darling! Come on Jonty! Buckets for us both."

The quiet water is disturbed momentarily by Dr. Metcalf as he dives off the jetty and swims a few strokes round the slow curve of the river.

"Come on!" Magda says to me. "You have this towel. I'm ravenous. I didn't have any breakfast before I left. Let's fry up the bacon I've brought."

Magda's father and Marigold, an actress, come later in the day. Magda's father parks his car in the field opposite and blows the horn for Dr. Metcalf to go for them with the boat. Magda's mother does not come. Magda was staying with her the previous night after having her tooth out.

Dr. Metcalf and I have been in the river shack alone together all night. On the bus journey we were both so tired we hardly spoke to each other. He sat with his arm along the back of the seat. It was as if his arm was round me though I knew really it was not. I liked this very much. I keep thinking of the journey now during this quiet day on the water. "A lazy day," he said when he invited me, "on the water."

The day is anything but quiet. Magda arrives in the mist. Her taxi driver gives a shout from the towing path and Dr. Metcalf rows across the secret water of the river to fetch her. I only wake up when the driver shouts. I feel all big and white-faced and puffy and ugly. I help them carry all the packages and parcels into the cottage. If only I could be a bit suntanned or else wake up pretty or dainty and not as I am in my slept-in clothes.

Some of the young men, Magda announces, are coming in a car later. She has masses of food she says. She has managed to get butter and cheese and real coffee and champagne and dried bananas. I am ashamed to be hungry. We sit on the jetty to eat our breakfast. I tell Magda I might be able to get her some eggs.

"There's a path up from the road but it's hidden in the long grass," I start to tell Magda about Gertrude's Place.

"But Darling," she cries, "how divine! You must tell me how to get there."

My evening with Dr. Metcalf was over very quickly. During the walk from the bus stop, across the river meadows, to where the boat was moored under the bank Dr. Metcalf was very courteous. He guided me from one firm patch of grass to the next. Enormous cream-colored cows, their moist breath sweet with chewed grass, gathered near the path waiting to be herded for milking. He showed me the room in the river shack where I would sleep. Because the small house seemed to sit in a bed of grass, and because it was so quiet, I was reminded of Gertrude's Place. The house, like her place, seemed to be asleep.

"I never heard the river in the night," I say. "I had hoped," I tell Magda, "to hear the water slapping against the jetty boards, but I must have gone to sleep without hearing anything." While we sit there, with our feet in the brown water, I think of the evening and of the way in which Dr. Metcalf sat close to me on an old sofa covered with an unhemmed cloth. He said that he was older than I was and that I had all my life before me. He said he knew this but all the same he wanted to kiss me. Could he kiss me, he asked. I said I thought people kissed each other without asking. This seemed to please him and he kissed me very long and very sweet kisses. I think of these kisses all the time now and I wonder if Magda guesses and, if she does, whether she minds.

Dr. Metcalf, after a bit, took me to the small bedroom which he said was mine. The bed was very low, he sat on the edge of the bed and held out his arms. I remember his kisses and I remember how he held me and covered me up. I must have gone to sleep without undressing properly.

"I never heard the river in the night," I say, "and I never saw the sunrise." Once again I feel that, because of my work, I am wasting my whole life sleeping it all away, waking up all pale and ugly and not able to have those hours back. Dr. Metcalf says it was a lovely sunrise and if I missed it, never mind, there will be plenty of other sun risings in my life. He smiles at me and my mouth longs for his.

Magda looks at me seriously and tells me that Jonty is right of course.

Magda's father and his actress arrive early. Even though not one of these people is in any way like Bulge and her mother I am suddenly remembering Bulge. Perhaps it is the outside lavatory, the earth closet with the wooden seat which I feel I must raise to make sure there is no snake.

When we were ill together, and isolated, Bulge showed me a picnic photograph of her mother and this person she called Chris.

"Is he your father?" I asked and Bulge explained that Chris was like a father but he was her mother's Friend. Her father died, she reminded me, while he was looking after sick people in an African village. Because of the boredom of being ill with only Bulge for company, and a few damp old books we found in the chimney cupboard, I stared for a long time at the picnic photograph. I tried, in the presence of *Clive of India, Bevis,* and *Nineteenth Century English Gardens* to make a book out of the photograph. I peered at every detail, the tartan traveling rug on which Bulge's mother was sitting and the kind of cake she had in an open tin on her lap. She was handing cake to Chris. The idea of cake made me hungry.

"What sort of cake was it?" I asked Bulge.

"I can't remember," she said. "Perhaps Madeira," she said. "Chris likes that." We were hungry all the time, both of us, Bulge and me. In the photo Chris looked tall. He wore plus fours. He was crouching fondling a little white dog. Bulge explained it was a Sealyham. Her mother always had a dog and it was always that sort.

Perhaps it is this picnic lunch which reminds me. If I compare my mother with Bulge's mother it is clear that my mother is below Bulge's mother in the comparison. My mother has never had a pet of any kind. When I consider this I have to realize that she does not like dogs at all and would be disgusted if she knew of Magda's habit of having the Red Setter in bed with her.

Perhaps it is the tartan rug which reminds me so unexpectedly of Bulge's picnic photograph. Because of being above Bulge in my comparisons at school, her hair, her cracked spectacles, her complexion, and the way in which she stood, bulging and biting her nails, everything being worse, I do not especially like thinking about her. This thinking puts us on the same level. I try not to think about her. Magda's father is very fond of his actress and touches her often. He is fond of Magda too and strokes her arms and gives her little hugs. For a long time he does not seem to notice me at all and then says he has heard that I am a Quaker and I say not a very good one I'm afraid and he laughs, throwing his head back, as he does in Theater when someone makes a joke during a partial gastrectomy, saying that's the best answer he ever heard and then goes back to not noticing me. I can't help dwelling on my good answer and I wish I could say something else which would be a good answer. No one really addresses any other remarks to me and, as I am hungry, as I always am, I eat a lot of the ham and the butter and the dried bananas. Food rationing does not affect Magda and the food she has brought is quite unlike what we are able to have at home or in the hospital. Magda's father has brought a paper bag full of peaches. He has them sent from London. I have never eaten a peach and concentrate my thoughts on hoping there will be enough in the bag for us all to have one.

Magda's three expected guests, the young men who come to her house parties, do not come and she is disappointed but thinks they might come the next day.

Cows have trodden down the river bank but Magda thinks it would be heavenly to sleep out on the grass. Her father and Goldy can have the bedroom in the shack. Magda arranges everything.

"There'll be a huge moon," she promises me, "and Jonty will find us a clean patch of grass." We carry our bedclothes out to the edge of the river.

I feel I should be happy listening to the river slapping gently underneath the weathered boards of the jetty. I am, at last, where I have wished to be. I breathe the river water and river mud smell and the fragrance of the crushed grass but it does not take away the unexpected sadness. For a time the moon is bright and the water, not shadowed by the banks and the trees, shines. From time to time something plops, with a small splash, into the water. I suppose it is a water rat. I am wishing for Dr. Metcalf, to be alone with him, in his arms, inside the blankets which are, like mine, rolled all round him. We are, all three, rolled-up bundles in a row, our feet down towards the water and our faces up to the moon. This is the same moon my father can see. In my loneliness now I try to think of my father and his moon but it is Dr. Metcalf I want. I am thinking of him and wishing for his arms and his kisses. I want to feel him close to me again as he was last night. I wish I had not slept last night.

Sometimes a solitary boat drifts by. Though I can't see them I know there are two people in each boat, unwilling to stop being together and not wanting the night to end. The moon has a ring of light around it. Dark clouds hurry across the bright face of the moon. Magda and Dr. Metcalf who were saying soft words, now and then to each other (they thought I was asleep), are quiet now. Perhaps I am the only person in all the miles of country not asleep. The cows, dark shapes on the other bank, move together. I can smell their grassy breath and hear when one of them lowers herself or gets up. I am glad they are not asleep.

There is a distant sound of aeroplanes. The engines throb as they come nearer. Like a heartbeat, on and on, coming nearer. They are German planes. I know this because of the throbbing sound of the engines. Far away across the water meadows pale search lights send their thin fingers, like long petals, across the sky. Magda says should we go inside and Dr. Metcalf says no, what difference would it make.

Bulge, when we were in isolation together, said that the Germans, if they came with the aeroplanes, if it came to a war between us and the Germans, the Germans could wipe out Britain with one raid. At the time I thought that the Chris gentleman must have told her that. I believed it. Later we all said it at school. "One raid and we'll all be wiped out. Really! The war, if it comes to that!" The Germans are not all that bad I wanted to say then. Not all Germans are bad. There did not seem, then, the words for this to be said.

Bulge's mother and Chris visited Bulge during our illness. They were so nice to me. Friendly and sitting on my bed and talking to me as if I had never been unkind to Bulge, ever. Bulge of course could have been as homesick as I was. Muriel, they called her Muriel, could have longed for her mother and this Chris. Her mother told me, "Muriel has some rabbits at home too," when I told her about our rabbits at home. Bulge was so nice to me. She never said one word about my not speaking to her. And she obviously had not said anything about the raggings she had from everyone. On the afternoon when her people came I hadn't got my spectacles on and, when her mother put her head round the door, I thought, for a moment, that my mother had come. I hid under the bedclothes when I realized my mistake. It was hard not to cry. It was then that this Chris gentleman sat on my bed asking me about my bandage while Bulge and her mother had their first hugs. I told him, "It's a middle-ear abscess," and he said he was sorry.

That night Bulge called out to me to fetch Matron because her pain was bad. "I think it's my appendix," she said, and was sick over her bedspread and the floor. I went down quickly, in the dark, to Matron's cottage. She came at once.

In my secret game of comparisons Bulge was placed high up, far higher than anyone else, for she had the school doctor at her bed in the night. I was envious and felt ashamed of being envious and tried to be helpful. Bulge was trying not to cry but her pain was too bad. Matron said to me to lie down and to try to go to sleep. She said they would have to take Bulge to hospital. They wrapped her in a blanket and took her in the doctor's car to Oxford to the hospital before it was too late. The tall grasses and the cow parsley along the lanes, I thought, would look like lace in the moonlight.

Matron, in her haste, left the light on and I tried to read the book Bulge's mother gave me, as a present, before she left. It was a school story about a girl called Treacle. The book was called *Treacle Wins Through*. I wanted to enjoy the book but I could not help thinking about Bulge crying and drawing up her legs because of her pain.

Magda's young men, the three expected guests, do not come on the next day either.

Dr. Metcalf and I go for a short walk to the farm nearby for some fresh milk. We do not have to cross the river.

"I was hoping to take you upstream," he says to me, "in the boat. There are wild swans there, further up . . ." I thank him and say in a small voice that it doesn't matter. On the way back he sets down the milk can and draws me to the shelter of a hedge. Quickly he holds me close and kisses me and then holds me away from himself.

"I can't give you all the love you ought to have," he says and he kisses my fingers, very lightly, brushing them with his lips.

"That's all right Dr. Metcalf," I say, hearing my own voice and words with surprise. I tell him that it's all right, that I've got a boy friend in the forces. In the air force to be exact. We walk on back to the river shack.

All day I am wishing that I had gone home and gone to Gertrude's Place. There was no way in which I could let her know I was not coming. She is probably walking down through the long grass to look down the long hill, as far as the bend, to see if I am coming up, walking, leaning on my bicycle. Two whole days off wasted. I thought I could be happy just being near Dr. Metcalf but it is not like that. I can't even look at him as I want to when other people are there. And he can't look at me, not into my eyes and my thoughts like the evening when we were down here alone. I want to be with him by myself. My mother, it consoles me to think this, might have gone on the bus to fetch the eggs and will have told Gertrude I am not coming.

Dr. Metcalf does not eat lunch. He seems thoughtful. I am afraid he might be depressed and sad and I try not to show that I am. Magda is decidedly peeved. She says so herself. "God I'm peeved!" she keeps saying it. The river is crowded with Sunday train-excursion visitors. Trippers, Magda calls them. She is obliged to put on clothes as so many boats are passing the little jetty. Young men, performing antics with punt poles, whistle and call out as they pass. Magda says she's had enough of the shack and we'll all go back to town and do I want to visit my parents because if so Daddy, as soon as he and Marigold are up and dressed, is going back to town and will give us all a lift and can drop me off at the bus station.

It is late when I get home after waiting hours for a bus and a train. As soon as I open the kitchen door my mother hands me a telegram. I have to return to the hospital at once.

"The telegram came yesterday," she tells me.

"I would only have been able to stay for the evening," I tell her. "I've had my days off."

My father says he will come to the station with me. We have to leave at once to be sure to get the train. He carries the small parcel my mother has made. It is a fruitcake she has packed and some hard-boiled eggs.

"The eggs are from Gertrude," she tells me.

Lois has washed her hair. It amuses me to see the turban she has made with the towel. I tell her that her turban is delightful and that I have brought some cake.

"We're on at midnight," she says, "a special shift." She does not explain further. "You're daft!" she says suddenly, "going with Them! She's as bad as he is. Can't you see? Those Metcalfs! No I don't want any cake."

"But you don't know them. They're sweet, both of them, and very kind." I eat a piece of the cake.

"Oh yes!" Lois says, and then with an accent, "Oh! yeah?"

"They're my friends," I say.

"Some friends!" She lights a cigarette from the new packet I have brought for her. "He's the reason for Smithers suiciding," she says, "it was because of Dr. Metcalf."

Smithers, the theater orderly, I remember him reading a poem he'd written. He asked me if he could read it. And then he asked me what I thought about it. He was very tall and pale because of always being indoors and in the artificial light of the theaters.

Because of the charge nurse coming in just then I was not able to listen properly. Smithers went on putting drums of sterile gauze on to the shelves and I went on handing them to him. I had not been able to understand the poem and, because the charge nurse did not leave, Smithers was not able to repeat his question.

I remember the poem and I remember his suicide.

"But Smithers!" I say.

"Exactly," Lois says.

Single Malt

❧

Suddenly I am reminded of my mother. Perhaps it is because today, in the distance, I saw a woman with her hair curled as my mother's used to be. This woman was standing with some other people further along the street. Because I knew it could not be her I did not go up there. However much a person resembles another person, and it is not that person, it is not of any use.

Perhaps I should, at some time, write down every single thing which I remember about my mother. Perhaps that is something I could do.

My mother, who always needed someone to tell things to, suddenly, after the death of my father, had no one. After three stormy weeks in a private nursing home she returned home to an empty house and had no one to tell her dreadful experience to.

She had to live several years alone.

. . . as he is now made partaker of the death of thy Son, so he may be also of his resurrection . . .

It is my evening off but I am not going out anywhere. A baby died today.

A baby died in my arms today.

The book I choose when staff nurse Ramsden says to me to choose any book I would like to have from her shelves is a foolish choice for me. I can never say this to anyone. My mother is fond of embroidery and would understand all the diagrams and the pictures in the book. She would understand the step-by-step instructions and descriptions; mount mellick, crewel work, Berlin embroidery, tapestry, gros point, petit point, ribbon work, and needle painting, bead work, black work, and all the stitches and techniques from the elegant oriental Tambour . . . I like the idea of the needle painting. Of course I can't give the book to my mother. It is a present from Ramsden and it is my fault that I chose it instead of some other book. I mean she had Wordsworth there and Keats, Goethe, Rilke and e.e. cummings and Dickens and others. That is the worst of being asked to choose.

It does not seem possible really, this evening, to go and see Magda. During the car ride after being at the river shack they all seemed to argue, in fun but not quite in fun. Dr. Metcalf laughed about Magda's single-malt gentlemen not turning up. "They knew all the single malt was gone," he teased her.

"They never drink all the single malt," Magda said. "You," she said to Dr. Metcalf, "you always have your tots and so does Daddy. Don't you Daddy?" I thought Magda might be going to cry but Dr. Metcalf was stroking her arm and I saw all the little lines and frowns disappear from her forehead and round her eyes.

I watched the hedges slipping by, the cow parsley tall and lacy all along the lanes. I kept wishing the bus station was not so far away.

Magda was sitting between us. Dr. Metcalf's arm was round the back of Magda and his hand, stroking her soft sun-burned arm, was very close to my arm. The back of his hand was against my arm. I told myself to bury myself then in the beauties of nature for ever. But then, like now, the phrase, the beauties of nature, had no meaning.

Magda's father, driving with a well-bred ease, had one arm round Marigold.

This evening I am putting my stamp collection in order, at least I am trying to. Some of them have come loose and have fallen out. I am unable to be interested enough to sort and arrange them properly. My head itches. I would like to brush my hair but Lois, who has gone home for her day off, has borrowed my hairbrush. I open my exercise books of pressed wild-flowers, meadow sweet, saxifrage, coltsfoot, lady's slipper, and star of Bethlehem. There is nothing I can do with them and, somehow, thinking about the grassy places where they grew makes me sad.

It does not seem possible to go and see Magda today, this evening. Not after the river shack. I wonder what they are doing tonight, Magda and all of them and Dr. Metcalf.

I put my clothes drawer straight, fold and tidy everything very neatly, and make up my mind to always keep my white blouse and my good pair of stockings clean, in readiness, in case I get invited somewhere. That is the kind of person I am.

Magda has not left a message telling me to come, as she usually does. Perhaps something has happened over there, at their place, since the river shack. She did have a tooth out. Perhaps an infection?

My stockings, my good pair, are really quite nice. It must be really special to have a man roll your stockings with nimble fingers so that when he puts them on your feet they unroll delicately and smoothly all the way up your legs. Once, in a film, I saw a handsome man kneeling in front of a very pretty woman and, this man, he could do stockings like this. I don't know many men and those I do know, for example, my father and Dr. Metcalf, I don't think they would ever do stockings. Though, perhaps Dr. Metcalf might.

The baby, the smallest baby I have ever seen, is called Roger Keith. He died in my arms. This morning.

"Nurse!" the charge nurse calls to me as I pass the end of Obstetrics. Ward 4. I am only on that corridor because the lift isn't working. "Have you got a clean apron on?" she bawls. I shout back that it isn't very clean and that I'm on my way to Pharmacy.

"Is there something you need from Pharmacy?" I go towards her. "They forgot our carbolic."

"Take it off," the charge nurse says, "your apron, take it off and put it on inside out. And be quick and come along in here.

Put your ration jars down there, yes, just down there by the door. That's it, turn your apron, quick as you can. Look sharp!"

The charge nurse is not one that I know. I don't even know her name.

"I'm not on this ward," I begin to tell her.

"I know. I know that," she says. "It's an emergency," she tells me. "I haven't a single nurse free, we're flat out, three heads showing and five just post-natal, and now this. Only keep you a minute. Quick as you can nurse, there's a good girl, you've got your sleeves down and your cuffs. Good!"

Propped up in the bed in the screened-off corner of the ward is a woman. Her hair is brushed back and tied up neatly with a piece of cotton bandage. She is very pale and she is weeping. She is crying without any sound, her tears are over-flowing as if straight from her heart. She is weeping as if she will never be able to stop. The charge nurse goes over to her at once.

"The chaplain is coming at once," she says in a low voice. The woman nods and still her tears pour down her cheeks.

At the side of the bed is a hospital cot, a little wire basket, covered with some folded pieces of flannel. The charge nurse picks up the quiet baby.

"Cesarean," she says to me out of the side of her mouth. "Nurse here," she turns to the woman in the bed, "nurse will be Godmother."

"But," I say, "but I'm not a . . . I'm a . . . we don't . . ."

"Never mind, nurse, whatever you are or whatever you do or don't do. Here's the Reverend himself." Swiftly she wraps the baby in a white cloth and gives him to me.

The tiny bundle is light in my arms. His eyes are closed and his little mouth is puckered. Already the finely made delicate lips are blue. As I hold him close I feel his tiny body make a feeble movement.

The chaplain bends his white head over his book. He moves closer as he reads. He asks me to name the baby. I glance at the woman. "Roger Keith," she hardly moves her lips.

"Roger Keith," I say, holding the baby towards the drops of water which fall like cold tears from the chaplain's fingers.

Roger Keith.

"I baptize thee in the Name of the Father, and of the Son, and of the Holy Ghost."

"Amen," the charge nurse kneels, so I kneel with the baby. The chaplain's words rush on:

". . . And we humbly beseech thee to grant, that as he is now made partaker of the death of thy Son, so he may be also of his resurrection . . ."

The small rustling sigh which was Roger Keith's breathing has stopped. The charge nurse takes him from me and replaces him gently in his cot. The woman in the bed holds out her hands to me and I feel their hot dryness. Her tears, like shining beads, force their way still from under her closed eyelids.

"Thank you nurse," the charge nurse has escorted the chaplain to the ward doors. "Whyever," she asks, "whyever are you taking your butter and jam and sugar down to the Pharmacy?"

"It's my morning-tea break," I say. "I'm to go to Pharmacy on the way back."

The lift is working now and I go down to the basement in the company of a long trolley rattling a dozen chipped enameled cans. The cans all have lids and they are all marked with numbers to show which wards they belong to.

"Sweet pees," the porter says to me. He lights a cigarette. Porters, with trolleys and dustbins and theater bins and laundry and these smaller cans, often smoke. They say they are allowed to because of the nature of their work. He is taking the urine from patients, soldiers, who have been having penicillin, to the lab. The penicillin will be extracted and used again. He tells me this and I let him even though I already know it.

"It's a miracle," the porter says.

"Yes, it is," I say and I almost ask him what kind of God there could be who would receive a child over whom the right words had been said and whether this same God would reject, really refuse, one who lacked this charm.

"Ladies hats underwear and dresses," the porter opens the lift to a row of bins. Pharmacy is just to the right and the Laboratory a bit further on. We go along the corridor unable to speak because of the rattling of the cans.

I suppose they will be having dinner now at Magda's, perhaps something which can be eaten on cushions on the floor.

"Hobbling along supported by academia." Magda, frowning and weary, once more, in the car during the drive from the river shack, accused Dr. Metcalf, talking about someone, a friend of his, a one-time friend of his, someone I have never met. "She's done enough," Magda said, "to make herself a footnote in the literary history of this country."

Dr. Metcalf laughed at this, at Magda's supposed anger. He raised his eyebrows in an amused look at me across the back of Magda's head. He pursed his lips at me as if to blow a little kiss in my direction.

"That's not true, is it?" His tone to me was playful.

"I'm afraid I don't know her," I said and I turned to stare harder into the hedges. Wild roses I wanted to say to them. Look you, dog roses, hundreds of little wild roses all along the hedges.

"Darling!" Magda said then. "Of course you don't know. Jonty had a Friend, with a capital F, who used to come. She said she actually thought our house was a sort of religious retreat. Can you imagine! A past pillar of the Ballet Rambert she wasn't slow on the single malt either. She ended up, my deah, in the school of stitchery and lace, an adventitious ornament, no doubt, with her big hands and feet."

They all laughed then. I couldn't ask what single malt meant. What it was. Something hard to get, I supposed, even for Magda for whom rationing did not seem to exist. Something hard to get so that it mattered if their friends were not slow on it.

Because I could not understand and because I did not understand the metaphor, if it was a metaphor, the school of stitchery and lace, I turned away to stare once more at the roadside and at the trees in the hedgerows.

"Darling Child!" Magda cried. "Jonty!" she said, "I do believe our Precious Child is jealous. Oh you sweet Darling!" She broke loose from Dr. Metcalf's arm and drew me to her sweet-smelling soft breasts and kissed me hard on the mouth.

"You are so sweet," she purred and continued to hug me and call me sweet for the rest of the journey. So it is strange, very strange, that I have not heard from her.

Diet Kitchen

"He didn't go, he didn't really go to the Front at all he shot his knee caps off and bled to death at his mother's place."

"Disgusting."

"I didn't know he had a mother."

"Yes, the poor thing—even though she's a prostitute."

"She must be quite old, I mean, if she's his mother."

"She is. But some men, they like Experience. Experience counts."

"That's right. Doesn't matter what sort of old bag. I mean looks just aren't in it. A man who's never done it doesn't go for looks, all he wants is a friendly vagina."

"I suppose he was illegitimate. Anyone got any butter left?"

"A bastard. Hm!"

"Yes a bass-tarrdd."

"Anybody got a ciggy?" Lois brings her coffee to the table. She is on night duty too. I slip the new packet from my pocket on to her lap. We always seem to be having our meal times at the same time. Without seeming to notice the *State Express* Lois does notice. She clears a corner of the table for herself and opens the packet.

"How clean you are, like a spring flower, a snowdrop," Lois said to me once. It was as if we were in another world then. We were walking in the rain and we stopped suddenly, looking at each other and laughing.

"Your hair!" she said then, "it's soaked but you look so nice, clean, green and white, they're your colors, a snowdrop. I'd like to paint you. Lois painted, water colors, in the room we shared.

We pinned up the paintings even after the Home Sister left a note telling us to take them down.

"Your tartan dress," I said, "it's so funny. I like your clothes, they make me laugh. Your hair," I said, "your hair's wet too. This rain!" The unexpected rain made the tartan wet so that it was smooth round her breasts. "Very sweet you are. Did you know you are very sweet!" I said then.

"Well of course if it's Dr. Metcalf you're talking about." Lois sends a cloud of smoke across the shepherd's pie and the baked apples.

It is Dr. Metcalf. Everyone's talking about him, everyone, that is, except me.

"They say he never got to the Front. He was crushed behind a lorry, an army lorry reversing. And the war practically over too."

"They say he was at the camp near Swindon. Ever heard of Swindon? Whatever made him join up now. Never got to any action. I mean if there is any now. It's too late. I suppose that's why. Pass the salt please."

"Did you know he was on morphia? Used to come to Lower Ground Radium for it and whatsaname, heroin. We used to hide the keys. On nights, you know, we hid the keys."

"Remember Foss? Wasn't Foss on Lower Ground Radium?"

"Yes, Foss was on there then. Charge on nights. Used to hide the keys in her bra. Ugh! This apple's sour! He got them, the keys, one night. When she was doing the linen cupboard. Put his hand right down her bra. Disgusting!"

"He didn't need to go. Have some of my sugar, I don't use it all. He only joined up to get away from his wife."

"And other people. Thanks, anyone else going to borrow some sugar? And other people. He's made eleven nurses pregnant."

"Could be twelve." Lois hardly looks up as she speaks.

"His wife's twenty years older than him. Or is it thirty?"

"He's got nine children all with different mothers."

"No wonder he wanted to get right away."

"And some there be who've got VD!"

"He did have VD, you know, and must've passed it on to goodness knows how many people."

"Should have gone to the clinic."

"He did under an assumed name but quite a few people recognized him of course."

"His wife's riddled with it."

"Not surprising."

"He wasn't a qualified doctor at all they've found out. He was just one big fraud. He was a greengrocer really with this prostitute of a mother. She worked in the shop and took the men upstairs."

"That's right! No papers."

"They found papers on him but they must've been stolen. He had Chatwyn Brown's papers."

"Chatters Brown? But he was reported missing ages ago! Poor old Chatters!"

"Yes. Well, Metcalf had *his* papers—on him!"

"They found a dead German's finger in his pocket, too, with a big gold ring on it. Couldn't get the ring off."

"I thought he didn't get to the Front."

"He didn't. Probably stole the finger from someone. Had to take the whole finger to get the ring."

"Disgusting!"

"Yes, disgusting."

"What d'you expect!"

"Sister Whatsaname on chests suicided because of him."

"Yes, and that's why Roberts ran away. Remember little Nurse Roberts? Ever such a quiet little person. Probably dropped her bundle by now. Anyone know what she got?"

"Twins. Could be twins, you know."

"Could be infected too."

"Yes could be. Would be tertiary, don't you see."

"Roberts hasn't gone yet. She's cutting it a bit fine. I mean it's obvious isn't it. I mean she's *showing*."

"And Smithers. Remember Smithers?" Lois looks for matches for her second cigarette. She glances at me through her cloud of smoke. Her eyes glitter beneath partly lowered lids. She looks away quickly.

"Smithers," she says, "on theater, he suicided. Remember? Lemmington Frazier's rectal orderly. He suicided because of Metcalf."

"Lemmington Frazier! That's Metcalf's father-in-law surely."

"Yes, he's on his tenth actress. Marigold Bray."

"You nursed her mother on Women's Surgical didn't you?" Lois inhales deeply, holds the smoke and lets it out across the table. "Didn't you?" she says to me.

"Yes," I say. "I did, Mrs. Bray, a hernia."

I often think of Mrs. Bray. I remember her telling me that she worked at the public baths. I remember all too clearly that I cried by her bed, behind the screens, the day Dr. Metcalf told me he was leaving for the Front.

"I don't want to lose you," I told him when he said he had to go. "I'm frightened," I said.

"Don't cry, please don't cry," he said.

"Don't you cry, dear," Mrs. Bray said, "he'll come back. Your boy'll come back." Mrs. Bray said something else too that day. She said a person has to love work. You have to love your work. She loved hers, she said, at the public baths.

I told her I had met Marigold at the river shack. "You know," I said to her, "Dr. Metcalf's place on the river."

"Oh yes, Edna, my daughter," she said, "only she don't call herself Edna any more. I'm hoping," she said, "as she'll come back and see me one of these days. I just have the one girl. That's what I mean about work. See? Enjoying your work makes you enjoy your life. Helps you to forget things as go wrong."

I am thinking now about Mrs. Bray's thin, sad face and how her eyes brightened when she talked about Marigold. I would like to talk to someone about Dr. Metcalf.

"Mrs. Lemmington Frazier," Lois stabs out her third cigarette. "Sweet. She's really sweet. Nursed her hysterectomy."

"Lemmington Frazier! Gives me the shivers. Dirty old man!"

"She had her veins done too. Mrs. Lemmington Frazier."

"Yes that's right, she did."

"Mrs. Lemmington Frazier used to come round the wards with that Red Cross trolley. Remember? Library books and magazines and writing paper."

"Yes and home-made face flannels and jam."

"She used to get chocolate and cigarettes for the men."

"The officers you mean."

"No, the men. She went round them all."

"Her daughter, Mrs. Metcalf, used to go too."

"Never!"

"Yes she did, all tarted up to kill. You can just see it next to the Lemmington Frazier tweeds! A sort of heather mixture."

"And the lilac twin set."

"And the pearls."

"And the lisle stockings."

"But really Mrs. Lemmington Frazier has very good taste!"

"Yes, if you like Henry Heath hats."

"It's supposed to be good for a doctor's career if he can get married to a surgeon's daughter. Specially an only one. Promotion eh? Luxurious! Straight to the top!"

"That's right."

"Wasn't Metcalf Lemmington Frazier's dresser?"

"Yes he was, that's right."

"Lemmington Frazier's daughter! She used to call him Daddy and there she was in theater, all gowned up, holding the artery forceps or a retractor. Supposed to be studying. I ask you! And nothing on under her gown. You could see *everything*."

"Yes. She used to leave when Daddy did when the dresser was sewing up. Other students had to stay."

"Must've waited somewhere for Metcalf, then."

"He probably ran out after her."

"But what about Smithers? Haven't seen him for a while, come to think of it."

"Yes, Smithers."

"Smithers? Smithers? Was he that tall one? The thin pale willowy one? Used to be the shave orderly?"

"You remember. Looked like he'd been in the sterilizer all his life. Steamed. That awful white skin!"

"Yes, of course, Smithers. Suicided because of Metcalf? But he was a *man*."

"Exactly." Lois says. "That's exactly it. He was a man."

The cigarette smoke is worse as some of the others are smoking now. I feel sick and am glad that the meal time is over.

"Lois," I said once, "Ferguson doesn't seem to like our being together so much. I think she feels left out. Could we?"

"Furgusun? Furgusun? Who is Furgusun?"

"You know Ferguson," I said. "I was sharing a room with her till we requested the swap. I think it hurt her that I wanted to share with you. It would have been easier for her if I'd asked to go back to having a single room. I was at school. We were at school together. You see? Could we include her. . . ? "

"Well, you're not at school now," Lois said. Trent heaved herself off my bed then and walked, half dressed, round the room on flat feet.

"Quack Quack and Quack. Quackitty Quackitty Quack Quack." We fell in a heap on Lois's bed.

"Your breasts," I said to Lois later when Trent had gone, "are indescribably soft."

"I know," Lois said, "Matron says I must get something done about them."

"Trent really can do ducks," I said, "she really can do ducks."

"She really can," Lois said.

"Ramsden," I say making an effort to keep my voice level, "my folks would be very happy if you would visit. Ramsden," I say, "when you have been to London, I mean, when you have had your holiday, I mean, I shall have my holidays then."

I renew my invitation to Ramsden to come and stay for a few days. Staff nurse Ramsden. We are in the lower ground corridor going in opposite directions. I have had my meal and she is going to hers. I have never worked with Ramsden. The others say she is very nice to work with. She is on Lower Ground Radium.

Ramsden says thank you and accepts. She seems shy. She often seems shy. It is then that she gives me the poems.

"I have no right to give you these," she says, "but here they are anyway."

"Thank you," I say, "thank you very much." I hold the little book carefully in both hands, with both hands together as if for a prayer.

"Look at them, if you care to, some time," Ramsden says, her eyes darker because she is shy. "When you have a minute. No!" she puts her hands over mine, "there isn't time now. Put them in your pocket. Put them away."

We both have to hurry.

"There is never time," she says. She explains that she has had to leave the Junior in charge as her second-year nurse had to go off. "She was really not well enough to be on duty." Ramsden has a reputation for thoughtfulness.

Wherever in my mother's house can staff nurse Ramsden sleep?

> *The feathers of the willow*
> *Are half of them grown yellow*
> *Above the swelling stream;*

I do look quickly into Ramsden's little book. It is all written in her neat small handwriting. Some of the poems are her own and some she has chosen.

The wireless is still on in the Lower Ground Men's Surgical. It is an officers' ward and the ordinary hospital rules do not apply. The lights are all on still and the officers are not even in their pajamas yet. Some are playing cards and others are sitting in the ward office with the Charge Nurse and her Junior. All very casual. They seem to be mostly convalescents. The wireless is loud, "In the Mood" is on. The lines of the poem seem to fit this music as it goes on and on;

> *And ragged are the bushes,*

and rusty now the rushes,
and wild the clouded gleam.

The words in my head are in time to the music. I even seem to walk in time to it. This music "In the Mood" is incredibly vulgar accepting, as it seems to do, entirely unacceptable vulgarity. I wish the poem did not fit and that I could walk to a different rhythm.

I wonder what other poems Ramsden has chosen. The Lower Grounds corridor is dark beyond the ward. The poem is about the autumn. It's the beginning of the autumn.

This summer belongs to us you said. You told me not to call you Dr. Metcalf. "Jonathon," you said. I was to call you Jonathon. It was hard for me to change. Dr. Metcalf I called your name and you said, "Jonathon, remember? Especially when we are loving each other. How can I be doctor?" you said. "Jonathon," I said.

For a few minutes just now in the corridor while I looked at Ramsden's poems I forgot, for just those few minutes what has happened to Dr. Metcalf.

The diet kitchen is awful. I can't stand the diet kitchen. It is on the Lower Ground corridor further on from Radium Therapy and the Officers' Ward. It is a basement really and is vaulted. It is not well lit at night. I suppose to save electricity.

I am in the diet kitchen. All round me are the horrible little trays and their food labels. I hate cutting and weighing pieces of bread. I can't stand the smell of the vitamin B extract. The smell of tripe stewing is as bad as the smell of boiling beetroot.

I am in the diet kitchen all alone. This is the place where Nurse Roberts, on day duty, can't stand the sight of the dried egg powder, not even the packets of it. A kitchen boy comes in with fuel for the boiler and the stove. He comes twice during the night. He works in the main kitchens where there are quite a few people including a crippled cook who can't talk. Trent told me once that she has to work at night and that she hides during the day because people are afraid when they see her. At least there is company in the main kitchens but nurses do not work there.

The kitchen boy is waiting. He stands very close. I can see his ginger eyelashes, each one individually.

"Well?" I say sharply. "What d'you want? You've stoked the boiler."

"Is it God's honor truth," he asks me, moving closer so that I can smell hard-boiled eggs on his breath. "Is it true," he grins, shaking his head and showing gap teeth, "that Sister Whatsit up on chests and Dr. Metcalf had to have an operation to get separated? Was they really stuck together like them," he jerks his head in the direction of the main kitchen, "like them in there says they was?"

"Of course not," I say, "don't be so silly! Here give me that!" I take the hod of coke and let it fall on his feet. His boots are thick and he does not seem to feel any pain. Either it's his boots or his stupidity. He stares at my tears. "What's up? What's the marrer?" He peers up into my face.

"Oh, go away!"

"Orright, then I'm goin'. Orright. Orright I'm a goin'."

"Don't cry nurse! There's nothing to cry about, now is there."

It's one of those Matron's office nine a.m. things. I am here in front of Matron's desk. She is sitting on the other side moving her freshly sharpened pencil to and fro above a timetable which looks like a checked tablecloth in front of her. She talks softly to herself as her pencil pauses. She frowns, shakes her head, and moves her pencil on, an inch or two, above the neatly ruled pattern.

Weekends have been the worst. Magda suddenly wants a garden Dr. Metcalf tells me. She wants all the rough grass at the back of the house cut and then mown into smooth lawns. She wants roses and fruit trees and vegetables. Weekends I have not been able to stop thinking about them doing the garden together. Magda wants home-grown salads Dr. Metcalf explains. "Come round," he says in his most gentle voice. "She wants you to come," he says. He wants me near him.

"All right," I say. I walk by their house several times but I don't go up to the door.

"The weekends," Dr. Metcalf says when we have a few minutes alone, "the weekends are full of planting Magda. Don't cry," he says, his voice very soft, his lips near my ear. "Don't cry. Please, please don't cry."

Matron says, "The diet kitchen and, let me see, night duty I think." She looks up from the big timetable which has, I know, because she has said so before, over four hundred nurses on it. "Plenty of fresh air every day before you go to bed." She smiles at me and tells me I am very pale. She likes her nurses, she says, to keep well.

I have never thought that I belonged to her. One of her four hundred nurses. My eyes fill with tears again.

"There is absolutely no need for these tears," Matron says, "come along nurse, dry your eyes. There is nothing to cry about. You know as well as I do that the rule about the doctor's corridor applies for the benefit of the nurses. Bomb damage aside, it is no place for my nurses. It has been brought to my notice that you have been seen there occasionally. No doubt you will have had your reasons and I am not going to question them. The corridor is absolutely out of bounds. The rule exists, nurse, because of those in our profession who are weaker." She smiles again. "I do not, for one moment, nurse, want to consider you to be one of them." She has made up her mind, she says, that I am to be a gold medalist. "You can do it! It's hard work but you can do it."

I watch her pencil write my name in one of the squares.

"The diet kitchen," she says, "is not a place of punishment. It is valuable experience." And working on my own, she tells me, is an excellent way of having a much-needed rest from patients and other staff. She smiles again. "We simply cannot have tearful nurses at the bedside you know."

"Yes, I know. Thank you Matron."

"I think that is all nurse. You will of course be, as part of your duties, dusting this office. I suggest you come in here either immediately before your meal time or immediately after it, between midnight and one."

"Yes, I know, between twelve and one, thank you Matron."

"You appreciate that this is considered a privilege. The dark polish is in this little drawer."

"Yes, thank you, Matron."

"You have weekends off. Also a privilege."

"Thank you Matron."

I must go round to Magda. I must go to the house and get my letter back.

An accident. The whole hospital is talking about an accident. About Dr. Metcalf's unexpected death. The diet kitchen, because of its dark emptiness at night, is worse than any other place. I have to understand that I shall never see him again or hear his voice.

There was, this afternoon, a memorial service for him in the hospital chapel. I meant to go but did not wake up in time. Lois also did not wake up for it.

"I do have my principles," she said. And how about we go to the pictures, Saturday. She's having the weekend off, for once, she said.

If Magda sees my letter she will be so terribly hurt. I must get it back. She must not see what I wrote.

I wrote everything to you Dr. Metcalf, Jonathon. I wrote everything about us both that is why she must not see what I wrote. They will send your things to her in brown envelopes. Everything found in your pockets will be sent to her sealed in these special envelopes. I have seen rings and photographs and money and letters put into these special envelopes. The things are sent to mothers and wives, to the next of kin as they are called.

My letter to you will hurt Magda.

I love you I told you in my letter. I want you to come back now. That's what I wrote to you. I told you I was crying while I wrote the letter. Why have you gone away? I wrote that too. Come back please. Come back now this minute. I've been up to your room. I keep on going up there in case you've come back. Your name's still on the door. It's locked. Come back before someone else has your room.

I am sick, I told you. Every morning since you left I am sick. Remember I was sick? I told you I was being sick when you said you had to go and you said you would come back soon. And we would be together. You said you would find a way for us to be together. I wrote about that to you too in my letter. You told me. Remember? You told me to wait and to be happy knowing you would come back to me. Remember? You promised me. You said, "Wait for me."

Magda must not see my letter. I never thought anything could happen. I never thought you would not come back. Oh why did you go? I never thought that you would not get my letter.

In the middle of the afternoon I wake up. It is only three o'clock. All at once I remember. You see, while I was asleep I had forgotten. Outside it is bright sunshine. A bit cold. I remember you like it to be cold and sunny. I'll talk to you while I get dressed. You like it sunny and cold don't you. I'm going to get the letter now. In a minute. But first I'll go once along the doctors' corridor in case you have come back. Are you waiting in your room for me? Sometimes when I was on the ward, you know, making beds or taking round the trays at tea time, I'd suddenly think you are waiting for me and I'd leave quickly. I'd take the lift and do you remember how sweet it was when you were there in your room? Sometimes I could only stay five minutes.

I'll always remember the time I stayed all night with you. You said there was plenty of room for us both on that narrow little bed. Please be in your room for me when I come now. Be waiting for me and smiling when you open the door. Please.

I have to go to Magda to get my letter back. You weren't in your room just now. I have to understand this. You aren't at the camp at Swindon, writing to me, either. There is a chance that you will come back wounded. You could be brought back, crushed with some bones broken, but not all that bad. Perhaps you are on the way back. Oh please be on the way back. Please.

What's the use? I must stop hoping.

Do you remember when you explained? It was such a sweet time for me, when you explained how you didn't sleep all night, that night of the fog, when you thought I should not sleep alone in the house with you, and you put the mattress down in Mrs. P's sitting room. She was so sour that night. I hated her and her room! As if it mattered what Mrs. P thought about us. But it was hurting Magda you were really afraid of and it was sweet when you said you wanted to protect me from your own feelings. Behavior, you said. When we talk about Magda you explain so well that if Magda was a perfectly horrible person it would be easier. I understand because I love Magda too but it is you I want to be with for ever. You wanted me and you thought you should not. I feel very happy knowing how much you wanted me.

Magda needs you, you explained. I understand that too.

But the night at the river shack, I reminded you. You were lovely and smooth and sunburned and your kisses very sweet. You said we should have made love that night. I went to sleep, I told you. And you said yes perhaps that was a good thing. Sleep is a protection you said.

I am almost at your house. The bright afternoon makes me look pale and hollow eyed. Ugly. I feel hungry but don't know what to eat. If you were with me we could go in to some place and have hot toast and tea. Perhaps they would let us have real butter and some jam.

It is awful to go towards that house and to know you will not be there. I wish you could be there to open the door instead of Mrs. P. When Mrs. P opens the door I hope she will let me in to the hall. Perhaps the brown envelope will be on the hall table. Perhaps I'll be able to take it quickly.

Why do you feel you have to go I asked you. The war is practically over. The war is everywhere, I know, but it is over. That's what people are saying. You are more use, you are really needed here in the hospital. The war doesn't need you now like the hospital does. Not like I do. I need you.

This is a terrible thing to say but how can I have proof that you are dead? Who can I ask?

I ring the bell and wait. On both sides of the front door the large clean windows are heavily curtained inside. The curtains are drawn. I ring the bell once more and wait.

Please, don't ever say that you can't forgive yourself. There is nothing to forgive. When I said that, "There is nothing to forgive," you looked relaxed and pleased. I loved you more than ever then. You said the hard little bed in your room on the doctors' corridor was now an idyllic place, that was the word you used, idyllic. You said that when two people loved as we have then it is as if that love is for ever. You told me to remember that.

No one is going to answer this door. It's no use standing out here. The afternoon is getting much colder. It's getting dark earlier now.

There is a queue at the greengrocer's shop. I join it to buy some Worcester Pearmains. One half of the shop is boarded up and an ARP depot is in the boarded place. The boards are painted ARP in red. The shop has looked like this for a long time. Today I seem to notice the boards and the red paint for the first time.

For a few minutes I forgot. It was biting the apple. Eating the apple I just thought about that.

It seems a long way back to the hospital. These mean little streets where we used to walk, hidden, because people we knew did not walk here, seem dirty and poor. I never noticed before though you once said they depressed you. You should see this street today. It is full of people, a long line of men and women, linked together arm in arm, dancing. Every day now there are street parties like this. They are like children in a school playground. Long rows of people dancing and singing. You know, the songs, "The Lambeth Walk," "Run Rabbit Run" and now it's "Knees Up Mother Brown." The women have got curlers in their hair and the men are in their shirtsleeves.

If you could see this dancing and rejoicing!

You said once how easily we accepted heaps of rubble. People, you said, got used to all kinds of things. It amazed you, you said, that this mess was all round people now and they did not seem to notice it. It's true what you said. There are heaps of broken bricks and slates everywhere and, at the end of this street, there is an old bomb crater which is not even fenced off. The people dancing don't seem to notice that some houses have whole fronts and sides missing. Some are tarpaulined and boarded up but others are showing pink and blue wallpaper, torn and discolored. Sinister really, but no one notices. You could say a house looked like a doll's house, opened, without the magic. They have been like this for a long time. Part of the hospital is still covered with tarpaulin. Remember? The far end of the doctors' corridor does not lead anywhere. The stairs and lift shaft at that end have all gone.

This dancing in the street is how the war has been ending these days. Did you know, Dr. Metcalf, Jonathon? Did I ever tell you how the war started for me? I mean really started. Not the declaration of the war. That was the terrible beginning. Terrible because my father could not and would not believe something which he had to believe. The war started one night with the post mistress and her son out in the village street outside my school. They were banging tin cans together and blowing whistles. It was the first air-raid warning. We all had to get up and sit under the tables downstairs in the dining hall. And, because the post mistress had no other noise she could make, there was no All Clear and we stayed under the tables all night. You have never told me Dr. Metcalf, Jonathon, where you were when the war started. Where were you? Were you married to Magda? I haven't had time to know enough.

They say it's an advantage for a doctor to marry the daughter of a well-known physician or surgeon. How did you meet Magda? I never asked you that either. There is a skinny black cat here. It's ugly because it's poor and alone. It's at the edge of these dancing people and it's trying to vomit.

Whatever shall I do with my life without you.

It is the weekend and I'm free. I have the weekends off now, remember?

I am at Gertrude's Place. Well not quite. The hens, I can see them plainly from here, are dotted all over the field.

"Gertrude is very ill," my mother said last night.

"I know, you told me."

"You haven't seen her for all these weeks, months. You've not been home to see us."

"I know, I'm sorry."

"You could go in the morning," she says, "first thing. You have to collect the eggs yourself and leave the money on the kitchen table. I'll give you change. Gertrude never has any."

"Yes, I'll go in the morning, first thing."

I am up the hill a bit from Gertrude's Place and I'm leaning on my bicycle. I wondered if I should ride it but it was all right.

The district nurse is pushing her bicycle up the field path. I ought to go down there. Perhaps I'll go back down in a minute. I have been up here at the edge of the spinney, for hours. Is it hours? It seems like a long time. It is all so quiet here. The nurse in her blue uniform looks small from this distance. I can watch her disappear into the house.

I have been several times to Magda's, missing my sleep, to try to get my letter back. But no one is there. No one answers the door and the curtains are always drawn. I suppose Magda is with her mother and father. Perhaps she is at the river shack.

I keep thinking about my letter and all the things I wrote in it. There has been no message for me from Magda. She must know about the letter, and about me, about us.

Gertrude is all small and shriveled yellow in a bed which was never used. She wanted me to have it once. I was early at her place. The fowls must have been out all night. I wondered about the fox. Fowls would have to be either out all the time or shut up all the time. It is something they can't do for themselves.

I watched Gertrude through the window. Her eyes were closed under a frown of pain. I watched and then I came up here.

I want to go back down there. I want to have Gertrude comfort me but how can I tell her everything when she is so ill. It should be me comforting her.

I think Gertrude is dying.

"I can wash Gertrude," I could say this to the nurse. But I can't say to Gertrude what I want to say. How can I go back over the summer and leave everything unexplained?

In the evening I can't stop crying. I can't tell my mother. It is only a simple thing I have to tell her but I am not able to.

"You must not be so upset over poor Gertrude," my mother says. "She is very fond of you and she would not want you to be upset like this. Try not to cry."

"It's not only that, not only poor Gertrude," I say. "It's because oh it's because I've been trying to write and I can't, it's just stupid, it's nothing."

My mother is knitting very fast. She started knitting at the beginning of the war and now she is always knitting. "No one," she says, "can write anything till they've had experience. Later on perhaps. You will write later on."

"Yes, of course," I say.

"You never play the piano now," my mother says. "Why don't you go now and practice something and leave the front-room door open. I like to listen."

"I haven't been able to sleep either," I say instead of saying the words I mean to say.

"You must have some of my tablets," my mother says, "they are yeast tablets and are very good."

"Thanks," I say and I put my hands up to my face because of more tears.

"You promised to play Halma," my sister says.

"Oh, shut up!" Immediately I regret my reply. I know she is trying to comfort me.

During the night there is a full moon, it makes a trellis of shadow and light on the opposite wall. It seems as if, instead of a corridor up here, there is another room. A room I have never seen before. L-shaped with a long passage leading to a place which shines as a river shines when moonlight lies across undisturbed water.

The tarpaulins have been taken off the bomb-damaged part of the hospital. This wing, at the end of the doctors' corridor, has to be rebuilt. There is no strange room there. Beyond some wooden barriers the hospital up here is wide open to the night. The corridor ends abruptly in space. The moonlight is on the wall of the huge clock tower which is a water tower. It is a reservoir for the water from an artesian well under the hospital. I feel afraid of the power and the force of the water in the tower. I can imagine, all too easily, the depths of the precipice in front of me. It is as though a neglected wound, which I already know about, has been uncovered.

All the doctors' rooms are locked and uninhabited. There are warning notices and barriers all along the passage. I have come up here one last time. The building work has started. Somewhere there'll be a watchman. Someone to keep people away at night.

The moon is wonderfully close to this ragged broken end of the corridor. I could step easily across this gulf straight on to the clean white moon.

The moon belongs to my father. He has always said it was his. If I was over there he would know without my telling him. It is only such a small thing I have to tell. Perhaps it is the small things which are the hardest to tell. They are the things which make all the difference.

It is because it will be so unexpected for him. What I need to tell him will be unexpected.

My father, when he comes to the station with me after my weekend at home, talks softly to me as we wait to cross the road. He admires the Clydesdale horses as a brewer's dray rumbles over the cobbles. He doesn't seem to notice the dried horse dung and straw blowing in our faces. The horses are fine he says and have I noticed how well cared for they are?

"How they shine!" he says, he can imagine the daily curry

combing and the polishing of the brasses. The dray is loaded but the horses, moving all together, are very powerful. "Look at their muscles," he says, "their muscles ripple under their skin."

As we walk to and fro on the platform, he says even if we are not seeing each other very often he is always thinking of me. They would, he says, like me to come home more often. He is going out to Gertrude's Place tomorrow, he says, he is going to do a few things for her.

"That's good," I say, "thank you."

"Is there anything in particular?" he asks.

"What d'you mean?"

"Are you worrying about something in particular?" His face is white in the autumn dusk.

"Oh no!" I say. "Not really. It's just that I don't like the diet kitchen."

"Quite a lot of life," he says, "is doing what we don't like very much."

"Yes, I know," I say. "I know."

There is a small sound behind me. I turn quickly. Perhaps it is the night watchman. There is someone in the corridor. A dark shape is coming towards me, a shadow in the red light of the little lamps.

"It's only me," Trent says. "I saw you pass the end of the ward." She's got night nurses' paralysis she tells me. She has long woolen operation stockings on over her shoes and an army blanket round her shoulders. She tells me it's freezing on Women's Medical. "It's that quiet," she says. "Kidneys. They're all on parsley tea," she gives a fat giggle. "They're your mob," she says, "you been fixing them lettuce again?" She takes my arm drawing me back from the edge.

"You lead," she says. "By the way," she croons, "has anyone ever told you, you're not cut out to be a corpse? No sex appeal!"

We waltz slowly back along the brick-dusty corridor.

"Do you come here often?" Trent, purring close to my ear, trips over the end of the army blanket.

"Goin' down!" Trent says in the lift. "A-wun-a-tew-a-tree-a-fower-a-faive-Tung Tung Tung Tung Tung Tung." She can make a noise, with her tongue and voice, sounding like the plucking of a double-bass string. While clapping in a slow beat she taps her foot in a rapid rhythm. "A-wun-a-tew-a tree a wun a woman band! Listen," she says. "Counter irritant," she says, "if things are bad make some other thing worse. Ching chang Chinaman givee good advice, don't pee until you have to. Busting! And that'll be all you can think about. Get me? And, just this, there's more than one pebble on the beach."

I shall go to Magda's once more. One last time and then not any more.

I can't stop thinking about you. I think about you all the time.

Today I found out just what sort of person Magda really is. I said, didn't I, that I would go once more to see if I could get my letter back, the one I wrote to you. I was so sure, you see, that it would be returned with your things, the things they call personal things. I have seen Magda now. It's like this.

"Mrs. Lemmington Frazier Metcalf does not wish to see anyone. She is not at home," Mrs. P says through the tiny space. She opens the door grudgingly so that I feel she is going to close it before I can say anything.

"It's only me," I say quickly, putting one hand on the door to prevent it from being slammed.

"You nor no one," Mrs. P says. "She's not in!"

"Oh please, please let me come in." I am surprised at my own voice.

"Who is it Mrs. P? Who's there?" I can hear Magda's voice from somewhere quite close. Perhaps from the stairs. She has a way of hanging over the banister. Remember?

"It's me," I shout. "Can I come in?"

"Of course. Precious child, of course you must come in!" Magda is dressed in that dressing gown made of bath-towel stuff. She wears this only when she is quite by herself or when she is ill, she once explained to me. You will know the dressing gown, she said it was yours once. Her hair, unbrushed, is loose, all tangled and messy. Her face seems swollen and when I look at her my own eyes fill with tears.

"Why haven't you come before?" she asks.

"But I have. Several times," I say.

"Mrs. P Darling! Will you be awfully sweet and bring us up some tea?" Magda puts an arm round me and guides me, hugging me, to the stairs. We go up together. Her action reminds me of you, Dr. Metcalf, holding me the night of the fog. Remember? I can't help thinking that she must have my letter hidden somewhere.

"Of course," Magda says, "I've been at Mummy's and Mrs. P's been away too."

There were no letters on the hall table, only the polished tray and other ornaments, all polished and cared for. No little heap of brown envelopes as I imagined there would be. She must have put the letter somewhere.

"I feel such a frightful mess," Magda says. "As you can see I've just let myself go. Awful!" She sinks down on the sofa and pats the cushions.

"Sit down," she says. Her eyes are full of tears.

"It's so awful, you see, he went orf with such a cheap and horrid person. That's what I can't bear and Mummy, of course, can't bear it either. It's hardest for her. Mummy's really quite ill over it."

So Magda does know, and her mother knows, and they think I'm cheap.

"I feel more awful than I know how to say, I . . ." The words are too difficult. Magda interrupts me with another hug.

"You see," she says, "this person is really awful, cheap and I mean really cheap and vulgar. And, you see Daddy's so clever, a brilliant surgeon, everyone says so but he's stupid too. He's made a lot of money. Mummy's used to being comfortable. Mummy and I try to protect him. What I'm trying to say is that this cheap little person is a gold digger. Like all the others," she searches for her handkerchief. "But you, not having the experience of people like that, won't know what I mean. He is already, in a sense, at the mercy of perfectly dreadful people who are waiting to get everything from him."

"You mean," I try to say something.

"You see," Magda says, "he keeps making an awful fool of himself. Didn't you think she was perfectly dreadful? The last one? You saw her that day on the river. Gloria or whatever her name was."

"You mean Marigold?"

"Yes, that's the one. It devastates Mummy every time—that's why I go over and stay the night with her every so often. She's dreadfully lonely."

"Oh I see," I am taking care not to look up.

"So incredibly vulgar and so grasping," Magda says wiping her eyes with both hands like a child. "They, those sorts of women and their relations would take everything, absolutely everything. The relations in particular hound Daddy. And where would Mummy be? She dreads a court case and she's terrified of the workhouse. Daddy's compromised himself more than once d'you see—and now this Marigold! It's all so ghastly!"

We are both quiet while Mrs. P sets the tray with the teapot and cups on a little table in front of us.

"Oh Mrs. P, toast! You are a dear!" Magda can manage an entirely different voice. She pours out. "You needn't wait Mrs. P thank you."

"Marigold's mother," I say in a timid voice, "is quite nice. I am sure she wouldn't, I don't think she is like that. I nursed her. Marigold's real name is Edna, her mother is Mrs. Bray. She is a nice person, very good and kind. Couldn't you go and see her?"

"Oh mothers can't stop their daughters!" Magda laughs. "You are so innocent and good," she says, "don't ever change!"

We drink our tea and share out the toast.

"Oh, I nearly forgot," Magda says, "you are perfectly sweet to write to Jonty. Poor darling Jonty!" Her eyes fill with tears.

"It's awful I can't stop this weeping," she says. "I see you can't either. They've returned all letters. I guessed you would've written. I've got your letter here," she leans back and stretches her arm across to her little writing desk. In here," she says, pulling open the little drawer. "Here it is, this is yours." She hands me my letter.

"You never put your name and address on the back," she says, "but I recognized your handwriting. Everything has been sent back to me."

I turn the letter over in my hands, almost stroking it, feeling the firmly closed-down envelope.

"Thank you," I say in a small voice, "yes I did write." My hands caress the thick secret letter.

"He would have loved having a letter from you," Magda says, "poor Darling Jonty. But as you see it never reached him. That perfectly dreadful place! It must have been awful for him and then no one being quite sure. It's all so stupid. Conflicting. A head-on crash?" She shivered. "Dead or believed missing. I can't bear it. Really I can't. I've been waiting at Mummy's and now here."

"Don't cry," I say, "please, Magda, don't cry!" The envelope is wonderfully smooth and unopened. Magda has given me back my letter. She has not torn it open to read it. She has not looked at it.

"There's some confusion. Where and which camp," Magda says, "everything's so confused. It's victory, I suppose." And she sobs aloud and feels around for her handkerchief. "In the front of that shelf," she says, "there should be some clean ones. Thanks Darling!" Magda puts her hand on my arm. "You see, Darling," she says, "I keep hoping he will come back. That it's all a mistake. I haven't given up hope. I suppose you realize that I'm heaps older than Jonty. That sort of thing makes people talk, d'you see, they say cruel things especially about women who are older. Jonathon—" she starts to cry again, "Jonathon, you see, I need him so much." I watch her shoulders shaking and I can see the dark-gray dirty-looking parting in her bronzed hair. I know I ought to help her.

"Shall I find your hairbrush?" I ought to look for her brush. "Shall I help you wash and do your hair? Let me brush your hair, Magda," I ought to comfort her. "Let me help you," all this I should say. Magda would comfort me, if she knew.

She sits crouched on the sofa with her face hidden in her hands. "You see, Darling," she says, "he wanted to be with Mr. Smithers. Smithers went about twelve months ago to a field hospital and Jonty felt he should go. But you see, Darling, it's not so simple. People, men and women, will travel the length and breadth of a country, at times, to be together. In one way it's as simple as that."

"But I thought, Smithers . . ."

"They worked together," Magda seems to have a note of defiance in her voice. "I'm waiting," she says. "One thing I'm certain of. When he comes back, *if* he comes back, I'm never going to let him go ever again. I simply can't live without him.

Her long tangled hair falls over her endlessly shaking shoulders. In a blind dazed sort of way I get up and stand for a moment in front of her. I can't see her face, only her shoulders without an arm round them. The bunched chintzy curtains and the cushion covers, with their crowded little flowers and acorns, and the hovering perfume all seem too much. I move silently towards the curtained door and open it and, with light little steps, make for the stairs and the front door.

"How much are the rings please?"

"Them's sixpence. All of them. There's nothing over sixpence."

"Oh yes, of course, it's Woolworths. I'd like a ring please. It's er, it's for drama, a drama, for a play in a dramatic society. I'm in a play, er, Shakespeare."

"Choose your pick. Them's all the same price, like I said, sixpence."

"I think I'll have this one. It's quite pretty isn't it?"

"If you say so."

All the lights are on in Woolworths and I move with the

throng of people. It is slow, this getting to the doors, and more crowded because, near the doors, there are counters with a few sweets and people are still coming in as the store is emptying for closing time. Out in the street there is an eeriness in the sad twilight. The hospital, with lights showing, seems like a huge ship for ever in harbor.

Nurse Roberts, little Nurse Roberts, stout in her winter coat, was down by the bus stop alone. I saw her there in the morning. Her big case on the pavement beside her. She was waiting for the early bus, the one we call the workmen's. It was raining, a light rain. When I saw her there I never thought then that she might have nowhere to go. I was high up closing the window because of the rain. Now I think, where could she go? Where can anyone go?

The wireless is on in the night nurses' dining room. This inescapable "In the Mood" music. It keeps on and on. Without wanting to I walk in time to this barrel-organ rhythm. Without wanting to I'm humming, without tune to this music. My voice in my head is an ugly croaking.

Lois is late. She comes in and sits down opposite me with her cup of tea.

Potatoes onions carrots, my ring flashes as my pencil pretends to scribble a shopping list.

"Night Fanny here yet?" Lois glances round quickly and lights a cigarette. She inhales deeply.

Someone turns off the wireless. Sister Bean, with the registers held to her heart, marches across between the tables. Her voice barks into the silence.

"Abbott Abrahams Ackerman Allwood . . ."

Lois, in her cloud of smoke, extinguishes her cigarette. "Whoever," she says, leaning low across the table, "whoever would ever have married you?"

"Arrington and Attwood. Nurses Baker Barrington Beam Beamish Beckett Birch Bowman D Bowman E Broadhurst Brown Burchall . . ."

"Nurse Burchall?"

"Yes Sister?"

"Nurse Burchall, Matron's office nine a.m."

"Yes Sister."

"Nurses Cann Carruthers Cornwall Cupwell . . ."

The Easter moon is racing up the sky. The stunted ornamental bushes look as if torn white tablecloths have been thrown over them and the buildings are like cakes which, having taken three days to ice, are now finished.

Tomorrow is Good Friday.

Next week I shall take the earlier train again and, before the journey is over, I shall speak to the woman.

It is more than likely that Ramsden would have white hair. Her hair was the sort of hair which goes white all over, all at once. Keats says, to *know the change and feel it*, I thought of sudden white hair when I read that.

The cardboard cover of the little book of poems which Ramsden gave me once, during the night on the Lower Ground corridor, is decorated with edelweiss and gentian, a circle of neat pen-and-ink flowers. Inside she has written in her neat small handwriting,

> *The best is not too good for you*
> *Und Ihrer Weise Wohlzutun.*

Ramsden, I shall say, *is it you? Much water has gone under the bridge*—this is not my way—but I shall say it carelessly like this—*much water has gone under the bridge and I never answered your letters but is it you, Ramsden, after all these years is it?*

CABIN FEVER

Nowhere either with more quiet
or more freedom from trouble
does a man retire than into his
own soul.

— WILLIAM PENN

SHIRT SLEEVES

I am still here on the twenty-fourth floor and when I sit in front of my mirror I can see, in the mirror, someone on the twenty-fourth floor across the street. He is sitting upright at a table and is in his shirt sleeves. I have no idea who he is.

"I should never have given you the book about Elisabeth Ney."

"Whyever . . . She was a sculptor and an artist . . . She . . ."

"She had a baby in that book without being married."

"Oh! Really!"

"It must have given you ideas . . ."

"Don't, do not be so utterly stupid. How can you be so stupid!"

"Keep your voice down. You don't want the others to hear you speaking to your mother like that."

Cabin Fever

Once when I am sitting with Magda in her white and gold upstairs sitting room I tell her that I hope I won't get wrinkles and frowns all over my face.

"But Darling Child!" Magda exclaims then, she is crouching in the hearth turning over little heaps of underclothes to air them (she always says what a cold person she is). "But Darling Child!" she says, "that's where character and experience are, in the lines and the frowns and the wrinkles. Your sweet round face is deliciously soft and smooth at present, you must try to preserve it forever. But even *you* will have experience one day and you must expect it to alter your appearance. Just look at Daddy, seven deep wrinkles on his forehead and two of the deepest frowns, ulcer frowns we call them, each side of the bridge of his nose. Those are for his nine actresses, Darling. Mummy has never caused him a wrinkle or a frown, d'you see? Look at him next time you are in theater. You mop him, don't you Darling, with the iced water while he's operating. Well, you count his frowns for yourself, you can't say he's not handsome. He simply, quite simply, is experienced."

How can I look at Lemmington Frazier as closely as that when he's all gowned up and I'm trying to dab at that angry red space between his cap and his mask with the iced swabs during the long and precise surgery. It's all I can do to try to stop water drops from falling on to his special spectacles and to take extra care not to let unsterile water drip down into the patient's wound.

It seems to me then that Magda is offering me experience. Several times she seems to be offering. And, because I love Dr.

Metcalf and want to be near him all the time I take what Magda seems to give.

I love Magda too. And then, in a rush of feeling, I tell Magda, "I can't live without you, Magda."

"Darling Child!" Magda hugs me and kisses me, and she seems to purr when she talks. "You don't have to live without me." Her perfume envelops me. It seems to me then that her perfume is richly purple. But of course I know that perfume does not have a strong color, I mean it's never purple.

MAGDA'S VISIT

I know now what Magda means that day when she comes unexpectedly to visit me at the Hilda Street Nursing Home. Her visit at the end of a long afternoon, on the day Helena is born, is unexpected and I have to try to take off Dr. Metcalf's watch, remove it from my wrist, under the bedclothes.

But I think she has already seen the watch and knows at once that it is his. She does not mention the watch at all. And she gives no indication that she has minded seeing it.

When Sister Peters says at the door that there is a Mrs. Metcalf to see me I am not able to think for a minute who this can be. I am not expecting anyone to come.

I know now, when I think of what Magda says then, about love in its purest and freshest, its most innocent and powerful form, I know now what she means then. The idea she says then, is of love existing between two people so that the only thing that matters is that they can be near each other. She tells me that the love I had was not dragged down, "mutilated" is the word she uses. Your love, she says, was not mutilated by anything, by money, ambition, property—"you know, Darling, divisions of property, mortgages on land and on houses, and no relatives intervening. It was," she says, "or rather, it is a love of the free-est sort and is a blessing." While she is saying this her eyes and my eyes are full of tears.

"Furthermore," Magda says, a few minutes later, "your love is completely untroubled by not knowing too much about the person you love and that is something you cannot expect to have for long."

Magda's visit, of course, makes me think about Gertrude. When I think of Gertrude now and how she, in her own honest way of thinking, tried earlier to draw me away from the fascination and the excitement of my new, in her words, wild and extravagant, friends. I also remember (I can never forget) how she, as she put it, tried then to go along with me, to humor me as if allowing me a full taste of the Metcalfs as if to tire me with them—when I am at her Place helping her with the fowls and then continuing this, when I am back at the hospital, in her letters;

> *I am afraid you will think I am interfering with your affairs. Can I explain that I want to avoid for you what I consider to be the Pit Fall ... It is strange how we each suffer or have to grope a way in this life we might have had so easily ...*

And then when for some long time taken up with Dr. Metcalf or Magda, or both of them, I do not go out to Gertrude's Place either on my bicycle or by bus I wait in the queue in the hall of the Nurses' Home for letters half hoping for and half afraid of having a letter from her. I have been writing to her and so must expect replies;

> *I should have written earlier in the week but expected you as your mother said you would be coming and would fetch the eggs ... I am very sorry you had the cold. I hope it's better. I am interested and a little amused where in your letter you write you wouldn't mind having a baby. Of course it's best to take out a license to have a baby really as unless anybody is really well to do and has a lot of money it's very difficult on ones own to pay for every-*

thing and have no one to rely on to help along. Also an
Unlicensed Baby is against Public Opinion still the most
powerful deterrent there is. But I don't see that its wicked
except as things are it has a stigma on its name . . .

When at last I do go, Gertrude is busy with the incubator in the bedroom which is never used as a bedroom. There is a billiard table in there and a harmonium where she plays hymns sometimes.

"Little chicks," she says, "hundreds of 'em all falling around over each other and under each other like lots of hands playing duets on the piano. You can have 'em all if you like to stay, to come in on the poultry with me. I'll make a nice room. I'll make this room nice for you." She pauses. "We can paste pictures, bright fashion pictures," she says, "out of a magazine on the walls. Put up a border of wallpaper too like we've done in the kitchen. That's nice. And you could sleep late, late as you like, till dinner time if you wanted. Or get up with the sun and run free in the field, up to the spinney, down the hill, wherever you want . . ."

But I am invited again, I tell her then, to a party. Dr. Metcalf and his wife Magda are having a party and they want me to come so I shall not be staying.

"I'll be going back to the hospital in the afternoon," I explain, "and on to their house in the evening."

Later Gertrude tells me, after some weeks when I go again to her Place, that perhaps it would be a good idea if these Metcalfs could be persuaded to withdraw themselves from my life. Could my father visit them she wants to know, could he intervene on my behalf explaining that he does not quite understand the matter but that he wants perfect happiness for his daughter. Gertrude says too that she can quite understand how my mother might be about to make things worse by trying to dish up different menfolk I ought to be able to attract. She says if my father is not able to go to visit these Metcalfs she is willing to go. She can put her bicycle on the train, she says, and she will take them some eggs and a couple of dressed fowls in a bag and persuade them not to invite me any more. What times are their parties she wants to know. She will go to the next one instead of me. She is not afraid to go inside their grand house . . .

I am afraid to even think of Gertrude in her black laced-up boots, her felt hat, and her heavy coat over the overall she never takes off, stepping into the splendor and lavishness of one of Magda's parties. I want to stop her from having this idea, to protect her from the fun they would make from her appearance, the ridicule which, though meant in a hilarious joking way, would hurt her and harm her. Their laughter, their exchanged looks and raised eyebrows and their small but extravagant gestures would completely submerge anything she would try to say. They would never see that they should not invite me unless they did not want to. They would not understand her on purpose. The way Gertrude is thinking is not their way.

The last time I see Gertrude to speak to I am quite unable to tell her how things are with me. After all the times of going to her Place, of looking forward to being where the soft green grass is right up to her door, of arriving to find her sitting at this door with her sardine tin of oil and the matches for singeing the boiling fowls after plucking, and the newspaper beside her with the coarse salt she uses to give her capable hand a better grip on the slippery entrails—after all this time I am not able to say to Gertrude that I wanted Dr. Metcalf more than anyone else and he wanted me. How can I tell her that I know already how things are with me and that I shall have no one to rely on, no one to help along . . .

⤳

CABIN FEVER

Playful spinsters and exuberant lesbians give birth and special seminars are held to discuss the phenomenon of these people wanting to keep their babies. Special committees are set up for discussions about the new infections which accompany new ways of living which are called alternative life styles. Years are earmarked for specific causes, the year of the child, the year of the aged, the year of the disabled—the year of the disabled produced some incredibly heavy swing doors . . .

How's business? people ask me. What do you mean? I ask. How many croaked? Any deaths? they want to know. How many, for example, died today?

No, I explain, they don't come for death, they come for living. They come for advice for living. The clinic is simply a place for . . .

How quaint! Do they pay? They want to know who pays and how much.

Everyone pays.

Everyone? Oh, you mean the government and the taxpayer. Specially the taxpayer, crippling, let me tell you my last income tax . . .

No I wasn't thinking along those lines, I tell them. What is your work? people ask me. What is it exactly that you do? they ask. They ask me and I have no clear way to answering. I see people, I explain. People come to see me. Consulting it is called. Appointments are made for consultation. What about? they ask. What do people consult you about? they ask.

I tell them that people want to ask about things which worry them. Like what? they ask. What sort of things and do they have to take their clothes off? they want to know.

Everything. People are worried about everything. All kinds of things worry people. I think I am safe in saying everything. And no, they do not have to take off their clothes, as a rule.

I am a shabby person. I understand, if I look back, that I have treated kind people with an unforgivable shabbiness. For my work a ruthless self-examination is needed for, without understanding something of myself, how can I understand anyone else.

Every day I am seeing people living from day to day, from one precarious day to the next, from one despairing week to the next, without any vision of any kind of future. It does not take me long to understand this because during my own small celebrations of passing moments I have seen the world and my own life, at a particular time in that life, from one narrowed day to the next, from cramped week to cramped week, at ground and hedge-root level, unable to see anything beyond the immediate.

Memories are not always in sequence, not in chronological sequence. Sometimes an incident is revived in the memory. Sometimes incidents and places and people occupying hours, days, weeks, and years are experienced in less than a quarter of a second in this miraculous possession, the memory. The revival is not in any particular order and one recalled picture, attaching itself to another, is not recognizably connected to that other in spite of it being brought to the surface in the wake of the first recollection.

It is during an evening passing unnoticed into nightfall that I am, as if late at night, feeling my way once more up and down and along the bookshelves in my mother's house searching for an unrecognizable name or initial on a discolored fly leaf. And then all at once I am remembering Dr. Metcalf, naked and handsome and shameless, leaning back in the cushions of a basket chair, facing the small westward window, high up, his whole body bronzed in the colors of the setting sun. Why should I think now, all these years later on, of his arms stretched out towards me? And why, after all this time, recall his smile contained in his whole body, even in the palms of his hands?

It seems now as if the urchin style, the razor cut, has some remembered significance as does the slow walking in the long wet withered grass of the autumn. It is as if both can be thought capable of bringing about essential change.

Remembered people appear and disappear disconcertingly in the tiniest nutshells of memory. Order is reversed. The longing for some particular way of living or for some particular person or place or possession can come back with a sharpness unparalleled by anything happening and experienced during the present time. Furthermore, understanding the loneliness and despair of knowing it is not possible to bring back a wished for person, and knowing that one person can never replace another, is understanding that this is what bereavement is. Bereavement has become a clichéd word but to feel bereaved and to know it when there is no one to turn to is to experience the kind of despair for which the only remedy is to lie on the warm earth *dissolving the long hours in tears.*

To be beside a little lake with wind-chopped waves in a deserted suburban park and to experience a bottomless depth of loneliness can sometimes lead to an unexpected order in the mind which, at the time, seems to have nothing in it but grief and disorder. And this too can contribute to essential change through the making of a deliberate decision.

Sugar

Last year on New Year's Day I spilled the sugar, twice. Not a great deal, but even a little sugar spilled seems unlucky, especially if spilled twice on one day. This year on New Year's Day I am here in this ugly overheated hotel, a few days earlier than I need to be for the conference. I have come earlier because I actually thought I would enjoy the freedom of wandering, as if with leisure, through art galleries, exhibitions, and museums. I thought that I might go to a concert, a play, the opera. The wish to see colors as I had once seen them with their magic names—cobalt blue, ultramarine, vermillion, and yellow ochre in my paintbox at school, and to see cloth painted in such a way that one might feel it, between the fingers, as cloth and not paint on board or canvas, can only be achieved by searching slowly through a gallery and not by brushing past masterpieces like an impatient housewife who has half an hour to spare, or as a bored delegate between papers at a conference.

Squirrels

I thought too I would like to see Central Park again. The little gray squirrels there, I remember, reminded me once of rats. They do not sleep, hibernate, during the winter as squirrels in other places do. I suppose here they have no tree pantries full of stored nuts. It is below zero in Central Park. The air is still and cold and the bare branches of the winter trees are in brittle patterns against the curiously light sky. The park is frozen into a silence which the noise of New York cannot fill. In spite of my hopes for leisure I have not been out to any of the cultural entertainment as intended.

Prunes

At about this time the prune plums back home will be intensely blue hanging secretly in the deepest green foliage; an enticing and surprising mixture of blue and green. The bloom on these small vividly colored plums gives the impression of a delicate mist hovering about the trees.

Magda

Perhaps I will try and remember everything I can about Magda. I thought at one time that I could not live without Magda and yet, at the same time, she was dreadfully in my way.

Magda says I saved her life. It is like this. She is brought into the Casualty Dept one night during an air raid. Her nightie has slipped off her shoulders, her hair is all over the place, and she is crying. She says she is dying, suffocating. It is asthma, an attack of asthma. While I am waiting for the RMO to come and, because I am the only nurse on duty, I feel I must help her. Not knowing what I should do I bring in an oxygen cylinder. As soon as Magda sees the big cylinder on its little wheels, its handsome dial and the mask attached she is better and she starts at once to say I have saved her life and I must, simply must come to her house on my next day off. I feel awkward and embarrassed when the RMO finally comes. I try to hitch the ribbons of Magda's nightie back over her shoulders . . .

"Since when, Nurse," the Night Superintendent says to me later, "since when has an empty oxygen cylinder been the treatment for asthma?" Just then even though the All Clear has hardly finished sounding there is another air-raid warning and I have to go at once to check the black-out curtains on the stairs.

Magda as it turns out is the Chief Surgeon's daughter. His only daughter. His name is Mr. Lemmington Frazier. At the hospital they say she is spoiled, very wealthy, and pretending to be studying medicine. Her mother, Mrs. Lemmington Frazier, takes a Red Cross trolley round the soldiers' wards. The trolley is piled up with books and chocolate and home-made face flannels and a sort of green jam. She gives to both the officers and the men. Sometimes the jam is red.

Magda is married to Dr. Jonathon Metcalf. She calls him Jonty. Everyone says it is a fortunate marriage for him because of Lemmington Frazier's very high reputation and position in the hospital. I discover quite quickly what his reputation really is among the other nurses.

Spilling sugar in this hotel room reminds me that on New Year's Day, last year, I spilled the sugar twice. The sugar on the blue napkins, a fine scattering like snow on a miniature mountain, recalls the dark-blue sugar bags in which I kept the sugar secretly hoarded immediately after the war when sugar was scarce and rationed still.

"The sugar," I said then, "a whole fortnight's sugar." And I added it straight away to my growing sugar weight. But that is a long time ago and before that time there is a time when small jars of sugar, jam, and butter are carried everywhere in little colored string bags.

The nurses all have string bags for their rations. It is Trent who replies to the question, when we are all sprawled, Trent, Ferguson, Lois and me across Trent's bed; what is the most important thing in the world and Trent says sex but not with any of you lot. Of course not I say. And we all get up then and put our aprons and caps straight.

Every year, faithfully over the years, at the beginning of October a letter comes from Betsy who was at school. This Betsy left school early and so was there only for two years of secondary school. She was not a boarder but came, red nosed across the fields, from a farm.

The letter is always the same, about her being in time for the Christmas mail and the number of cards and letters she received the previous year and how she has to answer them. She writes on several small sheets of note paper, schoolgirl's note paper still, closely written on both sides of the page in a hand which time and experience have not changed. It is clear that she still lives, but alone now, in the farmhouse. And it is clear that she loves her own handwriting. Her letters are descriptions of the repairs to the farmhouse, half the dining room replastered, new gutters on the south side, a new carpet in the sitting room because of the rising damp—in spite of fires all the year round. Six windows painted, two front doors, a garden door and the gate painted. And outside the dahlias are lifted, the onion bed prepared, the vegetable garden tidied, and all the borders and flower beds still to do . . .

It is a warm Sunday in March when we are invited to Drinkwaters farm to tea. Helen Ferguson, Bulge, and me. In our Sunday dresses and overcoats we set off to walk to the farm which is on the edge of the next village. Helen Ferguson thinks if we walk fast enough we could leave Bulge behind and she, not knowing the way, would be lost and we would go to tea without her. We can say Muriel couldn't come Helen Ferguson says as we walk as fast as we can, the mud clinging to our shoes, taking a forbidden field path. Helen Ferguson calls Bulge Muriel because it is her real name. I, privately, call her Bulge because she bulges. In my secret game of comparisons Bulge is far worse than I am in every respect, her hair, her stockings, her spectacles, and her shape.

Bulge, who says at the stile, that we should really keep to the road, persists in following us. Her face is red and she has stepped too deep in the mud. It is all up her stocking to the knee. "Cow pats and all," Helen Ferguson can't stop laughing. We can hear her calling to us to wait for her. She's crying. Helen Ferguson laughs till she nearly bursts. "I'll burst," she says.

We are always hungry at school and at a small shop, in the village, Helen Ferguson tries to exchange some stamps for jelly crystals. The shop woman is annoyed saying don't we know it's Sunday and she is closed and, even if open, she wouldn't have jelly crystals for us.

Bulge arrives at the farm all muddy and crying just when we are about to sit down to a table heaped with home-made bread and scones and butter, two kinds of home-made jam, and a chocolate cake, Helen Ferguson having told Betsy Drinkwater's mother that we would have to have tea straight away as we have to get back to school before dark. Mrs. Drinkwater helps Bulge to clean her shoes and she comes to the table and eats her tea without looking across at us.

Betsy Drinkwater, in her soft country accent, one which we mock every day at school, asks Helen to take a photograph. Betsy says she had this box camera for Christmas and has never had an opportunity to use it . . .

I don't, as a rule, ever look at this photograph now but whenever I do a curious sense of shame comes over me. We are standing, for the picture, in the trellised archway at the front door of the farmhouse. Betsy in the middle with Helen Ferguson on one side and me on the other, both of us replete. We are draped, hanging by the arms, round Betsy's thick shoulders. Our dark serge Sunday dresses, with their white Quaker collars, are too tight and, because of our positions of exaggerated affection, the hems in front are lifted up unevenly. We look as if we are very fond of her. Bulge is not in the photograph because Helen Ferguson told her to take the picture.

It is my pretended affection which makes me ashamed now and which makes me shrink from receiving the Christmas letter.

Perhaps it is the remembered boarding-school cruelty inflicted on the innocent victim. It is too the remembered tea table, the empty plates with jam-smeared knives and the tea cups spilled into their saucers which we left that day for Mrs. Drinkwater and Betsy to come back to when they were done with the milking and when the hens had been shut up for the night.

On the Monday, in English class, Bulge writes a description of the Sunday walk to Drinkwaters farm. She gets top marks and her piece is chosen to be read out to the class. As I listen I begin to understand that, while I was hurrying to get away from Bulge, to lose her in the mud and to get to the farm without her, I never saw the long-legged lambs running across the grass to their mothers. I never noticed the clear water from the swollen stream spreading and sparkling over the grassy banks. I did not see, either, that the fresh green leaves on the hawthorn, the catkins, and the pussy willows were beginning to show, and I must have gone round the curve of the hill, down over the wall of loose stones and past the sheep fold without seeing any of it, and without seeing a newborn lamb struggling to its feet by itself. In her piece Bulge does not say that she ran alone, crying, as she tried to keep up when we hurried on without her. She does not write that we laughed when she fell in the mud. Instead she fills the classroom with the coming spring, the warm March sunshine, the Sunday which was the birth day of the lamb.

Helen Ferguson's essay gets good marks too. Not for the actual writing which, we are told, is full of cliché and spelling mistakes, but for the nobility of the sentiments. Helen Ferguson has written a description of how she helped Mrs. Drinkwater clear the table, wash up, and dry all the plates and cups and saucers after the wonderful tea we had enjoyed, and how it had given her pleasure to show her gratitude for the kind invitation by helping with this task.

I have always in my secret game of comparisons tried to sit in class like Helen Ferguson sits, one foot a little in front of the other and, with a thoughtful expression, sucking the rounded end of my new pen. In spite of despising Bulge, in spite of how she looks, I begin to try to emulate her.

❧

The first night in this room I am disturbed, soon after midnight, by the sound of running water, overhead and down inside the wall cavity close to where I am lying.

It sounds, at first, as if a bath might be overflowing. There is a lot of water, a flood. If the flowing water forces a hole in my wall the room will soon be full of water. The windows do not open so there is no way out for the water. The door, I understand at once, opens inwards. It would not open against the pressure of the water as it deepens in my room. Water is a very powerful element.

It is very hot in the room, incredibly hot. It occurs to me that because of the heat the water might be boiling. An even more unpleasant thought is that, instead of water, it might be steam.

I think about other people. Are there any other people near? And can they hear this water running? And are they disturbed too? I try to think of the design of the hotel, but, as with the streets seen from high up, I have no sense of direction from here. I have no idea, for example, where this room is in relation to the rest of the building except that it is at the end of a long passage on the twenty-fourth floor. If this is the top floor then there can be no bath above to overflow. I had the feeling earlier that there are rooms on either side of this one but, on reflection, I remember that both the doors out there are service doors of some sort being rough wooden doors without numbers and without keyholes. An uncomfortable memory.

The ritual for falling asleep is different for every individual but the position for not falling asleep is the same. To lie with the arms folded behind the head is an indication and a warning. Some time elapses before the realization that this is the final retreat, that sleep is not possible. Sleep has retreated.

On this first night I remember reading somewhere that in

order to be able to sleep in a strange room it is necessary to clear the mind; "to empty yourself for sleep."

The sound of the running water is persistent, as if it will never stop. I feel the wall above my bed. The wall is warm.

The indecision, one of my faults, is the worst attack I have ever experienced. The sought-after isolation in a hotel room is frightening, especially the apparent isolation high up above the strange city with nothing on either side and the water pouring across the ceiling and down inside the hollows of the walls. I am undecided about dialing 9 for the front desk.

The Front Desk
It is an old building a gentle voice soothes and no it is not an overflow from a locked-up bathroom but is simply the heating system which, regrettably, is old fashioned and noisy.

The sound of the water running stops almost at once.

Black Clothes
While I am traveling my customary good humor disappears. I am unable to bear, after quite a short time, the small jolts of traveling. Small things like having my seat changed in an aircraft, as if it really matters. All the seats are going towards the same destination I kept reminding myself yesterday.

I dislike the crowds. I waste energy wondering which sort of crowd is worse, the crowd traveling or the crowd still at the airport. I try to tell myself that these people in the crowd are really the people for whom I am working. The object of my journey is to further my studies and research in the finding of beneficial methods and treatments for the ailments which attack, at some time or other, these people. Mostly the people in a crowd are not thinking of medical attention or of the possibilities of surgery at some time in their lives. For the most part, though most of them will require some sort of treatment at some time or other, they seem unconcerned.

Perhaps my black clothes are partly the cause of uneasiness. The fellow travelers are all in holiday clothes and are laden with brightly colored plastic bags stuffed with shopping, French perfume in grubby hand-worn packaging, wine glasses with gold edges and stems, boxes of chocolate-covered nuts, and enormous bottles of whiskey.

My black brief case and black clothes are out of place in the busy airport thronged as it is with families on their way to and from relatives at this time of the year. I have forgotten that people do, in fact, go to places for a holiday. Places which, for me, are simply unavoidable stops during a long journey. Suddenly my life seems confined and narrow in the presence of the pleasure seekers.

Perhaps one of the unexpected aspects of traveling is not wanting to be in the places where I am expected to be. And, on arrival, being impatient to go on to the next place only to discover a repetition of that same impatience.

Parts of the plane are sprayed with anti-freeze. We arrive in a light falling of snow and recollections of ice on pavements and snow freezing on top of ice packing on roads and footpaths. The cold is intense.

Being unable to leave my hotel room is my own wish to remain in the room. I will rest one more day and then make my way into the conference rooms, listen to the papers, and deliver my own. The conference is my reason for traveling, after all. How can I work for people, I ask myself, if I seem, like now, to dislike them?

Sometimes life seems to be all worry and suffering and at other times it has dignity. A certain age, work, and a kind of detachment seem to create this dignity. During the years I have been writing less and less in a diary because I began to feel that this writing extended anxiety and unhappiness. Dr. Johnson never wrote his history of melancholy because he feared it would disturb him too much.

Whether things are written down or not they dwell somewhere within and surface unbidden at any time.

The Nurses

⚭

"You know Woods. Sister Woods on Men's P.S. Well this morning Woods smacked a junior across the face for cutting the crusts off some bread and butter she was giving to a post-operative hemorrhoids, wiped the floor with her saying didn't she realize what happened to bread and butter, crusts and all, before it got to the rectum. And before thingamajig, forget her name, could say she'd done it because he'd had all his teeth out as well Woods swiped her one and because her teeth are the kind that stick out, no not Woods—silly! thingamajig, I'll get her name in a minute, it's on the tip of my tongue, Thomas? No, Thompson that's it, well, because Thompson's teeth protrude rather, the smack on her face made her bite her lip and cheek and you should have seen the blood. Blood everywhere. All over Woods as well. When Thompson did manage to explain Woods reported her straight away to Matron's office for being cheeky."

"Oh that's rich, cheeky, get it? *Cheeky.*"

"No, don't get it."

"Well, forget it."

We are all up in the room I share with Lois. We are high up on the eighth floor. From the window you can see the streets and buildings of the city, you can see the railway line and the canal. The water in the canal seems to shine all night. Water does seem to stay light all night. The best part about this view is that you can see the trees in the park and, beyond all this, you can see across to the fields and the country outside the city. We are here, as we often are, revising for a test. Nursing is like this. One test or exam after another. We are having some currant buns with butter. Lois spreads the buns with her nursing scissors and, when we have finished eating, she remembers she did a taxi driver's feet with them this afternoon.

Lois is short with a round face and a round forehead. She has blue eyes wide apart and a little mouth. We have been sharing a room for some time. She smokes.

Trent is big and makes us laugh with her impersonations. Trent is the kind of nurse we all declare we would like to have looking after us if we should be ill. This is the highest compliment one nurse can pay another.

Ferguson was at boarding school with me. We started training together at the beginning of the war. We used to share rooms but Lois and I, being fond of each other, asked to change rooms. I am afraid Ferguson might have been hurt by this. She has never seemed to lack friends. Having plenty of sex appeal, she says, helps.

McDougal, who shares with Ferguson, is with us on this occasion. I often feel sorry for McDougal.

Since my friendship with Dr. Metcalf and his wife Magda began, Lois and Ferguson seem somewhat put out. And now since things have changed greatly for me with the sudden death of Dr. Metcalf when he went to the war, to do war service when the war was really over, I am aware of Lois observing me closely. She seems at times a little spiteful and quite often displays a triumphant look as if she is enjoying all that has happened to me. Things never used to be like this between Lois and me. Quite the reverse, there was something mysterious, exciting, and special between us at first. The kind of thing—when you go into a room full of people, for example, the big dining room here at the hospital, and you look quickly all round to see if the person you want to be near is there and, seeing her, you cross quickly hoping that there is an empty chair at her table—that kind of thing. Or seeing something in a shop which would please her you go in and buy it even if it takes up all the money you have. I once bought the prettiest nightdress for Lois and she gave it to her mother. Her mother, I thought then, was the ugliest woman I had ever seen. But Lois said, at the time, that her mother had never had nice things. But all this about Lois and me is changed.

I try to re-enter the pages of my *General Text Book of Nursing* wholeheartedly, to learn and to revise, to take my mind off the more sorrowful and worrying things in my life. For a time gossip helps. I mean, when hearing things about Sister Woods and Sister Purvis it is possible to forget other thoughts for a time, but inevitably these other thoughts come back heavier each time than before.

"I can't stand the way Purvis stands over me when I'm poaching an egg."

"Can't stand poaching eggs, full stop."

"Can't stand old Purvis, I mean, talk about a battle axe."

"Yep. A battle axe all right. That's because of her D.U."

"A D.U.?"

"Yep. Haven't you ever heard of a disappointed uterus? Said to be the cause."

"Cause of what?"

"Battle axes, silly."

"I'm not so sure about the D.U. Did you know she hasn't any sex organs?"

"Go on!"

"How does anyone know a thing like that? I mean, it's a bit private isn't it? I mean, it's a bit much, don't you think?"

"Purvis has got them all right. You can hear them rattling when she's mad at someone."

"Like when you've ruined a poached egg. I don't think patients should have their own shell eggs. Takes up too much time mornings. What's wrong with the hospital scrambled egg? Good honest dried egg!"

"Everything. Just about everything I'd say. It's rubber."

"Well, about Purvis. Lemmington Frazier, right in the middle of a rectal exploration last week, stopped half way and said, "Miss Purvis," he didn't, you notice, say Sister Purvis, "Miss Purvis," he said, "this Vaseline's about as sterile as you are." And then he looked at Purv. over his mask, you know how he does, and said, "Perhaps I'm crediting you where no credit's due." I mean what could be plainer!"

"I don't get it."

"Forget it. But about Purvis and Woods. You know how their wards, Men's Private Surgical and Women's P.M., share a ward kitchen well, last night Fanny Woods was throwing saucepan lids at Fanny Purvis and *she was* in her own half of the kitchen. Definitely she was on her own side of the kitchen. Woods threw the lids right across the kitchen. You never heard anything like it. Talk about battle axes in combat."

"Whyever?"

"Well, Woods likes everything rinsed in cold water, every cup, plate, spoon, what have you, all put in cold water straight after being cleared from the trays. And Purvis says that's the wardsmaid's job not the nurses'."

"And, I suppose Woods insists on the nurses, on both sides, rinsing things?"

"Yep. They were having this argument and then Woods says does Purvis realize that *her wardsmaid* is stuffing her bag with toilet rolls and spam meant for the American officers who are still here. Every night, she says, Purvis's wardsmaid goes off with this fat bag full of stuff. That's when they start throwing things. We don't dare go in there because of the noise. And Woods comes rushing out crying and Purvis has an asthma attack after blowing her boiler like that. Blue in the face she was."

"That's right the RMO had to be sent for. He put Purvis on parsley tea."

"I thought parsley tea was for abortions."

"No stupid, it's raspberry leaves brings on an abortion."

"Yes. Raspberry leaves. There's a few people in this hospital could do with a dose of raspberry tea." Lois looks across at me with lowered eyelids. "Except it might be too late. I mean if it's too far gone the old raspberry tea can't do anything."

"Describe Leiter's Coils and how to reduce temperature," Trent says with her finger in the pages of the *General Text Book of Nursing.*

"Better look it up. Look up cupping too and the tepid bath, is it four sponges used or six?"

"Heavens, all these water treatments! However much you cover the bed with rubber sheets—everything gets soaked. And really what difference, four or six sponges!"

"Well you don't have to say that in the exam. And anyway there's no water in cupping and it really works. Purvis swears by it and Woods won't hear of it."

"I mean, shall we ever get to do cupping?"

"Yep. I've just said Purvis does it all the time for pneumonia, swears by it. She's an old witch with the Bier's suction cups and the meths. She flames the cups with burning blotting paper. You've never seen anything like it! Little torn off bits of blotting paper dipped in spirit, she uses the forceps of course though I have seen her use her bare fingers . . ."

"No feeling."

"Yep. No feeling. She uses the forceps when lighting the bits of blotting paper, drops the bits, one in each cup, and then, when almost burned away in the cups, quickly puts them on the patient's back or chest. Woods won't have a bar of this treatment but there's no need to say that in an exam. Don't forget the vaseline—to mention it in the exam, I mean."

"We'd better look up Trendelenburg's and Sim's positions," Ferguson says. "I get them mixed up."

How can Ferguson mix up these two when Sim's is left lateral and semi-prone and in Trendelenburg's the patient is on her back, head lower than her pelvis, legs flexed at the knees . . .

"You use straps, fastenings, in Trendelenburgs," someone says.

I can't help thinking about the money Ferguson owes me. I'm going to need all the money I can get hold of from now on. No more State Express 333 for Lois. I am watching her smoke from the last packet I can give her. And definitely no more lending to Ferguson. If only there was some way I could get back what she owes me. I can't help wondering if Purvis and Woods, when they were young, lent or owed money. People, it seems, either lend it or they borrow it.

~≈~

FORTUNE TELLER

The special thing about being on night duty in the diet kitchen, if there can be, at present, anything special about this, is the surprisingly sweet fresh air where the inside of the hospital flows from its subterranean depths to meet the outside world. Sometimes, at dawn, I go through the half-lighted basements of the hospital kitchens and come out to the ramp where the empty milk churns are taken away. I stand there devouring the cool air of the new morning. Sometimes I help myself to a bowl of fresh milk from one of the new churns delivered during the night.

From this ramp it is possible to hear the city clocks chiming through the dull roar which is the regular, unchanging breathing of the city. A thin trickle of sad tired people leaves the hospital at about this time of day. They are relatives unknown and unthought about, having spent anonymous nights in various corners of the hospital, waiting to be called to a bedside where they will not be recognized. At dawn they leave in search of that life in the shabby world which has to go on in spite of the knowledge that someone who has been there for them is not there any more.

This ramp, this is the meeting place where all the weariness and the contamination and the madness of suffering of both worlds, the inside of the hospital and the outside, come together. In this pure spaciousness of the fresh air I have to understand, every morning, that I am one of the ones, who, without having had a silent bed to sit by, has to go on in the world.

The night nurses have dinner in the Maids' Dining Room. We have dinner first thing in the morning when we come off duty; mince and cabbage and boiled potatoes followed, as a rule, by rhubarb and custard. Sometimes there is a steamed currant pudding and custard. Sometimes the meat is cold meat with beetroot. Breakfast, with the bouncing scrambled egg, is in the evening. So that we have some time out of doors we are not expected to be in bed till twelve noon. The rooms are checked every day at twelve. Sometimes the maid, Hilda, does this. She is easily fooled by pillows heaped under bedclothes.

Lois wants to look at the fair. A traveling circus.

"But there'll be nothing doing at this time of day," Ferguson says. We go all the same. Lois, Ferguson, Trent, and I walk on the damp sweet-smelling grass between the tents and the caravans and the cages of animals. A few people, like us, are strolling about peering at the private lives of the animals and the circus people. The grass has been trodden down heavily the night before. This seems to enhance its fragrance this morning, as if being crushed it is now all the sweeter, as if adversity can bring about something pleasant. I almost speak of this to the others and then I don't. I simply hope that this idea has some truth in it for me.

"Cross my palm, dearie," the fortune teller is sitting on a stool outside her booth. She has on a red and black shawl and is decorated lavishly, as if she slept in them, with rings on her fingers and ears. Her long black hair is loose. She is brushing it.

"Cross my palm with silver, dearie," she calls across to us.

"Anyone got any money?" Lois is looking at my purse.

"She wants silver," Trent says.

"Oh come on," Lois says, "you've got a shilling there, you've got two." She pokes a finger in my purse.

"Who's going?" I look at the others.

"It's your money, Wright," Trent says.

The sweet grass is intoxicating. I can feel the damp when I sit down by the fortune teller. She studies my hand tracing the lines with a black-edged finger nail. The others stand near, listening.

"You've a long life, dearie," the fortune teller says. She makes me clench my fist and she counts the creases below my little finger.

"You'll have three children, dearie, easy births. You'll be a mother before you're a wife, dearie. Romance is to be yours.

Romance will come your way. There's a tall dark handsome stranger in your life . . ." She stops suddenly and goes on brushing her hair.

"Short and sweet," Trent says as we move on between the tethered ponies. "That's all you get for a bob, obviously. Could be that she's off duty, like us, too."

"Mother before wife. Hm Hm," Lois lights her last cigarette and surrounds herself with a cloud of smoke. "Now what can she mean by that, I wonder? I just wonder." I can see Lois narrowing her eyes as she looks at me through the settling smoke.

"Come on," Trent says, "let's get back, the post should be in by now."

At the hospital, in the Nurses' Home, we queue for letters. There is a parcel for me from my mother. Records direct from the shop in town. The excitement of this is pleasant and a reminder of other surprise parcels in other days when it was possible to be entirely excited about something and to have nothing worrying at the back of the mind.

I hope, as I take the parcel and sign for it, that it might contain the Mozart piano concerto which has an octave leap in the first movement, piano notes an octave apart, not once but several times granting the satisfaction which a realization of the expected gives. This is how staff nurse Ramsden would speak of the octave leap. And in the second movement there is a tender reasoning in the music. Efficacious, this is not a word I use but I feel certain that Ramsden would apply it to the second movement of this piano concerto. Efficacious, the word is more than suitable for her voice.

Back up in the room which I share with Lois we try the records. The gramophone is in the wardrobe with a towel over it to muffle the noise. I am disturbed by the music, disappointed, not liking it at all. I have never listened to anything like it before.

"God!" Lois says, "Golly! What a row. Turn it off for God's sake!" I try one of the others. It is just as awful. "It's Bach," I tell

Lois, "unaccompanied cello, and the other is a string quartet by Beethoven. It should be nice, it's Beethoven."

"If you say so," Lois says. "Me, it's not my cup of tea."

"You might not like this music at first," my mother, without seeing my face, has sensed my lack of enthusiasm which I try to hide during my telephone call of thanks. "It is a sophisticated music. You will like it very much later on," she says, "only listen and wait. You must learn to wait. There is time," she says, "for all things but you have to wait till the right time. Listen and wait now." She tells me to bring my ration book if I am coming home, later on, for a holiday when I have finished night duty. "The butcher," she says, "has some nice hipponstek, but will need ration book." I tell her that I won't be coming home, that I am not due for any holiday. How can I go home from now on.

"Be sure to bring ration book when you come," my mother says.

Lois is having her bath so I get undressed and into bed as quickly as I can. The blending of discord and deep sorrow, deepening with each note in the opening of the Beethoven string quartet and the grave unaccompanied cello of Bach seem to have enclosed me inside a wall of heavy solemn thoughts. It is the first time I have heard a cello by itself for more than just a few notes. One piece of music will not replace another wished for piece. It is the same with people.

The deep bowls of milk I scoop from the churns first thing every morning are rich and creamy. This fresh milk should be beneficial for small delicate bones and for the muscles of a tiny heart.

Ration Book

Beatrice, Baba. Baba I must talk to you. You and I, Beatrice—
Baba, must have a little talk. Twice today, Beatrice, you have
kicked me. Beautiful Beatrice, the giver of blessings. You, Baba,
seemed never to be growing and now, all at once, you have
grown and you move. Will you be a pretty little girl, Baba, with
fair hair and brown eyes?

Now, the first thing that I must do is to get my ration book.
Yes, Baba, Ration Book. You, Baba, you do not know anything
about things like ration books yet. Ration Book is not for you to
worry about. I have to worry. How to get Ration Book is the
next thing.

Dr. Metcalf, I know you always told me to call you Jonathon
especially when you kissed me you said to call you Jonathon or
Jonty like Magda. How could I call you Jonty when that was
Magda's name for you? Dr. Metcalf, I must tell you that our baby
moves. If only you could be here to put your hand on me and
feel Beatrice kick, thump thump, here in my side. From the outside you can see her move, actually from the outside. *Actually see
her moving.*

But the ration book. I must get it. I can't leave here without it.

"Where's your ration book?" My mother's first question,
always. "Why didn't you post your ration book?" Her voice
indignant with her question on the telephone on different occasions. "You know very well that Mr. Shaw likes to have the ration
books. He needs them, particularly he needs them for the bacon.
And the butcher too, he must have the meat coupons. Have you
still got meat coupons?" My mother, intimidated by food office

officials and by the grocer and butcher, is always angry about ration books.

The women who work at the food office all wear head scarves. They keep their hair in metal curlers all day and cover them with these head scarves. When I get my ration book I shall have to go to the food office to get my green ration book which I can have because of being pregnant. The women, in their head scarves, sitting on the other side of the trestle tables, will keep me standing so long while they put their head scarves together to study my identity card and the hieroglyphic on the top right-hand corner which, I understand, means "assumed name." It will not be their business to discuss my change of name, my assumed name which I have taken because I am pregnant and not married. But they will discuss and they will look at me with a hard-eyed curiosity; and they will keep me waiting. Twice during ward report little Nurse Roberts fainted. Here in the diet kitchen I do not have to stand at report. If I have to stand a long time in the food office I am sure to feel faint and they will help me to one of their horrible little chairs and bring me rusty water in a cup.

You, Dr. Metcalf, you never had to worry about food rationing. You never had to know anything about the long lines of people waiting outside shops and at the bus stops. For Magda food rationing has never and does not now exist. She never has to queue for anything. The last time I saw Magda she was still hoping that the news of your death, Dr. Metcalf, was not true. I still have the same hope but because there are things pressing which I have to do I have to think about these things.

"Why are you so late?" my mother always asks. She is peevish with keeping a plate of dinner warm over a saucepan. She keeps my father's dinner warm like this, too, for when he comes in white-faced and tired from school.

"Why are you so late?" The question persists.

"The bus queue . . ." I explain, "so many people . . ."

"You must not always stand aside," she says, the irritation growing in her voice. She is anxious about me. "You must get the ration book and go to the food office for the green book," she says. "And then, always, you must go to the heads of the queue, right to the tip, and hold up your green book, so, and when all can see it you will be first on the bus. Rosa," my mother adds, "Rosa is having twins as you know and her mother-in-law, Frau Meissner, takes always Rosa's book and is every time first on the bus." I start to correct my mother.

"No s on head for queue and tip is not . . ." I am afraid she might make mistakes in front of the neighbors. It suddenly seems too difficult to explain that "always" and "every time" are not in the right places in her sentences.

Rosa and her family are among the first people to escape, with my mother's help, from Europe.

I am obsessed, Baba, with Ration Book. I cannot leave without it. I need it to get the green ration book for you Baba. You will benefit greatly . . .

It is part of my work at night in the diet kitchen to go round to all the wards to collect request forms for ration books belonging to patients who are being discharged. I usually do this in that quiet time of the night when I have finished dusting and tidying Matron's office. She keeps a little tin of dark polish and a soft cloth in one of the drawers in her desk. Dusting Matron's office is a privilege entrusted only to a few nurses she tells me when I am moved by her well-sharpened pencil to night duty in the diet kitchen.

"The diet kitchen," Matron says then while her pencil hovers and pauses above the colored squares on her big map of the nurses' experience and movement charts, "The diet kitchen is not a place of punishment. It is a valuable part of your training." And working there on my own, she tells me is an excellent way of having a much needed rest from patients and other staff. She tells me there is no need to cry and that I must have plenty of fresh air every morning before going to bed. When she speaks to me she talks of me as "one of her nurses." It is thinking about being considered by her as belonging to her which makes the tears keep coming. I had never thought that she might have thought of me as hers. She takes the opportunity then of explaining something I already know, that the doctors' corridor is out of bounds (her words) for the nursing staff. I have been seen there occasionally apparently.

"No doubt you will have had your own reasons," Matron goes on and she says she will not question them. She says that the rule is made to "protect those of our profession who are weaker." It is then that she tells me she has made up her mind that I am to be a gold medalist. "It will be hard work," she says, "very hard work but I know that you can do it."

"You, Baba, you come from there, from the doctors' corridor. No one knows this at all. But it is only fair that you should know it. That part of the hospital was bombed and is being rebuilt, Baba. It will never be the same there and you will never see it."

But the ration books. The office where I have to go for the patients' ration books is also the place where my ration book is. It is in the same subterranean corridor as the diet kitchen and the ordinary kitchens. The radium therapy ward is down there too and a surgical ward for soldiers, officers, mostly convalescent patients who are allowed out during the day.

There is a certain place along this corridor where staff nurse Ramsden and I met one night, each going in opposite directions. It is then that Ramsden, very shyly, gives me a little book of hand-written poems. Some of them are her own and some are poems which she has chosen. At the time, she says she feels she has no right to give me the poems but will I have them all the same. As we are both in a hurry she says not to look at them then.

Ramsden must be having nights off as staff nurse Burrows is in the office on the Lower Ground Men's Surgical. I see her there when I am on the way to the ration-book office.

As soon as I manage to get my ration book there are the other things I must do. I may do all this in one day and in that case shall not see Ramsden again. Often I have walked along the corridor and back simply in the hope of meeting her or of seeing her sitting in the office of the ward bent over the reports she is writing.

I think that, because of the shy and tender expression in Ramsden's eyes, she really likes to see me. It might be because of her being so much older than I am, and more senior, that she does not tell me that she likes to see me. Of course I would not be able to tell her what I am about to do as soon as I can get my ration book. I am ashamed that, in spite of all the suffering inside this big hospital, all I can think about is my ration book and what I have to do . . . Also, I do not like staff nurse Burrows because she is not Ramsden . . . I am sorry about this too.

Time has been going very slowly and yet it goes on in an inevitable way. My life seems to spread over an Age, an Eternity. I feel old. My life seems to be a never-ending time of having no one to talk to, of going for lonely walks in the mornings, early, before going to bed. I walk by the Metcalfs' house. I never see anyone coming out or going in. The curtains are always drawn. I think about Magda and wonder what she is doing, who she is with, and what she would guess if she knew about my baby. Yes, you Baba. Dr. Metcalf's baby and mine. In a curious sort of way, Baba, it is as if you are the Metcalfs' baby. Magda's and Dr. Metcalf's.

Every night in the diet kitchen I am tired before I start work. Every night I do the same things. I cut and weigh small pieces of bread and wash lettuce leaves and boil beetroots. I make up the trays and label them with names and illnesses, diabetes, kidney disease—kidney failure mainly. I stew prunes and beat up dried egg powder. I try not to breathe in the smell of the Vitamin B extract. I work alone. My body aches behind the buttons of my uniform. I think of little Nurse Roberts. As well as fainting all over the place she couldn't stand the smell of the dried egg. It was said she threw up just looking at the packet. I suppose she will have her baby by now. They say, at meal times, that you, Dr. Metcalf, are the father of Nurse Roberts's baby.

The smell of the dried egg and dehydrated potato powder makes me feel sick still. When I slice tomatoes I have to turn my head away.

Trent says, one day at breakfast, that though the war is supposed to be over, if a war ever really ends, she says, the dried egg will go on forever. When she says this she is chasing some scrambled egg as it bounces across her plate and we all laugh. Inside I am not laughing at all really. I am lonely. Alone beyond all words even though we all go together then, Trent, Ferguson, Lois, and me to queue for our jam ration. We all have to take a clean jam jar with a well-fitting lid and the Home Sister ladles the warm red jam from a zinc bath into each jar as we file past. She has the bath high up on a table which has been covered with a clean sheet.

When I go home to my mother's house for my nights off I go there by the Back Lane, from the bus, instead of along the street where the neighbors might see me. Mostly I go at dusk and this has not been difficult because the evenings are still getting dark early. How will I go there in the long light evenings of summer? How can I nurse my baby on the bus and then carry her on my arm to my mother's house? This was something I always wanted to do. It was something I imagined doing, something nice to do at some time in the future. I never thought then of it being like this. I mean, I never thought of making the journey with my baby secretly and without the pride of taking her home to be admired.

I never go to Gertrude's Place now.

Sometimes my father is waiting for me at the bus stop. Even in the rain he waits and we walk home together. He comes to the station when it is time for me to go back to the hospital. He tells me, on my last visit there, that they would like me to come home. He tells me that if it would be easier for me they will sell the house and move. "Buy another house—somewhere else and move," he says. I think of the walls of books in the house and of all the other things there, undisturbed, for years. They know all the people living nearby. My mother is sustained by the people she knows. I tell my father it is not necessary for them to move. I tell him I have other plans. "Thank you all the same," I tell him. He takes my hand and shyly kisses the space above the back of my hand.

We walk together up and down the deserted platform. I look along the empty rails to see if the train is coming and I try to think what are those plans of mine. It would be easier to be going to bed upstairs in the back bedroom at home and to have my father bring me the strange half cup of tea he always makes, with the tea leaves floating and with too much sugar, in the mornings.

"I don't want to go," I want to tell my father. I want to tell him that the diet kitchen is an awful place, that I don't feel well there, and that it is dark and lonely and that I shall be cutting up and weighing and arranging little bits of tasteless food all night.

"Always the same little pieces of bread and the same lettuce leaves for patients for whom there are no medicines and no cure." I can't help saying this.

"It is God's work," my father consoles. And, as if forgetting that I shall be obliged to leave the hospital soon, he says, "Every day new discoveries are made and if these patients can be helped with diets while the scientists, with their research, are providing new drugs then that is a good thing." As he talks his voice is full of hope. "Take school dinners," he says. "All schools are now providing dinners . . ." The train comes and our talk has to end. I lean out of the window to wave to him. He has walked, almost running, alongside as far as he can to the end of the platform.

He has not forgotten. I see him standing white-faced with one arm raised. He gets smaller and smaller and I can see him till, at last, the train moves round into the great curve. He has not forgotten at all.

There will always be school dinners now. I hear my father saying this often. He says children at school must have enough to eat. "Plenty of food and plenty of sleep." Those are the words he says. Sometimes he talks about the school dinners to strangers in shops. Perhaps on New Year's Day when he wishes people he does not know a happy new year and shakes hands with them.

Before the war my father arranges school dinners himself. He employs two women and pays them himself to come to school and to cook and serve the dinners. The children do not have to pay for them. He wants me to come with my mother to the school to see his dinners.

"Is like a dinner for a dog," my mother says peering into one of the enormous saucepans. "The smell!" My father is proud of the dinners and introduces us to the two women who are standing, their large arms bare, ready to serve as the children file past. My father is accustomed to eating a pile of bread with his own meals. He stands by one of the desks and cuts thick slices of bread and gives a piece to each child so that the gravy can be soaked up and not wasted.

"He gets up earlier and earlier," my mother complains to me later. "He goes on his bicycle to the markets to buy the meat and the vegetables," she lowers her voice. "People also," she says, "give him meat coupons and carrots. He is peeling himself." Because I can hear her tears in her voice I hesitate to correct her.

Baba? You there? Baba, you are very quiet and still. I am on my way at last to that dreary office on the lower ground floor. It is not far from the diet kitchen past the Radium Therapy, the Pharmacy and the Officers' Surgical. I don't need to tell you, Baba, because you have been everywhere with me for quite some time now. Though I have made a point of keeping away from Lower Ground Radium. Might be a dangerous place for you, Baba. As I was telling you I am on my way to get the ration books for the wards and to try to get my own ration book so that I can get the green one, Baba, for you. So keep calm Beatrice Baba, in there. Have a little rest and do not take any notice if I seem nervous or upset. I have thought of a way to get Ration Book. And, Beatrice Baba, I might as well tell you now that if I am successful in a minute, it will not be long before we leave the hospital. We shall be going to a place where I shall be house-keeper, "a mother's help." Don't laugh Baba! Do you laugh in there? Go to sleep!

"You'll need a signed slip," this woman says, "signed by Matron." The woman's only a clerk, for heavens sake. Who does she think she is! Really, Baba, if you could *see* her.

"Yes. Yes. I know. I've got it. The slip. It's up in my room on the night nurses' corridor. I forgot to bring it down."

"Signed by Matron, is it?"

"Yes. Yes! I'll come right back down with it. I'll be down with it before you go off duty. But I'd better get these round to the wards first."

"There's twenty-five. Sign for them here." She pushes a ledger towards me.

"Sure!" I say. "Heavens! You have been busy cutting out coupons. You must be bored to death." I examine the stack of ration books. Naturally mine is not among them.

"Just sign please."

These official administrators! Baba, I can't say this aloud but she is the most boring person I have ever seen. No style. Absolutely no style. I suppose she doesn't need any, sleeping all day and guarding ration books and cutting them up all night. If you could see her hair, Baba. Unwashed string. And her jumper is a hand-knitted hideous shapeless thing covered with yellow and purple blobs.

"You must be bored to death," I try once more. Must keep her talking, thinking about something else while she looks out my book.

"I am," she yawns.

"I'm on holiday," I say.

"I'm so pleased for you," she says without a hint of pleasure.

"When will you get your holiday?" I'm having to actually *chat*. This woman kills me. The awful thing is that I find myself longing for boredom like hers. Safe solid boredom instead of what I have to get done. In my head I'm telling her to hurry.

Hurry up do! Find my ration book, only hurry before you change your mind or before someone else comes in here. Quick quick find my ration book!

"This war!" I sigh, "I know it's over and all that but they say the shortages and the ration books will go on for a long time. You know," I lower my voice and lean towards her, "this war's had a terrible effect on my mother. She hoards bags of buns, those iced buns with currants, under her bed. Can you imagine!"

The clerk looks up at me. "She never!"

"Yep, she does. You have no idea." Ideas spring into my mind. "Mention the word 'ration book,' " I say, "in her hearing and she bolts off to queue wherever there's a queue. Sometimes she goes in carpet slippers, really old ones. And the mess under her bed. Rats, do you see? Awful!" I'm peering at the ration books in her hands. "Er, that looks like it might be mine," I say.

"You got your identity card on you?" she snaps.

"Sure!" I say feeling my uniform pocket. "It's in here somewhere. It's in my little Bible here."

She takes the little white Testament.

"There's nothing in here," she says.

"I must have left it upstairs," I say. "I'll bring it down later."

"Oh never mind! Your name's in here, in the Bible. It's a neat little book," she says. "I'm getting my holiday in about nine weeks time," she offers.

"I'll bet you're counting the days," I say. "Jolly nice!" I sit on the edge of her desk to show how relaxed I am. A cramp seizes the back of my thigh.

I can hardly take the ration book without snatching it. It is a long time since I held the book in my hands. I look at it without really seeing it. I hold it as if clamped with my fingers to the top of the twenty-five for the patients.

"Don't mix them up," the clerk yawns once more. "They're in order, starting on Lower Ground and going up, makes it easier and quicker for you."

"Oh ta," I say, "ta very much, thank you very much, ta! I'll be right back down."

"Tonight will do," she says, yawning straight at me. "It'll save you coming back. Bring the slip tonight." She starts to tidy her desk. "I'm getting off early this morning, a bit early," she says.

"Good idea!" I say. "I'll come tonight." I try to whistle as I go along the corridor but my mouth is too dry.

"Nurse!" I hear her voice calling me back along the corridor. I can hardly bear to turn round. She can't have my ration book back now. I go back. She has actually left her desk and is out in the corridor.

"You left your Testament," she is holding out the little white Bible. I manage to smile.

"Oh," I say, "you keep it. I'd like you to have it. I've got another."

"Thank you," she says, "thank you very much."

Upstairs the night nurses' corridor is quiet. My room is just as I left it. McDougal, who now shares with me, is in the Nurses' Sick Bay. It is thought that she has diphtheria. She is being barrier nursed. We have all had throat swabs taken. Mine is negative.

I wish I could show you the ugly Ration Book, Baba. I suppose you don't have open eyes yet. You won't have finger nails, Baba, till eight months. Baba, stay till you are full term and then you will have everything. Be a good baby and don't you worry about anything.

This is going to be quite a day for us. As well as Ration Book I have my trunk up here in my room. This used to be my trunk for school, it's called a cabin trunk. For ship journeys I suppose, Baba. I got it up in here just now, first thing this morning, without seeing anyone except the maid, Hilda, and she took no notice of me except to say did I know that the mice had got into McDougal's box of mince pies and she's taken the box away.

"Atta girl Hilda," I say to her, "atta girl!" It seems to me I am saying words I would never use as a rule. Perhaps I have heard Trent say "atta girl" when she is being funny. Today is no ordinary day. The mince pies, Baba, for heaven's sake, they've been around since Christmas.

I did not go to the night nurses' meal this morning and that is how I am able to bring my trunk up here without seeing anyone. To get your trunk, Baba, you are really supposed to put in a Requisition slip the night before, signed by Matron of course, explaining that you have been told to change your room. And the trunk appears later in your room. Well I want my trunk now so I ask the night porter to unlock the trunk room with his skeleton key.

"That'll be a kiss Christmas," the porter says. He jingles his keys.

"Sure!" I tell him. "I'll keep you to that."

The trunk room, Baba, is a very restful clean place. All the trunks and cases and boxes are arranged in alphabetical order on wooden racks. The floor always looks swept. I have a look first to see what Ramsden's trunk is like. I can see at once it is made of something expensive like pig skin. It has brass-bound corners and a sturdy bright lock. Ramsden has certainly traveled, all over Europe it seems. I peer at the partly torn off colored labels. All sorts of colors and all sorts of places and hotels. Exotic. Amsterdam, Brussels, Frankfurt, Paris, Rome . . . Ramsden, in her traveling, would have been sure to go on a steamer on the Rhine. She would have seen the miracle of the confluence—the apparently inexplicable appearance of the brown water of the river Main meeting and flowing with the blue waters of the Rhine. An unbelievable division—actually in the water . . .

"This one yours?" the night porter has my trunk by the door. He jingles his keys. He has to be off, he says, his wife, who works during the day, will be waiting . . .

"Oh sure!" I tell him, "thank you." And I drag the trunk into the lift easily.

I feel strange, for one thing I have started saying "sure" to everybody like a character in an American film. It would be easier, I think, to live a life in a film.

Hilda leaves a milk pudding every day in the night nurses' pantry at the end of the corridor. Because of you, Baba, and because I have missed the night nurses' meal time, I go off quickly to the pantry and spoon up nearly the whole dishful. The pudding is meant for all the nurses should they need something more to eat after going out and before going to bed. Not bad, Baba, the pudding not bad at all, a sort of loose blancmange, white and smooth and sweet.

"Atta girl! Hilda," I say to the vanishing shape of the maid as she goes along the passage to the top of the stairs. Hilda was once Matron's personal maid and is retired but kept on in the hospital to have somewhere to live. She looks after the night nurses' corridor. Some other elderly maids and nurses are kept on in the sewing room, Baba, where sheets are mended and uniforms are made—that sort of thing. Sometimes I think it would be nice to just sit in the sewing room unpicking (they would give me the unpicking to do) and, just sitting, unpicking, untroubled—and bored with my companions. I really do just want to be thoroughly bored, Baba.

Baba, you and I cannot be bored. Ration Book and Trunk all at once up here in my room . . .

Our headmaster at school always said he knew which boys and girls would hand in their *Golden Treasury of the Bible* (two vols.) on leaving school and which boys and girls would keep them as a spiritual guide for the rest of their lives. I put the two gray nondescript books, Part I a fat book of the Old Testament and Part II, slim, the New Testament, in the bottom of the trunk with *The General Text Book of Nursing* and the *Golden Treasury of Songs and Lyrics Book Fifth*. Shoes must go at the bottom too and flat, on the bottom, my Beethoven Piano Concerto, The Emperor. Some of my pressed wildflowers have come unstuck. It is a long time since I have looked at them. I put them back between the pages of the exercise book as quickly as I can. I seem to see, clearly, shining long fingers pulling stalks and holding bunches. I remember the sweet wet grass near the school where we searched for flowers. Saxifrage, campion, vetch, ragged robin, star of Bethlehem, wild strawberry, and sorrel. I must hurry. The flowers, the colors are still fresh, I can't help looking at all of them in turn, buttercup, King cup, cowslip, coltsfoot, wood anemone, shepherd's purse, lady's slipper, jack-in-the-pulpit, and bryony.

Whenever I think of my father, like now, I hope he is thinking about school dinners. I have all his letters. I put his letters in the trunk carefully. They have underlined quotations in them.

> *Wherefore I perceive that there is nothing better, than*
> *that a man should rejoice in his own works; for that is*
> *his portion: for who shall bring him to see what shall*
> *be after him?*

Ecclesiastes 3 v 22. He includes the chapter and verse because he always hopes I will look up the passage and read for myself.

My white blouse, my white blouse, which I keep for when I am invited somewhere, has to be folded neatly and my good pair of stockings, always clean and in readiness I put in beside the blouse. Then there is the little book of poems written out for me by Ramsden. For some reason I read the second verse of a poem and am surprised that though I liked the first verse very much:

> *The feathers of the willow*
> *Are half of them grown yellow*

I never read on to,

> *The thistle now is older*
> *His stalk begins to moulder*

and realize I have never really known the poem until now, and I feel sad in a quiet sort of way. I never read any of the poems to the end but only took the lines with the images I wanted.

Baba? Beatrice Baba? Will I sit reading poems while I nurse you in my arms? I remember my mother saying once that, before she had any baby, she imagined that she would sit by the window holding her baby and reading a novel. She said she understood later that the idea was not realistic and that it had come to her from something Goethe wrote.

Ramsden will have liked the poems she copied out in the little book.

> They have no song, the sedges dry
> And still they sing
> It is within my breast they sing
> As I pass by.

As I read I am overwhelmed with a wish to hear Ramsden's voice once more. I would like to ask her to read "The Song in the Songless" but she will be either asleep or possibly away still on her nights off.

The trouble with packing, Baba, is that even though it is necessary to hurry I keep opening books and reading bits here and there. It says here in my *General Text Book of Nursing* that a woman is said to be pregnant when she has conceived. You will take, Baba, ten lunar months or 280 days to grow. To calculate the date of your birth, Baba, you can be expected to be born nine calendar months and five days from the last day of my last menstrual period. This reckoning is correct, it says here, within two or three weeks. The only trouble is, Baba, which you probably know as well as I do, that I have forgotten when that last date was. All I know is that it is rather a long time ago. It says here too that *every married woman should be advised either to consult her own doctor or to attend one of the many excellent antenatal clinics provided, as soon as she knows she is pregnant.*

Obviously, Baba, this applies to unmarried women as well. It is a bit awkward this being unmarried but it is clear to me that as soon as possible we must go to a doctor.

When I have finished packing this trunk, Baba, your life and my life, up to the present time, will be contained inside it.

My trunk looks small in the deserted space of the front hall. It is not often that the hall is empty of people. Someone is in the phone box and someone is waiting outside, too preoccupied with the impatience of waiting. I have to go up to the next floor where there is a phone for staff nurses and sisters. I must hurry. I must get my taxi before the nurses pass to and fro in the front hall on their way either to or from the dining room. The night nurses will not have been called yet. I want to miss Trent and Ferguson and Lois. I do not want to see them just now.

I have to wait for this phone too. I wish really that I could be going home and not to a strange house. The awful truth is that I like to see my mother and my father but after about half an hour I want to go away again. I am quite unable to explain why this is. Of course I never say anything about it. I feel strangled in the back bedroom at home and more alone than ever, especially when I sit there looking across the back gardens of the other houses and watch two people, a man and wife, working side by side, in their own garden.

My taxi will come soon. I am promised the first available.

On the way downstairs I pass staff nurse Ramsden's door. I hear some music from her room, something which has the strength and the stillness of mountains and mountain lakes. Music with a tender serenity about it. I think I know the music, something by Sibelius, I think. Parts of this music were played at school by the school orchestra, every one playing at their own pace, not keeping together and not in tune. Ramsden must be getting up already though it is not time yet for the night nurses to get up. I have not been to bed all day and, though I shall be able to sleep tonight, it will be in an unfamiliar room and an unfamiliar bed.

I stop outside Ramsden's door and listen to the music. I long to tap on her door and to go in and hear her voice once more, to see her, to tell her, really, to tell her everything. But people cannot do things like that. I would like to hear her say "come in" in her rich well-bred voice. She must be in there because there would be no music if she was not there.

I would like to go right in there and tell her *Ramsden*, I would say, *I have to say "goodbye" I'm leaving* and then I would be able to tell her everything, even that Dr. Metcalf said I was to call him Jonathon—especially to call him Jonathon when we were loving each other... Of course I can't knock and go in to her room. I can't tell her anything. People, well-bred people and I want to be well bred, don't burden each other with their dreams and their mistakes.

It is not like Ramsden to listen to Sibelius though I think she would describe the music as having a haunting quality of loneliness. She might use words like "a mellow work of poetry." People say things like this about music but when Ramsden speaks you can tell that she really means what she says. Ramsden could say, for example, that this music has strength and ardor.

It is not like Ramsden to listen to Sibelius, if it is Sibelius. Perhaps she is listening with someone, staff nurse Pusey-Hall. They do go to concerts together. Of course I cannot possibly go in there while Sibelius is being played. It *is* the Andante from something by Sibelius. One of them, Ramsden or Pusey-Hall, might come out suddenly and find me just outside the door. And then there's my taxi on its way and my trunk down there in the front hall ...

"Well here's a shock!" I say excitedly as Lois, Ferguson, and Trent come up the stairs from the dining room and into the front hall. "Here I am," I say to them, "being moved all of a sudden." The three of them stand staring at me. Trent has taken off her cap and her hair is loose. They all have their string bags with their jars of butter and sugar and jam.

"Where on earth could you be moved to?" Lois narrows her eyes as she does when she is smoking though naturally she is not smoking at this moment. "Where on earth!" she says.

"The Accident hospital," I say. "Apparently, The Queens, the Accident hospital, is terribly short staffed and Matron's lending some of her night nurses." Ferguson looks at me in disbelief. Lois lights a cigarette and surrounds herself in her customary cloud of smoke.

"Sounds like your cab," Trent says. I am relieved to hear the horn.

"I'll give you a hand with your trunk," Trent says.

I feel hungry, terribly hungry in this taxi. I even think I could eat that awful tripe which cooks slowly all night in the diet kitchen.

In my mind I consider the contents of my trunk safely in the luggage part of the taxi. I have not forgotten anything, my exercise books with the pressed wildflowers, the saxifrage, the meadow sweet, and the bryony from school, all my books including my *General Text Book of Nursing* (1942) and the huge book of Embroidery I chose so stupidly from Ramsden's shelves when she once shyly offered to me to choose a book, any one of her books which I would like to have for myself. I have no idea why I chose a book full of embroidery designs and diagrams of needles in the act of making stitches, when I could have had poems, Rilke, for example, the Orpheus poems. In English of course.

I am lucky to have this taxi. With all the shortages, they are called the immediate postwar shortages, it is practically impossible to get taxis. I suppose it is some kind of providence which is helping me just now. I mean, what was it other than providence, which made me, when I ordered the car, say it was for Doctor Wright and that it was urgent. A childbirth, I said. Well you will be a childbirth, Baba, later on.

I really do feel terribly hungry. I have the ration book. The next thing will be the Food Office and the women there. I know what it is like at the Food Office and I have seen the queue there, right out on to the pavement . . .

But first the house at Clifton Way and I hope that there is something to eat there.

. . . Abbot Abrahams Ackerman Allwood . . .

. . . Arrington and Attwood. Nurses Baker Barrington Beam Beamish Beckett Birch Bowman D Bowman E Broadhurst Brown Burchall . . . When Sister Bean calls the register and gets to my name I shall not be there to answer. She will call twice and no one will reply, no one will reply for me.

It is only a short ride to the house in Clifton Way. I hope they will offer me something to eat. I am hungry.

Cabin Fever

∽

THE BREAKFAST BAR

Tomorrow, tomorrow I tell myself, tomorrow I shall, without hesitation, go down to the place where breakfasts are served. At street level there is an L-shaped restaurant, a breakfast bar, where people on the pavement can peer through plate glass at other people sitting among stacks of pancakes, flying fried eggs, and bowls of steaming porridge, butter soaked and overflowing. Between the customers, like small traffic islands on the counters, are the cups and saucers over which a hot jug hovers pouring, without splashing, the life-giving coffee. There is a special door for this breakfast bar. Hotel residents need not enter by the street door where there is always a queue of silent hungry people waiting, pausing impatiently on their way to their work.

Yesterday I said that the next day I would go down for breakfast. I remind myself now that all kinds of people are down there having breakfast. Women with intelligent eyes and Viennese accents, on museum or gallery research, speaking English slowly. Elderly men and women, married and living together for years, watery faced and red veined, knowing each other's preferences, speaking to each other without needing to, one addressing the waitress, unasked, on behalf of the other. Over all this hangs the fragrance of hair spray and bacon.

ROOM SERVICE
Because I am tired. Tired and travel shocked, too tired to dress

and make my way along to the lift and down the twenty-four floors, I'll dial for room service and have a pot of coffee and some croissants sent up, balanced shoulder high on the palm of the waiter's hand, the heavy tray, silver at the edges, drenched in white linen, bringing with it an unbelievable atmosphere, a sense of offering and of cherishing carried, from the place where it has been carefully prepared, all the way up to my bedside. And here it will be placed, set carefully on the space cleared temporarily as my notes and papers are moved with reverence across the smooth covers of the bed.

I shall lie back on the pillows and breathe in the fragrance of the coffee and of the croissants, their crisp golden warmth, hidden folded in the white table napkin. I shall handle the cutlery, heavy with good quality, and feel with my lips the china rim of the cup. Seen from the consolation of this masterpiece my notes are noble.

THE NOISE

For some hours there has been and still is an incredible noise immediately outside my door. Someone is drilling and hammering and trying to push a cable or an electric wire of some sort through a small space somewhere above my head and in the cavity of the wall behind my head. I have never in my whole life heard any noise quite like this noise. It is a wild and dangerous noise, a noise of discord suggesting pain and trouble, disorder and sorrow.

BROKEN GLASS

Someone out there has broken some glass. It is being swept up. The broken glass is being swept up in that methodical way in which broken glass is gathered carefully, with the slow sweeps of a small worn-out brush into a metal dustpan. Some larger pieces, I can hear quite well, are being picked up and dropped into the pan. Perhaps there are two people out there crouching over the breakage. Probably it was a light fitting of some sort. I remember now, when I think of the long passage, there are opaque white bowls fitted over the lights. If I do think about these bowls at all, with any kind of seriousness, it would be to suppose that they are made of plastic . . . Clearly, it is broken glass very close immediately outside my door. There is a murmur of subdued anger, a low growling in a gravelly American accent; one of them, crouching there, must have cut himself.

SHIRT SLEEVES

I am still here on the twenty-fourth floor and when I sit in front of my mirror I can see, in the mirror, someone on the twenty-fourth floor across the street. He is sitting upright at a table and is in his shirt sleeves. I have no idea who he is.

CABIN FEVER

There is no way of controlling the heat in this room. At times I find the heat overpowering. The heat induces dreams bordering on nightmare. Delirium in which harm is done;

> . . . *Willst, feiner Knabe, du mit mir gehn?*

> *Will you come with me, my pretty boy?*
> *My father, my father, and don't you see there*
> *The Erlking's daughters with long flowing hair?—*
> *My son, my son, I do see them sway:*
> *It is the old willows that look so gray.—*

> *Mein Vater, mein Vater, jetzt fasst er mich an!*
> *Erlkönig hat mir ein Leids getan!—*

> *My father, my father, I feel his cold arm,*
> *The Erlking has done me some terrible harm . . .*

This must be what is meant by Cabin Fever. I heard the expression recently never having heard it before. *Reise Fieber*, I know this, is something *before* a journey.

But the Cabin Fever. This is how I hear about Cabin Fever. Two people are on a holiday snowed up in the mountains, at the foot of a mountain. As the time passes the young man loses all inclination to go out. He sits huddled near the stove in the small hut looking out occasionally at the snow-covered landscape. You've got cabin fever his companion tells him. You must come out walking at once. So the two of them put on their ear muffs and their warmest clothing and go out. At an ice-covered stream they pause wondering whether to cross on the ice. The man asks his companion if it is safe to cross on the ice and his companion says yes it is safe because there are no beaver tracks in the snow. Beavers swish their tails under the ice and the movement of their powerful tails wears away the under surface of the ice making it perilously thin—though this is not evident from above. No tracks to be seen, this ice is safe. But the ice does give way and, at once, they are both soaked up to their chests in freezing cold water. This is how I know about Cabin Fever.

The heating in this hotel room is too powerful. The heat is unbearable and there seems to be no way of turning it off. The windows do not open. I'm suffocating.

I lie with my arms folded under my head, a position which demonstrates a resignation to sleeplessness. Perhaps the position of Islam, a word which means to resign oneself, to surrender oneself completely... to ...

It is too warm for either reading or writing. The indecision which accompanies me in every situation, for a time, keeps suffocation at a small distance.

The heat is suddenly worse. There will be no one at the front desk, down there, between two and three in the morning but I dial the front desk all the same.

The voice from the front desk is a remarkable voice, gentle, well mannered, soothing. *There is someone down there.* Immediately the room is cooler. Perhaps there is a switch actually in the office, something, some method of stopping the assiduous stoking of the gigantic boilers.

Perhaps if I had known more about thin ice, about the metaphor of the strength of the beavers' tails, more about what is hidden immediately beneath the skin, hidden behind the voice of excited enthusiasm or the melting gaze which seems to be, at the time, love—I could have known and understood earlier about things which cannot be known purely from the surface, from the outside appearance.

Closely Watched Hedges

⚘

"That you Daddy Doctor? Din-dins ready."

"Hallo! Mummy Doctor. Just coming. Must wash puddies first. Coming in a minute. Hm! Smells good your din-dins. Grub grub wonderful grub . . ."

The doctors are proud of their downstairs cloakroom opening off the hall just inside the front door. Daddy Doctor whistles, when he comes out, a sort of proud little tune.

The doctors explain that they met over a crucible. Their surname being Wellington they explain too that they are happy that they have a pair of Wellingtons. Mummy Doctor says that she always believed she could not live without a bicycle and a pair of Wellingtons.

The doctors ride their bicycles to the university every day when the weather is fine. When wet they catch a tram. They seem pleased to tell me things.

Mummy Doctor says she always thought Wellingtons were called gum boots.

"It depends," Daddy Doctor says, "on where you went to school. These, this little pair, are Wellingtons. And, you do have a bicycle."

"Yes of course," Mummy Doctor agrees.

The little girls drink their milk, their solemn eyes regarding us over the rims of their Beatrix Potter mugs.

"Daddy Doctor? More puddy?"

"Daddy Doctor has had more than enough puddy. What about Mummy Doctor? Mummy Doctor have more puddy?"

"Well perhaps one teensie spoonful."

The Mummy Doctor one offers to share the last of the apple charlotte, she has made, with me. "Dried apple rings," she explains. It is my first meal with the doctors. I shake my head.

"No, thank you. I really cannot eat any more."

The mummy one drips cod-liver oil on the living-room carpet and, whenever she cuts bread for toast, she makes crumbs in the knife and fork drawer.

I don't know where anything goes in the kitchen and I pick up a plate and put it down in another place. I feel big in my woolen smock, the only thing I can wear now. Under this smock my skirt gapes, expanded on an elastic with a safety pin. My socks are darned solid.

I have been here for two meals now. I have helped with the washing up and fastened the little girls' shoes, little button shoes to wear in the house only.

The mummy one explains that her sister will be coming to stay for her long weekend break soon. She explains too, when we are upstairs, that the daddy one likes to be called upstairs at bathing time.

"Daddy Doctor! Bath time!"

"Coming Angie. Coming Barbie. A and B. Angle, Bangle I'm coming up to the bath! Roar!"

Daddy Doctor comes up the small staircase, two steps at a time. He is laughing, he smiles at me as I try, in the small space in the bathroom, to not be in the way.

They are doing their utmost to make me feel welcome in their house.

They call each other Daddy Doctor and Mummy Doctor and the little girls are Angela and Barbara. Angie and Barbie. A and B. Sometimes Angle and Bangle. They are twins, four years old. They are very kind to me, the two doctors, and they trust me with their pretty little girls who like to change their frocks and have their smooth hair brushed several times a day. They are well behaved.

The trouble is, the only trouble is that I am lonely. I feel alone all the time even when I'm busy like now out shopping with Mummy Doctor and the twin pushchair which has a big waterproof shopping bag fastened to it. I can't explain to myself what it is like to be on the edge of someone else's shopping. I am trying to be enthusiastic and pleased. Being on the edge of the shopping, walking by the pushchair on the grass-edged footpath, is the same thing really as living in their house, being on the edge of the family.

Two doctors in one house, the Ph.D sort. Every morning they go off to the university to lecture and demonstrate; maths, equations, physics (hers), rocks, earth, boulders, and minerals (his). Sometimes, like today, Mummy Doctor takes an afternoon off to teach me the shopping. And, another afternoon she came home early and we all went to the doctors and sat together in the waiting room. The little girls whispered to each other, their blonde heads shining in the rather dark room. When I came out from my antenatal appointment the doctor came out of his surgery with me and chucked them both under their dimpled little chins. He is their uncle.

As I walk by Mummy Doctor I stare at the beaten earth of the footpath and I stare at the garden gates looking closely into the hedges as we pass. I'm not looking for birds' nests, I'm looking into the dark evergreen foliage and at the dusty thin branches and twigs and at the glossy thick leaves and the prickles of the holly. As we pass I say the names of the houses to myself, Chez Nous St. Cloud Prenton Sans Souci The Pines Holly House Barclay and Newton, names chosen and painted on to the gates or on little varnished boards screwed to the gates. Closely watching the hedges I am closed in by them and do not look too much at Mummy Doctor and her two little girls.

Watching the hedge closely it is as if I am about to be a part of the hedge or about to step away through it. A consolation perhaps to pay minute attention to something alongside the walk, as I might at one time have consoled myself at the river shack belonging to Dr. Metcalf and Magda, when I so much wanted and needed to be there with Dr. Metcalf by himself.

Mummy Doctor is not at all smartly dressed. She wears an old bluish coat and a round hat over her hair which is scraped into an unbecoming bun. I am wearing my school overcoat which is keeping up with my mother's expectations of good quality and lasting for years. The little girls have velvet collars on theirs.

The gardens in Clifton Way will be pretty with crocuses and daffodils later on Mummy Doctor tells me. I, meanwhile, am longing for my baby to come so that I can stop being a mother's help—for a while at least. It is much harder than I thought it would be. I can't think how I could ever have thought it would be a good way to live. Having to get away from the hospital somehow made me look, I see now, towards being somewhere else. I have a little room at the top of the stairs. The room is all right. There is a bed and a chair and a cupboard and the window looks out over the gardens. Just now the winter trees are bare, the branches making patterns, which daily become more familiar, on the pink-edged clouds of a perpetually gray sky. I am in the house all day with the two little girls while Mummy Doctor and Daddy Doctor are away at their university. I have telephone numbers for both of them. Tomorrow Daddy Doctor is going to come home at lunch time and I am to make a treacle pudding because it is his favorite pudding.

Mummy Doctor reminds me to wash my socks when we get home because, she says, feet stay warmer in washed socks. My feet are cold all the time.

We use my green ration book to go to the front of the queue and I collect the extra oranges we can have and the eggs. I carry the oranges in a string bag and try to be agreeable and pleasant but we are now in the streets where I used to walk sometimes with Dr. Metcalf, quite near the hospital. I thought that taking work and living near familiar places, places where I had been with him, would make it easier but it doesn't. I try to enjoy the sensation of the fresh cold air on my face but feel I want to cry. We have come to the corner where I ran to Dr. Metcalf once when he had his back to me and I surprised him. I remember how pleased he was to see me that afternoon and we went off alone together for a long bus ride. It was summer then.

Being in this street where I once was able to see him and meet him is not what I thought it would be. Being here and knowing that I can never see him again is made the more painful by this knowledge. The street, busy with people and without him, is empty. I try to listen to Mummy Doctor and to pay attention to the chatter from the pushchair during the slow and incredibly boring progress of the shopping expedition. On one side is a coffee shop where Dr. Metcalf and I had some coffee once. It was a terrible coffee, he said then, but it made us laugh. Mummy Doctor does not even notice this shop. Why should she? She has made up her mind to ask the butcher for something extra. She asks me if I like corned beef, perhaps. I try to remember what corned beef is.

Mummy Doctor and Daddy Doctor argue, for fun only, about who shall have the last drop of coffee at breakfast. Every morning there are two hand-painted saucers on the table. One is for real butter, a small square of real butter, and one for margarine. There is always a bigger square of margarine. Both the doctors are careful not to help themselves to the butter. Their knives avoid the butter saucer and, taking a tiny scrape of margarine, they spread it thinly on the crooked slices of toast. Both doctors talk and crunch their toast shamelessly. And, with quick upward movements of the chin, both catch any crumbs which might begin to fall. I spread margarine thinly on my toast too and the butter saucer is returned, after the meal, to the slate shelf in the small pantry.

Putting the butter and margarine out on the table at the same time is a way of not eating the butter. At the hospital we had to queue once a week for our rations. We all carried little screw top jars, one for butter, one for sugar, and one for jam, in a string bag. We never went anywhere without these string bags. Often we ate up a whole week's butter ration at one go and then ate the strong-smelling yellow margarine provided on the dining-room tables.

The untouched butter saucer makes the funny stories, the amusing anecdotes, at meal times, simply stupid. The little girls, at breakfast, often have a piece of fried bread each and they do not have butter then either.

During our meals which are, as they say *en famille* (but in this small house where else could I have meals?) they remind themselves of exotic foods they were accustomed to before the horrid war, before rationing. Daddy Doctor cuts his toast into little squares and moves little heaps about on his plate and remembers a particularly large and juicy steak which had two fried eggs and mushrooms on top of it. Even in their wildest imaginings of rich and plentiful meals they are not able to describe anything which could match Magda's pantry and her ability to disregard completely food shortages. And then Mummy Doctor asks Daddy Doctor does he remember Mrs. Whitey and Daddy Doctor says of course he does. They both begin to laugh.

"That Mr. Hilter!" he says in a squeaky voice with a cockney accent. He folds his arms. "That Mr. Hilter, if he puts my name on a bomb I'll get it. You get the one with your name on it. See? That Mr. Hilter! I'll get 'im first." Daddy Doctor laughs some more.

"Mrs. Whitey," Mummy Doctor, laughing, explains, "used to come once a week to do the floors. She couldn't say Hitler. Mr. Hilter, she kept saying Mr. Hilter. That Mr. Hilter!"

I have been here for three days and now while I am awake in the night it seems to me I have been here for ever and simply have no chance of getting away. If my baby would come now I'd be able to leave at once to go away to the nursing home. My baby can't be born yet, it isn't time. This evening I burn the potatoes and both the doctors keep on saying how much they prefer to have bread in their gravy instead of potatoes. The meal is only potatoes and gravy in any case, bread and gravy. I can see too, all through the meal, that they are trying to think up amusing little anecdotes to tell in well-bred voices. Even with all this I do not want to stay here.

I am cold in this little room at night. It is worse in this place, worse than anything I have ever known. I can't help hearing the doctors talking in low voices in bed, in their room. The Mummy one says the twins seem subdued, unnaturally subdued, she says. Are they sickening for something, she wonders. Perhaps, she argues, she should not have accepted the position in the department after all. Perhaps it was not the right thing to do. The Daddy one consoles saying that the children are fine, they are just a bit shy with a new person, it will soon pass, he says, the shyness. I can hear him telling her to enjoy the university and I can hear them turning over in bed towards each other.

Someone else's household is not the same thing as the one you come from, not at all. And working in a house looking after the children of the family is not at all the same as working in a hospital. For one thing there is no one here to work with and to talk to.

The little girls have piano lessons. A shabby old man comes to teach them. He has penciled in on the lines and spaces "F. A. C. E. 'face,'" he says. And "Eat Good Bread Dear Father. E. G. B. D. F." All the notes in the music books are labeled in pencil. He takes off his long black overcoat and his black hat when he comes and I make cocoa for him. Mummy Doctor says I am to give him something to eat. She makes a sort of ginger bread using hardly any sugar and no butter and no real eggs. She says to give him some of that and to have some myself. I can smell the dried egg inside the ginger. I still can't eat dried egg. This is a part of being pregnant. Nurse Roberts, at the hospital, was the same. They said just looking at the packet made her throw up all over the place. Trent said the dried egg would be with us long after the war was over, it would be with us for ever. They said Dr. Metcalf was the father of Nurse Roberts's baby. Roberts, they said, stayed too long at the hospital. She showed dreadfully. I mean everyone knew. At least I got away before I was really *showing*. At least, even if Trent and Ferguson and Lois guessed, they didn't really *know*.

The little girls take turns to sit on the old man's knee to play their notes. He guides their small rosy hands and lifts their delicate wrists with his splayed and yellow fingers.

Suddenly it seems that I am bigger. I feel clumsy and slow when I move, but the little girls never run away when we go along the street for a walk. They walk with dainty little steps and hold my hands, one on either side, with their furry little gloves which are attached to an elastic passing through their sleeves and across inside under their coats. This, I can see, prevents the gloves from being dropped and lost. I shall do this for my baby when the time comes.

The closely watched hedges are all along this street and the next and the next. The leaves are dark green and glossy sometimes shining wet and, at other times, marked with the dust. Looking closely at the hedges I can see places where the grass of a lawn shows or, beyond the lawn, the lighted windows of a front room or the stained glass of a front door. The hedges are old. They are the evergreens, the laurel, the privet, the rhododendron, and the holly.

⁓

On the afternoon of the first music lesson I could see that, after I had made the old man's cocoa, I could have some time to myself. Now, in this cold bed I can recall the bleak moments of something I began to understand. I thought that during the music lesson I would have some time to myself and I looked forward to a kind of freedom. I thought I would write something, a letter to someone. I listened while the old man, the music master, played something himself for the little girls to dance to. He played from Schubert, *Rosamunde*. He thumped on the piano and I could hear the little girls laughing and dancing, thump thump, round and round in the small sitting room. Upstairs in my cold bedroom I sat with my pen and my writing pad and suddenly there wasn't anyone I could write to.

Rosamunde, my mother despising the people in the house

next door (when I was a child) said every night that the only music those next-door people could play and listen to was *Rosamunde*, and only a part of the overture at that. She described it as an infectious music because people all liked it, a music which people who knew nothing about music could safely learn the piano arrangement and appear to be musical. "On cheap piano," she said, "and, worse, on pianola!"

These people next door made a tiny lawn on the slag which was the earth of our gardens. Carrots and sunflowers grew on this waste from the coal mine and sometimes a coarse tufty sort of grass. The neighbor people tried to *actually cut* their tiny lawn. Every night *Rosamunde*, a part of the overture, could be heard from their piano. And my mother despised their choice.

While I sat in this cold little bedroom remembering my mother I wished for her. Now, in bed here, it seems to have been a silly wish but, because I am cold and not asleep, I do wish, all at once, to be in bed in my mother's house.

If my baby could be born tonight, I could go away now. I could go in to the doctors and tell them I am in labor and need a taxi, at once, to the nursing home. But I am not in labor.

At bath time, in the evenings, Daddy Doctor comes upstairs and they all laugh and splash together and Mummy Doctor says they must not be too excited just before beddy-byes and I am not at all sure what I should be doing so I stand there trying to smile and to look like a part of the happiness. I feel clumsy and in the way. I wipe the floor and the next minute it is all wet again which is quite good really because I can wipe it once more and look as if I am doing something.

Now, in the night two things are in my mind. One is the awful remembering of how I felt and do feel, when the thought comes to me, that there is no one for me to write to. I had never imagined this. Especially I took for granted the letters I sent to Gertrude and, perhaps even more as my right, the letters she wrote to me. All our letter writing stopped when I told her I did not want her advice and when she wrote to say she felt she had betrayed my confidence (her words), and I did not reply.

The second thing is that I understand that I am living through each small event of the day to get to the end of each small event. For example, like the bath time, I start off by looking forward to the end of it, to the time when bath time is finished, bath cleaned, floor wiped, bath toys hung up to dry, and the little girls neatly in their beds and then I have to realize that this end to which I looked forward is nothing. I came to nothing, nothing at all. And straight away I am looking towards the end of the next thing. Like this evening when Daddy Doctor has to go back to his department for a meeting and Mummy Doctor says as we're going to be on our own we'll be cozy and eat our supper on the floor by the fire.

I can't wait for the end of this supper. It is some little pieces of boiled celery on toast. Mummy Doctor makes it. The celery is a bit burned and has a strong taste but it is not exactly that. It is more Mummy Doctor talking of where we'll put my baby's cradle and how she will make some little cot sheets and pillow cases out of some of my old hospital aprons and, though I long for the end of the evening, I can see too the prospect of my being here for ever in the house after my baby is born. I know that this is the arrangement but I have never considered it as I have to consider it now.

These are the heavy things in my mind.

It is strange too to think that I actually looked forward to Daddy Doctor being out for the evening when it is in fact easier to sit there while the two of them talk to each other. His absence contained, I thought, something I could look forward to like a promise of something nice because he would be out. When I think about my life before Dr. Metcalf left for the war (which was in reality over), I was always getting through time and things, working towards the hours when I could be with him. This habit kept up now, when he is not here to be with, is of course a way of living which does not offer me anything except an unbearable emptiness.

I do feel I want to be at home with my mother. I know this is stupid. The very stupidity of the wish is enough to make me start crying. I know that after a very short time in my mother's house

I always want to leave, to go on to some other place—somewhere else. Now, of course, there is nowhere else to go on to. I can't sit with Lois and Trent and Ferguson complaining about the food, the patients, the ward sisters, or revising for exams.

"Infection takes the line of least resistance . . ."

"The patient is placed with the head lower than the pelvis . . ."

"That's not Sim's position, that's something else. For Sim's you have the semi prone, on the left side, both knees drawn up, the right more flexed than the left . . . Remember?"

"Ah! yes I remember. Now name the varieties of catheter . . ."

I can't laugh now with the others when Trent pretends to bandage a chair with a many tailed bandage. And I can't go to Gertrude's Place. It is easy to remember the field sloping up, deeply green, right up immediately outside her window, sloping up to the sky which always seemed to be low as if to rest on the rim of the soft grass.

And of course I am not able to write to any of them.

～

THE SECOND ANTENATAL VISIT

"Are you, at least, were you, a gymnast, a gym teacher?" The doctor asks me on my next antenatal visit. "Your muscles . . ."

"No," I tell him, "a nurse. I trained as a nurse." This time I have come alone to my appointment.

"Ah Ha! All that walking, fast walking, back and forth," he gives a little laugh. "Walking not running. Nurses can only run for a fire, a hemorrhage, and a vomit bowl. Correct?"

I give a small smile and a nod. He says, when he has finished the examination, that everything's fine. He says he's booked a bed for me at St. Luke's nursing home. He suggests that I go, one afternoon, to see Sister Peters.

"Gladys will take you," he says, "they were at school together."

"Gladys?"

"Yes. Gladys, my sister-in-law. Three Wellingtons," he laughs, "and one little pair." He says the joke's wearing thin. It's clear that he loves his little nieces. "The little pair of Wellingtons," he says. I want to linger in his friendliness. I wish that he could remember me, not from my previous visit, I mean from when I was working at the hospital.

I almost tell him that I remember him. That in an exam once, a practical exam I pushed the monaural stethoscope towards him. Lois and I were in charge of the diagnostic instruments. He was supposed to diagnose a patient from her own description of symptoms and his own observations. The patient was simply pregnant. It was a trick question. A normal condition presenting symptoms. My pushing the monaural stethoscope towards him was the smallest movement, the slightest hint. Mostly, the doctors taking the exam, and being given that particular question, did not recognize the normal state of early pregnancy but diagnosed all kinds of hereditary conditions, tropical diseases, and even diabetes and kidney failure.

I almost ask him, while he writes up my card, if he remembers Dr. Metcalf. If, by any chance, he knew Dr. Metcalf. Dr. Metcalf would be older but they may have, at some stage, consulted or worked together.

I am dressed and ready to leave. Of course I can't speak to him about Dr. Metcalf. And of course I don't really remember him from a doctors' practical exam. It is just that I wish so much to remember him, to be able to talk to him, a sort of hope and a wish for some kind of conversation of remembering with perhaps something to laugh about.

"A shared practice," he is saying. "Next time you will see my colleague Dr. McCabe. She is very nice and will look after you well."

I remember McCabe. Some of the nurses called her the cold fish. They did the supra-pubic catheters themselves, during the night, rather than call her from the residents' corridor.

Dr. Heartless, Trent said once and we all agreed. It can be a disadvantage to know the doctors but when training in a large teaching hospital it is inevitable.

I walk back to Clifton Way instead of taking the bus even though I know it says in my *General Text Book of Nursing* (seventh edition 1942) that a pregnant woman who does housework and shopping does not need to take a walk every afternoon. I consider the hedges as I walk, the varying states of the bushes, some well cared for and others neglected. Since I am alone I do not need to study the hedges as carefully as I do as a rule. I notice the places where railings, sacrificed for the war, have been removed and I look into the laurel and the privet, the rhododendrons and the holly, evergreens in a series of repetitive quartets. There is one garden scattered with toys, a doll's pram on its side and three tricycles crashed together on the path. I like this garden and wish that it was my place with the children's toys all over it and a husband coming home in the evening.

When it is time to register my baby, though she will have to have my surname, I shall have her father's name, Dr. Jonathon Metcalf, in the place for *father's name* on the birth certificate. Who will see this certificate? I mean, my mother and father will not see it, neither will Lois, Trent, or Ferguson. And certainly Magda will never see it. The garden with the wild toys and this thought about the certificate make me reasonably pleased.

Mummy Doctor's sister will be coming soon for her short visit. Saturday is to be considered my free day, though this can be changed if necessary. Sundays I can have some time to myself in the afternoons. Sometimes I sleep the free time away and sometimes I walk out here to the far end of Clifton Way to this little park where there is a small lake. Just now I sit on the bench nearest the water and watch the small choppy waves as they hurry, in the wind, towards the shore. It is not at all sheltered here and the wind is cold.

I sat here, in this little park, once with Dr. Metcalf. Once, before I was to go home for my day off. The Red bus passes the end of Clifton Way, mostly anyone who is in the park is waiting for the bus. Dr. Metcalf was due at the hospital for Mr. Lemmington Frazier's theater list at nine and I was waiting for the eight-thirty bus. That day Dr. Metcalf said that because of me, because of his knowing me, it did not seem, any longer, as if the whole world consisted entirely of hemorrhoids. It was summer then. We laughed here on this bench and watched the ducks and I forgot I was waiting for a bus, and that in a few minutes I would have to leave him. When I remembered suddenly that I had to go on the bus without him, I cried and told him I couldn't go and I begged him to take the day off, to stay with me. Very gently he explained that he had to go to his work and that I must go on the bus. It was summer then but, without my realizing it, the summer was ending.

I began that day, from the bus window, to look into these hedges, closely watching the hedges for as long as they lasted. It is while I am sitting here frozen on this bench in the little park, on my way back from my appointment with Dr. Wellington G.P. that I make a decision. I have been sitting here for some minutes staring at the regular movement of the icy waves on the lake—it is more of a duck pond really. I decide to stop being such a sad and depressed person. It is not good for anything. And all my sorrow, no amount of sorrow can bring anyone, or any times, back. There is the possibility too that Dr. McCabe will either be on holiday or ill. She might even be dangerously ill when I start in labor and then I might have Dr. Wellington G.P. for my delivery after all.

I walk on alongside the hedges. Dib Dib, this Dib Dib will be with us soon. She is good fun, Mummy Doctor has said so several times. Dib Dib's visit hangs heavily above the house. I can't help wondering what her fun will be like. I think it will be best to go home for my day off this Saturday.

It occurs to me too that I have made some decisions, important decisions, in one afternoon.

⤫

FRAU MEISSNER'S BATHROOM WINDOW

"Your father's at the station. He went early on purpose to meet you."

"I came on the Red bus."

"Never mind. He'll wait for one more train and then come home. Frau Meissner is locked out of her house," my mother explains, "and Rosa has gone to town with the twins." Frau Meissner is, as usual, sitting at the kitchen table with a large cup of coffee in front of her. Rosa is mysteriously related to Frau Meissner who uses the twins' green ration books often, for her own purposes. Frau Meissner is one of the people my mother has tried to help from the time of her forced exile and her arrival as a refugee before the war. She often walks into the pantry and looks at various plates and dishes saying, *"Das schmeckt mir nicht,"* before taking her place at the kitchen table. My mother with an unusual good humor pays no attention to this.

I keep my overcoat on in the warm kitchen. My mother puts a cup of coffee on the table for me. I am not able to take my coat off in front of the visitor because she will see at once how things are with me. The coat is no longer all that much of a disguise, but I keep it on all the same.

"Good morning Frau Meissner," I say in a cheerful voice. I have come home for my free Saturday. I am keeping to my resolution not to be a depressed sort of person.

"What about your rations?" my mother asked when I telephoned to say I was coming home for the day.

"I shall be able to bring a piece of corned beef," I told her.

"It doesn't matter," her voice changed, "your father fetched some eggs from Gertrude."

My mother worries dreadfully that she will not be able to provide enough food. She is generous to all kinds of people. She tries to make people friendly by giving gifts of food.

"Frau Meissner is locked out of her house," my mother explains again. "The door slammed with her key on the table."

Frau Meissner spoons up the generous amount of sugar, she has taken, from the bottom of her cup. She leans forward and reminds me that she remembers that when I was a schoolgirl I often climbed, for fun, on to the coal-house roof and then from there climbed up into the house through the bathroom window. Her English is not very good.

"Barserum vindo," she says. I see the gold fillings in her teeth when she smiles.

"It vos a game wiz you zen," she says, "bot could you not do ziss for me now?" she asks.

"No, she cannot." My mother is bent over the sink showing displeasure in the rounded back of her flowered overall. Frau Meissner leans closer towards me across the kitchen table.

"Pleess?" She gives another gold-tipped smile. She tells my mother that her coffee was very good.

"Pleess?" she says and gives me an encouraging nod.

"You are not to climb up," my mother says quickly to me. I can see from her movements my mother is annoyed and agitated and afraid.

I, in my not being a depressed sort of person, say that of course I will climb into Frau Meissner's house and will unlock her front door for her.

"We'll go right away," I say as if there is no change in me at all from being the kind of person who used to do all kinds of things, like climbing on the roof, to being the person who keeps on her winter coat in an over-heated kitchen in an attempt to hide herself, to keep hidden within herself her secret.

The hedges on the way to Frau Meissner's house are the same as the hedges in the streets round Clifton Way. I look into the hedges as we all three walk by. My mother says she is afraid the coal-house roof will be wet and slippery.

"What if you fall?" her voice is low and angry. "And what if the window is too small now? You cannot do this thing! We should wait till your father comes home."

We walk on. Frau Meissner's house is identical with my mother's. I know the coal-house roof and the bathroom window.

I look up at the roof and on up to the small window with some misgivings. The bathroom window seems to be very small and very high up. I cannot take off my coat, that is certain.

I pull the dustbin closer to the wall.

"She should not climb now," my mother's agitation is evident. But Frau Meissner, her eyes bulging behind her spectacles, eggs me on.

"*Warum nicht?*" she asks. "She is, how you say a fine young vimmin. *Sie ist eine Valkyrie.* Wiz her strenz she can do anyting she vants. See her beautiful skin! She is healsy und stronk und yong. She vill get me beck into ziss house."

I put my whole effort into concentrating on being able to climb up from the dustbin on to the ledge of the coal-house door and up on to the flat roof. And then from there to place my foot on a particular bulging drain pipe and from there to draw myself up to the narrow window, to reach into the window, to open it fully, and from that move to the next move that of pulling myself up and into the narrow space.

When I am half way through the window the bath looks a long way down on the inside and my feet are no longer able to be supported by the pipe outside. I notice the greenish stains in Frau Meissner's bath. I am stuck. It seems I am too big to squeeze through the window. I should have taken off my coat. I try not to call out in panic. I make one great twisting effort. It hurts my side and I am afraid but I lean down and am slowly head and hands down into the bath.

"You should not do things like this," my mother says when we walk the shortest way home afterwards. I am sorry she has been frightened and I look closely into the hedges of the gardens. These are something the same as the hedges in Clifton Way but have more of the familiar about them. These are the hedges containing the secrets of childhood. I am relieved, for once, that I shall be at home for the rest of the day.

"I don't think Frau Meissner guessed," my mother says. "Do you?"

"No, I don't think she did."

"Do you hurt anywhere?" She is anxious. "Have you hurt yourself? Anywhere?"

"No, I don't think so."

"I don't think she guessed anything," my mother says once more.

"No, I don't think so."

"She is always locking herself out of her own house." There is a small note of complaint in her voice. "Your father has to go there so often now to help one way or another. Always something wrong."

"Yes," I say. We are alongside the familiar hedges. My mother stops to speak to some neighbors. She holds her scarf, which is over her head, with both hands under her chin. I push my hands in my coat pockets and push the coat out in front. It hardly meets but my hands in the pockets give a casual appearance. At least that is what I hope. I look closely into the hedge and wait for my mother.

My Mother's Hats

I waited once high up in a window. My head was wrapped in bandages. I waited for my mother.

I waited for my mother to come. From the tall window high up, I could, if I pressed up against the glass look right down to the street. I could see the tram lines gleaming along the wet cobbles. I could watch the trams and I could see the people moving along the pavement in both directions. I searched this movement for my mother's white hat. She had a white hat with a broad, soft brim. She said she would wear the white hat so that I could see her coming. She said that when I saw the white hat in among all the people I would know that she would soon be there. So I waited. Everyone else had gone home. My bandage was low over my eyes.

"What are these stalks of dry grass here for?" I asked the nurse. She said they were not stalks of grass but only the rough edges of the bandage.

"It's a bit frayed," she said, "that's all it is. A bit frayed but it's all right." The nurse disappeared through the door and I was alone at the window. The ward was empty, all the beds and cots were empty, and the screens, pushed together, were folded in to a corner. No toys had been left out. I pressed closer to the window. It was a long way down to the street. The winter afternoon was beginning to get dark.

"Your mother's not coming," another nurse came by, "you're not going home, you'll have to stay here," she said.

"I'll see my mother's white hat in a minute," I told the nurse. The nurse looked out of the window.

"I don't see any white hat," she said. "She's not coming, your mother. She must've forgotten you." The nurse and another nurse laughed then.

"She is coming." I couldn't say more because of the tears showing in my voice.

The hospital ward was closed because of scarlet fever. My mastoid dressing would have to be done in the out patients.

My mother had other hats. There was another one with a broad soft brim. A navy blue velour. Deepening the shadows round her eyes, it made her face fragile, increasing her delicate paleness. I liked this one very much.

"Why are you so sad?" I asked her once. "Is it the hat?" She said she was not sad and yes perhaps it was the hat.

There was too a small round hat. Light colored, a color as of peaches and the color wrapped in silk round the hat. A small veil went with this hat. A spotted dark gauze. My mother's eyes seemed to shine in the spider-web net as if they were caught there and pleased, all the same, to be caught. The soft peach of the hat was the same peachy lining, smooth and fragrant, of the fox fur when that golden vixen lay asleep and yet not asleep, alive and yet not alive, on my mother's gently sloping shoulders before a concert.

"Your mother has such pretty arms," my father said. The glass eyes of the fox were yellow, overflowing with tears which did not fall.

The white hat was the hat I was looking for. The people moved in both directions down there on the crowded pavement. A tram went screeching round the bend at the top of the hill and another tram came with a similar cry from the other side of the hill. Some horses pulled a brewer's dray up the hill. And suddenly there was my mother beside me, laughing. She had a new hat. A hat of fur encircling her head low just above her eyes. Her eyes were clear and bright and tender and laughing at the same time.

"Why do you cry so?" Her arms held me close.

"I thought you were not coming. I looked and I thought you were not coming."

"Don't cry! Of course I was coming."

Her cheek was cold and soft and smooth. I breathed in her scent and pressed my face to the soft smoothness and melted into it. I stayed against the softness of her cheek as if I could stay there for ever. As if I need never move away.

"Don't cry. See. I've brought a present."

"But it's not my birthday."

"It's a present for coming out of hospital. Hold it. Guess what it is. You can open it in the taxi."

"Aren't your legs cold?" My mother has finished talking to the neighbors.

"Yes."

"I suppose you can't wear a suspender belt now."

"No."

"Your socks look dreadful."

"Yes, I know."

In the hedge near the collapsing gate post there is a little piece of pink wool, thin like darning wool, caught in the green leaves. I have seen it before. I look out for it every time I come home. Because it is there and, because it is always there, I feel certain it means something which I have thought all along, that my baby is a girl. Beate, Beatrice, Baba, Baby.

For some reason my mother keeps the ugly scarf on her head in the house. It is a war-time habit this head scarf. Even though the actual war is over, in many ways it is still as if there is a war. As if the war will never really come to an end.

My Mother's Bathroom

The evening after I have climbed up into Frau Meissner's bathroom window, my mother, back in her own house does not take off her coat and her head scarf. She rushes into the rooms and opens all the windows, in spite of the cold, saying that the air in the house is not good. And she begins, at once, to do some cooking, chopping noisily and frying and breaking eggs, real ones from her bucket of water glass, into a basin.

While I am upstairs washing my hair I hear her angry voice, subdued but quite clear, complaining.

"Just treating the house like an hotel. Coming in and then straight away hair washing, just as if house is hotel." There is apparently another trouble too, a visitor has sent a parcel with a toilet roll in it.

"And I am always so careful about bathroom." My mother's hurt anger is accompanied by crashings on the stove. "It is not now the war time. Bathroom had toilet roll."

It always takes time for my mother's mood to change. My father, not knowing the disturbance of Frau Meissner's command, tries to explain that the war caused people to send parcels with toilet rolls in them, that the war caused people to feel that they should be good neighbors. I hear his voice talking like a boulder in the middle of the flying utensils. It is sad, he is saying, that people only become good neighbors when there is a disaster to be shared.

"Insults!" my mother says, but my father persists saying that he had been shocked during the Great War because people, in the streets, had been so excited in anticipation of bloodshed. He had never expected, he says, that people would look forward to killing. His deep voice talks on, consoling.

I stay upstairs trying to rub my hair dry in the cold bedroom. For some reason I remember the way in which my mother had thrown some red sausages, once, across the kitchen table saying that, even if there was a war, she did not require visitors to the house to bring their own food. The guest, blinking behind thick spectacles, gathered up her unwanted gift in silence and, in a touchingly clumsy way, tried to stuff the sausages, not wrapped up, into her handbag.

"Come down," my father calls upstairs. "There's a nice fire downstairs." When I go down my mother puts a hot plate of bacon and two fried eggs on the table in front of me.

"You must eat," she says, "before you go back."

The wearing of the head scarf in the house makes me think she is about to go out again but she sits on her side of the table knitting furiously.

"I am always so careful about bathroom," she says, not slackening her knitting speed.

"Soap too!" she says. "How could she do this thing!" She pushes the tablet of soap across the table.

"It's not bad," I say, "the soap's not bad, it's violet. Who sent the parcel?"

"Recha," my mother says, "she was here last week to tea. We helped her years ago. Remember? When she was refugee?" A tear runs down my mother's cheek.

"Perhaps that day you didn't have any in the bathroom, perhaps it was a sort of hint?" I remember Recha very well. She mistook the lending of a dress for a gift.

"No, not so. Everything was in bathroom. I am always so careful about bathroom."

I almost correct my mother; "it is not usual, in English, to leave out the definitive article . . ." so that she will not make this mistake in front of neighbors, but I think better of it. She is upset and I am, after all, terribly hungry.

Cabin Fever

The poet Shelley compared the mind in creation to a glowing coal. How can I best describe my own state of mind during this pause on the twenty-fourth floor of a hotel in New York? This pause, this not going out of the hotel, as I had intended, is much the same as sitting in a suburban train within reach of a woman who looked like Ramsden *might* look after all the years which have gone by—and then, repeatedly, not speaking to her. To come to the end of a journey, several times, without asking the intended question intensifies the pause till it becomes a scar.

When I think now of my mother I think of the idea I have often had. Not a new idea, I am sure many other people have thought about it. This idea is to write down all the things I remember about my mother. One thing, of course, leads to another.

It often seems to me now that earlier, at the time of my mother's hats, when women wore hats to please themselves, to please other women, and to please men, there were little pauses and spaces of mystery and respect between men and women. There was the exchanging of the small graceful nod, there was the lifting and replacing of a man's hat and the slight bringing together of the heels to accompany the hint of a bow. These small, hardly perceptible actions created a tiny pause between two people. In the exchanging of the greeting the broad soft brim of a hat could obscure, for a fraction of a second, the expression in a woman's eyes. There was, too, the bending over and the acceptance of a woman's lifted-up hand in order that the space immediately above the back of the offered hand could be kissed.

Long before the ugly head scarf, worn during the war and afterwards, there were the hats. The white hat, the navy blue velour, and the little round hat wrapped in the peachy silk. The hats belonged to gallant attitudes of devotion. The quiet unobtrusive actions of greeting suggested the deeper feelings which might be contained, unobserved, in the conventional and the acceptable. The little pauses were a part of the artistic methods of manners and of love. These were picturesque and, with restraint, passionate and had often a beauty and a power, a grandeur even.

My mother, during the war, often listened, without making a secret of it, to Schubert Lieder on her records. Whenever she saw photographs or pictures of Churchill on newsboards or on the front of the *Radio Times* she tore them up. I always hoped she would not do this outside the newsagent's when I was with her.

Later, much later, at the time of his death, she sat with a neighbor in front of the neighbor's television set and wept all through his funeral.

"I was deeply moved," she wrote in a long letter to me. A letter in which she described the funeral in great detail.

Closely Watched Hedges

DIB DIB AND DUB DUB

"Oh but surely, Dub Dub, Beethoven's violin concerto is old hat nowadays. Surely no one *discovers* Beethoven now. After all, we discovered him years ago. Remember our gyrations to the old wind-up gramophone!" Seriously they are talking about music. Dib Dib's toast-crumbed knife plunges across to the square of hitherto untouched butter on its little painted saucer.

They, the sisters, call each other Dib Dib and Dub Dub. They have used these names since they were small children and they are quite shameless with the names. In the street, in shops, and on buses and trains.

"Angle? Bangle? Love Auntie Dib Dib?"

"Of course they do. They *adore* you. You must know that."

"And you, Dub Dub, you know I absolutely adore them."

"It's Dib Dib's long weekend hols," Mummy Doctor explains to me. The house is full of pet-names which, of course, I do not use. I mean, how can I?

Dib Dib is house mistress at a boarding school for girls. She will come again during her long holiday when I have to go to the nursing home to have my baby. This way, Mummy Doctor has already explained, she will be able to keep her post in the university department. Dib Dib will be coming back when she is needed and there is nothing for me to worry about.

Dib Dib, for this visit, is to sleep on the couch downstairs in the doctors' tiny study. They have cleared all their books and papers off the couch on to the floor. When I am away she will be able to have my room.

Dib Dib is good fun, the doctors tell me.

I watch from my cold bedroom, at the edge of the window, early, when they are all out in the garden with their skipping ropes, their feet pounding the fragile frosted grass in time to the horsey-mouthed counting and chanting of skipping rhymes;

> *I am a girl guide dressed in blue*
> *These are the things that I can do*

and:

> *My mother said*
> *I never should*
> *Play with the gypsies in the wood.*

They are all out of breath in the cold morning air. The little girls have bells on the handles of their ropes.

The sisters do not look alike. Dib Dib, though much younger than Mummy Doctor, is much bigger. Very tall, with enormous thighs, she gives an impression of hugeness. When I look at her it seems as if I am seeing her without clothes on. She is big in that way. I think of her in the Trendelenburg's position.

The two doctors are short, shorter than I am and, in the presence of the visitor, seem even smaller. The little girls are small partly, of course, because of being twins.

Dib Dib has an appetite. In the kitchen she pops things into her mouth during preparation and has often eaten most of the meal before it reaches the table.

Boarding school, they explain to me, makes you hungry. I do not tell them I know this and that, in any case, I am hungry in their house. Dib Dib attacks the butter saucer as if without any thought that it might be sacred. The doctors, it is clear, would never actually mention anything about not eating up the butter.

Running on the spot and high knee raising follow the skipping. As I watch them in their physical exercises my bedroom seems removed, for the time being, from them. In a small house it is not easy to ever feel private. I wonder where, in this small house, can two people really have the secret things of their lives, the things which belong with being together. However hard I try I am unable to imagine the two doctors undressing each other, playfully, fondly, unbuckling and unhooking each other, drawing off and slipping out of their clothes, leaving their clothes scattered where they drop them. They must have undressed each other, taking turns to unbutton something and pull something off, at some time. At least once, they must have.

I did see Daddy Doctor, once, tugging at a jumper, pulling it up over Mummy Doctor's head inside out, the neck of it being too small and it was caught on her ears which are quite big. But that is not the same thing. They had come in from a walk soaked in sudden rain. He was helping her because she, in a hurry, was upset inside the jumper. At least I thought she was upset but she showed no signs of being upset afterwards and went to fill the kettle as if nothing had happened. Neither of them laughed. When I think about it I don't think either of them said anything. They each have thick sensible dressing gowns which they put on for the two steps in one direction to the little girls' bedroom and for the two steps in the other direction for the journey from their bedroom to the bathroom. Dib Dib comes up from the study downstairs in her Burberry raincoat. It was not worth packing a dressing gown for two days. Her muscles seem to have the faint odor reminding me of the school sports pavilion, a mixture of linseed oil and human sweat. It is not hard for me, in my mind, to put her up in Trendelenburg's, for examination only so that she does not have the benefit of an anesthetic.

"J'ai une petite few pensees extrorodinaire," Dib Dib confides in her sister while biting heartily into an enormous slice of breakfast toast. "Dub Dub, I mean, en français, *Doub Doub*." She washes down the toast with a long drink of the concentrated orange juice which is meant for the little girls and for me because of my baby. "*Doub Doub*," she says, "avez vous considered les dangereusements de TB? Je mean vous bringez an autre dans la famille?" The school French is pathetic. I look down at my plate.

"Alors! Non, Dib Dib. Elle est straight d'ospital so we feel considerably au secours, savez? Staff TB Testé vouz comprenez? A l'ospital they would know, n'est ce pas?"

To add to this way of trying to talk so that I shall not understand Dib Dib turns to me and tells me that what I need is a three-mile walk after breakfast and she will supervise it if I can be spared for half an hour. She raises an eyebrow in the direction of the doctors as if to ask their permission.

I don't think that I can walk three miles in half an hour I tell them. Not now. I feel the tears coming to my eyes so I leave the table and go to the kitchen and start on the washing up.

I walk slowly, closely watching the hedges, the laurel, the privet, the rhododendron and the holly, the evergreens. Dib Dib is alongside. We are on our way back. I watch the hedges, mainly the places low down near the earth, trying to think of something other than this walk. There is a cold wind which makes my face ache. My real tears can mix secretly with the tears made by the wind. I think the cold has made Dib Dib's face ache too because just before we reached the little park at the far end of Clifton Way, the place where I always pretend to myself that I shall see Dr. Metcalf again sometime soon, she said to "right about turn."

"I expect I am too slow for you," I tell her on the way back.

It is my bath night. My turn for the bath. Looking into the hedges I long for my hot bath and then the warmth in bed afterwards. Out here by the hedges my bedroom is a sanctuary with a number of hours to go through before I can get to it.

The doctors share their baths. This is supposed to be a secret and private thing—as if two people could share a bath in this kind of house, even with whispering all the time and hardly moving in the water, and not be heard. The shared bath means that they can have two baths a week. It is not really an economy. One bath a week between them would be a real economy. They did not have their bath last night because Dib Dib, with the cunning bred in boarding schools for girls of good families, was up in the bathroom first and the water could be heard gushing for a long time filling the deepest of deep baths. Steam even appeared under the door. Something I saw at the hospital once when Trent said she would take cold baths in the mornings since the rest of us were doing it; but never in this house have I seen steam actually coming out from under the bathroom door.

"I don't suppose the thought occurred to her. I mean she didn't think . . ."

"Yes, she did. She laughed on the landing. She called out and laughed and said, 'The wise virgin got here first.'"

I heard the low voices of the doctors, indignant and consoling, and the sound of their bed as they turned towards each other in chilled resignation.

In the afternoon Daddy Doctor says he will take Angie and Barbie to see the rocks in his department so that Dib and Dub can play at being sisters together.

Mummy Doctor suggests I have a couple of hours to myself. "A nice rest with a book," she smiles at me. I tell her, "Thank you," and go upstairs.

Really I do not need to be here at all today but, in the arrangements, this Sunday is not my day off. Stupid really to have to be here. Two hours is not long enough for me to go anywhere. I mean, it takes too long to go to my mother's house and back.

The gray sky presses down on the winter trees. It seems that spring will never come, that my baby will never be born. I put on my light and get one of my books from my trunk. It is an art book, Monet with reproductions of paintings; *Au Bord de l'Eau* and *Camille sur la Plage de Trouville* and others.

On June 28 1870 Monet married Camille-Leonie Doncieux. That summer was spent at the seaside resort of Trouville. Monet commemorated afternoons on the beach with a series of small paintings . . .

It is too idyllic for me to read. The word "married" swims in my tears. I long for such afternoons.

The afternoons at Magda's were nice. Sunny and warm. I think of Magda, like the time she was baking and making a mess trying to make a pastry for Quiche Lorraine. A luxury, because of the butter and the chopped up bacon and the mushrooms. An onion pie would be easy she said then, plenty of onions. The flour was all up her arms and round her on the kitchen floor.

"So sorry Mrs. P Darling," she kept on saying, and Mrs. P was sour and did not reply. Magda made more mess because the crosser Mrs. P was the harder she worked. Magda often made a terrible mess on purpose.

That afternoon, that was before Dr. Metcalf had ever kissed me, that afternoon Magda said she liked best the bit in the Hardy novel, she couldn't remember which, when they are baking apple pies.

"Practically out of doors, my deah, in a shed. So of course the flour on the floor didn't bother anyone a scrap." And then she went on to remember a Chekhov story in which the air is laden with the sweet smell of cherry jam, the jam being boiled in a copper out of doors. "Heavenly," she said, "to make jam like that."

Why can't I be with people like them. Why did it all have to change. Why can't I still be with Magda and Dr. Metcalf.

I can hear music from downstairs. They must be playing some records in the study. I open my door and go half way downstairs to try to hear.

"It's Albéniz. Tango," Dib Dib is saying. "I love it."

"An expressive counterpoint," Mummy Doctor starts to say.

"Oh Dub Dub! Always so mathematical. Why can't you be more romantic. Listen! Wonderful melodic music. Can't you feel the ductile movement . . ." Dib Dib's voice changes suddenly and she sounds as if she is crying. It is a kind of howl. She has burst into tears in the middle of the tango.

"Oh Dub Dub," she sobs, "it takes two to tango. I know it's a cliché, but it's really true, that statement. What's wrong with me? Am I really so hideous?"

I go down three more stairs. The gramophone has been stopped.

"Why can't I be married with a nice husband and children and a house—like yours," Dib Dib says between her sobs. "I'm so sick of being house mistress. I hate boarding school. I really do."

As I move quickly back upstairs I hear the low beginnings of Mummy Doctor's voice as she starts to comfort Dib Dib.

Back in my room I lie on my bed and stare at the darkening afternoon. There is a soft tap tapping at my door and Mummy Doctor's voice is asking me if I will make a pot of tea please and bring it to the study.

Weekends, the doctors wear shabby clothes. It is a sort of point of honor with them to wear crumpled ancient corduroy and Harris tweed patched with leather at the elbows. Mummy Doctor has a big jumper darned all over with the wrong colors, I mean the darning wool is not the same as the wool of the jumper. They stay in these clothes all weekend.

Because I am worried about my bath I ask, in my politest voice, half rising in my chair, to be excused from supper and am upstairs lying in my rightful share of the hot water while they are probably still hovering over the mathematics of sharing a hard-boiled egg, since I have said I do not want any, equally between three people instead of four.

As it is clear that I never help myself to the butter and, it is clear too, that they will never confront Dib Dib with any form of reproach about her taking such a lot, I feel quite safe to go downstairs very quietly, after they have all gone to bed, and eat a thick slice of bread spread with butter as thick as the bread itself. I help myself to a second slice and take it and the concentrated orange juice back upstairs to bed.

Who is to know whether Dib Dib, with her boarding school habits, did not have a midnight feast? Neither of the doctors will raise the subject with her. They will know it is a sort of boarding-school thing to do. They are far too concerned with their attempts at being well-bred, buttoned up, Trent would say, to ever mention the butter which was on the saucer. And as for the orange juice I have only taken my baby's share and have not touched the bottle belonging to the twins.

It is difficult to know real names from which the pet names are made. Dub Dub is nothing like Mummy Doctor's first name which is Gladys. I can only think it must have been some sort of game once upon a time, a make believe between them. But when I see them and hear them together I am unable to see any possibility of make believe.

Trendelenburg's position would be acceptable for both of them. Tilted so that the head is lower than the pelvis, with the ankles fixed to the lower flap of the operating table and the knee joints flexed exactly over the hinges. That way there is no danger of either of them falling into the anesthetist's lap; but of course, if it is for examination only, then there will be no anesthetist. This Dib Dib and this Dub Dub! If I ever do see Dr. Metcalf again. I mean suppose, just supposing it is possible and I meet him in the little park at the end of Clifton Way, past all the closely watched hedges, the laurel, the privet, the rhododendrons, and the holly, and if I do talk about Dib Dib and Dub Dub he will not begin to understand what I am talking about.

Already I am in a different world.

Cabin Fever

The constant sound of motor horns and sirens, fire, ambulance, and police is a kind of music in this city. This symphony of rising and falling noise and the endless voices on the television must be for a great many people what a mountain stream was for Wordsworth. Back home I have, instead of the screaming crescendo and the dying fall, the doves. They sidle to and fro, back and forth, along the edge of the roof above my window, endlessly scraping and tapping and rustling along the tremulous gutters. If there are doves or pigeons above the windows of this room I am not able to hear them.

Half asleep, wrapped in concrete and an indestructible nylon carpet it is hard to recall, because of the similarities in the present day hotels, which hotel, which town, which city, which country.

This hotel with an ancient hot-water pipe, unhidden and undisguised, passing across the ceiling and making its perilous descent just inside the bathroom door has retained its characteristics from an earlier time. The lamps have unreliable switches and the chairs are made of cane. Dust laden in the crevices they have faded chintz-covered cushions. The writing table is made of cane too. There is a shabbiness and a continuation of recognizable hotel towels, linen, furnishings, and ornaments which have not yet been replaced by nylons, plastic, and imitation marble.

Twenty-four floors down to street level, down on the opposite corner of the intersection there is someone living on the footpath. Gathered partly into a cardboard box and, partly sur-rounded by bags stuffed with rags and possessions, the person living there sits close into the space where part of the wall is at right angles to the rest of the building. Every few minutes I get up and go to the window to look through the blinds to see if there is any movement down there. Once, I saw the person crawl out, turn round, and crawl back into the heap. That was at dawn. Since then the streets and pavements have become crowded with ordinary people on their way, to and fro, busy with all the things they have to do. The TV announces the tem-perature at below zero and that there will be light falling snow with the danger of snow freezing in places on the roads and on the footpaths. Watching at intervals the life of the pavement person, the movements rather, as it can scarcely be called a life, is becoming an obsession. I am timing my restless visits to the window, it is only four minutes since I last looked out.

There are a great many of these people who live on the streets. It could be that there are, on all the floors of these tall buildings, people inside going to the windows and peering out to look and to watch the people living in their heaps of boxes and plastic bags. Perhaps these people, inside the buildings, are recording too the number of times they get up, harassed, to go over to look down the great distance to the street.

This room is so warm. It is hard to believe that the temperature out of doors is below freezing. I remember once before in this city taking a long bus ride out to an old monastery. It was cold on the bus. The intense cold crept from my feet through the bones of my legs and up my spine. As the bus traveled through dreary streets of apartment houses I found I was actually long-ing to be inside one of those uncompromising rooms. It seemed then that the pale sunshine, as it lay slanting weakly across the boards of a covered broken window, or where it touched on the dirty curtains of another window, might have put some warmth into the room beyond. There were frozen fenced-in and locked playgrounds and small poverty-stricken shops, open from before six in the morning till late at night. The bus, that day, slowly ate up the streets and spat them out behind.

I have lost count of the hours or days I have spent in my hotel room. Sometimes it seems as if I have just arrived and the porter, having placed my luggage on the rack provided, has explained how the TV is turned on and, taking his tip, has gone. At other times, like today, when the femme de chambre, ignoring my "Do Not Disturb" notice on the door, insists on changing the bed linen. She cleans the bathroom crooning as black mothers croon to their little children. I would like to ask her to stay and sing some more but I busy myself over my papers on the cane table and do not say anything. I make some self-conscious notes in a handwriting much smaller than my real handwriting. I write about things done on purpose and then forgotten about and about other things which are done unintentionally and which, when we think we have left them behind, chase us later. I thought as my pen hovered fussily over the note how it would be possible to live in the setting and through the events of an Ibsen play but as if written by Brecht or Pinter. Music: Gustav Mahler. I laugh aloud at Mahler and wonder why I laugh. The conference is certainly no laughing matter. The conference, it is emphasized, is not directly a confrontation with AIDS though it is clear that several of the papers and much of the discussion will be reasonably close to the most grave and pressing problems in society. In the program there are titles which indicate the nature of our study. *Symptoms of Panic Disorder. Cupboard Infections. A recent study of Closet Relationships.* Several surveys of Regional Inpatients' Units and the usual new discoveries about Diabetes and the manifestations of Anorexia. My own *Perspectives on Moral Insanity* contains various examples of present-day venereal infections drawn from my Thursday evening clinics.

All aspects of human life are being examined and a wide range of specialists are to be present; psychiatrists, physicians, surgeons, pharmacists, general practitioners, nurses, and social workers. I look through the names hoping for the familiar and it seems that there is not one person, not one colleague whose name I know, present at the conference. I read through the lists again, once more, surely there must be someone . . .

Once more the water runs somewhere in the cavity of the wall and through the exposed pipe in my room. The ugly water pipe is the only familiar thing and is of course, I am able to be reasonable about this, the cause of the memories which haunt. Long ago water pipes like this one lined rooms, passages, and corridors and, like this, were the then ignored source of heat and noise.

The Hilda Street Wentworth

✁

I should never have given you the book about Elisabeth Ney."
  "Whyever... She was a sculptor and an artist... She ..."
  "She had a baby in that book without being married."
  "Oh! Really!"
  "It must have given you ideas ..."
  "Don't be so utterly stupid! How can you be so stupid!"
  "Keep your voice down. You don't want the others to hear you speaking to your mother like that."

It is a cold day with the wind howling outside. I can see the dull green leaves of the trees shake as the branches toss wildly. Occasionally there are bright patches of sunshine and the jug of red tulips on the window sill suddenly seems alive. The light shines through the red waxy petals. The day seems to be one of warmth and sunshine changing suddenly to the grayness of rain lashing in the wind. Smoke is whirled from the chimney pots opposite. It whirls into space and blossom flies from some trees in a nearby garden. My mother has come to visit me. She has brought some lilies of the valley, her favorite flowers, in a small green vase shaped like a stork.

  Helena is in a little wicker cradle half hidden by a screen at the foot of my bed. I almost make a cruel remark that I suppose my mother is trying to pretend that the stork brought Helena. Perhaps the hardest thing is not having any visitors, I mean not having a husband or the baby's father to come.

The other women have husbands who are also the fathers of their babies.

"My baby's father is dead," I tell one of the women when she asks me. After that she does not say anything else. I lie far down under the blanket during the times when visitors are allowed. I try to read. I hope Helena will not go on crying. She has been drawing attention to us both and to the empty chair beside my bed. I have been reading where Virginia Woolf writes of "the clock which marks the approach of a particular person" knowing that I have no such clock.

Helena cries the whole day, the first day of her life, a heartbroken crying as if she knows straight away some secret awful thing about the world into which she has come.

"Why does she cry so?" My mother's eyes fill with tears. She holds Helena trying to quieten her. I see something about my mother then, something which must have belonged in her life and which I have never seen before. She tells me she has brought a present. I unwrap small pink knitted things. They look like dolls' clothes.

"The clothes are very sweet," I try to thank my mother. I did not expect her to come. Her journey will have been quite long and complicated. Two buses and a train as well as the walk to and from the buses. I try to thank her for coming.

Suddenly it is quite dark outside and snow flakes are whirling about against the panes of the tall window. I watch the snow. It settles on the green leaves and, melting, slides off the shiny surfaces. It is late for a snow storm. The crocuses and daffodils are in flower in the gardens, my mother says, the front lawn is pretty with them. I feel a fear about the snow instead of the half-remembered childhood delight when someone would cry, "It's snowing!" A journey is made so difficult when it is snowing. I think how will it be when I have to leave the nursing home with Helena. My mother is saying she is glad I have called my baby Helena. It will be easier for her to spell when she goes to school. She sees that I am looking at the darkened sky and the whirling snow flakes. She looks towards the window too.

"It's not settling," she says and she says she is sure it will be sunshine again in a few minutes. Before my baby is born I call her Beatrice, the *bestower of Blessings*. I feel her little round head in my side and I keep reading about Dante's love for Beatrice and how, in his poem, he sees Beatrice as being a guide through Paradise.

"No one calls anyone Beatrice nowadays," my mother says. She explains that Helena means light and that the name is considered to be the symbol of beauty. "And, in any case," she says, "the child must have a Saint name." She says do I realize that over a hundred churches in England are called after St. Helena because of a certain Helena who was made into a saint because, while she was on a pilgrimage, she dug up the True Cross in the Holy Land. "Imagine," my mother says, "her having the good sense to take a spade in her luggage." My mother says she has always liked the idea of a pilgrimage.

"You certainly made one to come here today," I say. Helena is actually quiet for a few moments and my mother looks at me again, the tears welling up in her blue eyes.

"No," I say as if she has spoken. "I can't come home to you. I don't want you to sell your house and move because of me. I shan't come so don't do anything silly."

Before she leaves my mother stuffs some pound notes into my purse.

I hold my baby. She is new-born and small and wrinkled with grief. I hold her close to my face and feel her soft skin. She smells clean, of Vinolia soap.

⁂

MAGDA'S VISIT

Magda's visit is a surprise. She seems tall in the doorway. Her arms are full of blue and yellow irises. She comes straight towards me.

"Precious child. Darling child," she sinks down on the side of my bed and holds me close in her extravagant embrace.

It is then while Magda is strewing her flowers all over the white quilt that I try to take off Dr. Metcalf's watch under the bedclothes. I do not want her to see the watch. I do not want her to see anything which might hurt her. But I think she does see though she does not show this.

Dr. Metcalf gave me the watch, his watch. I have been wearing it ever since he gave it to me except when I was on duty and had to have it pinned inside the pocket of my uniform dress. He gave it to me up on the resident's corridor on the fourth floor of the hospital. We were just leaving his room, both of us, to go on duty. He said he wanted me to have his watch so that I would always think of him.

"I'll think of you in any case," I told him then.

"I believe you really will," he said looking at me closely. His eyes seemed deep and thoughtful. "I believe you will," and he kissed me.

"The watch strap," I told him then, "has your scent."

"Has it a scent then? Do I have a scent?" he was laughing. We had to part at once, leaving the corridor separately so that we would not be seen together.

Always I am breathing in the scent of the leather strap trying to catch something of him.

"So. Is this why you stopped coming!" Magda leans over the cradle. She moves the small fold of sheet with one jeweled finger. "An angel," she says softly as if to herself. She is dressed exquisitely in black, very high heels and with something gold at the throat with pearls showing a little below the gold. Her hair shines. Red gold, the color of a fox.

"I've just come from the hairdresser, Darling," she explains. "It's more than half a year now and I'm still trying," she says. "And you, Darling Child, why didn't you come to me?"

Suddenly she is sitting close to me and talking about Dr. Metcalf in that low intimate voice she has. Jonty, she calls him as she used to. She can't get over his death, she tells me, this unnecessary death and the war practically over when he went. "That damned war!" she says. She tells me she dreams at night that she is with him at the Army camp near Swindon, that she is about to warn him, to stop him from being crushed by the lorry. "As if I could ever have saved him," she weeps silent tears without moving her head. The tears pour down her face.

"Magda, your make-up," I want to warn, but she searches in her handbag.

"I've got a hanky somewhere here," she says, "I'll put my eyes back in a minute." And then, laughing a bit while she's still crying, she shakes her head and says she's sorry and I feel I'm the one who should be saying something like that but I can't think of the right words.

In her handbag, Magda tells me, she has some seed pearls.

"These are for her," she nods towards the cradle. "Please," she says, "take them." She explains they were a present to her from Dr. Metcalf's mother. "In a sense," she says, "they are a present from him." She leans towards me with a kiss and somehow it is as if I am accepting the little necklace and saying thank you. As usual it is Magda who is doing everything. It is then she describes love which can be pure and fresh and unspoiled by all the squalid details of everyday living. "You may not believe this now," she says, "but I actually envy you!"

I want to ask Magda how she knows where I am and how she knows about Helena. I don't need to ask because she tells me the next minute that she saw two of the nurses, girls, she says she knew by sight but did not know their names. She asked them about me, at the hairdressers.

"I guessed the whole hospital would know," I say and I feel my face and neck all burning hot.

"Oh no, Darling!" Magda laughs. "Only two of the gels and they were absolutely discreet. I really guessed."

"Oh Magda!" I say. And she hugs me and kisses me again.

"Tomorrow," Magda says, "is the court case. Poor Daddy. But poor Mummy, even more poor Mummy." She tells me that Marigold Bray, Mr. Lemmington Frazier's tenth actress is taking him to court with all kinds of wicked accusations. The case comes up first in the morning.

"I expect the accusations are all true," Magda says. "That's the worst of it. Poor Mummy. I'll be there in court with her. Please think of us. Remember? I told you once that one or all of Daddy's *affaires* could ruin him, and Mummy too of course. It's the relatives who are so vindictive."

I think of gentle Mrs. Bray who worked in the public baths and who, on the day that Dr. Metcalf left for the Front, consoled me behind the screens in the ward telling me he would be sure to come back. Marigold's real name was Edna and her mother wished she would come and visit.

"I can't imagine Mrs. Bray," I begin. "She was one of my patients, very quiet and . . . She had a hernia . . ."

"Heavens no!" Magda says, "it's Marigold's husband and his brothers and family. You never saw such a bunch of crooks."

I have never before considered this kind of possibility that a whole unthought of family could become all at once something sinister. As if knowing my thought Magda says, "This is the awful part, d'you see Darling, that you find yourself involved without wanting to be, and this goes for Daddy too of course, with the most awful people. The kind of people you could never have imagined existing. How d'you think I'll look in court?" she asks making her face into a smile. "I mean, I'm dressed in a sober way aren't I, with just enough elegance don't you think? And not too much expenditure."

"Oh yes," I say, "yes dear Magda you will look . . ."

"The damned war!" Magda says again. "And that man Smithers! Oh why Smithers? Why did Jonty. . . ? " Once more her eyes fill with tears.

"I'm studying," she says. "I'm really trying to study. I'm going to lectures on Comparative Religions. Next week," she says, "it's Islam."

I can't eat my dinner after Magda has gone. I keep crying even though I'm hungry. I do not want Sister Peters to think that I don't like her meal and I ask her how she makes the gravy so that it is thick and dark. I try to ask her but I cry instead. Sister

Peters, trying to be kind, asks if I have a picture of Helena's daddy and I say I haven't. She wants to know if I have a letter or anything belonging to him that I could look at and I say no I haven't and I go on crying. How can I tell her that Dr. Metcalf is Magda's, that he belongs to her and she belongs to him? And because she has just been to see me I can't help crying. How can I tell anyone this?

Sister Peters moves me into a small room before the evening visitors come. She says I can have the room to myself. She says lots of women have a good cry after childbirth and she says I'm not to worry about anything. She fetches the pudding from the dinner tray. It is a little steamed ginger pudding with treacle and custard. It is very nice and I ask her how she makes all the little puddings like this. She explains that she has a whole lot of cups without handles and she uses them to make the puddings. While she talks to me she changes Helena and admires her and says she's very intelligent with a well-shaped head, long fingers, and aristocratic limbs. It comforts me to hear these things. I feel I want to tell Sister Peters that Helena is Dr. Metcalf s little girl. But of course I can't. Instead I show her the seed pearls.

Sister Peters admires the little necklace and says that it is probably an heirloom handed from one generation to the next.

"They were given to my friend," I explain, "and she brought them." We look at the seed pearls together. They nestle, glowing on silk, inside a pretty little box made of beaten gold decorated with tiny blue and pink enameled flowers. Sister Peters thinks they are forget-me-nots.

Sister Peters says I should have a tablet and go to sleep early. She says she will put Helena's cradle in her own room for the night. She tells me that her husband has just bought two hundred scrubbing brushes.

"He's sitting in the kitchen now," she says, "trying to work out a way to sell them and the two hundred buckets he . . ." She pauses. "Two hundred buckets," she says, "that came with the brushes. They're all flawed," she says, "there's something wrong with every one. He's got to find two hundred people who won't notice the flaw . . . Imagine!" Sister Peters gives me a tablet.

Though it was snowing a bit during the afternoon it is really the spring, seriously the beginning of the summer. The evening is light and is a daylight evening. I think of the loneliness of the long light evenings of summer.

The branches of the sycamore immediately outside the narrow window of this little room are tossing in the wind and the fresh new leaves are shaking towards me and away from me. The leaves seem to have nervous little faces they seem to be talking, passing on messages, just out of my hearing.

Magda looked as if she was on the way somewhere. She is trying to get on with her life. She looked dressed up for going out to some place. If she dressed simply to come to see me then she would be at home now, sad and alone, taking off her nice clothes and putting them away. Perhaps she had a practice dress up ready for the court case tomorrow. Perhaps she is putting on the old dirty dressing gown made of towel material. She wears it when she's ill or sad.

Was it Ferguson or Trent or Lois talking in the hairdressers? How could they explain to Magda what had happened to me since I never told them? Trent would never go to a hairdresser, come to think of it, neither would Lois or Ferguson. We always did each other's hair. And in any case it's practically six months since I ran away from the hospital.

What is it that hurts Magda most? It seems I am not the only one causing her the greatest pain. It is Dr. Metcalf for going away when he did not need to go, she says, when the war, which seemed to be never ending, was really coming to an end. Smithers. Smithers, she says, Dr. Metcalf, Jonty, Magda says, wanting to be with Smithers. She said once that a person will travel the length and breadth of a country to be with the person they want to be with. Is this, is it this which hurts Magda so much or does she understand it and resign herself? Islam, she used the word, means to resign oneself, to accept, to submit.

Smithers, which one was Smithers? The pale orderly in theater who looked as if he steamed himself every day in the sterilizer—in with the instruments—or was Smithers the shave orderly? Or was he Lemmington Frazier's rectal orderly? Was he all three? How can I forget certain things, Smithers for example, so quickly? I don't suppose it matters. Except that it was for Smithers, Magda explained once, that Jonty, Dr. Metcalf, went away. Smithers, I remember now, wrote poetry. I remember he once asked me to read a poem he had written.

The buckets all have something wrong with them, Sister says, they are flawed. Perhaps they all have a small hole somewhere or perhaps they don't have handles . . .

I lie in for the customary fourteen days and when I am allowed to get up for the deep hot bath Sister Peters says I can have, my legs are so weak I can hardly stand.

⋙

THE HILDA STREET WENTWORTH

"The little white collars. I love them."

"The little white collars?" My mouth is full.

"Yes. You know, the little lint collars you've made." Sister Peters' mouth is full also. She tells me I am the first person to do her castor-oil bottles like this. She has in the past, she says, had various nursing assistants but not one of them ever cleaned out the medicine cupboard.

I have washed and polished the glass water jugs too and Sister Peters is pleased. She says the medicine cupboard is a treat, quite different now, not swimming in castor oil for one thing and a lot more space now the empties have been thrown out.

There is a lot of castor oil in this place. It is given on white earthenware spoons. The oil floats on orange juice and this makes it easier to swallow. It is given before all the births. Many of the mothers think it makes for an easier birth, Sister Peters says, they don't really understand the orifices in their own bodies. And castor oil is not expensive. Some doctors prescribe it to accompany the normal enema.

"This cheese," Sister Peters says, "it's mouse-trap but it's not bad, not bad at all." She has a rabbit sitting on her lap. We are all, Sister Peters and her husband, Mr. Hoob Peters, and me sitting by the kitchen range eating all our cheese ration at one go. Sister Peters fancied a cheese and pickle supper. We have a whole square of cheese each and some new brown bread. I have one more week of my month, paid for by my mother, at the Hilda Street Wentworth nursing home.

"No pickles for you!" Sister Peters says to me, "they'll turn your milk. Hoob!" she says to Mr. Peters, "she mustn't have pickles."

"If we had strawberries," Mr. Peters forks the onion off my plate on to his, "you wouldn't be able to have them either."

"Bad for your milk." Sister Peters jumps up then pushing the rabbit off her lap. "Look at that, will you. Wet me right through." The rabbit, with her heavy under-carriage, hops towards a corner of the kitchen.

"She's due any minute, I'd say," Sister Peters nods towards the rabbit and tells Mr. Peters he should get on with the hutch. They are going to keep rabbits, like they keep the fowls, Sister Peters explains, to put towards the patients' food. She has to feed the patients well and it is quite a struggle to do this. That is why they are trying to grow the quick summer vegetables.

For the last three days I have been helping in the nursing home, carrying basins of warm water to the lying-in mothers, changing babies, carrying away basins to empty them, and preparing the hot baths for the mothers who are now able to get up for a bath. Not only do all the glass jugs on the bedside lockers sparkle but all the brass taps and window fittings in the big old-fashioned bathroom are bright and shining; especially in the late afternoon these taps really glow. I have polished them too. I have fed the fowls twice now for Mr. Peters and I told him I would like to weed his vegetables. I feel much stronger. I enjoyed cleaning the medicine cupboard, especially

I liked putting the neat little circles of lint on the oily necks of the bottles—something I learned to do at the beginning of my training. The white collars on the dark-blue castor-oil bottles remind me of staff nurse Ramsden. I never actually saw her cutting out these collars but I can picture her doing so, meticulously and in the perfection of a silent concentration. I am reminded of Ramsden too when I mix the deep hot baths for the patients who have had their fourteen days in bed. Ramsden, who could reach unspeakable heights in an intellectual conversation with staff nurse Pusey-Hall, ranging from music theory to deeply religious philosophy, sounded like a poet when she described the bathing of a patient in Obstetrics Ward 4. She said then that the warm soapy water should be deep and that the patient should be encouraged and shown how to give herself a thorough washing of the vagina and surrounding areas. Many women, she said, did not understand how to wash themselves and it was the duty of a good nurse to teach this.

In the sharp fragrance of the medicines and the antiseptic lotions, on the lower shelf, I felt restored and happy and Helena slept peacefully, for once, while I was busy.

I do not want to go back to the house in Clifton Way.

"I don't want to go back to the Wellingtons," I say suddenly to Sister Peters and Mr. Peters. "Can't I stay here with you and help with the work?" I ask them.

Sister Peters shakes her head.

"There's two reasons," she says. "One is simply that I can't afford to pay anyone, and the other is that I was at school with Gladys and she would be upset thinking that I've taken you away from her."

"There's never more than one reason, one real reason," Mr. Peters interrupts. "A person can't have two reasons that really matter," he says, "and this real reason is that we can't pay. You don't give a damn about the Wellington woman. You never liked her at school, you've said so yourself."

"All the same, Hoob, she'll think . . ."

"Bugger what *she* thinks! Vera here might like to sell the buckets and the scrubbing brushes, it's up to her . . ."

"Oh really, Hoob! Of course she can't. Do have some sense for once. Those buckets and scrubbing brushes, she can't eat them or live in them."

"I don't mind not being paid, really I don't," I say. "Please let me stay here, please. I can't go back there."

I help Sister Peters take the six babies round to their mothers for the ten o'clock feed before going to sit in the small room, which is almost like a cupboard, to feed Helena. I want to stay here with Helena. I feel I cannot face, in spite of all the kindness, that other house. Mummy Doctor has been to see me several times bringing crayoned pages for Helena from Angie and Barbie and some little clothes, pretty treasures, saved from when the little girls were newly born. And, one time, she brought a surprise parcel, some clothes she made in secret, perhaps sitting up in bed late at night in the quietness of the sleeping household with Daddy Doctor snoring politely on his side of the bed.

Daddy Doctor and Mummy Doctor, the Wellingtons, would never eat cheese the way we have eaten cheese this evening. Mummy Doctor would make a thin cheese sauce to pour over some boiled carrots or onions. Or, she would mash a tablespoon of grated cheese into a saucepan of boiled potatoes. Or, she would cut some cheese in thin slices, almost like paper, and toast it on very thick slices of bread. The cheese would be made to seem endless, the only trouble being that no one would know it was there at all.

The two doctors graduated together, at the same graduation ceremony. They very nearly didn't. To begin with Daddy Doctor was already a year ahead of Mummy Doctor—at the time of the sharing of the Bunsen Burner. He was demonstrating that day, when the crucible shone white in the intense heat of the blue flame, that a mysterious substance became heavier as it burned in air. Daddy Doctor, for a whole year, marked time with deep breathing and thinking about something else till Mummy

Doctor was up to where he was. Of course they were not doctors then and only one of them was a Wellington.

I do not really want to think of them while I am here in this place but I do keep thinking of them like this; Daddy Doctor and Mummy Doctor. The Daddy one putting his mind on something else and, with held breath, waiting till the Mummy one is ready. Their separate pillows, when I was in their house, were always indented neatly where their heads, well ordered, in separate hollows, had been all night.

The Peters' bed is hardly ever made. One of them is nearly always in it, mostly Mr. Peters, snatching a nap, as Sister Peters calls it. The babies are often born at night. Sister Peters says the only thing Mr. Peters is reliable about is when he says he's going for a sleep. Their bedroom opens off the kitchen. Sister Peters says it's best to be downstairs. She can bring troublesome babies down there at night.

Before I go to bed I go down to the kitchen, quietly, and set the six trays for the patients' breakfasts and I cut a neat plate of bread and butter which I cover with a clean damp cloth. I like the night silence of the Hilda Street Wentworth, everyone asleep for once. Sister Peters says that newborn babies mostly sleep well. It is only when they get home they start bawling their heads off. Back upstairs in my small room I write a letter to Mummy Doctor telling her I am not able to come back and will she please send on my trunk, which is all packed, to this address.

I packed everything (some things had not been unpacked) during the night I started in labor so that Dib Dib, when she came to stay, would have cupboard space for her things.

They are so concerned about health, the two doctors, accusing each other, with affection, of bringing home a cold. They gargle at night with hot salty water if they feel they have been breathed on in a bus by someone who seemed to have a cold.

Dib Dib, in particular, was afraid I might harbor diseases, something mysterious and infectious brought from the hospital.

Night Sister Bean once, during a lung hemorrhage, paused in her ward round to tell me that I should not take such a personal responsibility, that there are times when another responsibility takes over and I must learn to recognize that. She waited beside me at the bedside during the choking rush of blood and watched while I cleaned away the clots and removed, as quickly as possible, all traces of the hemorrhage. Afterwards she got down on her knees and, leaning on the bed, she drew the man's head on to her arm and prayed there beside him. She said to me to follow the prayer in my heart so that I would know it for another time if she was not with me. In between the words of her prayer she muttered to me that it was very important to nod and smile during hemoptysis as if everything was going to plan and was satisfactory. She said too to always remember that there were times when the proximity of a sympathetic nurse was the only remedy.

Night Sister Bean at the time I am thinking of—at that time—had been on night duty for thirty years. She was said to be a witch. They said never let her look directly at a blood transfusion. They said always stand between Sister Bean and the drip. If she looked at the drip, they said it would stop.

Sister Bean said that if a patient lay in bed with his arms folded under his head he was awake. No one, she said then, sleeps with the arms in that position. A person lying like that in bed should be promised a cup of tea. The nurse, she said, should tell him that she is going to make some tea even if she knows the tea and sugar ration tins on the ward are quite empty.

The patient, Sister Bean said, in the relaxation of knowing tea is being made will usually fall asleep in the time it takes to boil a kettle. In the event of a failure, he should be slipped a Mickey Finn.

At the Hilda Street Wentworth the patients all sleep well. If a baby is noisy in the night the cot is pulled away from beside the mother's bed and put in the bathroom or downstairs. A delicate baby enjoys the honor of being at the foot of the Peters' bed. Both the Peters will walk the floor with a fretful baby, all night if they have to, but this does not seem to happen often.

When Dib Dib was worrying about tuberculosis, it somehow

did not seem possible for me to explain to her and to the Mummy and Daddy Doctors that, in spite of being close to disease, I do not think I am anything but immortal.

If I post my letter first thing in the morning the doctors and Dib Dib (whose special leave from school is about to end) will receive it in the afternoon post.

When I set the Hilda Street trays I search the sideboard for the best spoons and I choose cups which are not chipped and which have saucers to match. I am pleased with the neat breakfast trays and I roll up the sleeves of the overall Sister Peters has lent me. With an extra high rolling up of the sleeves I feel efficient. I go to answer the front door with Helena tucked under my arm, dangling in her shawl, carelessly, as the midwives carry the babies.

"The head's on the perineum," I tell Dr. McCabe. She, with her black bag, sweeps past me and goes straight upstairs. We have just admitted an emergency, a multipara premature, a seventh child.

"Vera!" Sister Peters calls over the banister. "Mrs. Thingummy's worried about her rhubarb jam. Tell Hoob, will you, to go round on the bike and turn off the gas. Her back door's open. Same address as before."

Dr. McCabe isn't such a snow storm after all. She actually smiled when I opened the front door. She was not bad at my delivery either, though for the last part I was hysterical and had to be put out or under as they say. That was not McCabe's fault. It was me not able to handle childbirth as I thought I would be able to. The marks of the forceps are disappearing. Sister Peters says this every time she looks at Helena.

Everything is sweet and nice at the Hilda Street Wentworth. The lines of nappies and towels blow in the damp wind. Every day we hope for the sun. Two mothers and their babies will be leaving and two more patients will be coming in. Mrs. Rhubarb is resting uneasily after her seventh boy. She cries when I give her a bowl of warm water for a wash. She wished, she says, for a girl.

"What did you get?" She looks up at me, her eyes overflowing with tears.

"A girl," my voice an apology, sounding vague, as if I'm not really sure what I gave birth to. She understands, though, that I have a girl and weeps afresh.

"People often cry after childbirth," I console, trying to be wise like Sister Peters.

"I should know," she says.

"I'm the only one here with a boy," Mrs. Rhubarb says.

"They come in runs," I say. I've heard Sister Peters say this too. "All boys and then all girls. Uncanny. Really!"

The new baby gets called Rhubarb Jam by everyone.

It is sunny in the garden and for half an hour, a little gift of time, I thin out and transplant some tiny cabbage plants. My knees make hollows on the warm earth and the doves in Mr. Peters' dovecote, a ramshackle affair which Sister Peters declares should be taken down before it collapses, talk to and fro softly; a contented murmuring reminding of the tiny gulping noises when the new babies are feeding all at the same time. This gentle and sustained music is a reminder of the incredible contentedness which accompanies the temporary moments of pleasure while hunger is satisfied and survival for the next few hours is promised.

Because of working in the garden, whenever I have the chance, my legs and arms are already sunburned and I feel stronger every day. Only one thing disturbs my peace and that is that any day now I shall have to receive a reply to the letter I sent to the two doctors. I dread the arrival of the postman and, worse, a visit from Mummy Doctor.

The Hilda Street Wentworth is a large old house which has been partly converted. The previous owners of the nursing home called it St. Lukes, a name Sister Peters likes but forgets to use. She likes the notion, she says, of St. Luke being the patron saint for physicians and surgeons and the symbol of the winged ox is particularly pleasing. She intends always to say "St. Lukes" when she picks up the phone but before she knows it she has said, "Hilda Street Wentworth."

The rooms in the house have honey-colored floor boards and there are trees, fresh with the leaves of early summer, immediately outside the windows of the rooms facing the street. Some patients stay only for the fourteen days of lying in and others stay for the month. Those mothers who are up do most things for themselves and their babies, and they walk out into the garden to sit on the lawn with their babies and their visitors. I still find it unbearable when the husbands are visiting and I have to overhear the little jokes about plucked chickens and force myself to smile.

Sister Russell is here today as there are two patients coming in, probably on their way already. With each new birth two things happen to me. One is that I am overwhelmed every time with the strength and determination of the newly born individual and how each one resembles the one born previously but is, in fact, entirely different. The second thing is that I am unable to stop recalling my own experience. On that day Mummy Doctor made a milk pudding with some rice and jam. And, in order to have enough milk, she rinsed out the empty milk bottles with a tiny drop of water and added the milky water drops to her pudding. I thought it was strange that she should do this so calmly when I was starting up in labor. All that day and all the night I was slowly approaching Helena's birth day. I had the same thought early in the morning about a woman in the garden overlooked by the window in the Hilda Street Wentworth. This woman was hanging out her washing while I was walking up and down the long passage and pausing to look through the window while my pains came and subsided. It seemed, at the time, impossible that anyone could be so peaceful, at *this* time, as Mummy Doctor was with her drips of milky water and this woman, too, with her clothes basket and her hands nimble among the clothes pegs. I watched her going from clothes basket to clothes pegs to clothes line, a gentle rhythm of movement, interrupted only as she gave each garment a shake before hanging it on the line. This extraordinary peace was within calling distance of the confusion of pain and drama about to take place in my own body. It seemed to me then that the most vivid and beautiful thing I had ever seen in my life was a white sheet, folded and pegged, beginning to billow against dark-green foliage. I thought too, on that day, that the sheet was in a place where it was too damp and leafy for it to dry properly.

At the Hilda Street Wentworth we make a rice pudding or a blancmange every day. Sister Peters is never short of milk because, in addition to what she is entitled to have, the milkman comes to her last and leaves half a crate, or sometimes a whole crate of extra bottles. He is glad to off load them.

I work very quickly with the cabbages and splash some water on them. I can hear Helena crying in the kitchen. I have her little cot in there every day now. Trying to keep ahead with the work and trying to squeeze in little extra things like working in the garden I fully understand that I am, all the time, evading the burden which is on my mind. And this is the immediate burden of the doctors and my not going back to them as arranged. I am paid with a cheque every month and I fully understand that this way of being paid requires a month's notice on both sides when it comes to leaving or being asked to leave. If I look beyond the immediate there is the question of where can I go with Helena if Sister Peters refuses to have me stay. I know she would not *refuse* but it really may not be possible for her to manage to keep me. I am, for one thing, taking up the tiny room she likes to keep for use either for emergencies or for special reasons . . .

I am in the kitchen. Sister Peters and Sister Russell are upstairs. Both the labor rooms are in use and Dr. McCabe is on her way. Mr. Peters has been putting up some shelving which, he says, he picked up for peanuts. The kitchen is in a mess with tools and dust and plaster everywhere. I have Helena under one arm and I am stirring a big saucepan of soup made from the carcasses of two boiling fowls and some cut-up onions and carrots and potatoes. I cover the saucepan with a tea towel to stop the dust falling into it. Mr. Peters' drill is screaming and Helena, who is not yet bathed and fed, is crying when suddenly two stout women in navy blue out-door uniforms wheel their bicycles up to the back door. They come into the kitchen without knocking. One of them explains that no one answered the front door, and the other one says they have come to see me and my baby. Immediately I feel afraid of them. Mr. Peters turns off the drill and explains about the shelves. They ignore him and ask me what I am doing and why am I standing at the hot stove holding the baby and will I prepare her bath as they want to see me bath the baby. They will need to see the cot too—if she has one. I understand, at once, that they are Health Visitors checking on me. I understand too that Mummy Doctor will have been obliged to tell them where I am.

The two Health Visitors poke about the kitchen and examine everything. They look in at the Peters' bedroom and mutter to each other. I show them Helena's little cot, not too clean this morning, and pushed in behind the kitchen door. With great speed I prepare the small zinc bath which I now use for her. For the last three days I have bathed her in the kitchen in front of the range.

The two visitors sit, knees apart, skirts stretched, on kitchen chairs and watch me bath my baby. They watch me feed her. They each, in turn, pass a hand over her little round head and mutter in low sinister voices about the anterior fontanelle.

"You haven't spoken to your baby at all, not the whole time we've been here," one of them accuses. "You used to handling babies? Eh? You had several? Paid for your pleasure with pain eh? Didn't think of that did you? Can't have the one without the other, can you!"

Only this one. I want to tell them. Only this one.

Where's her daddy? they want to know next. Even though they will have all the details.

"He's dead, you say he's dead. We've heard that one before, haven't we?" They nod knowingly, lips in thin lines and chins pressed down and back.

I change Helena to the other breast.

"Oh Ho! That's a quick change. Not much milk, I see, losing your milk eh?"

They want to know why I am still in the private nursing home. Surely I was booked in for the two weeks only, just for the lying in and not the whole expensive month. "Who's paying?" they want to know. "Your mother paid, you say. Did she now! Private nursing home!"

"Did she now! That's a very generous mother you have, or is it your Gentleman Friend, is it? Is that who's paying?" They sit square on their chairs looking at me. One of them, as if struck by a thought suddenly, asks if I have my other children here with me.

"You seem very experienced," she says, "handling this baby, much too quick and easy with the baby. Can't believe it's a first. Are the others here with you?"

"That's enough!" Mr. Peters, in the corner with his tool box, stands up suddenly. "She's a nurse that's because and why." His voice is unlike his usual voice.

"Oh Uncle, there you are," I say, surprised at my own words. "Uncle I didn't know you were still here in the kitchen. Could you please hold Helena for a few minutes. I must see to the soup." My legs are shaking and I feel I will cry.

Mr. Peters holds out his dirty hands.

"Come to Uncle Hooby," he says. "Come along to Uncle Hoob." He takes Helena and holds her up to his face and then puts her up to his shoulder and pats her back gently.

"Clear up the bath quick, then Vera," he says to me. "Her ladyship, your Anti, will be down soon. Her and Sister Russell and the doctor will be through upstairs soon and they'll be down here looking for a bite of lunch." He turns to the Health Visitors.

"You two ladies like a bowl of soup?" He jerks his head in the direction of my enormous saucepan. The visitors scrape their chairs on the tiles as they get up; they do not want soup, thank you. They must be on their way. Thank you very much!

Mr. Peters jogs Helena on his arm and guides them to the door.

"Call in any time," he tells them. "Vera's stopping with us, her folks, for the time being. She'll be here for a while. Just you call in whenever you're passing. Always welcome! Bowl of soup or a cuppa tea. Any time you're passing."

He closes the door firmly on them and peers through the lace curtain.

"Bitch one and Bitch two, excuse my French," he says. "Pity!" he turns from the window. "Pity!" he says, "I've missed a sale. Should've flogged 'em a bucket and brush each." He walks up and down the kitchen still holding Helena. He keeps laughing, little laughs.

"Uncle!" he says. "Your mother," he says to Helena's wrinkled face, "she's a sharp one. Me, uncle! You've no need to worry with a mother like you've got."

Two things are on my mind. One is the afternoon post. A letter might come from Mummy Doctor in answer to mine. I am afraid to have a letter from her. She might come to see me. Both a letter and a visit, or one or the other, I am afraid of them. I would like not to have the letter or the visit. Simply I would like my trunk to arrive, by carrier, without either of the two doctors.

The second thing on my mind is really a nice thing, at least I am supposed to think of it as nice. Sister Peters tells me that one of the patients, a rich patient, who has her third baby now would like me to go home with her and to be a "live in" nanny. I can take Helena with me and I will be well paid. They live, Sister Peters says, in a beautiful park near Worcester, the house is a mansion, she says. Sister Peters says it is worth considering because of Helena's future. But, she says, it must be my own choice, what I do. I have a fortnight in which to make up my mind. Lady Poynter, she says, is really nice.

It might be Mummy Doctor and Daddy Doctor all over again. On the other hand it is a big house with extensive grounds, and there are other staff members in the house. For example, Sister Peters explains, I would have a nursery girl working under me. There is a cook too and of course there are maids and there is even a manservant and a chauffeur.

"Imagine the dinner service needed just for the staff!" Sister Peters sighs and breaks a cracked plate in half. "I've been meaning to do that for ages," she says. She was tired, she added, of trying to avoid giving that plate to one of the patients.

"Think about the position," she says to me. It would be easier if Sister Peters would say either that she wants me to go because she can't keep me or that she hopes I'll stay because I'm useful and she can't manage without me.

I keep thinking that the postman has come and I go repeatedly to the front hall to look for letters.

Rhubarb Jam has his own pram at the Hilda Street Wentworth. The eldest boy pushed it round and left it ready for when his mother and the new baby could come home. Mostly the babies do not have their prams here, just sometimes if a mother lives very close. Rhubarb Jam's pram is useful. Sister Peters suggests I put Helena in the pram and go for a little walk. She says to go to the park and back—just half an hour, she says it will do me good. One of the babies won't settle after her feed so Sister Peters puts her in the pram too. Two babies, like dolls in a dolls' pram.

"Bring back some dandelion leaves," she calls out after me. Walking with the pram with the two babies flat on the mattress, tucked in a piece of flannelette sheet and both of them quiet in the smooth movement is one of the nicest things I have ever done. I never imagined it would be like this to push a pram. It is a high pram with big wheels, a bit shabby, but the shabbiness makes it less conspicuous.

While I walk with the pram I give myself up completely to the soft sound of it on the pavement and to the feeling of the fresh air on my face. Both babies sleep immediately. I wish the pram was mine. I look at the houses and the gardens, at the sky and into the summer green of the trees along Hilda Street. The horse-chestnuts are in flower. I had forgotten the horse-chestnuts with their creamy candles of flowers. Hilda Street is a main road, navy blue and efficient, and the traffic is pouring westward away from the city.

When I pause to cross a side street I hear, in the distance through the faint roar of the city's breathing, the chiming of the clocks. An old woman pauses too and peers into the pram and tells me that I have beautiful children. Twins she supposes and very very young. So I tell her, "Yes."

"You will have your hands full," she says and I tell her "Yes." We smile knowingly at each other. She fumbles with her purse and drops two florins into the pram.

"Silver," she says, "it's an old custom for a baby boy. You have one of each," she says, "I see the pink and the blue. I can't give to one and not the other, can I." We smile once more, knowingly, at one another.

I am the mother, the mother of twins, a boy and a girl born, it is true, two weeks apart—almost three to be exact, but, here in the pram, twins. Back home music can be heard, something, an arrangement of the wedding march for the piano, by Liszt—piano music can be heard through the open french windows, the maid is making cucumber sandwiches for afternoon tea, and my husband, the twins' daddy, will be home from the office . . . Daddy will be home to bath you both tonight . . . Perhaps Daddy will be home early from the operating theater. . . He will leave his dressers to sew up . . . Not the office, the theater. . .

In the field at the edge of the park I hastily gather some dandelion leaves. I take off my cardigan and roll it up with the leaves inside and put the bundle across the foot of the pram.

In the afternoon post there is a letter for me. Sister Peters says, "There's a letter for you Vera." She has taken the post up to the patients, mine is on the kitchen table. Sister Peters has made the tea. She pours a cup for me. She says to leave the babies asleep by the back door.

I do not want to open the letter. I know it to be the reply from Mummy Doctor. Slowly I open the envelope. The letter is very short. It is from the Nurses' Insurance Company explaining in the politest phrases that a payment to a nurse in my circumstances can be made only once. With the letter is a cheque for four pounds.

"What's this for?" Sister Peters takes the cheque and holds it between one scrubbed red finger and her red thumb.

"For my food," I say.

"Aw! Go on with you! You don't owe me anything," she says.

"It's yours. Put it away for now and pay it into your bank quick before *Uncle Hoob* gets his paws on it."

Mr. Peters is trying to fix one of his new shelves. Sister Peters explains it came away from the wall as soon as the saucepans were put up.

"Everything slid off," she says. "I've laughed myself silly. Oh God! I'm that tired!" She tells me to run upstairs with a cup of tea for Sister Russell before taking the trays with the little teapots, all filled from the big teapot, round to the patients.

When I open the rabbit hutch, later on, to feed the rabbit with some of the dandelion leaves, I count six baby rabbits. In all eight births in one day at the Hilda Street Wentworth. A record.

When I think about it, I know I have never actually heard staff nurse Ramsden describe how a nurse should teach a patient how to wash herself, but it is easy for me now when I am thinking about her to put the concept and the words, which are in fact from my General Text Book of Nursing, into her richly serious voice, even though I shall never be able, ever again, to hear her speak.

How soon can a rabbit be pregnant again? Sister Peters wants to know.

❧

THE PRUNES AND THE PRESENTS

"But you must eat it," I say. "Sister Peters has poured her soul into this dessert. Her whole soul."

"Dear child, of course I'll force myself, if only for your sake." Lady Poynter's plump fingers curl round the stem of a second little glass of the delicate frothy Apple Snow. I tell her it is one of Sister Peters' special successes, made from stewed dried apple rings and powdered milk.

"It is indeed a triumph," Lady Poynter says. She goes on to tell me she is grossly overweight, that child bearing has completely ruined her figure. She is definitely going to start dieting as soon as she gets home.

"I'm hoping, we're hoping, that you will be coming home with me," she says, letting the words slide from the corner of her mouth. "You'll be a tonic," she says, "in our household." She takes a teaspoonful of the Apple Snow closing her eyes for a moment and then opening them to regard me earnestly; "All the fragrance of ripe apples," she says, "in one delicious mouthful."

When I look at Lady Poynter's pursed red mouth it seems as if in the experienced adult there can still be a baby feature. A red mouth wanting to suck.

"We do hope, very much that you will decide to come. We shall treasure you and Helena very much. You have no idea how much!"

I thank her and take second helpings to the two other mothers in the room. Nursing and lying-in mothers are always hungry. Food for the nursing-home patients is a constant concern. Private patients, in particular, must have good food, well cooked and nicely served. Whenever we are near the rabbits we feed them.

At the Hilda Street Wentworth the rooms are all named and the names are painted in faded pink and blue or green and yellow over the doors. Some are decorated with flowers and foliage, these painted backgrounds almost disappearing with repeated cleanings. So, on the upstairs corridor there's "The Rose Garden" and "The Meadow" each with three mothers and their babies. Sister Peters can have up to six mothers and their babies. I am causing her to have seven. My little room (unnamed) is really required if there is some sort of emergency. Sister Peters says that private nursing-home patients like the rooms to have pretty names and, for some women, the term labor theater would scare their wits out of them so she has the "Gooseberry Bush" and the "Cabbage Patch." She hardly ever uses the names herself, perhaps only when talking to a new patient or a husband.

It is disconcerting to see babyish details in the features of grown-up women. I pause, laden with trays on the landing at the top of the stairs, and, in the landing mirror, I straighten my own mouth into a grim line. I manage to reach the kitchen without dropping anything.

"Mr. Peters not back yet?" Sister Peters, still in her hat and coat, is prising the slats of wood from a small crate, a present from a grateful husband. "Prunes," she says, "that's nice. Very useful." She takes a glistening wrinkled prune and eats it explaining that she's sorry she's late back. She missed the bus, she says, because of nipping into someone's front garden after some dandelion leaves just as the bus was coming. The order, she says, from the markets will be delivered later.

"Mr. Peters," she says, "he should be here by now. You didn't give him that money? Did you? You didn't lend him the money?"

"What money?" I am pushing the patients' plates down in the big bowl of soapy water we keep in readiness in the old-fashioned sink.

"The money. The four pounds you got." Sister Peters is serving a plate of dark gravied stew for me and one for herself. "You didn't let him have it? He's a fool with money."

"No," I tell her, "I didn't give any money to him. I've still got the four pounds."

"Never lend him any money," she says. Her long hungry fingers seek out another prune which she hands to me. "He's a good man," she says, "but a damn fool with money. Well I can't *do anything*," she adds. "Sit down and have your lunch. Never lend Mr. Peters money. Just remember that."

We eat in silence, quickly.

"Last time," Sister Peters says, "we got a tub of butter and now prunes. With their first we got a whole Danish cheese. Imagine! Patients have their ways of being grateful. And that reminds me, there's some presents for you."

"For me?"

"Yes, for you, why not. You've done a lot ... There's a pair of stockings, pure silk, for you and a dress length and the cost of having it made up is to be covered. That's nice isn't it." Sister Peters unwraps the material.

"It's very nice," she says, "good quality. It'll suit you. It'll be the devil to iron, you'll have to have it just right, not too damp and not too dry. It'll hang well. Keep it for best. I'd keep it for best."

"Yes," I say. "I never imagined presents," I tell her.

The material is linen, a navy blue background with a pattern of pale green and white flowers. A better quality than anything I have ever possessed.

Sister Peters has saved an Apple Snow for me. She says it's really for Helena. "It's lovely," I tell her.

Upstairs, once more, I rush round with six bed-pans and the six little enamel jugs of the dettol and warm water mixture. These jugs, the little douchings are poured with the usual jokes about plucked chickens and being ripped to ribbons. There is no such thing, Lady Poynter declares, as self-conscious embarrassment while lying in.

At last I get to my room. Helena has been crying. I could hear her despair all along the passage. When I pick her up I see her little face is swollen red and puffy with crying. As quickly as I can I sit down, facing the window, to feed her. The traffic is pouring both ways on Hilda Street. Perhaps tomorrow I shall be able to go on the early bus to visit my mother. Perhaps tomorrow I shall know whether or not I ought to take Lady Poynter's offer.

It occurs to me as I rest, holding Helena upright and patting her tiny back, that the presents from the patients could all be for Sister Peters if I was not here.

≈

THE SLEEPLESS NIGHT

I do not know what is wrong with my baby. Every time I try to put her back into her cot she cries. I have never had a night like this with her before. I think she might be hungry and I try to feed her and she seems eager and then turns her head away and cries and cries. This crying, I can't stand it.

I am tired. I am afraid her crying will disturb the mothers and babies in the rooms just along the passage from my room. She is only quiet if I walk and rock her in my arms. Every time I think she is asleep and I put her carefully on her little mattress she lies quietly for a minute and then, as soon as I am in bed, she starts crying and crying. I pick her up and shake her.

I stand at my window. It is wide open. I can smell the night sweetness of summer grasses and leaves. Helena, quiet now in my arms, gives a tiny sigh and a shudder passes through her small body. She seems vulnerable as if at any moment she might stop breathing. But worse than this is the thought that I am the only person she has. She is defenseless and helpless and I am ashamed of the anger in my action. She will have felt it and there is not any way of telling her I am sorry.

"Baba," I say, "Baba please forgive me." I mean, can my words mean anything to my baby?

I am alone here, with my child, by the open window of summer.

Hilda Street is a main road, blue-black at dusk, it crosses Wentworth Street. We are on the corner of this crossing. At night the buses slow down for the cross roads. This slowing down and starting up is a kind of lullaby. Sometimes the buses stop for the Hilda Street-Wentworth bus stop. Sometimes lately, when I have been in my room, I have watched the buses with some anxiety in case either the Mummy Doctor or the Daddy one should, after receiving the letter I sent, be coming to visit me.

The long light evenings, the horse-chestnut trees, lit up with their flower candles, and the wet tires rasping on the wet road after a light summer shower have, in the last few days, brought back to me similar evenings. Evenings from last summer.

In spite of everything I am still the same person who raced ahead of Dr. Metcalf that special evening, that other summer evening, uphill, breathless and both of us laughing, knowing we were going to be together all night. We found, that night, a cottage where the woman had placed a Bed and Breakfast sign in the window. On purpose we went out for a walk knowing that we could return. It was not like being at the river shack, the Metcalfs' place, where visitors or Magda or Magda's father and his current actress might turn up at any time. With the walk we prolonged the secret long light evening, putting off, on purpose, the night we were to have together.

There was beetroot soaking in vinegar in a glass dish on the table, as well as the other things for breakfast, the next morning. He laughed, Dr. Metcalf did, and ate some of it to please the landlady, as he called her. She called him "sir" and said we should come again. "Any time," she said. "City folk," she said, "should come out to the country more, for peace and quiet, to enjoy themselves."

We set off, laughing still, down hill for the bus. A fox, crossing the path in the wood, stopped and stared before slipping off into the undergrowth. The sadness of parting was upon me before we reached the main road and I begged Dr. Metcalf to let me stay with him the rest of the day. "The river shack," I said to him then, "couldn't we just go there?" But he explained that the river shack was not such a secret place. It was, after all, Magda's and, at any time, she could take it into her head to go there. He reasoned about our work and how we should be in time for it. His reasoning, I thought then, is so much the truth and he is right about the reality of what we must do. I believed in him, then, completely.

The evening, without, it seems time passing, has become night. Something disturbs my baby. She cries and then stops crying and a bit later on she cries again.

All at once a memory returns and it is as if I am, late at night, feeling my way, once more, along the bookshelves in my mother's house. The shelves in that house are from the floor to the ceiling. Shelves full of books industriously read by my father and, with equal industry, brushed and dusted by my mother.

Often, at night, I went along the shelves taking down books and, looking inside them, discovered names and dates of previous owners and faded records of Christmas and birthday gifts. These gifts, often given and received by people unknown to me, provided endless speculation. People known only by names or initials on a discolored fly leaf, the date sometimes too far back to be believable.

This evening, earlier, horribly disturbed by screams from the Cabbage Patch (Sister Peters' name for the little labor room along the passage) I have been reliving at a too short distance the final stages of my own wild pains and hysteria. Crouching by the open window I am taking, with one hand, my own books, one at a time, from my trunk which was delivered quite late after supper and carried upstairs for me by Mr. Peters and the carrier. The trunk is here with no message, not one word from either of the two doctors in reply to my letter.

Holding my books, one after the other, reminds me of the times when I pulled books from the shelves at home to see which of them belonged to my mother, having been given to her at some time or other by a particular friend, signed with initials only, each discovery or attempt at discovery exciting the midnight curiosity. I change my position and move Helena to my other arm and continue this search for some trace of my mother in my own small store. Perhaps her messages and quotations chosen especially to be suitable for her gifts to me, these things, in her handwriting, I want to find now. Perhaps in the quietness after the earlier than expected labor and delivery, three doors down the passage, and Sister Russell's late departure followed soon after by Sister Peters' final footsteps going downstairs, in that wonderful silence which follows childbirth, I am making a curious attempt after what seems a long time to, somehow, be near my mother. To bring her close in some way. I can't help wondering what this alarming compulsion, this searching through the books, opening them with an unrealistic eagerness only to put them aside, can mean. I must have been looking at my books for more than an hour. Because there are so few it is a distressing symptom experienced alone and at an unearthly hour.

The Hilda Street Wentworth is quietly asleep. Even Helena, in the aching crook of my arm, is asleep. I am tired and sleep evades the welcome I could give. Often I stood beside a sleepless patient fingering with longing the smooth pillow and the cool sheet amazed that, in such comfort, the man could not fall asleep when, had our places been changed, I would have slept at once.

Perhaps there is a deeply felt wish which I must acknowledge. Perhaps I must recognize the wish to have my mother bend over my baby with all the pleasure and tenderness expressed in the words and gestures of cherishing which I seem to recall clearly as coming to me from her when I was a child. The gestures especially, the soft sound of scented hand cream being smoothed over and between her fingers before she bent down to kiss me, the soft coolness of her cheek felt lightly on my face as I turned to resume the pleasure of approaching sleep after receiving her caress.

Perhaps this time is the one time when the child turns back towards the parent in that curious bond between parent and child in which the child is always moving away.

My mother has seen my baby but only here, with certain restraint, in the room Sister Peters calls the Rose Garden where there were two other mothers and their babies. She has not come a second time.

I would like to take Helena home to my mother where she can, in her own kitchen, unwrap and exclaim, and where she can nurse the small perfect body in front of the kitchen fire and sing in that sweet, suddenly remembered voice which knows the music but is not able to reproduce it.

Why do I remember now, Dr. Metcalf, naked and shameless, leaning back in a basket chair beside the small westward window in the cottage, high up, so high up that, though dusk was filling the valley, the last color of the setting sun made his body golden as he waited for me and, smiling, stretched out his arms to draw me to him?

Why does the next summer have the same fragrance of the summer before?

I will take Helena to visit my mother. We can go on the early bus, the one we always called the workmen's. This decision is not so hard to make. I can be there before the neighbors wake up.

I have two things on my mind. One is that when I wrote to Mummy Doctor I returned her cheque, a month's wages. I scribbled all over the cheque and now I keep seeing, in my mind, the childish scratching of my pen all across her neat mathematician's handwriting.

The other is simply will I, would I, fit into the Poynter household? If only I could know beforehand.

❦

VISIT TO MY MOTHER'S HOUSE, THE BUS RIDE

"I didn't know you wrote poetry."

"Poetry?"

"Yes you left a poem here, last summer."

"Oh, did I?"

"Yes I showed it to Gertrude. Remember how ill she was? I showed her the poem. She liked it, said it was nice but she thought the hospital was near the canal, not a river."

"I took the bus to Worcester. There's a river there."

"There's no need to cry over Gertrude. She was very fond of you always. She would not want you to be sad and to cry over her."

"No, I know. I'm not crying. Really, I'm not."

When I look at the other people on the bus it seems to me that even the most hopeless sort of person knows what to wear. I mean, take Sister Peters and Mummy Doctor, they both look awful when they go out. Mummy Doctor, in particular, has no hesitation. She heaves on her greatcoat over whatever she has put on, a badly fitting skirt and jumper mostly, and considers herself dressed.

This morning I hesitated and changed my mind so often I was almost too late for the workmen's. Mummy Doctor never ponders uneasily on the landing wondering whether to start off downstairs or whether to go back into the bedroom to pull her other skirt out of the wardrobe. It never seems to occur to Mummy Doctor that she looks a mess. She even darns her stockings with wool which doesn't match. Sister Peters, who is always in a hurry, pulls a coat on over her uniform overall. She never hesitates either.

The summer morning is fresh and sweet in the mist when I leave. A cuckoo calls through the mist reminding of the fields at school and the long wet grass where, in soaked shoes, we searched for and gathered wildflowers. I wait under the dripping horse-chestnuts in Hilda Street opposite the nursing home. Helena, wrapped in a shawl, is quite heavy. I feel pleased that I did not put on the new silk stockings, that I have saved them for some future time when I might be invited somewhere. The early bus, the one we always call the workmen's, is almost full when it comes. I find a seat upstairs at the back.

The early morning mist promises a fine day. I can't help wondering about my mother. I suppose old conversations are coming into my mind as I try to prepare myself in advance for the visit. She is hardly likely now to recall the poem she found last year. I remember it starts: "Keep the Love . . ." I wrote it for Dr. Metcalf but, of course, never gave it to him.

Helena is six weeks old. I've had my six weeks check. Dr. McCabe is very quick with an examination, almost as if she is embarrassed. I have been at the Hilda Street Wentworth for just over six weeks. My mother will have things to say about this, that she can't have me staying there without paying and I'll have to try to explain that I'm helping Sister Peters.

"What d'you mean helping, doing all the dirty work which no one wants to do? You with your brains and your training . . ."

"No. No. I'm bathing the babies and . . ."

I look out into the mist. The front gardens and the old houses and the trees are still half hidden in the shreds of mist. The bus will turn off soon away from the ancient suburb and go into the heart of the industrial yards, the factories, and the iron and steel works. When Helena is bigger I'll be able to sit up here with her on the bus and point out the canal to her and the barges and the horses on the towing path and the place where artificial silk and rayon are made and where buttons come from and the old road, where I used to go with my father, to see the women working in the chain shops. But before all this there's my mother.

"A servant? What do you mean about working? A servant. I do not understand. A servant only."

"No, not a servant. I'm offered a post as head nanny to . . ."

"A nursemaid! After all your studying, after all your exams. How can you do this. A nursemaid!"

"It's a good position, I mean—place. It's at Poynter Hall, Lady Poynter is . . ."

"A *position!* and worse, a *place!* Just like an uneducated cook or a kitchen maid with nothing in her head. You doing this?"

"I would have people under me. Head Nanny with a . . ."

"Already you talk like one. "*People under me.*" It is too much. Head Nanny. How could you! Poynter Hall. Poynter Hall. Where is this Poynter Hall? This Lady Poynter. What is she? Some parvenu with money and vulgar feet and ugly overdressed children. Lady Parvenu with much money and no intelligence or culture. What about your music? I always wanted for you to go to Europe to study music. What about your music?"

"But first there was the war and now there's Helena . . ."

How shall I be able to discuss with my mother, as Sister Peters suggested I should, my future? It's too difficult either in imagination or in reality.

Daddy Doctor is in the bus. Up front, in the very front of the bus. Whatever can he be doing going so early on the bus, on this bus? He must have been sitting there, in front, all this time. I can only see him from the back but I know his coat, his light summer coat and the hat he wears. I suppose his brief case is down on the floor by his legs. I don't want Daddy Doctor to see me. If I get off the bus at the next stop I might not be able to get on the next one. The buses fill up and further on they only stop to let people off. I can't afford to miss buses. I must be early at my mother's house. Down the Back Lane, early, with my baby and into the kitchen before the neighbors are up.

I am hungry.

"For whom did you write the poem?"

"Who did I write the poem for? Oh, no one really."

"Poems are always written for someone."

"This isn't really poetry. Anyway, if you must know, I copied it out of a book."

Really, I must stop this. My mother is sure to have other things to talk about.

If I get off last when the bus reaches the terminus I'll be able to turn away to the window while Daddy Doctor passes to go down. Wherever can he be going to at this time of day, on a bus going in this direction? We don't go anywhere near the university. I must keep calm.

Helena's eyelashes are resting on her round cheeks. I put my face down close to her face feeling the wool of the shawl and breathing in the baby smell of Vinolia soap. The bus is full. The man next to me is too big for his half of the seat. I look out of the window and see people at the bus stops. We pass them without stopping.

Perhaps Daddy Doctor is going to my mother's house. In his quiet, well-bred way he will sit at her table moving the food she gives him from one side of his plate to the other. He will relate an anecdote, keeping his voice soft and, in a slightly amused way, will suggest to my mother that I go back with him to the doctors' house and the two little girls.

The question is how does Daddy Doctor know that I am going home to my mother's house for the day today. Does Sister Peters tell the two doctors everything? Does she telephone Mummy Doctor? After breakfast, with a cup of coffee in mid-air, in that space between the table and her mouth.

"That you Glad? Got a minute? Yes, she's going with her baby. Yes, with the baby, to her mother's place. Yes, just for the day.

No, not train, the early bus, yes the workmen's, yes that's the one. Yes, if he gets that one he'll be sure to meet her. It'll be easy. You'll have her back by evening. The trunk? It's not properly unpacked, just a few books out and some dried flowers, petals and stalks, yes a mess but nothing much. I'll get it back by carrier. Yes tonight, yes carrier. Don't you worry . . ."

Daddy Doctor is still in his seat at the front. Quite a few people are getting off now that we are passing factory entrances and side roads leading to the iron and steel works. If only he would be getting off at the next stop. He could be going to visit a factory. That's it. He is probably visiting in the capacity of advisor to any one or several of the artificial silk manufacturers. Or, he could be going to meet a group of students. Yes that's it, meeting some students to take them round the iron and steel works or down a mine.

Helena, seeming to like the movement of the bus, sleeps on rolled up in her shawl. My breasts, too full, ache. Of course Sister Peters would not talk to Mummy Doctor about me.

It will be a quiet day at the Hilda Street Wentworth today. No new patients expected yet and the present ones all able to get up to the toilet and for their hot baths and all able to walk about and do things for themselves and their babies. Sister Peters said it was a good day to choose for the visit, the beds being booked in advance, so if all keep to expected dates everything will be very tranquil there.

"What about your ration book? Have you brought your ration book?"

"I've a piece of corned beef and a pound of prunes, the prunes are a present from a patient . . ."

"If I had your ration book today I could get some extra cheese. Why did you not think to bring the ration book?"

My mother's first question, for some years, has always been about ration books.

We have gone past the factories and have left the iron and

steel works behind. A good many passengers have left the bus and a few people, office-girl sorts are getting on. Daddy Doctor has not moved from his seat.

From the top of the bus there is, for a long way, an exceptionally good view of the canal. It will be nice, when Helena is older, to explain to her what a roan horse is and that the barges are loaded with coal and that people live on the canal barges and decorate them with castles and roses in bright new paint.

I want to enjoy this ride. I have not been on a bus for a long time. It is Helena's first bus ride. Not far from the main road, just about here, there are some fields. The housing estates stretch for some way, new houses built by the council, council houses, and then there are the left-over fields with their tattered hedges. There is a sand quarry out across there too. The quarry is partly overgrown with grass. Just now there will be the long summer grasses and the scarlet poppies. I went there once with Lois, before I knew the Metcalfs. Lois danced on the edge of the quarry, high up. Looking at her from below, seeing her against the sky I thought then, in the excitement of knowing her more, that she was beautiful and that I would always want to do things for her and to give her the things she might want. I mean, I washed her stockings for her and I bought her favorite cigarettes, State Express 333, and sometimes, with pleasurable extravagance, I bought an Art Magazine. We were on bicycles that day coming upon the curious little patches of country which lie between the factories and the rows and rows of small houses. There is a small triangular farm near the quarry. We looked that day through the elderberry and the hawthorn at the cow and the pig and the chickens. There were children there too. We watched them playing in the dirt. At the time I thought they were quaint and had a nice life on their little farm. It is only today, on this bus thinking about them, that I begin to understand that the farmhouse is small and derelict and that they are poor and probably do not have enough to eat. I remember the white and pink hawthorn flowers and how I once decided to store them in my mind for ever so that I could think about them. I have always tried to store prettiness in my mind so that I will not forget it. I realize today that I have not been able to make use of this storage when I needed to.

I have been thinking about this journey for some days, this bus ride when I would be taking my child home to my mother and father for the first time. It is unfair that Daddy Doctor is sitting up there in the front of the bus. It's as if I am not free from the doctors' house. Not at all. Sitting there, like that, he's spoiling the journey.

"I tode 'em as she's been planting out them cabbage plants and that's why there's all dirt on her knees, I tode 'em."

Late last night. So late it's nearly morning, late last night I am in the kitchen putting the Hilda Street breakfast trays ready and covering the slices of bread and butter I have prepared with a damp cloth when I hear, through their partly open door, the low voice of Mr. Peters talking to Sister Peters in bed.

"She's not dirty, I tode 'em. She's been on the ground planting cabbages." For some reason when he talks in this half voice and half whisper Mr. Peters sounds more and more as if he comes from Yorkshire though he's told me several times he was born and bred in the Brickworks near here. "They make this note, see," Mr. Peters goes on, "they make this note of her knees, all the same, and when they come back they're going to get on her back about 'er knees. And listen here, Dolly, there's summat else, you can't let 'er go to that place."

"What place? Hoob, I'm dead tired, it's late." Sister Peters can't remember. "What place?" she keeps asking, telling Mr. Peters it's late and she needs to sleep. Mr. Peters tells her she knows full well the place he's talking about. "Poynters Park," he says. "Lady Poynter. *You know!*" He keeps on about me not going to Lady Poynter's place and that Sister Peters must stop me from going. Sister Peters keeps on with a terrible yawning and tells Mr. Peters that she's sorry about my knees, saying she thinks they probably were very dirty. I can tell she's tired and put out because she calls Mr. Peters Hubert instead of Hoob and she tells him that she can't possibly tell me what to do with my life. "I can't stop her going," she says, "and that's that!"

"You can if you've a mind to," Mr. Peters says. "You can do anything if you put your mind to it." Sister Peters tells him that it's up to me to choose and how can I, a mother with a child, go on managing without money. Mr. Peters says there are more important things than money. "She's nowhere near ready to go anywhere," Mr. Peters raises his voice. "You know that as well as I do. She ought to have three months and more . . ." Sister Peters tells him she knows all that but it would be a shame to miss a good chance. There may never be such a chance again. "Lady Poynter's good fun," Sister Peters says. "She gets on well with Lady Poynter. They're always laughing about something."

"You know as well as I do," Mr. Peters says, "she'll not be likely to be having afternoon tea with her ladyship. Any woman, and this goes for her ladyship, any woman as refers to her husband as "sir" ought to be let alone and that's my last word." Sister Peters tells Mr. Peters that nothing can be done to stop me from leaving.

"Yes there is," Mr. Peters says. "Tell her. You tell her you'd appreciate her staying a while longer. She'll stay. She likes it here. I tell you, Dolly, if she goes she'll regret it—you know what it's like in places like that. She's smart as a button but she's not tough. She'll never hold her own in a place like that. She needs looking after. And I'll tell you this, she's right valuable. I might make mistakes over buckets and horses, Dolly, but not with people eh?"

From the darkness in their room the Hodson baby starts crying. Sister Peters has been having him downstairs at night as he's fretful. I can hear Mr. Peters getting out of bed, and I wait with one foot carefully on the bottom step of the little staircase which goes straight up from the kitchens to the end of the passage where my room is. When the Hodson crying is at its loudest I go up the creaking steps as quickly as possible. I hear Mr. Peters telling Sister Peters that he'll walk Master Hodson for a bit and then make a cup of tea.

"It's all right Dolly," I hear him, from the top of the stairs, "he's quietening. Have a nap. I'll brew the tea."

Daddy Doctor is not spoiling the journey after all. He's getting off the bus just now and it isn't him. How could one man look so like another from the back and then not be that other person? This man as he passes me to go down from the top of the bus is not one bit, front view, like Daddy Doctor. There is no dreaded glance of recognition and no vague smile of the stranger. Nothing. When I see him getting up and coming towards me, I look down into my bag and, as he goes down the stairs, I look up quickly, sideways, through my hair. It is not Daddy Doctor. Absolutely not. Not at all. One person simply cannot be another person. This time, I am able to be pleased with this thought.

In the freedom, the wonderful freedom of thinking about things on this bus now that the person who is not Daddy Doctor has gone, it seems to me that I was afraid of Mummy Doctor somehow taking my baby over along with her little girls, apart from other things to do with being in her house. Another thought is that I have come now, during these last few minutes, to the conclusion that there is no need to discuss (Sister Peters' word) with my mother my going to Poynter Hall. This conclusion comes about because I like being at the Hilda Street Wentworth. The Peters seem to quite like me and find me useful. Unless Sister Peters tells me quite firmly to leave, it goes without saying I'll stay there.

I am pleased to discover something about myself and this is that once more I have been able to come to a point of reasoning and decision.

From the bus terminus it is not far to walk to the Back Lane.

❧

THE SURPRISE OF THE
SUMMER-FULL GARDEN

"Your father mends for other people, he mends every one else but not himself." My mother tells me she has been standing looking out for me. She stands complaining, the surprise of the summer-full garden, the lupins, the roses, and the big red peonies crowding behind her, at the front gate which is, as always, wedged permanently half open on the wet earth. A curving border of pinks leads the way to the front door, the little path is almost hidden. I have forgotten the garden in summer I tell my mother, I have forgotten the garden in summer.

"The pinks are for her." My mother takes Helena from my aching arms.

"The peonies! Your favorites!" I follow her along the pink-edged path. "The peonies!" I say.

"Your father is taking cabbages. He puts them on people's doorsteps, without asking he puts them there. He was going to meet you, he went early on purpose." With one long finger my mother moves the soft curl of shawl away from Helena's face.

"I came on the workmen's."

"Yes, yes he intended to be there."

"Will he go straight on to school then?"

"School, school? Why the school? Today is Saturday." My mother's long finger caresses the curve of Helena's soft cheek.

"Oh yes, Saturday of course." I am surprised that I can forget the days, not know what day it is.

The mist has lifted but the grass in the back garden wets our shoes. A cuckoo calls over and over again, muffled by small distance, like the one in Hilda Street. My mother buries her face in Helena's shawl. I look once again at delphiniums, light blue and dark, reaching up into the arms of the little apple trees, into the abundance of the small green unripe apples.

When my mother looks up at me it is as if my baby has inherited these jewels, my mother's blue eyes. My baby looks like my mother.

"She looks like you," I tell her.

"Your father will say she looks like his mother," my mother says. "He has always said this about babies."

"Only if they are related."

"No, not always."

She has picked some pinks. They are in a little jar on the kitchen table. They are for me to take back with me. "All babies look like someone," she says after a bit. She sits down with Helena and starts to unwrap her. Once again I am seeing something I have not known about before, in my mother, like the time she came to the Hilda Street Wentworth, the day Helena was born.

"How the child has grown!" she says. "Did you meet anyone in the Back Lane?"

"No," I tell her, "no."

Helena's eyes are intensely blue. I hoped once for brown eyes like Dr. Metcalf's. Helena's resemblance to my mother is striking and cancels any other resemblance.

"She is like you," my mother says. "She looks like you when you were a baby." She has made a little sleeping bag for Helena. It is of a fawn woolen cloth decorated with pink rabbits, embroidered by hand, and she has made soft cloth-covered buttons. Eagerly, like a little girl with a doll, my mother undresses Helena to change her on the kitchen table. I look on, seeing her doing the things I imagined her doing. I take the necessary items out of the bag I have with me but she has it all, in a little basket, baby powder, nappies—everything all prepared. She bends over Helena who lies kicking on the folded blanket. In their smiling at one another it seems, for a moment, as if they are exchanging the blue brilliance of their eyes.

My mother, holding Helena dressed now in the sleeping bag which is a bit too big, wants to take her next door to show her to her neighbor.

"But it's a bit early, isn't it, to go visiting."

"In a little while," she says. "Feed her first and I'll cook an egg for you."

I can feel my mother's excitement and pleasure mixed with her nervousness. She takes Helena and carries her to the door.

"What will you tell them?" I am eating toast solidly as if I haven't had anything to eat for weeks.

"That she is my grandchild. I shall say to them she is my grandchild."

I feel ashamed to be eating so many pieces of toast. I have another piece with butter and jam as if satisfying my hunger is my only concern.

My mother returns immediately. They are not up yet, she tells me. It is Saturday, of course they are not getting up early on Saturdays. Mrs. Bright was up, in her hair curlers still, my mother explains, and she adds that she was not invited inside.

"All in a mess there," she says, "and of course they have seven children!" She supposes they, the family next door, with seven children are not very interested in a baby.

"No, I suppose not," I say. A curious grief seems to engulf me. I am sorry for my mother, for her almost childlike eagerness to show off Helena, in spite of the shame I have brought, to some-one—and for her disappointment.

My mother displays an extraordinary resilience. She suggests we walk carrying Helena up the Back Lane to meet my father.

"We might even walk in the field a little," she says. "And later we will bath her and she will sleep and you," she tells me, "you must sleep too."

In her eyes is her disappointment and the reflection of a great hurt. I wish for my father to come now.

Go to sleep. Go to sleep. Go to sleep. My father comes creaking on bent legs along the hall. He crawls flickering across the ceiling crouching double on the wardrobe. Go to sleep he says. Flickering in fire light and candle flame. Flickering and prancing he moves up and down the walls, big and little, little and big, colliding in the corners with himself.

Go to sleep. Go to sleep. My father folding and unfolding comes closer. I'm the engine down the mine, he says. I'm the shaft. I'm the wheels turning and turning down down the mine. I'm the shaft. I'm the steam laundry. I'm a Yorkshire ham, a cheese, a Cheshire cheese, a pork pie. A pork pie that's what I am. I'm a mouse now, he says, I'm a mouse in the iron and steel works. I'm a needle and thread. I'm a cart wheel turning in the road, turning over and over turning and turning. I'm the horse pulling the cart. I'm turning the cart in the roadway. I'm the tired horse, the tired horse. Go to sleep. Go to sleep.

My father's voice is soft and softer. His voice, my father's voice is singing down through the years to me. I'm the tired horse he sings softly, so softly, the tired tired horse. Go to sleep now go to sleep.

It is my father singing to Helena. Not singing he says only groaning. Helena is sleeping. She sleeps, he explains, without him noticing. One minute her eyes wide open wide awake and the next minute fast asleep. I have forgotten the short *a* in my father's speech. When he says fast asleep she is even more asleep.

I have been asleep here in my mother's house sleeping away my whole life for two hours, for over two hours, while my mother and father have been watching over Helena. I wake weeping and do not know the reason.

Helena sleeps and when she wakes to my mother's face close to hers, she smiles with her mouth, her eyes, her whole face.

It is time to leave to go back to the Hilda Street Wentworth. My father comes to the bus with me. We walk up the Back Lane and he tells me again that they will sell the house and move and that I should come, with Helena, home. I tell him yet again that I do not want them to move and that if they do move I shall not come and live with them.

❧

THE SEASONS

The Little Celebrations and the Growing Sugar Weight

There is something I do and that is to make a little celebration, an occasion, a reason out of something quite small. As time goes by these little celebrations become more frequent since they are the way in which Helena and I go out together. I am, in reality, taking her out either in a small pushchair or else walking very slowly. Too slow for me is too fast for her. The walk is to the second corner in Hilda Street where there is an ice-cream shop, or we might go a little further to a funny little shop where broken dolls are mended; these are the things we do for our outings. These are the things I am looking forward to doing while I rush the trays back to the kitchen and slide the plates and cups into the big tin basin of soapy water. And then, while I am wiping them on the worn-out wet cloths which we use for drying up, my impatience to go out increases and I sort, as quickly as possible, the knives and forks and spoons into their compartments, moving my lips as if I am praying and not just checking and counting them.

With a sort of restrained eagerness we go out from the Hilda Street Wentworth to certain known and named corners before we turn back. Sometimes we go to a small park. Usually we bring back from these expeditions dandelion leaves and handfuls of grass for the rabbits. The places we reach before turning back are the witch's house, the garden full of toys, the churchyard, and the holly hedge. We are always back at the Hilda Street Wentworth in time to give the mothers their washing bowls and their afternoon tea. About every six weeks or so Sister Peters insists that I take a day off in order to visit my mother. These visits are not always the happiest as my mother insists on weeping over Helena saying her arms and legs are like sticks and that she needs to be looked after properly and why do I refuse to leave her at home with them.

On the bus ride back to the Hilda Street Wentworth I feel afraid and I try to measure Helena's arms and her little thighs with my fingers. She does seem very light in weight and I try to make her eat something from the packets my mother has given me. Helena is always sick on this return bus journey.

I feel afraid that Helena will somehow be taken from me.

I notice the changes in the weather especially between the fine days and the wet days because of the great rush to be out early with the nappies to catch the sun. And then there is the rushing out at the first sign of rain to gather in the partly dry washing. Mr. Peters has made some big wooden clothes horses which are propped up permanently as much out of the way as possible. The big things, the sheets and counterpanes, go to the laundry. Laundry is a big item on all the accounts. Cotton wool and cascara are on all the accounts too. Every patient is charged for a whole roll and a whole bottle. No one ever complains about these things and Sister Peters explains to me that it is a method of fighting the overheads, and that patients accept these items.

"Probably they never even read them," she says. "Did your mother," she asks, "did your mother complain about anything on the accounts?"

"No," I tell her, "no she didn't."

"A very generous lady, your mother," Sister Peters says.

The summers are encapsulated in the fragrance of boiling jam. Plum jam because Mr. Peters goes to the markets late on Saturdays and brings back cheap yellow plums. We pick over the fruit, the three of us together. It won't keep, Sister Peters says, and often at midnight we are at the stove stirring the golden boiling contents of the jam cauldron. A good rolling boil Sister Peters calls it as she tests for setting. She tells me to put the shining clean jars above the stove to warm. We use up the carefully hoarded sugar. Saving out the sugar from all the weekly rations has become for me a sort of hobby, perhaps like stamp collecting or like collecting fishes' eyes in matchboxes. I add to the sugar store a cupful or two whenever I can and I take great pleasure in weighing the dark blue bags. Throughout the year I record the growing sugar weight on a card pinned to the back of the kitchen door. On this door too are the marks I make to show how tall Helena is from the time when she first stands up to take her first steps and then onwards. She is quite a tall little girl. I enjoy recording her growth in this way.

Perhaps the summers in the garden are the best, idyllic and peaceful for short times when I am crouched small and insignificant on the earth, planting out tiny cabbages and cornflower seedlings, beneath the great dome of a summer blue sky lined at times with nests of pure white clouds and resounding with the contented murmurings from the dovecote which, in its repaired state, towers above the busy fowl yard and the increasing number of rabbit hutches. Helena makes mud pies in the dust and runs with both hands outstretched towards Sister Peters whenever she returns in her hat and coat from some bus journey or other. Helena, alert to the familiar sound of the side gate, runs across there at once both to Sister Peters and to Mr. Peters. They seem fond of her though often Sister Peters shakes her head saying things like, "That poor child," and "What is to become of this poor child?" and "It's all right now, Vera, but what are you going to do later when she's expensive?" At these times I lie awake at night wondering what I ought to do. Sometimes, as if sensing my uneasiness, Helena wakes up and cries and I go down quietly to the kitchen and make us each a piece of bread and butter, without disturbing the Peters whose bedroom door is never properly latched.

I snatch time for being in the garden. Sometimes, when Sister Peters suggests that I take some time off, I have a whole afternoon in the garden. I have come to need the safety and the privateness of being enclosed within the mellow brick walls; and I look forward, with a sense of comfort, to the coming of the blossom on the big old pear tree and to the yearly transformation of the vegetable garden from the dark rich forked over earth to the neat little rows of summer lettuces and radishes, spring onions and beans.

The pantry shelves, every summer, are like the pages of a book which is being written. Every day something fresh being added to what was there before. In the long light evenings of summer when Helena's face is a white, peevish half-moon at the edge of the bedroom curtain, I am in the yard, at a makeshift trestle table, with Sister Peters, preparing vegetables and fruit for preserving. Some of these are gifts from grateful patients and some are bargains brought from the markets by Mr. Peters who walks with the heavy baskets balanced on the handlebars of his bicycle. Tomatoes, carrots, green beans, plums, and black currants. We do the apples and pears later and, still later, the Seville oranges—an unusual yearly present from a previous patient. We make, using as little sugar as possible, a rough-cut marmalade. Sister Peters' own recipe. The evenings are already cold and dark by the time we are slicing the bitter fruit. The Peters, who never spend on a newspaper or a magazine themselves, send me upstairs to "scout for something to read," papers discarded by the mothers. Mr. Peters, in shirt sleeves, with his feet up at the kitchen range reads aloud to us the spicy bits from *The News of the World* and, changing his voice, from the "anxious blue eyes" problem pages in the magazines. Sister Peters and I work quickly. Drying our hands, we take turns to answer a bell or to pace up and down with a fretful baby.

The Rose Garden which, at one time, must have been a gracious, upstairs drawing room, has a large fireplace. In winter we have a coal fire there and the mothers, who are up, sit round the hearth. Husbands, at visiting time, join the fireside. It is then that I experience again the deep-felt wish to be part of a married couple, to sit by a fire in winter with the man who is my husband. So intense is this wish that I try to avoid seeing the mothers with their husbands, and if I write the word "husband" on a piece of paper my eyes fill with tears. The word "wife" is even worse. So much do I long to be someone's wife, with a cupboard full of knitting patterns and scraps of left-over dress material, that it hurts me to hear the word "wife" spoken. The husbands, with an ennobling sense of chivalry brought on by fatherhood, often help me by fetching coal to make up the fire.

"Watch," Sister Peters says, out of the side of her mouth, "to see that they are not too generous with the coal." So I develop a method of placing a coal ration in a bucket at the top of the stairs. I like the coal fire, the look of it, and, in spite of the extra work, I spend time polishing the grate and the brass fender and the brass top of the fire guard. At night, because of the cold, I wear my old hockey jumper in bed and long woolen stockings left over from school.

Sister Russell and Dr. McCabe often have quiet conversations during the second stage of labor. They are capable of discussing some philosophical or literary point while standing, one each side of the patient, holding up the heavy white legs and commenting, during the abstract discussion, on the position on the perineum, of the emerging head.

"I can see the head, doctor," Sister Russell says to Dr. McCabe. And to the patient, "a lovely head of hair, dark hair, dear, a lovely head, it won't be long now."

Usually this is a false declaration suggesting a more advanced stage in the labor. This is in order to encourage the mother, who is now in a panic and beyond any feelings of embarrassment at having both legs raised and pushed back, flexed at the knees, till the knees are on her chest in a home-made stirrups position. She pulls at the knotted sheet on the iron rail of the bedhead and screams, one scream following another, pausing only to give a weak smile and the repeated words of timid apology as one pain fades and before the unbearable force of the next.

"I declare this head of hair," Sister Russell says, "this head is a beautiful head, well shaped, dear. Now Push!" She encourages, "One more push, dear."

I have heard this often enough to know that the head is not yet visible. Along the passage, too close to the screams, I am holding a small block of wood behind a frozen pipe while Mr. Peters hammers the ancient lead, tap tap tap, gently, as he tries to close the crack, to mold the edges of the burst pipe, its ice protruding, together.

"Better go shut them doors," Mr. Peters says as the screaming starts afresh. He has brought up two kettles of boiling water as he has to thaw the bath outlet which has frozen solid during the night. "Life!" he says, "it's all pain and noise coming and all pain and noise going. Like teeth," he says, "take teeth, nothing but trouble. Trouble when they're coming. Trouble when you got 'em. And trouble, talk about trouble!, when you lose 'em." He goes on patiently tapping the burst pipe and gradually the sinister ice jewel, the unwanted ornament, is covered delicately with hand-beaten lead.

"There!" Mr. Peters stands back from his handiwork. "You'll

have to watch," he says, "it'll drip in the thaw. Get one of my buckets, it'll do till we get the plumber."

~

One bitter day in winter a colored postcard comes for me. It is from Magda. It is over two years, almost three years since I have seen Magda, since Magda's visit the day Helena was born. The card is written in ordinary ink instead of the flamboyant purple of the earlier letters. It is brief and with the same quality of telling. It is a sudden reminder of another world and the one-time excitement and longing I experienced in receiving her letters and invitations.

For a moment I am lost in reading the card:

> *Darling!*
> *No doubt you've read of Daddy's latest disgrace.*
> *I'm with Mummy in the South of France. Heavenly.*
> *We've taken a villa. Would love to see you. Any*
> *chance? Come!*

Magda's name is scrawled with almost the usual flourish. I study her name closely. The flourish is perhaps a bit weaker, perhaps a bit tired. I read the card again and turn it over to look at the expanse of blue sky and endless golden sands. Brilliant and empty.

"There's no date on it and no address," I tell Sister Peters and, for some unexplainable reason, I start to cry. "There's no date and no address," I say, "how can I go and see Magda?" I go on crying because I am not able to stop.

Sister Peters, her hands dropping flour, comes round the kitchen table. "You've got Helena in the pushchair," she says, "out there in the porch, go for one of your little walks, dear." She puts an arm across my shoulders without letting her floured fingers touch my jersey.

"Put an extra wrap round Helena," she says, "and have a little walk. There's a good girl. Just you take a little walk."

•

If when I walk alongside the big gardens, casual with trodden-down flowers, broken bushes, and scattered tricycles and dolls' prams, thinking of them as sacred places to which husbands return every evening, sacred in that closeness and trust which I long for and which I believe to be in every marriage, I console myself, even more now as I walk, in imagining that such a place, a large old house full of children and their untidy bedrooms, all surrounded by a neglected but safe and contented garden, will one day belong to me.

The particular garden, to which I am always drawn and which, particularly in summer, suggests all that I wish for, has today a snowman in the middle of the trampled snow. The lights are on and the long uncurtained windows offer a glimpse of the magic of the life within; the desirable warmth and harmony of a family, and the idea of having been especially chosen to make this family.

I walk too far with Helena in the pushchair, my mind being occupied with thoughts and the going over repeatedly, in these thoughts, the overheard conversation between Sister Peters and Mr. Peters.

"She's cried this afternoon, Hoob, like no one I've ever known, out loud, like a child, couldn't stop, like crying I've never ever heard." Sister Peters telling Mr. Peters, thinking I've already gone while I am still on the kitchen stairs with an extra little scarf for Helena. "She'll have to find some other life Hoob," Sister Peters' voice crossing the space from the stove to half way up the small staircase. "She'll never ever meet anyone here. And the child, she's . . ."

There's nothing to worry about," Mr. Peters is adamant. They're better off here than anywhere just now. And that little girl she's a little princess with us . . . She's a duchess . . ."

"No, she isn't," Sister Peters interrupts him. "She's left for hours strapped in the pushchair. She cries for ages because Vera's busy. She's pale to transparent with those blue shadows under her eyes. Vera's obsessed with the routine, the work she does and the child hardly gets a look. I'm worried Hoob really I am. The child could have TB or something."

The stairs creak as I try not to move. Mr. Peters flips the newspaper and clears his throat noisily.

"And listen to this Dolly, the couple alleged," he reads, "that they ate a hot Sunday roast in bed where intimacy took place before the murder . . . oops . . . where intimacy took place before the *double* murder . . ." He looks up as I creak on the bottom tread of the kitchen stairs. "Hey!" he says, as I step into the kitchen, "thought you'd gone for a walk."

"Eavesdropper!" Sister Peters shakes a finger at me. "Eavesdroppers never hear good of themselves."

As I walk I reflect that it is possible to know from a changing quality, a different sound or resonance in voice and a greater energy in speaking that people's real thoughts are different from those actually uttered. When my mother says that Helena is pretty and dainty her voice betrays the thought she has which is, in reality, that Helena is neglected and starved.

This resonance and energy and the changes in quality are particularly noticeable to me when I overhear conversations. So that when Sister Russell and Dr. McCabe talk about "clearly defined ideas in abundance," and "creating an unbelievable harmony in imagery," they might well be discussing a book or a play, but the intimate lowering and closeness of their voices during a delivery which is, after all, itself an immense thing, the emergence of a whole new person, shows me that there is something else of importance in their lives, something extra to their serious and necessary work, something extra even to their reading, something extra which I do not have.

I hardly notice the fast fading light of the afternoon and walk too far. And, when I turn back, the pushchair is facing a biting wind. I have to drag the pushchair in the wet snow which is now beginning to freeze again into thick uneven ice on the pavement. For a time this intense cold and Helena's small pinched cold face are my only concerns. I try to wrap the inadequate scarf round her face and I hurry as fast as I can home to the Hilda Street Wentworth. I shall be too late, I realize, to do the upstairs afternoon washing basins and the afternoon teas. My flying tears are only partly caused by the cold wind.

Sister Peters has saved a hot toasted fruit bun for Helena and one for me. She pushes extra butter in them while I take off our outdoor clothes. One of the mothers has left earlier than expected she explains. Instead of staying the full month she has gone home a fortnight early. Not only is there one person less upstairs, two if you count the baby, but there are a whole fortnight's rations which she did not want to bother with.

"The sugar," I say, "a whole fortnight's sugar."

"Yes," Sister Peters says, "you'll be able to save it out for your growing sugar weight. Not now!" she says. "For heaven's sake, child, have your tea first."

Because we are one less unexpectedly there is extra hot water and Sister Peters says to me to have a hot bath before I go to bed.

Having a bath and going to bed is one of the things I look forward to. Sometimes when I am getting up in the morning I think of bed time and how I will try to be as early as possible to bed. Bed time and clean clothes and clean sheets are all part of what I have come to look upon as the little celebrations especially when Helena is all dressed in clean clothes too.

When I was a child I liked cold sheets. Sister Peters, at first, does not understand what I mean when I tell her this.

"Oh," she says, after a bit, "you mean linen sheets, they would feel cold." I tell her I suppose that must be it.

"No one has linen sheets now, or only rich people," she says. And then she remembers some worn old sheets she has, put away somewhere. So we get these out and machine them sides to middle. I like doing this.

Helena, in her cot, has patched sheets and I have the old linen sheets, seamed down the middle and am reminded every night now of the seamed sheets of my childhood. It is a sort of comforting thing. In a way I imagine myself as half way between a child and a married woman. Because, I hope so much to be married one day.

❧

THE BIBLICAL DIGEST

"Matthew Daniel Samuel Ruth Sarah and now Elijah, a veritable Biblical Digest, don't you think?" Sister Russell and Dr. McCabe are taking off their gowns after delivery. The Hilda Street Wentworth is full once more.

Lady Poynter tells me after the birth of her fifth son, Elijah, that Sir Harold will kill her when she goes home with yet another stocky, short-legged bullet of a boy.

"Just like his father," she moans when I bring the new baby, washed and fragrant in new baby clothes, to her bedside. "Here I am mother of another boy!" she raises herself on one elbow. "Ripped to ribbons yet again for *this!*" she says. "You'll simply have to let me adopt Helena since *you* won't come to Poynter Hall, you stubborn girl!" She lies back on her pillow turning her face away from the soft little bundle. "We've enough heirs for the Works," she says. "I daren't take home another. You *must* let Helena come home with me. She's a dear little thing. Sir H will dote on her. He doesn't want another son with stubby fingers and a scrubbing brush for a head, he wants a—a little girl, a daughter to sit on his knee and play with his watch chain. He wants a pretty little girl with long, fine, fair hair and long legs, the long legs of chivalrous aristocracy, my dear, like yourself, my dear, and your little girl. Helena, you see my dear, would, later on, sit so gracefully on a horse. Her hair would be the envy of all the other girls and she would be our pride and joy."

I try to put the baby in bed beside Lady Poynter but she pulls the sheet up close to her chin.

"Sir H would give her everything," she says, "he'd have her *be* anything she chooses, he's all for education for girls as well as boys, She could be a lady doctor or a concert pianist—whatever she would want. A princess if she likes. Helena has your aesthetic lips, my dear, a delicate refined little mouth, whereas the boys all have buckets, much as I adore them, instead of mouths. Exquisite fingers you have and Helena too, my dear. Please *please* consider my request. At Poynter Hall, she could be anything and have anything—down at Poynter Hall . . ."

"Don't cry, Lady Poynter," I say, "please don't cry." Quickly I tuck the new Poynter baby into his cradle and I tell Lady P she really must try to lie quietly and sleep as I have to clear up the Cabbage Patch before lunch.

"Sister Peters likes the walls washed," I say in a soothing voice. "You know how much she values cleanliness." The truth is I am listening to Sister Russell and Dr. McCabe who are, in their well-bred voices, having a conversation which interests me. They are just along the passage resting by the deep window sill with their cups of tea, where I stood once, pausing in the intervals between pains during my own labor to watch a woman hanging out washing, as if that was all that mattered at that moment, a few gardens away.

Russell and McCabe, though reserved, seem to know each other quite well. Perhaps they have both been reading the same book or have been, possibly, to a play together. They are talking about the looking back on the supposition that it is possible to learn the pleasures of love without being obliged to become acquainted with the sorrows as well. It must be a book or a play as it is clear that neither of them are sorrowful with love. I wonder which book or which play. I wish I could know.

I take my pail of soapy water along the passage to empty it hoping to hear more but now they are on to the ineluctable changing of the season, the coming of the spring. Ineluctable is a word both of them would use. I have never heard it before and now, hearing it for the first time, it is as if, in spite of the bitterly cold wind and the shining wet blackness of the horse-chestnut trees on the other side of Hilda Street, the irrepressible new leaves are beginning to appear in little bursts of fresh green, shining with moisture as if unable to prevent their own appearance. Just as, in the same way, the green spears of first one crocus and then another are showing in the dark earth in some of the gardens.

When I hear Sister Russell and Dr. McCabe talking together I am reminded of staff nurse Ramsden and staff nurse Pusey-Hall. As now, I only ever heard then, snatches of what was being said. Sometimes I have an indescribable longing to have conversations like this with someone. There are times when I long for the company of another person, for the excitement of a deepening of understanding and the making of a lasting friend. I want to find in someone else the things which match with me. Mostly, most of the time, other people do not matter all that much but I could, if I had the chance, set great store upon one friend trusting that friend completely and needing him, or her, so much for what I think of as happiness—that is, a contrast in feeling from sadness and a freedom from anxiety, a state which I imagine then becomes happiness. The person I could become attached to in what they would have described at the hospital, Ferguson and Lois that is, as a neurotic way, could become tremendously special to me; a person of music and of poetry and of skills—not a neurosis—if a person whose fingers are nimble, either in embroidery or on the keys of the piano or in the deft changing of a complicated surgical dressing. Such a person was embodied in staff nurse Ramsden and I feel that Sister Russell and Dr. McCabe have these same qualities but these qualities are not there for me, not actually there in them for me.

All the same I resolve, up and down the stairs, in and out of the rooms, the Rose Garden and the Meadow, the Gooseberry Bush and the Cabbage Patch, to emulate Sister Russell and Dr. McCabe and what I remember of Ramsden. It is a long time since I read a book for one thing. And then there is another thing, my hair. My hair is awful. It's depressing me. I'm heartily sick of this Olympia roll, this long heavy hair brushed for ages every day and rolled up on a boot lace which I have to tie round my head with exactly the right tightness. Because I am in a hurry I often push my hair into a net. It's out of the way while I am working but when I see myself as I go by the long mirror on the landing I have to look the other way. Hair bundled up and sagging in a hair net is ugly, it is worse, much worse than a head scarf. How can I read a book or expect an intellectual conversation when I simply do not know what to do with my hair. I hate my hair.

One of the differences between Mr. Peters and Sister Peters is that Mr. Peters says an aitch with an H. Haitch he says when spelling Hilda Street on the phone. He likes Haitch P sauce. Sister Peters remembers to put it out for him. She does not like it herself but puts it in her rabbit stews and her other casserole dinners together with a big spoonful of camp coffee, an essence, she says, which helps to create the spectacular rich dark gravy. She says the special ingredients of the sauce, the dates, the molasses, the rye flour, the raisins, the tamarinds, and the other things must have been really hard to get during the war; but the sauce, she says, never lost its piquant flavor. Not her special choice of flavor, she says, but a favorite of the mothers and of course Mr. Peters.

"I'll go along with that," Mr. Peters always says whenever Sister Peters holds forth on the HP Sauce.

Mr. Peters has HP Sauce with everything. He is already having his lunch when I come down to fetch the trays for the mothers. "That Poynter Place, Hall, whatever it is," he is saying to Sister Peters, "is certainly being stacked up with livestock. Sir H and Lady P must be Roman Catholics or something, you know, assuring themselves of places in heaven. One brat after another!"

"I don't think so," Sister Peters says, "they are seriously trying to get a daughter." She arranges a plate judiciously putting on a bit more carrot and lifting off a fragment of meat. She explains that the wealthy, with good brass in their pockets, and the very poor have the big families. The boys, she says, will be useful in the iron and steel. Born with the iron works in their mouths. I can just see Sir H expanding. "All the same," she goes on, "he wants a girl. You must," she says to me, "consider their renewed offer to adopt Helena. Lady P is adamant about this. Listen! Why not let them have Helena for a few days to see how she gets on?"

When I pick up the first tray my hands shake so much I have to put it down. I am shaking all over.

"Hurry up do!" Sister Peters has the hot plate ready. "Hurry, dear, do," she says, "it's hot lunches today and I don't want them served cold. It's a very good opportunity for Helena," she adds. "You must think about it seriously." Her eyes fill with tears. "I wouldn't want for her to go away," she says, "but we do have to think of her future—and yours."

I take the first tray and as I start up the kitchen stairs I hear Mr. Peters saying that Sister Peters should keep in mind that the next time the old cow calves she may well drop a filly.

"You've got your animals and their verbs mixed," Sister Peters tells him.

"You know full well what I mean," Mr. Peters says. "When Sir Sauce gets his own little girl you know what'll happen to the adopted one . . ."

"Sir Sauce? Sir Sauce? I don't get it."

"Sir H.P.," Mr. Peters, with his mouth too full, is laughing. "Sir Harold Poynter Sauce." He almost chokes. "Haitch P."

"That's a below stairs sort of joke." Sister Peters' voice is cold and hard. "Really, Hoob!"

"And that's where our little girl will be," Mr. Peters says, "she'll be *below stairs* when Princess Poynter makes her entrance."

"Hurry, Vera! Hurry up do!" Sister Peters calls up the stairs. "Eavesdropping never does anyone any good. I've told you before. Eavesdroppers never hear good . . ."

"I know," I shout back and I go on upstairs, my own heavy steps making too much noise on the uncarpeted treads for me to hear the next bit of their talking.

⚬

TRENT'S VISIT

"She's you!"

"D'you think so? I suppose she is . . ."

"She's you all right. Well, how's things?" Trent, in black from head to foot, is standing in the kitchen just inside the back door. No one was about so she stepped inside, she explains, she's come to see me and is it a bad time to come she wants to know. Oh no, very good I tell her, we're slack at present, I say. All six mothers are up, walking about, carrying their babies out of doors to sit on garden chairs on Mr. Peters' little lawn out there. We have a cold lunch today I tell Trent. All very easy, the Peters are going out. See, I tell her, the trays are ready, plates all served and arranged with cold cuts and green salad, cold sideboards, Sister Peters calls them, corned beef mainly and some sort of meat loaf she makes with left-over roast, usually a leg of something or other cooked for hours in a big old tin we have. I am surprised and a bit embarrassed to see Trent so I talk too much. At least that is how it seems. After a bit I stop talking and look at Trent. She is looking at me. She says the trays look very nice, very appetizing and the idea of a blue cornflower on each one is sweet. You have to feed private patients, especially nursing mothers, well, I tell her. The flowers are all blue, I go on, because we've a run of boys, this often happens, all boys in the Hilda Street Wentworth or all girls. Funny, but that's how it is.

"It's been a long time," Trent says. "She's you," she says again, looking at Helena more closely. "I've never seen such a likeness, never ever. Peek-a-Boo!" she says to Helena who covers her face and peers at Trent through her thin little fingers.

"Ask your friend to have some lunch with you," Sister Peters, who is dressed for going out, says. Trent says thank you she would just love that. She draws a kitchen chair near to Helena's little high chair and sits down. Sister Peters, in her hat and coat, helps me to take the six trays to the mothers who have asked if they can eat in the garden while the sun's out.

"It'll save you the stairs for once," Sister Peters says. "Shall you manage the clearing up all right?" she asks me and gives herself a look of approval in the little piece of mirror we have over the sink.

"Of course," I tell her. "You'd better hurry," I say, "Mr. Peters has been waiting Ages."

"I know. I know," Sister Peters says and she's off.

"She must be three if she's a day." Trent nods her head towards Helena.

"That's right, nearly three and a half."

"Time flies," Trent says.

"It certainly does."

"You haven't changed, Wright," Trent says.

"Neither have you, Trent," I say. "Not a bit."

"Though we've both been through a thing or two," Trent says. "We've seen the world a bit, you and me."

"I suppose so."

"Your hair!" Trent says. "It's still the same."

"Oh my hair!" I say. "Can't do a thing with it."

"Have it cut," Trent says, "that's what they're doing now. Razor cut it's called, the urchin cut. It'd suit you a treat. Short hair. Everyone's going for it."

"D'you really think so? I haven't had a hair cut for years." Nervously I push at my hair, pushing it into the net.

"This meat," Trent says, "this meat's lovely. Really beautiful, this meat."

"Have some more." I offer the plate with the extras on it. Trent puts both hands, fingers outstretched over her plate to show she's had enough. I am not sure why Trent has come here. Quickly I gather up the bits of food Helena has thrown all round her chair and when I make the patients' tea I pour a cup for Trent. She drinks gratefully.

"Don't top it up," she says, "you'll spoil it. Good tea!"

"Yes good tea." I rush with the cups of tea to the mothers and bring in the trays as quickly as I can, two at a time.

"Don't rush because of me," Trent says. "I don't have to hurry away. How d'you like my Black?" she asks. She stands up and turns round slowly. She picks up her hat and her handbag.

"It all looks nice and new and smart," I say, knowing my

mother, had she the chance, would dismiss the clothes as cheap and not at all elegant, one of her favorite words. Trent seems pleased with her new things. Her shoes too are new and black.

She's in mourning she tells me, widowed, she says. Married three months and then all of a sudden, she says, a widow. She isn't nursing now, she tells me, not any more. She's selling ladies' dresses and accessories.

"Accessories?" I am wiping Helena, who is protesting, with a gray-looking face cloth. In front of Trent I am ashamed of the dirty color of the cloth.

"Yes accessories," Trent says. I can see that she has noticed the cloth. "Yes," she says, "you know, ornaments, jewelry, imitation pearls, imitation opals, imitation gold—things to go on black or with red or blue or gray or green, all kinds of accessories, necklaces, pendants, brooches, those sorts of things. And I help customers to choose perfumes and hat trimmings and collars and little scarves and whether to have spotted net or voile or chiffon . . ." I stare with admiration at Trent. How does she know all this? I never think about these things, about fashions. It's as if she has come here from another world. A place of pleasure and brightness and of choosing for oneself, a place where people have lots of clothes for different occasions. And not only clothes, they have accessories, all kinds of pretty things, kept in charming little scented boxes in special compartments in their dressing tables.

"Allow me." Trent teeters on high heels towards an imaginary customer. "Allow me, modom, allow me to show modom how to tie the teeny leetle knot in the teeny leetle scarf . . . to place the bow just heah on modem's . . ." Trent, in her special voice, demonstrates. We laugh. Tears come into my eyes with my laughing. I don't seem to have laughed for years, I tell her. We laugh some more.

"You can laugh yourself silly like this," I say, and I tell her I'm sorry she is a widow. Trent says she thinks it might be worse to be married for life to the wrong person than to be widowed. Did I know, she wants to know, that one of the girls hanged herself in her mother-in-law's kitchen? "No one you know," she says. "She came after you left, got herself pregnant, married secretly, though we all knew of course, got turned out, nowhere to go except her mother-in-law. You can picture it! No idea of the background. See? I mean, the men all look the same in pajamas or hospital blues, a man could be anything. The mother-in-law found her hanging dead, pair of stockings round her neck. There's no way of knowing," Trent says, "what you're marrying into if you marry pajamas."

Trent, who used to amuse us with her one man, vocal and tap, band and who danced me, one night, all along the bombed passage, the forbidden locked-up residents' corridor, where the doctors had their rooms on the fourth floor of the hospital, picks Helena out of her little high chair and waltzes, whirling round and round on the red tiles of the Peters' kitchen, singing; "A wun a tew a tree a wun a tew a tree a wun ah Danube so blue pom pom pom pom my heart is so trew pom pom pom pom," holding Helena up so that she is laughing and laughing.

"Remember your gramophone?" Trent collapses on her chair. "Stuffed up with a towel and shut in the wardrobe? I really missed the music after you left," she says.

"Did you?" I'm remembering all at once the Tango Bolero and Lois dancing naked in a strip of moonlight when we took down the black-out curtain once during a hot night. I remember too how she hid herself in a heap of bedclothes when the Night Sister came up to our room to complain about the noise. Later Lois came out naked still, straight into my arms.

"I really missed you when you left," Trent says, "you and the music and the poems. Remember? The Emperor? And The Serenade for Strings, I loved that." She puts Helena back into her chair and takes the plates one by one when I have done swirling them round in the big tin bowl of soapy water. My washing up seems more messy than usual.

Trent's black coat has wide shoulder pads and a belt of the same material as the coat which ties in front. My own coat, when I think about it, is my school coat which has not worn out. My coat is shabby, I have never liked it. I don't like Trent's coat either.

"The hem line," Trent says suddenly. "There's a new hem line, it's called the New Look," she says. "Lots of material, a new mid-calf length, they call it Ballerina, bright colors, lace all over the place and broderie anglaise, square necks and high waists, should suit you a treat, Wright. A square neck, not too low and a bodice of broderie anglaise. It's you Wright."

"Me!"

"Yes, you. Don't you ever think about a dress? Don't you ever go out to look at dress shops or anything? I'll bet you never go to a show or to the pictures. I'm right aren't I? You never go out. You used to like a film or a concert when you had the chance."

"I have plenty to do here," I can feel my mouth thin in a prim line, the way I don't really like my mouth. Trent is making me nervous and restless. I'm picking up knives and forks and then putting them down in the same place I pick them up from. I'm wishing I knew what to say. She's right I don't go anywhere and there's no music at the Hilda Street Wentworth. We have the news on the wireless and the football match and that's about it.

"You've certainly been left holding the baby." Trent gives a little laugh, not unkindly. "She's too quiet," she says.

"What d'you mean?"

"Your little girl, Helena, she's too quiet, too subdued. She needs to bash around with others her own age. She needs to go places with other children." Trent looks across at Helena who is sitting quietly in her little chair turning the pages of a picture book. Her thin little white fingers carefully lifting the pages one after the other.

"I do take her out," I say. I'm wiping the trays before setting them for the next meal. "We go for walks to the Botanical Gardens and sometimes we go to the ordinary park. We can't go this afternoon because the Peters are out." I feel awkward wiping the trays.

Trent nods her head. She wants to know what these Peters people are really like. I tell her they're nice, the Peters are both very nice. Trent wants to know what money they pay. "Excuse me asking," she says in her politest way. I tell Trent that the Peters have lost some money at the races. I tell her that they go to the races. Horses and sometimes dogs.

"Say no more." Trent hangs up the sodden cloth. She tells me I need to get out and about. "You'll rot here, Wright," she says, "without clothes, without money, and without friends. It's true, the patients are friendly and nice, I'll grant you that, but they're here today and gone tomorrow." Trent tells me she knows that childbirth is important and that the care of the lying-in mother is very necessary. "Important and necessary as they are, Wright," she says, "it all fades, every bit of it. Women don't live with their childbirth, they forget it. These mothers aren't your friends at all. They're nice enough but they'd have fits if you and Helena turned up, visiting, on their doorsteps. You'll never see them again and though they give you presents they aren't interested in you at all and, Wright, believe me, in the life you're living you'll never meet anyone."

"I don't want to 'meet anyone,' Trent. Really I don't."

"Everyone wants and needs a true friend, Wright, and you're no exception." She goes on to explain that being happy is only possible if you're with someone you can really trust. A person you can have a good laugh with or a good cry and who likes what you like and hates what you hate is a good friend, she says. "I'm in the same boat as you with customers," she says, "that makes two of us. The customers seem like friends when they're trying on clothes and asking, with complete faith in me, for my opinion. But when they're truly pleased with a cor-sage I've made, you know, something in real velvet, looking like the petals of an exotic flower, pinned on the bust properly with the pin not showing, off they go smiling and admiring themselves in every mirror they pass and I'm forgotten straight away. We're two of a kind all right. We really are two of a kind. You and me."

"Oh God!" Trent says after a pause. "Oh Goddy God!"

"Shall I make us some more tea?" I lift Helena from her chair and she fetches her little dust pan and brush and sets to work sweeping the kitchen tiles.

"She's you," Trent says, "take a look at that, will you. She's you all right."

"Shall I make us some more tea?" I fill the kettle.

"Have you got it to spare?" Trent wants to know. I tell her we had a whole tea chest of tea from one of the patients whose grandfather is in the trade. I tell her I'll make a little parcel for her to take home with her.

"Remember our bike rides?" I say. "Remember what a fool I was always lending Ferguson money?" I'm trying to make Trent laugh. "She was always borrowing from me," I say. Trent doesn't laugh.

"Ferguson," she says, frowning, "that one! How was it she used to go, *Can you lend me money for breakfast if Queen and Trent pay and you'll pay them and I'll pay you back later*, how could you, Wright, have gone on the way you did. That's how Ferguson was. Always saying she'll pay back and she never. She never!"

"We were at school together . . ." I start to say.

"That's no reason for her to bleed you," Trent gets up and brushes her black skirt with her hands.

"Have another cup?" I'm trying to keep Trent, to stop her from leaving. She disturbs but at the same time I'm holding on to her company. I am surprised about this and unable to help myself.

"Ferguson," Trent says, "that one! I suppose she's never sent you a penny. And she must have known."

"No," I say. "She owes me. I don't expect she knows."

"God knows what she owes you. She could have got your address from your mother. You'll never hear from her I'll bet. D'you hear from Lois?" she wants to know. I tell her that I never wrote to Lois. That I don't even know where she is.

"She's a tough one that Lois," Trent says, "a tough little lady but all the same she needed you to fasten on to. I used to watch you, the two of you, you trying to read and listen to music and her pretending to be doing both but just waiting her chance to get some thing out of you." Trent puts on her hat in front of the bit of mirror over the sink. "I could always read you like a book, Wright."

"I know," I say.

"I'd rather read you than her any day. I wonder who she's with and what she's doing. I've never written to any of them." Trent admires her hat, in the mirror, turning her head from one side to the other.

"Neither have I." I hold up the tea pot. "There's more tea." Trent sits down once more and pushes her cup towards me.

"Lovely tea," she sighs. "Lovely tea this. Black market tea eh? Remember Sister Bean?" I tell her yes I do remember Sister Bean. Trent changes her voice; "*Abbott Abrahams Ackerman Allwood . . .*" She manages to sound exactly like Sister Bean. "*Arrington and Attwood. Nurses Baker Barrington Beam Beamish Beckett Birch Bowman D Bowman E Broadhurst Brown Burchall . . .* How could we forget?" Trent resumes her ordinary voice and tells me that on the day after I left, when Sister Bean called the nurses' register, no one answered for me. "She called you twice," Trent says. She tells me that on the next morning at the end of the register Sister Bean called her. She changes her voice.

"*Nurse Trent?*" Trent sounds exactly like Sister Bean.

"Yes Sister."

"*Nurse Trent. Matron's Office nine a.m.*" Trent tells me that she goes along to this nine a.m. Matron's office thing and Matron asks her straight out does she know where Nurse Wright is and Trent says no she doesn't know but perhaps Nurse Wright's mother would know and Matron says yes that is a possibility. Then Matron asks Trent if she would like to tell anything, in confidence of course, she might know about Nurse Wright. For example if Nurse Wright is in some sort of trouble. She cannot, she tells Trent, let one of her nurses go into some difficulty or trouble without offering help of some sort. Trent doesn't know what to say and then blurts out that she thinks Nurse Wright might be going to have a baby. "Matron," Trent tells me, "doesn't bat an eye-lid. She just sits at her desk with that great calm she always has." Trent goes on to say that Matron tells her that it is a pity about a baby at this stage; later on would have been more appropriate because, Matron says, because she is sure Nurse Wright would have been in line for the Gold Medal.

And then, Trent tells me, Matron simply said she would be grateful if she, Trent, would come straight to her if she heard anything.

"So there you are, Wright," Trent says, "that gives you a picture of how Matron really is and what you might have been! Such a quiet little thing you are." Trent turns to Helena who has come to stand close to Trent's chair. "I'll have to be getting along now," Trent says to me. I nod and turn away, my eyes suddenly full of tears.

"You'll have to get away to some place," Trent says, "where people read and talk and where there's music—I mean, Wright, have you read any good books lately?" We both have to laugh at this. Then Trent tells me seriously, "Seriously Wright," she says, "you'll have to get Helena to other children. She needs company. I've never in my life seen such a quiet and, pardon my saying this, such a quaint three-year-old. I suppose you forget to speak to her. And here she is tucked away in a corner of this old-fashioned and, pardon me again, none too clean kitchen while you work yourself to death. I just know you, Wright! But you've got to think of her."

"Surely it's not that bad," I try to smile at Trent. "Oh, the tea." I jump up quickly to make the little package. "You will come again, won't you?" I have to ask Trent. But she shrugs.

"Don't know," she says. "I'm off to London in a couple of days." And she tells me that she's been offered an appointment in the London shop. "I don't know if I'll ever be back here," she says.

"Let's write then, shall we? Please do let's write."

"Yes, we'll write," Trent says. She's pulling on her black gloves, smoothing the fingers, one by one. "Wright," she says, "you must pick up your life after letting that rotten man and his wife ruin it, because ruin it they did. You must get back into what you are meant to do, Wright, I mean this. I really do mean this, Wright."

"Trent. I know you do, Trent."

I mean, I can't write to Trent and ask her who she married and what did he die of. Was it an illness, an accident, a suicide, or was he murdered? How can one person ask these questions of another person? Does Trent have any in-laws? I can't ask her this either. What are the in-laws like, I would like to know; and is there a sister-in-law she can be fond of. She did not say anything at all about any of this.

I have an address for her in London. As soon as she left, because I missed her so much I thought I would start a letter to her. I thought I would start a letter straight away to try to keep hold of her but I have no idea what to write. I am not able to imagine her life at all and how it will be in London. I feel I want to be near her and writing to her would bring her close but I have nothing to say.

The afternoon is going by slowly. I seem to have forgotten the things I would ordinarily be doing to keep ahead with the work. The mothers all brought their own tea cups to the kitchen. Back upstairs they are washing themselves and changing their babies in readiness to sit together, up there, in "the Rose Garden," to feed their babies. I can hear them talking and laughing together admiring and praising, being modest and proud at the same time.

Mothers during lying in seem to like to describe their husbands and their clothes in great detail. One of them hides in the bathroom till her husband has gone to sleep because she gets worn out with his passion. Another describes a little close-fitting hat she has, entirely made of the most beautiful feathers from the tails of Indian bantam roosters. This particular group of mothers has formed a little clique as schoolgirls do. They do not seem to need me though I have been very close to all of them in turn being the first, mostly to address the new mother, the new mother of the first born, as mother for the first time in her life. This is always a pleasure for me to be the one to say "mother" to someone who is mother for the first time and who, in those few minutes when I bring the baby, washed and fragrant and warm, to the bedside and into her arms, suddenly realizes who she now is. I have done this for all the six mothers here at present and because of this have special feelings towards them but I have to understand this afternoon, after Trent's visit, that these feelings do not exist the other way round.

Mostly the mothers in the Hilda Street Wentworth ignore Helena. If they do notice her it is when she has a cold and they are fearful like Daddy or Mummy Doctor might be that someone with a cold is sure to pass it on. It's possible that Lady Poynter might have been an exception.

This afternoon I do feel left out. I wish I could have gone for a little walk to the bus stop with Trent or even to the station to see her off. Helena would have liked that. Sister Russell is "on call" in case of some emergency but my going to the station because I feel like it is hardly reason enough to telephone for her to come.

Trent was here in the kitchen with me and the next minute she was gone. That is how it seems now.

Trent's visit brings back all sorts of things from an earlier time. Strangely not from the weeks and days leading up to the evening of the day when I packed and left. Seeing Trent again I am reminded more of my arrival, with Ferguson, at the hospital, the smell of the cold enamel tea pots in the nurses' dining room, the signing for keys to our rooms and then being shown how to make up the white caps, damping the stiff tapes with a wet toothbrush so that they would draw through the starch making the neat pleats at the back. Ferguson's first question, on arrival, was to ask when we would have a day off. The question was recorded on a note pad in Matron's office but no answer was given.

And then, up in our rooms, there were the black-out curtains, hanging permanently but looped up during the day letting the sad sunlight of the late afternoon lie in pale shafts across the bare floor boards. My school trunk, already in my room unroped and unlocked, waiting to be unpacked was a betrayal. The wildflowers gathered from the fields near school, pressed and labeled in exercise books, spilled across the floor as I searched for the special buttons for the uniform. All round me were these reminders of other times, the saxifrage, campion, vetch, violet, buttercup, King cup, cowslip, coltsfoot, wood anemone, shepherd's purse, lady's slipper, jack-in-the-pulpit, bryony, and the pretty celandine.

... I saw Lois first not in uniform but in a tartan dress. The material was shabby as if she did not have many clothes and always wore this dress. And once, quite soon after our first meeting, when I sat behind her during a lecture I saw the soft little curl at the back of her neck and the sideways droop of her head when she wrote some notes. This remembered Lois is not the same Lois I came to know later. The first time of seeing a place or a person can hardly ever be recaptured. This is the way of all friendship. The deeper and more intimate the more painful the discovery. Can I write that to Trent?

I can't write in a letter to Trent that we are both lonely. She has just told me that. Helena is a quiet child. I *know* she is quiet. I am not alone because I have her but I know how really lonely it is to be alone with your child. I look at Helena who is standing waiting with a ball. Something about my look upsets her and she starts to cry. When she cries her voice is hoarse as if she spends her life crying. I see her mouth go square and the tears seem to splash out of her eyes. She drops the ball and wrings her hands. I know I ought to gather her up and hold her on my lap and read to her and then go out into the garden to play ball with her. I sit at the table as if I am unable to move. I watch her crying. She stands by the kitchen door crying and crying and still I sit at the table, too miserable to move. Gradually the crying changes to a whimpering. She is no longer looking across at me.

Life, having come suddenly to a standstill because of a single remark which, cutting deep beneath the skin causing an unbelievable unexpected hurt, has to go on, has to go on with an equal change of pace, equal that is to the abruptness of the standstill. I, who never once in my thoughts felt need of harshness towards Dr. Metcalf and Magda, have now to soften for myself somehow the abrasive judgement with which I am left.

As I continue to watch Helena it seems as if she is wringing a whole world of sorrow through her small fingers without knowing at all the reason.

GAMIN

"Suits you," Sister Peters says.

"D'you think so? Really?"

"Yes," she says, "I wouldn't say so if I didn't think so."

I keep putting my hand up to feel my hair, the freedom of my hair, to feel with my fingers the strangeness of the short hair all round my head. Every time I pass the landing mirror, at the top of the stairs, I take a quick look at this different person who is me.

"It's the urchin," I tell Sister Peters.

"The whatter whatter?" She has both hands in the pastry bowl and I am peeling potatoes.

"The urchin," I say, "it's cut with a razor, a cut throat, not a safety, and the hairdresser's a man!"

"Good heavens!" Sister Peters says. "I bet it cost a lot."

"It did. The man, the hairdresser, called it gamin. He even sounded French."

"He never!"

"Yes, he did. And my hair lying all round the chair. You know, on the floor, seemed not to be mine, seemed as if it had belonged to someone else. For one thing it looked green."

"I suppose that was the artificial light."

"Yes, that would be it."

"Anyhow it suits you, it really does."

"Really?"

"Yes, I've told you."

I wear my linen dress, which is really my best, and I polish my school shoes, and I answer an advertisement in a magazine. A better quality magazine one of the mothers upstairs has. I apply for a post, not a position, in a progressive boarding school.

I leave Helena with my mother for a whole day and go to see the school and the headmistress and the glass cabinets filled with ceramics and pottery and other art works done by students. Through half-open doors I see little beds bright with colored blankets (the children bring their own), pianos in at least three different places, a harp in the headmistress's own room, and, in the dining hall, hand-hewn refectory tables and benches. The staff sitting room is hung with paintings, and someone called Tanya is at work on a mural, mainly nudes for which she is apparently well known, in the hall. All these things beckon me into another world.

Josepha, I am told, is to be my assistant. She is from Switzerland. Though she speaks English she does not say anything when we shake hands. The headmistress is called Patch by everyone. Myles, the Deputy Principal, is out somewhere with the dogs. And Frederick, another member of the school staff, is writing poetry and not to be disturbed.

I am shown the kitchens and the slow-combustion stove. Patch walks with me a little in the grounds of the school and asks me how soon I can come.

"Almost at once," I tell her. "Splendid," she says, "splendid."

On the way down to the main road I slip in the mud oozing from a large manhole at the top of the field path which is a short cut. I suppose the drains of the school are there. Drains have be somewhere. I wait at the edge of the cornfields for the bus to London and my train.

The next day at the Hilda Street Wentworth I feel I must leave for the school as soon as possible. I start at once to stuff my life back into my school trunk. And, all the time, I run my fingers through the freedom of my short hair. The urchin cut.

The Peters do not try to persuade me to stay. They tell me they really like my hair. When I describe the school to them they listen and nod with approval.

"I'll be buried in the country," I tell them, "and Helena will run wild with other children of her own age." I like the phrases "buried in the country" and "run wild." I imagine Helena laughing, rolling in the grass, and rosy with the fresh air. The phrases, the little phrases, suggest an entirely new life. I use the phrases repeatedly to Sister Peters and to Mr. Peters, to the lying-in mothers upstairs, to Sister Russell and Dr. McCabe, and, at home when I fetch Helena, to my own mother who says to me to leave Helena with her and to try the school on my own first to see what it is like. "She can run wild here," she says, "in the garden." And she says that she will take Helena to a dancing class in town. "How much was your hair cut?" my mother wants to know. She rummages in her handbag. "You could have had a nice perm," she says. "My Mrs. Crossley would have done a nice perm for you." My mother goes to this hairdresser once a week for a shampoo and set. Sometimes she has a henna rinse as well.

"I like my hair like this," I tell my mother and I take the pound note she holds out to me.

"Vera. Leave Helena here with us," my mother says.

"But it's for her that I'm going to the school. I'm doing this for her." I tell my mother that it's a good school. "Progressive," I say. "I'm to be Matron there. All the children have their own face flannels. They all have their own little hooks in the bathroom."

I am afraid that something will happen to prevent my going, that someone will stop me from keeping Helena with me. I tell my mother again about the bathroom hooks. These hooks are the kind of thing she would like and approve of but she doesn't seem to hear. She keeps on saying I should not be taking Helena away. In the end I shout at her and she cries and I promise to come once more to visit her before I leave for the school. My father puts his boots on and comes with us to the station to see us off.

The visit from Trent was in the spring. It is a day in early summer, the middle of May when I have to leave the Hilda Street

Wentworth to go once more to see my mother. I am wishing I could go straight to the school. Helena is four years old. My mother wants her to come for her four-year-old birthday.

We are in the hall. Sister Peters gives me a post-office savings book which she has been keeping for Helena.

"It's not much," she says. "I just don't know where money goes in this house!" She started the book she tells me with the money the Wellingtons insisted on paying me after I sent back their cheque all scribbled over. They came, both the Wellingtons together, apparently to try to persuade me to go back to them.

"You were in bed very early that night," Sister Peters said. "We chatted a bit and then they said they owed you some money and would I give it to you. That was all there was to it." The bank book has ten pounds in it.

In Helena's hat there is a folded five pound note which I, thinking it is a bit of paper, almost throw away. It is from Mr. Peters. He has written his name with an indelible pencil on the back. He says that people do this with Bank of England five pound notes, and that I should put my name on it or else go straight to the bank.

I cry then and tell them I can't take their money and Sister Peters says that's the least of it.

"Four years," she says, "is four years." And how is she going to manage? How is she, she wants to know, can someone just let her know, how is she going to face each day without having Helena run up to her the way she always does? To say nothing of the Help she is going to have to do without. She had not meant to break down the way she has, she says, but there it is, she says, four years is four years. We are both crying, howling I suppose it is and, when the phone rings we don't hear it and Dr. McCabe who has, she says, just inserted a duckbilled speculum upstairs, has had to come running down to the hall leaving, she accuses us, the patient up there in the left lateral stuck with the duckbill . . .

"Imagine that!" Sister Peters says. "Just imagine, duckbill!"

"I can," I say. "Duckbill." We listen to Dr. McCabe's seriously gentle voice as she speaks on the phone.

"Someone's on the way in," Mr. Peters says. "Out of turn, early. Someone's early. Could be," he says, "our very own Lady P, maybe she's on her way now for a girl."

"Or another boy," Sister Peters says, "sure to be a boy."

"Could be you're getting out just in time," Mr. Peters says to me. "And another thing," he says, "take no notice of this, I mean take no notice of what I'm saying, if you don't want to. What I'm saying is—leave that trunk of yours with your mother, at your mother's place. Just take a case to that school where you're going."

"Whyever?" I laugh. Mr. Peters laughs too, but not his usual big laugh with his head back, it is a little laugh in his throat as if he's a bit nervous.

"Oh Hoob!" Sister Peters says, "don't be daft."

"I know I'm daft," Mr. Peters says, "but it's been my experience as it's best to be able to carry, at times, by hand. To be able to carry by hand is better than to have to rely on being sent on. Hand luggage see? Instead of luggage in advance or sent after by Goods."

"Yes Vera," Sister Peters says. "Hoob's got a point there."

"Thank you," I tell Mr. Peters, "thank you."

Fairfields

⚮

Perhaps one of the greatest difficulties is the piecing together of people and events. This is often a blending together of the present with the past. One remembered thing leads to another. Some match with an exquisite naturalness and others have first to be hunted and caught and then fitted.

"*No man putteth a piece of new cloth unto an old garment, for that which is put in to fill it up taketh from the garment, and the rent is made worse.* St. Matthew, chapter nine verse sixteen." My father is telling me that not only is there a present and a past, there are several aspects of the present and several layers of the past. My father, during one of our little walks in the rain, asks me if the children in the school have enough to eat. He thinks Helena is a little pale. Does she have enough sleep he asks me. Immediately I reassure him praising the diet of raw cabbage and lettuce and, at the same time, trying to convince myself. I tell him, laughing, that at the school we have the awful problem of preventing the mothers and fathers of the children from arriving at the school to visit, both, on the same day. The mothers and fathers, I tell him, can't bear each other. My father stands still, the rain running off his oilskin in little rivers. He seems, as he listens, to be studying the wet ground. We walk on and I have to understand, as if from his silence, that there is no father to come and see Helena. And, when I tell my father that most of the children come from what are called broken homes, that is they have no home to go to, it is suddenly clear, though my father says nothing of this, that my position with Helena is no better.

"Fix a time," my father said as soon as he arrived. "Fix a time" meaning the time when his visit should end. This is something he has always insisted upon, that the end of a visit should be decided at the beginning. He has always wanted to know in advance the date and time of departure. He is staying for one week. He tells me, he has always avoided, whenever possible, a damp bed. During our walks he never tries to persuade me to leave, to return with him when the time comes.

When I am busy, my father walks alone or in the vegetable gardens with Frederick, the one we call Frederick the Great, and discusses agricultural methods with him. Tanya tells me later when I come in from walking back with him to his hotel down on the main road, that Frederick has told her that he thinks my father is an old fool but harmless. Tanya is in the middle of one of her Frederick rows. She has been up to his solitary room over the stables to seduce him, she tells me, without success. Apparently they have both been telling each other that they are no good at their subjects, poetry (Frederick) and painting, dancing, singing, and the piano (Tanya). Tanya wants me to hate Frederick too so that she can enjoy her own hating more. All he can talk about, she says, is his mother. Imagine if you can, she says, imagine him with his underpants down round his ankles standing there shivering and crying. "What if Mother could see me now."

All he can talk about, Tanya says, is his mother.

My father has brought with him a small bag of things which, in my haste to escape from my mother's accusation, her anger, and her tears, I left behind. In the bag are some small toys including a little wooden hedgehog and a tiny doll in a pink basket. Helena is pleased to have them. He brings too one of my mother's cakes made with insufficient ingredients because of persisting post war shortages of sugar, butter, and raisins. She uses up their rations, he explains, making cakes for people in the street at home. He has with him, as well, all Gertrude's letters written to me when I was at the hospital, some before I knew the Metcalfs, but more after I stopped visiting her because, more and more, I was visiting the Metcalfs. The letters are just as I left them in a small brown paper bag.

"Your mother has been having a great clearing up," my father explains. He tells me his desk is now out in the shed and I try to imagine the varnished yellow roll-top open out there in the damp. My father's treasures in the place where, every year, the rats get at his seed potatoes.

⁓

It is perhaps my father's unexpected arrival which makes me understand that Fairfields is unbearable. And it is after his visit that I write to Ramsden asking for her help, though I do not realize this at the time. That is, I do not realize it while I am walking in the wet withered grass of autumn, with my father, during his short visit. Perhaps it is, too, because of the things he brings with him.

Dear Ramsden, I write late in the evening after he leaves, *Dear Ramsden, I have no way at all of getting away from this place. Please Ramsden can you come? Please?*

I have no idea where staff nurse Ramsden is. It is several years since she wrote saying that she was still nursing and inviting me to stay in her little flat. I have no idea how to address her now. She may not be nursing still. Instead of working quietly alone, preparing syringes and needles for penicillin, in the sterilizing room, she might be on a concert platform, somewhere, coming to the end of a complicated piano sonata, turning to smile at an audience who are unable to stop their applause. Perhaps Ramsden is traveling from one concert platform to the next.

Another thing brought by my father is the little book of poems written and copied by Ramsden. The cardboard cover is decorated with edelweiss and gentian, a circle of neat pen and ink flowers. The night she gave me the poems we were in the subterranean corridor of the hospital, each going in opposite directions. She, with indescribable tenderness in her eyes, told me not to read the poems just then as there was not time.

It was Ramsden who said once, in that quiet way she had, that love was infinite. That it was possible, if a person loved, to believe in the spiritual understanding of truths which were not fully understood intellectually. She said that the person you loved was not an end in itself, was not something you came to the end of but was the beginning of discoveries which could be made because of loving someone. I have to understand now when it is too late that Gertrude, though she did not use the same language as Ramsden, was, in her own way, saying the same thing.

I do not remember seeing my father in shoes. He always wore boots. Ordinary black boots with long laces which he wound round the ankles before tying them. He walked firmly in the boots. At night sparks flew across the cobbles. He explained then that this was because of the metal tips. Heels and toes, he said. The metal, he said, prevented them from wearing out too quickly. At home, in his chair beside the hearth, he took off his boots and studied the soles before placing them carefully beside his chair. This intense silent examination was never explained.

"I'll put my boots on. Wait, I'll get my boots," my father would say at the last minute. "I'll come to the station with you." My father was always meeting a train or going to the station to see someone off.

It is cold and wet, the week my father comes to Fairfields to visit Helena and me. He seems quiet and sad and is, of course, out of place. Helena, who does not know him really, is shy. We walk together in the long wet grass in the rain, Helena trying to hide under my coat.

It has been clear to me from my first few days in the school that nothing has been added from students' work to the exhibits in the front hall for at least thirty years, so I do not spend time showing these to my father.

I concentrate on the gardens and grounds of the old house which, in spite of my unhappiness, I try to think of as special. I have had to learn during the summer that the cascades of roses and the beech trees, with their smooth trunks and nutty fragrance, and the meadows, deep with pink-tipped summer grasses sprinkled with the delicate blue and yellow of harebells and buttercups, cannot alter a mistake and that it is not possible to be lifted from sorrow by pretty surroundings. Sadness is enhanced by the sweet breath of summer fields and the sound of the cuckoo calling.

In this place all that I wished for, this being buried in the country and Helena running wild and happy with other children, is not what I thought it would be.

My father takes off his wet boots in the school playroom and examines them before putting them beside his chair. I fetch some of the older girls to talk to him. He wriggles his toes in his socks to amuse Helena. She seems frightened of his stockinged feet. He is surprised when Helena screams and screams and tries to hide from him. I feel irritated with Helena for being stupid when he is being gentle and kind. I tell her that her grandpa has come a long way to visit but her crying drowns my voice. She goes on crying. I leave her and warm fresh socks for my father.

My father is staying in a small hotel on the main road not far from our field path. He says the room as well as the bed might be damp. When we walk we talk uneasily because of this. The field path is steep and slippery with mud, the bottom part through the cornfields is easier.

I have seen the corn growing from its first frail stalks to its green softness and on to its waving golden ripeness, red splashed with poppies. Now the corn on both sides of the field path has been cut and the sturdy stubble, my father thinks, will survive the cold.

Patch invites my father to have meals with the staff during his visit. She makes a few remarks to which my father replies with a sincerity which seems to expose Patch's position as vulnerable with a doubtful suitability to be headmistress of the school even though it is her own. This is something he would never do on purpose. He offers his replies from unshakeable convictions, attitudes and standards. He sits at the refectory table, on a bench, and eats the brown bread and raw cabbage. He sits next to Olive Morris who tries to talk brightly to him when he admires her four children who are in the school. He has already seen her children gathered at the partly open door of the music room watching the dancing class in which, in Myles's words, staff offspring are not to be included. Tanya was conducting the class, pounding the piano and counting aloud for the dance. Tanya, because my father was present, had quickly drawn Helena into the class. Helena, previously uninvited, was unaccustomed but held up her little skirt, her fingers grasping the hem too tightly on either side. She skipped bravely to and fro, a little dance of her own, which had nothing of the rhythm and the movement required by the music. I had to turn away from the eager strained expression on Helena's white face. Without wanting to I had to see her small knuckles whiten.

At table, Olive Morris is trying to explain to my father, without actually giving the reason, why her four children did not dance during the morning. Because Olive Morris's husband was taken away to prison, in front of all of us, she is ignored in the school. Financially ignored, as well. Because she has four children here with her she is worked to death. I have not had a chance to tell my father this. As I watch Olive courageously talking in front of Patch I have to remember that I have only been paid once during the months I have been in the school and that was not a full payment, it was just "something on account."

Myles says nothing during the meal. When my father admires the two enormous dogs which accompany her, like hunting companions, she continues to be silent except for the smallest murmur one person can give another when obliged to acknowledge a compliment.

"Tanya," I say quickly, catching up with her as we are leaving the dining room, and while my father lingers to reply to Olive.

"Tanya, perhaps you could, for a little while avoid, for your mural, some of the subjects, I mean, er . . ."

"But of course Darling!" Tanya screams, "I'm painting fruit and sunsets at present and I promise, as far as my sexual habits are concerned, and those of the headmistress and her illustrious paramour," she jerks her head towards Myles who is by the long windows, "my lips are forever sealed."

Josepha (as it turns out, I am *her* assistant) is too busy to notice my father, though when he speaks to her slowly and carefully in German she smiles and answers him. She gives a little laugh and looks pleased for a moment and then hurries off to the pantry, where she always spends a lot of time banging the girls' dresses with a scorching hot iron.

Tanya's piano playing is terrible, everyone says so but, until this morning when Helena was allowed in the class, I have tried to hear her play as often as I could. There is no wireless here. At the Hilda Street Wentworth there was a wireless. It was on for the news and for the football pools and then switched off. Sometimes on my walks, then, I would pass a house and, hearing music from a partly open window, I would pause to listen.

I am hungry for music. I thought before I came to Fairfields that there would be music here. The harp in Patch's room has no real strings. Most days when Tanya is playing the piano for the dancing class I hang on to every crashing false note and, to be near, clean the windows in the hall.

"All that cleaning," Tanya says to me, when she comes out," all that cleaning, you're just guilt ridden, trying to get the guilt out."

I feel I have to finish the windows though, when I think about it, no one has asked me to clean anything. No one tells me to do anything. Josepha seems pleased if I am slow. She races ahead bathing the children or dressing them before I know what is to be done. Her only communication is her scowl.

Tanya says all kinds of things just when she feels like saying them. She does not say them in front of my father. I am in a curious state of almost telling him the things Tanya has already told me, as if I should tell him, but carefully, paraphrasing everything. It isn't as if he would not understand. He is shy and reticent, Tanya notices this, she says he seems to consider every word before he speaks. He is not used, she says, to people like her who rip off all their clothes if they feel like it and make remarks without weighing the consequences.

Josepha, Tanya told me one night, is at her zenith of sexuality when scrubbing floors and walls. "Gives her as good as an orgasm," she says. And, did I know, she went on that night, that Josepha makes Rudi sleep on the floor with only an old army blanket over him. "On the bare boards, mind you, while she's up on the bed all heaped up with blankets and beautiful Swiss cotton sheets. You should see the sheets," Tanya said. "Embroidered, pure white on pure white and well laundered, not our filthy old wash house here, but a proper laundry. Spends a fortune on laundry that one. Boy! Has that gurl got problems!" Tanya's attempt at an American accent makes us both smile. I said that I thought Josepha and Rudi were married. Tanya explained that Josepha's family won't allow the marriage. "Every time she gets a letter from her mother she scrapes another layer of paint off the wall. She's here," Tanya said, "because she can't have Rudi any other way. She can have him here and no word said. Not to her face anyway." Josepha and Rudi have moved rooms several times, Tanya explained. "Chasing an orgasm," Tanya said. "Patch, the mean old bugger, is pleased, though she'd be the last to say so, because they're doing up the rooms, bit by bit, that new distemper in your room is because Josepha thought bright yellow would be the color to make her come. They were in there less than a week. Didn't give themselves a chance did they."

Sister Bean always said that if a patient lay with his hands up behind his head it meant he was not going to sleep. It is the position, she always said, adopted by a person who does not expect to fall asleep.

It is when I find I am lying like this during the night that I get up quietly and carefully so that I do not wake Helena who has a small bed in my room. I tie my cardigan round the light and look

up the word orgasm in my *Pocket Oxford Dictionary.* The unfamiliar word is used often here at Fairfields. Orgasm. "Paroxysm
of desire or rage or other passion (Greek orgaō swell)."

I am seeing Fairfields and the people here as if my father's visit
has put them through a sieve. In my father's presence I see them differently. Perhaps a girl, living at home with her mother and father,
when she is married, begins to see her husband through her
mother's eyes and then experiences her mother's distaste as if it is
her own. Certainly a fault, like scattering bread crumbs on the carpet during meals, could be magnified in this way. Other faults, more
intimate, could become distorted making married life impossible.

My father, in his innocent visit, is removing all hope of a
desirable new way of living. I think of him in the cold bed at the
hotel down on the main road and hope that he is asleep.

Gertrude's letters have a strange power. When I look at the
folded sheets of rough paper covered with her sloping black
handwriting I know that, while reading them over again, I can
lose sight of immediate surroundings and be back once more
in her small living room, where the window, with its low sill,
looks out on to the slope of grass going straight up towards the
top of her field, a place where the sky seems to rest low and close
on the horizon. I can't re-read, now in the night at Fairfields,
these letters, because of the incredible loneliness and sense of
desolation which comes over me when I have to remember that
Gertrude is no longer alive. These feelings will not be comforted
not even by knowing that my kind father will be walking up to
the school, from his hotel, first thing in the morning.

If I think now about Gertrude I seem to see her looking westward towards the setting sun, the grass of the field to the side of her
sloping up in shadow, a deep, darker green heralding night fall. I
remember too the little round hill and the spinney and the road
climbing up, in summer, through the cow parsley and the purple
willow herb. And, in winter, the road narrow with the snow drifted
up into the hedgerows. I can think about Gertrude until I am held
in the magic palm of memory and I can feel sure that her place,
Gertrude's Place, is only round the corner from where I am. That

I have only to step outside and walk the smallest distance, turn a corner, and I shall be at the foot of the path, trodden through the long grass, leading to her door and on to the poultry speckled field with Gertrude, herself, sitting at her open door, as she so often sat, a partly plucked fowl across her apron and her face turned towards me, smiling. It is only then, in this point of remembering, that I can disregard the great distance in time and place and event and, in this forgetting, take the few steps which are needed and, putting out my hand to reach her hand, my whole self to receive the blessing of the welcome she never failed to give.

It is the cardigan scorching round the electric light shade which reminds me where I am. The ugly smell of scorching wool. I pull it down and turn off the light. From across the passage I can hear, muffled through the closed doors, the endless monotonous conversation in another language as Josepha and Rudi try to come to some sort of reconciliation. From further away there is the sound of a bath being filled. I have come to know that Tanya uses up the hot water during the night after one of her failed suicides.

It is like being on the edge of a precipice of falling crumbling sand, the precipice of the bad dream during a time of illness and high fever. Fairfields is not at all the place I thought it would be. I can't go home with my father however much I might want to. I always want to leave as soon as I am there. I can't stay at Fairfields either.

I will go with my father to the station when the time comes for him to leave. After he has gone I will re-read Gertrude's letters and I will write to staff nurse Ramsden and ask her to help me. But first the station with my father . . .

DISORDER AND EARLY SORROW

My father often arrived when it was raining. There are times now when I seem to hear his voice calling for a towel. He disliked having a wet head. Sometimes he kept the towel over his head in order, he said, to avoid a draught. Being in a draught was something he disliked too—perhaps dislike is too strong a word, perhaps it is better to say he avoided draughts, both for himself and other people. When he came in calling for a towel he always asked, as well, for a newspaper for his wet boots. Often it seemed that his ancient overcoat hung dripping in the kitchen without any possibility of being dry again.

My father's picnic at school is not easy partly because of the war and partly because of the rain. It rains all that day in autumn when he comes one Sunday, unheralded, to school. It is a surprise for me to see him standing amazed beside his motor bike and sidecar in the street outside the school. His amazement is over a threepenny bit on the pillion seat of the motor bike. He explains that he stopped for petrol about four miles from the school at a village. He says that the threepenny bit was the change. His ride, he says, must have been very smooth. He shakes his head marveling at the smoothness. He takes up the tiny coin to examine it and then puts it down once more on the cushion of the pillion. He says to ask my friends out to a picnic. "Get permission," he says, "we'll have a picnic."

"But it's raining," I say.

"It won't be much," he glances at the sky. This has always been his attitude towards rain, the fact that it will not be much and what there is will do good.

"It's doing good," he says looking with approval at the dripping beeches and at the puddles in the village street.

I invite Helen Ferguson and Amy, and I include Bulge who is back at school after her appendix holiday. I have to repay the present her mother gave me when I was ill I tell Helen Ferguson when she asks, "Why on earth do you have to invite Muriel?" For a moment I can't think who Muriel is because of always calling her Bulge to myself. She does bulge I insist, to myself in my own thoughts, everywhere. Her tunic pleats, her stomach, her behind, and even her eyes, everything about Bulge bulges. In my secret game of comparisons Bulge is far worse than I am in every respect. I almost explain this quickly to Helen Ferguson but my father is saying two can ride in the sidecar and two can walk and he will drive so far and turn and come back to pick up the two walking ones while the dropped two will walk on. "A sort of relay," he says.

"You see," I say to Helen Ferguson quickly, "her mother brought me *Treacle Wins Through* when I was ill that time. It's a boarding-school story, a lovely book—well, not all that good really. I must force myself to include her."

"Well then," Helen Ferguson says, "don't speak to her then. Let her come but no one speaks to her. Right?"

"Right," I say, not explaining what I now know about Bulge, that her father died being a missionary, and that Bulge has told me that people find fault with missionaries, blaming them for everything that has gone wrong, without pointing out the good things they do. Even Albert Schweitzer, Bulge has told me, people complain about him in spite of his hospital in the primeval forest. I let myself think for a moment of Bulge's mother and her gentleman friend who is so kind and polite to Bulge and even to me. And I do not say how thrilling and wonderful the *Treacle* story is and how pleased I am to have it.

Helen and Amy ride first and I walk in the rain with Bulge. Bulge starts off talking a bit. She tells me about a doll she had once and how she left this doll in the long grass by a bench in the park and then, remembering the doll in the night, she cried. And when she went, with her mother, the next day to look for it, it was gone. Bulge gives a shy little laugh as if to say she was silly to have cried like that over a doll. When she laughs she turns towards me and I see her cheeks bulge round while she laughs. I want to ask if she found her doll later, and what other dolls did she have, and what were their little clothes like. But, of course, not speaking I turn towards the hedges, as we walk, as if looking for natural history things. I look into the hedges closely as if knowing where tiny birds' nests would be. I make my close watching of the hedges seem as if it is some kind of hedgerow research, as if I am noting how many alders are in the hedge and how often an elm rises from the skirts of hawthorn and elderberry.

Bulge walks in silence then. Our feet splash on the wet road. It is partly because of Bulge telling about her doll and partly, I think, because of hearing my father's voice, after not hearing it for a long time, that I can't help thinking about Tulip. My arms are suddenly empty. This is one of the worst things about being at school.

I have a great longing to be at home holding Tulip, changing her clothes and rocking her in my arms and hearing my father's voice, downstairs, talking to my mother, soothing her at intervals in her misunderstandings.

I keep going to the pram to put my hand on the broken head. It's under a cloth. Every time I put my hand on it I can feel the three broken pieces move. They grate on each other badly.

Tulip, I said, don't, do not, sit there. You will fall backwards in the hearth and you know perfectly well what will happen. Of course she doesn't listen and she does fall and her head breaks in three places. She looks at me with her worried eyes. Tulip, I say, I did warn you. I'll put you in the shawl like this, all round your head, and I'll wheel you about in the pram. I'll leave you in the sun by the apple tree and I'll sit in the tree and watch over you. I'll spit on anyone who comes.

No one comes. I'm thinking about Tulip's solid little feet. I mean, she came without toes. I loved her little feet straight away. You have sweet little feet I said to her. Straight away, I said this. Marigold came with Tulip. Sometimes Marigold and Tulip whisper. We are a large family and desperately poor. Fatima, Fatty for short, is my baby in long clothes. Margaret and Patsy have hair which can be brushed and combed. Lovely long, soft, silky hair with ribbons. Margaret is fair and Patsy is a brunette. Margaret looks quite nice really with her new short bob. Her hair is in an envelope marked Margaret's First Haircut and the date.

What do you mean, first hair cut? Jap asks. How will she ever have a second hair cut? he asks. Jap is Japanese and is called Jap.

When her hair grows again, I say. He is older than the others. I am surprised at his silly question and tell him so. I tell him that I'm busy, that I have to fold the clothes. I go to the pram again and feel Tulip's head. In spite of the shawl and having the pram to herself she is no better. I can feel that the pieces of head are still not joined up.

Jap, I ask him, how many flowers did you sell today?

One daffodil and one snowdrop and that's only, he says. He sinks down in an exhausted little heap. Why Jap, I say, you're wet through. I undress him quickly and put him to bed next to Patsy. She was out in the rain all night and her clothes have to be put to dry too. I can hear Patsy, in bed, telling Jap that she is going to earn money for us by being a prostitute. She feels, she says, that she must save the family somehow. I don't catch Jap's answer. Perhaps he is begging her not to take this terrible step.

The next morning, unable to stop my tears, I place Patsy on the street corner. First she persuades me to cut the neck of her dress really low. It looks daring and her pink chest shows. She insists on lipstick too. She has borrowed Margaret's hair ribbons and her button shoes and little white socks. Her own are still wet. She stands there all day with her little handbag firmly on her round arm. From the apple tree I can see her leaning against the lamp-post. And I can see her babyish legs wide apart to help keep her balance. I can see her rounded cheeks and the expression in her eyes. She has always had rather startled eyes. I cry silently to myself because of her determination and courage. A few people pass but no one stops to take up her offer. Jap says he'll sell his flowers near her to attract customers. I put him and his little wicker basket of paper flowers in the gutter close by and then I hide by the gate to watch. The street is very quiet. No one comes by.

I check Tulip. There is no change. If only her head could be whole again under the shawl! Perhaps a few drops of scent sprinkled like holy water...

Did you earn anything? I ask Patsy later but she is too tired to reply. As soon as she is undressed and put to bed she closes her eyes.

Jap, I ask him, how much money did she make? I jerk my head towards Patsy who is lying very still in bed.

None, Jap says. Your father came by on his bicycle just as I was sure a client was approaching. Your father got off his bicycle. He dismounted. Remember how he throws his leg backwards over the saddle? What is Patsy? It is Patsy, isn't it? What is Patsy doing out here? your father wanted to know. I told him, she is a prostitute. Was it her own idea? he wanted to know. Yes, I told him, it was her own idea. Your father, Jap says then, said he would give Patsy a ride home. He also, Jap adds, offered me a ride too.

Tulip is still wrapped in her shawl. I am nursing her. Fatima, my baby in long clothes, is soft all over except for her head. Fatima, I say, not in the hearth, do not sit in the hearth. Fatima has fallen backwards and broken her head. She folds up well in the music case and will go to the hospital. I am nursing Tulip. Perhaps if I rock her and sing to her her head will heal tomorrow . . .

Bulge is saying she can hear the motor bike coming back. Her voice in the quietness of the gentle steady rain is a shock. I almost explain to her about Tulip.

It does not stop raining. We have our picnic in the rain. My father shares out the tinned sardines and the bilberries and explains that he meant to buy some bread. The dark-brown plowed fields slope up on all sides towards the low sky. My father, in his slow careful way of speaking, talks to Bulge. He asks her questions about our science experiments, about the results obtained when burning magnesium in air, and he is pleased with her replies.

I am not able to really understand this but my father seems to actually like Bulge.

The hungry hedges lean over the dismal road.

HELENA'S TEARS

The Peters do not write letters. I mean I've seen Mr. Peters lick the point of his pencil to note down the name of a horse or an address where something is for sale, cheap. Neither Sister Peters nor Mr. Peters would think of writing a letter.

To begin with, at Fairfields, I write to them almost every night telling them about the school. It's because I miss them, not having them to talk to. I make the most of the wholemeal bread and the lettuce in my letters, and I describe the avenue of beech trees and the stateliness of the old house. I don't write about the children and how they quarrel and fight in the sandpit instead of making sand castles. And I don't tell them how tired I am, that on some afternoons I lie in the long grass trying to rest without falling asleep. I would like to tell the Peters things because I find I do not really understand why the children, who have a lovely field where they can pick flowers and play, never do play. They fight all the time over one little broken spade. I can't tell the Peters that Helena tries all the time to hide in my skirt, that she cries if she can't see me. And I can't tell them that I have never been paid, that there is no such thing as Matron of the school. And if I try to put into words that I want to return to the Hilda Street Wentworth a terrible sense of hopelessness comes over me. If I write that Patch walks about the school with a fresh loaf under her arm, picking off the crust and eating it, singing sinister remarks in a contralto voice, which I have discovered is the prelude to trouble, it all becomes more unbearable. To write these things, to dwell on them means that I would relive them and in each reliving find them worse. I long for the safety and the happiness of the Hilda Street Wentworth. After my first few letters I do not write to the Peters any more. By the time my father comes on his visit I have no idea how either of the Peters are and whether the Hilda Street Wentworth is still as it was when I left. In my mind I am still dwelling in the picture stopped, in a sense, as it was while I was there, cheerful and busy, urging patients during delivery, running deep hot water for the first baths the new mothers are permitted to take and hurriedly eating big meals in the Peters' kitchen, laughing with Sister Peters about things like the home-made stirrups and the duckbilled speculum.

Some of the children have an infection and I have to get up in the night to clean the lavatory.

The upstairs lavatory of the Hilda Street Wentworth is old and decorated, like the heavy china chamberpots and bed-pans, with roses and green leaves and embroidered with a whole world of cracks and shadows, the rivers and foliage of a strange country mapped under water. The Fairfields lavatory has the same stained-glass door as that of the Hilda Street Wentworth. I reflect that, as winter comes, the upstairs and the outside lava-tories at Fairfields will need candles inside inverted flower pots to prevent the pipes from freezing. In the night, when I think of the winter and how cold and miserable it will be here at Fairfields, I can't imagine how I shall be able to stay here. During the long night when I think, too, of Olive Morris and her four children and their dreary future in the school, I can see that my own future, and Helena's, will not be any better.

The world is so big, my father says when I go with Helena to see him off at the station. But even, so he tells me, we all, when we look up, are seeing the same moon. We must remember, he says, to look at his moon.

I stand on the platform until his train is out of sight and am, for once, in the place, that of seeing off a train, in which he usu-ally is.

Helena holds my hand and, as we turn to leave the station, I see that tears are overflowing from her eyes. Instead of whimp-ering or howling aloud as a child does, she is crying quietly to herself as a grown-up person might cry. The tears are welling up and running over her cheeks as if they will never stop. When she looks up at me I see my own sorrow looking back at me. I see now, all in one moment, that in her reticence, her stupid shyness, she really wanted to be near her grandfather. She must have needed his presence and liked it. She must have liked to hear his voice and she must have been pleased to have his kind hand holding hers. I know from memories returning and returning during the nights when I could not sleep that it is the sound of his voice which recalls and comforts. It is not hard for me to long for the sound of his voice and for other voices which are no longer heard.

"Come along," I say to Helena. "I'll buy you a cake."

In the station buffet there are cakes under a glass bell jar. They are yellow.

We wait for the bus back to the cornfields and Helena tries to eat the cake. The dry crumbs stick to her cheeks.

Journey

✖

It's only you I'm concerned about. I am most con-
cerned when I see your Happiness in life threatened. I
want you entirely surrounded by love. I want every
cloud lifted from your life. Things are not ever as easy
as just wanting. Wanting all that for you has not given
it. I only now regret that I am sure I forfitted your con-
fidence and drove you off in a vain endeavor and was
3 to 6 months too late. I'm thinking you won't under-
stand what I've just written. It's only another way of
saying I expect you regretted ever confiding in me—I
want you to know you will always be very wel-
come . . . I am loving you and thinking about you every
hour. My best love to you always . . .

Gertrude's letters are written in strong black handwriting on
the paper she used for the fowls, for wrapping up the dressed
fowls which she sold privately to people who would pay the price
she asked. "That old red fox has had a wing offer one of 'em tell
mother," she would say about a badly maimed boiler. "Tell her
as I'm sorry about the wicked fox." Gertrude neatened the dam-
aged fowls with her dressmaking scissors. She often supposed
the fox to be a vixen with cubs. But, in her opinion, this did not
excuse the fox's habit of raiding and killing beyond the need for
food. Some women, she said, were vixenish same as foxes.

After my father's visit to Fairfields, the night after seeing him
off on his train, I open the small brown paper bag and re-read
Gertrude's letters. I read all through her wisdom and her kind-

ness, her persuasion and her love. And while I am doing this, for a small space of time in the long unhappy night, it is as if she is still alive and waiting for me to come to her Place. And then I write my letter to Ramsden:

Dear Ramsden I have no way at all of getting away from this place. Please Ramsden can you come? Please?

But it is not possible to still be at Fairfields should my letter reach staff nurse Ramsden and should a reply come to me from her.

"Fortnitt? Fortnitt?" Patch says during her sinister pacings between tables, in one door and out of another. "Fortnitt? Deah? But you must go today, deah. There's a bus at the end of the field path at three o'clock. Do leave today, deah. What's all this? A Fortnitt?" She's tearing crusts off a loaf she has under one arm, she's tearing off the bread crust and stuffing it in her mouth. As she walks she is watched by the children who have only their lettuce leaves in front of them. They watch with hungry eyes.

I try to explain that I am thinking I should give two weeks' notice before I leave. A fortnight . . .

"Fortnitt! Fortnitt!" Patch sings in the contralto we all dread. "By all means do go today. There's a bus . . . By all means . . ." She exchanges a raising of the eyebrows with Miss Myles who is, just then, with her dogs, passing the open door.

The girl whose bed Helena and I have at the women's night shelter in London, this girl who is having a propelling pencil removed from her bladder, the woman in charge tells me, hasn't a coat. "She does not have a coat," she says. She has been watching while I try to force my winter coat, the one which has accompanied me since school, into the hopelessly bulging case.

Why not, the woman suggests, leave the coat for this girl who has nothing she can call her own, not even her baby. "Lorst her baby pore thing. The things these girls'll do to theirselves! The things they'll try! It'll sort of show your gratichood," she says, "for having the use of her bed so to speak." The woman takes my coat and folds it over the end of the bed.

"But I'll need my coat later," I start to say, "I'll be needing it quite soon." But she has made up her mind about the coat and who shall, in the future, have it. After all the girl is in hospital and hasn't got anything . . .

There are several advertisements in the magazine, *The Lady* I think it is, the outside cover is torn off. While I drink the cup of tea and eat the slice of bread and margarine supplied at the night shelter for breakfast, I read quickly down the positions advertised. Skipping the flower arrangings and the dressmakings I come to one where a live-in housekeeper is required, "one child no objection." It says to apply in writing. The address is Glasgow. It means a long journey. A journey which will use up all my money. There is no time to write a letter.

Fairfields, which was only yesterday, seems a long time ago. Waiting all those hours at the final stop for the Green Line bus from Hertford was the silliest thing I have ever done. The long evening moved slowly into the night of soft dusty warmth. A few people walked by on the pavement where the slabs were still warm with the trapped sun. All those people had places they were going to. How could I have expected Ramsden to come? I waited not knowing whether she had ever received my letter. In the letter I told her everything that had happened, about Helena, about my leaving home, about my loneliness. I sent my letter to the last address I had from Ramsden several years ago, the letter in which she said she was still nursing and that she had her own little flat where I would be welcome. I told her in my letter that I would I wait for her at the terminus of the Green Line.

When I think of Ramsden I remember her shy kind eyes and my own eyes fill with tears. I have to understand that she might be anywhere at this present time. Unreachable, perhaps playing the piano on concert platforms in towns up and down the country. A curious feeling of having been rescued comes over me when I think of the policeman who, after passing me several times in the street, brought me and the case and Helena, who was asleep on the case, to this women's shelter. I would not have known to come here myself.

Helena has eaten her breakfast slice. It is time to leave.

"You can have the book if you want it," the woman in charge of the night shelter says as she collects the two small towels she lent me.

"The book?"

"Yes, the book. You can have it."

"Oh yes, the magazine, thank you." I almost tell her I don't want it, that I have read it but realize, in time, that she is giving me a present. I tell her again, "Thank you."

It is time to go. For some reason it requires an effort to leave this place. It is a place I would never have come to and now I have to make myself leave. Perhaps it is the idea of safety, the shelter is very much a shelter when compared to the streets and the pavements. I must leave. My mind is made up. I have the address. I must take a chance.

When I think about Gertrude I remember how she tried to save me from what she thought of as a pitfall. When I think about her I have to remind myself that she is no longer there, within a short bicycle ride from my mother's house. Remembering this makes me feel alone and helpless in the compartment especially as the train is rushing now through landscape made familiar by the fields and hedgerows and the small patches of woodland similar to those surrounding my school and, a bit further on, as we race through the rapidly unfolding countryside, similar to the place where Gertrude lived.

If, after thinking about Gertrude, I think about my father and how he would not have understood the truth behind Olive Morris's attempt to hide the truth and, at the same time, give an explanation as to why her children were not in the dancing class, it is because, like Gertrude, he would never imagine for one minute that any child would ever be left out, excluded on purpose, from something so pertinent to childhood as a dancing class. Similarly Gertrude, when she tried, as she thought, to save me, could never have imagined for one minute that the fashionable Metcalfs, Dr. Metcalf and Magda, could not be persuaded to refrain from seeing me, to stop inviting me, to stop all that she thought was happening, through them, to me. She would willingly have braved what she called the grand house and the well off folk to rescue me without imagining for one minute what those well off folk, as she thought them to be, were really like. Gertrude had no idea of the lengths the people, who frequented Magda's parties, would go to in their elaborate jokes and methods of ridiculing someone. Their intentions were for amusement and not for hurting but, for someone like Gertrude, the hurt would be deep and lasting and never understood.

All at once I am remembering my father's pleasure in his school dinners. I went to his school once and watched, with my mother, as the ragged children went, in single file, up to my father who offered the thick slices of bread for them to eat, soaked with the gravy, so that it would not be left on the plates wasted. It is all I can do not to leave the train now at the all too well-known station where he has so often seen me off on a journey or come to meet me on arrival. The train, hissing and steaming, stays here for some time. I lean out looking eagerly up and down the long platform as if it could be possible that he, sensing my travelings, could be there now to run alongside as the train starts to move again, slowly at first and then gathering speed resuming the journey, pushing, in his usual way, a magazine and a comic, a last minute final gesture, through the window. I look with longing at the familiar station slipping by. I have never thought before what it would be like to be so near the place I have always thought of as home and not go there. I think with longing of that first half hour in the house with my mother and her delight to have Helena with her. This delight which turns so quickly to her disappointment and anger over me and then the way in which this is followed by her ability to reduce me to an unwilling rage and to tears.

Because Helena is so sure we should be getting off the train she starts crying; a terrible howling, as I pull her down on the seat beside me. She cries till she is sick and I have to try to clean her with the inadequate drips of water which have to be coaxed from the faulty tap in the lavatory.

Later when she sleeps, rocking against me with the motion of the climbing and then speeding train, I feel a great tenderness for her and I cover her small relaxed fingers with my hand. I reflect on chance. When I left the night shelter I took two chances. The big one, to make this journey and a quick small chance which was to lift, as I went by the end of the bed, my school winter coat and put it over my arm. In a sense I did give the coat when asked, or rather, told to. The night shelter woman happened to have her back to me as we passed along the narrow hall and out down the steps into the street.

In the hoped for peacefulness, enhanced by the presence of the ugly coat, rescued and curled loosely in the luggage rack, I try to rest while Helena sleeps, but the darkening afternoon threatens a storm. Driving rain and heavy banks of cloud accompany the journey towards an incredible loneliness and the mistake I might be making in traveling at such speed into the unknown.

Cabin Fever

❧

My father used to say that learning something was not really of any use unless it was fitted to some other thing which had been learned. Perhaps a better way of saying this is to say that facts should be linked and everything should then be applied to where it belongs in human life. This is true about fiction, he said then, fiction places people where they belong in society. There is no such thing he said as a dated novel. The novel set in a particular time gives a picture of that time with all the details of life as it was lived then. In any case he said human beings have not changed except outwardly in fashion where clothes and food are concerned and in the equipment they have learned to use. Love and hate and revenge, ambition, jealousy and grief are all as they have always been.

But back to facts. To know the population of a town or a country is not enough. Other things have to be included, how and where the people live, what they wear and what they eat, what their illnesses are, where their drinking water comes from, what they grow, what their houses are like, what their work is, what their hopes and ambitions are, and what they fear most in their lives; all these things are only a beginning.

⌐≈⌐

MY FATHER'S MOON

Over and above all this my father would always remind me that if I looked at the moon, wherever I was, I was seeing the same moon that he was looking at. "And because of this," he said, "you must know that I am not very far away. You must never feel lonely," he said. He said the moon would never be extinguished. Sometimes, he said, it was not possible to see the moon, but it was always there. He said he liked to think of it as his.

At the Georges

⮾

"How can you say that! How can you say a thing like that!"

"What d'you mean—like that? Like what?"

"Saying that on the phone. How can you say that? And another thing, don't take that tone with your own mother. What will . . ."

". . . people think? There's no one here to listen at present. What did I say then? What's the trouble?"

"How can you say 'it's his wife speaking.'"

"Well, I can hardly say, 'This is his mistress here' to the plumber, can I."

"You're not his wife. You're not married to him. How can you do this to your own mother!"

"I'm not doing anything to you."

"And another thing, you can't call her Rachel."

"Whyever not? It's a pretty name. I like it."

"No one calls a baby Rachel these days. No girl can have this name. Rachel was the Queen of the prostitutes."

"Don't be silly. That's not true, it's silly, a silly made up . . ."

"Im Kloster, they always said . . . In the convent they said . . ."

"You're not in the convent now. And *if* she's a girl she's Rachel. It's a Hebrew name and it means 'ewe' and is a symbol of innocence and gentleness. It's a pretty name."

"Anyway you're not his wife. He probably will never marry you. Whatever will people think?"

"At present everyone thinks we are married so there's nothing to worry about is there."

"And another thing, you know what men are like. You'll be

turned out of the house on to the streets with two children. The house isn't even partly in your name."

"We're going to put the house in our joint names. We're going to get married too. It's not that easy. We'll have to go somewhere else and have a special license and be married in the Registry Office . . ."

"What about your family and witnesses?"

"Oh for heaven's sake, blow family! This is just something that has to be done, and as privately as possible. We'll get a couple of witnesses off the street."

"Oh. How can you do this to me, your own mother! You're an adventuress! How could I have had a daughter like this."

At this point my eyes fill with tears as I imagine how my mother will start to cry with the deep disappointment she has with me. I shall feel sorry for her and try to comfort her. It is remembering the way her nose goes red when she is upset, I can't bear remembering this. Also she's sure to have in her lap a partly unwrapped parcel of the new little pink clothes she has made and brought for my new baby, for Rachel. She will have made the long journey and be tired. I persist. "Look," I say and my own voice, echoing aloud, alone, surprises me. "Look, you'll feel better later. You'll like him. You'll like everything. I promise you, he's going to marry me. We want to be married. We're going to have an au pair girl and I'm going to study to be a doctor like you always wanted me to. Everything's going to be all right. Look, if you like I'll study music too . . ."

My mother, when she comes, is sure to be uneasy and unhappy. It will be her first visit to this enormous house. Helena will be shy and not give her the welcome she hopes for and she will be meeting the Georges for the first time because, of course, they have never seen each other.

"I don't expect the sister is at all pleased," my mother starts again. "How old is she? Seventy-five, you said. *Seventy-five.* When she knows, *knowing* might well kill her. She might well have a stroke. You'll spend your life nursing her. And what about him? *Fifty-eight? He's older than I am.* Vera, how could you! *He's older than your father.* Vera, how can you! You'll spend the rest of your life nursing these two people and being an unmarried mother . . ."

These conversations of the future, like past conversations relived, circle round and round, voiceless, leading nowhere. While I am preparing vegetables, dicing carrots, turnips, and parsnips for a bland soup with pearl barley, I can see clearly my mother's tears on her soft cheeks; and her lap strewn with tiny garments, a small hand-knitted vest tied with ribbons, little knitted boots, some pink and some blue, to be on the safe side, something she calls a matinee jacket, white, because it might upset a baby boy to lie in his cradle dressed in pink, even if the pink is of the most delicate and dusty sort.

My mother has never really believed that Helena's father is not still around.

"Why can't the father, the father of your—what I mean is why can't he do something?"

"I've told you he's dead."

"How can you say that, he was on the phone—I could tell by your voice, that's who it was."

"He's dead. I've told you."

Round and round in my head the words leaving no room for other thoughts.

"I simply can't understand you. How could you with your education and your background breed like a rabbit – "

"You're always saying that, for years you've said it. I've told you, rabbits have six, I only one."

"How can you speak to me, your mother, like that."

"Oh shut up and remember this. I'm never coming back home. Never!"

The conversations, without my wanting them, return and return.

There are other things on my mind too. One of the troubles about doing work which requires very little calculating thought is that it leaves the mind free to suffer in its own inimitable way. While I am washing the stone flags in the kitchen or the mosaic of richly colored tiles in the porch between the stained glass of the front door and the outside storm doors which are unlocked and folded back on each side every morning, I try to think clearly and work out in a private internal discussion the best ways in which to follow a hoped for plan of action based on certain facts and promises.

Some of these things are hypothetical because, to start with, promises made by other people are not always honored and I am not altogether sure of certain facts.

"How could you have been so stupid, Vera," my mother's critical voice echoing, possibly echoing my own unrealized thought. "How could you, Vera, have been so stupid getting pregnant as soon as you arrive, practically the minute you arrive! The brother can easily declare his innocence and the sister will believe him and both will be certain you were already pregnant before you came to them." I must try to silence my mother's unwanted voice.

Early on, as soon as I arrived here, it was clear that I had to understand that my need for survival was great and if something fell into my lap, an illness for example, there was a moral profit to be gained by making use of this in spite of a desperate request for silence on the subject. During that night my argument, which was once more an internal one, was that I must, as in the past, make the best use of my knowledge, take what comes my way and make use of that. It seemed then that I could have the moral profit of acting in such a way that I would help someone and simultaneously benefit my own life and Helena's hugely.

"How can you propose to spend your life with someone you don't know at all and who is so much older. Sixty, Vera, how can you!" My mother's voice, breaking with indignation, in my head as it has always done all through the years. "This man, Vera, is older than Daddy. You'll spend your life, your whole life, nursing, and nursing a relative is not the same as nursing in hospital. Not at all."

My mother has not yet come here for a visit. She will be coming. She will be coming, not just in my imagination, but in reality. Not even the prospect of being unwelcome will stop her. She will come because she thinks she must come. She will try to take Helena home with her. She will come, uneasily.

Knowing the Georges as I am beginning to know them I don't think she will be unwelcome. For myself I don't seem able, in my mind, to get rid of my mother's thoughts, her voice or her tears. And there is no welcome, at present, for her in me.

Another conclusion I have come to is that it is almost impossible to get married once you are living in the same house and sleeping in the same bed with someone, even if the bed part is a secret. It is impossible, in certain circumstances, to announce to friends, relatives, colleagues, and shop assistants that a marriage is intended. There seems to be no way of dealing with this. The only reason why I have not given my mother words about this is because it will be beyond her thoughts. Up till now this particular difficulty has never occurred to me. My mother will have no idea about this problem.

"I'll slip into my negleege, pardon my deshabbee," Sister Peters used to say on the occasions when she relieved me during the night when I had been up with a fretful baby.

"Go back to bed, Vera," she would say. "I'll walk the floor for a bit with his Highness. You get back to bed and get some sleep."

When I hang out the washing here at the Georges I am reminded of the walled garden at the Hilda Street Wentworth. In the spring there, the pear blossom filled the sky, overflowing the boundary of the wall, cascading in streams of pure white like the dress and veil on a silent bride. There is a gnarled black tree in the Georges' garden. Perhaps it too is a pear tree waiting for a wedding dress.

Every day when I take in the washing, as the weather gets colder, it is damp still and smells of the soot-laden fog.

I would like to see Sister Peters and Mr. Peters. Perhaps I can make some jam here. It would be like being at the Hilda Street Wentworth, not that I want to be back there. Not at all. Just to see them for an hour or so, that's what I would like.

"And another thing Vera, sixty-two is a dangerous age for a man." My mother at my elbow again. If only she would leave me in peace. "Men of that age," she's persisting, "men of that age like to be congratulated on having an affair with a younger woman. But people shake their heads, you'll see, over the girl and her uncertain future. Sixty-four, Vera, is an age when men make fools of themselves. I shouldn't be at all surprised if his sister thinks he's making a fool of himself mark my words, Vera, *She* will have her revenge. An elder sister takes care of a younger brother. You'll see, she'll have her revenge."

I go upstairs, two at a time, in the empty house. Helena is outside sweeping the wet bricks of the wash house with a small broom we found out there.

"You're to come home with me Vera!" my mother follows even when I take the stairs three at a time. "You're to come home with me. I've come all the way to fetch you. If you won't come, at least let me take Helena. What's all this going to do to her? Have you thought about that? You never do think! I regret every day of my life that I gave you that book."

"What book? Whatever has a book to do with this?"

"That book about that sculptor woman, Elizabeth something or other, Elizabeth Ney, she had a baby in that book without being married. And now you'll be having a second baby and no husband. I should have thought your nursing training would have taught you . . ."

I'm pleased the house is empty this morning, I hurry on up to the bathroom, which is not the servant's bathroom. I go there all the same as quickly as I can. For some reason I feel dreadfully sick. I would so like to see Sister Peters just now even though I know she would remind me soon enough that the Nurses' Insurance Company make the four pounds maternity payment once only and it's not just because of being an unmarried mother.

"What about diseases, Vera?" I hear my mother still as I bring up all my breakfast, thankful to be in the bathroom and not on the stairs. "Surely they taught you about diseases in your training, Vera." I look at my reflection in the bathroom mirror and wipe the tears from my eyes.

"A man in his position can't suddenly change," my mother's voice, at my elbow, once more. "A man of his age, if he has never had children, is not used to babies and children. You'll see, Vera, it's one thing to have a housekeeper who has a child. He can smile at the child and drop coins in her shoes now and then, but you do see, Vera, don't you, you'll be in an impossible position. Oh Vera! think of Helena. How can you do this to her! And, another thing when he has a child of his own, this . . . this Rachel, he isn't going to want the older child. Helena will be unwanted. Oh Vera, let me take Helena home. Your Daddy and I can look after her. She's fond of us . . . Vera, you can't, you cannot let Helena be *unwanted*." I wipe the basin after washing my face.

"And Vera," my mother again, "Vera, I'm certain the sister, his sister, is not likely to suffer fools gladly. She will quite rightly be annoyed at her brother making a fool of himself, making fools of both of them. How will she be able to go out socially with everyone knowing her brother, a professor at the university, has been—well, seduced is the only word I can think of? This poor innocent man! That a daughter of mine should be such a person to do what you have done. I can't believe it . . ."

After I am sick again I cry. My mother will be coming here later on for a visit. I won't listen any more to what she's saying in my head. That is, if I can manage not to. But the stupid, the really stupid thing is that I want my mother. I want my mother as she was, delicately scented, her hands hovering above an earache and her shadow, twice its real size, moving across the ceiling in the candle light.

I suppose there are times in a person's life when there is an unexpected need for the mother.

I wipe my face once more on someone else's towel in the Georges' bathroom.

Every time my mother, in my head, mentions Mr. George's age he is two years older than he was. I mean he has aged six years in a few seconds. How can I know what his age really is?

FLOWERS

When I thank him for the flowers Mr. George says the greatest pleasure from flowers is in the sending of them. He says the sender has tremendous pleasure because of enjoying the thought of sending them in the first place. And then there is the thinking, he says, the thinking about going to the shop to choose them. Deciding which flowers, in all the wealth of flowers, he says, deciding which flowers and what sort of an arrangement is an extra pleasure especially when the shop assistant seems very interested and pleased with his choice. He says too that he thinks it is an extra pleasure, extra because it is so unexpected, to write the name of the person, who is to receive the flowers, on the little card provided by the shop. The little cards are all pretty, he says, and this makes it hard to know which one to have. He says he has never sent flowers to anyone before.

I have never had flowers sent to me before. I am alone with Helena in the house when they are delivered. When I see my name on the small envelope I am taken aback but recover quickly.

"Don't," I say to the delivery boy, "do not lean your bike up against the paint work." My heart is thumping. I take the flowers through to the wash house out the back and put them in a bucket.

SNOW

"I'd like to have a gas boiler and I'd like to be a doctor," I tell Mr. George when he asks me what I want most in the world. I tell him that his question does not strike me as being a naive question at all when he says he is sorry for asking such a naive question.

"It depends on when and where the question is asked and why," he says, as if explaining things to himself. That is the kind of man he is. We have to lie very still, our bodies close, on the single bed. We have to whisper so that we are not overheard.

"Funny you having such a narrow bed," I say.

"I've always had this bed," he says. There is, of course, no reply to this.

"About the gas boiler," he says, "there's no reason at all why you should not have a gas boiler *and* be a doctor. A gas boiler!" He laughs a bit at that but does not laugh about my wanting to be a doctor.

Pale foggy fingers of light show in the sky outside Mr. George's bedroom window. It is almost time for me to be getting up so I go as quickly and as quietly as possible up to my own bed in the attic. There are two attic bedrooms. The other one is occupied at present. A discovery which I make surprisingly quickly will lead, I am certain, to the other room being empty soon. Helena will go on having a little folding bed in my room as I shall not feel disposed to move her into that other room in the circumstances. Not at present, anyway.

It is interesting to me to have discovered something about myself. It interests me, on reflection, as I slide between the cold sheets (cold, thin sheets, linen, soft with age and frequent washing, just as I like sheets to be) of my own bed, that I seem to prefer being kissed on the neck rather than on the lips. Lips are all right but the neck is better, much much better.

"This may prove to be purely an intellectual exercise," Mr. George says to me the first time we are in his bed together. "I hope you will not be disappointed," he says. I tell him I want him too much to be disappointed and he tells me he wants me terribly much. I tell him I often think of his pullover, the soft red-colored one, and that I love the way it wrinkles slightly at the back. He seems pleased and he tells me he loves me and I feel with pleasure the force of his love. "I love you too," I tell him and I mean it.

It is so nearly time to be getting up I do not have long to enjoy my own sheets and my exquisite memories. So busy is my mind with the strange way in which things have turned out that I scarcely notice the hardship of getting up on a cold morning in autumn. It is cold enough to be winter already, as the Georges say, with the early snow, a light-falling snow storm and then the freezing fog for several days in a row.

I wash, splashing my face with ice-cold water from the attic jug imagining I am like a peasant girl in a Tolstoy story. I even clatter across the stone flags of the kitchen as I think Tolstoy's peasant girl would have done. I like to think of myself as nimble and unafraid, able to do all sorts of things which the Georges do not seem able to do, like going up through the landing sky-light at the top of the main staircase to shovel snow off the flat roof. Between the attic gables there is a flat roof. The snow settles there and when it melts it seeps through in places causing mold on the ceilings. I wash my neck as well as my face with the icy water. It is something I have been taught to do.

Because of not having a house of my own I seem always to be living in the kind of house I would never be able to afford to live in in the ordinary way. Things are quite good in my life at present, very good in fact, at present, in terms of a spacious house, the kisses, and the sheets. There is an obstacle to start with, a hindrance, but fortunately I have a kind of patience and foresight to see that something will happen which will enable me to take rewarding action.

> There is a tide in the affairs of men which taken at its
> flood leads on to fortune ...

Because of the way in which things happen for me I think of this quotation, something we had at school, but mostly I remember it because Magda, whenever she hailed a taxi, and took it out of turn, always recited it. "Shakespeare, Dahling, when dear stupid Brutus is being tricked into an evil plot. It's called irony, Dahling, and you have to jump right in to the flooding river and take your chance, your opportunities. This taxi, Dahling, is gorgeously comfortable isn't it. Such a piece of luck getting it so easily. And all those people in the queue. Just look! I wonder why their mouths have all dropped open like that." Magda often hugged me in taxis.

Going up on the flat roof and out on to the fresh first fall of snow is the first thing I do here. Well, not really the first thing, it is a sort of first thing. It's like this, after the first fall of snow I go up there. Up through the roof trap knowing that the Georges see me as light and young and strong. The Georges, on that morning, make me feel that's what I am like. I shovel off the snow that morning early. There is not a great deal but what there is I shovel off, scraping gently and throwing it lightly over the parapet into the fog-pink sunrise. I love this snow. My cheeks burn in the cold air. My face continues pleasantly flushed all day and, in the evening, Mr. George notices.

Strictly speaking the first thing is my arrival. Really first is my arrival, not expected by anyone.

~~~

ARRIVAL

Really first is my arrival, not expected by anyone. No one knowing about my long journey, not knowing about my destination. To travel without being expected to arrive is something new for me. When I arrive, naturally I am not expected. It is late in the remains of the half light evening of summer moving into autumn. I am cold and wet through because of a sudden downpour. Helena is asleep on my arm and flopping over my shoulder. My other arm is nearly out of its socket with dragging my case the length of the street from the tram stop on the corner.

"I've come," I tell them when they come, lamplit, from the dark hall, leaning together to the front porch in answer to the doorbell. They, the Georges, both tall, bending over with concern, asking me, "What did you say? What is it you're saying?"

"I've come from London," I tell them. "I've come about the position," I manage to say, "child no objection. Live in."

In the subdued murmuring of the two soft voices, now near and now far away, I understand that they are suited, that the advertisement was placed months ago. It must have been an old magazine. I have to understand. They have someone. I sink down under Helena's weight on the steps and lean against the outside door. Above me their voices are gentle, like voices in a dream. They are sorry, they say, echoing each other, but they are suited. Suited, that is the word they use. They have someone. I cry then telling them I have used up all my money. Helena wakes up and cries. One of them lifts Helena up away from me. One of them is saying to close the storm doors and lock up.

"Lock up, now." The words from one to the other are hardly heard.

They tell me they are called George, these people. They hover, uncertain, in the kitchen. They make some hot milk in a small saucepan and pour it over bread broken up in two basins. Helena has never eaten bread and milk before and I am nervous that she will be rude to the old lady and refuse to eat. But Helena spoons up the new dish quickly and I do the same. There is hot water, they tell me, if we would like a bath and a bed which we can share.

Helena is very hot all night. Helena is feverish. Unable to keep awake I feel her through my sleep, her hot thin body next to mine, sinking in the feather bed. And I hear her coughing, a little dry double cough. Two coughs, cough cough, and a pause. I should get up to attend to her but can't wake up enough. She coughs, hot beside me, all night.

In the morning the sparrows are all round the edges of the gray light of the roof windows. The little black shapes of these birds are busily edging each other off the edges of the windows. The sloping ceiling of the attic room reflects the light of the coming day. Helena, awake, is lying looking up at the birds. She looks refreshed. The cough is not hers. Someone else is coughing. The dry double cough is coming from the other side of the wall, from another little bedroom up here under the gables.

I remember immediately, the people, the Georges, the two

kind elderly people, already have their maid. They have her now for several weeks. She suits them. She is in the other room.

The little feet of the sparrows skid across the skylight. Like Helena I lie watching the sparrows and listening to their chirping. The attic room appeals to me. There is a strip of thin worn carpet across the plain boards, some simple wooden furniture and a washstand with a jug and basin. Maid's furniture. The wish to stay in this room is overpowering. I long to be the maid who comes up here to the top of the house to rest her aching feet, to sleep the innocent sleep maids sleep when their work is done. How simple life could be for a maid, especially in a solid house like this. This is what I want. And then I hear once more that small restrained dry double cough through the wall. One maid is enough. The Georges will only want one maid.

They are brother and sister George, Miss George explains. She tells me repeatedly how sorry they are that they are suited. The housekeeper has two days off to go and visit her family. Would I like to stay two or three days? Miss George asks me. She suggests I try and find a place and in the meantime I am welcome to stay. "Stay awhile," she says, "till you get things sorted out. Doris," she says, "has gone, she's gone for the early train. She always goes before breakfast."

"Thank you," I tell Miss George that I am very grateful, I tell her, "thank you."

So I don't see Doris, the real housekeeper, straight away. The only thing I know about her is the sound of her cough.

"Now a *red* one and now a *blue* one." Miss George is bending over Helena at the kitchen table. She is showing Helena how to color some cut-out paper flowers. Miss George does not scribble with the crayon. She does not scribble round and round pressing hard, tearing the paper with the colored pencils. Miss George holds the crayon lightly in her long fingers and shades in the color in delicate strokes all slanting in the same direction. Helena looks on and is pleased. She tries to copy Miss George's precision. Helena's pale hand is small beside Miss George's hand which is brown flecked and elderly.

The first few days with the Georges go by very quickly. Miss George shows me the house, the damp linen cupboards, the sideboards of china and silver and the rooms full of books. I take Helena out with me and queue for fish and leave a neatly written grocery order which will be delivered. Miss George says it is fortunate that the grocer and greengrocer have resumed delivery even though the boys arrive at awkward times and tip everything out on to the kitchen table so that earth from the potatoes goes through everything. Her voice is never raised and her complaining is mild. I imagine how Sister Peters would shout from the upstairs landing, in the middle of a birth even, if she thought a heap of vegetables was being dumped on the table downstairs.

I discover straight away when I dust Mr. George's desk that he is Professor George. I try to make out his subject from various papers, a historian perhaps.

These Georges, they fascinate me. They make me feel I want to do things for them. And the little attic bedroom is a place I like to think about. I look at the floor boards up there and think how they will be warmed in summer. I want to be up in the attic sitting on the sun-warmed floor. I want to stay in this house.

There would be a moral profit in the possibility of getting rid of the present housekeeper. Moral because of the circumstances in which there would be a virtue in my telling certain things, a certain thing, that is, which I think I have discovered without even seeing her. I think I know something of the present housekeeper's predicament.

A message from Doris is telephoned by a relation. Hanging over the landing banisters I can see and hear Miss George's concern. She tells me later that Doris has another cold and will be away for a few more days. Miss George says that Doris never seems quite well, that, in spite of good food and an hour or so in the fresh air every day, she continues pale and unwell.

"I insist on her walk," Miss George says. She is not able to understand why Doris does not look better. I almost say then what I think about what Miss George goes on to call Doris's persistent cough. I listen and nod my head but do not say anything. Having made up my mind, in a sense, to be ruthless, to stop at nothing to keep the attic bedroom as mine, it is almost impossible not to speak, especially as Miss George adds that sometimes Doris is almost green in her paleness.

⌐⌐

THE OWNERS OF GRIEF

"Vera," Miss George says, "Vera you have been here a week, it is your turn and Helena's to have a bath."

"Thank you, Miss George," I say, "thank you."

These Georges, they are refined. I am still here with them. Helena is asleep in the attic and Doris is back, coughing in her room. Doris and I, during the day, do not have much to say to each other. I see her looking at me sometimes and am prompted to remark that I've had no luck with the advertisements. And Doris agrees that it is hard to find a place. She's lucky, she says, to have found the Georges. She has four children she tells me. They are at her mother's. I try to imagine what it must be like making the journey, going home to four children, all girls, and a grandmother, on her days off. I try to imagine what it must be like to be separated from the children and I wonder if the grandmother is full of reproachings as soon as Doris arrives.

"One awful place'll have me," I tell Doris. "It's a man and three grown-up sons and the house is really small and nasty. It smells, and you should see the bathroom! And the room meant for me is no more than a cupboard." Doris is sympathetic and says she wouldn't want to go there either and perhaps I should look around a bit more. She says Helena is tall for her age and is about the age of her second youngest. She says she hopes something else will turn up.

"If it doesn't I'll just have to go there," I tell her.

•

These Georges, they like nice things. They have delicate taste and polished manners and when they speak to each other it is with subtle thought and language. Just now I am listening to some music, cello. And I'm thinking how nice the bath was. I feel free because Helena is asleep upstairs and Doris is up there too, coughing. Doris goes to bed very early. Because of her cough she does not get enough sleep. I am sitting on the stairs, at the bottom of the main staircase, listening to the cello from Mr. George's study. Miss George went to bed some time ago.

I have been cheating the Georges. I have thrown away the advertisements, telling Miss George I was too late or that a child was unacceptable. The man with the three grown-up sons will be expecting me to come because I did not tell him outright that I was not coming. I have been working hard here. There is plenty to do as it is a very big house and Doris does not manage to do all that needs doing. All the same, two maids are not required.

My cheeks are flushed and hot after my bath. There was a light fall of snow, an early snow storm this morning.

"Snow in autumn," Miss George says as she takes her place for breakfast. She shivers. Mr. George asks me to fetch Miss George's shawl please. He smiles.

The sloping ceilings of the attic reflect the light of the snow-covered gables. As soon as I see this I get up and go downstairs. Mr. George has the stepladder on the landing. Both the Georges are anxious about the settled snow on the flat roof.

Mr. George is particularly pleasant to look at when he is wearing a dressing gown.

I have no difficulty, in the face of the Georges' admiration, in raising the roof trap and in climbing through to clear away the very small amount of snow. My cheeks are pleasantly red all day because of this.

This night starts well for me with my rosy face and the music of the cello. It is so long since I heard any music that my eyes fill with tears even though I do not know the particular piece. Mr.

George, coming out for more coal, asks me if I would like to come in by the fire. He explains it is Beethoven, a quartet. As I listen, the notes, one after the other, climbing, entering and combining, are all in my head. And afterwards, when it is over, I tell Mr. George that I have been to a quartet from school but never since. Mr. George is so nice, without meaning to, I go on talking and tell him about Ramsden, staff nurse Ramsden, and how I wanted once to tell her about the downward thrust of the cello and about the perfection in the way the other instruments come up to meet the cello. I tell him that I did not feel able to tell her that I thought someone had measured the movements of the notes controlling carefully the going down and the coming up in order to produce this exquisite mixture.

Mr. George seems interested and pleased but I am not sure if this is not just kindness and good manners. He suggests I come nearer to the fire. I sit on the floor near the hearth and closer to him. Very gently he touches my cheek saying that the snow storm has made me look well. He lifts my hair away from my face and says that the red cheeks suit me.

All I seem to see is his russet-colored pullover and his smile.

It is when he guides me upstairs in the sleeping household to his room where he helps me undress before taking me in his arms and then into his bed with him that he tells me he is susceptible to music and he hopes I will not be disappointed.

"I am susceptible," he says, "to music which seems to contain an everlasting youth. It seems to restore one's own youth." And he hopes he has more than just this susceptibility to offer. He wants me terribly he says but I can escape to my own room if I do not want to stay in his.

I tell him then that I have no wish to escape.

"You are a remarkable young woman," Mr. George says afterwards when we are lying close to each other in his narrow bed and I have been telling him about the nightmare of Fairfields, about Tanya, about the Metcalfs, about Lois, Trent, and Ferguson, and about my father and his moon.

"You are a very remarkable young woman," he says once more. "My mentor!" he says. There is something in his way of holding me which is powerful and, at the same time, restrained. He explains that he responds to music and that he feels, now, he should not have directed this response towards me. I tell him I wanted him to, that I am susceptible to music too but would never have thought of the words to describe myself. When I tell him I want him one more time, he says I am wonderfully shameless, and when I ask him what there is to be ashamed of he seems pleased and says he'll never forget my question.

Somehow it is, just then, as if the remembered reddish color of his pullover is blending with the glowing floor boards and the cherry-wood furniture of the attic bedroom, and I wonder why I should, during the sweet wild moments, consider this woolen garment and the attic chair, the woodwork of the wash stand and the floor boards.

How can I tell anyone of this, least of all my mother who would be reassured if a time comes when reassurance is needed.

The silly thing is that I miss Tanya, actually miss her. When I think about her, like now, I can see that there is something about her which makes her like Magda, or rather, which reminds me of Magda. Perhaps it is that they are both people of misfortune. They could be called owners of grief. When I think about that, I too am an owner of grief, but I am completely without the flamboyance which gives Magda and Tanya glamour. And of course money makes a great difference, the possession of money. Tanya and I are different from Magda. Tanya and I have no money.

How could I, just now, have considered that there could be anything reassuring in the fact that I am lying naked, held by Mr. George's arm, as he sleeps beside me. I am actually stupid enough to imagine that my being loved by him will reassure my mother. If I should try to speak of it to her she would immediately reply using some phrase which would not match with her ordinary way of speaking but would be, perhaps, the only way in which she could express her fear and distaste.

"You *are* a *fast worker*, Vera. How could you be so *cheap?* Cheap and wicked. And Vera, he's got *white hair*. How could you, a daughter of mine, do this . . ."

I would like to have my books. Often during sleepless nights I would take up one book after the other and look inside them at the fond inscriptions and read bits here and there. But my books are all at my mother's house in the trunk which I did not take to Fairfields. It would be a nonchalant thing to do to read in bed in the arms of a man who is both a stranger and a lover.

Some of my books are the lives of painters and writers and explorers. Somewhere in the book about Monet there is an account of the difficulties he had trying to paint the long tresses of river weeds streaming in the clear water. The water is so clear that the long green fingers of the weeds, moving just below the surface, can be seen easily but are impossible to paint. He says that once more he has taken up something which he finds impossible to do. In the end, he says, this is what he is always trying to do. This idea of trying, almost without meaning to, to do something impossible seems to fit closely to my own life.

There is consolation in reading about the lives of composers, sculptors, painters, and of people like Albert Schweitzer. In reading it is possible to take a long view over the difficulties and the suffering and the sorrow in these other lives and then it is almost possible to do the same over one's own life.

I do not have long to enjoy my smooth sheets and the sweet thoughts of the night. As soon as I am in my own bed it is time to be getting up. Helena is still asleep buried in blankets.

I look up the word mentor in my little dictionary: *Inexperienced person's adviser.* When I look up susceptible I find: *Impressionable, easily moved,* and *of amorous disposition.* I hardly notice the icy water in the attic jug. I wash and dress and go down quickly to the kitchen to boil the kettle for the Georges' early morning tea. They have a little tea pot each and have their tea served in their separate rooms.

⨠

MENTOR AND SUSCEPTIBLE

I am an inexperienced person's adviser and Mr. George is of an amorous disposition. Mentor and susceptible. I am susceptible too. Though both are words I would never have thought of using I like them, and I am always ready for Mr. George to chase and catch me, silently like a thief, on the stairs, in the pantry and behind the kitchen door for his quick secret kisses.

I am in bed early, really early, without supper. Oliver, that is Mr. George, is out to a dinner in a restaurant. He has been invited by his students, by some of them. Oliver, Miss George pronounces his name, Ulliva. Ulliva, she says, is very much liked by his students, especially by the young women. They are called the post grads, Miss George explains. She says at Christmas, every year, they have a party here at the house. "They do seem to enjoy themselves," she says, "they stay an awful long time, practically all night." She is not annoyed by this, I mean, she just seems perplexed.

I can't sleep. I'm jealous, I think I'm hideously jealous. In the hall when I help him into his overcoat, just before Miss George comes to see him off, I turn my face away from his quick secret kiss.

"Vera . . ." He has only time to say "Vera" in a low voice. Later, I tell Miss George I am going to bed as soon as Helena is in bed and, no, I do not want supper, thank you.

Also Doris is back. She is in her room coughing. Doris has been away with her second cold for eight days. I have been here for almost a month. I do not want to leave. Doris is here a day early. Tomorrow is Sunday and Sunday is officially her day off. Miss George says, when Doris turns up, that she should have her day off and that since I am here, if it is all right with me, I can work the day.

"Of course it is all right," I tell Miss George. How can I tell Miss George that I want to stay, that I don't want to try and find another place. I don't want to leave. I want this room under the gable. I have come to think of the sparrows on the sky light, every morning, as mine. I like to see Helena lying in bed, every morning, watching the sparrows. I suppose she is old enough now to think of them as hers too, and to remember them and their noise for the rest of her life. I want Helena to have some nice memories like this.

I suppose I was hoping this time that Doris would not come back.

When I think about not wanting to leave a place it reminds me that when I handed back the two uncompromising huckaback towels to the woman in charge of the women's night shelter in London, I would have stayed there if she had suggested it. It is a frightening thought. I suppose I might stay in a place like that simply because I have no alternative. It would, this kind of thing would, in the end, cause Helena to be without a real home, like being at Fairfields for ever.

Patch, on almost my first evening there when I am bathing the children, one after the other, in the top bathroom, wants me to have a little pause, as she calls it, to lie on her big double bed, where she is lying with her thick glass of whiskey, and listen to Wagner with her. It is when I take the first little group of children down to her room, where they are allowed to play on the rug with some building blocks after their baths, that she asks me. Staff offspring, Myles's phrase, do not share this privilege, this special favor. She asks me then what the music is and I tell her I think it is the Siegfried Idyll. She says the music was not intended to be for love between two women but it could be. It could be deliciously so and she says she hopes I will accept her invitation. Can I be tempted she wants to know.

I can see now things might have turned out differently at Fairfields. Patch starts to tell me then how Wagner came to write the Siegfried Idyll and I tell her yes I have read about the staircase music and that I must get back to the top bathroom to the other children waiting up there.

"Just top up my glass then, deah, will you, before you go." Completely unruffled, Patch holds her glass out to me and, while I pour, she strokes my wrist with one fleshy finger extended.

In this whole house, next to the attic bedroom, the best room, in my opinion, is the maid's sitting room. This room is between the kitchen, with its stone flagged floor, and the dining room, a room solemn with polished furniture, a sideboard laden with polished silver, and an explosive gas fire. Miss George handles the gas tap calmly with an enviable courage, Mr. George explains this on my first morning in the house. The maid's sitting room is all doors; as well as the kitchen and dining-room doors there is one into the main hall of the house and there is a small door, two steps up, to the back stairs which come up directly to the attics. These narrow uncarpeted stairs can be approached half way up by a little passage from the landing of the main front staircase.

The special thing about the maid's sitting room is its tranquility, a curious effect of the light which comes from a combination of colors, the ancient yellow-ochre of the thick tasseled table cloth, the cherry brown of the chairs, the wood worn smooth over the years, and the reflections from a small conservatory immediately outside the window. The tall window, hung with transparent lace curtains, looks directly into the deep green of the glass house.

Whenever I pass one of the open doors it seems as if the room has some magic about it, as if it is deep under water and unattainable. There is a little wireless in there too which I'm sure Doris never uses. All this makes me want this room. Of course it is Doris's and I never go in there. She does not seem to have any possessions strewn about, no books, no sewing basket, and, since she has no child with her, no toys.

I had hoped and hoped that Doris would not come back. I would so much like to stay.

Doris has stopped coughing at last. In the silence I should be able to sleep. I turn over and then I turn back. I can't help wishing for Mr. George, he is always so cautiously sweet.

I should not be put out that Doris is back but I am. She is back a day earlier than Miss George expected. Tomorrow is Sunday, Doris's official day off and Miss George has told her she can have it off. I wish Miss George would tell Doris she can have every day off.

"When's that flat-footed floozie going home? She's been here a week tell her she can flat foot it home—tell her she can buzz off allez voos ong. Scram!"

When I stay with Lois at her mother's house on the outskirts of the ugly side of Oxford, the motor-works side, her twin brothers, "Bob's yer uncle and Nick's yer Aunty," soon make it quite clear that I should not be there, almost as soon as I come to understand this myself. The deep regret that I am in this house with Lois and her mother and her grandmother and her brothers and not at home with my mother comes upon me as soon as I arrive.

"Will one of youse boys fetch Gran off the lav so Vera can go?" Lois's grandmother sits in the lavatory, which is immediately outside the back door, and conducts the conversations which are going on in the kitchen. Not even the half-expected initiation to certain mysteries each night can make me really ignore the unwashed sheets of the bed I'm expected to share with Lois.

"Cornflakes and toast for breakfast." Lois's mother puts her head round the bedroom door before leaving for work. She asks Lois why she is not wearing her pajama jacket and Lois says because she was too hot. The sound of the front door slamming behind Lois's mother is an experience bordering on happiness. But this and the hitherto unknown pleasure of being naked in bed beside Lois does not make up, in the end, for the boredom in a house which has no books and no music. I long for bookshelves and for the act of picking up something to read. It is like being cooped up in a small desert. In the mornings, while Lois is seeing to her grandmother, I clear up the dreary pile of plates and cups in the sink and feel I am caught in a wilderness from which there is no escape. Even when we are out in the small roads through the hills which surround Oxford, leaning our bicycles into the dripping hedges while we search for primroses, trying not to mind the rain, I am able only to think that soon we shall, because of the rain, be forced to go back there to watch this rain running down the kitchen window and to wait for the return of Lois's mother and the two brothers.

"Lois is my pride and joy," Lois's mother tells me repeatedly as if I am spoiling Lois in some way when it is Lois herself, who, unknown to her mother, is the more experienced. I leave a day earlier than arranged.

It is with an unforgettable relief that I put my bicycle in the goods van at the back of the train. The trains from Oxford crawl through endless meadows as if following the flooded rivers and the curving lines of mourning willows. These trains stop for long intervals at the wayside stations. The journey is slow and long enough for me to have a return of tenderness towards Lois and I am full of regret for not being nicer to her in that awful place she calls home with those awful people who are her family.

"Which is my towel?" I call out to Lois on the first evening. I can hardly bear to think of this during the journey.

"I have never been in a house before where everyone uses the same towel in the bathroom." I am sorry now for shouting my distaste, for displaying my dismay and anger, especially as Lois is fond in bed introducing me to previously unimagined experiments and sweetness.

When we are back at the hospital once more we shall be back on a deeper level of friendship.

Looking out across the dismal wet fields I think of a present I can buy for Lois. Something pretty, she has so few things. I look forward to the restful cleanliness of my mother's bathroom and to going over to see Gertrude and to shopping for something very nice for Lois.

All this, of course, is before I know the Metcalfs and before the great change which comes over Lois.

"What is the area of discussion? Eleanor?" Mr. George pauses in the kitchen doorway.

"The weather, Ulliva, the weather that is all." Miss George is standing by the scrubbed table where I am sitting on a chair weeping. I began to cry while I was scrubbing the table. Miss George has been asking me why I am crying. "Can you tell me?" she asks. I am hidden from Mr. George by Miss George. She waves him away. How can I tell Miss George that I can't face leaving to go as housekeeper to that squalid little house where there is the man and his three grown-up sons, that I don't like the way he looked at me, that there's nowhere in that house for me to be except in the living room with them or the scullery where there's no fire, that it's awful there? I can't stop crying and I can't speak.

"There there," Miss George says, "don't cry. You mustn't cry like that, my dear. There! Try not to cry so." Miss George shyly pats my shoulder.

The worst thing about not being asleep is that I'll be a wreck in the morning. It's the morning already. The sky's getting light. I watched the sky getting light that first night I was with Mr. George. That house where I went when I answered the advertisement reminds me of the time I went to stay with Lois. It's the remembering that makes all the unhappiness come back. And, I've simply got to find a place. I'll not be able to stay on here.

Mentor and susceptible, I watch the sky turning pale, drained of color, in the circle of the gable window.

Helena turns over muttering in her sleep. There is someone on the stairs. Perhaps Doris has been down already. Perhaps I've overslept. It's Mr. George. He comes at once to my bedside.

"Eleanor says you went to bed without supper. You didn't have supper."

I breathe in Mr. George's evening. He is still in his overcoat, his scarf loose and the coat unbuttoned. He is handsome in evening dress. I breathe him in some more, the restaurant, the food, the students, the fragrance of cigars and of exotic wines and, holding all this together, the cold air, the breath of frost, still clinging to him. He must have come upstairs to me as soon as he came home.

"Eleanor says you are very upset," he says, "she left a note for me."

These Georges. They always leave notes for each other, pencil on paper on the kitchen table, sometimes with funny spelling and little sketches.

I tell him he must not come up here. Helena will wake up. "You can't come up here," I tell him.

"Please come down then," he says. He says he's afraid it's all his fault. He wants me to come down to talk. "Please do come down."

I tell him I can't and that he has not upset me. It is something else. Just then Doris starts to cough. Cough cough, the double cough, the pause, and then the double cough cough. She is out of breath very quickly.

"Come downstairs, please, just for a minute." Mr. George touches my face and hair very gently and bends down to kiss me. Doris coughs and coughs. I have never heard her cough quite like this before. I take hold of Mr. George's hand and tell him he must go down at once. "Doris's cough," I say, explaining.

"All right," he says, "later then." He kisses me again, his breath is the breath of a stranger and, at the same time, familiar and desirable.

"Help me please," Doris calls as the attic stairs creak under Mr. George's careful tread. "Please!" Doris calls in her coughing fit. I get up at once and go as quickly as I can into Doris's room.

⁓

RITUAL

Miss George, straight after breakfast, wonders what we should all have for dinner. She stands, in an overall, at the kitchen table slicing the remains of the roast in order to determine whether there will be enough to go round. I am suddenly struck by the thought that, in all sorts of places, responsible people carve meat for other people. Sister Peters with her own sharp knife will be doing exactly what Miss George is doing, even to the time of day and the wearing of an overall. Cold sideboards, Sister Peters would make this announcement, usually on a Monday. Patch, at Fairfields, on the few occasions when there was meat—like the time Olive Morris's husband, before he was hauled away by the police, gave presents of dairy-fed poultry to the school (for which Patch received the bills)—she carved, placing judiciously a wing or a leg or a slice of breast on each plate. I never saw meat carved at the hospital or at school. It appeared on oval plates having been cut up out of sight. All the same, someone in an overall, wielding a sharp knife, would have carved it.

Before changing over to minced beef, the small ration during the war, my mother, at home, carved while my father asked a Blessing;

> God bless this food that now we take
> To do us good for Jesus' sake. Amen.

I suppose I am thinking about carving this morning because Miss George is in my way in the kitchen with the meat, the oval plate, and the sharpened knife. She is in my way, in her own kitchen, because I need to go through and out to the wash house with something I do not want her to see. In a sense I want to protect Miss George. You see, it's like this. Miss George's special skill is sewing and embroidery. Embroidery in particular. "My girls . . ." she often starts a conversation relating something from years ago about her girls in the succession of needlework classes. "Some of my girls' work." She has shown me the cabinet in her room, a display of some of the daintiest and prettiest things I have ever seen. "All hand embroidered," she tells me when she takes out the cloths and the little garments. It is years since she retired, that is why I want to protect her.

These Georges. There is something innocent about them. I must go through the kitchen quickly with the bundle of crumpled blood-stained sheets and pillow cases. I have them rolled in a sort of ball I need to get them out to the wash house without causing Miss George distress.

"What about a green aitch," Miss George pauses, the knife hovering, she leans towards Helena who is sitting at the scrubbed table. "And now," Miss George is saying, "what color will you choose for the e, and shall we make a little flower in the e? like this!" She puts her knife down and takes up a crayon. I hurry by them and, safely in the wash house, I turn the cold tap on hard and push the sheets down in the shallow sink to wash away the bright red blood clots and stains. The water reddens quickly. At once I realize I'll need evidence. Quickly I turn off the tap and let the blood patterned sheets float and bulge above the water. I shall have to tell the Georges. I'll tell Mr. George first and then he can talk to Miss George. These Georges, they are very delicate with each other.

I know I should not but I feel relieved and even happy when I am back in the kitchen watching Miss George as she teaches Helena to write her own name.

"Vera," Miss George says, pointing at the oval plate with the tip of her sharp knife, "will this be enough d'you think? With some beetroot and potatoes?"

"Oh yes, Miss George," I say, "more than enough."

Miss George is taking Helena with her this morning when she goes to church. Helena, pleased and happy in new long socks and with her little coat brushed and pressed, is going to Sunday School.

"Vera," Miss George says, "we have left Mr. George resting after his night of pleasure for long enough, please take him some tea at eleven or thereabouts."

"Yes, Miss George," I say.

"And Vera," Miss George says, "I noticed, yesterday, some withered flowers in the wash house. Perhaps you should throw them away?"

"Yes of course Miss George." The dead flowers are in a bucket out there, the white chrysanthemums and the bronze, and the expensive, out-of-season roses and carnations next to the sink now full of blood-stained sheets. "Oh yes Miss George," I say, "I'll see to the flowers."

If Miss George, in the mornings in her overall reminds me of Sister Peters, in the afternoons, at about half-past three, she reminds me of my mother. This is because most afternoons Miss George, tying a small apron round her waist, comes into the kitchen for the little ceremony of cutting the bread and butter for the four o'clock afternoon tea. Most days Mr. George is home, after his short walk from the university, for afternoon tea which they have together in his study. My mother in her Aryan period, just before the war, a time of Heidi hairstyles, beaded dresses, and twice weekly visits to the new Odeon cinema always, in a small apron, cut bread and butter for afternoon tea. The ladies then, visiting each other, kept each other company during this ritual.

How can I tell Miss George just before she leaves with Helena for the walk to church that I am afraid I might be pregnant and that Doris is asleep upstairs after the most terrifying hemorrhage I have ever seen.

As I take the stairs, three at a time, balancing the round tray with Mr. George's tea pot, cup and saucer, and milk jug nicely set on a clean table napkin, it seems to me that it's no wonder when the ladies meet in the afternoon, round the special little table cloths, that they talk endlessly about servants and their problems.

❦

THE LOG LIFT

The proximity of a sympathetic nurse is often the only treatment Sister Bean said once. The thing I remember most about hemoptysis, this frightening rush of blood, is Sister Bean kneeling, during the night by the patient's bed and the way in which she drew the man's head on to her arm, into the crook of her elbow really. She was so close to him, she leaned right over him, her arm under his head, close, not frightened of tuberculosis at all. And, all the time, she kept telling him that everything would be all right. She did this while I was clearing away the blood, wiping away the clots, and slipping off the sheet and the pillow cases to put on fresh ones. She held him close and prayed, and afterwards she repeated the prayer saying that I should remember it in case I ever needed to say it.

Doris has a jug and basin like the one in my room. I soak her towel in the icy water and wash away the blood as quickly as it comes. She can't speak except with her imploring frightened eyes. I nod my head to her and tell her that it's nearly finished and that she'll be better directly. I pretend to feel her pulse and count it and I tell her the pulse is strong. When Helena appears, half asleep, in the doorway I tell her sharply to get back in bed and play with her doll. "I'm coming in a minute," I tell her.

"Everything's going to be all right," I tell Doris.

"Don't tell *them*, will you," Doris says as soon as she can speak.

"No, of course not," I say. As quickly as I can I pull her nightgown off and I pull her sheets and pillow cases away rolling them into a sort of horrible bundle. The warmth of the clots through the rolled-up sheet makes me feel as if I've pulled part of her body away. I am shaking dreadfully. I fetch some clean water from my room and my spare nightgown. Doris lets me dress her in the gown and lies back exhausted. I tell her I'll get her some tea but she begs me to stay by her.

"Don't go down just yet," she says. She says she'll be better in a few minutes and I say yes she will be better.

"Tell me about your children." I sit on the edge of her bed. "Tell me about your children," I say. She is cold, she says, so I wrap her round with a blanket from my bed.

"Don't tell them about it, will you," she says once more. She starts to tell me something about one of her children but she is unable to keep awake. I watch her fall asleep. She sleeps like a child, with her arms up on the pillow on either side of her head.

"Keep my place for me," Doris looks at me. There is no reproach in her look. "You will keep my place for me, won't you," she says. "I'll lose my place, you see," she tries to explain to the two ambulance men. They carry her rolled in a blanket in what they call the log lift, the attic stairs being too sharply angled for their stretcher.

"I'll keep your place," I promise Doris. I tell her that she'll be better soon, that going to hospital is the best thing.

"I'm afraid," Doris looks back at me.

"Don't be frightened," I say, "everything's going to be all right." I follow the log lift down the attic stairs, along the passage, and down the main staircase to the front hall. I have pushed Doris's few possessions into her shabby case. It is dismal, the case, and very light.

I can't stop crying.

"It's because of her small luggage," I cry in the hall after the ambulance has gone. Mr. George, still in his dressing gown, puts his arm around me and guides me gently to the stairs. We go up together.

❧

THIRTY SHILLINGS AND KEEP

In the mornings after I have been sick I cry. I feel terrible and I keep hearing my mother's voice complaining, on and on, somewhere inside my head.

"There must be something not quite nice about him, Vera. If a man, however handsome and refined he might be, hasn't married by the time he's sixty, Vera, there must be something about him that's not nice . . ." I create replies telling my mother that Mr. George isn't sixty. "He's only fifty-eight," I tell her. And, without wanting to, I make up an answer for her; "Near enough, Vera, as makes no difference," in the kind of phrases she would never use.

In the mornings, straight after being sick, I lie down for a little while, the house being restfully empty. Mr. George always leaves early and Miss George goes for a walk. She has started taking Helena out for this walk. Often I lie down on Mr. George's bed, before I make it, and I think of him, about how good looking he is, and kind, and how I like looking at him when he's asleep. When I tell him this, one time, he says he isn't asleep he's waiting for me to wake up because he likes watching me wake up. One morning he leaves a book on his bed for me, not a new book, but it is for me. Inside he has written my name and a quotation;

> *You have first taught me,*
> *You have opened my eyes*
> *To the unending value of life*

The book is a collection of poems. He has penciled little initials, mine, by certain poems. Some lines in another poem are underlined;

> *. . . when thy mind*
> *shall be a mansion for all lovely forms*
> *Thy memory be as a dwelling-place*
> *For all sweet sounds and harmonies;*

In his small neat handwriting Mr. George has written *Eleanor* by this part of the poem, in ink, now faded, and I have to understand, when I read more of the poem, how much they have always cared for each other.

"He's fifteen years younger than his sister," my mother chips in, "fifteen years, and his mother dying when he was a baby! She, the sister, she will have been a mother to him. Brought him up like a mother, I would say. And he probably worships the ground she walks on."

"Yes, that's right," I tell my mother. My voice in the empty house startles me.

"Mothers often dislike their son's women friends." It is as if I am, through my mother's voice, heard only somewhere inside my head, voicing my own uneasiness. And then I tell myself I am not uneasy. I have only to think of the way Mr. George holds me and kisses me to know that he loves me.

"And another thing," my mother goes on and on, "how can a man, an educated man, ask a woman to marry him without any knowledge of her background? I've always said, Vera, academic men are never *practical*. I mean, has it occurred to this man yet that he might be the father of a child?" My creations in speech, haunting me throughout the morning's work of cleaning and polishing, surpass all the previous ones.

Something greatly in my favor, and I do need something to be in my favor, is the way in which Miss George and Helena have taken to each other. Helena follows Miss George everywhere in the house. Miss George is making a second little dress for Helena, this time of Viyella, pale blue with pink smocking. She is teaching Helena the piano, the alphabet, and something they call number.

Miss George is a very sympathetic sort of person.

"Whyever didn't you come straight to me and tell me before?" she says on the day when Doris has to be taken quickly to the hospital. Mr. George, on that day, tells Miss George what has happened as soon as she comes in from church, before she has even had time to take off her hat and coat. Miss George says then that Helena had told her, on the walk to church, that her mother was washing Doris, in the night, with a wet towel, and that Doris was crying. Her eyes are dark with pity and she goes, in the afternoon, to visit Doris.

I want Mr. George to tell Miss George how things are between us. Sometimes I allow myself a little dream of Miss George sitting in the window of the front room here, overlooking the street, nursing my baby. I imagine her rocking gently to and fro and singing in that way people do sing over a new baby. For some reason I am certain my baby will be a girl. I shall call her Rachel. It would be better if Mr. George tells Miss George. He is clever and gentle and furthermore Mr. George and Miss George know each other so well.

"Vera," Miss George says to me in the evening when she is back from the hospital and I help her off with her coat. "Vera, I take it you would like to come in to the position, that you would like to work here. Will thirty shillings and keep for you and Helena be all right?"

"Oh yes," I say, "yes, thank you, Miss George, that will be quite all right."

I want to tell Mr. George that I think Miss George knows. Every day I hope that he will speak to her. I want to tell him that I think Miss George knows everything, that she has known everything since the first time when I listened to the Beethoven quartet with him in his study. I think she knows on that first morning, after our first night, when I take her tea in to her.

That morning, I want to tell him, she was lying back on her pillows and, though she seemed to be asleep, there were tears all along her eye-lashes. When I think of these tears they were the largest, most glistening tear drops, the most tremulous of all tears—not shed but trembling as if about to be. I want to tell him that I think she was crying because of us. She did not open her eyes when I said, "Your tea, Miss George." She simply thanked me without looking at me. She must know already, I want to tell Mr. George, and so it would be better to tell her straight away.

On the other hand, if Mr. George knows about Miss George's tears, that morning, it might be impossible for him to speak now.

"I am worried about Miss George," I say that first morning when Mr. George gives me a fond little kiss in the hall early before he leaves for his lecture. "What about Miss George?" I ask him then. He kisses me again quickly and tells me he is sure Eleanor will approve, I am to leave it to him he says. He tells me he is very happy and he says a soft little "thank you" close to my ear and that he is looking forward to coming home.

It is during that day that the flowers arrive for me and I hide them in the wash house. Later on, when everyone is in bed, Mr. George tells me of the great pleasure he had in sending the flowers.

If I do belong to Mr. George, as he says I do, how will it be about the attic bedroom, the cherry-wood furniture, and the floor boards? And how will I be able to go on sitting in the deep watery green of the maid's sitting room? That wished-for shaded green of the conservatory mixed with the ancient yellow-ochre of the table cloth, will that have to belong to someone else? Where will I be, if I do belong to Mr. George as he says I do, where will I be in this house? At present I am all over the house, everywhere, both openly and in secret.

The days go by one after another. Some days I long to go out to meet Mr. George when I know he will be walking home from the university. I long to walk in the wind and the rain with him, holding hands, and showing the world that we belong to each other. Until he tells Miss George, we are not able to do this. In my thoughts I walk with him every day. After all thoughts are safe, neighbors and colleagues cannot see into them. All the same, I really do want to be seen with him by everyone. I want to be seen going through a door with Mr. George, one arm gently at my back, holding the door open for me.

Perhaps tomorrow Mr. George will speak to Miss George.

"The area of discussion, Eleanor." I can imagine Mr. George leaning forward to open the dining-room door and holding it open to allow his sister to go through first, one hand protectingly at her back. "The area of discussion today, Eleanor, my dear, is in a field which is new to us, something which we have not discussed before but which we must talk about now." I imagine the door being closed and then only the subdued murmur of the two voices in harmony without any words which might be usefully overheard.

I want Mr. George to tell Miss George. It is only such a small thing we have to tell. Perhaps it is the small things which are the hardest to tell. They are the things which make all the difference. It is because it will be so unexpected for her. What we need to tell her will be so unexpected.

The coming of a baby, the birth of a baby is inevitable. In this house we are all pointing, because of my new baby who cannot be put off, inevitably in a certain direction.

Meanwhile my trunk has come, the trunk I had at school, at the hospital, at Clifton Way, at the Hilda Street Wentworth, but not at Fairfields and not here till now. My mother has sent it by rail and the carrier, an obliging man, brought it up to the attic.

When I open it books and shoes and clothes spill out. Some of my pressed wildflowers have come unstuck and I put them back between the pages remembering the sweet, wet grass near the school where we searched for flowers. I seem to see clearly shining long fingers pulling stalks and holding bunches. Saxifrage, campion, vetch, ragged robin, star of Bethlehem, wild strawberry and sorrel. Quickly I tidy the flowers—violet, buttercup, King cup, cowslip, coltsfoot, wood anemone, shepherd's purse, lady's slipper, jack-in-the-pulpit, and bryony . . .

I am unpacking my life, for the time being, into this top room, at the top of this house.

Cabin Fever

⚮

All this goes on inside me, in the vast cloisters of my memory. In it are the sky, the earth, and the sea, ready at my summons, together with everything I have ever perceived in them by my senses . . . In it I meet myself as well I remember myself . . .

—Saint Augustine

⚮

THE STOREHOUSE AND THE REMEDY

My father had a deeply felt belief that the life he was living was simply a prologue to some other kind of life or existence. This did not mean that he thought people returned to earth as rich when they had been poor, or as animals, dogs or cats, or as plants or trees. He said that what had to be endured in life, as we know it, was not the only intention. I suppose he saw the changing of the seasons and the inevitability of birth and death as a resurrection and a replenishing. That the four seasons following one after the other, the waxing and waning of the moon, the heat of the sun, the falling of rain, the ebb and flow of the tides were all part of a pattern was an indication to him of a power greater than any human power. This belief, which he had, put a meaning on what he called the earthly life. It was not an explanation, he said. This storehouse of experience was a mystery. In spite of not knowing, human individuals went along living their lives baffled when they questioned. But mostly, he said, people questioned only on a superficial level if they questioned at all.

•

During the sleepless night when I read through my papers and lectures they do not, in the confined overheated space of the hotel room, have any meaning. I read aloud putting in pause marks and asides which could spring from the text. But this act of the will, which is a necessary part of preparation, does not enable me to add anything useful or fresh.

I am still here on the twenty-fourth floor. When I sit in front of my mirror I can see, in the mirror, someone on the twenty-fourth floor across the street. He is sitting upright at a table and is in his shirt sleeves. I have no idea who he is.

I am frightened. I have lost count of the days.

For a long time I keep my light on. Without the light the hot airless room becomes a tunnel lined with earth. It is treacherous with a system of exposed hot-water pipes. The room is a cave where a dog might turn round and round ensuring his safety before lying down to sleep. I have been round this room over and over again. There is no escape, no bolt hole from the lair. The only way out is into the long dimly lit passage which seems to lead nowhere. There is too the feeling that I am alone here on the twenty-fourth floor. Insanely high, swaying . . .

The abstracts, when I study them, are elaborate and pretentious. And the names in the conference program, though they are well known to me, probably belong to strangers.

The cure for cabin fever is to recognize the symptoms. In order to overcome the inability to cross the thin ice of the conference rooms it is necessary to collect all the images and the experiences as if they were treasures in a small storehouse. The cabin fever is the same as the pause with which I am familiar. It is the same thing, this cabin fever, as sitting at a bus stop, back home—when I am not actually waiting for a bus, watching the Easter moon climb the dark blue evening. It is the same thing as watching a woman in a neighboring garden calmly hanging wet clothes on a line during a time of complete self-absorbing drama. It can be regarded too as being the same thing as traveling by an earlier train, earlier than usual (also back home) on purpose to see again the woman who reminds me of staff nurse Ramsden. This cabin fever is like the intention to speak, it is the long drawn-out pause of intention.

I have never spoken to the woman on the train. It seems to be enough that I promise this for some future time. It is enough, for the present, to create Ramsden in my own image. It's like this, certain phrases of music recapture Ramsden clearly. It is as if we are walking together once more in the rain as it drips through the branches of the beech trees in autumn and I am listening to her telling me something . . .

I never walked anywhere with Ramsden except in my imagination. And the music now, which recalls her, is not the music we listened to together. The Schubert piano and cello is not the piano and cello music of those other times. Perhaps the ability of the cello to suggest the tender reasoning I heard in her voice is a part of the mysterious process of acknowledging something which is to be slowly unlocked at some time later on.

I am certain that a confrontation of recognition, a reunion, with exclamations and animated conversation, on a train would be like the hoped for ending to a particular kind of novel. I mean, how can anyone's life, in reality, at the present time, contain the fulfillment of expectation and the happy ending of a romantic fiction.

Betsy Drinkwater's yearly letter with its repetitions of household repairs and endless responsibilities towards onion beds and herbaceous borders has something inevitable about it like the changing of the seasons but without the sensation of a change in the air and without the different gifts which each season, in turn, promises. I am not able to see, in my mind, the writer of these letters, to match her life with the lives of the people I see daily in my consulting rooms, lives which do not, for various reasons, go beyond a daily experience of an incredible loneliness. I do not try to recognize her as she must be now. Betsy Drinkwater remains youthful for ever, the schoolgirl in an innocent uniform hurrying across the fields to school. When I am holding one of her letters in my hand it is as if I could never have had any idea of what was lying in wait for me.

I do not have letters to look forward to now. At one time letters brought that excitement which accompanies the deepening of friendship, the discovery of the self in relation to someone else. It seems strange that there was ever a time when I waited eagerly for letters. At present letters received and sent are mostly brief communications and reports about the human condition, about diets and about medication.

Occasionally a warm fragrance in the days approaching summer prompts me to suggest to someone, who is coming to keep an appointment, that they take the path through the pines from the station. It is both a short cut and a pleasant little walk. A remedy.

THE GEORGES' WIFE

"Die mit Tränen säen, werden mit Freuden ernten"
(They that sow in tears shall reap in joy)

"The smallest service done to the lowliest
possesses an eternal value."
— EVELYN PEARCE

. . . when thy mind
Shall be a mansion for all lovely forms,
Thy memory be as a dwelling place
For all sweet sounds and harmonies;
— WORDSWORTH

"Tell me about yourself, Migrant," the rice-farm widow says to me. So I tell my widow things about myself. When I tell her about Felicity and Noël her mouth is so wide open, as she listens, I can see her gold fillings. At that time, I think her whole fortune is in her mouth.

"You mean to tell me!" she says. "Oh, I can't believe . . ." she says, "that they, I mean, *together*. You can't mean that."

"Yes, that's right," I tell her.

"Oh, Migrant. You poor child, poor poor child."

"Oh no, your widowship, not at all. Nothing like that. They were very gentle and considerate. They were intellectuals, don't you see. The whole thing was more of an *idea*. And it was quite a joke thing between us, between the three of us, every time. Their very good manners, don't you know."

"More than once! Heavens, child!"

"Please, please—don't be concerned. Do not concern your gracious self; it was funny, really funny. They were, *unlike us*, so very polite."

"You mean, '*after you*' and 'Oh no, *after you*.' "

"Well sort of, not quite, but yes, rather like that."

"What an *experience* you had."

"I suppose so."

"You *suppose* so. My dear Migrant, do you realize that plenty of people would give their eye teeth . . ."

"But what would anyone *do* with someone else's eye teeth?"

The Roads

What are you thinking, I want to ask Mr. George. What are you thinking about, I want to ask him. Are you thinking about Miss Eleanor and whether she will be coming home soon, I want to ask him.

From Harold Avenue we turn left into Hammond and left into Goldsworthy, cross Goldsworthy into Bernard, and go on westward downhill, smooth smooth, to the park. My heels, the heels of my shoes, newly repaired, sound on the new surface of the road, like a trotting horse, a little trotting horse. Like a toy horse, Mr. George makes this observation saying, at the same time, that his feet are not making any noise on the road.

From the park it is uphill into Thompson and then a right turn into Koeppe across Princess into Caxton, then Warwick, and back along Queen. Queen Street is lined on both sides with old twisted trees. The long-leaved peppermints, they make a tunnel of shade and fragrance. In Queen it is like being in a green church or a small green cathedral. Does Mr. George think so too, I want to ask him. Would he agree about a cathedral? Is a little street in a suburb, I want to ask him, a place of worship and of prayer?

There is hardly ever anyone about in the streets in the quiet afternoons. Sometimes the days, depending on the time of the year, are either too wet or too hot, but we are there, all the same.

Sometimes I think of asking Mr. George does he remember when the girls were little and doing their spelling and arithmetic with Miss Eleanor. Does he remember now their piano practice, I want to ask. Does he remember the night porter with his springing hoop of keys at the hospital and does he, I want to ask, think of the farm, the derelict farm in the field by the coal mine. Does he, I almost ask, does he remember Dr. Metcalf and his wife, Magda, and does he remember Noël and Felicity. Gertrude too, does he remember Gertrude? How can Mr. George remember Gertrude except what he will have been told? It is likely he does not remember what I told him about her.

Do you remember the illness I had, I want to ask Mr. George. Does Mr. George remember my mother's reproachings over both the illness and the pregnancy, saying how is it that *as a doctor* I have been unable to avoid the particular illness, and *as a nurse* before that, stupid completely stupid about the pregnancy—just like a rabbit, breeding straight away, she said then, adding that she should never have given me the book about Elisabeth Ney, the sculptor because she, E. Ney, has a baby in that book without being married.

I remember my mother's repeated warnings about the illness. Mr. George would not remember them. They were not directed at him.

When I ask Mr. George if he remembers our long journey across the world, he says he is sorry he is such a silly old man and will I remind him. And when I ask him what he has had for lunch he does not know. And when I ask him what he does remember or if he asks a question himself, both his reply and his question are surprising to the point of being startling.

The Hour of the Wolf

I often wish for a mountain or even two. I have the feeling that a sky line with hills and mountains would put the landscape into some sort of proportion. I think, quite often, that a well-proportioned landscape could help me to have a more balanced view of my life. I suppose the same could be said about seeing the well-balanced and pleasing proportions of a man or a woman, a perfect stranger, in the street or in a shopping center.

Occasionally a warm fragrance in the days approaching summer prompts me to suggest to someone who is coming to my rooms to keep an appointment, that they take the path through the pines from the station. It is both a short cut and a pleasant little walk. A remedy.

The strange thing about living, I often nearly speak of this during a consultation, is the repetition. It is as though the individual enters the same experience again and again. The same kinds of people make the same demands, and the giver, blessed with giving, gives yet again in what turns out to be the wrong direction.

I am a shabby person. I understand, if I look back, that I have treated kind people with an unforgivable shabbiness. For my work a ruthless self-examination is needed. Without understanding something of myself, how can I understand anyone else.

Every day I am seeing people living from day to day, from one precarious day to the next, from one despairing week to the next, without any vision of any kind of future. I understand that I, at various times in my own life, have been unable to see anything beyond the immediate.

Every day the waiting room, outside my consulting room, is lined with people waiting. During the years I have become acquainted with all kinds of waiting rooms but have never waited in mine. I intend one day to be there early, earlier than the first appointment, to try out my waiting room as if it would be possible to be then shown in to my own consulting room . . .

Mr. George is not straight in his frame. There is a white space at the bottom of the picture. When I take the back off the little silver frame of Mr. George's photograph—just a head and shoulders with both ears showing as for a passport—I find a lock of his hair before it turned white. I don't see the hair at first but find it on the quilt and I can't, for a minute, think where it has come from. I hold it in my hand and then I understand Miss George must have put it there. It is a soft fair curl, perhaps from his first baby hair-cut.

Mr. George during the time I have known him has always had white hair.

If I miss Mr. George, it is something from before which I am missing. That is what he would say. But just now the glowing colors of the bricks in the path reflect in the soft breast feathers of the doves. It is likely that during the next consultation I shall heal myself. I shall try to put into ordinary words the verses from 1 Corinthians chapter 16 v.13 and 14

> *Watch ye, stand fast, in the faith,*
> *quit you like men, be strong*
> *let all your things be done with charity.*

"Be kind', my father always said. With kindness in mind, perhaps I shall suggest a little dwelling in thought on the reflection of warm brick colors and on the tender breasts of doves.

Sometimes I wonder whether, between the soft fair curl of baby hair and the white hair of an elderly man, Mr. George had brown hair. This is the kind of thing it would not do to ask Miss George. If she had wanted me to know she would have told me.

What are you brooding on, Vera, in your silence, what are you brooding on?

I suppose I shall be lonely, Mr. George, I suppose that, one day, I shall have to be alone. I shall be lonely.

I shall be lonely and alone without Mr. George, Oliver really, but I always think of him as Mr. George and that is the name I have for him. This way a continuity is not broken. Similarly Dr. Metcalf was always Dr. Metcalf. Silly, but that's how it was. In any case we do not talk now of Dr. Metcalf.

Everything changes. Slowly everything changes. I am tired. Because of being tired I am irritable. Mr. George can hear that I am impatient and it is as if he is crying somewhere quietly inside because of the tone in my voice. An old man, like a baby, is able to hear and to know the tone and he cries. If you go on being impatient and unkind, the feeling of remorse which follows is so powerful and terrible and there is no way of explaining that you are sorry. Remorse is irreversible and unforgettable and there is no way out from the pain of feeling it. There is nothing for me to do but to take Mr. George's hands in my hands and stroke them and kiss them in an attempt to say I will not be impatient again. And then to try, for ever, to prevent anything which will bring it back—this remorse.

In every old man I suppose there are glimpses of his childhood which he will have forgotten and which did not show earlier. They would have been hidden in the conventional mannerisms and *face* necessary for household, for work, and for community. These tiny transient appearances of certain behavior, of wish and choice, of dignity and affection which I can see, from time to time, in Mr. George reflect the shape, the pattern, the whim, and the fancy in the ideas on upbringing held by Miss George.

There are too some things which seem to frighten him, or threaten, perhaps reminding vaguely of small punishments of some kind. Small things like spilling a glass of milk or scattering crumbs or not finishing a sandwich . . .

"How can Faust go on after what has happened?" a student asked Mr. George during one of his lectures. Mr. George explained then that Goethe gave Faust forgetfulness. "Perhaps," Mr. George said, "perhaps forgetfulness is the kindest blessing. But whether Goethe meant this is another matter."

I sometimes went to Mr. George's lectures simply to be where he was, to be in the same room, *in an ordinary sort of way*, where he was. Naturally it was with Miss George's approval that I went.

This might be as good a place as any to mention that it is perhaps a curious irony that my mother visiting the Georges did not come as a reader of Goethe, *Faust* or *Iphigenia*, for example, in Goethe's own language and having, in addition, the ability to discuss with Mr. George his own favorite aspect that all guilt, in Goethe's interpretation, both human and that of the gods is avenged on earth. She came, not as someone who could, from her own reading and interest, offer detail from Goethe's own life—an example being, that as a young man he had insisted on his mother spreading out, for his choosing, three sets of clothing every morning—but she came as my mother, the mother of the maid and grandmother of the maid's two illegitimate babies and who had, as her best friend, the railway-man's widow, Mrs. Pugh, living in the small house next door to her own small house.

My mother could have quoted Kestner's response to *Werther, il est dangereux d'avoir un auteur pour ami*, but in the presence of the Georges she did not seem to be that sort of person. So much do people alter themselves and equally do not recognize their own merit in the eyes of other people.

The Georges, I know now but did not understand then, would have welcomed this other aspect of my mother had she chosen—felt able, I should say, to offer it.

Perhaps it is true to say that both my mother and I, usually from necessity, have been able to present more than one face during both favorable and unfavorable times. I think that this is probably an acquired skill developed from a hidden gift at birth, which for some may never be needed.

Once I told Mr. George that I was afraid he would leave me or that he would not want me any more and he, nursing me on his arm, told me that most people ultimately have the experience of having only the memory of love; except, of course, those who have never known what it is like to be in love, to love and to be loved. And even then, he said, most people will have some remembered cherishing or remembered feelings of cherishing towards someone else.

"I shall always love you and want you," he told me then, "but in the end we all do have to leave each other. Even when I do leave you," he said, "I shall have given you myself and you will be different because of knowing me. This is inescapable and it goes both ways."

When I think of this it is necessarily true of Dr. Metcalf and, in this idea of being different because of receiving certain intangible gifts, it is true too of my father and my mother, of Gertrude, of staff nurse Ramsden (even if mostly in my imagination), and of Miss George, and even of my father's sister, my Aunt Daisy, or Miss Daisy as her housekeeper companion, Miss Clayton, called her.

One afternoon I wait for Mr. George. I want to wait for Mr. George and walk home with him from the university, feeling the palm of his hand pressed against my palm and our steps measuring, side by side, together on the pavement, and feeling the damp air of autumn fresh on my face and in my hair but mostly feeling his hand holding my hand and both of us, in this way, making the declaration of belonging to each other. So I wait for him.

As I begin to write now a feeling of peacefulness comes over me as if I need not for inexplicable half-hidden reasons refrain from writing any longer. Three things emerge; one is that a mother always forgives. The second is that it is often not possible to write about events until they are over or sufficiently of the past, that they can be regarded as being in that twilight between the fact and the imagined. There are tremulous and fragile boundaries; thin invisible lines of hoped-for coherence through which the writer moves with caution aware, all the time, of an emerging nakedness for which conventional clothes are too transparent. And thirdly; secrets, if they are revealed completely, become mere facts. Secrets, if partly kept, can be seen as relating not to some kind of imitation but to something extra to real life.

On that afternoon I do slip out of the house secretly to wait for Mr. George on the corner where the trams stop and there is almost always a drunk, in an old coat, slumped over one of the smooth metal stumps which are along the edge of the pavement to stop people from rushing across the road in front of a tram.

I wait there in the cold darkening afternoon wishing to see him, fresh faced and smiling, his heavy overcoat unbuttoned and his scarf loose, coming down University Avenue. I think that it will be dark enough for us to walk without being noticed.

After waiting for what seems a terrible long time I telephone the house to see if he has gone home some other way. It seems silly and insolent of me to do this. Miss George answers, her kind elderly voice saying, "Hello" and then the number. I hang up on her three times before going back there alone.

I suppose waiting for someone I really want to see at different times during the years reminds me all over again of that time, a long time ago, when I am cold and pregnant and not at all sure how things will turn out for me. That day I remember clearly, in the evening, Mr. George telling Miss George about a student of his who laughs like the opening of the Bach cantata, the one with the exultant trumpet matching exquisitely with the superb voice of a boy soprano. Number fifty-two he thinks it is, "Praise the Lord Everywhere Throughout the Land," perhaps not exactly those words but that is the meaning in the triumphant music.

When I tell Mr. George later that I am jealous of the student and what was her name, he says he can't remember anything about her except her laugh.

"You must not be jealous," he tells me then. "You must always tell me how you feel," he says then privately in the aprons hanging on the back of the kitchen door, one of his favorite hiding places for catching me quickly as I am going through. "I must know everything about you," he says, "and I want you to be happy."

To look at the back of someone's neck is to see how vulnerable the person is. The back of Mr. George's neck is the same as it was when I first knew him. For Miss George that hidden and gentle place will have been hers to know at a much earlier time. The elder sister bringing up the younger brother, as she has done, her knowledge and her feelings might well be much greater than mine. I do not speak of this to Mr. George.

Bay Road, Hammond, Harold and Goldsworthy, Bernard Street, the park, Thompson Road, Koeppe Road, Princess, Caxton, Warwick, and Queen. Of these closely watched roads Goldsworthy is smooth and Hammond, because of the rough blue-chip metal, is uneven. Queen is fragrant and shaded with peppermint trees whereas Hammond has cape lilacs and plane trees which arch, dappled, overhead creating either a shelter from the sun when it is too hot, or from the rain when it comes. The delicate china blue of the washed sky, beyond the middle distance, created by the high, thin branches of the lilacs, is serene and impersonal. The leaves, turning, rustle and fall. They sound like approaching footsteps and then they collect in softly whispering drifts.

Some days Mr. George, not remembering, feels he is lost.

Watch the hedges I tell him, look closely at the honeysuckle, the hibiscus, the oleander, the rosemary, and the raging plumbago. Look, I tell him, at the roses, the white roses and the red. Look at the bougainvillaea, the purple, the pink, and the apricot, and, over there, the wistaria. You are not lost I tell him, I am with you.

Our walk is smooth smooth purring along Goldsworthy and smooth smooth down Bernard, westward to the park. Because of the new blue-chip metal Hammond is rough. From the back I can see closely the back of Mr. George's neck. The back of the neck, the nape, is vulnerable. From behind the wheelchair there is the close view of the back of the neck of the person who is sitting in the chair.

Sometimes I wake too early at that time described as the hour of the wolf. I think then of all the books and papers, the pictures and the cassettes, the dishes, the linen and the clothes, and the furniture in the house. I think of the shabby paint and the deep cracks in the walls and the ceilings. And then there are the places where the roof leaks. I go round in the dark, putting pails and bowls to catch the dripping rain water. This house has, between the corrugated-iron gables, a flat roof similar to the flat roof years ago where I shoveled off the snow, when I was young and not at all fearful of the height of the ladder, perched on the top landing, with all the flights of stairs curving down, below me, down to the front hall. A flat roof, we all agreed at that time, gives the most trouble.

A flat roof is the worst kind of roof—Miss George always made the announcement on wet mornings in that other house. She was sure the wind had brought all the soaked leaves from the surrounding streets into the space between the gables.

Suffering is like art we create it within ourselves. Noël said this and said it was written by Strindberg. Felicity, as usual, answered Noël with a second quotation; "Look," she said, "*at the ruin of the individual when he isolates himself* . . . "Strindberg again," Noël said.

It does not seem possible to avoid either of these truths. I am confronted daily in my consulting rooms with manifestations of both.

The raw inhospitable remains of the night are captured by the surprise of the morning. This soft patience waits outside the closed blinds where birds, unconcerned, squabble endlessly, perhaps going over the roosting disagreements of the previous evening.

Perhaps it can be said that the only thing in favor of blinds is the revelation when they are released in the mornings. This revelation is always forgotten during that hour when life is at its lowest ebb, that hour years ago when I was nursing; and in the stillness perhaps between three and four in the morning, a life, hovering, would slip away for ever and Sister Bean, for thirty years the Night Superintendent, would add to her bedside prayers, while still on her knees, a reprimand saying that nurses should remember that they were only nurses and should not think of themselves as being capable of controlling the Divine Intervention.

This revelation, when the blinds are released in the mornings, is in the daylight which is so steadily and reassuringly increasing as if suggesting that, with the rising of the sun every morning, everything will be as usual. And that all I have to do is to go out into the new day in an ordinary way, as usual.

Every morning with the orange juice, that is when I am squeezing the small oranges for juice, I put aside a glassful for Mr. George. A libation, you could call it that. And I drink my own share straight off and look up at the sky.

Every morning I understand that this is the only time when I remember to look, with suitable undisturbed humbleness, at the sky. As a well-proportioned and balanced landscape can help towards a balanced view of all that belongs to living, the high up, often clear limitless space of the early morning sky can be a reminder of my own insignificance. Feeling insignificant like this helps to bring about a measured sense of proportion.

This morning, during my homage to the sky, I see something I have not thought about for years. I see in the slow-moving, white masses of cloud, without any previous remembering or thought, the face of a ram. The ram which was caught by his horn on a branch of a small gnarled fruit tree in an orchard beyond the top field at Gertrude's Place. I was there with Gertrude very early as I had gone on my day off from the hospital to fetch black-market eggs for my mother. At that time, during the war, I was nursing and I went to Gertrude's Place, on my bicycle, whenever I could. As always the clouds seemed low, as they often do in the country, over the field. I felt that I could reach up and touch them with both hands. The sky there was often like this, especially when it was about to rain. We were walking round the field she wanted me to have and we pushed through the hedge into the orchard which belonged to someone else but which, Gertrude maintained, we could buy if I came in with her on the idea she had about me owning the field and the two of us having a pig there and a sty built. A few sheep, unconcerned, moved in gently closing circles together between the neglected trees. We came upon the ram by accident. Gertrude said that he must have been there, hooked on the low branch, for some time. She said she thought the tree was an apple tree. She said to look at the way the bark had been rubbed smooth with the ram trying to free himself.

The dignified gentle expression in the cloud ram's face matches, in my memory, the dignified patience in the eyes of the exhausted and starved ram imprisoned on the low twisted branch.

On that day, Gertrude showed me how to push and pull the ram to get him free. "His horns, the shape of 'em," she said, "are against him." She explained that an animal was not the same as a human. Lacking human imagination the ram would not have been thinking and anticipating the suffering of being trapped and slowly starving to death as a human being would. The ram, she said, would pause in his struggles and then resume them and a bit later on would pause once more and so on. But he would not think, she said, in between times, that he was trapped.

When, at last, we managed to free the ram he tottered and fell over and Gertrude said that, if I did not mind, we must have him up on his legs. So we tried once more and he started off after the sheep in a crazy sort of way. Gertrude said then that he would fall again and not be able to get up and he would die. He had that look about him, she said, but since he wasn't her ram there was not much use in us hanging about there.

We wrapped the eggs in threes, in sheets of newspaper and in pages torn from magazines. I wanted to tell Gertrude about a forthcoming party at the Metcalfs' but already, by this time, she was for urging me to let those people alone and had, more than once, offered to visit them to ask them not to invite me to their house and their ways. Gertrude had two dressed fowls as well for my mother, as usual. And, as usual, she explained that one of them had had a fox get to her but not all that much taken, just a wing and a bit of breast. She had neatened the damage, she said, with her dress-making scissors. "Tell Mother," she said, "I'm sorry about that old red fox."

It seems strange now to remember small things from years ago. Perhaps remembering them means that they are not so small.

Remembering the dignified gentleness in the eyes of the ram I think, too, of the dignified gentle patience with which Mr. George sits waiting either in his room or on the veranda. When he sees me his face lights up with pleasure, I suppose as mine lit up, as he used to say it did, with happiness, each of us, in the presence of the other.

One memory leads without real sequence to another. My mother, often quick to voice an opinion or a warning, said at the time when I was ill, unable to keep the fear and the indignation out of her voice, as when I was pregnant for the first time, "A doctor! And having such an illness. You should have been more careful. With your nursing too you should have known better. You cannot say I did not warn you. Always I said to you to walk on the other side of the road. I taught you to avoid the spots of blood in the snow."

The cough, when it came, seemed to start somewhere out of reach, persistent and irrepressible. Of course I thought, all the time, of Noël. I actually wished for Noël and Felicity to visit me.

The sputum mugs, with chipped enamel lids, disgusted me. It was not because they were unfamiliar. They were all too familiar. I detested them in the days when it was a part of my work to collect them, empty them and clean them. Describing their contents, either in speech or in writing, disgusted me. And I still detested them.

When I could, when I was allowed to walk about, I looked for places where I could leave unclaimed this terrible ugliness, on a high shelf in the bathroom, in the sluice room or behind the door of the boiler room.

"Where is your sputum mug?"

"I don't have any sputum."

Hides sputum, was recorded along with my temperature, pulse, and respiration.

"A mother has always to forgive," my mother's repeated words during her visits then.

It is sometimes said that events cannot be transformed into fiction until they are sufficiently over. There will be exceptions. There is too the idea that different elements can be woven together in the creating of characters and story. There can be a merging of the actual and imagined. It is necessary to cultivate the ability to keep the vision sufficiently apart from the real event. It is this ability to hold on to the vision while being involved in the event which helps to bring about the making of a fiction writer or a poet.

It occurs to me now that events are well enough advanced to enable an attempt at this transformation.

It occurs to me too that there are yet more people who have given themselves to me in their several ways, so bringing about changes in me. I am different because of knowing, for example, Noël and Felicity and even that small man, Boris, who visiting one night with his home-made lute, an exact copy of the original, provided a fragile music at the foot of the heap of black slag, the pit mound; a strange ugly place for the serenity of the lute and the self-conscious laughter of the three of them, Boris, Noël, and Felicity, as they repeatedly failed to reach the right notes in their singing.

Then there are the widows. Both giving advice and both, in their own ways, giving imitations of attitudes, mainly their own.

My mother's widow and my own widow.

Perhaps this would be a good place to note that I have to acknowledge that my clothes are more suitable for sitting in out-patients' departments than in any other place. I mean, I am never suitably dressed for a restaurant or a concert, a morning or an afternoon-tea party or the waiting room of an accountant or a solicitor—all places for which better and more attractive and fashionable clothes are required. This goes for my consulting rooms too and accounts for the fact that I often wear a white coat there, even though I know the trend (if I can use such a word) is to be dressed in ordinary clothes, perhaps something lacy or knitted, a floral dress obviously home made with puff sleeves or from the current gear, jeans, Reeboks, and a T-shirt with a slogan to put patients and their relatives at ease.

Eine Bemerkung

Perhaps, as on the previous page, this is as good a place as any for the inclusion of an observation, a glimpse from before, a little explanation, something of that sort.

"Addi," my mother remarks, "is fading away in unhappiness." She adds that this is merely *eine Bemerkung*, and, though it is serious, it can only remain as an observation because it does not do to interfere between married people. She was waited, she says to my father, for the right moment to tell him this.

I am under the table, far back where the table is against the wall. I am trimming the fringe of the green plush cloth with forbidden weapons. I can hear everything. Bert Rose is crying.

Bert Rose, a traveler in fat (mainly for fish and chips), and who grew up in the street where my grandfather, in public, disowned my father for being in prison during the Great War, because he was a C.O., has left the room for a few minutes to go to the lavatory. He whistles a small tune when he pulls the chain. I have noticed that people often whistle or sing at this particular time.

Addi, with dark shadows round her eyes and a paleness which, my mother says, is threatening, has left Bert Rose. He has no idea where she is and no idea, at all, why she has gone. Bert Rose cries some more.

Bert Rose and my father are friends. Bert Rose will have seen my father turned out of the house with my grandfather throwing a shilling at him. Bert Rose maintains that my grandfather was only ashamed because of the imprisonment, ashamed that my father was in prison, and not about the reason for his being there.

"Addi is, how shall I put it?" my mother says, "*ein Zigeuner-Mädchen*. You say she has taken her violin? She likes—no, enchanted is better, she is *enchanted* by the *Zigeuner*, and the violin, the endlessly sad music of these people. She will be back," my mother goes on, "she will come back when the gypsies move on. You will see. In any case," she adds, "she will be back for 'The Archduke' in the town hall next week."

Under the table my father's boots are planted on the linoleum. Bert Rose's boots, which are heavier, move and shuffle and I know that his big red hands will be shuffling across his red face as he tries to wipe away his tears.

My father suggests they go on their bicycles to Tinkers' Castle Hill. There is time enough. And Bert Rose says that he has seen a place there where a woman sells eggs and boilers—cheap.

"Bring a fowl and some eggs," my mother says.

Years later Gertrude, remembering my father and his friend turning up early at her Place that first time, tells me that she feels dreadfully ashamed that morning because, as she tells me, "I hadn't even washed me when—*there they was*—the two of them, these gentlemen, coming up out of the long grass!"

When she tells me this we are tearing up an old newspaper and wrapping up the new-laid eggs. Black-market eggs, they are called then.

I must explain something about my father. He was always seeing me or other people off at the bus stop or the station. "I'll come to the train with you," he'd say at the last minute, just before it was time to set off.

His coming to London to see off the boat train is unexpected. Because of this habit of his, it should have been expected. On that occasion Mr. Berrington, after consulting his watch, says that it looks as if the train will be leaving on time. He moves his folded raincoat from one arm to the other and holds open the compartment door for my mother and me to climb in. Then he shakes hands with my father. He hopes, he says, that my father will have a pleasant journey back to the Midlands.

"Stay on deck," my father says to me, "and then you won't be sea sick."

As the train begins to move my father walks alongside on the platform. The train gathers speed and my father runs smiling and waving. His white face, anxious and sad behind his smile, is the last thing I see.

I mention Bert Rose because it was Bert Rose who told Mr. Berrington that German was spoken in our house. Bert Rose was, at the time, fixing something electrical for Mr. Berrington.

Mr. Berrington, attracted to the language and its literature, became a regular visitor. He came every Sunday for the midday meal, and he and my father exchanged the texts of the sermons at their respective churches during the first course, and the weather forecast while the pudding was served. Mr. Berrington stayed on for his German lesson. Sometimes my mother went to Mr. Berrington's house, where his housekeeper provided afternoon tea with sugar bread, which my mother often brought home in a paper napkin in her handbag.

My mother looked forward, always, to the concerts in the town hall. She was accompanied by Mr. Berrington. Perhaps it says something for her neighbor, Mrs. Pugh (who did not share my mother's taste in music), that she never once commented on the concert going and never once said one word about Mr. Berrington's regular visits to my mother's house.

My mother understood that Bert Rose suffered.

"It is in the glance," she says to me one time later on when we are waiting for a bus. "It is the glance," she says, "the raising of the eyebrows and the small nod—all these—which are so intimate between one performer and another. Perhaps *especially* between the piano and the violin, in the 'Kreutzer Sonata,' for example. But Addi," she continues, "Addi achieves these private and familiar little communications even when there are three players, for instance as in the 'Archduke.' "

My mother explains the difficulties of different cultural backgrounds. Bert Rose, she says then, holds Addi in reverence but does not understand her.

It is only now all these years later, that on reflection, I am recalling my mother's inability to disguise her surprise and alarm when I tell her, in confidence, that Dr. Metcalf is like Levin, the landowner in the Tolstoy novel. This Levin, a nobleman, instead of simply giving orders, takes a scythe and, moving in line with the peasants, he mows his meadows with them. He rests with them and even accepts a share of their simple food. My admiration for Levin because of this, and because of the charming and romantic way he proposes to Kitty, is known by my mother.

"Dr. Metcalf reminds me of Levin," I tell my mother just at the time when I am being drawn irresistibly into the magic world inhabited by Dr. Metcalf and Magda. Gertrude, by this time, more knowingly than my mother, is anxiously trying to discourage me from following what she feels is the way to the greatest of disasters.

It is only now as I write this that I begin to understand that my mother would understand and fear for me something which she herself, during her own marriage, had experienced. An admiration and a reverence and a need for a particular person and for whom she was not free.

At that time my seeing Dr. Metcalf as being like Tolstoy's Levin did not suggest anything to me about either my mother or Mr. Berrington because, naturally, I was not thinking of them. I was thinking only of myself.

And, despite the complication in her own life, it was, without anything being said, clearly my mother's wish that she would, one day, hear the music for the opening of Act III of Lohengrin which accompanies the bridal procession of Elsa and Lohengrin to the Bridal Chamber, being played for me. Not liking or even approving of Wagner's music, I think she must have overlooked the fact that *Lohengrin* was one of his compositions.

All this is in the nature of what my mother would call *eine Bemerkung*, a remark, an observation which is perhaps a bit more than a casual remark or a casual observation.

My Mother's Visit

∝

"I think it is your half crying, Mrs. Wright." Miss George smiles across the table at my mother who, anxious for her share of the new baby, jumps up immediately making for the door, the hall, and the stairs as quickly as she can.

They, Miss George and my mother, decide as soon as my mother arrives to share the new baby, to have a half each, and they take turns to bathe and to change her and to carry her about. My share is naturally the feeding so I get to have an all-night share. Though both Miss George and my mother take a turn each during the one bad night we have had. Colic, they decided together then, and first one and then the other walked up and down with the angry little bundle while I lay in bed, pretending to be asleep, thinking about Mr. George and wishing that I could be alone with him. Such a silly wish really.

Everywhere there is the atmosphere of a house being given over completely to childhood. The pram is in the front hall and the baby bath is on the kitchen table. The cradle is moved from one best place to another best place. A fire burns in Mr. George's study and the clothes-horse laden with wet baby washing stands steaming there all day and every day. I light the fire there every morning when Miss George asks me to, saying that the weather is not showing any signs of clearing yet. My mother nervously suggests that it always rains, even in summer like this, when there is a new baby. Both women smile at each other.

My mother, it is clear to me, would rather be in her own house with Helena and Rachel. She has been upset by the choice of the name Rachel.

"No one calls a baby Rachel these days. No girl can have this name. Rachel was the Queen of the prostitutes," my mother manages to say when we have a few minutes alone together.

"Don't be silly," I tell her. "That's not true, it's silly, a silly made-up . . ."

"*Im Kloster,*" they always said . . . "In the convent . . ."

It's a Hebrew name I tell my mother. I am reliving an imagined conversation from before Rachel was born. It is a strange experience. "It's a Hebrew name and it means 'like a ewe' and is a symbol of innocence and gentleness. It's a pretty name," I tell her as firmly as I can, keeping my voice soft at the same time.

Miss George, as usual with her keen insight, suggests, when my mother returns to the table with the baby in the crook of her arm, held with all the remembered knowledge and tenderness I had seen when she first held Helena, that perhaps when my mother returns home I should go with her, taking the children, for a week.

"That would be very nice," my mother says trying, in her politeness, not to sound too eager to get to her own place in order to enjoy her grandchildren.

"Thank you, Miss Eleanor," I say. Later I ask her will she manage alone with Mr. George being away.

"I shall manage perfectly," she replies. "Life is simpler when one is completely alone. Of course I shall miss the children dreadfully, but a week is only a week, isn't it."

Mr. George is in Europe with a group of students including the un-named one, she of the Bach cantata, trumpet and soprano, laugh. I am at the stage of picturing Mr. George and Cantata holding hands secretly during a cultural outing, brushing shoulders and hands accidentally while gazing at portraits of royal princes and princesses and the Emperor Franz Joseph. I manage to picture her—almost immediately, because of her loud cascade of laughter, being forcibly thrown out from the sacred silence of some beautiful and ancient church or from a silent gallery of statues and monuments. This is only a temporary picture unfortunately. I feel certain that Cantata is absolutely stylish in loose artistic unwashed dresses and has her long hair tied back, leaving some strands of hair falling carelessly and deliciously across her unblemished face. She probably calls Mr. George Professor or Prof or she might have reached, with the long fingers of a thick-skinned egoist, towards *Oliver*. I have no one to whom I can denounce her.

The postman knocks with an expected package of literary journals for Mr. George. There is a letter for Miss George, from Mr. George, and a post card for me. I am pleased and comforted at once. It is from Weimar and is a picture of Goethe's *Schlafzimmer*, which has in it the narrowest shabbiest small down-at-heel bed you ever saw. I know at once that he has chosen this especially because of the resemblance to his own narrow shabby bed, his bed which has accompanied him from boyhood and which, he has said more than once, has been transformed for him by Venus into the couch of Adonis.

Goethe must have had another bed, probably a bigger one, because this one is in his *Gartenhaus*. This does not at all spoil the special message the card has for me.

My mother privately calling my new baby *die kleine Vera* or simply *die Kleine* instead of Rachel, says, as we pack to go away for the week, that my father will say that the new baby looks like his mother. This is something, she says, which he always says about a new baby. Even if you brought home a black baby, she says, he would say this. I am pleased to see my mother laughing. Quickly she folds things into the open cases.

Miss George sits in the window seat rocking the baby and singing. Helena is spelling aloud to her from an old-fashioned spelling list on a card. After the spelling she will recite the multiplication tables. Helena speaks as Miss George speaks. Exactly.

"You will never be able to leave them." My mother, in the train, is suddenly unable to enjoy the peacefulness when both children are asleep. "They are very kind people and well-educated but they will not let you go. You will be working for them for ever. She will never send you away and you will never feel able to leave him." My mother cries a bit. "She sees in you someone who can go on looking after him. People don't ever do things with complete unselfishness. Vera, will you never learn?"

"But where should I go?" I am afraid my mother will not allow herself to enjoy having the children for the week.

"Well," she says, "perhaps to study, Vera. Your father and I would be pleased to have the children. Please, Vera let us have the children."

I tell her then that I am not accepted in Edinburgh for medicine but that I am coming a bit later on to study medicine at my old hospital in the Midlands. I have been accepted there.

My mother does not say anything. Either she thinks I am pretending and making up the arrangement, or else she does believe me and, at the same time, is afraid that the children will remain with Miss George.

We continue the long journey in silence, giving ourselves up to the soothing rhythm of the railway train.

Miss George's Visitors

I have always believed that if you want something very much you will get it.

One of my wishes is granted. Something I really wished for is granted. It is hardly possible to believe at certain times that a wish will come true, but this one does. I do see Miss George, as I always hoped I would, sitting in the window seat half-hidden in the thick curtains, nursing my baby and singing to her in that soft crackling voice which belongs to old age, and is tuneless, and which sometimes disappears altogether even when the person is still singing.

"Where is thy mother, the slut?" Mr. George, coming home, bringing a breath of the fog with him, and bending over the pink shawl, says. He strokes the small exposed cheek and the tiny ear with one finger.

"Slut? Ullivar? That is no name for this child's mother, not even in fun or for a nick-name!" Miss George, in her reprimand, shows complete understanding. "Her name is Vera, Ullivar, please remember! And this child is Rachel."

"*You could tell her,*" I tell Mr. George in the evening. But I can see at once that he is thinking of his sister and of his sister's visitors; he is thinking of their hats and their gloves and their thin bread and butter and the wide scalloped tea cups, the fine bone china from which they are accustomed to sip their fragrant tea together in the afternoons. He is thinking of these ladies, of their choir practice and of their Sunday mornings and evenings at the church.

"Miss George always asks me to bring the children in during afternoon tea, to be admired," I begin to tell Mr. George. "Helena reads from her reading book and draws pictures." I try to go on to tell him that both children wear the dresses made by Miss George. Helena's has embroidery which is reversible and a ribbon which is pink one side and blue the other, and Rachel's gown is pure white with tiny white embroidered flowers at the neck, the wrists and the hem.

"Miss George really loves them, especially Rachel," I say. "And I'm sure she *knows.*"

"I know. I know." Mr. George tells me, as he always does, that he loves me and the babies, both babies. He always calls them "the babies" even though Helena is already six years old.

In the cherry-wood warmth of the small attic room under the summer-warm gable I cry quietly because I want to be with him all the time. To be his and not just on the edge of him and not just now and then. For the present the new baby is mine and only mine, with no questions asked, and having nothing to do with the name of George.

I carry in the heavy tea trays and the visitors admire my children and exclaim over their prettiness and their lovely clothes. Rachel, as the new baby, is passed round as all seem to want to nurse her. As always, I catch sight of Miss George's face, she is full of love and pride and is enjoying herself.

I have to understand that the structure of Miss George's life could never be altered beyond small changes which accommodate Mr. George.

Miss George has never asked who is the father of the new baby. She is too reserved and well-bred to make an inquiry of this sort.

When I stop crying I feel calmer and, as always, come to the same conclusions. I reach, at a certain point, the thought that there are ways in which I am both fortunate and unfortunate. One such thought is that Miss George will never ask me to leave. She will never *require* me to leave. I understand too that all people need to be loved and that to have someone to love is perhaps even more important. The only person in the world whom Miss George could love is the one man, her own brother, and she must be her own silent wardress and *not* love him. In spite of their difference in age, or perhaps because of it, the remembered childhood pleasures, the anticipations and the confidences persist in such a way that they cannot be ignored.

Then there is the love, a different kind of love but not all that different from the elder sister caring for the once small brother, the love Miss George has for Helena is another stroke of good fortune. I seem to see, as in a sort of vision, as if my tears have washed my eyes, Miss George, in her apron at the kitchen table carving. Her sharp knife is competent and delicate as she carves judiciously the hot roast, leaving more for cold cuts as being the most economical. Miss George, pausing, holds out the knife to Helena and, from the tip of the blade offers her, in advance, a trembling juicy fragment. An image and a memory to be hoarded.

It is to everyone's advantage that Miss George is amazingly healthy. I imagine her having an athlete's heart beat, unbreakable bones, and healthy bowels. It is likely that Miss George could outlive us all. If I look at this supposition calmly, I understand that this can be seen as a disadvantage which seems at times to be, in an unquestionable way, greater than all the advantages.

The Helplessness of
Brothers and Sisters

∽

"Your father has gone to his sister," my mother's first words always on a Saturday morning. "Your father is with his sister." For as long as I can remember these were my mother's words on Saturdays, a refrain encapsulating the inescapable need for tolerance, a statement, an expression of annoyance bordering on the desperate.

Because of my father's sister, my mother, for the whole of her married life, is not able to stand the sight of a rocking chair.

When I think of my father's sister and of Miss George, Mr. George's sister, I understand that there are enormous differences in the ways in which people conduct themselves.

My father stops visiting his sister quite suddenly. After all the years of the Saturdays, of going by train and bus to visit her, he stops going. He never explains to anyone why he no longer visits her house.

When she dies he is required, he says, to go over there, not having visited, for some mysterious reason, for a long time. He is obliged to go, he says, in the event of her death. He is required to clear up her things. His sister, having bought an annuity for herself with what my mother describes as my father's share of the money, does not have any money to leave to anyone.

The sad part about it is, my father says later, that there is a houseful of possessions, furniture, books, pictures, clothes, knives and forks and plates and cups and saucers and photographs, all of which were *treasures* to her but are unwanted by anyone else. He gives away what he can and has to have enormous bonfires for the rest. There is, for example, a whole cabinet of babies' dresses, carefully embroidered, some with smocking, and some trimmed with handmade lace by her girls at school. She has been a sewing teacher at the same school all her life. She was always very proud of the collection of what she called "my girls' work." The babies' dresses are, by this time, discolored and marked in places with iron-mold and mildew; some are actually rotten.

It is this extraordinary coincidence of a special skill which Miss George has, the sewing and the embroidery. Fine sewing and embroidery in particular.

"My girls at school . . ." She, like my father's sister, often starts a conversation relating to something from years ago, about her girls in the succession of needlework classes. "Some of my girls' work." Miss George has shown me the cupboard with glass doors in her room. It is full of some of the prettiest things I have ever seen. "All handworked," she tells me, when she takes out the table cloths and the tray cloths and the gowns and dresses for babies.

It is years since she retired, so naturally I want to protect her. Perhaps, in spite of what I really want, I do want to protect her and the life she has with her church and her visitors and the people she visits and, more importantly, with her brother.

These Georges, this brother and sister, there is something innocent about them.

There is an indestructible devotion going both ways between Miss George and Mr. George. Mr. George tells me one time, when we are alone, that it suddenly occurred to him that his sister was the one person who had known him for the longest time and that she was the only person who had ever wanted to hear him sing.

I suppose Miss George must have been about thirteen or fourteen when she was left looking after her baby brother.

My father told me that he had to look after his younger sister. Elder brothers and sisters, he said, must always look after the younger ones. He had to take his sister to the elementary school every morning. He was not fond of going to school himself. On one occasion, he said, he returned home telling his mother that the school gates were locked because the school had burned down during the night. This was before his sister was old enough to be taken to school. His mother said she would very much like to see a burned-down school so she put on her hat and coat and walked him straight back down the road to school where the bell was ringing and the children, in their separate playgrounds, were lining up to go in.

In taking his sister to school, my father when telling this would explain, he adopted a method of getting her there as quickly as possible. He hooked an arm round her neck, he said, and set off at a steady trot with her held fast in the crook of his arm, their metal-tipped boots sounding like little horses trotting along the pavement. Sometimes, he said, by accident they kicked and bruised each other's ankles. She wore, he remembered, a round, knitted cap with loose woolen tassels which he could feel against his neck. On arrival at the school he used to push her hard, it was a shove really, through the gate which had an archway marked GIRLS AND MIXED INFANTS in big iron letters. And then he would run off, as if unrelated to her, head down, his responsibility shed, to a similar gateway, arched in iron and marked BOYS.

My father's sister's housekeeper is called a companion. This raises her above the idea of servant. Here at the Georges I am not called a companion. Strictly speaking I am not a house-keeper. Miss George keeps the house and, as the saying goes, she keeps good cupboards. Her household linen is irreproachable and her methods for the care and the upkeep of the rooms are impeccable. I find it very satisfying to be the one to do the clean-ing and the washing. I prepare the food, the vegetables and so on, but Miss George carves the meat and makes decisions about what is to be served at the different meals. I enjoy waiting at table when there are guests and, especially I like taking in the laden trays, when Miss George has her visitors for afternoon tea and I hear their little phrases of admiration about Miss George, her room, and her tea-cakes. I like to see Miss George happy and she does seem so very happy on these occasions. She never fails, at a certain time during the afternoon, to tell me to bring in the children and there is an added pleasure for me when her guests praise my little girl and my baby . . .

During the week when my mother comes as a visitor Miss George does not have her usual tea parties. It is as if she is, thoughtfully, sparing my mother the sight of me bearing the heavy trays and handing round the cups of tea and the little plates and the lacy table napkins before being told that I can leave the room.

"They will do their own reaching," Miss George says. It is a little sentence giving me freedom.

My father's sister's companion is a true daughter of the canal barges, sharp-tongued, energetic, quick at mental arithmetic and spelling; she is knowledgeable about things geographical, historical, political, medical, and personal. She is a small thin woman with a pile of white hair and a voice. Miss Clayton and my father's sister (my aunt) get on satisfactorily together by frequent repetitions of that certain emotional release which follows on the heels of an all-time, all-encompassing row. These two, they have these rows all the time either when they are alone together or in the presence of company or even when there is simply an audience of one. These rows, violent and at screaming pitch, in an agitation of rocking chairs, come unheralded and end quickly in low-voiced soothing moans and endearments uttered from these same rocking chairs, which gradually subside on either side of the hearth. Sometimes there are accompanying tears.

Once you have cried in front of someone or if you have seen someone cry you are never quite the same with that person again. Miss George has seen me cry. Only once. She was shy and patted my shoulder gently, telling me not to cry. I was scrubbing the kitchen table at the time, and when Mr. George, who was mostly the reason for my crying, appeared in the doorway Miss George seemed to place herself between him and me and began to discuss the weather with him even though she had her back to him.

I have seen Miss George cry, though not crying in the way I was, having to sit down by the wet table, holding my face in my hands, unable to stop sobbing.

Miss George lying back, as if still asleep, on her pillows that other morning, when I took her little round tea tray in to her, had her eyes closed and, trembling all along her eyelashes, were her tears. It was that first morning after I had been all night in Mr. George's arms in his narrow bed, answering his rather shy response to certain music, music which, he said then, seemed to promise eternal youth.

"This may prove to be purely an intellectual exercise," he says to me that first time. "I hope you will not be disappointed," he says. He tells me I can escape to my own room if I do not want to stay in his. I tell him then that I want him, his nakedness and mine as close together as possible, completely and at once.

The reddish color of his pullover blends with the suddenly remembered glowing floor boards and cherry-wood furniture of the attic bedroom which I have, for the time being, forsaken and I wonder why, during the wild sweet moments, I should consider this woolen garment and the attic chair, the woodwork of the wash stand and the floor boards.

When, later, Miss George is sorting and throwing out clothes she says the russet pullover is not worth further mending, so I take it. I have it safely with my things. Miss George gives me some of the left-over wool and I darn it and, on cold nights, I wear it to bed as I used to wear my school hockey jumper for many years.

The tears all along Miss George's eyelashes that morning when she was lying as if still asleep, after the night of the Beethoven quartet, the night when I listened with Mr. George, by his fire, to the Beethoven, made me feel that she really knew everything and that it would be right then for us to tell her that we love each other in spite of the great difference in our ages and other insurmountable difficulties, namely because of our different and unbridgeable positions in society. These are not phrases I would use. They could be my mother's if she ever puts this opinion, which she holds, into words. It is something she is sure to do sooner or later when she is upset or angry.

But that time for telling Miss George passes and so do all the other times. Not being able to tell Miss George could become the most important thing in our lives.

Now, when I am either in outpatients' waiting rooms or in my own consulting rooms or on a journey to a conference or, by some miracle, with one or other of my grown-up daughters, the one-time importance, that of being unable to tell Miss George the one thing we needed to tell her, has shriveled, withered like the limbs of an old man when he no longer walks, or like the shelves of unused crockery and saucepans in a house in which most of the rooms are no longer used, because there are not enough people to sit round the table and no one is requiring well-aired and well-made beds. And perhaps most significant of all, since there is no one to sit in the garden, the garden furniture is actually carried indoors and stored in a room lined with books and where, at one time, the carpet used to be rolled back because the floor was considered to be the best floor for dancing.

Even on the occasion of his sister's death, when all the clearing up is finished, my father does not say what it is that made him stop his weekly visits after going on with them regularly for all those years, in the face of my mother's outbursts of anger and reproach.

My father often says that the people who are the hardest to love are those who need it most. I understand now that he saw his sister as being all alone, unloved, and what is worse, having no one of her own to love. And that is the reason for his journeys every week on the early train, returning at night exhausted after digging her garden or mending something in the house, very often something which should have been discarded and replaced. But what tired him most, my mother would argue, were the tirades of complaints and worries. My mother often remarked that her sister-in-law was like a dog with a bone. She would describe the dog worrying the bone, putting the bone down and taking it up again to shake it first one way and then the other way. She said her sister-in-law would even, like a dog, bury her bone in order to dig it up once more and start worrying it all over again. My father, after one of his Saturday visits to his sister, once asked me what he could suggest she should buy for inexpensive presents for her friends at Christmas because she was worrying about Christmas so much and it was then still only June.

It is only now much later on that I understand why, without saying anything to anyone, he stops visiting his sister. He makes this big change in her life and in his, because of me. A great part of her weekly tirade, for a number of years, would have been about me.

It is like this. I have not seen my father's sister (my aunt) for a long time when she calls unexpectedly to see me. Mr. George is at the university and Miss George has taken Helena to listen to the church choir practicing.

My aunt would have left home very early for the long journey, several hours by train with buses at either end.

Without touching her tea or the bread and butter I have cut for her she begins to explain in very carefully articulated words that, because of the way in which I am living and must have lived (this with a sidelong glance at the baby clothes arranged for airing along the fireguard) she has, in her words, been obliged to cut me out of her will, completely out of her will.

The surprise of this is not in connection with any possible gift being withheld, it is more to do with the fact that she has planned to make this journey for this particular reason, this special intention. The sudden intensification of my own feelings of loneliness is a surprise too. I am already alone. I am accustomed to the idea of being alone, but her words cause an extra emptiness, that of being removed from belonging to a family.

Immediately, perhaps with the aid of a cultivated practice of self-protection, consolation, and rescue, without really thinking, I tell her, "Please don't worry about me, I have been well provided for."

"Don't tell Dad," I say later when visiting my mother. The visit is one prescribed by Miss George. Mr. George is climbing mountains in the Tyrol with a group of students. Miss George describes me as looking peaky and in need of a change of air.

My mother says that it could be considered a great comfort for us both that the Georgian silver teaspoons I am meant to inherit from my grandmother via my father's sister will hang like a great weight round her neck . . . She pauses suitably in her finger-pointing pronouncement, to let all the possible horrors contained in this image be continued in the imagination.

"Don't tell Dad," I say again, not thinking that of course my aunt would tell him herself, rail at him, have him on the mat, worrying the subject—the dog worrying the bone—never giving him any peace, wanting to know who is providing for me, what sort of people does his daughter know and mix with and what dark world of sin is she being paid to inhabit.

Not thinking, I say again to my mother, "Don't tell Dad." She says she won't, but of course she does. As I should have known by then, she always tells my father everything.

And it is after this, though I do not at once make the connection, that he stops going to visit his sister. And I never see her again either.

It is only now while my mind is on sisters, Mr. George's sister and my father's sister, I see as *in the lives of the obscure, that being supplied first with gilt-edged notepaper and then with baby linen* and hiding out in a large house, remote from my mother and father, my training abandoned, and being nothing better than a housemaid is not what she had had in mind for me when I had been earlier safely, as in the promise of Isaiah, graven on the palm of her hand, cherished there and not forgotten. She comes all the way to visit me that day because of all that has gone before and because she is inarticulate and helpless in her inability to protect or even to reach.

Wheelchair . . .
Closely Watched Roads

✑

From Harold Avenue turn left into Hammond turn left into Goldsworthy and almost at once cross over turn right into Bernard going west downhill smooth smooth all the way down into the park. In the park there is hardly anyone about. The slopes of cut grass catch the sunlight and the shade. And the ancient trees, each one a benign sanctuary for the doves, the green parrots and the rosellas, do not change either with the passing years or with the seasons. The plane trees in Hammond and Dunbar have lost their leaves and the bare winter branches on the overcast sky of winter remind me of England and of the cold.

The nape of the neck remains unchanged. The nape of Mr. George's neck is not changed. Mr. George asks about Miss Eleanor and if she is busy with the children's spelling and their arithmetic. I explain that Miss Eleanor used to be busy like this. He is thinking, I tell him, of earlier times. Mr. George says, with his little laugh, that he is sorry for being such a silly old man. I tuck the tartan rug more closely round his knees and remind him that the two little girls are now grown up and that Helena is a cardiologist and that Rachel is an obstetrician. He says he remembers. The wheelchair purrs on smooth smooth on the cement path. Smooth smooth.

I ask Mr. George does he remember the night porter at the hospital and his skeleton keys on the small springing hoop which resembles a circular knitting needle. These keys which open everything, all the nurses' rooms, the rows and rows of change-room lockers, the poison cupboards, the operating theaters, the matron's office, and the storeroom where the oxygen cylinders are kept. These keys, they open the late pass door to the residents' corridor and the heavy gates at either end of the tunnel which joins the hospital to the Nurses' Home. So many keys. This porter is the one who, in talking about an air raid one night during the war and his wife being alone all night, during the air raid, takes my mind abruptly off the shortage of hair clips to the more important and serious side of the war.

Surely Mr. George remembers the night porter who unlocks for us at opportune times years ago.

I ask Mr. George if he remembers the Black Country farm and my stupid friendship during the time I am Resident Houseman at my old hospital. And does he remember, I ask, that he wants then to know is it Dr. Metcalf and his greedy, ugly wife all over again, and I tell him "no"; almost to the point of lies, I tell him "no." How could he or anyone think of Magda as either greedy or ugly or both.

And does he remember, I ask him, visiting me during my illness and how he stays the night at the Holly Bush one time and travels by Pullman the other time even when my mother prepares and offers a room for him. Does he recall the luxury of the Pullman?

I ask Mr. George if he remembers the voyage to Australia when we each take up an appointment together but separately. Does he remember, I ask him, all those shipboard rumors? I mean, I suppose then, that they are rumors. One is the midnight funeral—ceremoniously—but with a secretly insisted upon Union Jack. Then there is the closing of the children's play deck because of the smallpox scare. And then there is the expected, scarcely possible, arrival of a pianist, a violinist, and a cellist, a trio renowned for their interpretation of Schubert, being flown out to join the ship for a recital. Does Mr. George remember, I ask him, the woman who repeatedly declares she is robbed? Every few days she is robbed of her furs, her dinner dresses, her necklaces and pendants, and her Italian shoes, expensive Italian shoes. She is the one, I remind Mr. George, wearing a toque, a curious hat which he describes then as a sort of brimless inverted flowerpot. I remind him now that he thinks then that this sort of hat enhances a slightly wicked expression in the eyes.

Then there is the rice-farm widow's well-meaning but impertinent question; surely he does not and never will forget the wording of it.

There is some special quality about the light at a certain time in the afternoons which brings back recurring events and images connected with the particular time of the afternoon, one of these hoarded recollections being the sound of people returning to the house. The afternoon light changing makes Mr. George, on some days, ask if Miss Eleanor will be coming home soon.

What are you brooding over, Vera? What are you brooding over in your silence?

On the symptoms of Exophthalmic Goiter, Mr. George, on Exophthalmic Goiter.

While the piano music spreads filling the whole room I think of Ramsden, of staff nurse Ramsden, erect beside the polished glass shelves of syringes and needles as she prepares them for the three-hourly penicillin, a long time ago, during the war at the time when train-loads of wounded men arrived in convoy at the hospital. I always tried then to make a point of passing the ward where she was so that I could catch sight of her. It was better when I was able to actually walk behind her and staff nurse Pusey (was that the name?), as they walked, their uniforms rustling, in step with one another, conversing in low voices about books and music and possibly a particular concert which both had been to. Ramsden would be familiar with this particular harmony, she would know the presence of the sound of the Neapolitan sixth in Beethoven. I listen for it in the "Moonlight Sonata," taking my mind off my studying for a few minutes.

What comes after Exophthalmic Goiter, Mr. George wants to know when he changes the records. It is the Beethoven fourth piano concerto now, played by Artur Schnabel. How is it possible to think of all the things I must think of during this gentle expanding music.

Your study is more important, Vera. Mr. George stops the music even though we both prefer it. I have to think, I tell him, about various things, the circumstance, for example, of a large overdose of insulin or the symptoms of acute spinal meningitis or a description of a normal gastrectomy and then, in addition, a sort of poem to follow; cirrhosis, leucocytosis, orthopnoea, thrombosis, embolism, hematuria, endocarditis, mitral stenosis, erysipelas, and uremia. And then I tell him, there's more, the signs and symptoms for an early diagnosis of Pulmonary Tuberculosis and a close description and recognition of the onset of Anterior Poliomyelitis and then the question how should a doctor deal with a patient who has received a violent blow on the eyeball. Then there's Cyesiology, Cyesis . . .

At least, I tell Mr. George, I was not caught out in the exam by diagnosing a woman as diabetic when she was merely pregnant. We knew the trick questions, I tell him, when I was nursing; we knew every year that among the patients presented for diagnosis there would be one normal healthy pregnant woman complete with her "signs and symptoms" which could appear to be caused by something else.

Can you study, Vera, while we have this music? Mr. George wants to know. I tell him that I can. It is not the music which is distracting, I tell him, it is the changing light during the afternoon which makes me think of my mother when she sits, in spite of her next-door neighbor and friend, the railway-man's widow, with *Faust* open on her dining table reading aloud with Mr. Berrington whose desire it is to read Goethe in German. My mother and her student are as if caressed together in a shaft of sunlight, which passes slowly from one side of the room to the other as the afternoon goes by. They read aloud, each one reads aloud in turn from the same book, my mother gently, from time to time, correcting Mr. Berrington's shy pronunciation.

Galeotto fu il fibro e chi lo scrisse, Mr. George says softly, when I tell him of this small picture of which I am, I suppose, the sole custodian. He tells me that these words come from Dante's *Inferno* where Dante is in conversation with two adulterous lovers, Paolo and Francesca. Francesca tells him how the two sat together over an old Romance and then passed from reading to some other pastime. Her words, Mr. George explains, mean literally *a pander was that book and he who wrote it.* A pander, he goes on to say, is a go-between, sexually, a go-between. And in the same conversation Francesca makes the famous and much debated statement that there is no greater pain in times of sorrow than to remember times of joy.

"I always thought," I tell Mr. George, putting aside my books and notes for the music and his little bits of conversation, "I always thought, when I was little, that the telephone was invented on the day when my father tried to make me go into a telephone box to learn how to put the money in and dial a number. It's the same about the hoover." I go on, "My mother had her electric cleaner in 1934 and I really thought that was when the first ones were made."

I suppose it is an old idea that everything starts only with us, with each person, as if nothing was ever known or experienced before. I suppose this is especially true over the discovery of certain music and the disturbance of being in love with someone. I have no idea why I should at this moment remember the field at the end of the street and my father whistling from an upstairs window, at dusk, for me to come home. There is this boy, he is big and old and I do not know where he comes from. He says his name is Victor and I can go bird's-nesting with him. So I stand in the long wet grass along the hedge, one hedge after another, and this boy is crouching in the ditch. He keeps telling me to move my legs wider and so I try and do this and he is so close under my skirt that I am afraid he will see my knickers. "Go on," he says, "stand wider, you look up above and I'll look down here." We do not find one nest, not one, and of course no eggs and no baby birds. And then my father is whistling from the back bedroom window, calling me home. "It's like he's whistling his terrier," Victor says, grabbing my dress as I twist quickly one way and then the other and make off across the field, running as fast as I can. At the road I look back and there is no sign of this Victor.

The room where my mother sits with Mr. Berrington has a french window opening on to a piece of concrete which is meant to be like a small terrace but is concrete all the same. From the concrete there is a path and the lawn, geometrically divided by small flower beds, goes back to a small wild place where there are rosemary bushes and two apple trees, one with cooking apples and the other is the Beauty of Bath, the small, sweet, red-cheeked eating apples.

Whenever I visit my mother, and the weather is fine enough, I sit and read under these trees. Mostly, during the years, it has been reading for my work, the skeletal and muscular structure of the human body and the systems; the respiratory, the vascular, the nervous, the digestive, and the reproductive, not for nursing any longer but for my qualifications in medicine.

I have no difficulty, I tell Mr. George, in studying either in his house or when I visit my mother's. The only distraction is the distraction of his presence at home when Miss Eleanor and the children are out.

Desire and desire rewarded is a refreshment of both body and spirit, Mr. George says afterwards. A pause, *moments musicaux*, he says, and I remind him that this music suffers an inheritance of scorn. Not especially because of the music itself, it being, perhaps, the last private and secret words on the piano from Schubert, but because it is often ruined by people pounding on pianos which need tuning. My mother utters words and phrases which carry her scorn when she hears the neighbors on the other side (not Mrs. Pugh's side) play extracts on their awful piano *fortissimo* with all the windows wide open to the freshly cut grass of the small lawns and the sweetness of the summerful herbaceous borders.

Mr. George says that Blake was right when he wrote that *Desire gratified plants fruits of life and beauty there.* The Neapolitan sixth, he says, in music is matched by these lines of Blake's. It starts like this, he says, *Abstinence sows sand all over Ruddy Limbs and flaming hair.*

The Neapolitan sixth, Mr. George speaks of it at exactly the right moment, when we are resting against each other and can feel the beating of each other's hearts. My head on his chest rises and falls gently with each breath he takes.

The Neapolitan sixth, Ramsden would explain, in her well-bred voice, is a chromatic chord, a chromatic modulation, a slipping from one note in one key to another especially in, for example, Beethoven's Sonata *quasi una fantasia* op. 27 in E flat called the "Moonlight Sonata," because a critic described part of it once as containing the imagery of a boat gliding over a moonlit lake, possibly the famous Lake Lucerne. The Neapolitan sixth being a composer's device which is said to produce thoughtfulness and an emotional, romantic quality of sadness creating pathos involving a listener deeply.

I know that recalling Ramsden in this way, in secret, is the way for me to come back to the ordinary day and the return of Miss George to the house. Sometimes, more often than not, I wonder in what way does Mr. George come back into the ordinary things of the household. It is something I do not ask him. I am caretaker, the sole custodian, of all this too.

An Idiot Savant

∝

"Your father is gone to his sister's," my mother is standing on her path, her swollen legs hidden in pink and blue cornflowers. She tells me she's made the back bedroom nice with clean sheets and towels and she tells me that my aunt, my father's sister, died and my father, after not going there for some time, a long time, has this feeling that he must go and clear up her things. Miss Clayton, he'd said, was all by herself now, so he must go.

"The back bedroom is all ready for your visitor," my mother says, "and I've made up the couch for you downstairs." I tell her that Mr. George has taken a room at the Holly Bush near the station. He has to go back first thing in the morning, I tell her. And I tell her that I'll be staying in my room at the hospital. The Holly Bush is quite near the hospital too. "I'm operating," I tell my mother, "at seven."

Abbott Abrahams Ackerman Allwood . . . Often as I pass the nurses' dining room on the way to the small dining room which is for the doctors, it is as if Sister Bean, with the register held to her heart, has marched between the tables her voice barking into the silence after someone has hurriedly switched off the wireless . . . Arrington and Attwood. Nurses Baker Barrington Beam Beamish Beckett Birch Bowman D Bowman E Broadhurst Brown Burchall . . . If I pause on the threshold of this once familiar place it is almost possible to imagine I can hear the names being called into the reverence of silence commanded by Sister Bean. Though the place holds the memory Sister Bean is no longer here and a register is not called;

apparently the nurses objected to having to answer to their names being called. It is a change, a change which would have seemed impossible at one time. The nurses' dining room is full of strange faces and noise. I never hope, in the corridors or the wards, to meet a familiar face, Trent or Lois, for example, or anyone.

In the doctors' dining room, as usual, only Mr. Farrer and Miss Wilson are there. Both are reading while they eat and both, as usual, give me the smallest nod and go on with their eating and their reading.

"It isn't a repetition," Mr. George says when I meet him at the station, "it isn't a repetition, is it, of that fellow Metcalf? This isn't the same sort of thing is it?" Mr. George has come all the way from Scotland to the Midlands to ask me this question.

I take him to my room on the doctors' corridor. I tell him, not at all, my friendship with Felicity and Noël is nothing like my friendship with what he calls "that fellow Metcalf and his greedy wife, Magda." I tell him of course it is different. I am older now, I tell him. I am a doctor now and in my first resident appointment. I remind him that I am the mother of two daughters and that, above all, I belong to him, Mr. George.

"Where would I be without *you?*" I say.

"I don't know that you are any wiser," Mr. George says. "You are such a strange mixture," he says. "An *idiot savant*—perhaps it is that which is so lovable."

I explain, though he knows from previous tellings, how the hospital was bombed during the war and that the doctors' corridor, the whole wing where we are, had to be rebuilt. It's all so different now, I tell him, it's impossible for me in any way to reach back to a reconstruction of the actual place as it was.

However hard I try, peering at the spacing and the positioning of every door, trying to look beyond the new to the old, I am unable to say which would have been Dr. Metcalf's room, the door to Dr. Metcalf. I do not tell Mr. George that time after time I try, as it were, to put an invisible mark on one of the new doors as if to say *this is the place*, this is where I waited for him, wanting him, and a few times was sleeping with him on the little iron bed which was meant for one person only and was very narrow. But I'm lost in the strange new corridor and am never able to establish where his door was among these new doors.

"As a nurse," I laugh and tell Mr. George, "I was not allowed to come up here. I did get into trouble because I was seen here by someone who reported me."

"What does all that matter now?" Mr. George says drawing me close. "Nor does it matter which was that fellow's room. And, if you're sure this other thing, this couple—if I can use such an ugly word—is sufficiently unimportant to you . . ." I interrupt him with kisses.

I am pleased to be a resident at my old hospital, to come back there with a certain status and to have a room on this corridor and to have Mr. George as my secret visitor. He is quite right in all he says and his calling Dr. Metcalf *that fellow* seems to put him, Dr. M, in a suitable place, a place where he no longer, even as Helena's father, matters.

All the same I never ever go up to the doctors' corridor without trying to figure out exactly where Dr. Metcalf's room could still exist in all the newness of this part of the building. It is a sort of game with its own ritual of hope and resignation. The second part of the game is a slow walk further along the new corridor which, like the old bombed one, is long. I try to see the moon sometimes at the far end, where there is now a tall window looking across to the wall of the clock tower which is a water tower. The artesian well under the hospital and the power and force of this water supply provided a resilience to adversity and was invaluable during and immediately after the war. At the time of the bomb damage the full moon made a trellis of light and shadow on the opposite wall. It seemed then as if there was a strange room out there, L-shaped, leading to a place shining as a river shines when moonlight lies across the undisturbed water. In spite of tarpaulins and wooden barriers set up then the corridor ended abruptly in space, in a precipice immediately in front of me when I looked, hoping one last time, for Dr. Metcalf. The moon then was so wonderfully close I felt as if I could step easily across the gulf straight on to the clean white surface.

When I look at the moon, my father's moon, he always thought of it as his, it is incredible that I was not able then to tell him the small thing I needed to tell. And now for years Helena has run to him, straight into his wide open arms. He has composed a lullaby for her, he makes up stories to tell her, and, at times, he cooks a kipper for her over the open fire place. This is something he feels he can do when my mother is not at home. When the kipper is done he holds out the best bits, with the bones removed, on the end of a fork saying to Helena, "This is the best part. Eat this."

Even though I am warm in bed next to Mr. George, my head resting on his gently rising and falling chest as he breathes in and out in sleep, I think of my father at his sister's place, surrounded by her things, wondering what to do first, and Miss Clayton, alone now, at the tea table pricing the tomatoes aloud when he slices one to eat with his bread and butter.

Why must you always have someone to influence you? My mother's voice is suddenly in my head. These people will only make use of you, this Noël and this Felicity. What are these people? Is what we have here not enough for you on your days off? You are simply looking for a replacement for Gertrude. After all these years and with all your studying you haven't grown up at all yet and *you are a mother* . . . Here I imagine my mother's eyes, cornflower blue matching Helena's blue eyes, filling and overflowing with tears.

It's all a stupid repetition, her voice persisting, it's those Metalcups all over again.

Metcalfs, she always did get the name wrong.

Those Metalcups and their silly selfish wasteful friends and their extravagant and wicked parties. How could you, Vera, these new people, they're using you for their own relationship. And here in my head the tirade has to stop. Relationship is a word not in my mother's vocabulary. My mother would not think to say anything like relationship. This is my own word and it is not exactly mine, I have it from a Lawrence novel in which he uses the phrase a *meaningful relationship*.

"Is all that we have had together nothing now?" Mr. George, waking, asks me, interrupting my self-made conversation with my mother. "Do you forget?" he asks.

"I thought you were asleep," I say. The room, the Holly Bush room, which I had looked forward to, seems airless in the dark, too full with the double bed and the heavy wardrobe and chest of dark wood. The curtains too are somber and heavy. Earlier I was pleased because the windows look out over the street which, being near the goods yard of the station is used by the brewers. We lie in each other's arms and listen to a heavy dray being pulled by the Clydesdales. The waggon rumbles over the cobbles and, though I am not looking out now in the dawn, I can imagine the horses and their muscles rippling under their well-groomed coats. Of course it is not possible to talk to Mr. George about my new friends, Felicity and Noël. He is nervous of any friendship I might make. His nervousness and subsequent irritation bother me in an indefinable way.

"How can I ever forget," I say to him and I tell him I want to thank him for making the long journey in order to have a few hours with me. However could I forget that Mr. George and Miss George, these Georges, with their softly spoken gentle ways took me into their house after they had locked up for the night and were on their way up to bed themselves. They took me and Helena in, that night, even though they had no idea whether I was a good person or a bad one. They had no way of knowing. Of course I am not able to speak of Noël and Felicity and their strange lives. I can't tell him that when I have time off from the hospital I go straight to my mother's house and, as soon as I can, go on my old bicycle to the little farm. It is, I have to understand, a repetition of my journeys to Gertrude's Place years before. Perhaps all life is, like repeated phrases in music and in poetry, repetition. After all Elke, the au pair at the Georges with the laugh which is a mixture of a pure soprano voice and a trumpet being played triumphantly as in the opening of Bach's Cantata *Praise the Lord in every place*, is a repetition of Hilary who, some years earlier, was the forerunner in Cantata laughter.

"Do you still love *that fellow*?" Mr. George asks me, as though he has been lying awake for hours.

"Who?" I ask. I rummage in the half-light for my clothes.

"You know who I mean." Mr. George sits up in bed.

"Which one?" as if there are so many. I know Mr. George thinks I am being untruthful. I am tired and worried about being late for the list starting at seven in the general surgery theater. All night I have been afraid to sleep because of the danger of oversleeping. I am ashamed too because I have not even opened the letter from Helena which is sure to contain crayoned pages from Rachel. I have not even asked Mr. George about the children.

"I wish you could stay another night," I say to Mr. George. "Please stay, will you. Please." I am dressed and ready to leave. I know it is not possible for him to stay. But I ask him. "Please do stay."

I know that Mr. George would somehow seem all wrong in my mother's house. It is impossible to imagine him in the bathroom there, and which bedroom would be suitable? And then there are the neighbors. The neighbors would be sure to peer at him. He looks distinguished and this in itself puts him out of place. Even though the flowers in my mother's garden enhance everything they are not quite enough for the reception of Mr. George.

I take short cuts to the hospital. I think of Mr. George and Miss George, the brother and the sister, and I think of my father and his sister. And then, for some reason, I remember hearing Miss Clayton reading one long light summer evening, long ago, when I was upstairs in bed. I was still at school then and visiting for a weekend. Miss Clayton was reading aloud to my aunt;

> *When she rises in the morning*
> *I linger to watch her;*

> She spreads the bath cloth underneath her window
> And the sunbeams catch her
> Glistening white on the shoulders,
> While down her sides the mellow
> Golden shadow glows as
> She stoops to the sponge, and her swung breasts
> Sway like full-blown yellow
> Gloire de Dijon roses.

"It's you, Miss Daisy," Miss Clayton screams her interpretation. "It's you, Miss Daisy, swilling yourself down in a basin." She reads on;

> She drips herself with water, and her shoulders
> Glisten as silver, they crumple up
> Like wet and falling roses, and I listen
> For the sluicing of their rain-dishevelled petals
> In the window full of sunlight
> Concentrates her golden shadow
> Fold on fold, until it glows as
> mellow as the glory roses

Miss Clayton reading as the moon comes up the summer evening sky, reading Lawrence to my Aunt Daisy in her own voice and accent with the sing-song tones of the canals, her voice rising at the end of every line.

"It's *you*, dear," she screams, sending her pleasure and excitement up through the house. "It's you, Miss Daisy! *You* having a camper's *bath*!" Her voice vibrating singing up at the end of every phrase and the "a" in bath short and sharp, lemon sharp, as in the north and in the Midlands, this short "a" considered by my mother to be both ugly and *common*.

"It's a luverly po-emm, Miss Daisy, it's a luv po-emm, it's *ever so nice*," Miss Clayton shrill with the delight of the portrait of love and the warmth and stillness of the summer night approaching. "Oh Miss Daisy, it's ever so nice in't it. *It's like a painting*."

I think of my father visiting unknowingly this adoration of the rose, this Gloire de Dijon, this expression of beauty and love. And then if I think about it, there is the *meaningful relationship* as in the Lawrence novel but without all those stockings, a defiance of red, of coral and canary, Lawrence's stockings—perhaps without any thought about the legs to go in the stockings. I start to think and wonder about my aunt's legs and Miss Clayton's. It is as if they have never had any legs all through the years. My own stockings, like Miss Clayton's and my aunt's, are black.

The short cuts seem longer as if I had lost the way. The early morning, with the long day ahead, is inhospitable. Without sleep I am afraid I shall not manage the day. This is a raw and unkind time for parting. I have seen other people, at times, having an early morning unhappy cup of coffee, before parting for the ordinary things in their lives after being secretly together for a few stolen hours. I do not want to be a part of this.

Mr. George, alone in the dingy hotel room, will have to get dressed and wait alone at the station before his train leaves. When he said he would walk back to the hospital with me, I told him no, he'd make me late. I told him I'd have to run all the way and that I did not want to leave him having to walk back, his face pink in the cold and his eyes watering because of the wind. I'd feel conspicuous I told him, unkindly, having to part in the street like that. And then knowing he was walking all the way back to the Holly Bush. Alone and with the dreariness of being up and dressed too soon.

In the scrubbing-up room Farrer and Wilson are already gowned and waiting. They comment, with eyebrows raised above their masks, on the dark circles round my eyes and they make little amused remarks about what they describe as my rough *night on the tiles*. Both of them, it seems to me, have nice eyebrows. It is the effect of the eyebrows arched above the white cotton which is so striking.

"How many times?" Farrer asks.

"Seventeen," I say, and I turn off the special taps with my elbows.

The House Standing Open to the Spring

∽

Whenever the sun shines, even if it is only a pale and fading sunshine, my mother opens her front door and as many windows as she can. She calls it "the house standing open to the spring," even if it is some other time of the year.

Her cornflowers remind me of other cornflowers, just as when her garden is full of pinks and peonies and roses I think of other times when these were in profusion.

"Why do you always have to have some other place to go when you come home for a day off from the hospital and why always a couple?" My mother's indignation shows between her shoulders as she bends over the sink. "Have you forgotten already how easily people make use of you?" And what is it about these people? This couple?"

"Felicity prides herself," I tell my mother, "on being able to make a shepherd's pie and bake a cake in the time it takes to listen to Beethoven's ninth symphony on the wireless." I tell my mother she would like Noël, Felicity too, they are both cultured people. "I think they would like *Faust*," I tell her, hoping to please her.

The black-out shutters in the hospital, where I was nursing during the war, were put up every evening so that light would not show from the large building. Before the war with all the windows lit up, the hospital, it seemed to me, looked like a great ship forever in harbor. Two porters put up the shutters at night and another took them down in the mornings. The evening porters started on chests on the fifth floor and worked their way down both wings of the hospital, through obstetrics, gynecology, ear, nose and throat, orthopedics, the private medical wards and the private surgical, and so on. Because it was such an immense thing to get done they had to start about four-thirty, when the afternoon sun was pouring into the wards. So, it was like this, coming off duty at half-past five for an evening off before my day off; the sudden light evening outside, after being in the darkened ward, was a surprise to say the least. This forgotten unexpected light— it was something which lifted me from my tiredness then—this summer evening queening it still through the city and the suburbs, I could not get enough of it. I always sat upstairs in the bus, on the left, so that as we lumbered through the suburb, scraping the summer-green leafiness, it was as if I was right there in these green tossing trees for the whole journey.

As I sit now on the top left-hand side of the bus I feel, as I did then, the pleasure of the summer evening—having come from the artificial light of the closed-in general surgery theater in the same hospital where the black-out shutters used to be put up every afternoon years ago. Other memories follow out of sequence, the red cabbages on my father's allotment and how he left cabbages as gifts on the doorsteps of unknown neighbors in the street, the roan horses on the tow paths pulling barges laden with coal, and a gypsy who cursed the veins in my mother's legs causing her inflammation of the veins which she suffers from now.

Perhaps it is the Regency tea party which is uppermost in my mind with its promise of Queen Anne cups and saucers, hand-embroidered napkins, China tea with cream and yards and yards of chiffon . . .

"You must come," I tell my mother. But she is too shy to visit my new friends.

"There's going to be chiffon, you know, lovely light thin gauze, draped along the mantelpiece," I start to explain. But she continues to shake her head saying she couldn't possibly.

"It's going to be Regency," Felicity says, every time I go over there, bunching the light material in her capable hands. "Do bring your mother."

My mother is unable to trust these two, Felicity and Noël. She has this feeling of mistrust without even meeting them. Perhaps it is my enthusiasm for them which worries her and the fact that, as soon as I arrive home for my time off, I go at once, on my bicycle, to their place. I admire their knowledge of music and literature and their ability to conduct whole conversations in another language or within quotation marks.

"*Suffering is like art we create it within ourselves . . .*" Noël says. "Strindberg."

"Look," says Felicity, "*at the ruin of the individual when he isolates himself . . .*" Noël says, "Strindberg again."

They have the ability to turn a serious conversation or discussion into something apparently ridiculous and light hearted, changing their voices and their words, using words like perchance and *I pray you, methinks,* and *forsooth.* Or, they adapt the language from Shakespeare's stage directions, *exit running, attendants follow, exeunt severally, a trumpet sounds,* and *trumpet answers within.*

Both have been to Oxford, they speak of Balliol and other colleges with an affectionate familiarity which is enviable. When I ask them what it means to have read Greats they explain that they have studied ancient Greek and Latin, ancient history, and ancient and modern philosophy. "You will have had your beginners' books in medicine—surgery, obstetrics and psychiatry— just as we have had ours in our subjects," Noël says.

Felicity's dark gray Oxford flannels are mostly hidden under colored aprons. Noël is fragile, they tell me, and that is why they have this house in the field. He has a cough, I notice, and is always hungry, ravenously. Noël is the brilliant and sensitive one, Felicity says. Noël, according to Felicity, maintains that unless a scholar has had a classical education there were many writers whose work would remain obscure. He is, Felicity says, interested in Eliot's obsession with Heraclitus and Virgil.

"I'm afraid all this is above my head," I tell Felicity. And Noël says then that he suffers from the illuminated intelligence which sick people have. And then they sing together as they often do in the middle of a conversation, as if they are characters in an opera.

Den Adigen steht die Ehrenhaftigeit
im Gesicht geschrieben.
Nun, verlieren wir keine Zeit
augenblicklich will ich dich hieraten

"*A nobleman's honor,*" Felicity explains the meaning, "*is writ-*
ten in his face. Now, let's not waste time. I'll marry you." When
Felicity laughs, a tenor voice seems to sing through the well-
bred laughter. Their voices, when they sing, are pure and able,
sustained as if with deeply felt and understood tenderness and
love, as if nothing could go wrong with either of their voices or
with them or with me.

They introduce me to the plays of Ibsen. They like to read
plays aloud, taking the different parts themselves. In *The Wild*
Duck they make me read Hedwig because, they say, I am like
her.

When my father asks me one time on my days off, "Have you
got a nice book? What is that you're reading?" I show him the
book and I tell him I'm reading *The Wild Duck* and how Ibsen is
showing his audience how we all have a lie to live by and that it is
wrong to take away a person's life lie and put nothing in its place.

"We should all be completely honest," my father says. "No lies."

"It isn't exactly a lie," I try again, "it's more like a mask." My
explanation does not seem very clear; I leave it like that, though
I feel my father would be interested in the ways in which Ibsen
uses lampshades to show things about his characters, Hedwig's
approaching blindness for one thing. And how his characters
talk about one thing, meaning something else at the same time.
I resolve to listen more carefully when Noël and Felicity read.

"These people," my mother says, "are arty crafty." How do
they earn a living, she wants to know. And how do they pay their
rent? Decrepit as the place is they would not get it for nothing.
"They must get money from somewhere," my mother says. Her
silence after this remark suggests something evil in the lives of
my new friends. My mother, being forever unsure of her own
place in a society to which she has never managed to become

accustomed, bases her attitudes and opinions on those of a neighbor, a railway-man's widow, Mrs. Pugh, who is a dressmaker. Crawling round on the floor with her mouth full of pins while she adjusts a wayward hem, this neighbor, it seems to my mother, knows all there is to know about human life and how it should be lived.

"You don't never get no pleasure," the neighbor tells my mother often. And when the New Odeon Cinema reopens on the edge of the housing estate they, in out-of-date beaded dresses made by Mrs. Pugh, go to the pictures together, twice a week, when the program changes. They sit in the warmth in the rich golden splendor of gilt-edged mirrors, thick carpets, gold-brass light fittings, chandeliers, every one with a hundred little bulbs shaped like candle flames, gold-brass handrails, palm trees in polished brass pots, and voluminous red velvet curtains making secluded alcoves where patrons can rest after an emotionally exhausting film. In the interval they listen to the theater organ as it rises from its cave in the floor. Often there is the rambling nostalgia of music from the war years, a medley of tunes from "The White Cliffs of Dover," "Room Five Hundred and Four," "Roll Out the Barrel," and "Knees Up Mother Brown." My mother observes often that the theater organ is versatile. Mrs. Pugh and my mother also order afternoon tea which is brought to them, as in pre-war days, by maids in black dresses with white aprons and caps, afternoon tea with dark fruit cake on little trays, which look, my mother declares, like hand-beaten silver.

So when my mother agrees to accepting the invitation to the Regency tea party it is on condition that Mrs. Pugh can come too. They will catch the two o'clock bus and walk from the corner and I am to meet them at the field path.

It is true, they, my two new friends are artists. One of them makes a skirt for me from cloth woven by them both. Knowing how long weaving takes, a skirt length is indeed an enormous gift. Between them they are always giving me presents, something made by themselves. They, as well as calling me Hedwig, call me Persephone.

"Persephone!" one of them calls, when I am trying to ride my bicycle over the tufts and crevasses in the field. "Persephone, harbinger of spring and bringer of destruction, what have you brought for us, have you been to the shop?"

They are always hungry and if I bring cake made by my mother they fall on it, as they say, like wolves. They make things, bookshelves, pottery dishes, egg cups, cloth—"But all uneatable," Felicity says. "Bring some bread with you next time, we have lovely home-made jam."

They rent the place. It is one of those dilapidated farm houses remaining partly in ruins, in a small triangle of green meadow right in the middle of an industrial area which has grown up all round it. To one side is a coal mine and a brickworks and on the other side is the bone and glue factory. Rising immediately behind the house is an ugly slag heap, partly overgrown with coarse grass and coltsfoot. The meadow is low lying and enclosed by hedges of hawthorn and elderberry. There is a derelict wash house to one side of the kitchen door and next to this is a potter's wheel and a kiln built by themselves. They have a cow and some hens.

"Persephone," they say the first time I eat something there, "now you will have to stay with us!"

"But I can't stay," I tell them, "I have to go back to the hospital. I'm operating at seven in the morning." That is all right, they agree, I can be part of the time at the hospital and the rest of the time with them. "That way it will not be hard for your mother to find you."

My mother, knowing all too well every time where I am, asks me about Mr. George. She wants to know what he thinks about my going there. And shouldn't I be saving up my weekends or other days off to have them together so that I can make the journey to see how my children are. What kind of mother am I that I can take work so far from my children. I tell her that I am arranging for the children to visit during the school holidays. Miss George will bring them herself and travel back the same night by Pullman. This pleases and comforts my mother and she says that Miss

George could stay overnight and I say, well you know Miss George, she will want to get back to Mr. George. "You might have told me your arrangements, Vera," my mother says. "I know you need friends, Vera," my mother says in a softer tone and I know that she has it in mind to choose some material, so that Mrs. Pugh can make some dresses for Helena and Rachel in readiness for the visit.

Scrambling on the slag heap with a trowel and an old cricket bag we, Noël and Felicity and I, collect bits of poor quality coal from the black scree of waste. They have to have a coal search every day.

One day I find a cucumber in the road. "I got off my bike," I tell them, "right in front of a tram to pick it up." I find their pleasure and excitement over the cucumber touching. Felicity makes sandwiches which we eat, without washing our hands, out on the slope of the ugly pit mound.

It is not a long ride from the housing estate where my mother and father live to the farm. Because of them, Noël and Felicity, I seem to notice things more. They call it "being aware." They say it is not because of them. They say it is because I am "that sort" of person. I like this idea very much.

To go to the farm I ride my bicycle along the main road, where I often have to wait on the left of a brewer's dray to let people on or off a tram. The Clydesdale horses stand waiting, tossing their noble heads.

Going off the main road are quiet roads lined on both sides with the narrow terraced houses built for miners and railway workers. Their front doors, all with white donkey-stoned doorsteps, open directly on to the pavements. Every now and then, in between the jostled streets and houses, there are fields and hedges and some old farm buildings left over from earlier times.

When I first went there, that first time, it was in February. I stopped to peer through the hedge, remembering a family which had lived there when I was a child. I often walked with my mother along this road when we came home by train. Once, there were spots of blood in the snow alongside the winter-thin hedge. My mother, frightened of the illness, told me to cover my nose and mouth with my handkerchief. She said then to always walk on the other side of the road. We crossed over.

Another night when I was walking home with my mother we heard someone crying in the darkness ahead. There was a sharp fragrance of elderberry; my mother said it helped to hide the dreadful bone and glue factory smell. My mother called out to ask who was crying. We stood still in the middle of the road and, after a bit, a girl came out from the black patch which was the elderberry. She cried and told my mother she was Sylvia Bradley and her father had turned her out with only a shilling. We walked on together, all three of us, slowly. The smell of the bone and glue was stronger as we left the elderberry behind. With a heaving roar the blast furnace on the other side of town opened and the sky was red with the familiar glow. We heard the wheels at the mine shaft turning as one lot of miners went down the shaft and the other lot came up. Sylvia Bradley cried, saying she had nowhere to go.

My mother, who never let us play with the Bradley girls, tried to comfort Sylvia. She said to her to go home again and that when her baby was born everyone would be sure to love the little newly born child. "You will see," she said then, "they will not turn you out. Go back home to them. They will love your baby," she said.

Some time later on Emily, another of the Bradley girls, came with a shabby pram to collect some clothes my mother had put ready.

It is while I am parting the hedge that day to look through at the old farm buildings that one of them, Noël, calls to me to come in. Their kitchen that day is warm and sweet with apple jelly. The shining jars are still warm. On the table there is a little heap of red-and-blue-checked gingham covers cut round with pinking shears to go over the jars when they are sealed. Felicity, dripping hot wax on each jar, explains that they made the jelly with apples stored from the autumn. "Wrinkled winter apples," she says.

The February day is soft and mild and Noël, for my first day, writes the first line for a poem on a bit of paper,

The February night, the warmth the stillness

and gives it to me as we all three walk in the dark, me pushing my bicycle, as they accompany me part of the way home.

My mother feels certain that Noël and Felicity are in hiding. "They're hiding from something, those two. Why don't you keep away from there?" She says she'll speak to my father. I know she will because she always tells him everything. She says she'll telephone Mr. George but I am not so sure that she will.

As the day for the Regency tea party draws near I am anxious about the dirty state of the house. They seem to enjoy writing their names and audacious remarks in the dust. They leave unwashed plates and clothes everywhere and they never make their bed. They say that because the bed is so big, taking up all the space in the bedroom, they can't get round it to make it. I despise myself really for wanting to impose my suburban and hospital-trained standards on them. And especially I despise myself for buying a lavatory brush on the way there one morning. They never seem to notice that anything needs cleaning.

The little piece of meadow, left over, brings some prettiness as the seasons change. There are daffodils, the flowers of the hawthorn, the pink and white mayflowers—unlucky, Mrs. Pugh says to bring into the house, but Noël and Felicity laugh at that when I warn them. Then there are the buttercups and the daisies and, on the slag heap in patches, the sturdy yellow coltsfoot. There are wild roses in the hedges and the flowers heralding blackberries and then the glistening fruit itself, and, at last, the hawthorn berries, elfin bunches of autumn, and then the rosy wild apples, crab apples. There is something magical in coming upon a corner of the earth like this in the middle of the smoke and dirt and the night-time roar of the iron and steel works when the sky is glowing hot red, red orange, from the opened furnaces. And then there is the unforgettable noise of the wheels turning as the miners' cages are going down or coming up. And then the times of quietness between all this. Sometimes a stillness as of a smooth lake and a quietness, unbelievable.

"Don't they speak nice," the railway widow, Mrs. Pugh, is not able to hide the approval in the face of her disapproval and distaste. She stands with my mother, both of them balancing in their best shoes, on a tuft of grass at the edge of the mud. My mother, as a rule, looks up to and admires people, who, having been to Oxford, speak with that special resonance as certain vowel sounds are brought down through the nose, as if an "n" lurks somewhere within these words. The short "a" offends her, it is a kind of curse to be got rid of. She is quick to correct people, even strangers in shops. She approves of the dark gray Oxford mixture, the special cloth for the flannels, and the Oxford sandals saying that they are elegant, one of her favorite words, and go well with that special haircut which allows a heavy, if drab, wave to fall across an intellectual forehead.

The only trouble about their clothes is that when my mother and Mrs. Pugh arrive, my two friends are not wearing any.

Nervously I stand with the two visitors listening to the high-pitched little screams which belong to the way in which my friends talk and laugh. The smoke from the wash-house chimney rewards us with a sudden shower of sparks and soot. From inside comes the sound of a tin bath being shared.

"Always, but always, the accomplished acrobat. Not a muscle out of place. You delightful tormenting creature!" A laughing well-bred voice causes the visitors to look away from each other and to stare stonily at the generous surrounding of mud.

"Acrobat! Contortionist!" The two-toned laughter contains in its music the sounds of an exchange of playful slappings of wet hands on wet bare flesh.

"And whose little bottom is this?" Slap slap. "And whose little bottom is this?" Two more slaps.

"Who or what are these so-called friends of yours?" My mother's white hat, with its small spotted veil, is an inadequate protection.

"Them forrin or what?" Mrs. Pugh jerks her head towards the wash house.

"They're Bohemians," I say.

"It's not a question of which country." My mother's lips are in a thin pale line. I look away from her.

"Bohemian," I try once more. "You know," I say, "*A la Boemm*, as in art, in painting and poetry, that sort of thing, clay modeling, pottery." I wave a hand towards the kiln. Another high-pitched scream and a laugh interrupt my attempt.

"Well," Mrs. Pugh says, "I can't say as I know much about art but I like a nice picture now and again, you know sumthink pretty, flowers or a nice bowl of fruit or a sailing ship."

One of the inmates of the wash house has started to blow bubbles. The other is singing in that surprising voice, a voice full of feeling. I recognize the descent, Leonora's descent, the faithful wife going down into the dungeon. The singer changes character and, beginning with the penetrating cry to God from Florestan, gets as far as *O schwere Prüfung* before breaking into shrieks of laughter.

"Sounds like there's two of a kind in there," Mrs. Pugh purses her lips.

"Really!" My mother's speech ends as the wash-house door is pushed open and two figures, incompetently sharing a bath towel, step on to the plank which partly bridges the mud between the wash house and the kitchen. The two of them fly across in a flurry of pink nakedness.

"I'm going for the bus even if I have to stand and wait the whole two hours for it out there on the corner." My mother begins to pick her way across the sodden meadow. "They'll wreck your career, those two." There are tears in her voice. "Believe me," she says, "between them, those two, they'll wreck your career."

Unable to look at my mother's white hat, I take her arm to steady her across to the next little island of turf. This is the second time that I am seeing myself quite plainly. That first time I was working my way through bladders and stomach ulcers, gall stones and various surgical conditions, through the men's private wards and the women's private wards, a never-ending path to being a battle axe of a sister in charge of some God-forsaken place like Radium Therapy or the diet kitchen on the Lower Ground Floor, or worse, in charge of the ear, nose, and throat theater, with its two humorless and untender surgeons, always at war with each other, and on to the final triumph, that of being a District Nurse, enormous in navy blue, on a bicycle, visiting patients, admonishing husbands, and delivering babies on sheets of newspaper in overcrowded kitchens or bedrooms. Not knowing then that I was being, in the eyes of my mother, wrecked, I went forward towards the consequences, being rescued at the same time. Now a second wrecking or rescuing is in the tears on my mother's soft, carefully powdered cheeks. On a different level, a life of supra-pubic catheters and septic toe nails waiting to be removed and the decision to make between obstetrics and gynecology, general surgery, third-rate psychiatry, or general practice is ahead of me. I notice once more my mother stepping carefully to avoid spoiling her patent-leather shoes. I can hardly bear to look.

"I won't let them. No!" I say, "No, I won't let them. I won't let anything wreck . . ."

Before my mother can bring out the words, "It's that Mr. Metalcup all over again," Felicity, dressed, as usual with a red-checked apron over the gray flannels, calls to us to come indoors. The kettle is boiling and the tea will be ready in a minute.

My mother and Mrs. Pugh, with customary good manners, hesitate.

There isn't any chiffon and the cups and saucers are absolutely not Queen Anne. Even though I have never seen Queen Anne china, I know the tea cups are simply the usual ones, white with a thin gold line on the rim and a shamrock, a kind of trefoil or clover, in gold, at the bottom of the cup. Everything just ordinary. Felicity must have discarded the chiffon and the Regency idea.

Noël and Felicity, their wet hair brushed back behind their ears, are charming and wait on my mother and Mrs. Pugh with gentle movements. The kitchen is warm. They must have pulled out all the dampers, the fire in the stove is roaring, burning up all the carefully scrounged coal. An unaccustomed extravagance.

"Thank you very much, ta." Mrs. Pugh holds her cup and saucer high, level with her proud bosom. "Well, thank you very much, I don't mind if I do." She helps herself delicately to the bread and butter from Felicity's offered plate.

During the tea time I go outside and, crouching in the rain which has started, I plant out a few cornflower seedlings. I use a wooden spatula of the kind used for pressing down the tongue during an examination of the throat. I keep it in my pocket along with my watch, a small scalpel and my old nursing scissors. These things, together with my pen are my instruments. I cherish them and hope to add a number-eight catheter when one in good condition turns up. This habit of keeping equipment belongs to the war years. All kinds of essential things are forever in short supply. Doctors and nurses hide them. I have no idea, while I am working with the little plants in the mud, that the possibility of a number-eight catheter could ever cease to be of importance to me. I think of the surprising show of color the little seedlings will produce later on, and it occurs to me that, up to the present time, I have made remarks and carried out various actions, both simple and complicated, always without looking ahead to consequences surprisingly pleasant or otherwise. And that one of the aspects of both sowing and planting is that it is necessary to remember that the work is done with hope. While I am crouching there close to the earth, feeling the cold rain make its way round the collar of my old coat, another thought comes to me. Never once has my mother reproached me over my lack of a *good* marriage, as she would hope to think of marriage. Perhaps my mother, seeing me living safely and well with the Georges, is too polite, too aware of what might be impossible, to ask outright, "Why doesn't Mr. George want to marry you?" and, "Why is there no marriage since there is now the second child?" For some years (Rachel is now seven years old and Helena almost twelve), she has been seeing me remaining as the maid at the Georges. She has been an onlooker during my years of study carried out during this time of my *maidship*. And she has been looking on while I am, at the same time, *mother*, providing Miss George with a longed for, perhaps secretly longed for, rôle which, I suppose, should be my mother's and which I know she wants very much in spite of gossip among neighbors. It comes to me then, with considerable surprise, that this mother I have, this mother being forced into the position of onlooker, possibly knows, understands even, that Mr. George and I are lovers whenever there is an opportunity for us to be alone together. In spite of thinking this I am, in reality, unable to imagine that she would ever think about such an idea. And, of course, at present she is being forced to watch with an understandable fear (which I am ignoring) my friendship with Nöel and Felicity which, because of limited free time, is intense.

A small scene returns often when I am alone, like now in the mud with the tiny plants. It is the day when I leave the Georges, qualified and about to go to the train in order to travel back to my old hospital, not as a nurse this time but for an appointment as a doctor and to be known as the Resident Surgical Officer— R.S.O. for short. Elke is coming in through the front gate. The hedge of sweet briar is sparkling with rain drops after a recent shower. My two little girls are with her, they have been for their walk. All three have wind-reddened cheeks and bright eyes.

Elke, seeing me standing with the Georges on the rich colors of the mosaic in the porch, in that safe place between the storm doors and the delicate stained glass of the front door, calls out, "Ha! The rescued maid leaves Saint George and the Dragon." And, with her second-hand cantata laugh resounding she brings the children up the path. I kiss them both, one last time before I leave . . . for the time being . . .

For the time being I have to remember that the sun-warmed floor boards and the cherry-wood furniture in the attic rooms at the Georges are not mine any longer. Elke will have unpacked her rucksack there. A young woman comes in daily to be at Miss George's elbow during the little ceremonies of carving or serving afternoon tea, and to care for the rooms with duster and polish in addition to the special soap and hot water for the stone flags in the hall and in the kitchen.

"Did you see the ankles and the collar bones of the one of them?" Mrs. Pugh says, in the field, on the way back across to the bus. "I never did see the size of them, not on a woman anyhow, and not on Mr. Pugh neither, but then," she pauses, "Mr. Pugh, he was a small man."

My mother seems to be absorbed in keeping her feet as dry as possible. I walk to the bus with them pushing my bicycle with one hand in the center of the handlebar, something I have seen my father do with ease but which proves hard for me, and holding my mother's arm with the other. Feeling her arm tense inside her coat makes me long to be close to her, to tell her I am sorry.

"A good cup of tea," Mrs. Pugh allows, "for all that it was China." And then a fresh thought, "China tea! What with the expense of it, *them* having China tea!"

I hope my mother will make some remark about the fragrant cup of tea, one of her phrases, but she remains silent. "A course to my way of thinking China's nothing as good as real." Mrs. Pugh has the last word.

During the afternoon tea, Felicity and Noël, I can see, are contrite about their late bath. The water will have taken too long to heat. I do not need any explanation from them.

At home my mother, because I have not had tea, makes bacon sandwiches for me, using up all the bacon.

"For you to eat in the train," she says.

Instead of going to the station I go quietly round the side of the house to the shed and, taking the bicycle as quietly as I can, I ride off in the dark, without a lamp, to the farm.

There is a small car on the grass at the edge of the mud. There has never been a car there before. I hesitate. The smell of crushed grass mingles with petrol fumes.

"Persephone! What a surprise!" Felicity opens the door to reach for some coal. "Shouldn't you be at the hospital?"

"Come in. Come in," Noël calls from the kitchen. "What destruction do you bring? Anything to eat? Any victchooalls?"

I tell Felicity that, yes I should have gone back but I want to thank them for the afternoon. And, in any case, I am too late now for the train.

Felicity, insisting that I stay the night, introduces me to their visitor, someone I have never seen there before.

"Boris, this is Persephone." Boris, they explain, makes or rather re-creates ancient musical instruments. He has with him a fourteenth-century lute which he is going to play and Noël and Felicity are going to sing.

"A replica only," Boris says, looking modest.

I explain that I should confess to knowing nothing about the lute. No one pays any attention to what I am saying, but I persist in trying to tell them that I do not know the lute.

Boris plays his lute and Noël and Felicity, after a few false starts and much laughter and coughing, sing. Boris eats all the bacon sandwiches saying that being registered as a vegetarian, in college, means that he never has any bacon. Why don't Felicity and Noël keep a pig, he wants to know. He wipes his fingers on his little black beard.

"Your beard, Darling," Noël squeals between coughs, "is positively charming, exquisitely *pubic*." Boris bows and plays some more music and the other two sing some more. I feel excluded but smile and applaud. I am wishing I had not come back. I think of my warm bedroom at the hospital. During an interval in the music making, while Boris drinks Noël's supply of prescribed stout, I tell them I ought to be getting home.

"Why?" Noël says. "They do not know you've missed the train."

"That's true," I say, wishing at the same time that I had not said it.

Felicity digs about in the small cupboard under the stairs and pulls out two blankets and a pillow.

"You'll have to be up for the early train," she says. Upstairs in the little back bedroom I discover that both blankets and the pillow are damp. The scree of the ugly slag heap rises directly outside the small window. I am all too aware of the blackness which blots out any light or glow in the night sky.

I am so cold in bed. I nearly go downstairs to the fire to tell them that I've changed my mind, that I'll go home after all. I have this extraordinary thought that in a moment I'll change and be their equal and, with my explanation, escape will be simple.

Every now and then little bursts of well-bred conversation and high-pitched screams of laughter reach me, where I am lying shivering under the inadequate covers. I have never stayed here for a night before and it seems to be the silliest thing I have ever done.

"Has the sanatorium caught up with you yet?" Boris's voice is abrupt in the middle of the laughter.

There is a sudden silence and Felicity replies in a low voice, "Not yet."

"I see you've a new *messenger*. Does she bring in the goods as satisfactorily as Jules did?"

"Don't, do *not* mention Jules," Felicity snaps.

"Oh, Jules," Noël yawns. "Jules let us down badly. Very badly."

"I take it," Boris says in a light and playful way, "there was nothing in it, as usual, as there usually isn't for the Jules of this world. I think I said, didn't I, that Jules would be bound to let you down sooner or later."

"It was sooner rather than later," Noël says.

"Well," Boris says, "as usual you have found someone else, though her accent is *appalling*, someone else to bring in the bacon. Oops! pardon the pun, darlings."

I lie there listening to their huge and artificial laughter and, in my disappointment over Felicity, I long for my bedroom at home.

I can't help wishing for the sound of my mother's voice talking to my father and my father's deep voice replying. One of the happiest things about childhood, I have to realize now, was being upstairs in a warm bed, on the edge of sleep, and able to hear these two voices, like the voices of doves, comfortably talking to and fro, one to the other, to and fro, wonderfully peaceful and safe.

As little phrases of medieval music and the starting and stopping of the singing float, with the broken fragments of gossip, up the narrow staircase the small bedroom seems colder and more inhospitable.

"How on earth did you find this *angel*, uncompromising as she is?" Boris asks during a pause.

"*She* came to *us*," Felicity says. "Noël found her, or is *discovered* the right word, in the hedge."

"A hedge-ling," Noël says. "It was so simple. I had hardly to raise my voice. You have to agree, darlings, that there is something of the Lorelei about me, the quality of the Lorelei has never let me down."

"That is true," Boris says, seeming to consider, "I was always aware that you were attractive to *sailors*. But surely this one is not *naïve*, like Jules. This one, with all her lack of, how shall I put it, *class* is much more useful, *eddicated* as she is in the problems of ill health. She is a *medico* is she not? *Indispensable* in the face of illness."

"Jules was not at all naïve as you say," Felicity growls. "He took exactly what he wanted. I never in my life was confronted by such blatant cunning ways."

"It was *interesting* however," Noël says in a low tone. "Jules had *something*."

"In any event," Boris laughs, "*he got away*."

After what seems a long time I hear them go outside. Boris, with great noise, starts his car. I hear their voices shrill over the engine. Laughing and coughing they stumble upstairs.

"Art thou sleeping Persephone?" I pretend to be asleep when Noël pauses at my open door. "Persephone, sleepest thou—with the sweetest dreams?"

•

It is when I am trying to go down the stairs, trying to avoid the creaking steps, that Felicity follows me. She catches me at the kitchen door.

"Persephone, darling! You're only partly dressed," she says. "I *am sorry*," she says, "but you must be frozen. Come back upstairs to bed. Come into bed with us." With her large hands on my shoulders she turns me round.

"Persephone, mounting the stairs in tears?" Noël raises himself on one elbow, his shadow in the candle light grotesque on the uneven ceiling. "We simply must look after her."

"Come on," Felicity says, "you first, in the middle."

Unable to stop shivering, I feel their nakedness on both sides of me. I feel their warmth and their ardor.

"I caught her *escaping*," Felicity says.

"But we need her here," Noël, his arm reaching across me, explains. "Persephone, you must know how much we really need you. Felix and I do really need you."

"We are *seriously* trying to live among *real* people," Felicity says, "the miners, the brickworks, and the bone-and-glue people and their wives and children. You can't *leave* us now. We need your ordinariness."

"Besides all that, I am ill," Noël says, "ask Felix."

"Yes, Noël is ill," Felicity says. "And the Felix part, he pretends I am Felix. That is *not* his illness. That is just Noël."

"Where can I go?" I want to ask Felicity, but instead I stare at the mud and say nothing. I can hear Noël coughing in the tiny bedroom upstairs. He has the window as wide open as he can and still feels he is not getting enough air. Sometimes he has his soup at the window, leaning on the sill with a pillow, looking out as if to see some goodness coming to him from the grass or the hedges. I wish he did not have the cough. By this time we know he has TB and we know too that the cow is tubercular and will have to be taken away to be destroyed.

Noël talks all the time. He tells me about Felicity.

"Felicity," he says, "Felicity with the dance, with the dancing way of walking and the slim hips, the boyish hips. Does one call this boyish?" he asks. "Felicity-Felix-Felicity," he says, "with the tenor voice which must be answered, must be rewarded with passion. Passionately rewarded. Felicity-Felix in disguise, disguised with the clothes and the manner of the perfect housewife.

"Felicity is Felix," Noël, feverish hot, with his arms round me, insists. "Felix, Felicity-Felix," he says, "you must know . . ." He reaches then to Felicity who is on the other side of me. "The poor child is cold." Noël seems unable to stop talking. His cough is the only thing which stops him from talking. "Felix," he says, "did you know that earlier Persephone was mounting the stairs in tears. We must, both of us, warm and comfort her."

I lie still. I feel them moving closer.

"Let's warm her," Noël says. "Felix means happy," he says. He goes on to say that Felix is Latin for lucky and Felicity comes from Felix and if you are lucky then you are happy, like Felicity is happy.

"Noël," Felicity says, "enjoys the power of hallucination."

"*I am indifferent in the mornings but brave in the afternoons,*" Noël says. He wants to know which parson said these words. And how can I, he wants to know, like the smell of elderberry so much when it makes him feel sick.

"Everything," Felicity says, "makes Noël feel sick."

It is not hard for me to acknowledge that these two friends of mine are the kind of people my mother and father would find difficult to like. Between them they might discuss these two, but the discussion would be limited with my mother saying they were well educated and cultured and she would then express anxiety about the drains at the farm. And my father, having only one answer to a problem of this sort, would suggest prayer and the certainty of reconciliation.

My father admires Dickens and my mother has read *The Forsyte Saga* and *Lorna Doone* in English. They both like music (hymns, my father; opera, my mother). But they do not seem to me to be on the same level as my two new friends. Even Dr. Metcalf and his wife, Magda, in comparison with Noël and Felicity, seem shallow and uncultured. Even Dr. Metcalf and his gentle way of lending me books . . .

In spite of Noël's illness and my mother's increasing disapproval, the strong fragrance of the elderberry excites and pleases me and makes me rush, whenever I can, to the magical company of my two friends.

"What about Mr. George?" my mother says every time I set off on the bicycle. "What about the children?" she says. "You have some holiday, you should go to Glasgow to the children."

But I ignore her.

Between them, as my mother says on the day of the so-called Regency tea party, the day I plant out the cornflowers, between them, these two, she says, are wrecking my career if not my life. Between them, she says, these two are taking away what I have and are not replacing it with anything. I tell her that I do not agree with her but rather I see myself as being saved, encouraged towards all that is worthwhile and beautiful. If anything I am being rescued from having to go on solidly working my way through all the drudgery of human suffering and, as Noël says, encouraging suffering to continue by temporary alleviation and by encouraging new births. He sees me, he says, ending up in obstetrics; my black bag, complete with speculum and forceps, my only companion. Noël is very persuasive. He can see me, he says, attempting to deal with medical and surgical conditions for which there are no remedies except those surviving from folk tales and legends, in the outside leaves of lettuce and in infusions of parsley, raspberry leaves, and nettles. "Mythology," he says, "and witchcraft."

Before we know about the cow, Noël has obediently swallowed a whole mug of cream every morning and, for supper, has eaten a baked apple swimming in cream. Every evening the kitchen is fragrant with the baking of clove-studded apples.

"Where can I go?" I stand at the edge of the mud wanting to ask this question. Felicity wearing the little red apron over the loose gray flannels, the long-lasting remnants from Oxford, is singing and humming.

> *One more river and that's the river of Jordan,*
> *One more river and that's the river to cross.*

Mostly it is humming, she is not able to remember the words. My question is one I want to ask but I am afraid of the answer. Small things, like the uneasy humming and singing and an increased use of quotation in the conversation, make me feel that they want to be rid of me. At the same time they wait eagerly for any provisions I bring from the shops and, whenever I arrive with a baked custard, they eat it straight from the enamel dish in which it has been made, knocking each other's spoons and shamelessly scraping it all up. It does not seem to occur to them that my mother has me in mind when she makes the custards.

Behind me Felicity is rearranging the jars of jam and bottled fruit along the kitchen shelf. One lot, the strawberry jam, the best-looking of them all, has been ruined. The long-handled wooden spoon has been used for stirring some pale-blue distemper, an improvement for the kitchen walls slapped on by them both in turn. The tainted jam is uneatable.

> *hum de hum de ha . . . that's the river to cross*
> *One more river and that's the river of Jordan,*
> *One more river and that's the river to cross.*

Felicity hums and sings the few words over and over as she moves the jars restlessly. The two of them, Noël and Felicity, these two, have started recently to talk about me in the third person.

It's as though we're *married* to her, Noël starts off. There's *consummation*, he says. More than once, Felicity agrees. But, Noël says, the marriage has never been *solemnized*. God, Felicity says, that is a word I would *never* use. Ah, but the mother might, Noël pretends to shake a warning finger. *Her* mother you mean, Felicity corrects Noël. *The* mother, Noël persists in a drawling voice, the mother, don't you agree, would approve of a solemnization. A solemnization would be precious for the mother. She would then be able to discuss the *wedding* with her friend Mrs. Pudge and Mrs. Pudge . . . *Pugh*, Darling, Felicity interrupts. And Mrs. Pudge, Noël persists, would make suitable dresses; Noël starts to laugh, for us all, he coughs and laughs.

The idea amuses them and they go on with the joke. A wedding, they say, with invitations and table napkins to match the candles and the icing on the cake. And presents, they say, do not forget the wedding presents, we can make lists to send to guests in advance. A coffee table, Noël says; an alarm clock, Felicity says; the jug and glasses, Noël says; the table mats, his voice gains strength; matching towels, *his* and *hers*, *theirs* and *hers* . . . An oven mitt, Felicity says, another jug with glasses . . .

"We are the primary audience," Noël says, "for our authorship, we are the after-glow of our legend."

"Correction," Felicity says, "s*he* is the primary etc. whatsit, primary thingamajig—audience and *she* is the after whatever it is etc."

﹏

"You must write to the hospital," my mother says, when I am sitting in her kitchen, "and you must write to the children and to Miss George."

I notice with some irritation that my mother is not able to say the names, "Mr. George" and "Miss George", without a certain self-conscious tone and emphasis. When she says "Mr. George" it is as though she is opening his bedroom door and is, without entering the room or even looking round the door, sliding a cup of tea across the floor boards towards him.

"And another thing," my mother says, "your father has given away his winter coat again."

"Your Father Don't Ever
Use the Moseley Road"

∞

"Your father will be home directly," my mother says, glancing at the three-shilling alarm clock on the mantelpiece.

"You must write to the hospital," my mother says. I am sitting in the kitchen. She glances from the noisy clock to the window as if she has heard my father open the gate. "You must write to Miss George and to the children," she says.

"Yes, yes," I say and I tell her that there is no need to write to the hospital. Everything is known there. It is hard not to be irritable, but I am quiet in front of Mrs. Pugh.

"To your professor then." My mother is cutting bread and butter for my father's tea. "You must keep in touch with him."

"Yo'll need some things to take to that TB farm," Mrs. Pugh, who does not mince her words, as she so often tells us, says. "I'm not one to mince my words, yo'll need *things* to last a fair while. It'll not be a weekend visit, nor a week, nor a month."

Mrs. Pugh does her treadle-machining at home and brings her hand-sewing round to my mother's kitchen. Mrs. Pugh is making three nightdresses and a pink flannelette bed-jacket for me to take to the sanatorium. She wants to stitch some lace, a neat and pretty trimming, she says, on the bed-jacket. I can see it will not take her nimble fingers long.

There is a moist patch, a shadow, I have been told, on one lung. I am to be admitted to the City Sanatorium as soon as there is a vacancy for me.

In the following few days Mrs. Pugh sews a blue bed-jacket for me. She, first of all, goes shopping with my mother for the right kind of material. She hems two face flannels; "One in the wash," she says, "and one to use." She makes a green bed-jacket and soon after it is finished I receive a card telling me to come the next day for admission at one o'clock.

"A couple of years," Mrs. Pugh consoles my mother. "A couple of years and she'll be back," she says. And she measures me for a dressing gown against the day I'll be allowed up, out of bed, to walk on the terraces in the lovely fresh air coming straight off real country fields.

"I'll allow a inch or two here and there," she says, "against you putting on some weight." Mrs. Pugh tells my mother that they should shop for material together unless my mother happens to have a piece of stuff by her or something which she, Mrs. Pugh, could make over. "She'll need it warm," she says.

On the day when I'm supposed to go to the Annex of the City Sanatorium my mother asks Mrs. Pugh if she can spare the time to accompany us and Mrs. Pugh, looking as she would say, affronted, as if it had never occurred to her not to come, says, "A course! A course I'm a coming." She points out that visiting days are the first two Sundays every month and that she can't see anything in her life to prevent her coming with my mother to visit on those days. "They've give us the train times too," she says.

Mrs. Pugh goes on to tell us that two of her brothers were in the Annex one time and that they are now in Australia, where they are doing all right for themselves. She says that Australia, or New South Wales as she calls it (anything with Wales in it is bound to be all right), seems to be the right idea for a great many people nowadays.

"I've always been a one to have the habit of looking ahead," Mrs. Pugh says. "How about if I make a flannel underlining for Mr. Wright's raincoat seeing as how he's give away his top coat?"

Mrs. Pugh's tea being too hot, and looking ahead to the time for leaving for the bus, she cools it in the saucer and drinks from that. A custom which, because it is Mrs. Pugh's, is considered by my mother to be quite ladylike and acceptable, though she never tries it herself.

"Your father don't ever use the Moseley Road now." My mother adopts Mrs. Pugh's phrasing in her letters, in spite of the care with which she has always spoken English. Her Viennese intonation, the musical up and down of her speech, is influenced too by the high-pitched tuning, as of indignation, from the Welsh in Mrs. Pugh's voice. "He don't never want to pass the farm ever again," my mother writes. She writes that Miss George is bringing the children down from Glasgow for a visit, but that it is not considered wise to bring them out to see me.

> *He comes home by Mount Pleasant now and the Lane even if it is longer that way and it makes him later home. It's so as not to pass the farm he comes the longer way. Do you want, do you want to have your Daddy come? Even though he's nervous about hospitals he will come if you want. He could come to see you the Sunday, as I'll have the children if you like him to come. Let us know what you want when you write. Mrs. Pugh and I are coming Sunday 1st.*

During the next few days I have the feeling of homelessness which I know already, only too well. I actually look forward to visitors' day which will bring only my mother and Mrs. Pugh, both of whom, after the first few minutes, when I unwrap something made by Mrs. Pugh, will be dreadfully boring.

It is Mr. George I want to see. Every day I hope that he will come.

"It would be nice if you could learn something useful," my mother says. It is as if she is suggesting that, like a prisoner, I should learn a trade while I am locked up. It is the first visiting Sunday of the month.

"But I already have," I say, stupidly near tears. "I have, I studied. I'm a doctor, I mean . . . what else?"

"Yes, yes," my mother says, and she hurriedly says she did not mean to upset me. "I mean something extra that you could do while you are getting better." She and Mrs. Pugh are sitting on the wooden chairs close up to my white counterpane which the nurses call a bed mat. These bed mats are removed at night and folded up. The long ward, which is a hut really, is curved and open along one side. It is quite cheerful at night with the red blankets.

"I mean," my mother says, still in the same reverent whisper, "if you could learn to sew, like Mrs. Pugh, that would be nice."

The cough seems to start from somewhere out of reach and it continues persisting, irrepressible, until I have to spit and cough again and yet again, and later I lie back exhausted, flat in the flat bed, in the long flat hut in a place perhaps flatter than I have ever known a place to be. From my bed I look out over a flat view, flat to the gray horizon where some dejected horses stand, all facing the same way. Mrs. Pugh says it's because of the weather the horses stand like that. It's a riding school she explains for the mentally defective, a failed horse stud, a knacker's yard. It was the same when her brothers were here, she says. The same. Even the horse riding for the idiots.

While my mother and Mrs. Pugh let their attention wander, restfully watching other patients and their visitors or, with small discreet movements, sort through their own shopping bags, I too go off in my thoughts to Gertrude's Place. I have the extraordinary feeling that I could walk out of this ground-level ward and find, directly outside, the path through the deep grass and cow parsley, which would bring me to the back door where Gertrude sits plucking fowls, singeing feathers, and burning quills with the little flame she nurtures in an old sardine tin beside her chair . . .

"It's not possible to go back in your life," my mother says, as if I have said Gertrude's name aloud. "Let me see," she says, "it must be twelve years since Gertrude died."

My mother listens while I tell her that I feel well enough to walk to Gertrude's Place. She reminds me again that it is at least twelve years. I try to explain that I am getting better, knowing that all the patients share this optimism. It is part of the illness. I want to tell her that the next cough will be the one to clear away, once and for all, the debris. I stop talking and try not to cough.

With an indescribable terror I picture the hemorrhage which will, if it does not kill me, rid me of the diseased areas in my lungs and allow the quiet unseen healing to commence. I do not try to describe this to my mother.

I put myself down for needlework classes and, on the first day when I am allowed to get up, I go along to the sewing room. It is a place of gossip. The women there are mostly nurses who have been ill and are now considered to be cured. I am given unpicking to do, a nurse's uniform dress, faded and soft with washing and about to be made over as a fourth or spare uniform for someone. Fourth dresses are like this. The feeling of the worn cloth makes me remember my own fourth dresses, years ago when I was a different person. I cry a bit and understand that, though I am older and more experienced in all sorts of ways, I am no different.

I long for Mr. George to come. I wait for a letter from him. He writes that he will come. He will put up at the Holly Bush and will visit me.

I am afraid that I won't get better. People don't really get better from this illness. No wonder my mother wanted me to avoid the places where there were signs. And though I want to see Mr. George I feel too tired to write a letter back to him. I have an apathetic tiredness and forgetfulness and a waiting for food and not wanting the food and not wanting to talk either to the nurses or to the other patients, I do not like any of them though I know really that they are all nice people.

For some reason the River Jordan song goes round and round in my head. And though I remember all too well Felicity humming and singing on that day as she moved, without purpose, the jars of jam and bottled fruit, I go back in my mind, to school and to being in the school sanatorium with a girl called Yvonne. We sing over and over again:

> *The animals came in two by two*
> *The elephant and the kangaroo*

One more river and that's the river of Jordan
One more river and that's the river to cross.

I sing one line and this Yvonne girls sings the next line. In isolation (the top floor), we are by ourselves with an eye infection and not allowed to read. All our books have been removed. We sing and invent games and lean out of the window calling out to anyone who passes below. I am interested in the creamy pink and white soft flesh which is this Yvonne. It seems to me then that she is made of better material than I am made of. It is as if she is the result of generations of good breeding, not just in manners but in the making of her body, as if years and years of very good food and comfortable warm luxurious rooms have produced her. I try not to stare at her when she washes herself in a china basin the nurse sets out on the floor. Another thing is that Yvonne scarcely seems to notice my body when it is time for me to wash. In my mind I compare what I imagine her mother and father to be like with my own mother and father. Both of mine, at different times, have suffered from poverty. Yvonne and I exchange addresses, we each have a little address book. And, though we are not meant to write either, we scribble in each other's holiday address. Yvonne's address surprises me because it is with a Miss Playfair not with a Mr. and Mrs., not with a father and a mother. The surname is not even the same as Yvonne's. This gives me considerable pondering which is almost as good as reading for the evening.

Not being allowed to go to the bathroom we have to sit on china pots. It is then I see the creamy hugeness of Yvonne with admiration which is tinged by my own terrible embarrassment at having to squat on the pot in the presence of someone else.

"And who does this Mr. George think he is, just who does he think he is," my mother visiting is not able to keep her voice soft. "And worse," she says, close up beside my bed, Mrs. Pugh is not with her this time. "Just who do you think you are, a film star or what?" She has brought a cake and a bag with chocolates and some flowers. I hardly notice the flowers and am not able to say later which, out of all the flowers, are from my visitor. I feel it is disloyal of me not to know whether my mother brought lupins or roses. And what is worse I have lost my way in the seasons. I have no idea what people in the outside world are thinking or doing or wearing. My mother always wears the same coat. Perhaps she hangs it up in the shed when she gets home. What time of the year is it?

"How can you Vera? How can you put the children out of your mind as you have done? You could at least write them half a page to thank them for their drawings . . ." My mother's voice remains close in my head after she has gone. I can hear the tears in her voice as if she is still beside me. "And what good have they, these so-called friends of yours, done? What good has it done you, them calling you a poet and taking everything from you? You can't say I didn't warn you Vera. If I said, Vera, that they would take all you had and not replace it, they have given you *something* and it's not very nice, is it. That's why you are here in this awful place. Your Daddy doesn't sleep thinking of you in here, not getting on in your own life as you should be."

Be fair, I want to tell my mother after she has gone to the train. Be fair, this spot on my lung could have come when I was nursing high up on the balconies of the fifth floor, where the air was supposed to be fresher and cleaner and where fresh eggs, cream, and nourishing soups appeared every day, sent up from those subterranean kitchens where I had once worked, hiding my first pregnancy. I want to run after my mother to tell her it was not from *them* or from my work that I have the moist patch, it could be just as easily an infection picked up during one of the long damp journeys on the bus or the train.

I want to tell her too that I want my children, I want to hold them and feel their soft smooth skin and to hear their voices. I did not even try to tell her that the hardest thing is being away from them, that I want to be there at their bathing and to see them wake up in the mornings.

It is true, I want to tell her, that I did not listen to her, that I was drawn in by Noël and Felicity, that they were, as she would say, making use of me, that they needed *someone*. And how could I tell her about these friends, that they called me "poet" and that we were lovers. How would my mother understand this without being hurt by it. I think of my mother's solitary journey. She would not be able to say all she knows and thinks even if Mrs. Pugh had come this time. The nurses call me doctor and tell me to come up out of the pillow. The nurses disturb me as they come round, as they always do, after visitors, with two big black metal trays. They collect all the chocolates, the biscuits, the sweets and the fruit so that the patients who do not have visitors can have a share of what is brought in.

"You must write to your professor at the hospital," my mother says as she is leaving. Of course I must. He has written me a kind letter. I have no energy and no wish to write a reply. Another letter from Mr. George lies unopened on my locker. Elke, or the other young woman, will be at Miss George's side while she, Miss George, carves the meat. Elke! How could I have allowed Elke, or anyone, to take my place in that household. Elke, drying my children after their baths. Elke, sitting up there on my cherry-wood floor.

Felicity and Noël. I want to know where they are and if they know where I am. *Felicity, I wonder, will you come to see me. Felicity and Noël please please come to visit me . . .*

Sometimes, like now, my thoughts are too heavy. While I was studying I thought that when I qualified everything would be different, that I would be raised in some way because of passing my exams and because of being able to understand the work I would be doing and in the knowing more about human life. And I thought I would be wiser myself and on the same level as other people instead of the wrong level. But is it not like this. I make the same mistakes. I want the same things I have always wanted and always I am on the edge of other people. Patients and illness are on one side of life and romantic beauty and ideals seem to be removed to another unreachable side. And then there are the obligations, the special obligations special people have towards each other. If I am to be outside or only a part of a special obligation it is not enough.

I want to be the giver and the recipient of the whole and it seems that I never shall be.

The cough when it comes seems to start somewhere out of reach, it is a small cough and persistent. If someone else had the cough within my hearing I would be intolerant. It is my way of coughing, as if I am not coughing, which would irritate me if someone else was the one coughing.

The sputum mugs, all shabby and chipped, make me feel sick, they are ugly in the way they are made and ugly in their reason for being there. I know that there are all kinds of sputum and that the nurses are trained to observe the amount, the color, the odor, the tenacity—whether it clings to a patient's lips or is difficult to spit out. I am shy of this being watched. I know that they want to know whether it is coughed up early in the mornings or after a meal or after any kind of exertion. I know all the descriptions of sputum; *abundant or scanty, clear or opaque, muco-purulent, bloodstained, or rusty.* It might be *frothy*, it might look like *the juice of prunes* or *like egg yolk,* or, in my diagnosis, *like sago grains.* It can come up, if it does come up, *in coin-shaped masses lying on the bottom of the vessel into which it is expectorated. This occurs when cavities are present.*

The ordinary sputum cup has a little antiseptic placed at the bottom for the sputum to fall on. Patients who are allowed up have a pocket sputum flask made of blue glass with a screw-top lid and this, in order to avoid soiling the pocket, should be provided with a separate removable calico pocket . . .

For disposal, sputum may be poured over sawdust which is afterwards burnt.

It is all too familiar for me, this ugliness of the illness. This ugliness belonged earlier to other people and now it seems to be my possession.

Whenever I can, when I am allowed out of my bed, I leave the sputum mug in the most out-of-the-way places. There are not many such places.

"Where is your sputum mug?"

"I don't have any sputum."

Hides sputum, is recorded along with my temperature, pulse and respiration.

There is no music here, only the sound of coughing. Endless coughing of the hopeless sort.

At first I do not understand that I am wishing for music. When my mother comes I almost tell her about the music, that I am missing it. She tells me she has brought me something to read. She has brought, she says, *Lorna Doone* and *The Forsyte Saga*.

"But I read these at school."

"Never mind! You can read them again." My mother goes on to say that she enjoyed them more the second and even the third time round.

That night, when Noël and Felicity have gone to bed, that night after their talk about a wedding, as if they want to hurt me by their talk, I am not able to sleep. I go downstairs and out into the field and see the moon. I have forgotten about the moon. My father always said that he thought of the moon as his moon. When I looked at the moon, he always told me, I was seeing the same moon as he was seeing, however far apart we might be. Just now in this place I am not all that far away from where my father is. It seems to be a great distance because we are not able to speak of the things which would make a bridge across that space between my earth and his moon.

I look up at the moon and set off walking across the field in the dark. When I reach the hedge and the road, I follow the road not choosing any special direction. Simply I am walking away from Noël and Felicity, these two, who are my friends.

The familiar fragrance of elderberry and the steady muffled snoring of a city, apparently asleep but awake with nocturnal industry remind of the carelessness of childhood and enhance the reality of what it feels like to have no place to go home to.

My mother no longer walks this road, the Moseley Road, with me. There is no fluting voice with gentle warnings about spots of blood in the snow and no wise consolations for a girl crying in the black shadow of the elderberry. No *other* girl, I should say because I am the one now, the one crying here at the side of the empty road wanting my mother.

On the day when the doctor comes to see Noël the towels and sheets are dismal, hanging gray and low, almost dragging across the mud. I watch the doctor, through the mist, as he leaves his car and picks his way across the wet field. He is a small man in a suit which has a waistcoat. A looped and golden watch-chain shines on the worsted cloth. His spats are the color of field mushrooms. His shoes are well polished. He carries a small case and, with a light step, crosses the mud, balancing on the plank and goes straight into the house without knocking.

"Which one? Which one are you with?" the doctor asks me on his way out. He glances, as he speaks, to the upstairs window which is now hanging by one hinge, Noël having wrenched it out of the frame in his desperation for more air.

"Which one?" the doctor asks again, jerking his head in the direction of the wrecked window. I look down at the mud. Immediately he apologizes. He says he is sorry, he begs my pardon in an old-fashioned sort of way. I imagine him begging pardon before the performance of an internal examination. It would be a performance. He puts his case down on the doorstep and scribbles quickly on a small pad. Tearing off the page, he hands it to me and tells me to report to the City Clinic for a chest X-ray.

He crosses the mud and stops on the first tuft of grass. "Is there any way," he says, "is there any way that you can get away from here?" he asks. "It's not a place at all to live in. No place at all. It's filthy and there's no drainage." He moves on then, as if dancing and balancing on the drier bits of ground. As he goes, I hear him muttering, "And wherever is the drinking water coming from?"

I notice every detail about the doctor because he seems to represent all the safety and cleanliness in my mother's house when I was small. He reminds me of the doctor who came, his hands warm and sweet with the scent of carbolic, to my bedside once, with one of my mother's best teaspoons in a clean napkin, to examine my throat when I had measles. I want to run after Noël's doctor. I want to tell him I can't stand the dirt any longer. I begin to cry, I can't stop the tears running down my face.

There is no sound from the upstairs bedroom. No coughing and no complaining. And then I hear Felicity coming downstairs.

"*You must take another road,*" Felicity appears in the doorway. She leans on the door post. Her handsome face is more care-worn than usual and seems thinner and deeply lined especially round the mouth. "*You must take another road,*" she goes on, "*if you wish to escape from this wild place.* I am paraphrasing Dante," she says, "Canto 1, page 9." Felicity yawns, as if bored in advance on seeing me. The pale sun offers no warmth. The wet washing hangs motionless. Though the mist is dispersing the cold rises through my shoes.

Felicity yawns in a well-bred way into the mist.

Felicity sees them before I do. She sees the two people, in dark coats, pausing in the narrow space between the elderberry and the hawthorn. She sees them pausing and peering across the field. Then I see my mother's white hat and my father's white face.

"They must have come on the bus and walked from the corner," I say. I want to run over the wet grass to the opening in the hedge. I want to go over to them, but I stay as if nailed to the rough wood of the kitchen window sill. I do not look a second time across to where they are.

Unperturbed, Felicity comments in a low voice about the ludicrous, the unforgettable and *ludicrous*, a white hat with an old bottle-green winter coat. She continues her recitation;

"*Wherefore I think I discern this for thy best that thou follow me; and I will be thy guide and lead thee hence through an eternal place . . .*"

I look up quickly as Felicity speaks and yawns, for a moment I think she is asking me to go away with her. I love and admire Felicity. Her face has no smile, only the tired sad look.

"All you have to do Persephone, *Darling*," she says, "is to substitute "them" for "me" and "they" for "I". Dante, *Darling*, same page probably. In an English translation naturally. You should go with your illustrious and suffering ma and pa." And then in a voice suddenly harsh, she says that an ambulance is coming for Noël. I want to comfort Felicity, I want to tell her that I know how weak and ill Noël is. I want to tell her too that it will be better for him to be properly looked after. Felicity jerks her head in the direction of the cow saying that something, whatever it is they use for animals, will come for her. "Do they have animal ambulances?" she asks. When I look at the cow I feel ashamed that I have never paid attention to her condition. I have never noticed how sharply her bones show all over her emaciated body.

Felicity is not allowed to travel in the ambulance with Noël. We watch as Noël is carried, gray faced with his eyes closed, to the ambulance. He opens his eyes and turns his head and says, with his handsome smile, "*Exit, pursued by a bear. Enter the Shepherd. Shakespeare.*" And closes his eyes.

Felicity takes all the money I have and races off across the field to be in time for the next bus.

I wait all day for Felicity to come back. I scrub some potatoes and bake them in the kitchen fire to have something hot for her. I wait all evening for her to come home. Several times I go out to look into the darkness, wanting to hear her voice calling across the field. I listen to the rats scrabbling in the walls of the kitchen. Felicity does not come. I gather as many things as I can push into one of the hessian sacks used for potatoes and cabbages and I set off for the road. Once there, it is easier to walk and I drag the sack. Because of the great size of the enormous pit mound it seems to be moving alongside, keeping up with me, an ugly black hump, a deformity hiding the moon for a long time.

My father opens the door. He has opened the door so often for me during my life that it seems to be quite natural for him to open it in the middle of the night. He has pulled on his trousers, his night shirt is only partly tucked in. My mother is half way down the stairs which come down to the hall immediately inside the front door. She is pulling her coat on over her night dress.

My father, with all the years of good manners stored up inside him, takes the sack gently as if it had the same quality about it as a fashionable leather suitcase complete with straps and keys and labels.

"Put the kettle on," he tells my mother, "and give the fire a good rake, it'll soon come up."

My mother cries a bit at the kitchen table, while my father rattles about in the coal place for suitable small bits to bring up the fire.

"You'd like a nice bath," he says to me. It is then that I remember almost the last thing Noël said the day before. He said that he was going to emulate Socrates by having his ultimate bath early so that neither of us, Felicity or I, would have the trouble of washing him after he was dead.

Because of her opinion of Mrs. Pugh, my mother understanding that Mrs. Pugh *knows*, agrees that Australia has great possibilities. Though for me any possibility of this sort is too far away for any consideration. The future is something vague and unattainable since something frightening and impossible has presented itself and there is no way round it.

The Widow and the Migrant

"Tell me about yourself, Migrant," the rice-farm widow says to me. So I tell my widow things about myself. When I tell her about Felicity and Noël her mouth is so wide open, as she listens, I can see her gold fillings. At that time, I think her whole fortune is in her mouth.

"You mean to tell me!" she says. "Oh, I can't believe . . ." she says, "that they, I mean, *together*. You can't mean that."

"Yes, that's right," I tell her.

"Oh, Migrant. You poor child, poor poor child."

"Oh no, your widowship, not at all. Nothing like that. They were very gentle and considerate. They were intellectuals, don't you see. The whole thing was more of an idea. And it was quite a joke thing between us, between the three of us, every time. Their very good manners, don't you know."

"More than once! Heavens, child!"

"Please, please—don't be concerned. Do not concern your gracious self; it was funny, really funny. They were, *unlike us*, so very polite."

"You mean, '*after you*' and 'Oh no, *after you.*'"

"Well sort of, not quite, but yes, rather like that."

"What an *experience* you had."

"I suppose so."

"You *suppose* so. My dear Migrant, do you realize that plenty of people would give their eye teeth . . ."

"But what would anyone *do* with someone else's eye teeth?"

We use these special names for each other, Widow and Migrant. Straight away, before the ship begins to roll, we use them, at the table, on the deck, in the bar, and during conversations, which Mr. George says, contain the language of the prelude to our, hers and mine, curious flirtation.

Widow and Migrant, sometimes adding "the," the Widow and the Migrant, so that we distance ourselves into a third-person narration. Particularly we do this during our daily shopping in the ship's shop, choosing expensive unnecessary clothing, gifts, and perfume.

"Would the Widow like this?"

"The Migrant ought to have one of these. No, I tell a lie, the Migrant should have two. Make that half a dozen." The widow opens her sequined purse and keeps it open dangling over one arm.

I have to admit, privately to myself, that I am surprised straight away at this distinction I possess in my ability to be someone quite different if an occasion demands a difference, the putting forward of a changed self. I reflect on this change, this ability, every time I have a shower in the widow's own bathroom. I have to understand that I was conscious of the need for a change in my demeanor as soon as I boarded the ship. If I pause and look back I can see that I have been capable of putting this sort of armor, this shell, a kind of protection, at various times during my life. I have to understand too that if I do not like this quality in myself, Mr. George, as well, might dislike it.

As the weather becomes warmer, I fret for my one pair of shorts packed without foresight, unreachable in the hold. At the appropriate time the ship's shop overflows with a summer display.

"You'd best have some of these," the widow says, making a competent selection. "Australian shorts are properly cut and tailored. You can't possibly be *seen* in English shorts."

Meanwhile, Mr. George, who is nearby in a long chair reading about the *unexplainable glow of legend* and *how a man cannot hope to live longer than the ultimate worth of his possessions*, glances across with, what is to me, an unfamiliar sort of smile. Neither of us have ever met anyone like the widow before. Mr.

George's new way of smiling and his public devotion to reading are, in part, a little mask to hide his uneasiness about his new appointment and this long journey towards it. I know this, for my own thoughts insist on leaping forward to possible strangeness and difficulties in my work and, at the same time, I am worrying whether Helena, when she starts the term at her boarding school, will be happy. And I wonder if Miss George is managing well enough with Rachel. Elke, the au pair with a triumphant and fearless laugh, seems very suitable. I try to hope that the children are happy and I rest in this hope.

Straight away after meeting the rice-farm widow I think it strange that there should be, all at once, another widow in my life making now a total of four if I count Gertrude and Magda, though it is never clear if Dr. Metcalf died on active service as a result of an accident or whether he is somewhere alive still and living with Smithers, the poetry-writing Theater Orderly with whom Dr. Metcalf was in love and, it was said, went to the front when the war was practically over, in reality, in pursuit of Smithers. If, after all this time, Dr. Metcalf is still alive Magda cannot, even though she is alone, be classed as a widow. And the fourth widow, the railway-man's widow with her pronouncements and her ability with the sewing machine, being as it were the chosen property of my mother, does, like the others, slip out of my mind in the presence of this new and even more powerful widow.

"I always take two napkins," the widow says, "one for the mouth and one for the lap." After a pause during which we are fully occupied with cold cuts on rye, new and unfamiliar for me, innovative I want to say but, because of the heavy grain, the word sticks, the widow says, "And what about your gentleman?" She untangles a bit of beef from what she calls her partial, her *unsatisfactory* partial.

"Oh please, *not* gentleman," I manage in a scattering of cress.

"Well, Migrant, your professor then. How does he respond to Beethoven, I mean not just the last five quartets, let's say the first and second symphonies?" The widow signals the steward and asks for coffee. "I mean," she continues, "they are a downright statement of passion which cannot be denied. And then again what about the drums in Beethoven's seventh?" While my widow talks I think of the time when my mother took me to a concert and, because of worrying about the people who might be late and not allowed in till the interval, I did not hear the music at first. I remember now the way in which the drummer hurled himself into the music. At the time it is a revelation.

"Body and soul," my widow is still talking about the seventh symphony, "and exercising great restraint at the same time." She has come to the drummer now and is talking about restraint. "Has your gentleman, your professor, the power of restraint?" I almost tell my widow about my mother, that she is no longer the same as she was, now that she has her own widow, Mrs. Pugh.

"Has he, your professor, ever mentioned a response to the symphonies?" she asks. Mr. George joins us at the small table. He, from being on the deck a great deal, lying back in a long chair, reading, has a healthy suntanned look. The widow, without any hesitation about making personal remarks, says that Mr. George's white hair and the suntan go well together. That the combination makes him look more distinguished than ever. She goes on to say that she would like to see him in a specially tailored, white, raw-silk jacket and that we should have one made during the voyage. There is no chance then for me to try to answer the widow's questions. She could even ask Mr. George himself. She seems to be that sort of woman. She will ask anything she wants to know. Mr. George acknowledges my widow's compliment with a smile. It is not the kind of smile I want for myself from him but, at present, any look or smile would make me feel better—a look or a smile from Mr. George, that is.

I often reflect on the idea of "widow," of being a widow and, that being a widow means that you are something special, that you have been selected and publicly chosen at some time in your life. The idea of being chosen means that someone has made a sensitive choice of taste and touch and has been drawn irresistibly—even if you live alone later.

The word widow and the idea of widow suggest black clothes, a soft spreading bosom and a lap, overfed and overweight. Included in the idea of widow is shining silky material, if not black perhaps a subdued violet or the color of a gentle petal, a mauve cyclamen perhaps. These images of widowhood do not fit exactly with my rice-farm widow. She never wears violet, and black only for funerals. Black would need something sparkling and hideously expensive, she explains, or else something fresh and tender and youthful.

The kiss the widow gives me, when we are just through the double doors leading from the deck to the top of the brass-bound stairs which go straight down to the dining rooms, is not a cool-lipped brushing of a powdered cheek crumpling against mine. It is a compelling kiss, masterful and tender at the same time, with a perfume on her breath of sophisticated exotic drinks and an overpriced suntan lotion with a foreign name.

She's been in the sun all day, she tells me then, on the top deck with nothing on except a wisp of cotton to protect her nipples. Then there was a bit of a party, she explains, and when she told the Purser that if she went on drinking she'd be under the Captain, she thought she had better leave. "It's my Big Mouth," she says.

"Come to my cabin," she says, so I go.

When I was thinking about all the widows, counting them up, I included Gertrude but, in fact, she was not a widow.

"To all intents and purposes, Gertrude was not really a widow," I say. But my widow is not listening, she is ferreting about in her cupboards, her cases, and her special boxes. She has something she wants me to wear if she can find the accessories, she says.

Gertrude wasn't a widow, I am remembering exactly as my mother tells me that time when I ask her. It is as though I hear my mother's voice through the throbbing of the ship. For some time we have been plunging as well as rolling. Quite a different movement from the smooth sailing at first.

"Gertrude," my mother explains, "had a husband but you won't ever have seen him. He was a farm laborer," she says, "with ten shillings a week. He walked miles to his work before it was light in the mornings and would have been walking back by the field paths in the evenings. You would already have left Gertrude's and been on your way home."

My mother says that they, Gertrude and her husband, did not have much to say to each other and, she says, they slept each in a shabby chair, one on either side of the hearth. It is not hard for me to imagine them both in the ragged armchairs, one on either side of the fireplace with the kettle humming softly on the hob between them. And where, every now and then, a hot cinder would dislodge and fall, with a small flare of light and warmth through the broken bars of the grate, breaking their sleep.

Gertrude, my mother says, used to declare that the cat they had for seventeen years used to prick up her ears and set off at a certain time through the grass and the weeds to meet Gertrude's husband. It did not matter which field path he had taken when setting out for the long slow walk home, the cat never failed to take the right direction and it would come back with him, treading lightly where he trod, pausing if he paused and *measured* in that the cat did not outstep him, but like his own shadow following him, she would not arrive home before he did.

It seems incredible to me, at that time, that my mother actually seems to know more about Gertrude than I do.

"You can't count Gertrude as one of the widows in your life," my mother says. "She died before her husband died. Everybody at some time or other knows a widow," my mother goes on, "and not all your friends are widows. Miss George," she says, "is a spinster and so is your Aunt Daisy. Neither of them can be widows."

I think of other nurses at the hospital. I think of Trent and remember that she was a widow, proud of her black clothes, but only briefly. And I wonder about Lois and if she ever married; and then there was Ramsden. What about Ramsden?

"It does not look," my mother says, "as if you will ever be a widow." She is bending over the washing-up bowl with her back to me at the time, so I do not know what her face is like when she is saying this.

"I'll have to go to the toilet or else my back teeth'll be under water," my widow, with an armful of clothes, beads, and chains dangling from her fingers, comes up from a final box interrupting my unexpected memories.

"Put this on," she says to me, "with this head band and the beads, lots and lots of beads," she says, "and you'll love the fringe when it settles around your legs. See what I mean?"

It was like having to listen to music alone, the rice-farm widow tells me, or reading something and having no one to talk to about what you've read. "It's not having anyone to tell things to," she says. "Wealth and prosperity," she goes on while I watch her pulling out more clothes. She's changing for dinner. "Wealth and prosperity are nothing unless you have someone to enjoy them with." She was not, she says then, one of the usual fat overdressed women, obliged to travel round the world using up the money their husbands had made, working themselves to an early death in the process.

"I did all the work myself," she says.

She has thighs as straight and as muscular as an athlete half her age might have. She makes me stand, she invites me, I should say, to stand barefoot on her stomach. She asks if I can feel her muscles and I tell her yes I can.

I thought, I tell my widow, that it would be so wonderful to be with Mr. George day and night, day after day and night after night during the voyage. I tell her that is not how we have been able to travel, to arrange our traveling, I explain. His university has arranged his ticket and my hospital has arranged mine. When I say ticket I mean passage, I begin further explanation but the widow interrupts.

"Officially you are not together," she says, "and before you left both of you thought that this would not matter. Unfortunately," she continues, "*husband* and *wife* stupidly do matter even on board ship unless you are the bold type and neither of you is bold and," the widow says, "scandal in Acadeem is greatly enjoyed. I can just imagine," she says, "the university wives in their hats and gloves at their tea club whispering . . ."

"He traveled, my deah, with a woman who is not his wife . . ."

"Who on earth is she?"

"She's supposed to be a doctor if you please . . .

"She's got children, I've heard she has children . . .

"Yes, she's left her children, would you believe *with his sister!*" My widow changes from her sixth-form schoolgirl voice to one of immediate understanding and sympathy saying that, during the war, people made allowances, boy friends going overseas, that sort of thing. But that now, twelve or thirteen years later, propriety has returned, decorum and the pleasure, during plain and dull times, of gossip.

"Does he," she asks suddenly, "does your gentleman professor admit to paternity?"

Her question surprises me. "It would only be for one," I tell my widow, trying not to show that her question has been a shock. "It was such a short time," I tell her. "I could, for all they knew, have been pregnant when they took us in. Helena was four. D'you see, they, Mr. George and Miss Eleanor, they never asked me anything. Later I told Mr. George every single thing about my life."

I tell my widow then about the snow I shoveled off the flat roof, about the Beethoven quartet by Mr. George's study fire in the evening, and about Mr. George liking my red cheeks, red because of the cold earlier when I was on the roof.

I tell her about Mr. George's narrow iron bed and the tears trembling along Miss George's eyelashes the next morning when I take her little round tea tray into her room and she is lying there as if asleep still, only I know she is not asleep because she is crying.

"There never has been," I say, "a time which was the right time for telling her. But Mr. George, he knows."

"If you ask me," my widow says, "she, Miss George, she knows it too."

After a bit she asks me how old I am. I tell her that I'm thirty-four. She says do I realize that at thirty-four or -five a woman has reached her sexual plateau. She is, at thirty-five, at her highest level of sexuality and therefore at her most desirable.

On the way down to dinner the widow says to me to come to the bar first.

"Migrant," she says, "I'll shout you." I'm not sure what she means but I go with her all the same.

The ship is a so-called one-class ship for the purposes of the voyage. Some passengers like Mr. George and my widow have very spacious and comfortable cabins and people like me share, usually four people to one cabin.

The widow, my widow, should have had a fellow passenger but she must have missed the ship. The widow rejoices. She has her own bathroom.

"Feel free, Migrant," she says, tossing a thick first-class type bath towel to me. I do not mind at all going with her to her cabin and I am very glad to use her luxurious bathroom as the three young women, with whom I share, seem to spend all their time locked in the bathroom doing things to their immature legs or to their complicated hair.

"Thank you, Widow. Much obliged, your Widowship," I say adopting a tone of voice which causes her to laugh. I like to make her laugh.

The widow is used to the word widow. She uses it all the time and mixes a great deal, if scornfully, with other widows. As she says herself, there is no escaping them or migrants on board ships like the one we are traveling on. I never thought of myself as a migrant but that is what I am. A migrant, if only temporarily, my appointment like Mr. George's being for one year with possibilities of extension. Mr. George's is more in the nature of an invitation.

I tell my widow that it is because of Mr. George and Miss George that I have been able to study and to qualify in medicine. The widow bets all the same that my mother and father would have turned themselves inside out to put me through and would not have required me as a maid or for *other services*. I have no reply to this.

I am still trying to get used to this migrant thing.

MIGRANTS QUEUE HERE MIGRANTS CHEST X-RAY
NO MIGRANTS PAST THIS POINT
MIGRANTS REPORT HERE

and so on. I am still trying to get used to all this I tell her.

"Your father," the widow says straight away, when she sees I am crying by the rail on the top deck. "Your father," she pats me on the back, a thump it is really, more of a correction than a consolation, "your father can't accompany you all the way in your life. There are definite times, are there not, when you would not want him." She is on her way, she says, to bat the guts out of all the other widows in a deck-tennis tournament. She would have preferred, she adds over her handsome shoulder, a game of quoits, the sharp-edged, ankle-biting iron sort. I hear her low rumble of laughter, gradually disappearing, all the way to the other end of the ship.

Often during the voyage I feel a curious sense of isolation in spite of all the people on the ship, and in spite of the presence, if at a distance, of Mr. George. And even the widow seems removed when the emptiness settles like a mist all round me. The ship, a substantial and portly sea-going duchess, seems to plow bravely on an unknown course. When I try to speak of this to Mr. George, when we meet at the rail, he laughs and says that ships are making this journey all the time and that I feel as I do feel because we are making the voyage for the first time. There is nothing in the sea to show us the way, I tell him and he laughs again and says have I forgotten who was the mentor on another first-time occasion.

"How barren Crete looks," I say to the widow when all the passengers are pushing to be at the rail to photograph a thin distant line of land which has appeared as if from nowhere. "Just a few flat houses and some skinny trees and scrub. The people there must be very poor and ignorant."

"I'll bet," she says then, "they know a thing or two we don't know." She says to wait till we get to the Great Bitter Lake, Port Said, and Suez. "But this sea," she says, "I had it from your gentleman, your professor, this morning, this sea is the special sea where Odysseus swam for nine days, nine days on end, mind you! There's a thought."

The ship at anchor, rolling slightly waiting for passage through the Suez Canal, seems as if suspended and lost. Bereaved, as if without hope of reaching a destination. When I stand at the ship's rail, up on the top deck, the expanse of water, disappearing into a sky of the same colorless opaque quality, seems to provide a visual but silent response to my loneliness. This quality matches the sound of the Arabic music heard faintly in Mr. George's cabin during the day and the night. It is a thin wailing song from within the raised paneling or, if imagined as being from the fringes of the land, it is a solitary note, sustained on a single breath, crying in the reeds. It is a sound refined and filtered from one remote culture to another through the mixture of materials, the steel and the brass, the timber, the glass, and the fumed oak in the massive structure which is the ship.

A ship is a closed unnatural world in which it is not possible for us to live as we would like to live, Mr. George tells me during the time I am with him in his cabin. I never stay there all night and some nights do not go in there at all. He tells me that later we shall be together every night and go, each of us, to our work and come together every night without impediment of any sort. He tells me he is impatient for this. Taking me in his arms he says he is sure he does not have to remind me of all that exists between us during the years I have been with him and with Miss George. Gently he tells me how much I mean to him and that anything that has to do with me and my life is his concern and is more important than anything else.

"How would you like fat-head for a nickname?" This detail from a conversation, overheard, coming into my head during Mr. George's tender embrace surprises me. I feel his quick little kisses on my hair, my forehead, and the side of my neck as he holds me close. I try not to remember sitting with my widow, earlier, on the white-painted chairs by the swimming pool, the Tavern Bar, conveniently as my widow says, immediately behind us, both of us submerging our freshly applied lipstick, *chameleon cerise*, in the deep whipped cream of her favorite Brandy and Benedictine coffee, brought to us without it being ordered, in tall, fluted, silver-rimmed glasses.

I pull Mr. George down on his bunk, pulling him close and trying to unfasten our clothes and discard them quickly.

"If anyone called *me* fat-head," the indignant voice continues in my thoughts, in the clipped overtones of outrage and shock and the need for imitation horn-rimmed spectacles to be removed and breathed on and polished with a handkerchief, "I would," the voice rising goes on, "I would certainly not be able to think of them as *friend*, would you?" I mean, think of it, *fat-head*." The reply from horn-rimmed's companion, at the time, is lost in one of the widow's long rumbling coughs during which she laughs, snorts, wipes her eyes, chokes, hiccups, and throws away her slim cigar.

"How about shit-head, darlin'?" she manages at last, but politely only just loud enough for me to hear. And then she is shaking with suppressed mirth and we quiver together close on the wrought-iron and I feel a desire for her which is overpowering. She looks into my eyes with an intensity which is at once kind and loving and fierce. My eyes fill with foolish tears.

"Later," she whispers. And then, in the accents of the fat-head shock and the imitation horn rims, she says, "Afterwards we shall both go on a water diet, cold bathings, cold douchings, and cold water to drink . . ." With an added, "Scooze I," also horn-rimmed and a little too loud after a lengthy characteristic burring coughing fit mixed with hiccups.

"Is it your new friend?" Mr. George asks a few minutes later. "I suppose," he says, "it's an excitement, the new friend."

"Look at the menu, child," the widow says. "*Migrant! You don't want curried wings. There's nothing on a chicken's wings. Bring two porterhouse steaks," she says to the steward. "Make that three," she says as Mr. George, approaching our table, pauses at the empty chair. "Make 'em rare," the widow continues, "with fried potatoes and salads. Baguette or rye?" She turns to Mr. George, holding out the little basket and smiling with approval. I glance at Mr. George sideways. This is something I have never done before. He has not been on deck all morning and when I knocked on his cabin door only Mr. Street was there making up the cabin, as he said, his breath sweet with whiskey. Street is Mr. George's cabin steward. The widow knows him and has warned Mr. George not to give him his tip, which should be about two pounds, till disembarkation.

"Or he'll be slumped drunk inside the cabin against the door and you'll not be able to get in," the widow says when giving this advice. Her own steward is called Smith and he had his two pounds early on with the promise of another two later. Consequently the widow gets additional services like having deep hot baths run for her and two warmed towels handed round the door when required. A woman does out the cabin I'm in and the widow says there's no need to give her anything unless I have an old jumper or a dress I can't wear any more.

"There is so much to learn about ship traveling," I say, in order to say something after Mr. George has seen my sideways look at him.

"I'll go along with that," the widow says as our laden plates arrive. "And people too," she says, "there's a lot to learn about people and a ship's a good place for learning."

I look down at my plate and try to concentrate on the steak. Without wanting to I am remembering the night, what little remained of the night, before I left Mr. George's cabin for my own. I am unable to forget Mr. George's words.

"That woman, that vulgar woman, her talk about music, for one thing, is the kind of rubbish put on record sleeves to enable people like her to talk as if they enjoy music and know something about it. How can you, Vera, be so taken in by someone like this?"

I try to tell him that the widow is only trying to be friendly and that I'm not being, as he says, taken in. I try to explain that I need friends, especially on board the ship since I have left everyone, my children included. Especially my children.

I am surprised then, well amazed really, when he tells me he has spoken to Miss George by wireless telephone and that all is well at home.

"Did you speak to the children?" I ask him and he says, yes he did and they spoke to him.

So that was why I was unable to find him on deck, he must have been in some office or other making this fantastic telephone call from the ship.

"The children," I say. "You heard their voices?" Mr. George tells me yes he did hear their voices and, he said, that Helena wanted me to know that she had on a pair of my silk stockings, the honey-colored ones from Marshalls, and that her legs, she thinks, look nice in them.

With the beating of the pulses in my head and neck drowning the thin nocturnal Arabic wailing, which is their music, imprisoned as it seems to be within the woodwork of Mr. George's cabin, I do not cry until I am under the blankets in the bunk in my own cabin.

The widow is telling us that we'll both have to learn to eat meat, to really eat it. She glances at our unfinished plates and jerks her head towards the table next to ours where a clean-looking family with three children have ordered steaks. "Even a whole T-bone for the little boy who only looks about seven," she says.

"You'll have to learn to eat more meat," she says once more. And then she tells me that I'll have to know how to choose it and cook it. She says she'll teach me the cuts of beef and lamb. She says no one, but no one, can live in Australia without this simple knowledge. Mr. George appears to be not taking much notice of my widow's remarks. I feel responsible for his silence. I am not accustomed to being in what amounts to a social encounter with him. I wonder if other people feel this sort of responsibility. In the silence while we are cutting up and moving little amounts of food about our plates I notice the people on the other side of us. Probably two married couples, an ugly but useful phrase, which is painful for me, but which cannot be disregarded, all four are picking at salads and staring about with bored mournful expressions. They pick a bit and stare, another pick and another stare, slack mouthed with what looks like unhappiness. I seem to see these reflections of unhappiness in all kinds of places, in the narrow passages, on the decks, in the communal wash rooms where women, in passing, smile with forlorn hope at themselves forced by the mirrors to see themselves often from more than one angle. Especially too, there are reflections in the shining brass door fittings which distort heads and bodies. Engraved on the brass floor plates are familiar factory names from the Midlands in England. Why these names, familiar as they are, but without any personal connection, should make me wish to be back there visiting Noël and Felicity, or my mother and father, or going back to earlier times, visiting Gertrude, is unexplainable. In the continued silence of the meal I remember seeing the factory names from the bus or the train. These brass things are simply a part of the ship, nothing more, except that they come from the place where I come from.

I am surprisingly unhappy that Mr. George is staying on at the table. Though I am not a bereaved person I have my own share of deep wounds to which I am responding in secret. I suppose, if I think about this, so is Mr. George. I am surprised that I am able to suddenly think this about Mr. George. Outwardly neither of us reveals anything. No one can guess, on seeing us, that something from before is still between us. Even my widow, who seems to see through everything. Though I feel afraid and perhaps relieved at the same time that, before the next landfall, she will drag the whole sad story from me.

"A real conversation stopper," my widow says, when Mr. George leaves the table with a polite little nod after, I suppose, giving up the idea of waiting for me. "Your gentleman," my widow goes on, "your professor certainly is a man of few words." I say that we should excuse Mr. George because he is preparing lectures for his new appointment.

"Migrant!" the widow says, "never ever excuse a man for anything and do not have milk in the coffee. Powdered milk, as *you* should know *ruins* everything. Plenty of sugar," she says, "but no milk." She orders the steward to bring two Napoleons in warmed balloons. "Men must make their own reasons and excuses," she says. "Never excuse a man," she says again, "a man, like an illness, can separate people, can break a friendship . . ." The widow stops talking as the tears spill stupidly down my face. I tell her that I know I'm silly. I tell her that I keep meeting myself on this ship, that I want to leave, to get off this ship. Would it be possible to get off and go back, say, from the next port? "I must get off," I sob, "I want to go back to my children." I tell my widow about Mr. George having the telephone call without my knowing. My widow does not say anything. She holds her brandy beneath her appreciative nose and, ignoring my crying, advises me to do the same.

"It's like an inhalant," she explains, "think of it as a menthol camphor or a friar's balls."

"Friars' Balsam, your Widowship." I regain some sort of composure and feel ashamed.

"Yes, you're right," my widow says. She tells me to think things out for myself, a journey is a good time for this. She says, that for many years, she seemed to have existed purely to keep accounts, to pay wages and to answer letters, to telephone the vet, the doctor, the manager, the shearing sheds, the kitchen, and to prepare reports for agricultural journals and conferences, *and* to order and prepare endless meals.

"Sometimes in unbearable heat," she says, "going over the books at night looking for the mistakes." She was a sort of machine until one day she took it upon herself to make changes. She tells me how she learned to take short cuts during her most busy times. She only used the china which would go safely through the dishwasher. She put away her silver and her antique dishes. "I used to put my husband's biscuits on a saucer," she says, instead of the gold-edged special plates for cakes and biscuits. "On a saucer," she says, "an old saucer just as if for a cat!" The gold-edged antique china had to be washed by hand so she stopped using it. The gold, which she loved, had been washed off some things, she says before she realized what dishwashers did. She is referring, she says, to her dinner service.

"All my gold edges are plain white now," she says, "but the cupboards are still crammed with good china and of course all my silver is put away in the bank. Change over from rice," she says, "to sheep, and change from silver to stainless steel. Easy!"

I try in the dining room, where we are the only ones left, to imagine what her house and her life are like. I almost confess that I have never seen a dishwasher and that, in any case, I would call it a washing-up machine.

You can be a widow in more than one sense, she tells me, you can be widowed from one style of life to another, from one set of household duties to another.

"I must have been one of the first with a dishwasher. You should have seen it. Huge." She pronounces it Hooghe. "All white enamel, took up the whole kitchen, also had hoses in the sink. Guess!" she says, "who left the hoses out on the floor." The enamel chipped off, "flew all over the place, bits in your hair, in your dinner, in your bed," she says. "And the noise! While the darned thing was on you couldn't hear a thing and it took for simply *ages.*" She went on to say that rice farming needed water and sheep required big paddocks. She widowed herself from one and moved to the other, she explains. If you get married you go where your man goes. "A great part of living, but I preach," she says, "is adjusting advantageously to change."

During the night the ship, as if with her tremendous and hidden heart pounding, after pausing, resumes authority and pursues her mysterious course.

"You had better go," my widow says gently. But I do not want to leave. We are in her cabin. Closed in and safe. My widow has explained that my tears earlier were travel shock, that when the ship is at anchor in the middle of nowhere it is usual, on a first voyage, to feel as I felt.

"I want to stay," I tell her. "Please let me stay in here with you."

When later I go along to Mr. George's cabin I remember the warm sweet bread and milk which was my first meal, mine and Helena's, in the Georges' kitchen. I remember the soft sounds of their voices, the two perplexed people, as they talked to and fro. And then Miss George, warming some milk in a small saucepan, broke some bread into the two little white basins. She poured the milk over the bread and let the basins stand for a few moments. I was nervous that Helena, unaccustomed to the strange mixture, would be rude to the old lady and refuse to eat it. But Helena spooned it up quickly and I did the same.

That night I simply arrived on their doorstep, late, after their locking-up time, exhausted and hungry, having used all my money for the railway journey only to find they were, as they said, *suited.* The advertisement I was answering was in an ancient magazine, apparently. It had not occurred to me to notice the date.

The Georges had found a maid already. They were suited.

There was hot water enough, they told me then. If we would like a bath the water was hot and there was a bed which we could share.

Why should I remember the sweet warm bread and milk now? It is almost ten years since that night. I have been with the Georges ten years.

Mr. George opens to my small knock. "Mentor!" he says, "and susceptible." He holds out his arms.

"Your father don't ever use the Moseley Road now. He don't ever pass the farm now." My mother is adopting more and more Mrs. Pugh's way of speaking. My mother forgets that she has given this information before. She forgets that she writes it in every letter. "He comes by Mount Pleasant and the Lane," she writes. "It's a bit longer this way and he's late home."

As I read, my eyes fill with tears so that her careful handwriting is blurred on the page. The pages of her letter are lined and fixed together at the top where they have come off the cheap pad all together.

My widow, never telling anyone where she is, does not receive letters at any of the ports.

"What's the matter now?" my widow, on the long chair beside me, sits up. "Oh, it's nothing," I tell her, "it's nothing." It's the names of the streets, the familiar names, but how can I tell her anything so silly. The familiar names bring everything back to me with an unexpected rush. I even long for the sound of my mother's voice, some of which springs straight from her letter. The familiar street names, two of them quite unlike the suggestion they carry, Mount Pleasant and the Lane, go alongside empty warehouses and yards and waste ground where the chain shops had been at one time. And the Moseley Road is the road which goes by the hawthorn and the elderberry, by the little meadow and the derelict farm. The sudden memory of the farm buildings, the small kitchen, and the even smaller bedroom and the ever present mud, all round the place, make me feel that if I could just step ashore, just now, I could walk there.

It is likely that my father and mother will avoid that road forever.

"Smocks." I try to tell my widow something, knowing that whenever I cry she will always find out the real reason for my tears. I tell her that both of them, Noël and Felicity, used to wear smocks over their Oxfords.

"Oxfords?" my widow pauses, with her lips pursed for the lipstick she is trying to find in her handbag.

"Yes, dark-gray flannels."

"Flannels?"

Trousers, I explain to her, worn at Oxford, a special cloth, a special woven cloth, dark and of a very good quality. I tell my widow that Felicity and Noël, in spite of having large hands, were very nimble; "their smocking was beautiful especially when done in green silk on unbleached calico." I remind my widow about Noël's illness and how it raced ahead. I remind her that my own illness followed. And I cry a bit more.

While my widow touches up her lips and puts her eyes on I finish my mother's letter. My mother writes that the photographs I sent from Naples have arrived and that she has shown them to Mrs. Pugh.

It looks like a nice young man, very good looking, she's got for herself on that ship, my mother writes what Mrs. Pugh has said. They have been trying, my mother goes on, to guess his age and what he does for a living. She wants to know too what Mr. George thinks.

The photograph is of my widow who was dressed for the Captain's Table fancy-dress ball at the start of the voyage. For this event she is, because of experience, completely prepared and is wearing a sombrero, thigh boots, a flattering jacket, and a shoulder belt packed with cartridges. She tries, at the time, to persuade me to dress up too but I tell her that Mr. George does not like parties.

"If you ask me," the widow says, "that man wants to eat his cake and keep it." She turns away saying, over her shoulder, that she'll be keeping company with the pack of widows on board and I am not to worry.

This is not the first time that I have noticed the way in which words seem to fall lightly, with scarcely any enunciation, from her lips. It is almost as if she is not saying them. This time, because she has actually turned away, I want to run after her saying I'm sorry, sorry.

It is a way of speaking which I have come to dread since it seems that, through my clumsiness, the widow is offended. I would never intentionally offend my widow. Often she seems to adopt this speech which, when I think about it, is essentially without syllables, when Mr. George is present, and it is then, when I hear her almost swallowing or breathing in her words, that I am uneasy. The uneasiness seems to be Mr. George's fault at first, and then it occurs to me that it might be something uncomfortable in the widow herself which causes her to perhaps feel inferior in some way, so that she drops words instead of saying them, often bringing her voice up at the end of sentences as though a question is being asked rather than a fact stated. She could even be doing this on purpose knowing that the slack-mouthed speech can be dismissive, keeping a companion or an acquaintance at a distance. In particular, it does seem as if she alters herself in the presence of Mr. George. The other uneasy thing is that my widow does not like to accept even a small thing like an apple saved from the dining table. A refusal in the lightly spoken phrases can be very painful for me because I seem to have very little, in the material sense, to offer.

We go ashore in Bombay, the widow saying it is the last land we can step on before the long passage across the Indian Ocean to Australia. Some white women with shrill English school-girl voices are offering little tours in their own cars to raise money for a charity. These "guides" come flocking on to the ship.

My widow buys me a lace table cloth from an Indian woman at the side of the road. To one side there are some gaunt dead trees, their branches decorated with vultures perching while others circle slowly, high above the towers where people place their dead relatives and friends. A ritual of funeral which seems unthinkable; the English memsahib explains that it is, at the same time, natural and sensible. "If you think of the climate," she says.

"There's a thought," my widow squeezes my arm. She is pleased, as she puts it, that we are not hampered by my gentleman, and, she says, did I notice how lovely the lacemaker was, such beautiful gentle eyes and how clean and fresh she was in the middle of all the roadside dust. My widow seems to get on with the English memsahib very well. I anticipate, with a sort of pleasure, her moments of mockery which are sure to follow.

"The very next time you feel like howling your head off for nothing," my widow goes on to remind me to remember the Dhobi laundry and what it would be like to have to work there day in and day out. "But I preach," she says. "Scooze I! And," she adds, "*Hello! All those ladies trying to sound like the Queen!*"

In the evenings I sometimes wander about the ship reflecting on and comparing my own life with the lives of the other travelers. There is the fat woman who dies. I am quite unable to imagine her life even with the gossip that she was, once upon a time, the most striking Madam in the red-light district of Poona. She has to be wrapped and sewn up in a hessian bag for a midnight funeral. She slides in a secret launching along the silver path the moon makes on a sea, so silent and smooth the surface seems solid as if beaten from precious metals. The Union Jack which, with her last words it is said, she insisted upon, stays afloat, rippling, long after the unwieldly parcel sinks.

The way in which the shipboard corpse is handled reminds me of the log lift ambulance men use when passage for a stretcher is not possible. The widow and I have some small amusement in seeing the Union Jack salvaged by a hand, invisible from the upper deck, casting hook, line, and sinker with an enviable accuracy.

I think of the Anglo-Indian teacher on his way to a country school in New South Wales. He is looking forward to it with pleasure. He will be provided with a house there. His whole family are with him. They are all, in the language of my widow, tinted folk, and are immediately blamed for bringing smallpox and other infections on to the ship. The little Indian teacher, father of several thin careworn children and creased with anxiety, rushes about the ship. He is frightened for his sick child, overpowered by his mother-in-law, and ignored by his passive and pregnant wife, who repeatedly changes her saris as if nothing concerns her. An ominous sign is that the special games deck for children is closed. He is at once accused by the nervous passengers. I imagine them, the whole family, banished to their cabin, an overcrowded, miserable hell in the middle of this wide sea and beneath the dome of the blue sky, both suggesting a freedom which is unattainable from a ship—except in the gaze of longing.

The story about the trio being flown out to join the ship changes from the Schubert trio in E flat major, piano, violin, and cello to the Saint Saëns septet, opus 65, for trumpet, piano, double bass, and a string quartet, two violins and viola and cello.

"Rumor abounds aboard ship, scooze the clichay," my widow says.

Several Indian Ocean weddings are announced. And the woman in the toque is robbed for the third time. She is heard declaring everywhere that she has now lost everything. But everything. The last of her furs, her jewels, and all the gifts she was taking home, including two enormous dolls from Naples.

"If she ever had them in the first place." My widow has her own opinions on shipboard robberies as well as on the Captain's weddings.

"Just take a look, willya," she says. "Just look at them, Darby and Joan. Imagine! Their choppers both sides of the bed."

I am in the Tavern Bar with my widow. We are perched on the high stools showing off our suntanned legs. I think of the weddings and wish that I could have one of them.

"Have you ever noticed," my widow says, breaking the small silence, "the salty taste on the wineglasses?" She goes on to say that it is a known fact about bars that traces of urine are often detected on wine glasses.

No one notices our legs.

"Why don't you read or spend some time in contemplation of the sea?" Mr. George says, when we meet at the rail. We are high up at the stern watching the furrows of white foam which express the inexorable forward journeying of the ship. Seeing the fresh clean sea sliced in this way makes the speed of the ship seem greater.

How can I, Mr. George wants to know, without irritation in his voice, waste the voyage, the experience of the voyage, by being so much of the time with this extraordinarily vulgar and nondescript person. "How can you, Vera, descend to whole conversations about, for example, the cuts of meat? How can you be manipulated, Vera, by someone whose interests are purely superficial and acquisitive?"

"Don't," I want to tell him, "please don't." How can I tell him that I am lonely, that I want to be with him completely, that I am missing my children and am on the edge of tears the whole time except when my widow makes me laugh or makes me feel special by choosing me. How can I speak to Mr. George about my widow's tender words in the privacy of her cabin. I want to tell Mr. George that I am seeing myself, reflections of my own life, which I do not want to see, in the lives of the other passengers. I want to ask him how will the woman in the toque face her family and her friends without the presents which are so important to them. And what about the little teacher man who is more Indian than Anglo. What waits for him and his uprooted family?

"Do you think," I ask Mr. George, "that the little school house in the country will have drains? And will there be a water tap?"

Mr. George is puzzled by my questions, so I keep to myself the thoughts of the scorn which might be the next thing the Indian teacher might have to face. And I do not mention the successful and popular Madam from Poona and her question-able reception in her deep sea bed.

I tell Mr. George that I am stupid, silly really. I tell him that I am missing him dreadfully. And he says that that is *really silly* because he is there on the ship. He teases me a bit about the widow and says he is not able to compete. He does not see me often, he says.

"Perhaps I am too possessive," he says. We rest against the rail, he has his arm round me, and he explains that he finds that he refuses to accept an unchosen friendship and that I must try and understand that. He has a present for me, he says; he has it in his luggage for me, but will give it to me straight away even though it is meant for later.

The book Mr. George gives me is by a man called Peter Green and is a biography of Kenneth Grahame. I read of *the herb of self heal of which he had always a shred or two in his pocket* and I resolve to emulate Kenneth Grahame. As I read it, it seems to me that Miss George must know this herb, perhaps under another name. And, if I go further back, Gertrude too. Miss George in particular with all that concerns her, me, for example, my children, and her own brother, caring for him all through his life as she has done. All through the years too, she has maintained a serenity in her household so that it becomes for me, during my years of studying, a haven, a place of retreat and sanctuary, where my children are well and happy, their cheeks rosy with the warmth of well being, good fires and food and fresh air. A place where household matters are smooth and efficient. A late realization, perhaps, in the middle of a long journey, in the middle of my life.

I think of my father, at the beginning of this long journey when I visit them, my mother and my father, before setting out. I forget all too easily about the herb of self heal.

The picture of my father seeing me off is still vivid. He is forever running alongside the train and, when he comes to the end of the platform, he has to stop running and there he stands, his face white and anxious and one arm still raised in a farewell of tender optimism, getting smaller and smaller as the southbound train pulls away, rounding the great curve away from the railway station.

It is true to say, I tell my widow later, that in the presence of Miss George and her smooth household there is an atmosphere of discretion and peacefulness. This peace seems to me to depend on the Georges together and the children. For a great part of the time I explain I have been away from that household but always looking towards it.

An Uncompromising Landfall
and the Beehive

❧

I did go back there, I tell my widow; I go back to the farm very early the next morning while it is still dark. I am worried about my bicycle, I tell her, and I want to fetch it. I describe the mist to my widow and tell her that it makes the whole place seem different as though I have come back to the wrong place. The pit mound disappears in a wreath of mist and is transformed in the first light of the dawn as the slag shines with moisture. At first I think it is coal miraculously surfacing and, from the habit of thrift, feel as if I should have a coal search on the mound before doing anything else. Of course I know really that coal can't come to the surface by itself and that there is not much coal to be found in a slag heap. But the paths of light coming up across the sky seem quite magical and it is as if some sort of vision might appear in that desolate place. There is no one there and the place seems strange as if it had been left for a long time. In the half-light things suddenly show up for what they are, a heap of dug potatoes and the broccoli, beaded with tiny water drops, ready to be cut. The kitchen door is open as I left it. The fire is out, but the hearth and the potatoes I put to roast are still warm. I wrap up the potatoes in a bit of newspaper and stuff them in my raincoat pocket. Why waste them, I think then.

I am nervous that Felicity might come, or someone else might come. I go on telling my widow, my mouth stuffed with fried onions, I suddenly have the idea that Felicity might have come back, that she is in the bed upstairs. She might not be nice any longer. There is a sinister side to Felicity and I am afraid. I find two sacks and put potatoes and broccoli in one. And in the other I squash in as much of the hand-woven cloth as I can. I have to tear up a sheet to wrap up the cloth to keep it clean. And, this is the awful part, I have to hack and cut at the cloth to get it off the loom. I feel terrible about Noël's loom. I have to walk with the bike because of the two sacks.

When I reach my mother's house I am sweating terribly and shaking and I realize I must be ill and I feel afraid to go with the doctor's note to the chest X-ray place. I feel certain then that I must have an infection, a patch on my lung. My mother says why am I being so stupid and childish, it's because I haven't had any breakfast. This, from her after all her warnings, and then the breakfast she makes, does make me feel better. So a bit later I go to the farm again, even though my mother says not to. This time I gather as much as I can lay hands on and stuff into the two sacks; books, some of them mine, and kitchen things, cups and cutlery, mostly paid for by me in any case. All the time I am there, I feel that one or both of *them* will return and I have the strange overwhelming belief that it is life and death which is making me do this thing. This kind of robbery.

"It's not in character," my mother says, when she sees me coming up her path. "You're like a gypsy," she says. "Didn't anyone on the road say something and you with that old kettle tied to the handlebar."

We give Mrs. Pugh some of the potatoes. She never touches cauliflower, she says, and especially not the purple-headed sort. From the woven cloth Mrs. Pugh cuts out and tacks in that day three waistcoats, especially tailored for ladies. That evening she tries them on for a fitting with one of her grand customers and sells them with the promise of special silk linings, olive green, gold, and cherry, which she has by her, as she says, for a price which, when she tells us, takes our breath away.

"A course," Mrs. Pugh says, "we'll have a share, the each of us, and there's no need at all to tell any of this to your Dadda. It's a woman's business, this is, which a man don't have any understanding about at all."

"You moll you!" My shipboard widow is delighted with the story. "You Moll Flanders!" she says.

It is almost straight after the waistcoats, I tell my widow, that I go for the chest X-ray and Mrs. Pugh sews the things for me and the card comes for my admission to the TB farm as she calls it. I did not have to wait at all for the bed.

"A course," Mrs. Pugh says, "that's on account of you being one of them. They look after their own kind," she says. "They look after their own kind, they do; if it was me or your mam we'd be waiting till Christmas."

"You'd think," my widow says, on hearing Mrs. Pugh's reported opinion, "that it's well worth it to study all those years to get a hospital bed!"

The widow heaves herself over to brown her back. "To think of you," she says, "sitting here on the deck hiding quietly every morning behind the *British Medical Journal* with all that stored up inside you like that. When I think," she continues, "when I think of you, from what you tell me, you don't seem to be a person capable of understanding even the advertisements in a women's fashion magazine let alone a medical journal." She sighs. "So naïve you seem to be." The widow pronounces it nave. This is something she does on purpose like calling Burgundy B'jundy and Proust the way it is spelled.

"All this that you've been telling me," my widow says, "it's better than the book of the film." This sets her off growling and laughing and then she coughs her way over to the ship's rail and flings her little cigar overboard.

"I'm giving 'em up. No worries!" she says. And then she is suddenly serious, wanting to know what I am.

"What exactly are you?" she says. Am I the sweet English sixth-form girl, she wants to know, or am I a very clever intelligent woman hiding behind a clear youthful complexion and a remarkable and convincing innocence.

When I tell my widow the difference in our ages, Mr. George's and mine, is something like twenty-two years, she is quite calm about it saying that in her book, it's better to be a sugar daddy's plaything than a slave for a princeling and his progeny. We are both amazed at her astute observation and what she calls her superb use of the vernacular, every bit as good as Shakespeare, that we go off at once to the bar to perch once more on the high stools to see if anyone will be captivated, as she says, by our legs. My widow, in particular, has very shapely legs.

"Haven't you ever noticed your own?" she asks me, when I mention hers. It is while we are there in the Tavern Bar, very close now to our destination, that my widow in a low voice warns me about gold diggers who might flatter an aging man and get his fortune away from him and, at the same time, deprive me.

"Aging men are terrible fools," she says. "They can be made fools of so easily." She says that we must watch out for parading pick ups among our fellow passengers. I point out that Mr. George does not have a fortune.

"He has a very handsome face and demeanor," the widow says. "He's very nice looking, distinguished, *and* he's an *intellectual . . .*" She breaks off to say that the ship's shop has a charming display of enamel. A special sort of enameling with patterns outlined in different colors. "It's called *cloissoné*," she says, "it's something we must see and, if we like it enough, must have."

The widow tells me later that she is, as she says, unable to make me out; she tells me that I am quietly dignified at times and, at other times I howl like a baby. I tell her that I suppose she is right.

There are times, she tells me, when we have to be dignified, or try to be, because of circumstances and the circumstances themselves often preclude dignity. As we so often are, we are both amazed at this spontaneous shrewd wisdom, so well expressed. "I like to think," my widow preens herself, "that during our long voyage, I have initiated you, helped you in some way."

I have to tell my widow that my destination, I explain I don't like this word, that the place I am about to reach, frightens me. I tell her that I am not at all dignified and controlled as she suggests, and, holding in my hand the little enameled brooch which she has just given me, I begin to cry.

"Listen!" the widow says, "hold your noise, as your Mrs. Pugh would say. When I said just now that you had a nice complexion and intelligence I failed to say that your hair is awful, it's terrible, it's pathetic, everything that can be wrong with hair is on your head. Listen!" she says, "why don't the two of us duck in now and get us a hair do."

Later, when we are standing in a long line, with all the passengers, on the deck, waiting for the routine fingernail and forearm examination by medical officers from Customs before disembarking, my widow, jerking her head towards the wharf and the sheds, tells me that the first people to arrive at this place took one look at the nondescript uninviting landscape and starting swearing. "And," she says, "they went on swearing and we've been swearing ever since."

My widow, I notice, is starting to inhale and swallow her words. "They went on swearing and we've been swearing ever since," she repeats what she has just said in that particular way she has, of not enunciating the consonant with the vowel, as she does when she is not quite at ease. She usually goes from this way of speaking to what I call her fruitcake voice. I wait for it trying to think if I have upset her in some way.

"It's called a Beehive," I tell Mr. George, as we stand together, at the ship's rail after the medical examination and he is able to leave the queue and come across to where I am waiting. I pat my puffed-up pile of hair.

"They call it a Beehive," I tell him. "That's what my hair is called. Beehive."

"I expect the style suits your friend," Mr. George says. His left hand trembles as he places it alongside my right hand on the rail. We look across together at the uncompromising landfall.

Ship and Wheelchair

❦

It is at times like this, when in some sort of suspended state, perhaps on board ship, or walking steadily behind the smooth purring of a wheelchair, there is the half-remembered idea of having my father's two hands next to mine on the throbbing rail of the ship. There is the possibility too that, as the rail of the ship rises slowly above the horizon and just as slowly sinks below the horizon, he may be the next person to walk towards me on the deck giving the impression that he has walked on the waters of all the oceans in order, as has always been his custom with buses and trains, to see me off or to meet me on arrival.

It is during moments of glancing memory like this, that it seems easily possible to step a little to one side and be able to walk from the end of the road, where we lived and on to the worn narrow field path which made a short cut to the main road and the row of little shops there, grocer, greengrocer, post office, and chemist. The field path seems now to have made a link between childhood and the responsibility which comes afterwards. I began, in this responsibility, to carry home fourteen pounds of potatoes, seven pounds in each of two bags.

Then there were the conspirational closings of the bedroom door during discussions between my mother and my father's sister, my aunt, about the Christmas dolls, the picture books, the new dresses, and the prospect of being taken out to tea in a tea shop where there was a lady violinist, whose name my mother knew, and a gentleman who accompanied the lady and her violin on the piano.

And then there was the time when this sister came and cried and cried for a whole afternoon and my mother with her limited English then, tried to comfort her. I wished so much that day that my father would come home early and *dismount* from his bicycle and whistle for us to come out to meet him at the gate. But he was, that day, taking his boys from school down the coal mine. He was always taking his boys round a factory, down the mine, or to the Municipal swimming baths.

"Does he have doubts about paternity, your gentleman?" the rice-farm widow, my new friend on the ship, asks me more than once. "Does he admit paternity?"

"It's something we don't talk about," I begin to tell her. And then Mr. George comes. The next person to come towards me on the deck is not my father stepping lightly across the washed boards after walking on the waves to see us off through Suez.

"Rumor has it," the widow says, "that this will be the last ship to go through Suez. Imagine," she says, "all the apples in subsequent ships going rotten. Imagine, this journey through Panama and round the Cape!"

Before following the two of them, my widow and Mr. George, down the brass-bound stairs to the dining room, I pause to allow myself to catch once more a tiny glimpse in my mind of the place where the field path comes out on the main road. At this place there is a house where a hairdresser lives. She cuts people's hair in her own front room, and while you are sitting there, in a sheet, with your hair pinned up in a topknot, you can see the people emerging from the field path and waiting to cross the main road. The bus stop is at this place too, immediately outside the hairdresser's house.

My aunt, when she comes on the bus to visit, cloched in beige velour with a grosgrain trim and her nervous fox fur, its little legs dangling, slipping to one side on her narrow shoulders, climbs down from the bus and comes towards me telling me, straight away, that I am growing too fast, that my dress is too short and too tight, and asking me how did I come to crack, already, one of the lenses in my spectacles.

All this belongs to another time and is pushed back there when I reach my widow at the table, and she reminds me again, while Mr. George is reading the menu, that the world is a place of couples.

"The whole world," she says, "is for couples."

The Plagal Cadence

❧

Your father must have been coming home by the Moseley Road. Your father has been run over and killed by a lorry in the Moseley Road. They say he died at once, but a policeman said he died in the ambulance. Your father, my mother writes, must have been coming home by the Moseley Road. She writes that she had to go to identify him. He is lying, she writes, on a bed, a sort of stretcher when they take me in to see him. He is all covered up except for a small part of his face. He does not look as I know him to look. I have never seen an injured or dead person before. They tell me he has a lot of injuries all over his body. The place on the Moseley Road is spread over with sand but his blood shows through. Mrs. Pugh is asking why your father was coming by the Moseley Road since he don't ever use that road. I am telling Mrs. Pugh I don't know why he was coming home by the Moseley Road instead of Mount Pleasant and the Lane. I know Mount Pleasant and the Lane is longer, but he would not have been in a hurry. There is no hurry for either of us and Mrs. Pugh says there is no hurry for her either. We shan't ever know, Mrs. Pugh says, why he was coming home on the Moseley Road.

Mr. George is listening for the plagal cadence in the Gregorian chants when I arrive at his apartment. He has this nice university flat near the campus; I live at the hospital.

He pulls off the headphones and takes me in his arms and I feel his heart beating in his warm chest. I cry about my father's death. The letter has taken about a week to reach me, I tell Mr. George, so I have to understand that all this time my father has been dead and he says that is so and that my father will be buried already. The voices, without ebullient pride, sustain their harmony in the headphones lying on the table. I imagine the singers in clothes made of rough cloth, standing, their feet cold on a stone floor and, for a moment, the apparent detachment from our lives and way of living seems desirable and comforting.

Die mit Tränen säen, werden mit Freuden ernten. "They that sow in tears shall reap in joy," my mother translates for me. Her letter is, as usual, a mixture. Herself over-laid by Mrs. Pugh. She writes that though she knows my father will not be coming home, she watches the clock expecting him, "any minute now."

My father's life-long belief, that the life we have is simply a forerunner for something else (he called it "everlasting life"), rescues me. I imagine him gathered up safely off the Moseley Road, safe and comfortable for ever and peaceful. I think I can even know the place by the elderberry bushes where the road curves. I can see the road clearly in my mind and this place is where he will have been lifted up. When I tell Mr. George this he says the Moseley Road might be quite different, quite changed now.

We have to go out for groceries. We have three nights together, a whole long weekend, after what seems to have been an endless separation, a fortnight during which we have both been under the strain of our new work. As Mr. George says, our time together is very precious.

My beehive is a mess. I try brushing. My head itches dreadfully. Brushing makes it worse. I simply do not know what to do with my awful hair.

These apartments, I tell Mr. George, are so noisy, you could have records and not bother with headphones. The headphones cut out the noise from other people he explains. And then he tells me, all in a rush, that he has been looking forward to this weekend tremendously and that he does not want us to live apart. I understand that I have been, selfishly, as usual, simply thinking about my own difficulties in a new appointment. I almost always think about my own sense of being alone and I forget about his.

Mr. George says that he thinks we should look for an apartment where we can live together. He says too that he will need to accept and give invitations and that he wants me to be a part of this new life. I say that I think I shall be good at this and that I can quickly become a hostess and inherit a dinner service from a department store. I am making the mistake, I tell him, of trying to see the whole of our lives in one long weekend, trying to cram in a whole future at once so that I can't breathe. He says we must live a little bit at a time.

In the greengrocer's, overcome by the fragrance of the peaches, the plums, and the nectarines, I buy a heap of fruit and another of vegetables. Mr. George is studying the grocery part of the shop. He is out of place in front of these crammed shelves. He is not his usual neat self, his pullover is wrinkled, and he has deep creases in his face which is red from too much sun. His shoulders sag and, twice, on the way back to the apartment, he pauses to have a rest.

"Perhaps I should learn to wear less," he apologizes, "it's the heat. I am the only person wearing a woolen pullover."

Catching sight of myself reflected in a shop window, I tell him that I'm not much of a dish myself, in fact I'm more bedraggled than he is, and that when we have taken the shopping home he is to have a rest while I go out to find a hairdresser.

My summer frock, my English summer frock from several previous summers, is rumpled, washed out, and ugly. My sandals are shabby too. I look a mess, I tell Mr. George; in the bright sunlight everything we have looks old and worn out. In the face of Mr. George's fatigue and my mother's letter it seems selfish to be considering things like hair and clothes. My widow is miles away. I wish for her, for her energy and her advice, and, in particular, her way of regarding things, and the way she could laugh.

I never talk about my widow to Mr. George. I had to understand, on the ship, that he did not like her. It was strange to have to learn this when I have known him for a long time and when I have always presumed that I, being loved by him, know all there is to know about him.

Mr. George has a shower and I leave him to rest while I go out again. It is a surprise when Mr. George, as I am leaving, says that he thinks I will be missing my new friend and that shopping will not be as pleasurable without her.

"Precisely this gift you have," he says, "of being able to have friends, which are not perhaps of the supreme or ultimate choice, is a gift which you must always use because it is a help to you and, in turn, can be of use to other people too." He adds that he does not have this gift. He even regrets this.

It is like having a Blessing from Mr. George and I feel cheerful when I go out in to the afternoon which is still full of sunlight and blue sky. There is something about the clear brightness which makes me feel shy and conspicuous. The shops have a flimsy temporary appearance and I have no idea which one to avoid and which one to enter. Twice I nearly walk into a veranda post. There is no one alongside to give my arm a pinch and to say, "You must have this," and "For heaven's sake don't, *do not* buy that color."

Ahead of me on the pavement is a young woman with two children, clinging one on either side of her. I remember seeing them as passengers on the ship. I pretend not to see them, they reflect my own shyness and lack of confidence. I recognize, unwillingly, myself in them. They walk, all three, close together, uncertain and tired, looking without seeing at the unfamiliar shops.

I feel suddenly afraid that I shall not find either a hairdresser or a dress shop.

When I think of the ship's shop and the daily overwhelming display crowding the smallness, I am amazed to realize how someone must have ordered and packed the incredible quantity of merchandise especially chosen to satisfy the needs of passengers in their boredom. I wish that I had allowed the widow to buy me a dress when she wanted to. I could have chosen anything then. She wanted to give me one more present, she said then, and I refused it. The cut of a dress or a jacket, she told me, matters so much. She said that in choosing a dress it was necessary to know the kind of seams and the exact positioning of the seams. "Seams in the right places and little slashings offering glimpses of the body, not usually seen; like the underneath part of the breast can be very sexy," she said then. And she described the fold and the fall of the material against the hips and the thighs and, especially, good fitting was essential on the shoulders.

"Honestly," my widow said, "your wardrobe's a mess. You don't seem to care one bit about fashion. You have a way of looking, not poor exactly, but as if you are unconcerned about money. You look as if someone throwing out their old clothes has let them fall on you. And then, at the same time, you are elegant. You do have a natural elegance but you simply don't know how to make the most of it."

My widow is right. I have not the slightest idea how to make the most of myself, especially with clothes. I think of her presents, the shorts, the little black handbag scattered with sequins, the scarves, which she promised would be tender, and the *cloisonné* brooch and suddenly it is as if she is telling me to go straight in to the next dress shop with the idea of choosing something with a low neck and without sleeves, either in white or with the clean colors of the *cloisonné*, and to forget how terribly English and shabby I am.

I can't think why your father did not die in his sleep, my mother writes. *It would have been so much better for him.* I carry her letter squashed in my pocket. I always felt my father would live for ever. That is the impression he gave. I suppose he had this feeling about himself and has passed on the idea, because I too think that I shall go on living—and not as an old helpless woman, but with the same strength and energy I have now.

For years it seems I have talked to and listened to my father in my head. I have always thought of him as being there at home whenever I should go back there. I remember that when he saw me off on the train, when I was leaving for the ship, he reminded me that he was getting older. He said that on no account was I to rush back to Britain in the event of either my mother or him being ill. He seemed then to have far more sense of the enormous distance which I only found out about as, slowly, that distance was covered. He said too that people who made this particular journey, at a certain time in their lives, often did not return but stayed in the new place. He gave, for an example, Mrs. Pugh's two brothers. It is only now that I seem able to take this in.

It seems, in my life, that my father has shown me everything, especially things like being able to feel the quality of the air, and to see what he described as lovely scenery or a fine view.

I understand now, I tell Mr. George, that I never thanked my father for the gifts of looking and feeling.

"I think," Mr. George says, "that he would not have expected you to."

Mr. George runs his hands over my clean short hair. He says he likes it cut this way, that it suits me. He says he likes my new dress. It is the first white dress I have ever had.

"Broderie anglaise," I tell him, "that is what these small embroidered holes are called."

Mr. George says that the dress, in a charming way, resembles a petticoat. And in the evening he helps me to take it off.

Your father didn't know he was going to die today." I re-read my mother's letter. "*Not knowing,*" she writes, "*he left a piece from his breakfast against coming home hungry.*"

For years, I can think now and remember, for years I have seen my father carefully put aside something from one meal to save it for the next.

If I have for all this time talked to my father in my head, asking his advice and telling him things, there is no reason why I should not go on asking him and telling him. After all, it has always seemed to me that when I pray *Our Father* it is *My Father* I see.

During the previous week Mr. George has, as a surprise for me, bought a record player. He has borrowed from the music department in the university the records of *Fidelio*. Mr. George has this quality, which I lack, of knowing something and not telling it until the most suitable time.

I do not mention the dinner service, but during the music I think about it. I think about saucepans and cutlery and a set of wine glasses. I am excited and I want to talk about these things to Mr. George and to ask him about the people, *the couples*, the people described by my widow. Because of not talking about this I am not able to stop talking about Florestan's cry from the dungeon and the part, in the story, where the prisoners, having been given the freedom of the daylight and sweetness of fresh air, emerge.

"I know," I tell Mr. George, "that people say that Beethoven wrote for human voices as if they were musical instruments and that, because of this, the opera is ungraceful, but I don't agree, not at all!"

I manage, in the magic of the music and the little enclosed world of our weekend together, to make a mint sauce. My haircut makes me feel neat and quick. I wash the mint and chop it finely and put it with some sugar and vinegar in a cup all in the time it takes for the *Fidelio* overture on a seventy-eight.

Another nice thing about our weekend is that Mr. George suggests that we go for a walk in the evening after dinner. He says that in this way we can put off going to bed and have a longer time to look forward to the night.

"Let me help you out of your Edwardian underwear," Mr. George says, when we return. It is our second night together out of the three, and once again, he helps me to take off the new dress.

Wheelchair . . . Roads

Once more I explain to Mr. George that Miss Eleanor has not gone out and that she is not expected home any minute. I explain that she simply is not here any more.

"Shall we think of something else?" I say. "Can you try to remember something else?" I ask him.

I am wishing for Miss Eleanor too. After all this time I wish for her. I wish for the sight of her approaching, tall, angular, energetic, her complexion clear and her light blue eyes always intelligent and always kind. I think of her hair brushed and scraped back and fastened in a bun on the back of her neck, the only style she allowed herself. It suited her.

At eighty-one she wondered why she was so healthy and again at ninety-one and even at ninety-seven . . .

I am wishing for the sound of Miss Eleanor's voice as Mr. George wishes for it.

One of the happiest moments in my life which I have never forgotten is because of Miss Eleanor. It was when she offered me thirty shillings a week and keep for Helena and me. This included two hot baths a week for both Helena and me and days off in a row so that I could make the journey to the Midlands to visit my mother.

Wheelchair in Hammond Road. Wheelchair rumbling over rough blue-chip surface. The moon rising quickly is a half moon, perhaps a little less.

"Can you try to remember something or someone else?" I try again, my heels clattering as I rush the wheelchair rough rough on the blue-chip metal.

"Are those your heels, Vera?" Mr. George wants to know. "Vera, are those your heels?"

"Yes," I tell him. "Yes."

"Horsey Horsey don't you stop," Mr. George seems to be singing, "just let your feet go clippety clop." Was that song, he wants to know, before the war or during the war or after the war? I tell him I have no idea. I had forgotten the song, a silly song, and it is something strange about memory, Mr. George's memory, that a song like this one should come into his head just now.

The storm clouds have parted enough to allow the red and purple sunset to deepen the color of the winter trees. The flame trees in particular are vivid, the red flowers bunched in between the yellow berries of the crowding cape lilacs. The blue chip is speckled with bruised and bird-pecked berries and the cape lilac branches are starved on the winter sky. The dusk comes quickly. There is not much light from a moon on the wane.

Mr. George tells me, when I ask him, that he has no idea at all what he had for lunch and this worries him until I remind him that it is Friday and we had fish and chips.

"Yes, it was a nice piece of fish." Conventional good manners come to his rescue. He remembers in his well-bred way, knowing that he should remember.

At the corner of Hammond and Goldsworthy we wait in the pale-moon silence to cross the quiet road. We notice, as always, that the noisy birds, the parrots, the magpies, and the doves, are quiet at last. Mr. George tries to remember a line from the poem "Margaret."

"Wordsworth," he says, "*to my heart convey* . . . What comes next, Vera, what comes next?" And I tell him; "*so still an image of tranquility.*" And he says that is the line he wants.

We cross Goldsworthy and go on down Bernard. I remember the poem is one of the poems marked by Mr. George, in pencil, with Miss Eleanor's name. The book was always beside his bed. Once, when we are tidying up, Miss Eleanor and I, Miss Eleanor says to leave the book on the chair where it is. "He likes to linger in its glance," she says then.

Yesterday, Rachel writes, *I attended a natural childbirth. It was in the woman's own house, a home birth, as she requested. I ended up sitting with the husband on the floor, each of us in a fisherman's oil skin. A beautiful baby, a boy nine and a half pounds . . .*

While I am thinking of the letter and wondering whether to explain to Mr. George about Rachel being submerged in the waters of childbed, Mr. George begins to tell me that, this morning, he means to go over to the British Museum but is a little late getting out of the house . . . Meanwhile, overhead, there is some stirring among the settled birds as if a fresh argument is being raised, even if half heartedly, over some roosting difficulties.

Shall I explain to Mr. George that it is now the evening and not the morning and that he is not going to any museum? Shall I, instead, talk to him about Rachel? This Rachel. This pink tiny nymph of a daughter, this Rachel delivering an enormous child for an unknown woman. A woman unknown to us. This Rachel, the tiny neat little girl reared in pink and white embroidery and learning to speak with Miss Eleanor's clipped and precise accents. This little girl who, it seemed, grew behind my back, to become tall like Mr. George and Miss George.

For some reason just now I remember showing Mr. George a photograph of Rachel sitting disheveled and sweet in her pram. I tell him I like the photograph very much. He likes the photograph too and holds it with reverence smiling at it. As I watch him looking at the photograph I see that I have to realize that his eyes and his smile are not directed at the child but rather on his own sweet briar hedge, which is a full flowering background surrounding the pram. He is completely absorbed in his own impenetrable hedge . . .

When I actually see the direction of his gaze and knowing, as I do know, that Rachel is Mr. George's daughter, *as only I can really know,* the sudden understanding is like the flash of awareness which accompanies learning something new from a textbook or even a literary work or a fiction. A rite of passage, a celebration of learning as if, in this moment, I have studied a long book. It is a sudden vision of the kind after which a person can never be quite the same again.

One morning I open the door into the fragrant steam of the bathroom and there is this child rising tall from her bath to reach for the towel. There she is, all at once it seems, grown up, tall, long-limbed, and graceful, rounded and smooth and a delicate shell pink, her skin glowing with youth and the hot bath, and she is quite unaware of her own fresh loveliness. She seems then untouched and untroubled. When I think about this now I understand that I was never like this, or if I was once, perhaps briefly, on the edge of this innocence and smooth youthfulness, the time came and went by without my noticing any of it, without my noticing my own body and how I might look as a young woman. I have no idea . . .

"I have no idea," I say to the back of Mr. George's neck. "I have no idea," I say, "what I was like, years ago. I mean, a long time ago." The wheelchair runs smooth now on Bernard Street. Really guided only by my fingertips. I hardly need to make any effort.

Mr. George wants to know what it was I said, so I tell him once more about not having any idea of what I looked like when I was young. Mr. George's rug is slipping, so I stop and tuck it round his high-pointed knees. He seems to ponder my remark.

"Look!" Mr. George says. "There are the fresh new leaves coming on the plane trees." And when I look up and along the deserted street I can just see, in the half light, the green leaves bursting out along the branches. The whole street is miraculously arched with a delicate green leafiness. The whole length of the street. It is just like Mr. George to be the one, the one out of the two of us, to notice first that the plane trees are coming into leaf.

As I walk, smooth smooth, with the wheelchair I think I will try to stop living in the way I am living. I am forever trying to get through what I am doing, to get one thing after another finished and *out of the way* only to find, of course, that there is nothing in particular waiting for me.

I must try to remember to think about Mr. George seeing the leaves.

Sometimes I would, at her invitation, look through some of Miss George's treasures. A photograph of Mr. George as a boy dressed in a heavy tweed suit and with a certain puffiness about the eyes. Miss George particularly is proud of the expensive good quality tweed. I search the childish face for the man. I read eagerly, then, to find very little about Mr. George on his old school reports carefully kept by Miss George without, I suspect, his knowing. Hardly anything is on the reports, his height and his chest measurements from one term to the next and English Literature seeming to be the only subject reported on. When I remarked on this to Miss George she would give her little laugh and say that her brother never cared for any mathematics or science.

A newspaper photograph survives of a queue of people in London in the early 1930s. Mr. George is pictured quite clearly as a young man, a member of the Fabian Society, Miss George explains. They were protesting against something called the means test, she says. It was during the Great Depression, she adds, feeling sure it was because of the means test and to do with education cuts.

I would like to talk to Mr. George as I used to. I always asked him everything and I told him all that was on my mind.

I want, just now, to ask him if he remembers being pleased with the Pullman when he used to travel to visit me. The luxurious Pullman with the rich paintwork and polished paneling and the white embroidered antimacassars and the firm upholstery and the pictures of castles and their battlements from all over the British Isles.

Did he look forward to visiting me, I want to ask him. But I do not ask him because he might not remember. In the same way I do not ask him if he remembers the sudden fresh green leaves of the plane trees in London and how he once wrote to tell me he was pleased to have found some accommodation within walking distance of the British Museum.

"What do you remember?" I ask him one more time as we turn into the next street. "What do you remember, Mr. George?"

"The fear of conception, Vera, the fear of conception," Mr. George replies.

Waiting Room (The First)

These days I live with the need to have something lined up to do next. The way in which I live reminds me of a joke; there are two goldfish swimming round and round in a goldfish bowl and one fish is telling the other fish that there's no time to chat as it's one of those "get things done" days.

I make little lists because I might forget what I am doing, or more importantly, what I am going to do. Like going to the doctor's to see if my moles are cancer, like throwing away left-over food, old clothes, letters, and other papers, especially receipts and bank statements saved over a great many years in case of a possible taxation audit (random).

It's when I am sitting in waiting rooms that I take stock of the way things are, of the way I'm living and of the way I used to live. I compare my life with other people's lives in a rather superficial way. Not comparisons about money but rather on the quality of roof beams, joists, floor boards, and the sizes and shapes of windows.

I go back in my thoughts quite often. One time I actually try to remember all the names of the hospitals in the city where I lived for years in the English Midlands. There was, at that time, the Hospital for the Diseases of Women, the Sick Children's, the Ear, Nose, and Throat, the Skin Hospital, the Fever, the Cancer, the General, the Accident (Queens), and the Queen Elizabeth. The QE was Maternity as well. I manage to stop the litany before going on to the names of streets, churches, schools, and shops, though the names of houses come to mind—Sans Souci, Barclay, The Hollies, Padua, St. Cloud, and Prenton. Naturally the hedges follow, the closely watched hedges, the laurel and the privet, the rhododendrons and the holly, evergreens in a series of repetitive quartets.

Those hedges from another country have given way to the honeysuckle, the hibiscus, the oleander, the plumbago, the white and pink climbing roses, the wisteria, and the geraniums. There are too the street lawns, the box trees, the plane trees, the peppermints, and the cape lilacs. But perhaps it is the blue metal, the smooth and the rough, which I notice the most when we are walking. The habit of closely watching the hedges is not lost, if anything it is more intense, and intensely too, the roads. The roads are closely watched; Harold Hammond Goldsworthy Bernard the park Thompson Koeppe Princess Caxton Warwick and Queen and back Queen Warwick Caxton . . .

I need a shrink, I say to myself, and go on to say that shrink is not a word I use. The use of it, even if not said aloud, is an indication that I need someone with specialist training.

Really this place! All I seem able to do here is to stare at the other people. We all seem stupid sitting here with a conventional obedience which is expected of us.

The chairs here are all joined together, fixed, making a square space in the middle where children can play. There are some little chairs and a low table for the children. I forget about myself for a bit, when I see a small child staggering about with a big plastic bucket. He has thick dark curls and a pale face and I pity him throwing up so much that he has to take a bucket around.

What's the matter with me, I think then, because "throwing up" is a phrase I never use; neither do I say "around" instead of round. I dismiss all this immediately when I see that the child is loading up the bucket with all the toys, the building blocks and farm animals, provided for *all* the children to play with, and is hauling them off to the safe harbor between his squatting mother's possessive spread-out legs.

A man sitting diagonally opposite gives his urine specimen to his wife to hold and she takes it and goes on reading her magazine holding the thing as if she was a specimen-glass holder, as if it is meant that she should just sit there, holding this specimen glass while he sits back stroking his chin and raising his eyebrows in every direction in turn round the waiting room; *see here everybody, meet the wife, my specimen-glass holder.*

The receptionist behind the curved desk has a commanding view of the whole room. When I look at her it is clear to me that she would prefer a dress shop in a not too classy department store. A place in which she could "peek round the fitting-room curtains saying with emphasis, "it's *you* dear" either for a dress, a blouse, or a hat. It is probable that the pay is better in the Outpatients' Clinic and the hours less barbaric, especially since the decision not to have the clinic open at all on Fridays. I notice every time, without really meaning to, that she wears mostly red dresses or blouses with low V-neck lines exposing the healthy unworried skin of a woman approaching middle age and a suggestion of a similarly healthy and unworried bosom, more or less out of sight.

Certain days are set aside for walking sticks, crutches, and wheelchairs. On these days I remind myself often to count my blessings and to remember that there are people worse off etc. For one thing I am only accompanying a patient and am not a patient myself. Without meaning to, against my will, I notice that some of the patients have a perpetually grieved look and some seem actually to be parading their disability. They exaggerate a grieved way of walking with one shoulder higher than the other, the body turned inwards on itself and the head tilted to one side. They seem to have the special skill of taking up the whole width of any place and then there's no way of getting round them like when you're waiting to go down in the small elevator to the Lab for blood tests. Sometimes people, like these people and unfortunate, will take up all the room in the aisles in the supermarket. Walking on two sticks, lurching first to one side and then the other, they make it impossible for anyone else to pass or even reach round for a tin of dog food, a cereal, or some soap powder.

I suppose all this sounds cruel and without sympathy. It is not meant to. I might be on two sticks myself one day. Such thoughts, like everything else at present, are very out of character. Like this morning when there are no oranges to squeeze I am shaken to discover how much the disappearance of a small ritual can disturb me and cause an inability to go on to the next thing—just because one insignificant part of the morning routine is missing.

When I ask Mr. George what he had for lunch he does not remember and when I ask was it nice, what we had for lunch, he says that it was very nice and, because it was nice, it is a pity that he does not remember what it was.

It is a pity, he says, to forget something nice.

An occupational therapist, with knitting needles pushed into her hair which is dressed in a firm gray bun, approaches. She has cut, she tells me, some pieces, squares and circles, of foam cushion material. She gives them to me saying that she knows relatives and friends enjoy being involved. She says that making little chintzy covers for these is a nice way of spending the long afternoons. She calls her pieces soft splints for pressure areas. She smiles with real pleasure.

I want to tell her that I don't have long afternoons except in my consulting rooms and I am not able to sew there. I nearly explain that I can't sew, it's a bit like not being able to dance, I mean ballroom dancing, it is always an embarrassment to say, "I can't dance." It is the same with sewing.

I can imagine all too easily the sense of futility which would all too quickly obliterate the hopefulness accompanying the giving of these chintz covers to some of my afternoon appointments who do, indeed, need occupation and direction but who have, at the same time, the ability in the face of offered activity to make the activity seem useless and unnecessary. This attribute is of course a symptom of the cause which might not be cured by the covering of soft splints with fragments of a cheerful material.

I take the pieces all the same and squash them into my brief case.

The Second Waiting Room

※

Then there is the wheelchair. I have to attend to the wheelchair.

In Wheelchair City all the years of clinics, of examination rooms, of X-ray departments, of physiotherapy cubicles, and the desks in reception halls pile up as if I am going from one to another and to the next and the next. The wheelchair-engineering-department waiting room is, in reality, nothing more than the corridor lined with various orthopedic appliances and devices and, of course, wheelchairs to suit every need.

I ask the secretary, when she telephones with the appointment, if I could come and fetch the new foam cushion myself. No, she says, the patient and the wheelchair have not been seen for over six months. Both must be brought in for the appointment.

It is during the time of waiting that I imagine my widow standing alone in a well-watered plot, a green place in the middle of the wheat paddocks. Her house sprawls behind her, a cool well-painted place, held by seams of green like an extravagant embroidery on a background of varying light and shade as the clouds move across. I remember my widow telling me she took short cuts. She made sandwiches, I suppose, instead of cooking dinner. I remember her ordering for me at table on the ship. She had ideas. One time the two of us have a fruit platter, all different kinds of fruit cut up and arranged in a design. Fresh pineapple rings, mango, paw paw, banana, peeled and sliced peaches, strawberries, and a scattering of frozen raspberries and blueberries lightly sugared. With this we have a white, crisp bread roll, some fresh butter, and a glass of white wine each, very cold.

I can make a fruit platter instead of the dinner. For some time I have been buying too much food. I have been preparing too much food unwittingly and throwing it away. A roasted leg of lamb, a whole chicken, a large handful of Vienna sausages, two lots of topside mince—actually made into dishes with macaroni (one) and rice (the other)—and countless carrots, onions, potatoes, green and red peppers, mushrooms, and zucchini. You name it—I've thrown it away.

Courgette, it occurs to me just now, is a pretty name for a certain type of housemaid or a little dog or for a prostitute with an unblemished record. It is because of thinking of my widow that I have these ideas about courgette being a pretty name.

"Have you ever noticed," my widow asks me one day on the ship when we are in our usual haunt by the swimming pool, "that women when they are naked are unable to resist looking at each other's legs."

I tell her that we are not naked.

"As good as," she says. And she tells me to come to her cabin. On the way she jerks her head towards the Lounge Bar where there is a little knot of passengers.

"The war's been over, how long?" my widow says. "The war's been over twenty years," she says, "and that woman's still telling how she was bombed out, how she lost everything in the bombing in London, in Hackney, South-East."

I tell my widow that I have noticed her and that every day she finds a different listener for her unforgettable dreadful experience.

"You should never ever," the widow replies, "stick on one thing like that. All she's doing is feeding the bad time and making it last for ever."

Remembering this now I think it is the kind of thing Gertrude would have said. I remember too how easily we, by the end of the war, accepted heaps of rubble. All this mess which accompanied our living, broken bricks and glass and slates everywhere and often, at the end of a shabby mean street, a bomb crater or a boarded-up shop. The people, when the war was over, linked arms in great long lines in the streets and danced "The Lambeth Walk" and "Knees Up Mother Brown" and "Run Rabbit Run." The women with curlers in their hair and the men in shirt sleeves did not seem to notice that some houses had whole fronts and sides missing. Some were tarpaulined and boarded up but others showed pink and blue wallpaper, torn and discolored. These houses looked like dolls' houses, opened, but without the magic. It is easy now, in the wheelchair waiting room, to recall all this, especially my loneliness then which seemed to be reflected by a small thin black cat, ugly because it was poor and alone, trying to vomit at the edge of the ruined buildings alongside the dancing people. I was alone and pregnant and sick. I remember now that, when I tell my widow about this dancing after the war, she reminds me that at the *outbreak* some people, *bloodthirsty*, danced in the streets. She reminds me that she was in London herself then and, in an attempt to go home to Australia, was held up in Cairo. When she tells me about Cairo she explains all over again how body hair was regarded as something undesirable and a special body-hair-remover woman, in a sort of yashmak, turned up once a week to attend to all the ladies in the house.

"Can you imagine!" I almost hear my widow's growling laugh which invariably becomes a cough. "She used some sort of honey paste. Honey and almond. Marzipan!"

"Couldn't we be married now on the ship?" I ask Mr. George one evening when we are leaning on the rail on the top deck. "Like those other people," I say. "The Captain is marrying couples." I tell him, "There are weddings almost every day . . ."

I can see at once the whole idea is distasteful to Mr. George, the idea of being conspicuous in this way and being a part, as he says then, of something cheap, a vulgar superficial celebration instead of something private and tender. Shipboard life, he says then, is not natural. It is an enclosed world in which everything is somewhat heightened and exaggerated. A ship is not a place for the making of decisions except, of course, those made in the course of duty, by the Captain.

As I watch Mr. George being lifted up now by two competent men in biscuit-colored work coats I understand something about myself and that is that housekeeping and shopping have become something of an act of the will.

The biscuit-colored men make some alteration to the new cushion. They lift Mr. George a second time and the therapist replaces the old cushion with the new one.

It is exactly how Mr. George is that he is the one to notice two magnolia flowers, the color and the texture, he thinks, of fresh cream, high up in the rough-leaved tree. I tell him I am not able, any longer, to climb into the branches of a tree. Does he remember, I ask him, that I did, once upon a time, climb up for a flower which, from below, looked perfect.

He says he is sorry he does not remember and will I remind him.

That's it, I tell him, I simply climbed up for a flower. I do not tell him that I discovered then that the great flower, which was pure and white from below, was sunburned brown and withered and beginning to go rotten.

The Third Waiting Room

Now I am acquainted with another kind of waiting room. This is a silent place and I am the only person waiting.

There are two young receptionists behind a high gray and silver counter. They are both young and pretty. They have well-developed telephone voices. They, on appearance, seem disdainful and apparently without thoughts but having the power, unspoken, not even known about, to cause a client disturbance and a careworn feeling beforehand about what to wear for the appointment. As I said, they do not know they have this power. It is not their fault.

The walls are gray, decorated with a pink pattern. The carpet is thick and gray. The elevator glides without noise behind automatic doors, which are the same gray as the walls making it difficult to see which is the way out. Some paintings in gouache and gold leaf hang in strategic places. The imitation marble tubs sprout growths of realistic fleshy leaves. On the whole it is a restful place. Secretly I touch the leaves, knowing them to be artificial.

I understand perfectly why I am waiting here. Ordinarily I would never sit in a place like this. And, ordinarily, I would never be in the position of seeing the fine beads of perspiration on a stranger's upper lip as he studies the papers on the table in front of him when we are alone together in his office. He is particularly careful not to make mistakes.

In this reception hall there are no surgical appliances, no lists on the walls about the importance of vegetables, about menopause support groups, the need for bicycle helmets, and the dangers of smoking. There is nothing about this place to give any evidence of the particular problems and the kind of consultations dealt with in this building except the revealing little outbreaks of moisture on the forehead and the upper lip which accompany concentration during consultation.

I am too early for my appointment having misjudged the distance, the traffic flow, and the number of intersections with traffic lights moving, one lot after the other, through four changes.

I am sorry to have to be the one to tell you . . .

I take out Mrs. Pugh's letter to read it again.

> *I am sorry to have to be the one to tell you, as how your Mam passed away very peaceful early this a.m. Your mam she came to the gate to tell me she felt cold. I feel cold your Mam tells me and I tell her now you go straight back to your bed and I'll fetch you over a nice cup of tea, nice and hot. Well I fill the hot water bottle and I go down to the corner to the phone box to ask the Dr. to come but by the time he come She is gone and he did come straight in about ¼ of an hour he was at the door. Shes gone I tell him straight away. You will be glad to know she went that quick and from what I know no pain. I must tell you that you writing your wedding to her give your Mam great happiness. There is ½ a letter she'd wrote you I will put in the post as you will be glad to have her Blessing. She does not know a Miss Gladys Moore she tells me when she 1st has your letter. This Miss Moore her who came in off the road to be Witness at the Registry or the other name. She does not know it either. I know she would hope them to be Good Friends*

to You. Your Mam is the best Friend to me all the
years. I want you to know we been Good Friends.
I don't have Her to talk to now . . .

It is several years since I received the letter from Mrs. Pugh.
I keep it with other letters in my handbag and, at times, when I
am too early in a waiting room, I take it out and read it again
and feel comforted that my mother is safely dead and buried.
She had to live some time longer than my father. While he was
alive, she told him everything. She had to manage without him
for some years.

I do not know Miss Gladys Moore and I do not remember
the other person's name, a man. Both very kindly made themselves late for work that morning by stepping, at my request,
into the Registry Office at ten-past-eight. Mr. George and I
were first off on the list to be married that day. This Miss
Moore, she enjoyed it the most. She said she loved weddings.
She was the happiest one there and her eyes shone. And she
kissed me.

When I am here in this cool quietness it is clear to me that there
are a great many people who would never need to wait here. They
would never experience the discreet harmony of armchairs, low
glass-topped tables, and untouched magazines. At intervals with
tiny sighings, the receptionists lift the receivers from the muted
telephones. The receptionists' faces are empty of emotion, enough
emptiness to enable them to spend whole days, weeks, months,
even years in this place. The softness of their youthful complexions
and of the pink and cream of their clothes merges with the general
soothing quality of the room which cushions the hardness of the
enormous building and its many floors devoted to human well
being. The individual is often not able, beyond a certain point, to
look after, completely, his own body and his own possessions.
Consultations about health and about possessions require complete trust between client and consultant.

I understand perfectly that it is because of money that I am
waiting here.

My Widow's House

It seems to me when I think about it and I do think often, like now in this waiting room, that I never saw the homestead again as I saw it that first afternoon when the sun, already low immediately above a blurred and distant horizon, sent long shadows from the trees at the near end of the paddock.

When we arrive that afternoon, my widow and I, the house is nestled in green, in a well-watered plot, she says, like she imagines the place in *Electra* where Orestes fulfils his destiny and slices his mother's lover in half during a barbecue.

The place is green to the windows and the door. Green hedges, green painted gates, and green, dark-green sad pines close together, a green embroidery stitched with firm green seams into a corner of the pale bleached land.

The house is really two houses held together with paint and the verandas, which are the best part of the house. She is forever painting the place. Start at one end, she tells me, paint right through and start again. She oils the floor boards and keeps some rooms clean and aired for guests.

She has what looks like a little village of houses for the men and their families and there are sheds for itinerant workers. She shows me as much as she can before it is dark. The silence is incredible. I tell her I love the smell of her land. And when darkness falls it is a black impenetrable darkness and it comes quickly with a cold wind as in the desert.

Like my mother's house, my widow's house stands open to the spring, to all the seasons, the doors propped open with ancient flat irons and the cast-iron ornamental claws, which were once bath feet. My widow pauses on the threshold to satisfy herself that the scattered droppings are from possums and not from rats.

All night the pines sigh outside the open window. The next day we change the shelf paper in the kitchen and the storeroom.

"Print," the widow tells me, "especially the pages of the specials in the newspaper, keeps the cockroaches away. Epsom salts are good," she says, and scatters the shelves with the clean white crystals. "Imagine!" she says, "the cockroaches after their dose."

Golden Fleece

"Loquats," my widow says, "you never tried them? Try one now. They are like lamb's-wool, gold tipped, caught in the deep branches of the tree when they are ripe."

My widow has had, as I have, too much to drink. She surpasses herself, she says, in poetic imagery. She never thought I would come, she says, and she is unable to hide her delight. "You have come! Dear child!" she says.

"Come out into the paddock," she says. The kiss the widow gives me at the edge of the paddock is not a pale, cool-lipped brushing of a powdered cheek crumpling against mine.

The Dorian Sword

It is a well-made Dorian sword. My widow stands with the rifle. "Throw off your buckled cloak," she says, "and grasp it firm." She then comes gently up behind me, slowly putting the rifle in position, telling me in the most loving and persuasive tones to look a little at the beauty of it and to handle this beauty. And, raising it for me, she tells me to look along the well-cared-for barrel. She tells me to shoot.

"Of course you can," my widow says, "and of course you want to. It is just the same here as it was on the ship, isn't it?"

Weight

"I've always been about nine stone ten," my widow says during the tenderness of a rest on the unbuckled cloak. We watch, together, the thin smoke drift from her dark little cigar. I breathe in this smoke. I breathe in her refreshment. *I do love you, Widow,* I say.

"I thought," she says, "that you would not come. I thought, after all this time, it would be too difficult for you to get away."

I explain that I am having a short holiday, that I have finished my appointed term at the hospital and have set up in private practice. I tell her I intend to stay in Australia and I explain that

Mr. George has gone to Scotland for a visit and will be coming back. "I daresay we shall have a lot of traveling to do because of the girls and Miss George," I say.

"Well, air travel and all that, easy even if expensive," the widow says. "And Migrant, even if we don't never see each other again, *I don't dislike you!* How's that for a double negative?" Together we contemplate the peaceful blue sky.

"But about my weight," she says, "I put it on and then lose it and revert to my birth weight, nine stone ten or eleven, give or take a pound." She confesses to having broken a toilet once in Italy. "A very cheap place it was, you understand, Migrant."

Her third husband paid for it.

Later I am still contemplating the wide dome of the blue sky and my widow is studying minutely the quality of the earth.

A First Husband

"I was married," my widow tells me, the day she is trying to teach me how to sit a horse. "I was married straight out of boarding school and we went straight to Europe for my *finishing.* The parents, both sides, insisted. The custom, you see, with the well-to-do. One property making a marriage with another. You knew from Christmas parties, from about the age of six and on to teenage tennis weekends, more or less, whose wife you'd be and which house would be yours. It was a bit like being in the cattle sheds at the Royal Show.

"Terrible eating habits in boarding school," she says, "packets of biscuits between meals, whole packets, that sort of thing. Fat with spotty faces, but mostly fat."

My widow explains that a first husband should always be acknowledged like a first publication of something, even if it's not particularly good. She has been married three times and has made several pastoral changes and additions. If she thinks of her husbands at all, she thinks mainly of her first one. She has always maintained that it is necessary, in life, to be capable of change and to move along with changes. She has herself gone from rice to beef and then to sheep and wheat and sometimes wheat and beef, give or take the poultry. She has owned and lived in different places. We leave the horse.

The Third Husband

"For my third wedding," my widow tells me, "I had a gray dress, rat gray. I did not see the color properly until I was actually through the ceremony. Gray, color of rat, I said to myself, and stuffed it behind the wardrobe in the hotel room."

She tells me that her third husband wore a four-button virgin alpaca jacket, $1,995.00, a cable-stitch hand-knitted cashmere cardigan, $1,925.00, narrow velvet corduroy trousers, a steal at $395.00, and ostrich gloves at $700.00. The gloves might have been emu. Not counting his underwear, his shirt, his hat, his socks and shoes (genuine python), and the gold in his teeth, he stood at $5,015.00. It was pounds actually, she explains, but she has put it into dollars, roughly, to give an idea of the value now.

"For entertainment at the Breakfast," my widow says, "we had a woman performer who used her dress as a musical instrument. With weddings," she goes on, "it is best to stick to convention. White, vanilla, or parchment for the first, *café au lait* for the second, and gray for the third, pearl gray not rat. I errored there, Migrant, just as you are going to error with that black. If you insist on black you should add something pink. This cheap little pink scarf, perfectly hideous on its own, will do something for your black. You need a little tender glow with black."

"I can't make up my mind," my widow says in the evening. "Simply can't choose between outfits, the Gertrude Stein or the Shirley Temple." She stands disheveled and disconsolate with clothes all over the bedroom.

The Kiss

"Oh! For *Heaven's Sake*, Migrant! What's all the fuss, it's only the two of us for dinner. A coupla snags on the barbie out there.

Kiss me! Migrant," my widow says. "Oo's got a kiss for Aunty?"

We have both been quenching our thirst, foolishly, with beer.

Mornings

The light here, in the early morning, is as if washed. A small cooling wind causes the net of green branches and leaves immediately outside the widow to sway and tremble. In this light even the untidy bedroom scattered with discarded clothes has its own order. The light comes dust freckled and leaf shadowed on the unwashed window. It makes a tremulous pattern which moves gradually down the wallpaper on the opposite wall as the sun rises higher in the morning sky. We do not hurry to get up some mornings.

Other mornings we are off to some distant place, some corner of fencing the widow wants to inspect. No one in the world (including Mr. George) knows where we are. And always when we return, the homestead looks different.

Sounds Which Remind

On my last morning at my widow's house there is a grinding noise from outside, a persistent groaning and straining as of trees being uprooted. It is a reminder for me of the tanks passing through the village, where my school was, during mobilization at the outbreak of the war. And then I think of Mr. George and the straining and creaking of the branches of an old tree outside his window and how he does not want the tree cut down. He says the noise reminds him of the creaking of the timbers of a great ship.

One thought leading to another; my mother is a widow for some years before she dies and is strictly eligible to be on my little list of widows. In thinking like this I am paying homage to her. Perhaps here I should acknowledge the enormous changes she was capable of, I mean how differently she conducted herself in speech and mannerisms when reading Faust with Mr.

Berrington, compared with later on when her widow, Mrs. Pugh next door, was practically her sole companion.

Being capable of change, as my widow says, is tremendously important even if some things never change in spite of surrounding changes. An example being my mother never changing the way in which she walked. She placed her elegant feet, toes pointing down, one before the other, never stumbling or making an awkward ugly movement. Always, in my mind, I see my mother's well-bred feet fitted precisely at the heels, her ankles poised in good quality shoes, well made and not needing to follow the dictates of fashion. Similarly, my mother, reared first on Caruso and then on Tauber, would say that the contemporary tenor sounded as if he had been eating too much red meat but she would, in spite of this opinion, be able to listen with pleasure to the qualities in the voice of a new singer.

My widow tells me the noise is because the tractors are moving off to make the miles of firebreak. I am amazed at my widow and her apparent carefree nonchalance, and I ask her if she is not at all overcome by so much land and at having to manage the men and the seasons.

"Migrant," my widow says, "I don't manage the men and the seasons. They manage me."

Ramsden

"You don't mean to tell me," my widow says, "Migrant, you do not mean to tell me that this woman, a mature woman, a staff nurse or charge nurse, as you call her, actually wore ankle socks over her stockings. Bobby-soxers!"

We are having a couple for the road, my widow's words, before leaving for the long drive to the airport.

I tell my widow that it might have been in my imagination only. I tell her that, though certain music recalls Ramsden vividly, the cello concerto of Boccarini and some cello of Vivaldi, I never actually heard this music with Ramsden. And, as for the neat ankle socks when she is walking in a storm of rain beneath massive beech trees, I do see her clearly wearing these socks under the dripping trees, but it's only imagined. I never walked anywhere with Ramsden, only perhaps several respectful yards behind her along a hospital corridor, and even then she would be walking with another staff nurse, the two of them rustling in conversation with *each other*. I tell my widow, "I tried to explain to Ramsden, at least I *wanted to tell* staff nurse Ramsden about the downward thrust of the cello and about the perfection in the way the other instruments come up to meet the cello, but I never did tell her."

"So you told your gentleman about it, instead." My widow's tone changes and she is breathing in her words hardly enunciating them. "I bet you did! Just as soon as you could!"

"You are the only person," I say quickly, "to whom I have said that I had this thought—that someone had carefully measured the movements of the notes controlling the going down and the coming up in order to produce this exquisite mixture." As I am telling her this I am not sure if I am being truthful or not. But this ceases to matter when she says, in her ordinary voice once more, that it is a known fact that women are better together at measuring and controlling. I am grateful for the emphasis.

In the car I explain that, during the war, we all did wear ankle socks over our stockings. The habit was both an economy and a way of keeping warm.

Still the Third Waiting Room

I am still sitting here waiting in this gray and pink reception place, the third waiting room. It surprises me that I am alone here, the widow, my widow, being naturally close in my thoughts. It is because of my widow that I am here.

I did not walk anywhere with Ramsden and when I see her that time, sitting near me in the suburban train (except for her white hair she looks the same and is within reaching distance), I intend to speak to her and, with that strange feeling that there will be another time for my intention, I let that chance go. Similarly, I intend to visit my widow. Once more, I let a chance go . . .

I do not go again to visit her after the first time. There is always something to prevent me from taking that particular direction, which is more complicated than simply crossing the enormous continent. It is as though I have been moving on and away, wrapped up in what I have to do and absorbed in what concerns my work and me. Perhaps it is simply that I let the intention and chance go—yet again. Perhaps this is what I am like.

My widow writes to me one last time. A letter I still have every intention of answering though I understand I have let that chance pass too.

In this last letter she is about to leave for distant places on the other side of the world. She means to concentrate on France and Spain because of her recent lessons in French and Spanish. *"Japanese next and then I'll go to Japan . . . Ginza here I come, but first Paris and Madrid!"* Her exuberance touches me because I have not replied to earlier letters.

> *All my life, Migrant, I've been able to change with the changes but this time I'm beat. If a tree is uprooted or the wires down . . . If a tree falls, I'm scared. And I've got no one to scream to if I almost step on a snake. You might wonder why I travel so often,*

the widow writes. She had always thought, she writes, that without the obligations and the constant work of looking after someone, that she would really be free to enjoy the farm, that she would be free to go off all day if she wanted to. Free for a shoot or a swim and without having to get back home quickly but, as it turns out, all this freedom is hollow and lonely and the place has become alien, an alien place.

> *I am alienated from the place by the place. I'm nervous here. I hardly ever sit down let alone lie back watching*

the clouds as I do on board a ship or even peering from
a plane. I guess, Migrant, that's why I travel. You will
come, Migrant?
     You will come again, Migrant, won't you, soon?

I pause in my re-reading of the crumpled letter which lies with others at the bottom of my handbag. It seems that the property is a place to worry about. A fallen tree is frightening and not simply a source of firewood. She dreams of disasters, of thieves, of land supposed to be hers but not resembling her land. She dreams that sinister people are camping in places where she might unexpectedly come upon them. She pictures herself swimming and trapped alone, at dusk, by a root hidden under water. She imagines a woman sitting in the hollow of the land, with her geese, on a filthy nest hatching goslings. She thinks of this as the nearest approach to happiness a human being can hope for, to be at one with life, she writes. She writes that she thinks she is going mad.

The accountant tells me to travel. He says the money is working very well for me. And he says it is up to me to make the money do what Mrs. Ruperts would have wanted for me. *He* suggests *travel.*

The uttering of her name in his calm and rather pleasant voice gives me, as it always does, a shock. During that time I was with her we always called each other Widow and Migrant, using these names frequently in third-person narrative as though we were both impartial and devoid of an excess of emotion. And then, often, we each enclosed the other in some special word or phrase of endearment.

Her death was special and in character in that she, my widow, was the only one killed in an accident when the bus, filled with tourists, went off the edge of a road in the Pyrénées. I imagine her, with a crowd of widows, singing on the bus, buying souvenirs, speaking lately learned French with extra gestures and stammerings intended to sound as French as possible and, most likely, making for herself a special Friend in the crowd, not necessarily a widow but someone with certain qualities of need.

It is years since I have seen my widow. She will have died enjoying herself. I nearly say this aloud to the accountant to take his mind off my shabby unfashionable clothes. He wants me to know that I have enough money and am able to spend some, he is trying, tactfully, to tell me this, on clothes.

When I think of money I think of it in terms of the way I was brought up. It is as if I shall hear forever the voice of Mrs. Pugh, my mother's widow, saying, "more money than sense" and "tek care of the pence and the pounds 'ull tek care of theirselves" and "a fool and her money is soon parted," like the refrain in an ancient ballad, telling a well-known story, or in a modern popular song, in which comment is made on some human disaster.

Church Bells

∞

I had an aquarium, just a small one, in here for some time. And then, one day, a patient starts screaming. She tries to cover her breasts, her pubic area, and her face screaming that the expression in the eyes of, as she says, the most hideous of tropical fish, reminds her of her husband and the way he looks when he is about to climax.

I tell her that I'll get the firm to fetch the aquarium straight away. It is only rented in any case.

This small waiting room, furnished with shabby chintz and tattered magazines, has in one corner a stained machine complete with paper cups and a particularly tasteless instant blend. This waiting room is mine. When I sit down in here for the first time ever, during all these years, I hear the church bells. The bells cannot be heard in my consulting room which is, of course, sound proof. The bell ringers are practicing and the repeated and reassuring peal is carried on the wind. It is like hearing the church bells across the fields when I was at school years ago. The whole school, on Sunday mornings, took to the field paths to walk to the Meeting House, which was in the next village, and which had no belfry and no outward call to worship. These bells, recalling those other bells bring back the summer morning mist, the soft voice of the cuckoo calling across the fields of wet grass and the sweet breath of herded cows waiting near a gate. This mist heralds, what we called in England, a fine day.

When I think about the third waiting room I have no way of knowing the hopes and expectations of the receptionists there. I can see for myself, from the results, the care with which they have dressed themselves and attended to their hair, and the ways in which, with cosmetics, they have transformed their young and innocent faces to the artificial, either the demure or the knowing. But there is no way of knowing their expectations or their ultimate realization of what their lives have to offer. In spite of the confidence inspired by being encapsulated in exquisite pink and gray tones and the impersonal elegance of carefully chosen cream or white blouses, authoritative tailored skirts, and high heels, the minute lines of discontent begin to form, unseen, causing the sweet rosy mouths to become thin lipped and slack with the beginnings of a realized unhappiness. A number of such people will experience some kind of waiting room sooner or later. Statistics show this.

My widow always maintained that a woman should never lean forwards over a mirror or a man.

"Lie on your back, Migrant, and hold the mirror up," she tells me this several times. "Hold the mirror up and a decade will slip back into your pillow. Lean forward," she warns, "and you'll need two porters to carry your bags." Perhaps I shall be able to pass on this advice at some time.

My own receptionist is fat and untidy. One of her legs is shorter than the other. She has an ugly limp. She has a mustache and an inordinate curiosity about people. My patients confide in her and her appearance consoles the nervous especially those who do not know what to wear for their appointment. She comes breathless, apologetic and late, a swirling mid-calf pandemonium of clashing colors laden with strips of black lace heavy-like braid, her floral armpits wet.

"*Ach! Ich schwitze,*" she says, in her mother tongue, and sits in the waiting room to rest her feet, gossiping as if waiting for a consultation herself. She likes, in her own words, a small dose of *Schadenfreude* and to enjoy the remains of human nature. She used to smoke but managed to give it up when I was obliged to have a "no smoking" sign on the wall.

Sometimes there is a small excitement, during which her Teutonic love of order and discipline and an unexpected gentleness in her ability to carry out this criterion of behavior are very useful.

I remember the widow asking me, during my one visit to the homestead, why I continued with my work and why had I changed from surgery to general practice. When I try to explain to her about the helplessness experienced in all forms of medicine, I remember Noël saying something about the ultimate choice I would have to make between being a surgeon, a physician, or what he described, with unnecessary unkindness, as a cheap psychiatrist. He, at that time, was cynical with a rapidly advancing illness of his own. He said then that I would be attempting to deal with medical and surgical conditions for which there are no remedies except those surviving from folk tales and legends . . . "Mythology," he said then, "and witchcraft."

At the time, I try to explain to my widow, that some things manifest themselves openly—an eye for example, dislodged by cancer, lying on the stained gauze when the dressing is removed—yet other things are wrapped up, remaining unseen in hidden wishes, in blame and remorse and in accusation.

When I contemplate my work like this I can see that cause and effect are more easily seen in outward harm, and the secret unseen flight into illness is the one which does not show itself clearly and is knitted to a destiny, from which there is no escape, and which contradicts all cherished ambitions and hopes.

The jeweled and pleated elegance of the doves strutting on the path is not disturbed when tempests of self-doubt, panic, and fear approach my door. The glowing colors of the warm bricks are reflected in the serene breasts of the doves. A pleasant image. A remedy.

I have to tell my widow, when she asks me, that I have no explanations. I do not pass on anything from my work but carry it myself in my experience. There is a great deal that has to be known and, at the same time, it must stay hidden in the heart.

To the questions, is there a Balm and is there a Physician? my answer is, yes. There is trust, there is courage, and there is kindness. These are the ingredients. And anyone can be the Physician.

I suppose homelessness, the sense of not having a place of sanctuary to return to, can come at any time, even in such separate places as the Great Bitter Lake where a ship might wait for a passage through the Suez Canal, or in the quiet suburban streets where the winter trees are finely drawn on the cold rosiness of the winter sunset.

Perhaps the homelessness comes about because of the lack of immediate links with immediate surroundings. The Great Bitter Lake because of the silence and the strange colorless calm water, and the suburb which shares the same lack of concern. The traveler is the more susceptible to this apparent emptiness and might concentrate on some detail close enough for minute examination, the whitening of the knuckles on the hands clutching the steady rail of the ship, waiting at anchor, or the innocence of the nape of the neck exposed and vulnerable.

In an unfamiliar park, one time, when Mr. George, half-remembering, asks me, "Where shall we eat our sandwiches?" I have no answer suitable. In the unfamiliar park the ugly toilet block seems to be the only building and, beyond that, no consoling view of any kind.

The church bells are repeating and repeating, still, their expected measured and exuberant movement of sound; the next falling sounds ringing out over the first falling sounds. The sustained pealing fills the afternoon and my waiting room. The light is changing.

Our walk is smooth smooth humming and purring along Goldsworthy and smooth smooth down Bernard, westward to the park. Because of the blue-chip metal Hammond is rough. From behind the wheelchair there is a close view of the back of the neck of the person sitting in the chair. The back of the neck, the nape, is vulnerable.

Bay Road, Harold, Hammond and Goldsworthy, Bernard Street, the park, Thompson Road, Koeppe Road, Princess, Caxton, Warwick, and Queen. Of these closely watched roads Goldsworthy is smooth and Hammond, because of the blue chip, is rough. Bernard slopes, Queen is fragrant and shaded with the old trees we call the peppermints. Whereas Hammond has cape lilacs and plane trees which arch overhead, the sunlight dappled on the green leaves. These trees meeting overhead, as they do, create either a shelter from the sun when it is too hot, or from the rain when it comes.

There is something about the changing light of the afternoon which reminds Mr. George of that time of the day when people start returning to their houses.

"Is Helena in yet?" he asks. And a little later; "Is Rachel in?" I remind him that Helena and Rachel are both living and working in London and that they are coming to visit at Christmas. He expects, he says, that Miss Eleanor will be home shortly.

I do not remind him any more that Miss Eleanor will not be coming, that we can no longer expect Miss Eleanor to come home. I leave it as if it is still the three of us, Mr. George and Miss George, the Georges and me.

Queen Street Warwick Caxton, cross Princess into Koeppe down Thompson to the park, we are on the way back. Thompson like Goldsworthy is smooth smooth . . .

"Is Father in?" Mr. George's question surprises me. The thought of a possible father for Mr. George takes me completely by surprise, that there was someone, that there was a father I know nothing about and have never thought about. A father, someone he will have known and expected home. Someone he called "Father." A whole fresh experience lies in the small question. Miss Eleanor, she too, will have called this man, this stranger, "Father." They will have been together. How were they when they were together? Brother and sister and Father.

"What did you say?" I ask Mr. George. In his quiet dignified way he tells me he is sorry, he is a silly old man and has forgotten what he said. He is holding a white paper napkin and, with great care, he spreads it out on his rug and then begins to fold it.

I watch the hedges closely as I walk, the honeysuckle, the hibiscus, the oleander, the plumbago, the white and pink climbing roses, the wisteria, and the geraniums. There are too the street lawns with the box trees, the plane trees, the peppermints, and the cape lilacs.

Perhaps because of Mr. George's small question, the surprise in his three words, reminding of another entirely different place, these hedges give way, for the time being, to that series of repetitive quartets, the evergreens, the laurel and the privet, the rhododendrons and the holly.

The hedges, the streets, the gardens, the houses, and the people, the couples. We, Mr. George and I, are a couple.

"We do not seem to be like a couple," I say.

"Vera, what is it you are saying? What did you say, Vera?" Mr. George wants to know.

"We do not," I tell him, "seem to be like a couple."

"Why do you bother, Vera," Mr. George replies, "with such an ugly word?"

A Note About the Author

Elizabeth Jolley is one of Australia's most celebrated authors, with a formidable international reputation. Born Monica Elizabeth Knight in England in 1923, she was brought up in a strict, German-speaking household and attended a Quaker boarding school. During the Second World War, she left school to train as a nurse. She married Leonard Jolley, a university librarian, and, in 1959, with three children, they emigrated to Western Australia.

Although Jolley wrote all her life, it was not until she was in her fifties that her first book, *Five Acre Virgin and Other Stories,* appeared. Over the next twenty-five years, she published fifteen novels, four collections of stories, and four books of nonfiction. She won every major Australian literary award, including the *Age* Book of the Year Award for *My Father's Moon* and *The Georges' Wife.* Her work was translated into every major European language. In the United States, several of her novels were selected as *New York Times* Notable Books. *Cabin Fever* was excerpted in *The New Yorker.*

The Vera Wright Trilogy, recognized as Jolley's masterpiece, was originally published in separate volumes, *My Father's Moon* in 1989, *Cabin Fever* in 1991. *The Georges' Wife* (1993) was published only in Australia. The present Persea edition offers North American readers this concluding volume for the first time.

Elizabeth Jolley died in 2007.